DUNCTON STONE

Moledom

WHERN

Wharfe

ABOD

Beechenhill

Dark Peak

Cannock

Rollright

Caer Caradoc

THE WEN

Severn

DUNCTON WOOD

Thames

Fyfield

Avebury

Buckland

UFFINGTON

The Stones of Seven Barrows

Based on Mayweed's map found in Seven Barrows

WILLIAM HORWOOD

DUNCTON STONE

Volume Three of
THE BOOK OF SILENCE

HarperCollins*Publishers*

HarperCollins*Publishers*
77–85 Fulham Palace Road,
Hammersmith, London W6 8JB

Published by HarperCollins*Publishers* 1993
1 3 5 7 9 8 6 4 2

A catalogue record for this book is
available from the British Library

ISBN 0 00 224174 9

Set in Linotron Caledonia by
Rowland Phototypesetting Ltd
Bury St Edmunds, Suffolk

Printed and Bound in Great Britain by
Hartnolls Limited, Bodmin, Cornwall.

Moles who appeared in *Duncton Rising*, Volume Two of *The Book of Silence*

WARNING: *If you have not read* Duncton Tales *or* Duncton Rising *you are advised against reading the character descriptions below as some of the plot of the previous books is given away.*

ARUM	Loyal helper to Thripp.
BARRE	Newborn Senior Brother Inquisitor sent by Quail and Thripp to help cleanse Duncton Wood's Library. Killed in the Chamber of Roots.
BODEN	One of Thripp's most loyal helpers.
BRIMMEL	Female and smallest of Privet's pups by her Brother Confessor. Died young.
CHATER	A journeymole and mate of Fieldfare. Killed at Caer Caradoc.
CHERVIL	Thripp's powerful and charismatic son.
CLUNIAC	Son of Elynor and a doughty follower who helps Pumpkin.
COBBETT	Librarian at Beechenhill who sets Privet on her quest for the Book of Silence.
DRUBBINS	Elder of Duncton Wood and close friend of Stour. Killed by the Brother Inquisitors.
ELYNOR	Elderly female follower who becomes friend and help of Pumpkin.
FALLOW	One of Chervil's guardmoles. Son of Feldspar.
FELDSPAR	Chervil's personal guardmole. Father of Fallow and Tarn.
FETTER	Senior Brother Inquisitor sent with Barre and Law to cleanse the library of Duncton Wood. Intelligent and cruel.
FIELDFARE	Middle-aged Duncton female who befriends Privet. Mate to Chater from whom she is separated on her journey to Seven Barrows where she helps lead a group of rebels.
GAUNT	Mentor (i.e. senior delver) in Charnel Clough.

GLEE	Female albino puphood friend of Rooster in Charnel Clough.
GREAR	Aggressive last leader of the Ratcher moles. Son of Red Ratcher and therefore one of Rooster's brothers. Rooster kills him at Crowden.
HAMBLE	Crowden warrior and puphood friend of Privet and later colleague of Rooster on his campaign against Newborns to the east of moledom.
HOBSLEY	Elderly follower who escapes into a coppice named after him north of Caer Caradoc. Privet and several others stay with him.
HUME	Delver from Charnel Clough.
HUMLOCK	Blind, deaf, mute puphood male friend of Glee and Rooster in Charnel Clough.
LAW	Newborn Senior Brother Inquisitor sent by Quail and Thripp to help cleanse Duncton Wood's Library.
LIME	Privet's sister by Shire.
LOOSESTRIFE	One of Privet's female pups by her Brother Confessor.
MADOC	Newborn female (known as Sister Hope) from Bowdler who becomes follower when she is befriended by Privet.
MAPLE	Duncton warrior who accompanies Privet and Whillan to Caer Caradoc. Set to lead the followers against the Newborns.
MUMBLE	Privet's only male pup by her Brother Confessor.
MYRTLE	Mate to Turrell of the Moors. Not to be confused with Myrtle, Furrow's mate, both friends of Maple.
NOAKES	Enterprising follower, originally from Gurney. One of rebels under Spurling at Seven Barrows.
PEACH	Mate to Spurling.
PRIVET	Scribemole born at Crowden in the Moors. Daughter of Shire, granddaughter of the Eldrene Wort. Is in search of the Book of Silence and has had pups by her Brother Confessor during a period at Blagrove Slide, from where she escaped to Duncton. Entrusted by Master Librarian Stour to continue the search for the lost Book.
PUMPKIN	Stour's library aide and a brave but reluctant leader of the remaining rebels in Duncton Wood.
QUAIL	A high ranking Newborn Brother from Avebury.
RED RATCHER	Vile leader of the Charnel Clough grikes and father of Rooster, who killed him at Crowden.

ROLT	Brother Rolt is sympathetic Newborn assistant to Privet's Brother Confessor at Blagrove Slide.
ROOSTER	Son of Samphire and Red Ratcher.
SAMPHIRE	Abducted from Chieveley Dale by Red Ratcher by whom she has Rooster.
SAMPION	One of Privet's female pups by her Brother Confessor.
SKUA	Senior Brother Inquisitor under Quail, and effectively his second-in-command. A pitiless persecutor of follower and Newborn alike.
SLANE	The Senior Brother Inquisitor responsible for the Ludlow strettening.
SNYDE	Hunchbacked scholar and deputy Master Librarian in Duncton Wood who has gone over to the Newborn side.
SPURLING	Follower, and escaped library aide, from Avebury. He is leader to a group of refugees from Buckland. His mate is Peach. Joins Fieldfare on way to Seven Barrows.
SQUELCH	Quail's obese son. His extreme depravity is redeemed only by his wonderful ability to sing and make melody.
STOUR	Master Librarian of Duncton Wood and most famous in moledom. Goes to the Silence taking the Six found Books of Moledom to their resting place beneath the Stone.
STOWE	A loyal follower, and Elder at Bourton in the Wolds.
STURNE	Keeper in the Duncton Library and asked by Stour to bravely pretend to be a Newborn, whilst still aiding the follower side. A friend of Pumpkin's, the only mole who knows his secret.
TARN	One of Chervil's guardmoles. Son of Feldspar.
THRIPP	Charismatic leader of the Newborns, originally from Blagrove Slide. Has turned against Quail.
WAYTHORN	Son of Turrell from the Moors.
WEETH	A Newborn from Evesham turned follower. Assistant to Maple.
WHILLAN	Adoptive son of Privet. Father is Rooster, mother Lime.
WORT	The Eldrene Wort was the notorious persecutor of Beechen and grandmother to Privet.

CONTENTS

PROLOGUE

Forgive me, mole, but, yes . . . I have been avoiding you. These molemonths of summer past I have wished to be silent and unavailable. Yet I have been aware that you were asking after me. Now you have tracked me down and find me much aged since last we spoke. You left then with my tale of Duncton's rising against the Newborns incomplete. No doubt when you returned to the Stone to hear the rest of the tale a day or two later, as we arranged, you were disappointed and alarmed to find that I had gone.

Indeed, I've heard you were angry, and then concerned, and set off in pursuit of me through the tunnels and glades of our once summery wood. But by the time you caught up with me a little wisdom had caught up with *you*, and you left me alone. You thought – and you were right – that it was best to leave things until I was ready to continue. Well, I freely confess I have not wanted to talk again to you until now that September's come. A long time it's been and though the sun's been warm my old fur's grown thin, and I have shivered even on the hottest days. Now, as autumn looms, my bones ache with the morning mists. Yet here I am at last, willing to talk to you once again, and tell you how it was that the Book of Silence finally came to Duncton Wood.

You have waited well and patiently. I fancy from your face, and even more your eyes, that you have learned much since you first came up into the High Wood and persuaded me to tell you of Privet, enabling you to scribe down the Book of Tales and then that of Duncton Rising.

How long ago it seems since you and I first talked – longer even than the tales we talked about! Does time play tricks when a mole grows old, or does he enter a new reality? Whatever . . . you seem to have learned a little more about life, and faith as well. And courage too, I'm sure.

No, no, tell me not of what you've learnt! I do not need to be told – I know; I feel it, I have heard it from others, and I see it in your face.

1

Now, mole, you've been a good companion on my journey back to the days of which I have told you, the kind that any wanderer would wish to have: attentive, intelligent, concerned, and, above all, trusting. You have dared let yourself be led by me, who am but an old mole now, and one few find time to listen to, let alone wait about for. For that I am grateful, and for your willingness to scribe down the words I speak, that others in times to come will be able to learn of these things as well.

Why then have I been so unwilling to talk to you again until now, and finish the tale you persuaded me to begin? You must know the answer to that question if you are to understand the last part of the tale I want to tell you. I have been unwilling because . . . because I have been afraid. I am old, I am ill now, and I fear death. I see now that this telling of a great tale to you, which concerns the final coming of the Book of Silence, is the last journey I shall ever make. I, who have journeyed so far in my life, and seen so much of moledom, and heard so many moles tell their tales, can now travel only in memory. I know that each word I speak to you now, each memory I evoke, each place I describe, each character I depict, each moment of history I recount, is one more step I shall never retrace. In speaking now to you I talk away the last moments of my life.

Yet now I see that if the mole is to know the Silence he or she must make this final sacrifice: must cast off the past, turn away from memories both good and bad, and face unflinchingly the present moment. Now, now, *now* is when we live; and we must strive not use our past as defence against the present. So as I talk to you and whisper out this tale that others may know it, and journey through its light and shade, I denude myself of all defence against the present terrible moment, the 'now' I have avoided all my life, the now which all moles seek to avoid. The now which Privet sought so long to flee from but which her whole life led towards.

I do not expect you to understand easily. You are young and can see the trees ahead, and the Stone beyond them, and the light beyond even that. Or think you can. It gives you hope, as well it might. But I . . . why, my sight is dim. I have barely strength now to raise my head to look for what I can no longer see.

Yet, strange as it may seem, I sometimes think I see more clearly than I ever did before. I see the trees, I see the Stone, I see its Light. Not as you may do, beyond yourself, there somewhere in the future, but here and now, about my frail paws, about this decayed leaf-litter on the ground, aye, and here within my heart.

2

So I am afraid because my life is ending. Just when I begin to see things that have eluded me for so long I feel a dread of the Silence I yearn for. This is what drove me away from the Stone where we first met, and where my telling to you began. Uncertain of myself, ill and lonely, I wandered off through the wood these long summer days past, avoiding company, seeking shadows, staring into tunnels that once, when I was young, I scampered down, but which today put fears into me, and strike me dumb.

Miserably, I came over here to the Eastside, ignoring the pleas of friends to move into less austere quarters, or to rest in my burrow when the winds blew cold and the days began to shorten. I have been rude to some and silent with others.

Until today. Until now . . .

The autumn leaves have begun to fall about me and perhaps in their going I sense something of my own departure. No, no, don't protest! It'll be a relief, believe me. Aching bones are not much fun, and nor is failing sight. But despite the tiredness that autumn's brought, I've rediscovered something of my old spirit, the same spirit that took me on many a journey, and makes me one of the few moles living who remember a life that to others is already history, if not legend!

Now I have a desire to see the Stone one last time, but I must confess I need somemole's help to get me back there, the last journey I shall ever make. It is not quite as simple as putting one paw in front of the other and tottering back upslope to the Stone itself. That I could just about manage by myself.

No, no . . . the journey that I wish to make must take in some savage moments of history, and confront some moles whose nature and confusion might easily put me off my course, if not subsume me entirely. This is where you come in. I need your youth and optimism. I need your faith. I need the hope that you still have. Then, too, I do not wish all I know to die with me. You and I began a journey together, a journey which without your coming I doubt that I would have started. Now I am ready to end that journey, and I wish to do it in your company. So if you'll listen, and scribe down what I say just as you did before, I'll be able to tell you of how Privet came back to our system, and how the Book of Silence was found. A story which will take us back to Duncton Stone in the way I most wish to return to it.

But be warned! I'll not be willing to stay in one place. I'll want to venture into this tunnel, or that burrow, and I'll need help to do so.

3

I'll want to look at trees I thought I had forgotten, and venture into tunnels I thought were lost. I'll be a nuisance! I'll be demanding! I'll be . . . bad-tempered. And worse of all to a scribemole like you, I might not even have the strength to finish my tale!

Oh yes! That could well be how things turn out, and it's no good pretending otherwise. If you want to reach the end of this tale you might well have to journey the last part of it without me. I mean what I say! Indeed, it may well be that *that* realization is what the coming of the Book of Silence is all about: that finally we must cast off our past, our memories, even our companions, and make the last part of the journey alone. Is it that which makes me so afraid? Is it that which makes the Silence so awesome? Is that why I have called you to my flank?

But let's face that when we have to. Meanwhile we'll find comfort in each other's company, and resolve. But you'll have to cajole me! And find good worms! Or make me a scrape if the weather grows bad. Which it does now, for look at how those trees sway in the blustering wind. Feel the chill breeze in your fur. Sense how winter approaches through the veil of autumn. For it's with winter that this last part of our tale must now begin . . .

PART I

Wildenhope

Chapter One

January. Chill, still, air. The bleak landscape of Mid-moledom; leafless trees, silent grey rivers, the streams and brooks that fed into them already frozen. Only the black flight of starving rook and the sharp bark of lonely fox gave life and sound to a melancholy world from which all colour, all joy, all pleasure seem to have fled. A January like no other before and – the solitary wanderer grimly hoped – like no other ever to come again. For this was moledom cast down not just by a freezing winter but by the freezing of hope as well. No wonder that the journeying mole stared along the route ahead, and back over the path just trod, with a shivering spirit, and a disconsolate eye.

No safe haven for him. No warm tunnel in which to hide from his pursuers in safety, no welcoming burrow in which to rest; no cheerful companion or offering of food and friendly conversation.

'No respite,' muttered the mole, whose face, though lined and scarred, held clear determined eyes, which told of a fugitive who knew his business, and was never going to let himself be caught without a struggle.

'We go on,' he said.

The 'we' he spoke did not mean he had others with him. Rather, it was as if by using it he might for a brief moment enjoy the illusion that he had company, to encourage him on along the bleak and bitter way. But this was no weak mole, nor one who, beyond a temporary pause to summon up new energy to proceed once more, gave any impression other than strength, experience, and purpose. This was a mole on a mission he was determined to fulfil, and even if that January had been yet chiller, yet bleaker, he would not have been diverted from his onward path. For this was Hamble, lifelong friend of Privet, stalwart companion of Rooster in the struggle against the Newborns, and now journeyer to Duncton Wood.

But while it is true that he looked like a mole with a mission, the truth was that he was not yet sure quite what it was. He knew at least that he would not willingly raise his powerful and forbidding paws in violence again, unless it be to defend himself against unfairness, or protect those who were vulnerable against the oppressive Newborns. No, his active fighting days were done, for Privet had pointed him in a different way, strengthening his commitment to what he had already begun to believe; that if moledom was to find peace and harmony once more then the way forward was for hardened warriors like himself to renounce fighting and seek other ways to achieve just ends.

It was this hard-won knowledge that had sent Hamble away from Caer Caradoc before Longest Night with Privet's blessing, to make his way as best he could to Duncton Wood, where he hoped to find a new direction for his life. The fighter turned pacifist, the warrior turned philosopher; the mole whom the years had made wiser, and whose inner goodness and strength – given so loyally to Rooster from whose violence he had finally felt he must turn away – must now find a different fulfilment.

Alone, but not lonely. Not yet. Hamble had had mates enough over the years, in the way that itinerant fighting moles do: a brief encounter, a night of comfort, a sharing of a day or two, and then the quick farewell and moving on. No, Hamble's constancy had not been for these encounters, but for Rooster, whose destiny as Master of the Delve he had early sensed and passionately believed in, but for whom he felt he could now do no more; and for his oldest, dearest friend, Privet, whose strength and purpose were so great, so sure, that Hamble willingly obeyed her instinctive sense that he should journey to Duncton Wood.

So he was off alone towards it across winter-bound moledom, to try to see what he might do in the Stone's service against the Newborns, themselves in thrall now to the vile Quail, who was determined to impose his brutal will upon all of moledom, as the Newborns had begun to impose it already upon a few important systems, including Duncton itself.

Hamble had slipped away from Caer Caradoc, been forced to lie low when harsh blizzard winds swept across his path, and now, mole-weeks later and with Caradoc's hill still darkly lowering up behind him, he was off on his way again towards Duncton Wood. Or rather, this was what Hamble *intended* to do, and would have done, had not his route that bleak day put him in the way of a small group of moles being forcibly marched not far from the path he was on.

This track follows the stream that rises on the eastern flank of Caradoc and leads first east and then south down to the once-pleasant system of Rusbury and thence via a place whose name is now notorious: Wildenhope. Under the Newborns this had become a centre of correction and punishment, having been utilized by Thripp originally for the purpose of conducting retreats upon the austerities – acts of cruel self-discipline, denial and abstinence. Since Quail's emergence as Senior Inquisitor Wildenhope had been corrupted into something far worse and there Inquisitors were taught mental and physical torture, and given rewards, mainly of a sexual nature.

Hamble did not know or recognize the place. Beyond it the stream forms a confluence with Eaton Brook at what historians now call Craven Rapids – the name is not used locally, and the whole area is now generally referred to as Wildenhope.

The rapids are simply a faster flow where the two streams join and fall over steeper ground into a dangerous race of white water and jagged rocks. It is not a place to linger by, and a mole wishing to continue his easterly journey does well to turn north and take the two-foot crossing above the rapids, whose malevolent roar is audible a long way off.

Of all this Hamble knew nothing, though while captive with Rooster and the others at Bowdler he had heard that not too far off was a Newborn killing field (namely Wildenhope) at a place near moving water. Which would make sense, for he knew more than most of the Newborns' killing ways, of strettening, snouting and the Inquisitors' preference for the punishment of drowning.

Nor was Hamble sure why when he awoke that day and could so easily have continued upslope into safety he chose to go back downslope over the white frozen ground. Towards danger. Except that some instinct for mole in trouble, and some new-found sense of where his next task might be, led him back to the main route he had left.

Even before he got there he could scent alien mole, and when he did he saw that the frosted ground was covered in tracks from Caradoc heading on downstream; they were fresh, and some of them bloody. It did not take him long to catch up with the moles who were making them, who turned out to be ten captives led by four large, bullying Newborns. The numbers might have seemed disproportionate and escape for the captives easy, but they were all lame or in some way injured and showed no spirit to put up a fight.

Hamble followed the unhappy group at a distance, as much out of a desire to help if he could as from curiosity to see what was going to happen to them, though he already had a grim idea. It was easy enough to go unobserved since the way was narrow and the vegetation

9

along the stream's bank plentiful. The air was so still and cold and the frost so thick that Hamble was not surprised to see that the stream on his right flank was frozen along its edges where the water was stagnant among the reeds. Only in its centre did the water still flow, black, cold and very uninviting.

The noisy, jocular march of the guardmoles, who seemed to think they were on the way to a celebration, was in contrast to the slow and abject gait of the captives, some of whom had increasing difficulty moving at all and needed the help of those few who were more able. One alone seemed to have more spirit than the others, though he was weak enough, and he asked continually that his ailing friends be allowed to rest, or stop and eat; and he asked too, with evident apprehension, where they were being taken.

To this the guards made a variety of replies the general tenor of which was, 'Somewhere you lot will not need to worry about food and sleep!'

It was around this more spirited mole that Hamble formed a rough plan of action whose success depended entirely on his being able to use surprise to disable the two guards at the rear of the group. If he succeeded, with the help of that mole he might then frighten off the other two guards and get the captives to safety. It was not a plan Hamble much liked, but needs must, and since it was obvious what was going to happen to these moles he knew he must try to help them if he could.

So indeed he might have done had not events pre-empted any plan he had, and made it unworkable. For the route suddenly dropped over a bluff to the clearer ground of water-meadows now frozen over, with no cover at all. There was the ominous roar of water further on, still out of view.

Its threatening sound seemed to warn the captives that if they were to escape their fate, now was their final chance. The spirited mole made a brave assault on one of the guards, while two others of the captives made a dash for it, but it was all over in moments, before Hamble could intervene. The two moles were simply grabbed and after a few buffets pushed back into line, while the more lively mole was taloned hard in the face by the guardmole he had attacked. Then, and most brutally, another guardmole came, shouting in anger, and taloned him again, as he lay on the ground.

Hamble prudently pulled back behind cover, for he was not a fool and knew he was no match for those four. Moments later, after a brief and dismissive examination of their fallen victim, they left him where he lay and led the remaining captives on across the meadow.

The moment they were out of sight Hamble went to the mole, who had not moved since he had fallen. Blood was spreading over the white ground from terrible injuries to his head and flank, and his limbs trembled, though whether from cold or in the throes of death Hamble did not know. Yet when Hamble touched him and spoke gently his eyes opened and he stirred.

'I am not a Newborn,' said Hamble. 'If I can get you into cover there might be a chance.'

The dying mole waved a paw dismissively and shook his head. 'We cannot let them be so,' he whispered; 'I came to Caradoc in peace. Moles must do what they can to stance up to them.'

They were his final words, for though Hamble asked his name and where he was from, and tried to revive him, he breathed but for a short time more, his blood still flowing after his body was still. Then even his blood began to congeal and freeze.

'You did what you could!' said Hamble respectfully, looking at the mole. He was middle-aged, not strong, a librarian perhaps, fooled into coming to Caer Caradoc like the others. The others . . . Hamble followed down the way, the roar of tumbling water growing louder all the time.

The track was now open and stretched without cover to the edge of Wildenhope Bluff, and then dropped down to cross meadowlands, and he was just in time to see the party disappear over the ridge ahead. Risking the possibility that they might come back and see him, Hamble followed on to the ridge and creeping up the last few paces peered over and downslope to see what they were about. The killing of the mole had not caused Hamble to change his mind about inter-vening – moles were not going to be able to 'stance up to them' if they got themselves killed making futile gestures. Having survived so long he knew when prudence made more sense than valour; and anyway, the germ of an idea had come into his head, suggested by what the dying mole had said; just a thought . . .

So Hamble was a silent witness to what happened by Craven Rapids that morning. Four Newborn guards and nine anonymous victims. One by one they were led over the frozen meadows to the confluence of the streams. There they were pushed to the edge of the bank and brutally taloned down into the icy torrent below. Briefly they disappeared from sight, for the bank was steep and the water furious, but then Hamble saw their bodies floating up to the surface in wild water before being tumbled over and down again to disappear finally

11

into the race of white water flowing south. It was quick, efficient, and final, and Hamble watched it all with growing numbness and shock.

One after another they were taken, some too weak to protest, others putting up a final valiant effort to fight their captors before they too were taloned into submission and hurled over the steep bank into the rapids. Each time they disappeared from sight beyond the bank, and each time the currents spewed them up again, their paws flailing in a semblance of life before they were swept away to icy oblivion.

Finally, their work done, the guardmoles chatted some more, ate a little, indulged in some brief horseplay on the bank's dangerous edge, and finally headed back upslope past where Hamble was hidden, to return to Caer Caradoc.

Hamble did not dally when they were gone, but nor did he set off to find a crossing-point, for he wished to see at close paw the spot where the executions had taken place.

'Aye,' he muttered darkly as he approached it, 'if I'm to do what I intend then I had best see all I can for myself.'

As he approached the bank the roar of the rushing waters was almost like a wall of sound, and the sight of the currents and whirlpools where the two streams met was enough to terrify anymole. He stared sombrely down into the rapids into which the nine moles had been thrown, and he could only hope they were dead before they reached such cruel waters; only as he turned away did he notice the sweet-rotting smell of death, foul enough in his throat to make him retch. He looked down the steep bank and saw a sight that, fight-hardened as he was, he could not easily have imagined – nor ever have wished to do so.

For the bank was steep indeed, no doubt gouged out by flood waters, dropping almost vertically into the rushing stream. Whether there was some eddy, or submerged silty shoal, he could not tell, but there, some under water, some clinging in their death contortions to the crumbling wall of the bank, were several mole corpses. No wonder then that the guardmoles had tried to hurl their victims out bodily into the stream, for the poor wretches below had not gone far enough into its main flow, but rather slipped and slid to the very brink and then, if not yet dead, found themselves trapped in this little treacherous odoriferous nook of death. Unable to clamber back up the sheer slippery bank, unable to burrow, unable to swim for it, many must have lingered on to die amongst the corpses of their fellows.

'We cannot let them be so . . . Moles must do what they can to stance up to them.' So had the mole they had murdered along the way spoken, and seeing what he saw now, Hamble was resolved to carry out the idea that mole had inspired.

'As the Stone is my witness,' he whispered, 'I shall kill no mole, unless it be in self-defence, but I *will* go where I must to gather evidence of what the Newborns do. And I will make it my task to tell others what I have learnt so that moles in the future shall know what happens when some believe theirs is the one true way, and think less of those who do not agree with them. For as sure as night follows day, once moles believe they have right on their side then some among them will lead others into the path of "just punishment", whose end I have witnessed today, and whose stench makes me retch now. I'm not a religious mole, Stone, nor have I been a good one, but so far as I am able from this moment I shall be witness against the Newborns and encourage others to be the same.'

Hamble had found his new task and having done so resolved to abandon his idea of over-wintering in some safe place, and decided instead to set off for Duncton Wood in a roundabout way forthwith when and where the Newborns would least expect journeyers, to find out all that he could about their killing, their organization, and their plans. As for explanation of whatmole he was, should he be stopped and questioned he decided to appoint himself the survivor of a patrol, all other members of which had been killed, whose task was to track down and bring before the Inquisitors that most infamous of moles at liberty – Hamble, friend of Rooster! It was not lost on Hamble that this search for himself, which Privet had started by sending him to Duncton Wood, might be nearer to the mark than most might suppose. Whatmole was he, after all? Only now was he beginning to find out.

So it was that Hamble of Crowden began his winter journey across moledom, a mole just a little past middle age who had seen much of life in one way, and now desired to see more of it in another. His life had not so far, as he himself had whispered to the Stone, been of a religious turn, and nor did his appearance – grizzled, tough, serious, doughty, strong of limb and slow to passion – suggest it would be now. But few moles that stark winter dared even venture out in the Stone's service, and fewer still can have had the potential to serve it so well as Hamble.

13

Chapter Two

Spring came to Hobsley Coppice towards the end of March, and quite suddenly. One day the air was chill and dark, and the trees and vegetation all leafless and bleak across the icy ground; and the next dawned warm and mellow, and even as the last snows melted and dripped away it seemed the delicate snowdrops and sunny aconites were up and about all across the woodland floor.

All of which was not a moment too soon for the six followers who had been so long safely hidden as refugees with the ageing Hobsley, but now wanted to be up and away with their plans, and projects, and journeyings. For with the stir of life underpaw that a new spring brings, and the buzz of life overhead, a mole is inclined to raise his snout with excited eyes and stare towards dreams and hopes in the far distance, giving little thought to the difficulties of crossing the middle ground between. All, that is, but Hobsley, the seventh mole, who had seen enough springs to last a lifetime, and wished for nothing more than to stay where he was and enjoy the coming warm days in peace and leave a troubled moledom to itself.

Of the others, Maple and Weeth were the most eager to leave, for their intentions were specific and well worked out. The question of whether Maple would continue to act as Privet's protector – which naturally he had offered to do – had long since been resolved by Privet herself.

'You have fulfilled your task in getting me to Caer Caradoc in safety, and out again,' she said. 'Besides, I have Rooster at my flank now, and Whillan too, and Madoc as well. If we are to go back to Duncton Wood, they will see me safely there.'

'Humph!' Maple had said, being persuaded though not quite satisfied that his task now lay in trying to build up resistance to the Newborns, beginning with the moles in the Cotswolds whose confidence he had already gained.

'Well then, we'll travel with you until I'm satisfied you're clear of Caradoc and its influence, and only then will Weeth and I think about how to lead resistance against the Newborns.'

14

But both moles remained uneasy about Whillan travelling on with Privet. She might have gained a new serenity and wisdom since leaving Duncton Wood, but where Whillan was concerned her judgement was suspect. It was as if she knew she should make it easy for him to leave her flank and journey as some youngsters must if they are to find true adulthood, and yet she would not. His life meant so much to her that she could not quite let him be free. This would not have mattered if Whillan had been more secure, more normal, than he was. But a mole who loses an anonymous mother at the moment of birth and has no known father, may well feel a reluctance, even guilt, to leave the foster-mother who raised him. How deep and troubling their strange tie, how hard, it seemed, to break.

It might have made all the difference if Rooster had confessed his suspicion that he was Whillan's father. Or so Privet and Weeth, who both believed this to be the case, argued. But Rooster himself was not so sure this would have done Whillan a favour, true though it might be.

'Will get in way of him finding his delving path,' he said, and refused the offer to talk of it, except once.

'*You* tell him then, you do it,' he said to Privet and Weeth in exasperation one day when they mentioned it again. 'You think, I feel. Am delver and only know feelings. Doesn't feel right to tell. If it does to you, *you* tell.'

But neither mole had, and as the winter had passed by Whillan's paternity seemed less important than before.

Meanwhile Whillan himself was full of resolve to break free from Privet – once he had seen her safely back to Duncton. None knew this better, nor more unhappily, than Madoc, whose love for Whillan was overshadowed by the knowledge of his desire to become independent. The fact that she understood so well his need to do so, which he had declared the first time he talked to her, made it no easier for her to bear. Their love had been born in danger, and had blossomed in the darkness of cruel winter, but with the coming spring she saw again the pain of restraint in his eyes, and feared that however bright the blossoms of their love, its fruit would never be.

Yet love is often optimistic and these fears and shadows were lessened by the hope that she was wrong, and that somehow on the journey back to Duncton Wood Whillan's restlessness would ease, and his need to escape for a time alone would be appeased for ever. Perhaps she would have his pups . . .

But that hope, at least, had been dashed by the time spring came, for she had not got with pup and as neither was slow to make love, she began to feel that the Stone had decided this was for the best. A time of uncertainty and travelling is no time to get with pup. Not that Whillan did not ask, and show disappointment when she said that she would not pup now. Yet his confusions were many, and she saw there was relief as well. If travel and doubt were poor auguries for starting young, so was a reluctant, vacillating father-to-be.

Although Whillan did not speak of such things outside their warm tunnels – nor even much inside them – Maple and Weeth guessed well enough what was on the youngsters' minds.

'Just as well she's pupless,' said Maple, not without sympathy, 'for a gaggle of youngsters would be nothing but a hindrance on the journey ahead.'

'Ah, true!' exclaimed Weeth warmly. 'But a *nice* hindrance. For what is life, if not for rearing young? Why do we seek to resist the Newborns if not to make a better world for youngsters to be born in?'

'Have you ever had a mate, Weeth?' asked Maple.

'I have had . . . moments,' replied Weeth. 'Love as such has not yet visited me, but opportunities have been few. There have been moments this winter past when I have envied Whillan his Madoc, and her her Whillan, and thought it would be good to retire to a warm burrow and the embrace of so charming a female. But I am content: I have my task, which is to serve you and the cause of all true Stone followers.'

'Don't you ever wonder about love?' asked Maple quietly.

'Well, I can see you do, sir!' said Weeth. He liked to call Maple 'sir' now and again, though Maple never asked that he did.

'Warriors don't have time for love.'

'I'll remember you said that!'

They grinned at each other.

'It has been good to have two lovers here in Hobsley Coppice,' observed Maple at last.

'It's been odd,' said Weeth. And then, responding to Maple's quizzical look he added, 'Peculiar, strange, the odd chances of destiny, and inevitability.'

'What are you talking about, Weeth?'

'Suspicions I can't yet express, things of which even after months of observation I cannot be certain; *things.*' Weeth had too much good sense to reveal his suspicion that Rooster was Whillan's father to any other mole than Privet.

A mole less balanced than Maple might soon have become irritated

16

by this kind of talk, but then Weeth was inclined to these musings, and Maple knew him well enough to appreciate that he only talked when he felt like it.

'Rooster,' said Weeth cryptically, 'from so far, and he is so . . . unsettled and unsettling, yet I do believe he is at the centre of it all. An uncentred centre, a non-delving Master of the Delve, yes, yes, no wonder moledom's in disarray.'

'That's Thripp's doing.'

'But which came first? The disarray or Thripp?'

'And what has *this* to do with two young moles in love?'

'Oh, *that*? Everything, I think, everything.'

'It's a pity Whillan and Rooster don't get on, then.'

Weeth laughed, and said in his cryptic way, 'Sir, you may be a fine, though unproved, general, but in the matter of moles' hearts take the advice of your subordinate.'

'What is it you know?' said Maple.

'I know nothing, I suspect much, and I blame the Stone for all of it! As for advice, I am not yet ready to give it.'

Sadly, Maple was right: Whillan and Rooster did not 'get on', or rather Whillan was unable to feel easy with Rooster or even understand the intimacy between his foster-mother and the delver, despite the discoveries of his own delving need he had made in the tunnels and chamber beneath the risen Stone. Like all young moles, especially those who have just discovered the joys of love, he could not imagine, nor did he wish to believe, that moles he perceived as old could actually make love. The very thought repelled him that Privet – *his* Privet – the mole who had raised him and who ought now to be declining gracefully into a respectable maturity of age, might do it, so to speak, with Rooster. No, no, it was not possible, it was disgusting. Yet he could not deny that Privet and Rooster spent nights together as well as days.

'But they can't . . .' he explained, 'I mean not that . . .'

Madoc laughed at his outrage. 'It's no different than us, my love!'

'It is! It is!'

She laughed again, not quite taking Whillan seriously. 'Some moles do it till they die,' and she giggled, thinking this a little ambiguous. But Whillan was in no laughing mood – the less so because he was beginning to think that Privet and Rooster really did do what he found so unacceptable.

'It's just wrong and . . . and . . .'

'You're jealous of Rooster, that's all.'

17

'*Jealous!*' shouted Whillan, very irate indeed. 'Me jealous of him?' But he was so angry he could say no more, and rushed out of their tunnels to stomp about on the surface above. Then, as many times before, he went down and lost himself amidst the delvings beneath the risen Stone, which calmed him and made him return to Madoc later, contrite and apologetic.

But it is harder to say quite what Rooster felt about Whillan, or why. Never an articulate mole on matters of the heart, nor one ever to express real anger and dismay about any other mole than himself – unless it be in the far distant years when Privet's sister Lime had so successfully lured him to her burrow, and helped bring on all their heads so much grief and trouble.

No, Rooster's anger was mostly an expression of the confusions and guilts he felt about his terrible past when he was only saved from a violent drowning in the Charnel at the paws of Red Ratcher by his mother Samphire, and destiny placed upon him the seemingly imposs- ible burden of being Master of the Delve. And then . . . not to live up to so great a task, to lose Samphire, to desert (as it had felt) his puphood friends Humlock and Glee and leave them to die desolate and outcast deaths, and finally to lose Privet; these had added furrows to his face, and left scars on his heart. While the desertion of his old friend Hamble at Caer Caradoc, so long threatened and in response to his violence, had shocked him into that state of self-abnegation in which the Newborns had found him, and with which they had come near to destroying him.

But at the heart of his discomfort was the fact of Whillan's unnatural ability with the sounding of the delve. Even experienced delvers he had known at the Charnel were rarely able to reach out and touch a delving line with such unconscious ease as Whillan. Rooster had known he himself had such abilities, and they had become far greater when he was trained . . . but that a youngster like Whillan should have so sure a touch puzzled him. He had instinctively said little of it to Whillan, and as the molemonths went by in Hobsley Coppice he felt sure this was right. There are some journeys moles make better if they travel without set directions, and powerful as Whillan's talent was it might easily decline and wither if a mole he did not like showed interest, or dared to give encouragement.

Privet agreed, but could not understand it all. Far worse, so far as Rooster was concerned, was the sweet longing that Whillan's sound- ings, and the existence of the delvings in the Coppice, put into his own heart. Whilst he still had no doubt that he could not – must

18

not – delve ever again, the delving need remained, and Whillan, unconsciously, exacerbated it.

'My dear, being here with you is like sleeping at the edge of a storm,' said Privet one night. 'What is it?'

'Whillan.'

'What of him?' If Privet was a little short it was not just tiredness, but the same irritation that Madoc felt when *her* beloved spoke of Rooster.

'He was in the delvings beneath the risen Stone. Today. Again. Angry.'

'What about?'

'Didn't ask! Not for me, all that. He sounded them. Privet . . .'

'My love?' She came closer and held him to her.

'Remembered Glee and Humlock, remembered the days when they were. Whillan should be a delver. Would have been.'

'Teach him then. Tell him now. I'm sure if you—'

'No, no, no. Stone will tell him right way. But – like shadows of trees, Whillan and I.'

'Shadows?'

'One great, one growing. Sun shines, shadows reach. One needs protection of other to grow. Now needs the great one to fall. Me and Whillan are those trees. He's a *delver*, Privet. Where did he come from? Why was he sent?'

He said the word 'delver' as if it were a curse – which to him it was.

'Rooster's afraid for Whillan. Don't want him to suffer my life. But . . .'

'But he suffers already?'

'Sometimes. He doesn't like me. Why should he? I don't like me!'

Rooster did not quite laugh, nor quite cry. Privet felt both emotions in him in the darkness.

'You will delve again one day, my love,' she said sleepily.

'No,' rasped Rooster.

'You promised.'

'Didn't.'

'To make me a home. One day you said you would.'

'Yes,' said Rooster miserably, 'did. But didn't say when.'

'You will one day because . . . because . . .'

Privet slept and Rooster stayed awake, eyes open in the dark, his paws restless.

'. . . because you'll need me to,' he whispered at last before he slept as well, words he only half-knew he said, whose source was a place of wisdom deep in his heart, lost in the silence all moles possess but few have the strength to reach.

Even before the spring thaw came, Privet had sensed that the little group of moles of which she had been the quiet centre was beginning to break up. Certainly Maple and Weeth would not stay with them long once they were clear of the influence of Caradoc, that was agreed. But though the rest would remain with her until they reached Duncton again, she felt an unspoken withdrawal from everymole, including Rooster. It was not a feeling she liked, for she felt she was being disloyal to friends, but increasingly she needed space to explore her deepening sense of the Stone's Silence.

But this feeling of . . . of *removal* – and how exasperated she was that she could not find quite the right word for it – had been building up ever since their journey from Duncton, which now seemed so long ago. It was as if, despite herself, an invisible wall was being created around her through which she could see moles and moledom clearly enough, but from her side of which their world seemed muted and in some ways inconsequential. She was, she felt, in preparation for something, but what she knew not.

The 'removed' world she began to find herself in was not by any means one of peace and tranquillity – a fact which historians of the time know well enough from the record she kept of that winter interlude.* It is less *what* she scribed that revealed the conflicts and doubts – not to say fears – in her mind than *how* she scribed it, for in many places, and especially just before the departure from the Coppice, her normally neat script declines into a disjointed untidy scrawl as if she already sensed the grim nature of the task the Stone was setting her. In places these records even changed to Whernish scrivening as Privet began to wrestle with the philosophical and spiritual problems of Dark Sound.

We can only guess that Rooster's proximity and the sense of love and security he engendered within her gave Privet the courage to turn her snout towards the challenge only she in all of moledom had then seen might come. But we may believe too that like anymole who

* Privet's records are preserved now in the Library of Duncton Wood. They were originally retrieved and edited by Cluniac of Duncton as *The Hobsley Coppice Archive* and form part of the Collected Works of Privet of Crowden. But Bunnicle of Witney's *Privet: Before the Silent Storm* offers a fascinating and now generally accepted interpretation, drawing heavily and most usefully on Cluniac's definitive text.

sees the approach of darkness and is reluctant to face it, she hoped it might 'go away' – and no doubt that hope was fostered by the arrival of spring in mid-March, and the prospect of 'escape' once more into the world outside.

So it was that each of the moles had good if different reasons for welcoming the coming of spring, and entered into a last few days of preparation with excitement. Indeed, such was the busy-ness and jollity among them all that a mole might almost have thought they had just been given their liberty after a period of imprisonment. But perhaps that is the sense that a blue sky and balmy winds, and the hurry and scurry of new life overhead and underpaw puts in all moles when spring comes.

This sense of a new beginning was increased all the more by Maple's decision to delay a day or two longer, just to ensure that winter really was over and they were not caught out in the open along the way by some sudden final freeze-up of the kind so malevolent a winter as they had just lived through might spitefully throw at them.

On the final night they all gathered for the last time in Hobsley's chamber, and talked and talked. It was like the night of their arrival, and each had his say and told his tales. For all of them there was no more impressive memory, nor greater testimonial to how far they had come, than when Rooster talked for what felt a final time about friends he remembered from the days of his training as a Master of the Delve. How relaxed he was, almost expansive, and how well he seemed to have put his past behind him.

'But miss them, miss them much. Mole must learn to do that and not die. Miss Gaunt, my teacher; miss Samphire, my mother; miss Glee and Humlock, my friends. If ever I delve again . . .' And how hushed the moles were when he said those words, how surprised *he* was that they slipped out! '. . . then will delve my love of them into delves for ever. Can never see them again, but can delve their voices and their being; can make them heard by others; can make them remember.'

'I hope you will one day, Rooster,' said Weeth, speaking for all of them, and feeling that their time with Hobsley would have been worthwhile for this unexpected turn alone. 'There's many a mole will be grateful if you do!'

'Won't, not now,' whispered Rooster, 'but glad to think for a moment that I might!'

The next day they said goodbye to Hobsley and his Coppice by the risen Stone at which they had first foregathered. Privet spoke a prayer or two, and tendered her scribings of the molemonths past to Rooster to secrete in the delve chamber below – a task he performed with Whillan's help, both forgetting their differences in the good cheer of the moment. Old Hobsley said his farewells tearfully but confessed readily enough that he was looking forward to a little solitude once more.

'You take care, Hobsley!' said Maple.

'Aye!' echoed the others, feeling, as they embraced him and said their individual farewells, that they were saying goodbye to days and nights of a companionship, and an interlude of peace, which they might well have cause to remember with nostalgia in the difficult months ahead.

They set off in the early afternoon, following Hobsley's clear directions, and intending to travel to the south-east as fast as they could. The journey was tiring but uneventful, a time to adjust themselves to a different pace of life, and to all the exciting sights and sounds of spring. Although the ice and snow had gone days before, except for isolated pockets on higher north-facing slopes, the ground was wet with thaw, and ditches and streams high and noisy with meltwater. Their fears of Newborns were constant and real, but they were forced to be wary too of predators, especially from the sky. For now the white-billed rooks flocked and flew, their raucous cries all about the huge treetops in which they made their nests, their black-eyed gaze greedy and spiteful; but worse were the silent wide-winged flights of tawny owl at dusk, with their hunting stoops at travelling moles, and their shrill and frightening calls at night.

But by the time the party reached Wenlock Vale, and the formidable prospect of ascending the looming Edge beyond it, they had grown used to the hazards of travel once more, and the initial aches and pains of journeying had gone. It was here that their first challenger and contact from mole came when an aggressive male charged out at them as they unwillingly crossed part of his mate's territory. She had, it seemed, recently given birth to young; with apologies, and blessings in the name of the Stone – the Newborn Stone – they passed hurriedly on their way. He stared after them suspiciously, and Maple felt that the sooner they were up and over the Edge and able to separate the better. A party of six moles at such a time was too large to pass without question and comment. Twice more they were challenged in the Vale, and that was twice too many for Maple.

'The sooner we get away from here the happier I will be. None of those moles may have been Newborn guards, nor even practising Newborns, but they'll want to keep any Newborns who visit them sweet. You can be sure that news of our passage through will reach some officious Newborn sooner or later. We've got our fitness back and have taken it easily so far; now we're going to have to push harder. We'll tackle the Edge itself tonight.'

A subdued hush fell over the group, for they had reached the foot of the Edge that afternoon after an uncustomary daytime trek, and as night fell its vast west face seemed to loom higher and steeper above them.

'Better sleep,' growled Rooster behind him, 'better rest.'

Which they all did but for Weeth, who was first watch, close and hidden in a scrape near a deserted two-foot way.

Maple woke them all just before dawn, and they began the climb in earnest as the sky above their heads, reluctantly it seemed, allowed streaks of dull grey to break into its darkness. They trekked upward all day with barely a break, finally collapsing into temporary scrapes at dusk to sleep.

But it was only next day, when the top was reached and they moved out of the trees and on to the gentle east-facing slopes of the Edge that they really began to feel they had left the Newborn threat behind. Naturally there would be danger ahead, but now surely they were beyond the immediate influence of Caer Caradoc, and the time was coming for Maple's and Weeth's departure north for Cannock, while Privet and the others continued eastward towards Duncton Wood by as obscure a route as they could find. Ahead and below them stretched another wide, flat valley along which the River Flade flowed southward. Beyond was a further rise of higher ground in whose undulations and remote valleys they could hope finally to lose themselves.

'Hopefully, we can journey by way of systems untouched by Newborns as we did in the Cotswolds on the way to Caer Caradoc,' said Privet.

'But the Newborn missionaries seeking to spread their creed probably set off for their destinations at the first sight of spring, as we did,' said Maple. 'That's a good reason for Weeth and I to find out what's apaw in Cannock now, before others get there. Then we'll turn back south for the Cotswolds.'

'One day perhaps,' said Privet, looking round them one by one. 'One day we will all be together again in circumstances very different from those we face now.'

There was a sudden brief fading of light across the face of the long wood behind them, and a cold rush of wind through its trees, and Maple said quietly, 'Say a prayer for all of us, Privet, that we may one day return to Duncton Wood safeguarded.'

She nodded, smiling, then, lowering her head in thought she said:

> *'Peace to our going,*
> *Peace to our intent;*
> *Peace to our journeys,*
> *Peace to our paws;*
> *Peace to our arriving,*
> *Peace to those we meet;*
> *Peace to our doing,*
> *Peace to those we face;*
> *Peace to our returning,*
> *Peace to allmole,*
> *To allmole, Peace.'*

Privet gently embraced Weeth, whom she had grown to like and respect, and as he held her he said over her shoulder, 'Guard her well, Rooster, for there's only one Privet.'

'Only one of all of us,' said Rooster, eyes warm.

Great Maple took her in his paws and held her close, so warmly and so tightly she gasped and protested in a pleased kind of way.

'The Stone is with you, Maple,' she whispered, 'and you are ready to lead others now. The day will come when Duncton moles speak of you with pride and pleasure.'

'I hope so!' laughed Maple. 'Be careful and remember that if you face a mole Rooster and Whillan can't handle I'll come to your aid!'

Their farewells were warm and affectionate, but there came the moment of final parting, and then the smiles were a little sad, and the eyes concerned.

'Farewell, Maple!'

'Goodbye, Weeth!'

'And good luck, good luck . . .'

Then Maple and Weeth were gone among the winter-worn grass, off back towards the top of the Edge, to begin their journey north to Cannock, and the start of a campaign whose objective was nothing less than to bring about the fall of Newborn strength and power for all time.

Chapter Three

Rooster was the last to watch after them, and indeed, it was not until they were long gone from sight that he turned back to his friends.

'You look as if you want to go with them!' said Whillan in the jocular yet uneasy manner he often seemed to have with Rooster, as if trying to mollify him in some way. Rarely had two moles found it so difficult to be relaxed with each other; but for once Rooster's response cut through everything to a deeper level.

'Was thinking,' he began, continuing after a moment's pause, '. . . was wondering. What it would be to be Maple. Good. Easy. Honest. Strong. In right place.'

For a brief moment Whillan saw the lost mole in Rooster, a gentle mole whose heart was filled with longing to be at one with himself and life, one who believed that others – at the moment it was Maple, but it might well be any other mole – had attained a state which he had not, and could not. With a pang in his own heart Whillan saw and understood, and felt an unfamiliar surge of warmth, love and sympathy for the strange and mysterious mole his foster-mother loved. That so . . . so *magnificent* a mole (Whillan could think of no better single word to describe him) could feel so worthless! It put his own doubts and fears into perspective and he felt suddenly humble, and relieved.

It was the kind of insight young emerging moles sometimes have when forced by some chance or circumstance to see the world from another's point of view; then they see themselves afresh, and more clearly, and, if only briefly, know themselves for the overly self-absorbed moles they so often are.

'In right place' Rooster had just said, and now Whillan felt he had found the courage and opportunity to try to speak more personally to him. Rooster was still staring after their departed friends, but now his huge front paws and talons were fretting at the grass and soil.

'That's when he feels the delving need,' Whillan said to himself, remembering this from what Privet had said.

'Rooster,' began Whillan tentatively.

Rooster turned to him and Whillan knew it was the right time to speak.

'Rooster, I was thinking, well, wondering—'

'Rooster!' Privet called, cutting across the moment, 'I wanted to talk to you. I . . . oh, I'm sorry, I didn't mean . . .'

Whillan turned from them both, his heart closing again, the moment gone.

'It's all right,' he muttered, and fled, angry for exposing himself. Rooster and he were just not ever going to be able to talk. 'And why should we?' he asked himself wildly; 'why?' He stopped and looked back briefly and caught sight of Privet and Rooster together, companionably as it seemed to him, and he turned away to stare downslope over the great vale across which they must soon travel. Worried, Madoc came over to him, but he ignored her too, to brood and stew and seethe about nothing he could put a paw on, except that it felt like *everything*.

'Stone, get me away from this, all of it. Yes, including Madoc. *All* of them. Get me away!' It was as bitter and desperate a prayer as he had ever made, and only later, when Madoc came close to him and his mood softened, did he pause to think how terrible it would be if the Stone answered such impulsive and negative prayers.

'Stone,' he began, but he could find no words with which to unsay such a prayer, so he just frowned and whispered instead, 'I don't want to be parted from you, Madoc. Never. I don't know why I get so angry.'

'It's past,' said Madoc, 'it's over.'

But she still felt the chill that had struck her heart when Whillan had said, 'I don't want to be parted.' How close she held him that day, as they waited for dusk to fall; how little she wished to yield him up to the world beyond, and the dangers that came from journeying.

But Whillan was wrong to think Privet and Rooster had been stanced 'companionably' when he had looked back at them – 'uneasily' was the better word.

'I want to talk to you,' Privet had said, and how much she had.

'Know,' Rooster had replied, 'and don't want to!'

To talk? Or to know?

'But Rooster, it's time Whillan knew you're his father. Whatmole can tell what lies ahead? We are going to be separated, of that I'm sure.'

'Know!' said Rooster more emphatically, thumping his right paw on the ground. 'Know he wants to talk. Maybe he was about to try.

26

I was trying. You interrupted. You want me to talk? Let me, let him, in our own way. Not interfere. Let go, let go, Privet. Then you will be closer.'

He reared and growled and frowned down on her, and if she had not known him better she might have been afraid. What she *did* feel was surprise and dismay. Surprise that he was ready to talk to Whillan, and say something about being his father; dismay that in her eagerness to see them talking she had prevented their doing so.

'But know there's danger here,' said Rooster suddenly, looking around the rough grassland where they had halted. 'Can't talk to anymole now. Best to rest a short time and then move. Not now, talk. Not now, think. Now we must go.'

'We agreed not to go until dusk.'

'Now,' said Rooster, a little desperately.

'Where to?' asked Privet.

'Not there!' declared Rooster, pointing across the vale they intended to traverse.

'But that's our way.'

'Our way,' muttered Rooster, frowning, 'maybe it is. A mole can't undelve a delving in the stars. That will be. Must be. But danger's there!'

'Rooster, we should talk,' tried Privet once again. There were times when she felt he was a mountain whose top she could never reach. He towered over her now and slowly turned away and when she called his name he took some paces from her.

'We'll go at dusk. Want to be alone.'

She watched as he climbed back upslope a little and snouted at the ground, until finding some tunnel or burrow he had seen before he dug his way down and out of sight.

'To brood, to fret, to continue to be confused,' Privet whispered miserably, turning from where he had gone to see Whillan stanced alone staring down at the view, and Madoc still some way off from him. Privet sighed. 'We're meant to be a party of moles travelling together but suddenly we seem like four individuals who have met by chance, and cannot agree on a common destination,' she said to herself. 'Oh, Stone, why have I grown so tired? Why do I yearn so for your Silence? And why do I feel so afraid? Stone . . . Why have you given me this burden of thought, and worry, and thinking about things that probably don't exist? Like the Book of Silence.'

She repeated 'Book of Silence' without pleasure, remembering how, long ago, when she escaped Crowden and reached Beechenhill, the old librarian Cobbett had suggested that finding the Book of Silence might be her task.

'Some task, Stone!' she muttered wryly. 'How can I ever find it? Where do I look?'

But there was no answer, not in the whispering breeze in the grass about them, nor in the wind that fretted at the branches of the trees in the wood they had passed through. Nor any at all from the distant vale below.

'I want it all to stop,' Privet continued in her thoughts, 'to be at peace, as moles should be. Moledom is so beautiful, so perfect, if moles could but see it. We are but part of something far greater and grander than ourselves, which is of the Stone's making. Why cannot moles see it and stop their rushing, and fighting, and dissatisfactions? Really . . . really Whillan and Rooster are no better than the Newborns in all their anger and confusion. I wish I could just rest! I *am* tired, but I shouldn't be, after all that time over-wintering at Hobsley Coppice: but I am!'

She stayed where she was on the surface for a long time, trying to rid her mind of her worries and doubts and feeling very detached from the three moles travelling with her. She was vaguely aware that on the slopes below Madoc had made a move towards Whillan and the two eventually made up, if that was what young moles did, and found a place below ground to rest until dusk. Then Privet was out on the surface alone, blissfully so, and she watched the progress of the spring day all around and above her as if each tiny gradual change – a cloud moving, a blade of grass quivering, a brief moment of birdsong – was part of a change in her. For a time she found a strange peace. There would be time to tell Rooster and Whillan what they needed to know – what Weeth had told her. Time . . .

It was only in mid-afternoon that she was roused from her waking stupor by the sudden emergence of Rooster from his temporary burrow some way above her. He set off downslope immediately, passing her by without a glance, and only stopping finally a good way below to stare as she had, and as Whillan had before, at the vale below.

His passing by her brought about a complete change of mood in Privet; she felt uneasy, restless, for there was something about his appearance that meant . . . meant *something*. She could not quite decide what. As she puzzled about this she was interrupted by the sudden emergence of Whillan alone from the burrow in which he had been resting with Madoc. Looking for a moment like a startled squirrel as he peered about the surface – Privet could not tell whether he had seen Rooster – he finally fixed his gaze on her and came hurrying up.

'There you are!' he exclaimed irritably, in the voice of one who feels the other has gone missing deliberately. Then more reasonably, 'I felt suddenly uneasy; I hadn't seen you . . . we should have been watching over you . . . I think we should move on.'

As Privet smiled and protested that she could perfectly well watch over herself, Whillan looked up and about as if he scented something in the air.

'What is it, my dear?'

'I . . . don't . . . know,' he whispered, moving round her and upslope towards where Rooster had been below ground, as if following a trail.

'That's where Rooster was . . .' she began. He set off for the place.

'No, Whillan, don't go there!' Now her voice was urgent. 'No . . .'

For she guessed now what Rooster had been doing, and realized why his appearance had seemed odd. His talons had been dirty with soil, his face and his fur dusty and besmirched. He had been delving! *He had been delving.* Though Stone knew at what.

'Whillan, you mustn't go down there!' she cried out, running upslope after him and trying to restrain him from venturing down where Rooster had been. But it was too late, Whillan was already on the way down, and despite her protests, continued until he was out of sight.

Why she was so fearful of his finding what Rooster had done she did not know, but she dithered in a state of dismay and trepidation, looking first downslope towards where Rooster stanced so still, then at the entrance nearby, and then down towards Rooster again.

Slowly, inevitably, he turned to look upslope at her, rising in alarm when he saw where she was and guessed what she was about before roaring out a terrible 'No!' Though he was a good way off, his shout was violent enough to shake a mole to his paws, loud enough too to bring Madoc up from where she was hidden. Then Rooster was charging back upslope. Privet, uncertain for a moment what to do, turned impulsively to the tunnel entrance and darted down to find Whillan.

'Mustn't go there!' roared Rooster. 'Nomole must!'

Privet supposed she had to warn Whillan that Rooster was coming, and the sound of her paws pattered urgently ahead of her.

'Whillan!' she called, or tried to. But the echo softened her voice into a caress of diminishing sound, as time seemed to slow; her sense of urgency left her as she continued along the tunnel towards a huge portal from which light seemed to shine, and shadows play. She passed through it into a chamber in which Whillan was stanced, peacefully gazing round the walls. The floor itself was covered in loose soil and stones, and in one corner of the chamber, the darkest place, a bigger pile of debris lay.

'I could hear you calling, and Rooster, and all the sounds of day,' whispered Whillan, awe in his voice at the sight of the extraordinary delvings on the walls. 'I can hear him coming now. He made it, didn't he?'

'Yes, this is Rooster's delving,' said Privet, her voice hushed as she stared about.

These were no ordinary delvings of the traditional sort, and nor were they the angry, jagged creations such as a mole like Rooster might be expected to make. They were deep and gentle, like dappling light through summer trees, and they seemed to shine and shimmer. The sound they made was soft and whispering, and distantly familiar, like a long-forgotten scent of someone dear, or the fragment of a song or tale caught on the wind.

'Sound the delving!' said Privet suddenly, quite carried away by the beauty that encircled them.

'I have already! I will again. Listen . . .' Whillan moved to one side, reached out a paw and touched the wall low down where the line of a sinuous soft delve seemed to emerge from the rough soil.

'It's a mole,' said Whillan, 'it's a mole I feel I know . . .' and he sounded the delving, now here, now there, and Privet heard the mewings of a pup, and the whisperings of mother-love, and the dark sounds of menace kept at bay from a growing mole, much loved and well-guarded – and by more than a mother. Nomole can be reared without threat and danger – nor should they be, for the experience of fear and the exploration of doubt expand a mole's perception of himself towards the reality of his life's path, which will be, *must* be, through light and dark, and dark and light.

So in this extraordinary delving around the chamber's walls Rooster had hinted at darkness along the way of the young mole whose life he seemed to have created, and Privet was amazed. There were the stumbling joys of first steps taken, and first food found, and the gambolling delights of early explorations beyond the encirclement of a mother's body, beyond the birth chamber, beyond the first tunnel to the next and beyond all that to the surface . . . of a wood. Oh yes, the wood was there, sighing above, whispering below, and bit by bit the mole advanced with the months and early years of growth as far and no further as the dark and looming shadows that lurk in wait beyond mother, beyond the birth chamber, beyond on the surface above, and then beyond the furthest tree.

Now Whillan was near the end of his sounding, and nearing the darkest corner of the chamber where the debris lay. Still the young mole journeyed on in Rooster's imagining and the shadows were more complex and the light brighter in places, fragmented in others; while beyond, in the darkest place – undelved as yet – was the full menace of the world, now looming up, now falling back to voids of fearful darkness.

'No! No!' cried out Privet, sensing the young mole nearing a place from which Rooster's delvings could not save him. For the delving was unfinished there.

'Listen, listen!' cried out Whillan in reply, for all the delving made *him* see was the light, broken and wonderful, a light alluring which nomole would deny; a light before which even the deepest void seems surmountable.

Then from out of the deep came the thunderous running of a mole, louder and greater and more formidable the nearer it came. So that as Whillan's paw reached the last of the delvings the mole erupted from the void their journey had reached.

'No!' roared Rooster. 'Not here, not see, not sound this delving never, never make it be. Must not make it be.'

It was a cry of despair, the plea of one who is afraid for another he loves, the warning of one who knows he cannot help.

'No!' said Rooster, putting his great paw out to stop Whillan sounding, but too late, too late – all was done. That young mole was gone out into the void, and he was calling for help that could not seem to reach him.

'No,' shouted Rooster again, his face contorting into a pathetic self-loathing as he stared at his paws and talons as if to accuse them, and so himself, for what he had created. Then he raised his great paws and did what Privet had once seen him do all those long years ago at Hilbert's Top: he began to destroy the delving he had just made.

Never in the time he had known Rooster had Whillan ever confronted him directly, despite all the anger and annoyance he engendered. But now, Privet saw, a confrontation was in the making, for Whillan was plainly outraged by Rooster's actions.

'You cannot destroy it!' he shouted – or rather roared, for Whillan seemed to be overtaken by a spirit more powerful than his youthful self. This was rage, and unequal though he might be to stopping so

31

large and unpredictable a mole as Rooster from doing what he wished it looked as if he intended to have a good try. He rushed over to him and pushed between the flailing paws and the wall they were destroying. Rooster hurled him to one side and continued to rip at the delving, bringing down showers of dust and soil. To Privet, who was on the far side of the chamber, it seemed that the struggle between the two – for no sooner had Whillan recovered himself than he sprang back, only to be hurled aside once more – was conducted in a storm of dust, or the haze of fog: vaguely, and in a seeming slow-motion. All the time Whillan raged, and Rooster roared.

Privet did try to intervene at last, but both turned on her, forgetting their dispute for an instant, and shoved her away again, their eyes seeming to see her not as Privet but rather as a puny irritation that had stumbled across their mutual wish to struggle with each other.

All this time, to add to the confusion, the delving sounded out the dying cries of the mole whose life Rooster had created, and who now retreated, as Whillan did, before Rooster's onslaught, until the cries faded into the terrible darkness of the void. Bruised and battered by Rooster's buffets, Whillan did not respond with violence, but only stayed his ground as best he could as Rooster beat him back, until he was cornered in the darkest place, and the young mole's cries faded far behind him into darkness. Rooster, with nothing left to destroy of what he had made, could only stance up hugely, and stay his taloned paws before they struck down on Whillan's body.

'No more!' And there was command in Whillan's voice, and a sense of right. 'You cannot destroy the delvings—'

'Made them. Can destroy them. No good, no more,' cried out Rooster. '*Have* destroyed them.'

'The delving was beautiful,' said Whillan quietly, 'the most beautiful thing I ever saw, or touched. You had no *right*.'

'Made it,' whispered Rooster brokenly.

'Yes, you made it. And you destroyed it. A delving is a thing for ever, or until the Stone decides its day is done. A delving is like kin. Does a father have the right to kill his son?'

'Father? Son?' repeated Rooster wildly, much distressed. He turned to Privet and looked at her with terrible appeal.

Whillan had fallen silent before his own words and all that could be heard was the panting of his breath as he stared at Rooster, mole to mole.

'Anyway,' muttered Rooster, suddenly contrite and reaching out his paws as if to embrace Whillan in the gentlest of ways, 'delvings not all destroyed. That was only the beginning. Mole left home. Moles always do. Listen, Whillan, there's silence after the void of journeying. Didn't mean to hurt nothing and nomole, never ever. Didn't know what to say. Don't know now . . .'

'No!' cried out Whillan as Rooster drew him closer. 'Never . . .' and he suddenly pushed past Rooster from the dark void he had reached, and past Privet, and ran from the chamber down the tunnel to the surface as if from his worst enemy. The sound of his paws receded from them as if to a place from which they could never return.

'Know what mole he is,' said Rooster. '*You* know,' he added savagely, looking at Privet.

'I know what Weeth *suggested*,' said Privet judiciously.

'*Know*,' said Rooster. 'Know it now. Certain now. Not just son in body. In spirit too.'

The chamber hummed with the dark sounds of loss and uncertainty. And suddenly overhead there was the patter of many paws.

'Rooster!' gasped Privet. 'There are other moles about.'

'Yes,' growled Rooster, 'they have been coming all my life. Found me now.'

'Rooster . . .'

But there was the sudden running of paws at the entrance, and another mole than Whillan came down.

'Yes,' said Rooster, whose delving had been his way of working out the truth he sensed – that he had discovered his son when it was too late to help him as he entered adulthood. Too late.

The rush of paws approached the chamber.

'It's Madoc, know her sound,' said Rooster, moving to Privet's flank.

Madoc came into the chamber, blood on her flank and her eyes full of fear and distress.

'The Newborns have come,' she said urgently. 'They've got Whillan, and have sent me here to get you.'

'Newborns?' said Privet faintly.

'How many?' said Rooster grimly.

'Too many,' replied Madoc. 'You must come now or they say they'll kill Whillan.'

'We'll come,' said Rooster quietly, 'now we're ready to come. End is beginning now.' His voice was soft with the relief of it. 'End is here so we can live again.'

Chapter Four

The ugly shouts that met Rooster as he emerged from the tunnel with Privet and Madoc up on the east side of Wenlock Edge were accusatory, and very menacing, and the scene was altogether grim. More than ten moles surrounded them, mostly young and powerful, with paws jabbing, and faces sneering and triumphant.

'It's him! It *is* him! By the righteous Stone, it is the miscreant Rooster!' they cried.

More moles were gathered some way off downslope with Whillan prostrate on the ground between them, bloodied and still.

'Don't even try,' said an older guardmole with weary authority, as Rooster tried to go to Whillan's aid, 'don't even think about it.'

Rooster struggled for a moment or two, and more so when one of the moles grabbed Privet and another Madoc – but all were quickly overpowered.

'Very wise, Brother Rooster, very sensible,' said a thin, unpleasant mole, who seemed in command.

He turned to another behind him and said with evident satisfaction, 'So you were right; it is the mole we have been searching for in the holy name of Elder Senior Brother Quail and at the command of the Convocation of Caer Caradoc.'

'I *thought* it was, Brother Adviser Fagg,' replied the other in a smug and unctuous voice. 'When I saw the party pass over our system four days ago, I said, "*They*'re fugitives *they* are and that great ugly one looks like Rooster, the one the worthy brothers have been looking for . . ."'

'Yes, yes, Brother, you have done well – your name and that of your system will be commended to the Elder Brothers,' said the 'Brother Adviser', a title which Privet and the others had not heard before. 'But you said you observed six moles in the party and so far I see only four. You others, search the tunnel below.'

Three guardmoles were about to do Fagg's bidding, though with some reluctance it seemed, when a forceful-looking mole detached himself from those surrounding Whillan and said, 'A moment, if you will!'

The guardmoles stopped obediently, and Fagg looked annoyed.

'I really think, Brother Commander Thorne—'

'I really think, Brother Adviser Fagg, that we should not waste effort or risk lives unnecessarily. I am happy to leave matters spiritual to yourself, but kindly leave matters military to me. Searching burrows that may contain enemies is not always as easy or safe as it looks . . .'

Thorne nodded to two quite different guardmoles, older than the ones Fagg had deputed for the task. 'There are tricks and traps for the unwary,' he said dispassionately. 'From what *this* mole says, or does not say, I doubt that there are moles below, but it pays to be careful.'

A respectful hush had fallen over all the moles. Brother Commander Thorne knew how to impose his authority, and Fagg, as was clear from the narrowing of his eyes and the petulance of his mouth, did not like it.

Everymole waited while the search was made. Eventually the two guardmoles re-emerged. 'Nothing, sir, nothing at all.'

'Humph!' said Thorne, signalling for Whillan to be brought to him. When he came the others saw there was something angry and determined in his eyes which suggested he might not be quite so badly hurt as at first it seemed.

When the Brother Commander said quietly, 'Well, Brother, it seems you were telling the truth,' Whillan obliged with an impressive lie.

'As I tried to tell you, they left us two days ago,' he whispered falteringly, 'to head for their home system.'

'Which is?'

'Munslow,' he replied promptly, naming a system Hobsley had mentioned which lay to the south.

'Their names?'

'Lakin and Cripps,' he said, almost too quietly.

'Lakin and who? – And don't *you* reply!' roared Thorne, pointing his paw at Whillan but addressing his question to Madoc.

His eyes glinted darkly and it was plain he was not entirely convinced by Whillan's willingness to talk. But had Madoc heard the name Whillan had made up clearly enough to maintain the lie?

'Well, Sister, share the name of your other former travelling companion with us.'

35

'Why should I?' said Madoc stoutly, seemingly playing for time. 'I won't.'

'Oh, you will!' said the Brother Commander grimly. He nodded at the moles holding Whillan, one of whom raised his talons and set them but a thrust away from Whillan's eyes.

'No!' cried Whillan pitiably as Rooster roared and struggled, and Privet simply stared in horror.

'Well now, I think you had better tell us, or we will assume your friend here was making up the names and trying to be clever.'

'He's not my friend!' shouted Madoc dramatically. 'But Cripps was . . . oh . . . I loved him!' It sounded frantic and hysterical, but as Madoc began to weep, apparently for revealing her beloved's name, the Brother Commander broke into a roar of laughter.

'Well, well, Brother Whillan, it seems you told the truth after all.' The raised talons were lowered and the look of relief on Whillan's face was genuine. 'We will send word for guards to catch up with your friends in due course – there is a Crusade apaw across moledom now from which no follower will escape, nor any blasphemer go unpunished. But, Sister . . .' he turned suddenly on Madoc again, '. . . why did *you* not go with the mole you say you loved?'

'He does not love me,' wailed Madoc.

Thorne seemed convinced, and switched his attention to Rooster, whom he contemplated for a time. Madoc moved closer to Privet, while Whillan was allowed to stance down and attend to his wounds. They had won some kind of victory in protecting Maple and Weeth, but it was obvious that their position was serious, and possibly fatal, with Rooster's surely the worst of all. Perhaps in those moments of silence all of them were wondering what other untruths they might get away with, and if there was any point in trying. But the same thought seemed to have occurred to the Brother Commander.

'Now we have established that you are all our prisoners, and that we wish you to tell us the truth, I had better say that I do not want to waste further time trying to tease information out of you. The moles Lakin and Cripps may be so named, and may have parted from you two days ago – or they may not. I am inclined to believe you. But it is not of great consequence in the light of the capture of Rooster – a mole who has led the Caradocian Order a pretty dance and whom Elder Senior Brother Quail will be well pleased to have secure again.'

Thorne said this with respect in his voice – and the manner in which he looked at Rooster was serious but not unpleasant. Indeed, in other circumstances he might almost have seemed a reasonable mole, an impression strengthened by the way he turned to Whillan and said, 'I personally have no wish to harm you, or punish you – I leave that to the brethren of the Stone whose task it is.'

He looked at Fagg and the three moles nearest him with some distaste, and Privet and the others concluded from the smooth and glossy appearance of these three, and the familiar cold look in their eyes, that these were guardmoles on the religious side, while the others were military moles under the leadership of Thorne.

'However, the fact that we find you in company with one so notorious as Rooster bodes ill for all of you, I fear – but again that is not my concern. Indeed my only interest until yesterday was getting to Cannock and assuming command of the defences there – but acting on information received we heard of your passage up to the Edge and diverted our own journey in pursuit. Enough of explanations . . . my name is Brother Commander Thorne. Whatmoles are *you*, and whither are you bound?'

It was Privet who answered. 'You won't have any need to detain the two youngsters,' she said.

'I'll be the judge of that,' said Thorne, again not unpleasantly. It seemed that he expected them to try to protect each other.

'Well, anyway . . . my name is Privet and I was delegate to the Convocation and claim its protection for myself and those with me.'

'And whither were you bound?'

'*Are* we bound,' said Privet sharply. 'To Duncton Wood.'

'Ah! Privet of Duncton Wood, and in the company of Rooster!' declared Fagg with evident satisfaction. 'Sister Privet's reputation precedes her. A Whernish scholar, corrupted by her ancestry and studies. A mole reared to sin and lusts, and concubine to Rooster. Yes, a most useful catch, Brother Commander, and one that will enhance all our reputations. This is a matter for the Elder Senior Brother himself.'

'And you other two?' said Thorne quietly, looking as if he doubted Privet had been – or was ever likely to be – anymole's concubine.

'Whillan of Duncton!' growled Whillan.

'Madoc of Gwynanst,' said Madoc.

'Brother Adviser Fagg, we had better talk of this privately,' said Thorne.

The two Newborns drew to one side and had an animated and not entirely amicable discussion about what to do with their captives. At first the Duncton moles could not understand why such an authoritative mole as Thorne should even listen to one like Fagg, let alone be swayed by him – and for a time it seemed he would not be: as the argument grew more serious Thorne's voice became deeper and more resolute, and Fagg's became thinner and more annoyed. But finally, when he began to refer to 'the Elder Council shall hear of it if you do not . . .' and 'Elder Brother Quail *expressly* asked allmole to watch out for the mole Rooster and would not be pleased if . . .', Thorne fell silent and attentive. At last the discussion ended, and Thorne approached them.

'I am persuaded that it will be in all our interests for us to make quite sure that we deliver you into the paws of the Elder Council alive, in one piece, and complete. The Brother Adviser here, who is the spiritual mentor deputed to travel with my command, has clear authority in this matter and he is naturally concerned that since the mole Rooster escaped so dramatically from the Convocation he might try to do so again. He feels in need of support if he is to get you moles back into custody. So be it. My guardmoles will do their duty, and so will I. But I am reluctant to take you all the way to Caer Caradoc and have therefore agreed to see you safely to Wildenhope where you may be easily held until instructions are received as to what to do with you.' As he spoke the name 'Wildenhope' a curious unease showed on the faces of his subordinates, which was in contrast to the pleasure on Fagg's; judging from the horrified expression on Madoc's face, all this reflected something of the reputation of the place.

Thorne ignored the reaction and continued: 'It will make all our lives easier if you do *not* try to escape or anything of that kind – and I hope I make myself quite clear when I say that if you do then my guards will take extreme measures to stop you. In this I will be acting within my powers as Brother Commander – even though my good friend and Brother Adviser would prefer it if you all reached Wildenhope alive.'

Here he smiled wickedly and some of his guards grinned at the discomfiture of Fagg and his two colleagues. Clearly there was no love lost between the military and religious wings of Newborn authority.

'To discourage you from thoughts of escape I shall instruct my guards to split into four groups, each of which will be assigned to one of you. You will travel apart from each other and be given no opportunity for conferring. If one of you even tries to escape the other three will suffer punishment. I hope I make myself quite clear – I have no wish at all for any unpleasantness, and nor do I want any delay. While you are in my paws you will be well cared for and treated with respect. I have no doubt that if when I pass you over at Wildenhope, I can report you have behaved well, it will be taken into favourable consideration.'

He smiled briefly, every part of him the image of a confident and fair-minded mole, and turned to organize the guardmoles. In the few moments they had left together Privet whispered to Rooster, 'My dear, we must believe that the Stone's will is in all this, though how or why I cannot say or begin to guess. But we must try to tell Whillan what we know or suspect of his birth. That at least he must learn.'

'"No conferring," the Brother Commander said, and he meant it!' barked one of the guards.

'Am here, always!' cried out Rooster as Privet was led away from him. Then to Whillan and Madoc he cried out, 'Always! There is light beyond the void; Rooster knows!'

Was it true? *Could* it be true? Or was it the forlorn hope of a mole who had once been given a great task, perhaps the greatest, but had failed to live up to it? With final despairing looks and words of encouragement the four moles were taken off separately by their guards – the smallest groups of two apiece for Privet and Madoc, while Whillan had four guards and Rooster was accorded the dubious honour of no fewer than seven moles to watch over him. But then, whatmole could even think of trying to escape if it meant punishment for all the others?

Now the clear spring sky of late afternoon, and the fine view across the vale to the east where they should have been travelling, seemed to taunt them all, and leave them to dwell upon, or avoid, as their temperament dictated, what might have been.

What Rooster's thoughts were beyond the bleak offer of hope implicit in 'there is light beyond the void' was anymole's guess. As they were led off southwards he travelled with head low, his great paws thumping the ground and crackling the husks of winter-dead plants beneath them, ignoring his guards altogether.

Some way behind him went Madoc, to whom the spring had brought health and comely beauty, which might have been why Thorne had assigned two older, grizzled-looking guards to her, lest younger ones be tempted by the attractions of their charge. Her eyes were brave but bleak, and if she looked behind her occasionally and saw Whillan, they betrayed no recognition. Perhaps her pretence of loving another – the fictional Cripps – now meant that she could not acknowledge the mole who might have given most comfort, and whom she wished to console.

Of them all, Whillan was having the most obvious difficulty. The battering he had received earlier to make him reveal if other moles were about meant that he now limped, and since one of his eyes was badly swollen he was forced to tilt his head awkwardly to see the path ahead more clearly.

A long way behind them came Privet, the only one able to see all the others, and with an aching heart she discerned Whillan's difficulties, guessed the turmoil in Madoc's thoughts, and imagined the dark confusions that must now have returned to Rooster's mind. And yet . . .

And yet those last words of his, 'Rooster knows!'

'Oh my love,' Privet whispered to herself as they went along, 'you have journeyed further than any of us into the darkness which most moles avoid, which lies beyond the shadows of their mind. Where fear and confusions meet, there you have been; and where each step a mole takes heads him further from the safety of his own self. And now . . . Whillan, your son, caught as you have been. Perhaps because of you.'

How hard Privet had tried to make Rooster talk; but he understood things best in the inarticulate deeps of his great heart, and expressed himself not through words but through the delving arts he had so long eschewed.

Until now, that is, down there in that scrape of a chamber where he had made a thing of beauty and compassion beyond words – a delving which he had not intended anymole ever to see. A delving which miraculously created life, out of what he had learned of Whillan's past through the winter years in Hobsley Coppice. It is one thing, Privet mused, to scribe down facts that have been gathered and ideas learned, and a history surmised, but quite another to make a delving that could sound out another's life, and predict the darkness that lay ahead.

She remembered again what she knew of Whillan's terrible beginnings in the cross-under beneath the roaring owl way to the south-east of Duncton Wood. *Had* she ever talked of that to Rooster? She did not think so. Could Whillan have done? The two moles got on so badly that she doubted it, even if Whillan knew much himself. Why, the Master Stour, who was the only mole present around the time of Whillan's birth, never said anything more about it, as far as *she* knew. Yet there in the delving was all of it . . . the desperate last flight to Duncton of Whillan's mother, Lime, the fatal attack by rooks, and the birth into death of all the litter but for Whillan himself: all had been there, all somehow felt and resurrected into a tragic beauty by Rooster.

40

'Oh Stone, protect him, guide him, let him live, for in his talons, and by his suffering for others, he strives to do your work!' she prayed, passionate and vehement in her faith that the Stone would not allow Rooster's life to be taken. If her prayer was answered, all this they were going through might have meaning and purpose.

Night came upon them swiftly and by the time Thorne had brought the different groups to a halt, and settled them into places where they could rest securely, dark clouds were looming in the sky and the air was growing oppressive with an approaching storm.

Privet's two guards treated her with firm courtesy, finding her food, and settling her into a tussock of grassy undergrowth with the words 'It is going to rain – you'll keep dry here, miss!' One or other of them watched her at all times and from their discipline and the respectful way they spoke of Thorne it was obvious that they were well trained – and well led.

'It would be nice just to talk to my companions,' said Privet, trying to look as peaceable as possible.

'No way, I'm afraid,' said one of the guards, 'it would be more than our lives are worth!'

'You seem a little afraid of Brother Commander Thorne.'

'You could say that,' said one of the guards, 'but there's not another I'd want to serve under. He's—'

'What is he, Brother?' said a thin voice from out of the still darkness. It was Fagg, eyes sharp.

'Strict, sir, he's very strict.'

'I'm glad to hear it,' said Fagg without warmth. 'Discipline does nomole harm! But I would not advise you to fraternize with this mole. She is not as harmless as she seems.'

'Only a female, sir.'

Fagg's face curled into a chilling sneer. 'And past her best if you know what I mean!' He laughed in the way moles do when they feel it necessary to put others down. 'Watch over her well!' he ordered as he left.

When he had gone one of the guardmoles said, 'Yes, well. Sorry about that, miss.' He sounded embarrassed.

'These religious Brothers,' said Privet quietly, 'all seem a little afraid of females.'

'They would be, wouldn't they?' the guardmole observed judiciously. 'They're not used to females. Not brought up with them. Not healthy, if you ask me.'

'And you were?'

41

'I'm old enough to have been, yes. The Elder Senior Brother never meant for males to be alienated from females for life.'

'You mean Thripp when you say—'

'There'll only ever be one Elder Senior Brother to me, just him,' he replied with quiet passion.

'And me,' said the other. 'It goes for all us who serve under Thorne. Why, Thorne himself owes his position to Thripp of Blagrove Slide!'

'How come?' asked Privet, glad and surprised the guards were so willing to talk.

'Spotted his talents. Saw he was interested in strategy and leadership, not religious matters. Some are born to worship the Stone with deeds, some with words. Thripp said that, and he didn't mean by it any criticism of those who are into words, like the brothers.'

'What did he mean?'

'He meant there's more ways than one of touching the Stone's Silence. No one way's exclusively right.'

'So why are Stone followers like me to be persecuted then?'

'Ah well, you've got me there, miss. I mean, I believe the Newborn way is right and that orders have got to be followed. That's what *we* do. But fairly, and we only get rough if we have to.'

'True Stone followers would say that there's no need *ever* to "get rough", as you put it.'

'They might say that, but they would be wrong and no disrespect meant. Before the Elder Senior Brother gave his teachings and proper leadership, moledom was in a right mess.'

'Was it? Not in Duncton Wood it wasn't.'

'That's not what I've heard, again begging your pardon. He said that the lessons learnt in the War of Word and Stone in our grandparents' time were being forgotten.'

'And what lessons were those?'

'Tolerance, respect, making time for the Stone, family and kin, keeping a clean snout – that kind of thing.'

'And Thripp taught that?'

'I only heard him once, more's the pity. When he spoke, you listened. He could make rocks weep and flowers open before their time!'

Privet laughed.

'Oh, I'm serious,' said the guard, mildly offended.

'It's not you I'm laughing at!' said Privet. 'It's just that I never expected such things from a Newborn guard holding me as a prisoner and taking me to Wildenhope to be judged by Quail.'

42

'Quail's a different mole altogether from Thripp,' said the guard darkly. 'Why do you think the Brother Commander's so eager to get away to Cannock? Mind you, it's obscurity for him, more's the pity.'

'Obscurity?'

'Well, I shouldn't say it, but Thorne's the best we've got. You can feed the commanders Quail favours to the roaring owls as far as I'm concerned. What mole was it neutralized Siabod? Thorne. Whatmole was it avoided real conflict with Rooster and that not so long? Thorne. What mole kept the peace when Quail's lot wanted violence? Thorne! But since Quail's taken control things have changed. I reckon he would eliminate Thorne if he dared, but he's done the next best thing and sent him north to obscurity.'

The guardmole fell silent, taken aback it seemed by his sudden outburst, and peered quizzically at Privet.

'Humph! You make a mole talk, you do! I can see what Fagg meant – you're a dangerous mole.'

There was a long rumble of distant thunder.

'Here it comes!'

And shortly afterwards the rain did come, heavily and with driving winds so that the two guardmoles squeezed in with Privet for shelter. She had felt strangely comforted by their conversation, and humbled too – some of the Newborns at least were decent moles after all, and their words confirmed the impression of Thripp she had formed at Caer Caradoc: he was not by any means all bad, and nor did she believe he was all finished either. Now each of them must seek to fulfil their task, once they had found out what it was.

'What is my task, Stone?' she wondered.

The storm seemed to circle about them through the night, but the only lightning she saw was distant, and diffused by cloud.

'I know what my task is,' she admitted to herself in the darkness, and she was afraid, terribly afraid, for it was one nomole would help her with, not even Rooster. Her fear completely overrode the apprehension she felt about what was to happen to them at Wildenhope, however terrible it might be. She felt comforted by the warmth of the guardmoles' flanks on either side of her and sometime between a distant flash of lightning and the dark sound of thunder, she drifted into sleep.

When dawn came, and all the moles were instructed to move off once more, the storm had passed by, but the rain still fell. It was persistent, though not heavy, and it came out of the low grey base of clouds swirling only a little way above the trees of the wood that ran the length of the top of the Edge. The ground was now wet and slippery, and as the day wore on the moles followed one another in silence, tired and depressed, the way ahead seeming interminable.

In the afternoon they turned upslope through a gap in the wood, whose trees dripped dankly on either side of them as the route ran gradually to the crest of the Edge itself. As they neared it their ears were assailed by a roaring sound which they took to be wind driving up the escarpment's face from the west and stirring the trees. Certainly a fresh breeze blew and nagged at their wet fur; it chilled them, and kept them wanting to move.

But the roaring was more than wind: it was the rush of water. Despite the lowering, murky sky the view down to the vale below was clear enough, if grey, and they saw that the river they had crossed much further upstream before ascending the Edge with Maple and Whillan was now white, and full, and angry. In several places along its course temporary streams of flood-water, yellow-white, flowed down into it, swelling it; as they picked their way along the slippery path and could see it more clearly they saw that it grew angrier and more dangerous the further downstream they looked.

One of Privet's guards stopped momentarily and pointed a talon downvale into the distance, where the river's torrential flow was lost in rain and what seemed swirling mist in the middle of flat meadow- land on the far side of which the landscape rose into wet haze. Some- times the mist shifted and the dark and lowering line of an ancient river terrace could be seen downstream on the far side of the vale.

'Wildenhope,' muttered the guard; 'Stone help us all!'

Chapter Five

It was April and Hamble had reached the last stage of his long journey from Caer Caradoc. But the mole he was with was reluctant for him to leave . . . 'So you're going to Duncton Wood, Hamble? Well, yes, you'll not mistake it when you see it! Half a day's journey and you'll be in sight of it, and as near the place as you'll ever wish to be. It rises dark these days, on the far side of a roaring owl way nomole in his right mind would try to cross. What rose glorious in the morning sun when I was a pup is now enshadowed by moles who are not likely to be removed in my lifetime. No, no, it's not a place to visit. But you'll not be the first mole who felt the need to at least go to just look at it, to remind themselves of the great things we have lost and will never find again. Oh, but I shall miss you, mole . . .'

Hamble listened to the old mole patiently, though he was anxious now to get away and make the final trek to the system he had travelled so long to reach. The time had come to end the journey begun when Privet had sent him away from Caer Caradoc, which had become, he found to his surprise, a kind of personal pilgrimage. How little he had known himself in the days he was with Rooster. How much he had discovered since; how much more there was to find out.

His friend's name was Purvey, and Hamble had found him living alone and frightened among the ruined tunnels of Cuddesdon, to the east of Duncton Wood, a place of prayer and scholarship founded a century before in the glorious days when the followers had defeated the forces of the Word, and made Duncton a centre of reverence and freedom once more.

Instinct had driven Hamble to Cuddesdon after he left Rollright in early spring, and curiosity too. The instinct he no longer tried to fathom or understand, but followed with an easy and wry good humour.

The curiosity arose because a mole – a Newborn indeed – he met along the way mentioned 'ruined Cuddesdon', revealing that 'Newborns do not bother to occupy it now, it being wormless and somewhat off the beaten track and quite inconsequential'. But Hamble remembered Privet mentioning it to him when they had talked at Caradoc, and the journeymole Chater had told him a little of Cuddesdon and his last visit there before he had died.

Why, Chater had nearly been killed by the Newborns who had taken it over, and it was said not one of the quiet and ageing scribemoles who lived in a brotherly community had survived. So when Hamble realized he was near it, and knowing he did not yet feel quite ready for the dangers of entry into Duncton Wood, he had made his way to Cuddesdon and climbed its desolate slopes to see the place for himself.

There he had found the mole Purvey, who had survived the Newborn massacre by virtue of being away from Cuddesdon for a few days in a nearby system. He had had the terrible experience of coming back, discovering the mutilated bodies of moles he knew and loved, and then being forced to retreat when he realized that Cuddesdon was occupied. Whatmole knew the terrors he suffered in the moleyears that followed? Like a forlorn pup without a home, he had lurked about the streams and banks of the vales below Cuddesdon, unable to go to the only place he knew, yet without another sanctuary.

Then, that spring, when the Crusades had begun again, Purvey had seen the Newborn Brothers leave in haste; he ascended the slopes of Cuddesdon, and ventured timidly into tunnels that had once echoed to the soft pawfalls and gentle chants of the brothers who had raised him, and taught him all he knew. There, skulking still, fearful of the Newborns' return yet unwilling to leave the place again, he had lived alone through the spring years, the sun, the high song of the larks, the budding of dog's mercury and the flowering of yellow celandine all beauties he could not enjoy.

But he had prayed for the Stone's help, as reverent followers will, for comfort, for strength through his time of trial, and for deliverance, and to occupy himself he had collected what fragments of texts and books the marauding Newborns had left behind. He sealed them up in the deep chambers where over the years the Cuddesdon brothers had hidden away the few texts and folios that told their short history, or which various of their members had been inspired to scribe, along with a few copies of texts that had been donated to them by Master Librarian Stour of Duncton Wood. As the libraries of moledom go this was modest indeed, but it was all Purvey had to guard, to protect, and to give him reason to go on living, and hoping, and praying.

Then one April day he thought the end had come. Up the slopes came a mole fiercer-looking by far than any Newborn he had yet seen:

46

scarred, tired, frowning with the effort of the climb and looking keenly about, as if for a fight.

Purvey had hidden away from him, retreating as the mole expertly quartered the sorry tunnels, snouting about and finding, no doubt, signs of Purvey's habitation. The old mole had contemplated fleeing, but surveying the vales below, in which he had earlier spent so long hiding, he could not bring himself to do so. This was his home, and here he would stay whatever the consequences. And in any case, was he not guardian of the Cuddesdon texts? Should he not therefore be prepared to stance ready by them, and defend them as best he could, however powerful the mole he faced? So Purvey had turned back from flight, and crept to that secret place where the texts lay hidden; there he waited, shaking with fear, praying, yet determined to do what he could.

There it was Hamble found him, as sorry and fearful a mole as any he had ever seen, a mole he could have cast aside with one paw had he wished.

'Mole,' growled Hamble, 'be not afraid of me. I know not whatmole you are, but whether you're a Newborn hiding from the rigours of the Crusades, or a follower trying to live them out without getting caught up in them, I'm not going to harm you.'

'Not harm me?' Purvey had repeated doubtfully. 'Not try to destroy the texts, not—'

'What texts?' asked Hamble, not unreasonably, though texts had been the very last thing on his mind. Food, more like; sleep; and calming down this frightened mole.

'I didn't mean to mention them!' said the mole, now even more agitated. 'I mean to say, I didn't mention them. There aren't any. You're not going to harm me, you say! Hmmph! You don't look very friendly to me.'

Hamble laughed and said, 'Mole, I'm tired and hungry and in no mood to try and persuade another I mean no harm. You'll just have to find out for yourself, won't you?' He thought for a moment that he might ask more about the texts which, plain as a hawthorn in blossom, lay beyond the badly sealed portal behind the mole. Not much of a guard, but a brave mole for trying!

'Well then,' muttered the mole, squeezing uneasily past Hamble and leading him up towards the surface, 'I'll find you some food. I expect you've a long way to go and won't be staying long.'

'Nice to feel wanted,' said Hamble, following him. 'Nice to feel welcome. I might just settle down here . . .'

His guide looked back at him, eyes wide, unsure whether he was serious or not. Then he led him back across Cuddesdon's rutted surface, down through tunnels and then into a chamber that despite the holes in its roof, and the collapsed portions of its walls, looked as if it had once been serviceably delved.

'It's all too much for me to repair, but it's dry enough, if you know where to avoid the rain. Now, it's food you want, isn't it?'

Hamble ate the worms the mole found in silence, frowning, aware that his every move was being watched nervously.

'So this is Cuddesdon?' he said at last. 'It seems deserted but for you.'

The two moles looked at each other.

'Relax,' said Hamble, 'I'm a follower and whatever you may—'

'Well, I'm not Newborn, that's certain,' said Purvey with some asperity. 'I hate them! But I am frightened of them too. My name's Purvey. Lived here before the massacre. Came back after it. Have lived alone since.'

He spoke in short bursts, telling as sorry yet typical a tale of those times as Hamble had yet heard. And he added more to it when he discovered how far Hamble had trekked, and that he had met a mole called Chater, of Duncton, who had been at Cuddesdon but a day or two after the massacre.

Then, when Hamble had eaten and rested, Purvey insisted on taking him from one place to another, to show him, to tell of the experience and share the grief he had borne alone until now.

'This was our communal chamber . . . and here was the scriptorium where I learnt to scribe when I came as a young novice. And here . . . here I found the bodies of some of the Cuddesdon brothers, unidentifiable. And here . . . and all down that slope, down as far as the river below . . . I believe they were strettened and died. Most of the texts scattered and ruined. All gone when I came back. All finished. And now . . . now just me, just my memories to prove Cuddesdon was a very reverent, holy place. Just . . .'

Hamble let the mole cry, that much he had learnt to do in his travels. These days many moles cried, for loss, for betrayal, in the belief that the Stone had abandoned them. He looked at Purvey, all thin and haggard, and guessed him to be rather younger than he looked.

'Not much above my own age!' thought Hamble in wonder.

Days passed, spring advanced, and Hamble did not leave. Purvey no longer wanted him to, indeed he was almost pathetically anxious he should stay, and had been appalled when Hamble revealed that it was his intention to infiltrate Duncton Wood.

'There'll be no followers left alive there now, not one,' he warned. 'I heard that Newborn Inquisitors moved in last Longest Night, and everymole hereabout knows there was a Newborn cell in Duncton moleyears before that. Should have driven them out. Aye, the Master Librarian failed there.'

Though Purvey went on somewhat, making up for the long moleyears when he had nomole at all to talk to, yet Hamble did not mind. He was glad instinct had turned him this way, glad to pause awhile, glad to let his own dark memories find some kind of peace.

One bright April day he felt the time was right to ask Purvey about those texts he had been so eager to guard when Hamble arrived, and which, he knew, he occasionally slipped away to look at.

'Well, I suppose there's no harm in telling *you*,' said Purvey, almost conspiratorially.

'Better show me,' said Hamble.

'Could do. Will do. Would like to.'

With which he led Hamble off across the surface. With a dig and a delve, a heave and a shove, he soon broke through his own roughly-sealed tunnel that led to a deep chamber. As Hamble entered it, and his eyes adjusted to the dim light, he found his heart thumping with an excitement he had never felt around texts before. This was not an ancient chamber, but it was the best preserved he had seen in Cuddesdon, and to his eyes there seemed a lot of texts ranged about the shelves.

'Dear me, there used to be far more, but not here, you see. They were on open shelves for general use, which is why we lost so much. The ones here, the only ones that have survived intact, though I was able to save some good portions of a few of the others, and fragments of many more, are mainly original texts put here for safe-keeping. We don't have any treasures here, I assure you! No Lost Books or any of that sort of thing!'

He moved to the shelves, his voice more animated than usual, and touched various texts as he talked.

Hamble was filled with sudden emotion, remembering just such a scene as this, moleyears before, when he was young, and had talked to Privet in the Crowden Library. She, too, had touched texts with love and he had always envied her ease with them. To her they were friends, to him . . .

49

'Mind you, this might interest you. It's a text we were always proud to have, you know. Here . . .'

Purvey lifted a volume and proffered it to Hamble, who took it uneasily in his big rough talons.

'Of course all libraries have a copy of it, haven't they?' said Purvey. 'You can see the paw is a fine one, very fine. If we have a treasure at all, it's this, and the volumes that go with it.' He paused, looking at Hamble quizzically.

'I'm sorry,' said Hamble awkwardly, 'you see, I can't scribe. Never learnt. Can't ken, never learnt that either. I . . . I've no way of knowing what text this is.' He gave it back as awkwardly as he had taken it, his eyes a little troubled, feeling his ignorance like muck in his fur.

Purvey ignored Hamble's evident discomfort and laying the text on the ground between them, opened it.

'This is the first volume of Woodruff of Arbor Low's great account of the history of modern moledom, *Duncton Chronicles*,' he said.

Hamble eyed the folios with diffident curiosity, a little fearful and over-respectful, but also with the look of a mole who wants something he cannot have.

'Would have liked to scribe and ken texts, but where I was raised, in Crowden up in the Moors, all our time was spent protecting what we had from the incursions of the Ratcher moles. The females like Privet and her mother Shire did the scribing and book-learning.' He stared at the text and finally reached out a blunt talon to feel the scribings he could not interpret. 'Duncton Chronicles, eh? That's a story I only ever had told me; a great story.'

'Not a story, Hamble, a *history*. And not so long ago either. We're both being thrown about by the same tides and currents of life and death as Tryfan and Henbane, Rune and Mayweed.'

'But it starts with a mole called Bracken . . .'

Purvey nodded and flicked back to the beginning of the text. He snouted at the first folio there, ran his paws over the scribings, and then began to ken the words aloud: '"Bracken was born on an April night in a warm dark burrow deep in the historic system of Duncton Wood, six moleyears after Rebecca. This is the story of their love, and their epic struggle to find it . . ."'

Hamble stanced down, growing more easy by the moment, and said, 'Go on, mole, go on. Ken some more for me . . .' and Purvey did.

His voice grew more assured and confident as he continued, and

Hamble breathed more deeply and steadily as he forgot his 'ignorance' and allowed himself to journey into the history that Woodruff had scribed down a century before.

Two moles, tossed and turned, as one of them had rightly observed, by 'tides and currents of life and death', sharing now their common heritage. Two moles in Cuddesdon, cast together for a time, learning together, going forward towards an understanding of the Silence, their ways different yet shared there and then.

'You'll ken some more tomorrow, eh mole?' said Hamble when Purvey had grown tired, but not so tired that he did not think to stop just when Mandrake, evil genius of Duncton in the days of Bracken, was about to do terrible things.

'I want to know what *happens*,' Hamble went on sleepily. Then, after a long contemplative silence, he said, 'I'd like you to ken the Chronicles to me at least until we get to the part concerning the mole my heart goes out to almost more than any other mole from those times.'

'And whatmole might that be?' asked Purvey.

'Mayweed,' said Hamble, 'great route-finder, humble mole, magnificent!'

Purvey laughed and said, 'It'll take a time to get to him. He doesn't appear in Woodruff's history until a good way into the second volume.'

Hamble shrugged and closed his eyes. 'I'll just have to stick around a bit longer then, won't I?'

'Yes,' said Purvey softly, trying to hide the gratitude he felt. He stared at Hamble as the big mole fell asleep, his scarred, rough face more gentle in repose. Why had he come to Cuddesdon? What was the Stone preparing for him in Duncton Wood?

'And why,' mused Purvey, 'do I have the feeling that this text was brought here years ago for just such a kenning as this, to a mole who needs time to be told this history, to be prepared?'

So it was that Hamble came to Cuddesdon, and stayed there for longer than he had expected, preparing himself for the trials to come. Until at last, in April, he had woken one day and known he must leave for Duncton. Purvey had kenned the whole of the Chronicles to him, and along the way taught him a little of scribing; now, in a rough and ready way, Hamble could scribe his own name, and that of Crowden, the system where he was born.

'Hamble of Crowden,' he would scratch out into the earthen floor of a tunnel, staring at it with real pleasure and thinking that nothing had ever given him a better sense of who he was.

'And what are you going to do now I'm leaving?' he asked of Purvey.

'You know perfectly well, Hamble, I'm going to scribe an account of Cuddesdon, as far as I know it, right up to your coming. I was trained as a scribe and a scribe I shall be. Stone willing, by the time I finish my self-appointed task I'll be too old to care much for the tribulations of this world. The Newborns will have power over all moledom, you'll be long gone, killed in some skirmish or another – though, mole, you *could* stay here . . .'

'No, Purvey, I couldn't. Privet sent me to Duncton, and now I must go there. As for being killed in a skirmish, I won't be. And nor will the Newborns survive for much longer. The Stone will see right done. As for you being too old to care, I don't believe it. Mark my words, one day there'll be young moles climbing back up this slope, come all the way from Duncton, because they've heard from me there's a timid scribe of a mole up here, who kens a text better than most, and has things to teach them, like he taught me. And I'm talking of more than just scribing down my name and home system.'

Purvey's eyes lit up as he imagined such a glorious dream becoming reality.

'Youngsters coming here, to learn?' he whispered. 'Cuddesdon alive once more? Its tunnels repaired, its texts out of hiding, and scribing and scholarship hereabout once more?'

'Why not? Pray for it and it might be,' said Hamble, giving his friend a last hug and turning downslope and westwards.

'I'll pray for *you*,' said Purvey, tears in his eyes.

'Pray for dreams, not battered old warriors like me,' called back Hamble.

'It's "battered old warriors" like you who make the dreams come true,' whispered Purvey with affection, and with hope.

Less than two days later, though it felt to him like a lifetime, Hamble found himself safely ensconced on a valley terrace on one side of a roaring owl way, looking across it at the rising mass of Duncton Wood.

As it happened, it *was* as dark as Purvey had suggested, for the morning was a cloudy one, and the air gusty and wet. Hamble knew himself to be a very different mole indeed from the one who had left Privet at Caradoc the previous December. He was fitter, he had lost that weariness with life that had beset him in his last molemonths with Rooster, and he knew now he would never strike another mole again in his life: his paws had found peace along the way, and peace-loving they would remain.

'But that's not to say I can't advise others how to carry themselves and use their heads to save their bodies,' he muttered to himself, casting an expert eye on the lie of the land between where he had stanced down and the high part of Duncton hill ahead of him.

He knew that the way into Duncton was by the cross-under which lay almost directly below him, but he also guessed it would be close-guarded by Newborns. So, too, would the more obvious nearby routes over the roaring owl way.

'Hmmph!' he muttered to himself. 'I'll set off anyway, but go a long way round. Yes . . .'

And so he did, taking his time, waiting for the midday lull in the flow of roaring owls, easing his way down the far embankment, swimming across the water-filled drainage dykes with easy strokes, and then up on to the pasture ground beyond. He stared upslope, waited patiently for twilight shadows to appear, and then using all the skills that years of eluding Newborns had taught him, he made his way steadily upwards, until at last he heard the gentle roaring that could only be one thing: the wind in the ancient beech trees of Duncton's High Wood.

'And may the Stone be with me,' he whispered as he went on up to them, his heart thumping – not with fear of the Newborns, but with the awe he felt, to have reached so famous and so revered a place, and to know a new life of service to the Stone was now beginning.

Chapter Six

Since the Night of Rising, a few days after Longest Night, when the followers had fled to the Ancient System, the winter years had taken their toll of Pumpkin, now their reluctant leader.

But it was not just the winter, cold and bitter though that had been. It was the Ancient System itself, which nomole forced to spend a night there, let alone as many as the followers now had, could describe as the ideal sanctuary. For should not a sanctuary be hospitable and warm, a place of respite from the chill winds of life beyond?

It should, but the Ancient System was not. Nomole now really knew (not even Pumpkin, who knew more about the history of Duncton than most) why the tunnels and chambers of the Ancient System had been deserted by mole. The story went that there had been a schism in moledom in mediaeval times when Scirpus, student of Dark Sound, had split with Dunbar, then moledom's holiest mole. Scirpus had travelled with his disciples to the north, to ill-starred Whern, where he had become the proponent of the infamous Word, the dogma which centuries later so nearly led to the extinction of the peaceful followers in Bracken's and Tryfan's day, as told in the *Duncton Chronicles*.

Moles said that with the coming of schism the Stone frowned upon Duncton's fabled Ancient System and it became wormless, and its inhabitants were forced to leave. Certainly Dunbar and the scribe-moles and spiritual seekers departed from Duncton, and the system fell into decline. The remaining inhabitants founded a new communal centre down in Barrow Vale, which lies beyond the slopes that lead to Duncton's High Wood, and so modern Duncton came into being. Gradually all real knowledge of the tunnels of the Ancient System that lay below the High Wood was forgotten, and the fact that they emitted terrible Dark Sound to any who ventured into them – no doubt as a result of deliberate delvings by the last of the delvers who lived there – meant that they became feared.

The only vestige of the old life that remained, though a vitally important one, was worship of the Stone itself, which moles could reach across the surface without the need to venture into the fearful tunnels. Not until Bracken's day was the Ancient System lived in once more – first by Bracken himself, later by Mandrake, and later still and at different times by followers seeking sanctuary for a period, or curious about what lay below the High Wood.

Of all the moles who ventured there after Bracken only Mayweed, Tryfan's friend and one of moledom's greatest route-finders, sought to explore the tunnels systematically. Indeed, it was said that he went further than that and scribed a map of the tunnels of the Ancient System. This map was of particular interest to Pumpkin, library aide and local historian that he was – or had been before the Newborns came. He had searched in Duncton's Library for clues to its where-abouts, or some proof of its existence, but with no success.

Then last Longest Night, or just after it, he had found himself leading the rebel followers away from almost certain massacre by the Newborns at Barrow Vale, and lacking the strength or skills to lead so mixed a party, which included a number of elderly moles, into a fight with trained Newborn guardmoles, he had taken them instead to the one place the superstitious Newborns would not go, the tunnels of the Ancient System.

'And how I wish I had found Mayweed's map in the days when I had a chance!' he had said often since. 'How much easier our life would be!'

'But you've said again and again that it probably doesn't exist,' said his friend Elynor, the redoubtable female follower who with her son Cluniac had helped Pumpkin lead the others into the Ancient System.

'Yes, yes, so I have, my dear, so I have. But you know, so much else of those days when Tryfan and Mayweed were alive which moles only talked about, I was able through my private researches to estab-lish as fact. And there is documentary evidence, dating from only a few years after Mayweed's departure from Duncton, that such a map *was said* to exist. Nothing more, though; but how useful it would be now!'

'You can say that again, Pumpkin!' muttered Cluniac, the bright-eyed youngster who had proved his worth again and again in the moleyears since Longest Night.

They were stanced down, as was their habit, in a communal chamber they had delved on the northern periphery of the High Wood, choosing the place for its distance from the major tunnels, whose Dark Sound oppressed and harried them too much to want to live nearer it. Even so, as Cluniac spoke, he looked over his shoulder as if to acknowledge that even in that cramped and distant chamber Dark Sound threatened them.

By Pumpkin's time the art of delving the indentations and subterranean forms that generate Dark Sound had been lost, it being a skill known only to Masters of the Delve. Consequently the only places where moles were likely to come across it were in ancient tunnels and chambers in the systems once occupied by mediaeval moles, such as Duncton Wood and, most notoriously, the Scirpuscun chambers of Whern, where Scirpus established the Order of the Word, and was responsible for some of the grimmest Dark Sound ever known.

Those who have never experienced Dark Sound find it hard to imagine how deeply it affects a mole. It reaches into a mole's heart and mind, and plays upon his individual fears and flaws. Thus, the same Dark Sound will seem different to each mole, such was the skill of the Masters of the Delve. He whose deepest fear is drowning might hear (or think he hears) the rush of water through a tunnel; while one who fears more being crushed by the rising and twisting of roots on a windy day, will imagine he hears the strain and stress of roots, and might even think he sees them.

Since few moles are without fear or flaw, most are affected by Dark Sound, which, in its worst forms, can affect all the senses, and bring about paralysis and death. Clearly, so potent an art was not one used lightly by the ancient Masters, and generally only where there were places or texts or other relics so holy, so precious, that they needed protection from intruders. In one or two cases, the most famous of which is that deep place of Silence beneath the Duncton Stone where the Stillstones and all the Books of moledom but that of Silence itself had their final resting-place, there may be additional protection – in this instance by the Chamber of Roots, the passage through which was fraught with physical danger.

Indeed, the only moles ever to pass alive through the Chamber of Roots and out again were moles blessed by the Stone, whose hearts were pure, and whose faith was absolute, if not always, at least at the time of their entry there. Which points to something more: the nearer a mole is to the Stone in spirit, the less he has to fear from Dark Sound; the further away he is, the more likely he is to be affected. No wonder then that Pumpkin and his friends found sanctuary in the Ancient System, and the Newborns, far from the peace and love of the Stone as their sectarian dogmas had led them, thought it so dangerous to venture into the tunnels beneath the High Wood.

But that all said, and moles being but moles, Pumpkin and his friends had found it no easy thing to dwell so long in and about the High Wood. Their waking hours were filled with fearful fancies and horrible hallucinations from which again and again they needed rescuing – a task which too often devolved upon Pumpkin himself, for he was blessed of the Stone, and found it easier than most to go into the midst of Dark Sound and lead back to safety those who had ventured too far.

Cluniac, too, was well-favoured, for young and inexperienced though he was when he first came into Pumpkin's life, his faith was strong and his courage great. It may have been, too, that his very inexperience allowed him into places all others but Pumpkin found difficult, and that in later years, if he had tasted greater fear and discovered his flaws, passage into Dark Sound would prove harder for him. All of this meant that the followers' explorations of the Ancient System were sporadic and incomplete and that the dark, deep tunnels, with their twists and turns, held enough dangers for them all that Pumpkin naturally wished he had the map which Mayweed was said to have scribed.

He tried to scribe one of his own, but it proved a paltry thing, and somehow, especially after a day of winds had stressed and shifted the roots below ground, the tunnels seemed to change, and new ways to open up and old ways to close, and the Dark Sound drifted from one place to another as if it sensed moles might get used to it if it did not shift and change as the roots did.

So far as there was a pattern to the tunnels it seemed to be that they all finally led to the Chamber of Roots, those on the larger eastern side of the High Wood (the Stone rising near the western edge) entering it via the Chamber of Dark Sound. To the east there was a large and deep communal tunnel that led from the slopes right under the High Wood, emerging at the edge of the Wood near the northern pastures.

This tunnel, or Main Tunnel as the followers came to call it, was not always easy to follow, for the Dark Sound sometimes entered it and there were stretches, generally darker, deeper, and narrower, where the sound was never far away and a mole went quietly lest his pawsteps echo and return a thousandfold, like the tramp of an army bent on death. From such places Pumpkin and Cluniac had often had to rescue others who, suddenly confused, barely able to do more than crawl, had huddled down or, worse, wandered off into adjacent passages.

The tunnels themselves were astonishingly well preserved in these

57

central reaches, and of the mediaeval arched style in which, by some alchemy long lost, the delvers had found flints and other stones below ground to use above portals, or to mark a tunnel's turn. In many places the walls were still etched with the original talon-marks of their makers, and were as graceful, or as stolid, as the talons were thin or thick. But such differences from one stretch to another served only to add a richer texture to the whole, and a harmony, as if to show that these great delvings were made by a community at one with itself.

Here and there were chambers and cells, many mysteriously delved up the walls far higher than a mole could reach. They stretched up towards the rutted root-bound roof, the cracks in which were the general source of light in the Ancient System; these indentations twisted and swirled, bent and retreated, so that a mole could not long look at them without his head seeming to swim as the walls did, and his eyes losing their focus. Then it was that the Dark Sound might start, catching the stress of his breathing, or the scuff of a nervous paw upon the ground, and he had to flee before the darkness of his mind overtook him.

'But how did they delve such things, and so high?' Cluniac asked Pumpkin on many occasions. But Pumpkin did not know – that was a mystery only a Master of the Delve might satisfactorily explain.

The winter had proved hard, and though the Newborns had not attempted any systematic pursuit of the followers, their patrols were always about and Pumpkin and his friends felt the constant stress of having to be careful about where they went and what they did. Then, as spring advanced and the weather improved, the Newborns began regular sorties into the High Wood.

March was a terrible month. Three of the elderly followers died, suffering perhaps from the cold and the inadequate diet that the High Wood soils provided, and one had been killed by Newborn guards. This more than anything had distressed Pumpkin, and though he did his best to appear cheerful and optimistic, privately he suffered much.

'Will we be rescued by moles from beyond Duncton Wood?' he was often asked. 'Will a time of peace return when we can go back downslope to Barrow Vale, and the tunnels we loved?'

'Yes! That day *will* come!' he would tell them, but how much it cost him to say it! How uncertain were his prayers to the Stone! How much he felt it had failed him!

If he had any consolation, though a cold one, it was that Sturne, now Acting Librarian in the service of the Newborns, was even more isolated than he was. Pumpkin alone knew the truth about Sturne, and how Master Librarian Stour, before his death, had entrusted him with the future of the Library, and the care of texts that between them they had managed to hide away from the Newborns' cleansing.

Day after day, molemonth after month, right through the winter years, Sturne had had to stay at his post, pretending to be one thing so that he might protect the others; so too that he might inform Pumpkin of any dangers or changes he should know about. But their meetings were difficult, for nomole could be allowed to know the truth about Sturne, none at all.

So it was that Pumpkin had continued his lifelong habit of going to the Stone alone – to pray and contemplate he said, but also now to give him opportunity to slip away across the dangerous surface of the High Wood, and meet Sturne in some fretful shadowed place, or draughty tunnel, and exchange information.

How little these two old friends guessed how much these meetings meant to each other. Pumpkin, friendly, modest, worried, great-hearted, was reminded that Sturne was far more alone than he, witnessing painful things among the Newborns, and forced to tell terrible lies, which offended him deeply. No, Pumpkin could not have carried on alone for long in such circumstances.

While Sturne, unbending, unsmiling, his face etched with severity and too much scholarship, compelled to seem a traitor to all he believed in, was given the chance to pass a few hurried moments with the library aide he trusted and admired and, yes, *loved*, more than any in the world, the only mole he had ever dared call a friend. The mole with whom, in better days, he had spent the festival days, like Longest Night or Midsummer's Eve, when he felt lonely. Then he had thanked the Stone with all his heart that he could, in his severe and uncommunicative way, share the hours with good Pumpkin.

These two then were partners in the strangest secret in Duncton Wood, each a support to the other, though their time together was snatched from the jaws of the Newborns themselves, and passed always too quickly.

'Must go, Sturne, must go now,' Pumpkin would be the one to say, for Sturne could never bear to initiate their partings.

'Yes, I suppose you must, Pumpkin. But, mole, be careful, I . . . I would not wish any harm to come to you. You are needed in Duncton by others now. Much needed!'

It was the nearest Sturne ever got to saying *he* needed Pumpkin as much as any mole. As for touching his friend, well, he could not bring himself to so overt an expression of friendship. But Pumpkin could and did, patting Sturne's paw and saying, 'There'll be help come soon, now that spring's here. You'll see!'

How long the feel of Pumpkin's thin paw on Sturne's remained after Pumpkin had gone, as he stared unmoving at where his friend had been; and how often in those terrible moleyears did Sturne feel the fears and rushes of emotion that came when he thought – though he quickly blocked it out of his mind – what it would be like if Pumpkin were taken, if his dear friend were to find himself again in *their* paws.

No, no, Sturne could not bear to contemplate for long so dreadful a thing, before tears began to prick at his cold eyes, and a lump came to his throat.

'No!' he would whisper harshly, as much to the emotion as the nightmare that provoked it. 'No, it must not be!'

Yet several times it nearly was, though Pumpkin never admitted it. For those journeys to meet Sturne *were* dangerous, and it seemed only a matter of time before Pumpkin was caught again. Twice it nearly happened, and a third time, at night, he was chased all the way back towards the Stone, only eluding his pursuers at the very end when, by some chance, they headed off in another direction.

Then he had lain panting at the Stone, thanking it for his deliverance, until Cluniac joined him and together they had returned to the followers.

'Did you pray all night?' Cluniac had asked innocently.

'All night, Cluniac,' lied Pumpkin, yawning. 'Yes, all night . . .'

But it had been no 'chance' that had led to the Newborn guards being diverted. For what Pumpkin did not know was that it had long been Cluniac's habit to follow the old library aide across the Wood, and to watch over him secretly against just such dangers as that particular night had brought. Nor did he suspect that Cluniac had finally observed that meetings with no less a mole than Sturne were the reason for Pumpkin's mysterious and dangerous disappearances. At first he had deduced that Pumpkin must be a traitor, for allmole knew that Sturne was Newborn. But after a time Cluniac had come to realize that the unbelievable was true: Sturne was a follower, and his acceptance of the Newborn dogma a pretence.

How tempted the young mole had been to confront Pumpkin with his discovery, but instinct told him not to, nor to confide in anymole-else, not even his mother Elynor. After his discovery Cluniac felt greatly in awe of Pumpkin and Sturne, astonished that moles he regarded as old and frail should be so steadfast and courageous. He understood then the true nature of the Duncton spirit, and saw with his own eyes the kind and calibre of mole who had always emerged from Duncton Wood when they were needed to uphold the followers' traditions of tolerance, love, and faith in the old ways of worshipping the Stone.

Sometimes then, though Cluniac never admitted it, he would himself pray to the Stone, asking it to protect Pumpkin and Sturne, and others like Privet, Maple, Fieldfare and Chater, who had left the Wood for a time to see what they might do to conquer the Newborn.

'Stone, give me such courage. Teach me to be a true Duncton mole. Help me support Pumpkin in every way I can . . .'

So the days had gone by, and April had come, and Pumpkin saw as yet no answer to his prayers, nor any hope in the warmer sun and the return of spring. Yet still he crossed the surface to see Sturne, whose news was still of brutal Crusades, and disaster, and massacres, and all this time, unknown to him, Cluniac followed in the shadows, ready to do his young best to protect Pumpkin, with his very life if need be. For the day was surely coming when the Newborns would no longer tolerate the survival of the rebel followers in the High Wood, and begin to flush them out.

Finally, that day *did* come. In mid-April it started: surprise patrols, shouting through the wood, the sudden rush of guardmoles from out of nowhere, the eerie thumping up on the surface by Newborns who had deduced that such simple tactics would produce terrifying Dark Sound underground.

A shadow came over the followers' spring as Pumpkin, Cluniac and the fitter of the others desperately tried to keep the followers together, and protect them from their own mounting fears and doubts.

'If we give ourselves up, like some of them have been shouting at dusk, they'll surely treat us fair . . .'

'I can't stand the strain any more, Pumpkin, sir, I just can't . . .'

'It's no good, Pumpkin, it's never been any good; it's all hopeless now . . .'

These last were the final words of an old Eastsider, worn down first by the winter, and now by being harried from tunnel to tunnel. He could take no more, and one April morning as a sun that might otherwise have seemed beautiful rose through the dew-gemmed High Wood, he died in Pumpkin's paws.

Then, two days later, two foolish followers, disobeying all instructions, ventured out on to the southern pastures in the hope of finding better worms than they had fed on in molemonths past. They did not

61

return. Their cries were heard, the hulking forms of guardmoles were seen, and then they were gone, and Pumpkin spent his last strength persuading Cluniac and one or two young moles from trying to rescue them.

It almost broke Pumpkin's heart, and for the first time he could find neither words nor example to encourage the followers and give them hope. They waited in vain for their two friends to return, but nomole came until four days later when some guardmoles appeared up by the Stone, thumping and shouting.

'We know you're there, and we know your numbers. There's . . .'

The brutal voice told how many there were, mentioned many names, and spoke of the chamber on the far side of the High Wood where they had hidden, but which Pumpkin had forbidden them to return to against just such a discovery as this.

'Your friends died lingeringly and horribly, for they were sinners and suffered just punishment. Crush a mole's snout slowly enough and he'll tell you anything. By the end they had nothing left to say. Give yourselves up! Give yourselves a chance to live, for you'll not be punished. But if you resist the true path longer you'll one by one go the way of your two friends.'

Aye, April became a dark time in the High Wood, and Pumpkin had no way of alleviating it, for he felt as dark and oppressed as any of them. Even praying by the Stone became nearly impossible, and very dangerous, for the guardmoles were often posted there, and twice more he was nearly caught.

'Don't risk it any more, Pumpkin!' Elynor begged him. 'For all our sakes don't! Things *will* get better; you've always said it, and now I'm saying it.'

But he was not cheered, for he could no longer believe it, much as he wanted to.

For three more days he barely moved, and scarcely tasted the meagre worms that Cluniac put before him. Then, finally, he slipped up to the surface, 'Just to see the Stone, just to keep my spirit alive . . .' and at a nod from Elynor, who knew that part of the secret at least, Cluniac followed after him.

But he did not go over towards the Stone Clearing, but instead, as Cluniac had rightly guessed, he headed towards the Great Library, no doubt to try to meet Sturne. But Pumpkin never got that far. Somewhere along the way his luck ran out. Two guards reared out of the shadows of some roots and challenged him, and all he could do was turn back the way he had come, running for his life.

'Mo-ole, we're going to get you . . .' the guardmoles called with playful menace, for what could a scraggy old mole like the one they had surprised expect to do against them! He could not hope to run far. So they tracked behind him, upslope towards the Stone, laughing, shouting mockingly ahead of him, hoping perhaps to bring out other followers and so increase their catch, enjoying their moment before they turned pursuit to capture.

Poor Pumpkin's breath began to fail him a good way from the Stone, too far to hope to reach it, or rather one of the tunnel entrances about it that might afford him better opportunity of escape. He had often thought of this moment and such plans as he had made depended on reaching such an entrance.

'Must try,' he panted, glancing over his shoulder and seeing how big the guardmoles were, how fierce, how close. 'Must try my very best!' And if anything gave him a little extra strength it was that they mocked him, and made him angry.

Then, suddenly, a greater shock, and a sadder one. He saw, out of the corner of his eye, Cluniac, gesticulating him on, Cluniac . . . In a flash he knew whatmole it was had helped him before when the guards nearly caught him. Cluniac had watched over him, but oh dear, oh dear . . . it was too late now.

'I order you to run for your life, mole!' cried out Pumpkin, stopping dead and turning to face the guards. 'Go now!' Pumpkin almost wept, for Cluniac did not, would not obey. Instead the youngster came to his flank to confront the guards with him.

'And an entrance so near!' muttered Pumpkin, afraid for Cluniac, not himself. 'You're a fool, Cluniac.'

But the guards had stopped, wrongly suspecting they might have been led into an ambush, assuming that such paltry moles as they saw upslope of them were capable of such a thing.

'Let's make a dash for it,' whispered Cluniac, 'the nearest entrance isn't that far. It'll be our only chance.'

'A dash!' panted Pumpkin. 'At my age!'

Yet, brave and resolute as ever, he turned back upslope towards the entrance and was almost to it, with Cluniac close behind him, before the guardmoles realized what was happening. Then, with a roar of rage, they came crashing upslope after them, ambush or no.

With a scamper and a scurry Pumpkin and Cluniac tumbled through the entrance and down a short passage into a dusty and echoing tunnel which they had used from time to time to hide in. Full of Dark Sound this one, leading to nowhere near the Main Tunnel that might have given them respite. No, this ran to the darker centre, where nomole might venture.

'We can but try!' cried Pumpkin, and so they did, the guardmoles already through the entrance and rushing down towards them before they began moving again.

Terror lay ahead, dark shadows, cries and screams, and the thunder of paws: cloying, gripping, paralysing Dark Sound clouded Pumpkin's sight as the tunnel narrowed ahead and ended. They had turned amiss, and were in some grim, vast chamber, talons of sound about them and behind them the guardmoles advancing, unaffected it seemed by what dismayed the two followers. Pumpkin slowed once more, knowing he could go no further, and Cluniac had stopped already, paws to his ears as the Dark Sound rushed over them.

'Well, you two bastards, we've got you now,' said one of the guardmoles from the huge arched entrance behind which the darkness seemed to Pumpkin to slip and slide, to mount and mill, to swing and become impenetrable.

'Come on!' he continued, with heavy patience. 'You've done the best you can and now let's get you out of this bloody noise.'

'And fast,' said the other, his snout growing grey in the gloom, 'it's beginning to get to me.'

The guards, much bigger and stronger than either of them, grasped them roughly beneath their shoulders, the pain of being gripped in so tender a place bringing a gasp from Cluniac.

'Come on!' said the first guard once more, suddenly angry. 'Out! Fast!'

So, helpless, beset now by pain and echoing sound, they began the short trek back to the surface, and Dark Sound fading, the echoes in the chamber behind receding, the . . .

Voices. Deep and rhythmic, yet far-off. A distant song.

'Listen, Cluniac!' whispered Pumpkin, and even the guardmoles listened, more affected by this it seemed than the Dark Sound that had so tormented the followers.

'Come on, on you go!'

Deeper now the chorus of voices chanting, louder than they had ever heard them, yet distant still. Deep, purposeful, marching . . .

'Cluniac, can you hear them, can you hear?'

'Yes,' whispered the younger mole in wonder, 'yes, I can, Pumpkin. But it's too late for us. Others will know it though, others . . .'

The chant continued, swelling now, deepening, and then fading as the guardmoles hurried them away and they reached the slipway up to the surface, and final captivity.

'Help us!' cried out Pumpkin, turning to look back.

'Help us, Stone!' called out Cluniac into the receding darkness.

Marching paws, the chant almost a melody now, rich in the ancient tunnels, the song of moles on a pilgrimage through time, trying to reach forward to help those who lived long after they themselves were gone to Silence. Their voices preserved for ever in the Dark Sound – no, in that place that lay beyond it.

'Stone!' whispered Pumpkin finally as the guardmole's rough paws pushed him ahead and up the slipway towards . . . towards . . .

Behind them the chant swelled, ahead the light of the dusk seemed almost to shine, then dim again as the way was blocked by one of the most solid-looking and frightening moles Pumpkin had ever seen.

'What the . . . !' began the leading guard, his paw-grip on Pumpkin weakening.

'What is it?' grunted the one behind him, with Cluniac. And then . . . 'Stone me! What mole is *he*?'

Deep, deep the chant of moles behind them, as if the Ancient System was a community again, and on an unstoppable march towards the Stone.

'Let them go,' growled the strange mole, 'and get out of here. OUT!'

The guardmoles needed no second bidding. With time's great army of followers behind them, and the reality of this fierce unknown mole blocking the exit ahead, they wanted to get away from these dread tunnels and these mysterious moles. The intruder pulled aside, frowned and growled again, and the guardmoles were up and gone past him, crashing away through the wood above, the sounds of their flight subsumed by the extraordinary chant that now filled the tunnels.

Pumpkin stared at the stranger, then at Cluniac, and then turned back into the tunnel, towards the song. It came on to them in waves, so powerful, so glorious, that all three were struck still by its sound as three moles might be who turn a corner and are caught for a glorious and eternal moment by the rays of a rising sun, with a prospect of a moledom ahead with all its vales and valleys, fells and moors, trees and mountains flooded by light and peace. So the chant enveloped them, and knew them, and gave them the sense of the Stone's grace. And then it faded, slowly, reluctantly, back into the lost tunnels whence it came, leaving only the whisper of hope, and the trace of a promise yet to be fulfilled.

65

'Did you hear it, Cluniac, did you hear it, mole?'

Silently Cluniac nodded. Then together they turned to face the fierce stranger whose coming had saved their lives. His face bore the scars of past fights; his paws were huge; his talons blunt. His eyes, which had blazed fiercely at the Newborn guards but moments before, now seemed diffident, almost shy.

'Whatmole are you, and whither are you bound?' asked Pumpkin, as Duncton-like as he could possibly be. Proud yet humble; brave yet frail; alone and yet with the sound of a great heritage and beloved community behind him.

'Bound?' repeated the mole. 'I'm bound *here*, to Duncton Wood. And if my observations of the last few days are right, you are the library aide Pumpkin, and you, young mole, are named Cluniac. You've things to learn about not being seen. A crow with one eye could see you right across the wood, rustling and hustling about as you both have been! Aye, you've things to learn and I've come not a moment too soon by the look of things.'

'But whatmole are you?' asked Cluniac, in awe, yet affronted that he had been watched and knew nothing about it.

'My name's Hamble,' said the mole, 'and I'm of Crowden in the Moors. Privet sent me. She thought you might be in need of help. She was right.'

'Privet?' whispered Pumpkin, his voice faltering. 'Scholar Privet? H . . . Hamble? The friend from her youth on the Moors?'

'The same,' said Hamble, smiling.

Pumpkin stared a moment more before it all became too much for him: the pursuit, the Dark Sound, the capture, the communal chant, being apprehended and then rescued. But more than that, hearing that *Privet* had sent this great mole to them, to help them, to help . . . And poor Pumpkin, who had led the rebel followers alone so long, sniffled and snuffled, his mouth trembled and all he could say was, 'Privet sent him, Cluniac. I always said help would come one day. I always said . . .'

And all he could do was burst into tears, and sob his heart out while Cluniac held him, as a son might hold a father who had fought alone long and hard for his family and now was alone no more.

Chapter Seven

'Wildenhope!' whispered Privet to herself, staring at its distant dark shape. Then, from the valley far below, came the ominous roaring of water.

'And how will we cross the river?' asked Privet.

Below her, surrounded by guards, Rooster had also stopped. Between them was Madoc with her group and Whillan with his.

'With difficulty,' said her guard.

As if he heard them, though he was too far off to have done so, Whillan turned and looked up to Privet. Beyond him and far below her was the white-grey rush of the river they must cross and she felt sudden desperate fear as if she sensed a danger she could not name. Indeed, so powerful was the feeling that quite involuntarily she pushed forward to reach Whillan, and for the first and only time her guards had to restrain her. The moment passed and the parties set off once more, but Privet was left with an aching unease which would not go away.

By the time they reached the bottom of the Wenlock Edge escarpment it was dusk and Thorne and Fagg decided it would be better to cross the river by daylight.

'It will be easier then, miss, so there's no need to fret. Maybe the rain'll stop and the river's flow ease off a bit.'

'Maybe . . .' said his fellow guard dubiously.

There followed a troubled night in which the rain did ease a little, but the roar of the nearby river grew louder. Everywhere and everything around them seemed to drip and run with water, and Privet felt chilled to the bone.

At dawn came the signal to move once more.

'I thought we would wait until full daylight,' said Privet.

'The Commander's probably thinking that the sooner we get across the better – if the river floods we could be stranded this side, or worse,' observed the friendly guard at some point when dawn light came.

It was cold comfort, for nomole likes a flooding. Water is one thing, a flooding is another, for however well a mole can swim, the power and rush of a flooding can overcome the strongest. A grim look had settled on to the faces of Privet's normally affable guards, and the only comfort was that they stayed protectively close to her as the party sloshed its way over water-logged meadows towards the river they could hear but no longer see. How they would actually cross it Privet could not imagine, for there was no sign of a roaring owl way and a nice safe stone bridge which might have led them comfortably high over the raging water. Privet had never wished before for signs of two-foots and their structures, but she wished for them now. Looking back the way they had come she saw that the top of the Edge was obscured by grey cloud, and now the rain began once more.

They came down at last to the field before the river itself, at which point they not only lost sight of it beneath its banks, but its roar became muted, replaced by the shriller sound of rushing water in the drainage ditches that crossed the fields all about. They turned south, parallel with the river, to cross the first of several ditches by means of swaying planks on unstable and rickety two-foot structures made wet and slippery by the rain and, worse, the occasional upward splash of water from the torrents they bridged. Privet disliked these crossings, but they were generally short enough to scurry across in one quick movement, being careful to keep eyes firmly fixed on the pawhold ahead and never straying past and downward to the water itself. Only once did Privet do that and she momentarily froze; the rush and dash of water below was so mesmerizing and terrible that the guard behind had to talk her on step by step until she was safely across.

It was midday before they turned once more towards the river, taking a route along the very edge of the dyke they had just crossed. Ahead was a clump of shrubby trees through which the river seemed to take a curving course. They cut in among these trees to slightly higher ground and for a moment Privet had the illusion they had left the river behind, and were safe once more.

The separate parties had slowed and bunched up, so that for the first time since the journey started Privet was near enough the others to see them clearly, if not quite talk. All looked tired, their fur bedraggled and their paws and snouts muddy. Rooster, huge and fearsome, seemed to tower over the guards around him and he looked round for a moment and gestured towards her and frowned, which might have meant anything from complete despair to a determination to escape. The moment passed and they plodded off once more through the trees, past two-foot structures, over a large concrete dyke by way of a sturdy flat bridge of the kind Privet would have welcomed earlier, and then finally out of the trees to the river's edge.

It was then she saw sweeping up from the bank a structure of a kind she had seen on her journey across Evesham Vale before Caer Caradoc, but never been upon. It was, Weeth had explained, for cows and sheep to cross from one pasture to another and had been all muddy and trodden down at either end where the livestock had grouped and waited. This one however was ruinous and abandoned, its entrance fenced off to cows by barbed wire. The structure was still whole on either bank, but where an elegant span might once have been there was now only a great girder of rusting metal, its centre sagging down towards the torrent that raged just below. To make the prospect of crossing it especially grim the girder had a leftward twist, and swayed to and fro in the wind, and up and down.

'Right!' said Thorne firmly. 'There'll be no dawdling and no rushing. One at a time, go steadily, concentrate on the next step, and count. That's the way to do it.'

'Counting keeps your mind off it,' whispered Privet's friendly guard, his paw touching hers reassuringly, 'we came this way and there's nothing to it!'

'Wasn't roaring then,' said his companion unhelpfully, 'wasn't flooded.'

Privet could have wished that she was among the first to go, but they went in the order in which they had travelled and her fears about the crossing had time to grow and fester and feed upon themselves. When the third mole across hesitated, she hesitated with him; when the fifth slipped and nearly fell, she slipped too, and half screamed in fear – a cry lost in the remorseless roar of the river below.

Whether out of sympathy or a moment's forgetfulness in the successive dramas of moles crossing, the guardmoles allowed their charges to come close enough to shout words of greeting and encouragement to each other over the noise of the river, and nothing was more comforting to Privet than that. Rooster was already near the girder, ready to cross behind one of his guards so it was Whillan and Madoc Privet saw best, and both seemed well, if tired, with Whillan now a little recovered from his beating.

Rooster set off firmly, making it look easy, and giving Privet a little more confidence. But halfway across, where the girder dipped down lowest to the torrent below, he stopped. Unaware of this the guardmole ahead continued, but the one behind paused, eyeing Rooster uneasily and knowing perhaps that here at least, without the others' support, he was no match for the great mole.

Rooster seemed oblivious to them all, but only stared for a moment at the dangerous waters below and then very slowly and strangely gazed around him and then upward, eyes wild, snout raised, mouth half open. Then, most terribly, he looked back at them, on his face the expression of one who never expected to see them again.

'Something's wrong!' cried out Privet, forgetting her own fears. 'Whillan, something's wrong . . .'

Whillan pushed forward shouting something Privet could not quite catch, but as the guards restrained him Rooster seemed to come out of his strange trance; he shook his head, and proceeded to cross without further hesitation, into the grateful paws of the guards massed ready for him on the other side.

'It was the Charnel Clough!' shouted Whillan to Privet. 'I think for a moment he thought he was crossing out of it again. Did you see the way he looked back here as if we were his friends Glee and Humlock he left behind? Did you?'

As Whillan was pushed up to the girder to take his turn at crossing it Privet thought, 'Even after so long he has not forgotten them. Friends lost. His whole life has been loss.'

Certainly Whillan's imagining, if that was what it had been, had the ring of truth about it, as if he understood something of Rooster's mind as only family or a friend might.

As Whillan crossed, and more guards, and then Madoc, the number watching from the far side grew, whilst those around Privet decreased, until only her two guards and Brother Adviser Fagg remained.

She might have been all right had not Fagg come close and whispered maliciously, 'Not nervous, are we, not worried about falling in?'

Privet stared at him, while her guardmole friend could only look on in despair.

'We are?' sneered Fagg. 'Well, nomole cares if dried-up bitches like *you* die, nomole at all. But don't worry, I'll be right behind . . .' His eyes glittered, and in them a mole might have seen the reflection of the river raging past.

'Brother Adviser,' said the guardmole, trying to intervene.

'You lead, guardmole, you lead . . . and I'll follow,' said Fagg, and there was nothing a guardmole could do to countermand a Brother Adviser's order. His friend went first, Privet next, and Fagg too close behind, his every word of hypocritical encouragement – 'Careful!

70

Watch that bit! Oh, dear, you nearly slipped!' – unheard by anymole but Privet, adding to her fears and turning her paws all awkward and stumbly; the rain got in her eyes, the wind tried to pull and push her from the swaying, slippery girder, and the river surface seemed to boil and break beneath and send waves of water up towards her.

The moles on the other side sensed something was wrong, though from where they watched they could not have guessed that Fagg was maliciously turning a difficult situation into a dangerous one. Behind him the last guardmole, the friendliest, leaned out from one side to another to see what help he could offer, but Fagg blocked his view, and all possibility that he might do anything.

The fear that Privet now began to feel was unlike anything she had ever known – indeed, she might have wondered if she had ever known fear at all until now. From the first moment she put her paws on the girder and felt it twisting and shifting beneath her, its hard, weathered surface offering so little grip to prevent her from slipping towards the maelstrom below, she felt panic coming upon her, and knew she would have trouble controlling it. But as she edged along the persistent voice of Fagg behind caused her to lose concentration, and think thoughts and do things she was trying to avoid. When he said, 'Don't look down or you'll panic,' she could not prevent herself from looking down, nor from feeling the panic tighten her paws, restrict her breathing, and . . . 'Watch that bit there!'

'Which bit? Where? Oh dear, oh . . .' The fear was becoming palpable, a black and numbing cloud closing in upon her and blocking out all sight and sound but the swaying stretch of girder ahead, and the blurring rush of water beneath which gave the illusion that her next pawhold was moving away to her right, and she could not breathe, could not place her paw, and she was being drawn over and over and must slip, was slipping now, would fall, on and on the screaming voice of fear was hers and nomole was there, none to help and . . . and Privet began to freeze where she was, her eyes wide with fear, and her breath coming out now in short audible gasps of pain as voices shouted at her, behind and in front, but she felt out of reach of any aid they might bring.

She did not – could not – see how Fagg was now being perilously restrained from further interfering with her by the guardmole behind him, while the one in front had turned, which was no easy thing on the narrow wind-buffeted girder, to try to reassure her.

But now on the far bank Rooster reared up, and Whillan too, and both were struggling with the guards in their efforts to clamber back on to the girder and give Privet what help they could. In Whillan's case the struggle was unequal, for the guards were as big as him, and he was outnumbered. But Rooster was throwing guards off himself like a giant mole breaking through dry undergrowth, whilst all the time he was roaring and shouting in Privet's direction.

But it was Thorne who assessed the situation, and perhaps saved it. He barked out several quiet commands – first to Whillan and those around him, which stilled them, and then to Rooster's guards, who fell away from a struggle they were beginning to lose.

Then as Rooster shook himself finally free Thorne said, 'You go to her, mole, and calm her . . . now!' And turning towards the river-bank he gave such a sudden and authoritative order to the guard in front to 'clear the way' that the mole turned forward again and scurried to the safety of the bank in moments.

Rooster needed no further encouragement and set off rapidly along the girder, but if Thorne thought he was going to simply talk Privet over to safety, he was mistaken. It was not in Rooster's nature to do the simple thing, nor, as in this case, the safest one either. Muttering to himself and glaring at both the girder and the river below as if they were living enemies, he charged down towards Privet with no concern for himself, and not much for Privet either – his objective was Fagg.

The Brother Adviser, restrained behind by the guardmole and now borne down upon by Rooster, notwithstanding that the terrified Privet was in the way, now seemed very alarmed indeed.

When Rooster roared, 'You! Off! Out! Leave! Away!' he looked quite terrified. The guardmole understood at once and leaving matters to Rooster he retreated to where he had started from and watched from the safety of the bank, with amused astonishment tinged with awe.

Quite what Rooster meant by his monosyllabic and threatening cries of 'Off' and the like was unclear, unless he was advising Fagg to jump into the river below. Certainly Fagg contemplated this as the lesser evil, but one look at the broken, crashing water told him that way was death.

In the time it took him to think this through Rooster had reached Privet, and Fagg looked as if he felt himself safe from actual assault. In this he was mistaken; before he knew what had happened Rooster had clambered around Privet with an agility amazing in one so large, and had reached the hapless Brother Adviser himself.

'Off!' he cried again, and putting his huge paws to Fagg's quaking flanks he turned him bodily round and shoved him violently in the

72

general direction of the bank from which he had come. How Fagg succeeded in not falling off into the river is one of those mysteries that the moles who witnessed the incident could never quite explain, but as it was he rolled and slithered along and finally tumbled off and down on to the crumbling river-bank whence the guardmole very nearly failed to rescue him before he fell in. With a desperate heave and cry, and with his body muddy from the bank, he finally slumped half conscious in the wet grass, his flanks heaving violently from the effort of escape and the fearful shock of so nearly being taken by the river.

Above him, precarious on the girder, Rooster glared malevolently down before turning back to attend to Privet. Those watching saw him transformed from the embodiment of outrage and menace, ready to kill if need be, to a mole as gentle and patient before another's fear as possible. He slowly approached her, ignoring his own safety altogether, and eased himself on to the dangerous lower side of the girder, no doubt to block her view of the river below, whilst placing a comforting paw upon her back.

Then, putting his rough old head close to hers, he began to talk quietly to her with words of reassurance, caressing her back as he did so, pointing at last to the distant bank. She nodded her head, slowly began to move forward, paused again, waited for him to come to her once more, and finally set off without faltering to the other side.

Ever unpredictable, Rooster stayed where he was, staring now into the rushing water beneath, while beyond him the remaining guard-mole and the barely recovered Fagg waited uncertainly.

Suddenly Rooster cried out, 'Whillan! You *see*! You *know*!' and his voice rolled and rumbled with the river's roar.

Privet reached the bank at last, eyes bright, her fear quite gone.

'Whillan should go to him,' she said, going boldly to Brother Commander Thorne. 'Some things should be done as they were meant to be.'

The guards looked at Thorne, who shrugged philosophically as if to say, 'I don't understand these followers and Duncton moles, but there's something about them that makes a mole think; and anyway they're hardly going to escape from *there*!'

He nodded at the guardmoles around Whillan and they pulled back from him. For a moment he stanced alone and unmoving, looking from Thorne to Privet and finally to Madoc.

'I know what he sees,' said Whillan quietly. 'He may need . . . company.'

Then he was allowed to clamber back on to the girder and go to Rooster, right in the centre.

'Is it like the Charnel Clough? Is that what you see?' He had to shout in Rooster's ear to be heard above the roar.

'Know! You know now. Need to know that. Don't know why.'

Together they stared down at the water, and to those that watched them they might have been two old moles contemplating a pleasing view of a warm summer's evening. But the onlookers could not hear their words.

'Cliffs there!' said Rooster, pointing towards wet grey sky. 'And *there*, dark, breaking, ending,' he added. 'Charnel's green with moss and grass, like no green I've seen again. Was my puphood in that colour, was all hope, all I knew. Whillan, you're a delving mole.'

'Me?' said Whillan. 'I can only scribe. Privet taught me.'

'No, no, no,' cried Rooster. 'She taught you to delve. That's it. Many ways to Silence, so allmole can get there. You can. You'll delve.'

Whillan stared at the river and felt no fear, only sudden love for this mole he did not understand.

'When I left the Charnel Clough I said goodbye to puphood. All that was gone. Left moles I loved behind.'

'Glee,' said Whillan, 'and Humlock.'

'Them both. One small, one big, one white, one blind, one and one were all my world. Miss them always and for ever.'

'Rooster,' cried out Whillan, unafraid, 'you must delve again. You *must*. That's what you left the Charnel Clough to do.'

'Did many times like what you saw. Secret places. Hidden. Destroyed most of them. But the delving need does not die, not like the past, not like what I left behind. You're . . .'

'What am I?' asked Whillan, still not knowing.

'Want to say it,' said Rooster, 'want to show you, want many things I cannot have or do. Whillan, you never do what I did and make it impossible to go back. Never, Whillan. You never kill a mole, you love when love's before you, you cry when tears are there, you shout at the Stone or with it, and you live in the light I lost. You do that, mole? Mole?' Rooster placed a paw on Whillan's and stared at him fiercely. 'Yes?'

To love, to cry, to shout, to live?

'Yes,' said Whillan quietly, feeling that though he did not understand all Rooster's words, and but few of the things to which he referred, he understood this: that nomole, not even Privet herself, had ever tried so hard to give him something that really mattered as

74

Rooster tried now. And the love in the giving, and the receiving, lay in the trying. Whillan felt Rooster's love, and in that he understood at last why Privet loved Rooster so, and why in their love the Stone's Silence found expression. It was enough.

'We better go back to firm land,' said Whillan with an adult smile.

'We better!' said Rooster, with a laugh.

'And captivity.'

'Privet says the Stone's in everything!'

'Then we had better start praying it's in this!' said Whillan, before leading the way back to where the guards waited to take them into custody once more.

'You Duncton moles are . . . different,' observed Thorne later that day to Privet, 'and in your way, impressive.'

'Different but normal,' she replied, 'and anyway, Rooster is not of Duncton.'

'Nor is the mole Madoc,' said Thorne grimly.

They were resting for a short time; after the tribulations of crossing the river, they had rapidly escaped up to higher ground, from which they had watched the water-meadows slowly flood as the river rose higher and spilled out on to them. The approach to their crossing-point was already blocked by flooded fields on either side, and still the rain fell in dark swathes across the vale. If they had not crossed when they did, they would not have crossed at all. The river ran through the middle, yellow-white and powerful, a terrifying sight. It was a pity, Privet thought, that Brother Adviser Fagg had not delayed on the far side a little longer still, but 'her' guardmole had helped him across, and he was much humiliated and was now, all too evidently, the bitter enemy of all of them. But these thoughts were replaced by fears for Madoc, now that Thorne specifically mentioned her. Had he come especially to Privet to talk about her? Perhaps.

'She is a harmless mole,' said Privet carefully. 'She was doing her best to convince us of the error of our ways. She should not be held captive.'

'Oh, I agree,' said Thorne with a twinkle in his eye, 'but not for the reason you give. I know perfectly well what mole she is – one of Bowdler, I believe. One of our guards recognizes her.'

Privet said nothing.

'Her life will not be worth living if I return her to Senior Elder Brother Quail. And yet if I let her go – assuming that I could – I betray my own beliefs. A pretty dilemma, Privet of Duncton Wood.'

75

'How will you resolve it?' Privet turned and looked into his eyes and wondered how it was that the Stone had put such a mole on the opposing side.

'You're a scribemole, they tell me, the first female one I've ever met. You might tell *me* if there's a simple resolution to such problems.'

'Usually,' said Privet. 'And prayer is the best way of finding it, not discussion.'

Thorne smiled. 'Rooster is like nomole I have ever known,' he said quietly. 'They say he is a Master of the Delve. Do you know what that means?'

'Yes, I do.'

'When I saw you together poised over that river it seemed to me that you knew each other well. You seemed as one.'

'You observe well, mole,' said Privet.

'A leader must. Now tell me, what were Rooster and Whillan talking about so intently out there, where none could hear?'

Privet shook her head and they were silent for a moment, then she said impulsively, 'I spoke with Chervil once in such a position as this. We were his captives, though that was not the word we'd have used.'

'You know Brother Chervil?' Thorne was both surprised and pleased. 'I knew him well once upon a time.'

'And Brother Rolt?'

Thorne looked surprised once more. 'He was our teacher when we were pups.' He hesitated and then said, 'You are a mole of many parts it seems, Scribemole Privet.'

'If you must give me a title call me *Keeper* Privet, which is how I am known in Duncton Wood.'

'How do you know Brother Rolt?'

'Oh, well, it's a long tale that, too long to tell you now. And anyway, Brother Commander, I am not sure you should be talking to me. The good mole Fagg is glancing this way and does not look happy.'

'I can deal with him,' growled Thorne.

'But can you deal with those he answers to?'

Thorne shrugged non-committally. 'So tell me, if you won't talk of your past acquaintance with Brother Rolt, what did you make of Chervil? I suppose you met him in Duncton Wood? His father – the Elder Senior Brother I mean – sent him there.'

'For his own good, I imagine. To escape Quail's influence.'

'You lead me on to ground as dangerous as that we crossed today.' His voice hardened. 'The followers cannot win this struggle against the Caradocian way. You know that, don't you?'

76

'The Stone will win it,' said Privet. Though she smiled, her glance was hard.

'And if we lose it?'

'*You* will lose it, if you do what you know to be wrong.'

'I know that taking the mole Madoc to Wildenhope is wrong,' he said very softly. 'Some of Quail's underlings in Wildenhope are unspeakable. They do things for which I would kill my guardmoles if I caught them at it. There is a mole called Squelch . . .'

The expression on Thorne's face turned to utter disgust.

'Yet you fight for them!' said Privet.

'I fight for the Stone. I fight for Thripp of Blagrove Slide. I fight for what is right.' He spoke calmly, even matter-of-factly. 'But who will fight for you?' he added suddenly. 'Does Duncton still produce leaders as great as it did with Bracken and Tryfan in the days when we were threatened by the Word?'

Privet thought of Maple, and wondered if indeed *he* would ever be called 'great'. Maple seemed inexperienced compared with this strong and self-assured mole. Yet there had always seemed to her something *certain* about Maple, something solid.

'Moles will emerge when they are needed,' said Privet. 'Perhaps Rooster, and I, and Whillan, and . . .'

'You were going to say Madoc,' he said, smiling again.

Privet gave him a sharp yet not unfriendly look. He was, of course, quite right.

'Well anyway,' she continued with a little frown, 'you may be sure that even if *we*' – she waved a paw in the direction of the others in a way that might have included Madoc – 'do not survive our coming meeting with the inquisitorial Brother Quail, there will be many others who will uphold the values in which we believe, and which Duncton moles traditionally represent. I hope *you* may meet them. I hope you may listen to them as you listen to me. You are a mole, Brother Commander Thorne, of the kind who might be surprised at how much you would feel at home before the Duncton Stone.'

'And you are persuasive, if I may say so.'

'Thank you!' said Privet, tartly. 'So will you let us all go free?'

'No, I won't.'

'So I'm not *that* persuasive then.'

Thorne grinned amicably. 'You have not said one harsh word about me. Nor about the Caradocian way.'

'Whatmole am I to judge another? It is not just history that has taught me that, but life itself.' She looked away from him, wanting to talk; and she felt that fear, mortal and terrible, that had come on her occasionally in recent times. 'You know,' she went on softly, 'the time will come when you realize that for these few days you have had in your power—'

'My care, you mean.'

'I am happy that you use *that* word. In your care then, you have had one of the most remarkable moles of our generation. Rooster is a mole whose paws can express through delving the essence of the Stone's Silence. No sect, no faith, can or should try to contain such a mole as him. Now then . . .'

As she spoke on Thorne felt himself surrendering to the grip of her words in a way he had only experienced once before, and that was when he had heard Thripp himself speak, a long time ago. Something about her words – no, something about *her* – reached beyond the barriers of reason and prejudice that surrounded all moles, to touch some sense of truth within his heart. As he had once believed Thripp had spoken profoundly of the need to reach out towards the Stone, so now he felt that whatever Privet said was right, because *she* was right.

But that was not all, not the only thing that contributed to his sense that there was something indeed special about the moles whom circumstances had put into his . . . care. For he had spoken at different times with each of them, and each had told him to let the others go, saying that they themselves did not matter. He found it hard to imagine such selfless courage among a group of four Newborn moles.

Madoc had spoken most movingly about why the others should be let free, ending her plea in a way that made it obvious that she knew all too well what might happen to a young Newborn female like herself when it was known she had gone over to the other side. *There* was courage.

But Whillan of Duncton had pleaded most persuasively for the others' lives, and the fact that he had thereby betrayed that his relationship to them all, and especially Madoc, was a close and special one which they had tried to hide, Thorne did not count against him. Thorne regarded the whole situation he was in as distasteful, and if he had his way he would have let them all go. Except that he did have a feeling, made paradoxical by their apparent harmlessness, that they were important, and whatmoles they were and what they represented was subversive of the Newborns, and deeply so.

Rooster had been the least articulate of them, yet in his awesome and frightening way, the most disturbing.

78

'I am nothing,' he had said, 'but others are all. Hurt them and you hurt *you*. Don't. Let them go. Don't hurt. Punish me, not them. They are the Stone . . .'

Now finally Thorne heard Privet speak, and knew in his heart that he listened to a great mole. 'Why have circumstances put these moles my way?' he mused, when he took his leave of her to let her rest. 'I was sent into obscurity and found . . .' But he could not yet put into words the feeling that he had found a way towards his life's task . . .

By the time the moles had rested up, and recovered from their ordeal of crossing the swollen river and its flood plain, the rain had eased; but the weather had not improved, for instead of a downpour obscuring their vision and splashing at their paws they now had to screw their eyes against a fractious and bitter wind that carried flurries of stinging hail and rain into their faces, and chilled them to the bone.

They had climbed up on to the bluff of land which marked the western side of the river valley, and they knew that it was this same bluff, a little lower perhaps, which formed the grim destination of their forced march: Wildenhope. But such was the lie of the land that they could no longer see so far, even had they tried to stare against so painful a wind; all that was visible ahead was a succession of thorny hedges and barbed-wire fences through which, endlessly it seemed, they now journeyed.

Had Thorne and his guardmoles not been constrained by the presence of captives and the Brother Adviser and his minions they might well have set off at a rapid pace and made Wildenhope before nightfall, but this could not be. In fact it was Brother Fagg who was slowest of all, much affected it seemed by the shock of his near-fatal tumble from the bridge. Not that anymole dared say so. Instead they all pretended that the frequent stops were for the benefit of all rather than mainly for Fagg. The Duncton moles continued to show the same stamina and fortitude they had before, and the grudging respect they had earned earlier was now open and sincere among the guardmoles, especially for Privet, who plodded on steadily without any faltering or complaint. The guards themselves would certainly have let the four moles talk and be together more, but Thorne's discipline and resolve were absolute, and it was not allowed.

But though Thorne did not give one hairbreadth in the policy he had adopted for getting his prisoners to Wildenhope, he had doubts, and regrets. He was to say in later years,* 'Privet and her friends seemed unafraid of what might happen to them at Wildenhope, with the exception of the mole Madoc, who I believe knew all too well. Some of my guardmoles believed that this lack of fear was born of simple ignorance – surely nomole who had any acquaintance with that dreadful place of punishment and elimination could possibly feel unafraid. But I believed – as I believe now – that their fearlessness came from their fundamentally different and more healthy view of the Stone and what it offered a mole.

'As Newborns, I and my guardmoles had been raised to view the Stone as a source of judgement and retribution. The disciplines it offered were designed to stop us sinning, for sinning we had been told was natural to mole, and temptation great. Do wrong and the Stone will punish you; do right and it might reward you. This was what our creed had reduced itself to.

'But the Duncton moles viewed the Stone not as a paternalistic enemy, but as an equal, a friend – forgiving, loving, joyous, celebratory. It was there to help, not hinder; and a mole did best when he or she strove to turn to the light of life and believe that everything was possible. I personally had no idea then what was to befall them, or how terrible it might be; if I had then I might after all have made it possible for them to escape. But I was a different mole then, and I did not. I wanted only to discharge my duty and be gone.

'Meanwhile, as the time passed and we drew nearer to Wildenhope, even my guardmoles slowed their pace in their reluctance to deliver Privet and the others to the brothers; yet the sense of faith and optimism amongst our charges grew almost unbearable. To us, then, they seemed like pups going to the slaughter; to them it seemed the Stone spoke with love, and put a courage in their paws that put a shame in ours. That last night I did not sleep at all, but doing the rounds of the four moles I found all of them, even Madoc, fast asleep.

'In the morning I asked Privet if she was afraid and her reply I remember word for word now, as I was to remember it in the months and moleyears ahead: "Of what should I be afraid when I trust in the Stone? Only of myself, and my own fear: *that* I do fear deeply, for it is hard for a mole to be worthy of the Stone's trust. Very hard. And I am afraid for Rooster and Whillan, who I love more than anymole; and for Madoc, who took all her courage in her paws to come with

* The quotation is from a private document found in the Cannock Library, scribed in Thorne's own paw.

us. This journey to Wildenhope, and the one that shall follow it, has been coming for many a moleyear, for decades perhaps. It is no accident that we four moles find ourselves on this fatal and unwelcome path, nor that it is you who are in charge of us. As for my fear, I am comforted by the fact that many Duncton moles before me have faced greater dangers and worse trials than mine, and survived with life and faith intact, and found a peace and Silence at the end of their troubled paths. Well now, mole, why should not I find the same, or you? So my fear is bearable . . ."

'She said this almost with a smile and I felt the inadequacy of my own purpose and faith before hers. I also felt, as I had once with Elder Senior Brother Thripp, that I was in the presence of a mole whose life was touched by the Stone's Light. It was then, at that moment, that I impulsively asked for her blessing and bowed my head to a mole who was my captive, and felt her touch on me. If she really felt fear she did not show it, but I felt it, deeply and unforgettably, and on her behalf. I felt it as savage and remorseless as the winds and rain that battered us, and the flow of the flooding river whose roar from the valley below filled our ears.'

So did Thorne later scribe of his feelings and actions in the fateful hours when Privet and the others were drawing near to Wildenhope, and to all that happened there.

That afternoon, the last of their journey, the path turned westerly and to their right, away from the edge of the bluff they had been following and for a time they lost all sight of the river. They entered rough and hummocky ground, and eventually took shelter in some scrubland.

That night the Brother Adviser sent one of his subordinates forward to alert Wildenhope to their approach, and to the importance of the moles they had arrested. There was a hard climb through rough ground the following morning, the weather still as bad as ever, and then they turned a corner and found themselves looking down a slope to a wider and more important path than the one they had been using. It ran west towards the dark mass of Caer Caradoc which was now all too plain to see, lowering in the distance, and east downslope towards a dark, humpy stretch of land beyond which the ground fell away once more to what they guessed would be the river and its valley.

But what took their attention was the group of ten moles on the path below, waiting for them in the wind and rain.

'The moles we'll be giving you over to,' muttered Privet's guard without enthusiasm. 'Guardmoles of Wildenhope.'

Thorne called the parties to a stop and unexpectedly summoned the captives to him, so they were together again for the first time since their capture.

'You had best say your goodbyes to each other here,' he said gruffly, 'for you'll get no other chance. Once they take you over from me you'll be isolated for good, so say what you want to each other now.'

It was the best he could do, and Privet and the others took advantage of it. While their guards looked away a little shamefacedly – though Fagg stared at them coldly all the while – the four moles embraced, and spoke blessings and prayers. It was a brief and precious time, and perhaps it was only then that they began to realize the danger they were in, from which there might be no escape. But it was all over in moments; Fagg shouted for them to proceed once more and the guards led them downslope to the waiting moles.

'Whatmoles have you there?' cried one of the Wildenhope guards. How powerful he looked, how pitiless his glance.

Thorne spoke their names, the wind snatching the words from his mouth and scattering them across the open fields.

'Lead him away! Get on with it! And her with you lot, and him, yes, him.' The captives were transferred to different custody.

'They'll give you no trouble, so there's no need to treat them rough,' said one of Privet's guards.

'They'll give us no trouble? Too right they won't,' laughed a Wildenhope mole, 'too bloody right. *These* moles will soon be giving nomole trouble!'

'You'll need Brother Quail's authority . . .' began Thorne, trying to protect them a little.

Fagg, who had been talking in an animated whisper to one of the Wildenhope moles, turned with a look of cruel triumph in his eyes.

'And they'll get it!' he said. 'The Elder Senior Brother Quail is in residence at Wildenhope *now*, so they'll get it very soon! The Stone's wrath does not wait for mole!'

Thorne said nothing, but only stared as his charges were led away down the path out of his control and beyond his help. He watched in silence as they disappeared.

'Where to, sir?' asked one of the guards.

'Cannock, where else!' he said sharply. 'Where we should have been long since. Cannock! Let's get out of here.'

'Yes, sir.'

'And may the Stone have mercy on those moles.'

'Yes, sir,' said the mole who had been Privet's special guard. 'But sir?'

'Well, mole?'

'Permission to stay awhile, sir, and follow at a safe distance.'

'What for, dammit?'

'She might need a bit of help, sir, if you know what I mean.'

'No might about it. But she's got better help than you or I could ever give.'

'Sir?'

'The Stone, for goodness' sake. The Stone's with her.'

'Do you believe that, sir?'

'I want to, mole, I want to. Now, lead us out of here, we've got a war to wage, and Cannock's where it's going to start.'

'Yes, *sir*.'

They turned upslope once more, and where one body of Newborns had met another, one touched a little by the Stone's Light, the other caught by evil shadows, nothing and nomole was left, but for the pawprints in the soft ground, and the cruel blustering wind, and the relentless rain.

Chapter Eight

It is one of the marks of successful tyranny that its practitioners can turn events and personalities, even time itself it seems, to evil advantage. In the period of his success Brother Quail was able to do this with devastating ease. So when Maple and the others effected Rooster's escape from Caer Caradoc and got clean away it was not quite the disaster for the Newborns that followers of the Stone liked to believe.

Tyrants like nothing better than an excuse to blame and punish, especially those who like Quail claim to act in the name of the Stone, investing themselves with the power to be its worldly judge and executioner. The Convocation of Caradoc was looking for ritual blood to spill, and having lost Rooster's it was happy to adopt as substitute the moles Quail falsely named, blamed and sentenced as the perpetrators of the plot to let Rooster go free, all in the same breath and that same evening.

He was tempted to include Thripp's son Chervil in his accusations – had not Chervil shown sympathy to Rooster during his confession? – but this was going too far too soon, and Thripp himself was present. So lesser moles were arraigned, tried and held for future punishment, most of whom had shown the spirit of resistance to the new order under Quail. It was an easy way of ridding Caradoc of Thripp's few remaining supporters, and among those arraigned though not yet killed were Arum and Boden, who had been so loyal to Thripp; of such confidants Brother Rolt alone was spared, perhaps because Quail felt he might be of use later, and that he was so demonstrably honest that his punishment would not be popular.

As for Rooster, and those who had escaped with him, Quail declared with absolute confidence, 'They shall be found in time, for no shadow, no dark corner, no obscure tunnel shall be dark or obscure enough to hide them.' He let it be known that the mole who found them would be well rewarded, and none could doubt this would be so.

For our knowledge of the subsequent events at Caer Caradoc,

84

through to the arrival of Privet at Wildenhope the following spring, we are indebted to the very remarkable records organized by Snyde, Duncton's former Deputy Master Librarian. It is one of the ironies of Newborn history that the records which were kept with the intention of glorifying its achievements have become through time the source for its greatest indictments. And in Snyde, whose appointment as Brother Record-Keeper at the Convocation was made by Quail himself, tyranny found a fatally perfect scribe. It may be that Snyde still harboured ambitions to succeed Stour as Master Librarian of Duncton Wood, but as official recorder of the Convocation he discovered his true role in life, and one he fulfilled with near-genius.

Twisted, embittered, sexually frustrated, intelligent and highly adept as a scholar and scribemole, and manipulative too, he was the right mole in the right place doing the right task. Anymole who has made the journey to Caer Caradoc, and viewed the huge and orderly collection of records that Snyde and the veritable army of minor scribes he eventually formed have left behind, sees the work of an obsessive collector of facts and data. Perhaps no period in mole history has been better or more completely recorded, as Snyde, exploiting the position chance and circumstance had given him, extended the web of his recording scribes, until almost every meeting of Newborn moles, however small, however inconsequential-seeming, felt incomplete without one of Snyde's moles present to scribe down its deliberations.

As for the policy meetings of Newborn Senior Brothers and Inquisitors, it was Snyde himself who recorded these, soon becoming a kind of background presence essential to all such meetings, where unobtrusively and without comment, he scribed down all he heard. Indeed Quail himself began to relish his presence, perhaps feeling that what he was saying and doing *should* be recorded for posterity, so important and 'historic' did it seem. Eventually Snyde's presence at a meeting seemed almost to legitimize it.

The trouble was that Snyde could not be everywhere at once, and so it was necessary for his subordinates to be increased in number and be always at paw to record events. In this he was only following a tradition begun by Thripp himself back at Blagrove Slide, where, in earlier and better days, the records had been kept with the sole purpose of ensuring that the background of young moles coming for training – birthplace, parentage, siblings, previous religious history, and kinship – was not forgotten. What was forgotten was the original

85

purpose of these records,* but as is often the case in well-organized systems the bureaucracy continued and the solution became the institution.

The growth of the Inquisitors under Quail meant that such records began to have new and more sinister uses, though difficulties in transporting them from one system to another limited their development. However, the emergence of Wildenhope as the main centre for the detention of miscreants and doubtful moles, once Caer Caradoc gained ascendancy, meant that inquisitorial records began to accumulate there.

The arrival of Snyde on the scene, used as he was to ordering texts in a large library, brought a new dimension to Newborn record-keeping. As a historian of the Modern period he was acutely aware of how the lack of good records hindered historical research and commentary; as a Newborn convert he sincerely believed in the greatness of his sect; as a mole he was obsessively inquisitive and prying; and as a librarian he loved nothing better than acquisition, and more acquisition. It was less the knowledge that mattered, and what the texts contained, but more the texts themselves and the pursuit of completeness, as if in the world of records he might find an order and security, and finally a control, he could never find among moles, or hope, in his personal vileness and unpopularity, to impose on others.

In appointing Snyde his official record-keeper Quail had unwittingly appointed a monster to a task he would make monstrous – his obsessive energy and secret endeavour turned ordinary scribes into a ruthless team of enquiry, and a hotchpotch of twisted records into the greatest collection of testimony and verbatim evidence of evil and tyranny that is ever likely to exist. Snyde was truly the spider at the centre of a web whose extent only he knew, or could ever hope to use.

Through the long harsh winter years that followed the Convocation of Caer Caradoc, Snyde and his minions busied themselves; first at Caradoc, then at Bowdler and finally at Wildenhope creating the structure of his system – vast, orderly, chillingly clean chambers into which the records of life outside, of Elder Brothers' meetings, of confessions, of inquisition, and of secret plots and counterplots would

---

* In his early days Thripp is believed to have hoped that such background records of the brothers, when set against their subsequent actions, would prove a useful guide to the importance of influences. He subsequently lost interest in such ideas as he came to view dwelling on the past as a hindrance to fulfilling the present. But the fact remains that Thripp set a precedent for recording meetings which Quail, using Snyde, so fatefully extended.

flow, and be stored for posterity. Once the Crusades started in spring he was ready to send out his spies and recorders in the form of the Brother Advisers, attached to every part of the Crusade – a representative specimen we have already met, in the vindictive and self-serving form of Fagg.

The Inquisitors certainly knew the worth of what he was doing, and he made sure of this, thus ensuring they would sanction him and his workers to record all they did. Equally, Quail saw to it that his own achievements were recorded by Snyde, who as spring approached had so gained Quail's confidence that he seemed almost like his twisted shadow, following him wherever he went and attending his meetings discreetly, silent but for the sliding and scratching of his scribing talons on bark.

But if these moles thought they knew the full extent of what Snyde was doing they were mistaken – they did not; nomole at that time did. For in addition to the 'official' records of inquisition and Newborn affairs, at some time in that period Snyde began to collect records to gratify his own peculiar interests and private obsessions.

These began with the obscene and filthy scribings that Squelch, Quail's obese and deviant son, one day showed him – records of certain activities, of intercourse with young unfortunates placed in Squelch's power for 'correction', so foul that even now few have ever been allowed to see them. Censorship may be a bad policy, but there are some things so corrupting, so evil, that it is surely better that they are not generally available to mole. Such were the scribings Squelch tentatively proffered Snyde, and it is better not to think too much about the heavy excitement and the eager lustful way the deformed librarian kenned them, his excitement mounting much as the normal passion of a young male in love with a female might mount in spring. We have already witnessed Snyde's necrophilic lusts at Ludlow, where he found filthy climax and fulfilment with the corpse of the guard who had been strettened. But generally Snyde was more fantasist than doer.

But what Squelch did, Snyde kenned, and the two began a relationship whose fervour and most passionate expression found its life in the pornography of the text. This was Snyde's first acquisition for his private collection, and it took him into dark tunnels of deviance and infamy in which sexual torture and cruel fantasy vied with the voyeuristic darkness and acts of obscenity and the necrophilia, real and imagined, already referred to. Snyde had a snout for such things, and the moles who indulged in them, and if the word 'great' can be associated with such an enterprise, his collection of such textual obscenities remains the greatest and most complete in moledom.

But much of the time Snyde was concerned with recording mundane trivia of the kind only an obsessive would bother with, and whose value or interest emerged only at later times. Thus did he depute a mole to set up a system of records of all who had reason to visit Wildenhope, whether as prisoners or guards – or as Newborns on the official business of arraignments and inquisition. So it is we know precisely whichmoles were held in Wildenhope from shortly after the end of the Convocation right through until . . . but a chronicler must beware of going forward too fast and revealing in the wrong sequence the infamous and historic events of those times.

It is enough to say that Snyde's records make it possible to construct a very full account indeed of affairs at Wildenhope as they affected Privet and the others, and to describe in as much detail as is appropriate the true horrors of that chilling place of punishment, death, and manipulation of minds, which is what Quail and his Inquisitors made it. But as we do so it is hard to forget that at our shoulder limps the deformed shadow, and pokes the weaselly snout, of Snyde, a scribe-mole of flawed genius; while beyond what we ken from his public record is a more private one, material for which his narrow, lustful, deviant eyes continually seek out, but which, thank the Stone, we will but rarely have to sully our minds and memories with.

Wildenhope has sometimes been compared to the Sumps, those deep and treacherous tunnels in the Cannock system which the moles of the Word used as a place of confinement and punishment when they moved their government of moledom there. Certainly it was used for a similar purpose, and the horrors of torture and inquisition were a feature of both. But Wildenhope was on a bigger scale, and much less obviously a place of evil and oppression. The bluff of land which held it was inconspicuous, and the tunnels themselves clean, spacious and well-ordered – more so than at Caer Caradoc. The surface was rough pastureland, which dropped away east and south to the wet meadowlands that bordered the river on one side and its tributary on the other. It is the kind of ground that youngsters spread across in summer when it dries out, worm-rich and easily delved but offering no permanence because of its vulnerability to flooding. All, that is, but for a raised pathway across it to the spit of ground where river and tributary meet and drop away steeply in cascading rapids.

When Privet and the others were brought to Wildenhope they were taken across the surface far enough to look across this wet ground,

88

flooded now by the rain that had hindered them so much. They could see the raised causeway emerging from submerged fields on either side, and past it the river-bank beyond whose edge the yellow rush of water could be seen.

'The water doesn't stay long on the surface,' one of their guards observed to another, who was unused yet to the place. 'It drains away, adding to the river's flood. The river is bloody terrifying close to, I can tell you! A mole looks down on to moving, rushing death!'

After this brief glimpse of distant terrors the four moles were taken below ground into wide, featureless tunnels. From here each was led a different way and, their separate protests ignored, for naturally they wanted to be together, they were placed in rough sandstone cells, lit from above, and well guarded. The only sounds were the distant roar of the river, the quiet and disciplined chat of the guards, and the occasional moans of other prisoners, heard but rarely seen.

Had the four moles been able to compare notes, they would have realized that they had been placed in near-identical cells. Each was round with a portal which widened upwards, making it impossible to get in and out without an awkward struggle which automatically drew the attention of nearby guards; and each could only be reached down a long tunnel whose entrance was close-guarded. They were set deep below soil level, in underlying sandstone, so that escape by tunnelling was impossible.

But to describe these extraordinary cells simply as 'lit from above' is to fail to convey any idea of the single feature which their unfortunate occupants soon came to regard with the greatest dislike. For the cells had no roofs, and the walls rose narrowly and inclined inwards, so that the perimeter at the top was only half that of the base. Above this non-existent ceiling, or hole as it appeared to those below, was the much higher roof covering all the cells, which were in effect small roofless chambers within one greater chamber.

This was not all. The main roof was fissured and open to the sky, and even on dull days such as that of their arrival the light appeared bright, blindingly so, to those peering up from below. Around the perimeter of the top of these strange exposed cells were routeways patrolled by guards whose heads, in featureless silhouette against the light beyond, would appear suddenly above, as they checked the presence of each prisoner in the cell below, who thus could not identify who was spying upon them. Since the guards rarely spoke, and never from above, the prisoners had the feeling, which soon became obsessive and deeply unsettling, that they could see nothing of the world, but the world could see them. Not for one moment could they feel private or unobserved, except at night, provided it was moonless and without stars. To add to the sense of isolation and helplessness thus created was the way the prisoners were fed – worms were dropped down from above, usually thin and inadequate, always sporadically and without even the comfort of regularity or routine.

Nor were the moles allowed out to the surface for grooming and ablution. Instead they were taken separately and in silence out of their cells, along a tunnel downslope into a cold damp chamber at the far end of which an underground river swiftly ran. Here they had to drink and wash, and then go to the furthest and darkest part of the stream, where it disappeared into rock, to pass water and faeces into the flow. It was clean, effective, and chilling, and left a mole feeling as icy and bereft mentally and spiritually as physically. Each prisoner who first came was warned against trying to escape or drown themselves by diving into the stream, though what might happen if they did nomole said. The threat was enough.

We know now that some hundred and twenty moles could be held in these extraordinary and efficient cells at Wildenhope, though few were ever there very long. Most passed through a system of holding, of sapping strength, or re-education, and of release or summary execution in the manner which Wildenhope was to make its own, and to which, regretfully, this account must shortly come.

The existence of a few long-term prisoners was rumoured by moles who dared speak of the place in any detail – former guards were expressly forbidden ever to mention it, but inevitably some did – and there were tales of moles forgotten except by guards, and now made pale and weak and withered by time. Perhaps some remembered the horrors of the Sumps of Cannock Chase, where many were so abandoned, and imagined the same of Wildenhope. There were terrors enough to make us hope that so cruel a place of loss and abandonment did not exist in the sterile labyrinths of the Newborns' Wildenhope. Certainly there was a continual supply of young males and females, ready, available and unwilling to satisfy the varied appetites of senior and privileged Newborns, such as Quail's son, Squelch.

This was the place into which Privet and the others entered, and where without word or promise of release they were summarily incarcerated. There, alone and seemingly abandoned, each had to wait, and struggle with the nightmare in which they found themselves as best they might.

They naturally did not see, and could not possibly have known, that the area of cells was but one part of the excavations, albeit one of the cruellest. Elsewhere, in higher tunnels delved in wormful soil at the western side of the bluff, were the administrative chambers of Wildenhope. Here the guards relaxed, and the mole who was responsible for the day-by-day running of the place gave his orders and meted out his discipline. This mole, the Governor, was always a Senior Brother, who for the period of tenure of his office was referred to by title rather than by name.*

But with Quail's ascendancy the Governorship lost some of its power for a time, simply because of Quail's decision, following the Convocation, to move his own administration and that of the Inquisitors to Wildenhope, which was rather better placed than Caer Caradoc for supervising the kind of Crusades that he had in mind for the coming spring and summer.

By chance this move had taken place but a short time before the capture of Privet, Rooster, Whillan and Madoc, so that there was no delay between their arrival and Quail's knowledge of it, since he was already at Wildenhope. Present too, and by now almost a prisoner himself, was Thripp, along with Brother Rolt, the one remaining aide allowed him, who had been at his flank in Caer Caradoc and had given Privet and the others such assistance, along with Boden and old Arum.

Many historians believe that it had been Quail's wish, with the help and collusion of Skua, to eliminate Thripp at Caradoc, or perhaps to 'disappear' him at Wildenhope – where the coincidence of the Governor being Tern, an ally of Quail, seems a peculiarly happy one for the Quail contingent. But Quail appears to have abandoned his murderous intent, at least for the time being, probably because the continuing popularity of Thripp amongst the brothers would have made it dangerous, perhaps fatal, for Quail to move against him too soon.

Then, too, though Thripp's present frailty made him a virtual prisoner of Quail, yet we know it to be true – as we have already indirectly seen – that he was by no means a spent political force. Plots and counterplots were the order of those days and Thripp, though physically weak, appears to have been much engaged in them. The one mole now had real power, the other a true following, and the two

---

* Snyde's records obligingly give the names of all the Newborn governors of Wildenhope, drawn from what sources nomole knows. The Governor during Privet's incarceration was Brother Tern, elder brother of Inquisitor Skua. The most infamous governor of all was, of course, Quail himself . . .

represented a schism that put the Newborn heart asunder for those few, those very few, who knew of it.

At the time of Privet's coming to Wildenhope the struggle had come to turn on the loyalty, or otherwise, of Chervil, Thripp's son. The question was, of course, loyalty to whom: to his father and an old idealistic dream, or to Quail, and a new, tempting reality? At the Convocation, as we have seen, Quail was already in the business of testing Chervil, for whom he had a natural dislike and distrust, given his paternity. Yet in the highest councils of the Newborns, now almost wholly supporters of Quail, two things about Chervil could not be denied: one was that he had shown no liking or inclination to sympathize with Thripp and his softer ways (as they were perceived); and secondly, that among the younger generation he was unquestionably the ablest and most charismatic mole, commanding the respect and affection of his peer group in a way that went beyond the fact that he was Thripp's son – though that helped.

Quail, who in Chervil's younger days had been appointed his mentor, had long recognized this. In truth, he had held Chervil in high affection and esteem, seeing in him all the potential for strong leadership and powerful command that was lacking in his son Squelch. When Thripp had commanded that Chervil be sent to the obscurity of Duncton Wood, beyond Quail's influence, the bald-headed Inquisitor had been hurt and furious, and had conceived a hatred for the Elder Senior Brother out of proportion to the act.

Chervil's return to Caradoc had therefore been monitored carefully by all the Senior Brothers, partly for the malicious pleasure that came from knowing that if Chervil favoured one of the rivals he would cause dismay to the other, and also because in terms of the resolution of the power struggle, if he lived up to his potential as a youngster, much might depend on him.

But Quail need not have feared – Chervil's reputation for toughness preceded him. Quail's spies sent back reports of the mole throughout the moleyears he was away and his moral rectitude and ruthlessness in pursuit of the Caradocian way could not be doubted. Quail had been especially pleased that on his coming to Caradoc it was to him and not Thripp that Chervil first paid his respects. True enough, he went to Thripp soon after, as any dutiful son might to a father who was ailing, but Quail's spies left him in no doubt that the meeting went badly. Old Thripp had tried to win his son's support and foment disunity, but Chervil had stayed firm. By this Quail was well pleased.

He was less happy however that Chervil kept his own counsel and was disinclined to come out against his father – which would have greatly eased Quail's elimination of him. Instead he stayed, as Quail saw it, insolently independent, as if he had his own eye on ultimate leadership.

'Which I have no doubt he has,' said Skua matter-of-factly, 'but what's the harm in that? Eh, Brother Quail?'

'It's insubordinate, Brother Skua,' replied Quail, eyes narrowing evilly.

'It's natural,' observed Skua. 'He will be a useful ally, and finally a useful subordinate.'

'He would do better to show respect,' growled Quail, not altogether unpleasantly.

'He might – but then perhaps he is only waiting for his father's demise. Many of the younger brothers would look askance if he publicly supported you against his father so soon. Watch and wait and be patient, and the young pretender will be yours to command.'

'And what do you say, Squelch?'

It was a peculiarity of Quail's conduct of affairs that he liked to have his loathsome son Squelch nearby, though moles no longer thought it peculiar, they were so familiar with it. Perhaps since Quail indulged nomole-else it did not matter that he indulged such a one as his rotund and pathetic son who emitted the sense of evil inadequacy as stinkhorn fungi drip foul-smelling poison that only the lowest and filthiest of creatures are attracted to. It was Quail's habit to turn to Squelch with a question or two at moments of doubt, usually rhetorically, though Squelch was capable of, and often gave, a perspicacious reply.

'Me? I say nothing today,' said Squelch on this occasion, 'because I choose to sing.'

His father laughed and said, 'You sing then, and sing well, for I must decide about Chervil.'

'Chervil's my friend,' said Squelch, 'and he you never ever harm, not ever. Never, never, never . . .'

The last word became almost a hysterical high-pitched scream before, disconcerting only to those who had never seen such a performance before, Squelch modulated his tones into the perfect pitch of his falsetto singing voice, and he sang a song of how green spring leaves held the glory of summer sun for too short a time and then withered, and were scattered by the autumn winds.

Quail beamed with pride. Whatever else his strange son might be, however disappointing, he had a genius for song, and when he sang, inappropriate though the moment so often was, he touched the hearts of those who heard.

Yet he had spoken a truth of which both Quail and Skua were well aware: whatever else Chervil was or might be, he *was* Squelch's friend, perhaps the only friend he ever had. They had been raised as youngsters together and shared in those secret talks and games that good friends know while they are innocent and incorrupt. How often had young Chervil defended his awkward friend; and how often had young Squelch turned the sound of skylarks and the hum of bees into the music of his lovely voice, and lulled the stronger and sterner of the two towards a gentler world that Thripp's harsh testing ways might otherwise have stolen for ever from Chervil's black and glittering eyes.

It had been Chervil who had pleaded Squelch's case to both Thripp and Quail, saying that he could never hope to be a disciplined brother as the rest of them would be, but that he had a gift for song and melody that was, surely, of the Stone. This was a little before puberty, and just before the harsher training of the youngsters was to begin.

'Training will kill him!' Chervil had said to his father and his tutor. 'He's not made for it . . . there's something better for him than that.'

It had been the last time Chervil had been able to fight for his puphood friend. Soon after he had begun his own rigorous training, while Squelch had been allowed – uniquely in the Caradocian order – to roam, to dream, to indulge, to sing.

'Is it what you truly want? Eh, mole? Is it?'

So had Thripp asked him one day, when Quail was there. And Squelch, already approaching adolescence, had darted an intelligent glance from one to another, and then smiled and said, 'Elder Senior Brother, may I speak to you alone?'

It was a surprising request, for Squelch had never before stanced against his father, but Thripp, not entirely willing, granted it. The two talked all morning, though what about none ever knew but Brother Rolt, Thripp's attendant. Afterwards Squelch was granted leave of absence from training as and when he wished, and was given the task of creating songs for Newborn rituals, such as those brilliantly performed at the Convocation. In all other matters he was to be free to do as he wished, answerable only to Quail.

Soon after this Chervil began his training, and later still he was sent off to Duncton by Thripp. Now he had returned, and one of the minor curiosities of Caradoc was to see how he treated his former friend – the one a mature and impressive leader in the making, the other a corrupted obesity who had grown into a monster who despoiled male and female youth, yet made songs of a beauty moledom had never heard before.

The answer had been that Chervil had far outgrown his former friend, and did not talk to him or show him respect. This was an aggravation to Quail, who regarded it as part of Chervil's disrespect to him. Yet still Squelch wanted Chervil's esteem and love, and reacted to any threat, real or imagined, to his old friend and protector, violently and with dismay.

So . . . 'I will not hurt him, as you put it,' Quail had to say. 'Why should I? He's a mole who will lead the Caradocian order one day!'

'We hope,' insinuated Skua.

'We do,' said Quail. 'If he behaves himself, and demonstrates his loyalty to me rather more than he has so far done.'

Which he certainly soon would, and in a most cruel and terrible way.

And then, most auspiciously, the mole Rooster was caught once more.

'And others too, I hear,' purred Quail, smiling on Fagg.

'Three others, Elder Senior Brother. Two youngsters of no consequence named Whillan and Madoc, and a third, the female scribemole and librarian from Dunction, Privet.'

'Ah, yes . . .' whispered Quail, 'I think my good friend Snyde knows *that* mole.'

'I do, Master,' said Snyde, 'and warn you against her. Whillan I would kill without delay. A troublemaker. Ignorant. As for Madoc, never heard of her.'

'I have made enquiries, but . . .'

Squelch giggled. 'I know *her*,' he said. 'She's one of ours, of Bowdler, lovely, curved and Welsh. I'll have her if I may, father, for my very own.'

'You may,' said Quail with teasing ambiguity, and how they all smiled, and how their eyes and teeth shone in the evil light of their council chamber.

Chapter Nine

The arrival of Privet and the others at Wildenhope did not cause quite the stir among the Newborns that Duncton historians have subsequently liked to imagine, and not as much as Brother Adviser Fagg, wishing to advance his career, had hoped. Privet herself was then almost unknown to Quail and his Inquisitors and in truth she was more curiosity than threat, for how could a female threaten the mighty brothers – even if her ability to scribe, and her reputation as a scholar, aroused interest?

Nor did Rooster's return into captivity attract as much interest by that spring as it would have immediately after his escape. The years of winter had passed by, moles had moved on, and now the long-awaited spring Crusade absorbed the Newborns' interest. In any case, those that remembered his confused and abject confession would almost certainly have failed to see the courage and pathos of it, marking him down instead as a mole past his prime. How could so strange and aberrant a mole be a threat to the Newborns?

As for Whillan, he was a mere youngster, and the Inquisitors were well-used to the recalcitrance of youth, and knew that the right discipline applied in the right way moulded most wills to correct behaviour. Thus, whilst the danger they were in was great, interest in them was at first minimal.

More obviously serious was Madoc's plight, for she was Newborn-trained and had dared to escape Bowdler and go her own way. She who as a Newborn female had been almost worthless, was now worth nothing at all. But she was young and pretty, and having erred deserved punishment – and females such as she (as Thorne had rightly perceived) could be both punished and made use of if given as a reward to deserving brothers or guards. The fact that Squelch had already claimed her for 'his own' boded ill.

This terrible fate, from which moles never emerged without emotional as well as physical scars – if they emerged at all – was one already decided for her long before the unhappy party reached Wildenhope, and the question was simply whatmole might have her first. The second and third were of less import, and the last few of no import at all. By then all the hope would have long since fled from poor Madoc's heart and eyes, and if there was life left at all in her used and abused body she would be cast out of Wildenhope and left to wander as a half-demented creature, and die lonely and afraid of the nightmare memories of a cell in which a succession, endless and vile, of corrupt males came to take their brief reward of her. Yet, though this was bad enough, there was a worse fate, and its name was Squelch. He had the run of such moles as Madoc, male and female, and if his lust was hungry, and his sadistic muse titillated, he might indicate that such and such a one be brought to him. This he had done.

It happened that Madoc's coming to Wildenhope coincided with a brief unwelcome lull in Squelch's and Snyde's symbiotic pornographic explorations. For only if Squelch did, could the other ken; Squelch the private doer was needed to service Snyde the secret fantasist record-keeper. But it seemed that nothing much had been doing of late.

No normal mole, raised to love and natural feelings, who delights in the shared touch and caress that innocent love may bring, can begin to understand why moles such as Snyde and Squelch find pleasures in clandestine deviant performance and aberrant observation, let alone collude in so foul a thing. But so it was, and at that time each was on the watch for the other's secret pleasure. Certainly Snyde had let Squelch know that it would give him useful instruction to be able to witness for himself, and scribe down, the things that Squelch did to a mole unfortunate enough to fall into his power.

So it was that just at the moment Madoc was brought to Wildenhope, Squelch was on the look-out for a mole who was deserving of fit punishment. We have no intention here of describing even in outline, let alone in any detail, what Squelch did to Madoc. It is enough to say that the very same evening of her arrival she was dragged to a cell rather different from the ones already described, in that it was down a deep tunnel that reeked of the odours of violent torture and death, made dreadful from time to time by the mortal moans and screams and helpless lost groans of moles brought to final confession and murder.

That Wildenhope even *had* such a quarter has until recent years been in dispute, and in defence of the Elder Brothers few of them even suspected its existence; even the Governor himself, his being an appointment temporary and by rotation, often never knew. Yet culpability must be upon the souls of those most senior for never asking questions and investigating to discover what happened to certain unfortunates who disappeared, and why it was that of those that arrived at Wildenhope some were never subsequently accounted for. Or if these questions were too much to expect, some of the Senior Brothers might have wished to ask why it was that the bodies of moles, often young, often horribly mutilated, were found along the banks of the treacherous river that was Wildenhope's western boundary. The river might at times be violent, as it was that fateful spring, but a river never put a mole's eyes out, and a river never tore the talons from a strong mole's paws; and no river ever ripped from a male . . . but enough is enough and of that we will scribe no more.

Not only was Madoc's cell in a less savoury place and nearer the tributary stream than those of her three friends, but it had a roof in which a vertical hole had been tunnelled straight to the surface, which allowed a curious round shaft of light into the centre of the cell. In addition, and disconcertingly, there were peepholes, just out of reach in three of the walls, which taken together meant that no part of the cell was free from being spied upon. That they *were* peepholes Madoc had no doubt at all, for the moment she came into the cell she heard a scuffling some way above her behind one of the walls, and looking up saw movement at one of the holes and an eye, black and shiny, staring at her. She moved out of its line of vision, and after more scuffling sounds it reappeared at another of the peepholes, as black, as shiny, and as filled with cold curiosity as before.

But Madoc had more than prying eyes to worry about. Apart from a quick word of comfort Privet had been able to give her on their arrival at Wildenhope, and a final embrace from Whillan and whispered words of love, as despairing but undying as they were real, Madoc had nothing to cling on to but hope; and hope dies quickly in the heart of a mole brought to such a cell as that by guards who prod her obscenely, and mockingly tell her that some very unpleasant things will soon be happening to her; threats which were confirmed by the stains and desperate scrabbled scratchings on the walls and floor of her cell. But Madoc had no need of any of this to put mortal fear into her and widen her eyes and set her heart beating in a near-uncontrollable panic as she was pushed into the cell and left to wait – for she knew already Wildenhope's reputation and had seen what was left of moles who survived the place, and had looked into the icy eyes of guards who had worked there. Madoc had no illusions – she knew that the chances of seeing Whillan again, or sharing time with

Privet, or ever completing the journey to Duncton Wood, were now negligible. All life as she had known it was over, and her venture into freedom now finished.

'Yet I did it, I did get away!' was all the comfort she could whisper to herself, 'and I met moles who treated me as a mole should be treated! And I loved and was loved in the way the Newborns deny, but which all moles should know at least once. Oh Stone, you granted my wish to live, to love; now give me courage to face what comes without losing faith in you, or the memory of moles I have been proud to call my friends.'

The eye at the peephole blinked at this prayer to the Stone 'so sweetly sincere' as the watcher, Snyde himself, was to describe it in the scribing-down of all that took place in that cell.

If the light in the cell brightened for a brief moment, and if the Stone gave the sense of its grace to that murky place, it was while Snyde blinked, which is why he never recorded it. Some things Snyde did not see.

'Oh Stone, Privet said you would help a mole if a mole will only help herself. She said your power comes from faith, and that even a mite of faith, even less than a mite, if it is felt in the heart, and expressed with truth, will bring forth from you all the power a mole needs – so Stone, I have faith in you, I really have. Help me now. Help me be true to my friends. Help me find a way through the trial, and Stone be with me.'

Privet! Snyde smiled with pleasure at this reminder of Privet and her current plight. Abandoning his secret occupation for a moment, he scurried down the tunnel to the main one from which the punishment cells radiated, just in time to find Squelch waddling along and peering pleasurably into each of the cells as he passed them by, to find his latest victim.

'Brother Squelch!'

'Ah, Brother Snyde! Welcome. But be peaceful, for such joys as you are going to watch and record are best taken slowly. Hunger is a greater pleasure than satisfaction; unsatisfied lust more joyous than fulfilment. Or did you not know that?'

'I know it, I know it,' whispered Snyde impatiently, 'your pleasure is a few cells down from here. Now, in saying her pathetic prayers Madoc mentioned a mole called Privet and I would like to learn what she knows of her.'

'The same Privet of Duncton we heard mentioned before?'

'The same.'

'I may ask her of it.'

'You must!'

A brief look of displeasure crossed Squelch's shining, benign face. 'There is nothing I *must* do, Brother Recorder Snyde. But let us not squabble over titbits when a feast of pleasure lies before us. Back to your spyhole, mole, while I go to the portal of desire!'

He made a flourishing gesture with his paw, if any gesture by so fat and greasy a mole could be called a 'flourish', and Snyde hobbled obediently back to his watch.

We have already made clear that the foul details of Squelch's inter-course with Madoc in that cell, fully recorded by Snyde though they were, will not be permitted to besmirch this text. We will say only this: Squelch heaved himself with some difficulty through the narrow portal of the punishment cell and presented himself to Madoc. She smelt, and knew, the greasy scent of his body even before he entered the place, and her nightmare came true when he did, and she screamed – a scream that only fuelled his lust, which fed entirely upon the fear of his victims.

She looked into his piggy, smiling eyes and knew that her life was about to be forcibly and irrecoverably changed. He touched her as the guards had done and she shrank away until her rear was to the wall. Then foully and sickeningly he abused her, so that her body felt it had been tainted and stained for ever, even before from out of the odorous, sweaty folds of his flesh there appeared that pink and shining thing which was all, for now, his vast and shapeless form became. Trapped, nowhere to turn, she struggled violently against his slippery yielding bulk, unable to get a hold, unable to escape. Then she was turned by him and submerged under him, as he clumsily mounted her, and entering her, tried to steal her very soul and self-respect for ever.

And all the while a solitary eye stared down from the peephole upon the sorry, murky scene.

But just as Snyde had not seen the brief glimmer of the Stone's Light when Madoc had prayed before Squelch's coming, he was blind to the grace of light, of hope, and of insight that now entered into her heart.

It is a fact of moles' spiritual life that often when hope is let go, and the tunnels are at their darkest and deepest, the Silence is heard, and the way ahead to Light made clear. We must, it seems, give up the hopes and expectations that link us to the past, to move freely forward. Such moments may be rare, but they are always recognized, if not for what they truly are, then at least as something special which should be harkened to. Such a moment came to Madoc then, and the thought it prompted took her utterly by surprise. One moment she was pushed and shoved to the void of self-abnegation and the next she found herself thinking in wonderment, 'I am going to have his young.'

Oh yes, she knew with certainty that from this vile act upon her the very thing she had failed to achieve with Whillan would follow, and in knowing that all fear fled her, and she knew that Squelch could not, would not, harm her more, and she would be free of him. Knowing this, she felt a terrible pity for him, that he was so hideous and his act so unforgivable. It was what had formed him – much trouble and lacklove in his past – that made her feel pity.

'Forgiveness is not so hard,' Privet had said once, 'provided you can forget yourself.'

For better and for worse Madoc knew that this act would leave her with pups and they, for all their horrid paternity, would be more important for a time than anything. Above, about her, over her, into her, Squelch quivered and slobbered the climax of his stolen act. And all Madoc could think was, 'One day I shall tell them what he was, except he *isn't* this. Nomole is this. All moles are of the Stone and we must strive to see the Stone in them, however foul they are.'

Many moles, and even some historians, insist on disbelieving that Madoc can have experienced such thoughts and feelings. Yet so she herself has scribed, but it helps that she repeatedly expressed utter astonishment at her final detachment from the horror of it all. 'I can only say,' she said, 'that I felt pity, and amazement that of all moles and all acts, this was the one to get me with pup!'

Squelch finished, his voice a squeaky scream, his paws fat and flabby at her flanks, his shafting excitement shrinking back into the folds of furry flesh whence it had briefly come.

'Sing,' she whispered, immobile on the floor, her strength utterly taken. 'Sing to me.' It was, she knew, what he did best – and that would be all she ever told her pups about him. The song, the beautiful song he would sing, and never the circumstances. Why should pups know their father for a monster, when a part of him is perhaps something more worthy?

'Sing?' whispered Squelch, heaving himself off her and wishing that Snyde was not privy to this part of their dialogue as he realized to his surprise and horror that his victim felt no more fear, nor even pain; not even disgust, only pity.

'Yes,' she commanded, turning to him and looking into his eyes with a sympathy he found exquisitely unbearable.

'What about?'

She took his paw and put it to her flank. 'About what you might have been if you had not been made what you are.'

He was gifted to understand what she meant, and spontaneous tears rolled down his cheeks.

'Sing?' he sighed.

'Sing for the sake of your unborn young.' she whispered so the voyeur could not hear.

'My young?' he sobbed, feeling her flank and forced to a vale of shame and self-pity he had never visited before.

Then sing he did, in that beautiful high-pitched voice, a song to the life he had made but which he would never – must never – know. And Snyde heard, and stared, and scribed, but did not understand the smallest part of the tragedy and triumph he was witness to.

When Squelch was done he was quite drained, and then Madoc knew she must talk to make him know her, make him want to save her, and tell him of things which, if he had tried to torture out of her she would have resisted telling to the last. Things which seemed a betrayal, but which, she knew, in a way mysterious and as harmonious as his song, the Stone willed him to know – as well as that anonymous observer who watched and heard all they did together.

Of Privet she spoke; of Whillan; and of Rooster. All, all she told, of their different loves and struggles and finally of how it might be that Rooster was Whillan's father, and Privet his aunt. In all of Madoc's story it is these revelations which remain most inexplicable and contro-versial. None can doubt that she was an intelligent and resourceful mole, so that the claim of naïvety cannot be sustained. She must have known, or guessed, the terrible use to which Newborn Inquisitors might put such information. Some describe the revelations as an appal-ling betrayal, for which Madoc had to suffer appropriate punishment. A few point out that from this 'betrayal' all that was good that happened after really stemmed.

But judgements are an irrelevance when the Stone's Light shines. All we can do is accept reality for good and bad, and trust that if a mole claims that it was the Stone that directed her to speak as she did, then she is telling the truth.

It is not hard to imagine the feverish excitement with which the spying Snyde heard these revelations. Knowing the modern history of Duncton as uniquely well as he did, in which the pattern of the

Stone's Silence was in all things, he understood what Squelch could not: that if Rooster and Privet were blood-related through Whillan, and one was a Master of the Delve and the other a scholar and scribe-mole of rare ability, then it might surely be in Whillan that the future for the Stone followers lay. In him, therefore, was the greatest danger to the Newborns. From which the starkest and simplest decision followed – the mole Whillan was better dead than living.

'He must die, Elder Brother Quail, he must be stopped!'

Oh, yes, after it was all over Snyde had barely paused to thank Squelch for letting him witness the punishment of Madoc before he was busily off to Quail to tell all he had heard, and to stress that the recently-caught Privet, Rooster and Whillan might have more significance for the Newborns than had been thought.

'If I may say so,' continued Snyde, turning and ducking his twisted head as if pre-empting criticism and doubts from Quail, Skua and the other Elder Brothers before whom he spoke, 'there is a kind of fatal pattern to events regarding Duncton – I hesitate to use the word "harmony" for moles as wrong-headed as the followers – and this matter of Rooster, Privet and Whillan makes me feel very uneasy. Rooster escapes dramatically, and now appears as a captive once more; Privet, a harmless-seeming mole turns out to come from the Moors and to know Rooster of old; the mole Whillan is son to Rooster and his mother is Privet's sister. And here they all are, together, *harmless-seeming*, but reminding me of times in Duncton's recent past when the kinship between moles was intertwined with events, and harmless-seeming moles proved far more formidable than their foes gave them credit for.'

Quail's bald head wrinkled at the thought, for by now he had a great respect for Snyde, and knew him for a subtle mole well versed in the labyrinths of history, and, therefore, of treachery and the work-ings of the Snake. Skua, too, looked thoughtful, his instinct telling him that there was a truth in Snyde's words, even if its precise nature and implication were hard to define.

'So?' whispered Quail. 'What do you suggest?'

'The mole Whillan is the danger,' hissed Snyde, feeling the exquis-ite delight of the machinations of high council, coupled this time with the personal and malicious pleasures that came with hurting Privet through her foster-son, whose abilities in scribing, whose obvious intelligence, whose very body, whose *potential*, Snyde had long hated. 'In the Duncton tradition it is always youth that comes to the fore and saves the day. *Whillan should be disappeared.*'

'He has sinned sufficiently to warrant it,' said Skua, eyes glinting.

'And what does Brother Chervil think?' purred Quail, whose face suddenly had the relaxed and purposeful confidence of one who has seen the way forward, and is waiting his moment to reveal a decision made while others continue to talk.

Chervil frowned, his eyes flicking with distaste from Snyde, then to Skua and Quail with respect. He was the youngest among them, but there was nothing youthful about him. He had matured since his dialogue with Privet on the journey from Duncton and now looked formidable indeed. Quail might be more frightening and powerful, and Skua more threatening, but when Chervil spoke his words had authority, and an appeal to allmole that made even those two listen with interest and respect.

'I think the mole Whillan should be rather more than "disappeared",' he said with conviction. 'He should be seen to die, and his death should be made known to the Duncton moles who still call themselves followers. As for what Brother Recorder Snyde calls "patterns", I defer to his assessment. I sense he may be right. I think however that if we are to win the hearts and minds of the remaining followers to our Newborn way we should be seen to be as publicly merciful as we are firm with moles like Whillan. We may take with one paw, but we must be seen to give with another. Therefore the mole Privet should be spared. But Rooster . . . now there we have a problem, Brothers. If we kill him we risk him becoming a martyr to the followers' cause. If we let him live we risk him rallying followers to his flanks.'

'Therefore,' said Quail, interrupting forcefully as leaders sometimes must, 'we must neutralize him.'

He paused just long enough for the Elder Brothers to look at each other, and wonder aloud at the point he had raised before he pushed his shining head forward, asserted his authority with a glance, and said, 'There is a way of doing that I think, once and for all, But it will mean bringing forward to tomorrow the punishment of the blasphemers we had planned for a few days hence.'

'You mean all of them?' said Skua.

'Yes, that is what I mean,' replied Quail decisively. 'Let the punishments be on the morrow, and let the judgement of Whillan and its execution be the final one. The moles Privet and Rooster may witness it.'

So Whillan's elimination was agreed. But as preparations began for that awful event, a mole went hurrying from the Council chamber, unremarked, and the brother he went to find was Rolt. This was one interview that Snyde and his spies did not record, even if they knew the burden of what was said: Privet was in captivity, and on the morrow her son would die, and Rooster in some foul way be 'neutralized'.

Learning which Rolt went hurrying to Elder Senior Brother Thripp, in the obscure part of Wildenhope in which he was confined, and told him of the recapture of Privet and the others, and how their fate had been decided.

As Thripp listened to what Brother Rolt had to report the tremor ceased in his body and a fire of hope and faith came to his eyes. And this, strangely, is what he said: 'She is come then, come back to me, and our prayers have been answered. Now, Rolt, now is the time for us to think, to pray, to act. You must take me to her in the cell where they have her. Take me now!'

He spoke almost feverishly, as if Privet's coming to Wildenhope was an act of willing return to him personally, rather than part of an involuntary process of captivity and finally punishment.

'It will be dangerous, Elder Senior Brother, very dangerous.'

'Ah, but there will be a way, the Stone will show it to us. It is the least I can do for her.'

'But I have told you, Arum and Boden are to be punished along with others of your followers tomorrow. In any case, Master, you are still too ill to be wandering around Wildenhope avoiding guards and seeking prisoners in cells whose location you do not know.'

'Am I, Brother Rolt? Am I not better? I think I am! Bold is best, and there are still many who will follow me, or at least turn a blind eye to what I do. Come, let us hasten to her. I owe it to Privet now. She has been the only joy of all my life.'

'You are too ill, Brother,' pleaded Rolt, faltering before the purpose and passion of the mole he had served and loved like no other in his life; he knew as no other could what Privet alone had been to Thripp once in years gone by in Blagrove Slide. 'Instruct me in what to say to her.'

Thripp suddenly smiled, and for a moment he looked almost young and well again. 'Why, Brother Rolt, if I knew what I was going to say, I would willingly tell you. My head aches, my bones and muscles ache, my very soul aches as they have for moleyears past. I would like nothing better than for you to go for me, but there are some errands a mole must run for himself. And anyway, *now* is the time of curing and healing; now I see a way. My ailment has been of mind,

105

not body. My dearest . . . my Privet, is my cure. Come, now, let us go together and put our trust in the Stone.'

With help from the devoted Rolt, Thripp rose slowly from the litter where he lay and went with difficulty to the portal of his chamber. As he came out into the tunnel beyond it a guard on duty snapped to attention.

'Forgive me, Elder Senior Brother, but you're not meant . . .'

Thripp silenced him with a stare that seemed to cut through to his very heart.

'I do forgive you, mole. Now, Brother Rolt and I have a short journey to make, and a cell to find, and *you* will see us safeguarded there and back. We go on the Stone's business.'

'The Stone's business?' repeated the guard, spellbound by Thripp's gaze, and voice, and being, as so many had been before him.

'Oh yes,' said Thripp, 'its most holy business.'

'Then I will, I will,' said the guard, his training and his loyalties quite deserting him, as for the first time in his life he had the feeling that he was playing a part, however minor, in a mission for the Stone, and that the mission *was* a holy one.

'How do you do it, Master?' muttered Rolt admiringly. When he wished it, Thripp could charm a worm out of a rook's cruel bill.

'Faith, Rolt, and passion and conviction, that's all you need, and the world is yours. In combination these are most fatal qualities. Of them all faith alone is what moles need. Now . . . is Privet really here at last?'

'She is, Master,' repeated the good Rolt.

'I am . . . afraid. Will she know me? She knew me not at Caradoc!'

'I made sure she could not quite see you, Master. But now she will see you face to face, and surely she will know you.'

'And then . . . ?'

Rolt shook his head and stared at the thin, ill form of his Master.

'Then? Elder Senior Brother, I cannot tell.'

'Well then, we must find out.' And Thripp went forward with a lightness in his step, such as he had not shown in many a moleyear.

Chapter Ten

Privet suffered the inevitable roughness and ribaldry of the Newborn guards well enough; she could tolerate such behaviour, and coarse comments about her being 'too withered and thin to take a mole's fancy'. Such slights would almost have been a comfort if they had not also got Madoc in their paws, who most certainly was neither too withered or thin to avoid their unwholesome attentions. But as she suffered doubts and agonies for Madoc, so too did she for Rooster and Whillan, who since the probable truth of their blood relationship had been realized, had come to mean even more to her, separately and together, than before.

The cell they put her in was at least clean, and once there she was left alone and unmolested. But the guards' silence was unsettling, as was the fact that the cell was roofless, and the bright light that came down from the high roof beyond, and the occasional silhouettes of moles whose faces she could not see as they peered down on her, left her feeling vulnerable.

Her only recourse was to prayer and contemplation of the sorry situation they had got themselves into, though this was made hard for her by the steady distant roar of the river. From the first moment she had heard it on top of the Edge it had upset her, as if in its never-ending tumult was a warning, an omen of some coming event that she ought to ready herself for. She had faith in the Stone, never more so – a faith that had been greatly bolstered in their present predicament by her conversation with Thorne, who unwittingly confirmed what she had always believed – that the Newborns claimed the allegiance of at least some moles who, at heart, would not thwart the followers' desire for freedom of worship and liberty of thought and speech, if only a way could be found of reaching into their hearts with the power of love. How *that* was done was the Stone's business! But meanwhile a mole must live in hope.

Which proved difficult as the tedious hours wore by; the night seemed never-ending, morning passed slowly, and still no word of any kind came, nor even food. She was hungry and thirsty, and even

107

the strongest mind needs food and drink to sustain its balance. Her first meal, such as it was, was thrown down to her in silence from the parapet above late in the morning, and though she called up for word of what was happening, and that she was thirsty and must attend to her natural needs no answer came back immediately. But later, when she was eking out the little food they gave a voice said from above, 'If you must foul your cell, do so, but you'll be taken to drink and wash and groom in good time.'

She was taken later to a low extensive chamber in which a chill stream ran, and there drank and did all she must under the insolent gaze of two silent guards.

'Right in, submerge yourself, and don't let the force of the water take you, for we'll not be in a hurry to save an old crone like you.'

She was wet, cold, and desolate when they led her back to the cell, and already dreading the long wait she now expected before mole spoke to her again. She felt her strength already seeping from her, and reality slipping towards the unreal life of isolation and horror.

'Stone,' she began to pray, as she was pushed back into the cell, 'give me the strength to survive.'

But survive as what? The mole she had always been, journeying from place to place, from system to system, in search of new moles, new tasks. *That* mole?

'No, Stone, not that any longer. Give me courage to be the mole for whom you have set a task that journeying mole can only vaguely see, but which frightens her, and brings a panic to her breast. It is near now, this task, and you must try to help a weak mole, all withered, all crone-like now! You must help that mole cast off her old self that she may have courage to venture forth to the task she knows awaits her.'

For a long time then Privet was silent, and still, and there was peace around her in the cell, and purpose, and sometimes her eyes half closed, her mouth moved and whispered fragments of thought as if she were searching through her mind and heart to find the true way.

'Stone,' she whispered as the afternoon waned into twilight, 'it was the Book of Silence I came looking for, so long ago when I was young. It was for that I left Duncton. And now it is towards it that I reach, frightened and alone, for none goes with me on this path, none at all.'

Tears trickled down her face; exhausted, hungry, and feeling terribly alone, she closed her eyes and slept.

Pawsteps approached along the parapet above, coming down

through the evening light. Whispered voices, whispered echoes. Guards slipping away from their post, compliant. Three moles approaching, and a head looming over the parapet to peer down at the exhausted Privet.

'This is the mole, this is the one.'

'The mole Privet?'

'Yes.'

'She has . . . aged. Her haunches are thin, her coat bedraggled with time.'

How soft the voice, how gentle.

'We have all aged, Master.'

'I must go down to her.'

'It may be the last chance, Master. But, remember, time is short.'

'So . . . this is Sister Crowden.'

'*Was*, Elder Senior Brother: she is Privet of Duncton now. Remember, you have but little time . . . I will watch out for you. The guards will be biddable for but a short time.'

Thripp slowly descended the winding way to the level of the portal into the cell. His eyes were bright, and his step firm, though he felt it prudent to stay near the wall, lest he needed support. His heart thumped in his chest. He peered at a guardmole, who studiously ignored him and then moved discreetly away. Then, with some difficulty, he clambered over the narrow threshold and found himself stanced before the sleeping Privet.

'Sister Crowden! Wake up, Sister Crowden!'

Whatever deep dream or dark unconscious place Privet was in was cut across by that old familiar authoritative voice. She stirred, she struggled to wake, even as she heard her own voice say obediently, 'Brother Confessor . . . I . . . I did not mean to sleep . . .'

For a moment before full waking she felt safe, she felt joy. Then loss, and fear, and all the years since Blagrove Slide crowded in and she awoke.

'Brother Confessor . . . it is you . . .'

She found herself staring into his clear eyes; he had aged, and grown thin and troubled.

'Sister Crowden . . .'

'My name is Privet now,' she said, wanting to reach out to him, this mole she had once loved. This mole had shown her ecstasy. This mole . . .

'What is your name? I never knew it, never.'

Even as he hesitated momentarily she recognized the thin body, the greying fur, the gentle voice. In Caer Caradoc had she seen and heard them.

'Thripp,' he said. 'I am Thripp.'

'Thripp! I should have known when I saw Brother Rolt again. So you are Thripp?'

He nodded as if it was a curse. 'The years have . . .' he whispered as he reached for her.

And the years since then might not have been as, for a time, they held each other close.

'Thripp . . .' she whispered.

'Privet . . .' he said.

Two moles in awesome pilgrimage, whose paths crossed once before, and crossed now, and would again, each knew, one more time.

'There has been no other,' he said. 'Never another Sister Crowden, Privet of Duncton, only you.'

'One other for me,' she whispered, 'one other love.'

Their voices were whispers, their tears conjoined, their time thus too brief.

He understands, she thought, *as Rooster does.*

She judges not, he knew.

'Master,' cried out Rolt from above, 'there's little time . . .'

They pulled apart, staring, amazed.

'Our pups, Brother Confessor, you promised they would live. Rolt said . . .'

'I kept my word as best I could.'

'As best . . . ?' Her voice trembled. She wanted to hear it from him.

'One did not survive, but three still live.'

'Which?' Her voice was sharp now, almost hard, the voice of a mother, readying to protect her young.

'The one that died was Brimmel . . .'

Privet sighed with pity and dismay. So many years had she held on to the memory of her four young and now she must take her leave of Brimmel, whose bright eyes she remembered looking into hers.

'Not . . . ?'

'Painlessly,' said Thripp. 'She did not suffer. Loosestrife lived, the liveliest of them all, and little Sampion.'

'You used the names I gave.'

'I did. And the male, Mumble, I called him that as long as I was able. A strange name, Sister Crowden, but who am I to question the names so erudite a mother gave her young? When he became a

110

brother we changed it to something more suitable.'

They looked at each other and almost smiled. 'Chervil, my son,' whispered Privet.

'It is so,' he said.

'I have spoken to him,' she said. 'Of them all he is the one I knew as an adult.'

'The others . . .'

'I would meet Sampion and Loosestrife if I could.'

'May the Stone grant it to both of us. I last saw them as pups. I think that Rolf told them your true name . . .'

'Master! Pawsteps!' It was Brother Rolt's voice from above. The sounds echoed down into Privet's cell and then faded. 'We must not stay long.'

'Sister . . . Privet . . . listen to me and try to trust me.'

'I shall,' whispered Privet, hoping she could.

'We know of your love for Rooster, and of his relationship to the mole Whillan. But we have little power here in Wildenhope. We shall do what we can, but you must trust us as you trust the Stone. They shall live, but in ways and places you may not like. They shall live on.'

'Let my life be forfeit before theirs.'

'On your life mole all moledom may depend.'

'But I am only Sister Crowden!'

'No, mole, you are Privet of Duncton Wood now, and time will prove you to be greater than us all. Try to forgive me, Privet – for all I have done to you.'

'It is for the Stone to forgive, only the Stone. Hear its Silence and you will be forgiven.'

The sound of more pawsteps . . .

'Master, we must go!' called Brother Rolt urgently.

'What were you to me?' wondered Privet aloud.

'I am Thripp, and that is all I am. Neither Brother Confessor nor Elder Senior Brother. And you, Privet of Duncton Wood, born of Crowden, daughter of Shire, granddaughter of the Eldrene Wort, you gave me all that has been worthwhile in my misguided life.'

'And our son?'

'Our son, our only son, Chervil, may the Stone guide him . . .'

Chervil . . . Thripp . . . all turned in Privet's mind and she knew the Stone's task was almost on her. Her son Chervil and Thripp and Loosestrife and Sampion lived. The walls of the cell turned, as the season, as her task.

111

'Chervil will one day be worthy,' she whispered. 'Our son will be worthy.'

'I wish it could be so, but . . .' said Thripp, uncertain.

The last light faded even as these words were said, yet they stared through the darkness at each other in silence, as if they could see each other now as they had never been able to through the long years since their parting.

'Privet,' he whispered to her, as if he had never said the name before.

'Thripp,' she replied.

'Now, come, Master, come . . .' called Rolt.

And the last Privet heard was Thripp's voice saying, passionately, fervently, and with that same resolute conviction that had inspired a generation of moles to follow him, 'There will be a way through this darkness, there will be a way . . . May the Stone help us find it in time. Trust in what happens to the others, Privet, and guard yourself, for on you now all depends.'

She heard his pawsteps departing as other, heavier ones hurried near.

Then in the black depth of her cell Privet prepared herself for the morrow; she whispered the names of all her young, the one that had been and those that lived still . . .

'Brimmel, and Sampion and Loosestrife and Mumb . . . and Chervil. And you Whillan, you as well, my dear.' And a fearful joy was in her heart as beyond them silence called her, and she knew how she might go to it.

Chapter Eleven

The captives could hardly have known it, but the rain through which they had journeyed to Wildenhope had stopped almost since their incarceration. But the sky had stayed for the most part lowering and grey, and the river full, and dangerously fast.

Not that the respite from rain helped them, for when one dawn soon after their arrival they were brought up one by one to the surface by guards, it began to spit down again. Rarely can moledom have known so gloomy and dispiriting a scene; the succession of moles, many ill or suffering the effects of torture, and others demented by isolation alone, were brought together on top of Wildenhope Bluff that morning, and told to keep their snouts low and their eyes cast down. Those that succeeded in glancing about quickly saw moles much like themselves, oppressed and with little hope. It was plain enough that punishment was in the air, but most seemed too broken-down to care.

Privet, Rooster and Whillan managed to catch sight of each other in the crowd and nod a gesture of encouragement – but of Madoc there was no sign, and nor was she there, as Snyde's list of the victims that day shows. She had, in fact, been detained below on Squelch's orders, and her name and arrival expunged from the records. Madoc now no longer officially existed at all. While huddled among the broken moles were Thripp's old aides Arum and Boden, their bodies defeated, but faith in Thripp's way still shining in their eyes.

All was grey, all oppressive, and while they waited a cold wind sprang up from the west, forcing guards and prisoners alike to turn their snouts eastward towards the spit of land which marked the confluence of the river and its tributary from Caer Caradoc. The river flowed shiny grey across the sodden landscape, except where the smaller stream met it and made a race of white and yellow water, which surged and sucked and ran on all swollen and murderous southward to a curve and then shot out of sight.

Despite the warning to keep their eyes to the ground the continuous dull roar and sheer force of the river drew a mole's gaze, furtive at first but then grimly fascinated, as a helpless mole might watch the preparations of the creature about to prey upon it.

The Elder Brothers finally appeared, all of them, the great and the good of the Caradocian Order. Quail now unchallenged at their head, Skua at his left flank, and other older ones gathering round him. While to their rear and at one side, less conspicuous than he had been at the Convocation at Caer Caradoc, was Squelch, beaming and content.

To the other side and more prominent was Chervil, not quite part of the favoured group. His face was set in a dark impassive glower, and he was flanked on one side by Feldspar, his guardmole, and on the other by Feldspar's two stolidly powerful sons, Fallow and Tarn. Snyde's record of this grim event makes the following subtle comment on Chervil's presence: 'At the Convocation in Caradoc, Chervil, son of Thripp, had also appeared flanked by these guards. But on that occasion they looked as if they were his captors; at Wildenhope they looked as if they were his bodyguards, obedient only to him.'

In the interim Chervil had won the three moles' confidence and loyalty, and their presence served to increase the impression of power and authority he manifested. This was reinforced by his obvious health and strength – his eyes were glittering bright, his black fur glossy, his powerful talons shining – and light seemed to favour him so that he had the fascinating appeal possessed by many consummately powerful moles.

We may well imagine the glances Privet gave him, knowing as she now did what he was to her. But not a single sign of feeling towards him did she betray, not fear even. She must trust the Stone, and that meant giving up fear as well as hope. She must trust . . .

The impression of power Quail conveyed was more direct and brutal than Chervil's, and perhaps more immediately chilling. He, too, benefited from the presence of acolytes about him, in particular the sharp-snouted, mean-eyed Skua. If the grey light of the day seemed to enhance Chervil's strength, it made Quail's bald head and cold eyes almost lurid in effect, and the myriad of lines and creases in his features were curiously frightening, as if even age dared not quite disfigure him yet was creeping up to take him unawares.

Snyde took a stance some way from the main body of moles, and on a little rise of ground, the better to view proceedings and report on them. He had come with two of his most trusted minions and after a brief consultation they both discreetly melted into the crowd of moles, one among the victims, the other among the Elders, where, no doubt, they would observe, eavesdrop, and report back later to their mentor.

It is to one of these perhaps that we owe our image of Rooster who, as striking as ever, was the only one it seemed who was not so over-awed as to be biddable and still. He moved restlessly, his shaggy grotesque head (as it seemed to the observer) jerking and shifting, his eyes here and there, unable to simply look down, or just stare at the river. And sometimes he groaned, or mumbled, and his paws patted and squelched at the wet ground.

The Elders waited in silence, until at last, slowly, aided by Brother Rolt, Thripp himself appeared. His fur was lustreless, his pawsteps shaky, his head atremble, and his eyes, peering from beneath a worried frown, looked a little lost, a little helpless. It did not seem possible that this sick old mole, once so great, had been able to talk so clearly and passionately to Privet the night before. Yet there he came, right past her without a word, muttering angrily as he caught sight of his son – *their* son.

Chervil turned impassively towards him, staring with a studied insolence which seemed to say, 'Your time is done, old mole, your brief moment is past, your life is run. The future is for moles like me.'

Thripp seemed almost to wither with dismay before this look, and he stumbled, turning pathetically to Rolt for physical support without which he might have fallen.

Certainly no such help came from Chervil, who stared coldly at his father's discomfiture, and then whispered to Feldspar, who nodded at whatever was said, and then smiled in a cruel way as they both glanced at Thripp, before giving their respectful attention to Quail and Skua.

With Thripp's arrival the waiting was over, and the Newborns' lengthy ritual of accusation and declaration of punishment began, led by Brother Inquisitor Skua.

'It is my solemn duty to pronounce condemnation, and sentence with commendation, upon eleven brothers gathered before us here today; and to pronounce condemnation and sentence without com-mendation upon a further seven brothers gathered here. And upon two more brothers, who have forsworn their vows and shown no remorse unto the Stone, there shall be condemnation and sentence severe, and the Curse of the Elder Brothers that these two shall be deprived now and for eternity of Silence and the right to hope for Silence.'

115

Skua's voice had grown gradually louder and harsher as he spoke these words, and his eyes, as sharp in their look as his snout was in form, stared unremittingly at the condemned. Quail's face was blank throughout; he even looked slightly bored; but Chervil's expression betrayed a hint of malicious pleasure at the grim ritual.

Meanwhile the guards had arraigned the prisoners in a row, with the single exception of Rooster who, no doubt in expectation of his giving trouble, was held separately by four strong guards. But it did not take an especially numerate mole to work out that eleven and seven and two made twenty, and that left three to go. Whillan looked a little fearfully around at Rooster and Privet as if to say, 'Well, we know who the three so far unsentenced are, don't we? But maybe . . . Maybe we'll get off with a warning.'

The bitter wind, and the cruel roar of the river, did not hint at anything so easy as that. Nor did Skua's face.

After this pause, calculated perhaps to give the prisoners time to think such thoughts as appeared to have preoccupied Whillan, Skua continued thus: 'The three remaining miscreants shall suffer the just punishment of those whose blasphemy is original without the inter-cession of vows, though broken, or innocence of Newborn ways. These three stand accused of a sin so grave that its punishment is put beyond our jurisdiction, lest by punishing them we sully and besmirch our clean paws.'

'How then shall they be judged, Brother Inquisitor?' intoned Quail, in the kind of voice that made it obvious that he knew very well how they were to be judged.

'By their own hearts,' responded Skua.

For some reason which was beyond the present comprehension of Privet and her friends, this response brought a collective sigh of horror and pity from both accusers and accused, which was, in truth, the most frightening thing that had happened yet. The only thing worse than a horrible and cruel punishment is imagining what it might be, and from the way allmole there now looked at Rooster, Whillan and Privet, it was quite plain that nomole there would wish to be in *their* place, not even those who seemed likely to be about to die in whatever vile way the self-righteous and cant-ridden Brother Inquisitors had contrived. But this part of the ritual had not quite finished.

'How shall they be sentenced, Brother Inquisitor?' intoned another Elder Brother.

'By their own mouths,' responded Skua.

'How shall they be punished, Brother Inquisitor?' said Chervil.

116

'By the eternal suffering of their spirits,' hissed Skua.

'And if they judge not, and sentence not, and punish not of themselves?' whispered Thripp in a quavering voice.

Skua turned to him triumphantly and said, 'By the brother that asked of the judgement shall they be judged; and by he that asked of punishment shall they be punished.'

It was towards Chervil that moles now looked, for he had been the brother to ask about punishment. He, it seemed, might be the one to carry out the sentence.

But now, for the first time, proceedings did not go quite according to plan, for Thripp, encouraged perhaps by his little intervention, now spoke again.

'Brothers, it is usual on these occasions to call upon moles to witness punishment,' he suddenly said, even as Skua opened his mouth to continue the ritual.

'There are none easily available,' said Quail sharply, visibly annoyed, in the way moles in charge of a public occasion sometimes are by some old buffer interrupting the smooth flow of things.

'They are not necessary,' added Chervil coldly.

'Oh! But they are!' said Thripp in a firmer voice. 'It is the custom to have witnesses, not from mere tradition but because justice must not only be done, but must be seen to be done by the ordinary brothers and sisters of moledom.'

Quail sighed and said, 'The former Elder Senior Brother speaks the truth, showing that we all have something to learn. His knowledge of Caradocian custom and tradition must be respected since he established it. On this occasion let us listen to him yet be mindful that all can be changed. Fetch witnesses.'

This was perhaps as gracious as Quail could be in the circumstances, and Privet, who still had faith that all might finally be well, could only hope that Thripp had a reason behind his request.

The witnesses, when they came, were a motley bunch, with two or three females among them, dredged up no doubt from the lower regions of Wildenhope, for such an infrastructure as that certainly needed minions to keep it going. These, it seemed, were they, and very reluctant about it they were too, barely daring to glance in the direction of the Senior Brothers, but looking with some sympathy it seemed at the condemned.

The custom satisfied, Skua now carried matters rapidly forward, mixing incantations and accusations, prayers and condemnations in a most confusing way, which left justice far behind. Until at last, with the morning advanced, and the spitting rain now turned into a depressing drizzle, the first accused was called forward for execution of sentence. The name of this hapless mole was given as Brother Normand, though that particular name was 'herewith ordered to be struck from the Book of Brothers' Names'.*

Brother Normand might once have been a strong enough mole, but like so many of the others he was now thin and haggard, and his eyes were pinched with pain. He came slowly forward, half dragging his hurt limbs, half pushed by his two guards, and he did not raise his eyes to look at Quail, whose task it was to pronounce the sentence.

The wind hissed among the stubbly grass of Wildenhope Bluff, and the distant river roared, as Quail said, 'You are guilty of blasphemy and the breaking of vows, and judged beyond saving. In the name of the Stone you will be taken from here by your guards and punished in the fitting way. From the blood and the waters of your mother's womb you came, guilty of Sin in the original, from which the Stone offers its full and eternal salvation. You have betrayed its trust beyond redemption, and will be returned now by your brother guards unto the blood and the waters of moledom itself.' Quail's voice was strong and terrible, and a shudder of chill horror went through the gathering, and especially the witnesses.

The final part of the ritual now took place as Skua came forward and intoned what appeared to be a cruel formality: 'If any there be would stance in the place of this mole and beg his liberty let him come forth. If it be not granted then that mole too shall receive the punishment.'

Before so cold-eyed a set of Elder Brothers and so ruthless an Inquisitor as Skua, it would have been a brave and foolhardy mole who came forward then. The wind blew, the river roared, and none came. The last chance of the mole who had been Brother Normand was gone. As he uttered a feeble, and hopeless, 'No!', his guards put a paw on either side of him, turned him towards the river, and hustling

* It is one of the great losses to Newborn research that of all the Newborn archive material rescued from Caradoc and Blagrove this Book is one of the few that are missing. The indefatigable Bunnicle of Witney has argued convincingly that the Book was destroyed or stolen by moles wishing to keep secret their former status as brothers. But see Cluniac of Duncton's chilling theory (in his *North of the North, and Other Adventures of a Traveller*) which proposes that a group of Newborns, led by a Brother Inquisitor, whose survivors and offspring settled in an unidentified system 'North of the North' has possession of the Book of Brothers' Names, which they retain as an icon to evil glories past.

him down the slope of the Bluff they led him along the raised way across the flooded meadowland. It looked almost as ordinary as a mole setting off from a system, but this journey was final and from it the mole would never return.

Brother Normand was taken to the spit of land which ended in an embankment above the river, with the tributary rushing in on the right flank. Sometimes he seemed to falter, at others he looked back wildly at the watchers on the Bluff, his eyes wide with mounting fear and despair, his mouth opening in what might have been cries for help, which could not be heard at that distance above the river's roar.

The end when it came was sudden, peremptory, and sickening. Indeed those watching – and it was impossible not to, and therefore impossible in some way for the watchers not to feel the guilt of responsibility for what they witnessed – could scarcely believe what they saw. One moment the mole had reached the end of his last trek, and the next the guards on either side of him had grabbed his paws and with a heave he was able to resist only momentarily, hurled him into the raging torrents of the river below.

'So in the midst of life we are in death,' cried Skua in ghastly exultation; 'to whom can we turn for help, but to you, Stone, who are justly angered by our sins. To you then we turn for judgement and just punishment. We entrust our Brother Normand to the talons of thy punishment, that thy cleansing blood of retribution and thy waters of wrath may drown the snake of temptation that has entwined his heart and spirit beyond the help and recall of his Elder Brothers. Take him, and do thy will with him.'

To this pitiless litany was Brother Normand cast into the river, disappearing from sight as he fell below the lip of the bank, before long moments later, Skua's words chasing after him on the wind, he suddenly reappeared in midstream, turning and struggling in the rushing water before reaching the fiercest of the turbulence and white water where tributary and river met in murderous affray.

There he was sucked down, tossed up, turned helplessly this way and that, before going down one last terrible time, limp, paws helpless, snout submerging, body battered, lost for ever to the living world. Then the waters where he had been closed on themselves in waves and spray, and were gone out of sight around the river's bend.

The guards stared after their victim, their strong young forms silhouetted against the torrent beyond, and then turned to take the path back to the Bluff where the shocked watchers stanced. Nomole spoke for a moment, nomole looked at another, but some

119

wept silently, and one of the witnesses sobbed quietly to himself.

'Next!' cried out Skua with busy relish, turning to the next terrified victim as if he were a recruit to a Newborn Crusade.

The brother was brought forward by his guards.

'Now, Brother Retter, you have sinned, most grievously sinned and your time of reckoning has come. Elder Senior Brother Quail will pronounce sentence . . .'

And the nightmare of drowning began once more, to meld in with the one that followed, and then the next, and then another once again. A nightmare journeying to death, and not only for the victims but for those who watched. Nomole is untouched who witnesses such murder as occurred that April morning at Wildenhope. Those who were innocent before are left innocent no more, those who had confidence in life emerge with their confidence shaken; those already brutalized, as Quail and Skua were, end up more brutal still. Life once taken is irrecoverable, and all the witnesses to that day, however free of guilt, became part of a collective shame. It was as well that the sun did not shine, nor the birds sing, nor anything but the killing waters move that long morning: for what happened then was an affront to light, to song, to any hope at all.

A mole might think that a certain boredom would set in by the fifth or sixth victim, or the tenth, or the fifteenth, but it did not. Rather, tension rose higher and more unbearable as the line of waiting victims grew ever smaller.

The atmosphere had somehow darkened with the twelfth victim, the first to be sentenced 'without commendation'; and it darkened still further with the nineteenth and twentieth, for these were the two Skua had pronounced were to be 'deprived now and for eternity of Silence'.* The names of these two are known to us. Brothers Arum and Boden, the only victims so far to show that the spirit of revolt was alive, for they cried out Thripp's name and asked for his blessing, and muttering, with raised paw, he gave it, while their dear friend Brother Rolt could only weep, and look away.

Whether or not the Newborns had the right to so deprive moles of Silence seemed of little consequence – the Inquisitors believed they

---

* Snyde's record states that 'the sky was lowering and pale, with strange streaks of lighter cloud. But, as the punishments neared their climax, and the Duncton moles' sentencing drew nigh, the sky darkened rapidly, and cast the scene on the Bluff in gloom. This was deemed most fitting, as if the Stone itself had cast the shadow of its vengeance upon the Duncton moles.'

had. Nor did anymole come forward to vouch for them when Skua finally enquired if any wished to. With heartbreaking cries of faith in the 'true Newborn way' the two moles were led separately between the flooded meadows to the river-bank and hurled into the torrent, disappearing from sight for a time as the others had done, and then reappearing as mere flotsam, beyond anymole's help, as the waters swirled them away for ever.

It was with sickening relish that Skua and Quail now turned their attention to the remaining prisoners, Privet, Whillan and Rooster. They were unceremoniously pushed forward by their guards, some way apart from each other. Privet was still and quiet, Whillan furious, scarcely believing what was going on, and Rooster dangerously angry on behalf of the other two.

'Not them. She's all right. Not Privet, not Whillan. Good moles, can't you see?' He muttered and ranted these sentiments and more, pushing and shoving against the restraint of his four guards to such effect that with a nod Chervil drafted in three more guardmoles to help. The more that gathered about him the more menacing and powerful he seemed. Whatever happened, this was not a prisoner who would easily go to his death, or let the others go either.

In contrast to his father, Whillan looked weak and helpless. It is true he had matured since leaving Duncton Wood the previous autumn, even more so since the escape from Caer Caradoc, and his mating with Madoc. But the guards deputed to him were older and more physical, and perhaps the rough treatment he had received initially on the Edge, at his capture, and the hard march to Wilden-hope, had taken their toll. He looked young now, tired and vulnerable; but his eyes blazed with intelligence and just outrage and he stared at Skua and Quail defiantly.

And then there was Privet, so still compared to either of the two moles now caught up with her in circumstances of tragedy whose repercussions will echo down the ways and tunnels of moledom's history for evermore. We can well believe Snyde's report of a looming darkness over that sad scene, and another witness has left us a memor-able description of Privet in the moments that marked the end of all her past life, and her acceptance of a task whose nature she was now beginning to comprehend more fully.

'Her eyes,' that brave witness later scribed, 'had been lowered until then. Now she raised them, and it seemed to me that they reflected those pale streaks that made the darkened morning sky so strange. At Quail she looked, at Skua; at Chervil she stared and at Thripp. At

121

all of us she seemed to look, her eyes growing more clear and light the deeper they looked into the palpable evil of that day.

'Anymole could see she was losing all fear for herself, and of the death that might be hers. It was poor Whillan she loved, and great Rooster she wished to protect, and now she began to see the only way she could do this. To me, her eyes were the portals into the heart of a mole who knew she must reach out with love; not to those she loved the most, but to those who were the most evil there, whom she had least reason or inclination to love.

'Sometimes I wonder if that morning really grew dark at all as their sentence was pronounced, or was it rather that the light of Silence that began to come then to Privet of Duncton, simply made it appear so . . . ?'

So Privet seemed to some that morning, and now she waited for Quail's pronouncement of their sentencing with a resignation that suggested she guessed already what it must be.

'The Brother Inquisitor has told you three already that in the case of moles who are not in the true way of the Stone we Elder Brothers prefer not to sully our office by sentencing you ourselves. In such cases Elder Senior Brother Thripp has ordained that where three such miscreants are arraigned only one of them shall suffer punishment. But one of the others must choose which that mole shall be.'

Here Quail paused, to let his words sink in. Whillan stared in puzzled disbelief; Rooster groaned and struggled; the eyes of Privet grew more bright and awesome.

'Of course,' continued Quail with studied and terrible matter-of-factness, 'if you cannot collectively decide who is to make the choice of which mole is to die – then we are empowered to choose for you . . .'

He smiled cruelly, and glanced at Skua and then at Chervil. Both nodded, as if to confirm what he had said. Then Quail hunched forward, the bald skin at his shoulders wrinkling into folds as he raised his head a little and stared down at them.

'Therefore, choose.'

'Choose,' whispered Skua, his voice as deathly sterile as an icicle.

'Choose,' whispered other Elder Brothers, 'choose.'

'Choose,' almost sang Squelch, giggling. 'Oh yes, you must.'

'Choose, choose . . . choose!' sneered the guards, and even some of the witnesses, even some of *them*. There was a madness come that day. Their voices died away and only the distant roar of the river remained, and the harsh shrill of evil in moles' hearts.

Whillan turned and stared at Privet, and then round at Rooster. His flanks trembled, and his eyes were wild.

Perhaps Quail hoped for discussion among the three, a discussion that could only be a punishment in itself – perhaps *that* was what the Elder Brothers had hoped. But Thripp? Had he really prescribed such a law? If he had not, why did he not say so? A mole could only think from his silence that he had, he really had.

'Privet,' said Whillan quietly. 'She is my choice to choose whatmole will die. She herself must live.'

'Must be,' growled Rooster, suddenly chuckling at what seemed to him life's comedy. 'Can't be anymole-else. Whillan knows. Always was her. Always will be. I love her, so does *he.*'

In Rooster's way it was a speech of love, and of pride too, for a mole could tell he was proud that Whillan had spoken first, and chosen as he had. Of course it must be Privet who would do the choosing, foster-mother of one, beloved of the other.

'Then it must be the miscreant Privet, whatever she herself says!' exulted Skua, evidently pleased with the way things were going. What would moledom make of a scribemole too cowardly to offer herself for punishment? Oh yes, Elder Senior Brother Quail had done well to remember so obscure, so subtle a law as this one. By it would Rooster one way or another be destroyed, and Privet too. Nomole could live in the normal world after making the choice she must now make. She would be pitied yet reviled. As for Thripp, he *had* promulgated this law, even if it had never been intended . . .

'So choose which of your fellow miscreants should die, and which should live,' said Quail. 'I await your decision with interest. We all wait with interest!'

There was contempt and triumph in his eyes, and morbid fascination in many other moles'.

'Choose?' repeated Privet, her voice quite clear and steady.

'Yesss . . .' sighed Skua, 'thy will be done!' And he even laughed, silently and mockingly.

'Choose,' said Privet musingly, quietly now, and then fell silent.

'If you do not do so, Sister, they must both die.'

'I have chosen,' said Privet. Her eyes were pale now, so like a pale luminescent sky that many there averted their gaze rather than stare into them. Then there came to her face a look of relief, and she suddenly seemed younger and seemed struck with wonder, as if she had found what she had been seeking for so long. She turned to the two guards on either flank, and so calm yet powerful was her gaze that they seemed to fall away from her as she stepped forward towards Quail.

'You see, Elder Senior Brother Quail, finally we must all choose. It is not difficult, especially for a mole who bit by bit has lost everything, as I have. Here, this morning, we have witnessed the brutal darkness which will always be with mole, and we know it, even you Quail, and you Skua and—'

'Do not address us so, Sister!' said Skua sharply.

But Quail raised a paw to silence him. For the first time that morning he looked interested. Sister Privet, it seemed, had surprised him.

'Go on,' he purred.

'There comes a time when we moles must stop seeking the Silence of the Stone as if it is beyond ourselves, or beyond the present moment, or beyond the present place. We must choose to simply . . . stop.'

'So which mole have you chosen?' asked Quail, frowning now and beginning to feel a fool.

'Oh, *that*!' said Privet in a voice that dismissed the impossible choice he had posed her as if it was nothing at all. Then she added, as if realizing he did not understand, 'It really is not important, Quail, which I choose, or whether I choose or not. If it were I would not do it, and as it isn't I will not pretend it is.'

'Choose, mole,' said Skua fiercely.

'The choice I have made has been much harder than so simple and ridiculous a thing as choosing between moles I love. I love all moles, even you, Quail, even you, Skua. Perhaps even Brother Confessor Thripp as once he was. You think to undermine me by making me choose between moles you know I especially love. You do not understand that the choice would be as hard or as easy whichever two moles you presented me with! I would die for each of them just thinking about it, as I have died in my heart for those moles your beliefs have killed today.'

'Choose, Sister!' roared Quail, suddenly angry, his smooth exterior beginning to break down. 'You have talked long enough.'

'I talk because I am afraid of the choice I have made, mole. I talk because I fear the journey I must begin. I talk . . .' For the first time her voice faltered. 'I pray that one day, when the Light of the Stone is manifest to moledom, and your little puny darkness is gone into the past, I pray I may be able to talk again.'

'Choose!' said Quail with open venom for this mole whose strange quiet words held the others about him spellbound, and insidiously attacked not only his authority, but, astonishingly, that of the whole Caradocian Order. Though how, or why, few could yet see.

'Choose?' said Privet finally. 'Oh yes, I choose! I choose Silence!' As she said the word even the roar of the river seemed to cease and not a single guardmole tried to intervene as she went first to Rooster and then to Whillan and embraced them tenderly. Then she turned back to Quail and said again, 'I choose Silence, and pray the Stone will help me, for surely no mole can.'

'Silence?' shouted Quail, perturbed but not yet understanding the profound decision Privet had made. 'Silence? That is not the choice we mean!'

'You choose *that*, and both of them shall die!' cried Skua, almost spitting at her, and thinking that by 'Silence' she simply meant to try to avoid the issue by saying nothing.

Yet three moles, apart from Whillan and Rooster, already seemed to understand the possible significance of what she had done. One was Thripp himself, who looked at her now with profound surprise, and strange hope, as if in the way she had chosen to take he saw, as other moles might not, the only possible course of action, or rather non-action, that those still resisting the Newborns all over moledome might follow. He looked like a mole for whom a lifetime of prayer had been answered.

Brother Rolt's response was more emotional and personal. He knew what the path of Silence might mean for a mole, and perhaps he had contemplated it for himself from time to time, but had shrunk back from so final a sacrifice. Now tears rolled freely down his face as he stared at the thin, unassuming simple figure of Privet among those aggressive and angry moles, and understood that nomole would be more alone than she in the place she had now turned towards.

One other mole responded in a way that suggested he understood what Privet had done. Squelch. For he now began to sing quietly, a strange and haunting song that told of a solitary heron, grey and black as that Wildenhope morning, which opened its wings and rose slowly over the rushing waters of life, and left them behind to begin a journey to a distant and long dreamed-of land.

'Well?' roared Quail, simply not believing that a mole could defy him (as he saw it) in so simple and direct a manner.

'You have been warned, Sister Privet!' hissed Skua again.

But Privet had said her last and Silence *was* her way now. She stared at her interrogators and at the sky, and when Whillan whispered ambiguously, 'They won't let you do it this way,' meaning perhaps they would kill her, she stared at him too. Not without love, not without concern, yet, in truth, not with much interest either. These moles, what*ever* moles they might be, she was beginning to leave behind. She had rejected responsibility for them, and left them to find their own way. She had stopped striving for them, realizing at last that a mole cannot do it for another, it being hard enough to do it for herself – even assuming the Stone wanted a mole to strive at all, which she was already beginning to doubt. But her mouth moved in silent prayer, for guidance perhaps, and she was restless to be away from that place of troubled moles and be by herself at last.

Many who hear this part of Privet's extraordinary story attribute to her a kind of cowardice, in that she did not show enough concern for the danger, all too real, in which she had now placed both Whillan and Rooster. One saved, argue such moles, is better than none. Why could not Privet see that? But she had seen and sensed a greater truth; that a day had to come in the long decades of struggle towards the Stone's Silence when a solitary mole must have the courage to commit herself to Silence, *whatever* it might mean. That the day, the moment in question happened to be when one of the two moles closest to her might have benefited from her help was no longer the point.

It is in the nature of that great commitment she had made that it cannot be deferred. This afternoon will not do, tomorrow is too late, whatever the implications. This was the truth, brutal though it was, on which Privet had acted, and because it was without concession or caveat it was so inexplicable, so infuriating perhaps, to many of the moles who witnessed it.

So, at Wildenhope, the irresistible force of the Caradocian Order under Quail met the absolute and immutable resistance of a single mole, who did not yet know that she was more than mere mole, she was the immovable object which was all that remained to thwart the Newborn darkness. And her strength was Silence.

'There is no other course for us to take but to sentence both these moles, Whillan of Duncton and Rooster of Charnel Clough,' pronounced Quail finally, attempting to regain the initiative. 'They will—'

But even now he was interrupted, this time by Rooster, who since Privet's announcement of commitment to Silence had become a changed mole. He no longer resisted his guards, and he ceased to cast his eyes all over the place and weave his great head this way and that. Rather, he had greeted her decision with a kind of cheerful laugh

126

and a shout of 'Yes! Right! Oh yes, Sister Privet!' 'Sister', moles must suppose, intended ironically. In short, he appeared to understand and approve what Privet had done.

But soon his pleasure had given away to consternation and mounting alarm and the reason was all too plain: he began to realize that both he and Whillan would be committed to the river as the other victims had been. For himself, he seemed not to care one bit, but for Whillan . . .

'No, no, no, not him. He's *needed*. He is future things, in his paws will be all of us, all of this. The pattern of him is like a delving on what's to come. He can't die.'

'Well, mole,' snarled Quail, cutting him short, 'you should have thought of that, and so should *she*.'

'He's—'

'Silence him!' commanded Skua of the guards. 'Now!'

Sickening blows rained down on Rooster's face and flanks and even his huge back buckled under them, and all that remained were his grunts and groans as sentence was passed and Quail spoke once more of the cleansing of the waters of the earth, and of its blood.

It was, then, to be the river for both of them, and only now did Whillan seem fully to comprehend what was to happen to him. In mythical tales of great moles of the past, victims approach their fate heroically, and their loving kin are noble in their sorrow. It would be pleasing but inaccurate to say that this is what happened, and Snyde's report, supported by the accounts of other witnesses to the tragedy, confirms the simple truth: Whillan was as frightened and afraid as any young mole with all his life before him would be when about to lose it. While Rooster, impervious to fear on his own account but vulnerable now to any threat to Whillan, sought to rise yet again and roared out his anguish.

It was only when he was brutally silenced once more that Skua's voice was heard to intone the last and cruellest formality: 'If any there be would stance in the place of this mole and beg his liberty let him come forth. If it be not granted then that mole too shall receive the punishment.'

But nomole came forth, none begged liberty for Whillan, and only the wind's whispers, the river's roar, and Rooster's moans broke the silence.

It might have been expected that Whillan would immediately be taken forth towards the river-bank for sentence to be carried out – indeed another guard joined those already at his flanks and began to

127

lead him away from the assembly when Quail, thinking perhaps this was a good moment to complete sentencing of Rooster, raised a paw to stop them.

'We will sentence the mole Rooster now as well,' he said, pausing suddenly in thought as a new idea seemed to come to him, one which appeared to give him smug satisfaction. He gestured Skua to him and they conferred briefly, until the Brother Inquisitor nodded and resumed his place, unable to resist casting a malicious glance at Chervil as he did so.

'Tell me, Elder Brother Chervil,' said Quail with quiet menace and eyeing Whillan as he spoke, 'would you say these moles are guilty of sin?'

'In the original or in the present?' responded Chervil, frowning.

'Both, Brother, both,' said Quail impatiently.

'They are guilty,' said Chervil.

'So their sentences are just?'

The other Elder Brothers and some of the witnesses exchanged glances, recognizing that Quail was testing Chervil in some way. The latter's dismay at some of the goings-on at the Convocation was well known and his loyalty to Quail had long been in doubt, given that he was Thripp's son. Yet he had acquitted himself loyally since then, even if he was sometimes a little too much his own mole.

'All the sentences have been just,' said Chervil.

'Then, Elder Brother Chervil, you will not mind carrying out the sentence on the mole Whillan of Duncton Wood.' It was said icily, and all eyes were on Chervil as Quail spoke.

But if Chervil did mind he did not betray it, and nor did his words suggest anything else but the self-righteous vindictiveness of the Newborns against followers of the Stone: 'You have said that Elder Brothers should not have their paws sullied and besmirched by the shame and blood of these moles, Elder Senior Brother; but forgive me, I do not wish to disagree with you . . . It would seem an honour to be the agent of the Stone's justice!'

Chervil's face seemed almost to glitter with satisfaction, and he looked round at the tough Feldspar as if to invite him and his sons along as well.

'Well, so be it, so be it, Brother,' beamed Quail. 'Let us be done with this sorry business and these moles. Brother Inquisitor, may we take it that the sentence upon Rooster of Charnel Clough is the same as for the mole Whillan?'

Skua nodded.

'Then take it as spoken already, and proceed to the last formality. Let us have done with them both.'

'If any there be would stance in the place of this mole,' began Skua immediately, as impatient now to come to a conclusion as Quail, the real fun being over and the stance that Privet had taken having left an uneasy feeling among them all – 'and beg his liberty let him—'

'There is!' a voice cried out suddenly. 'There is one ready to stance in the place of the miscreant Rooster!'

Surprise and astonishment showed on the faces of almost all present, the exceptions being Skua, whose look was one of complete dismay, and Quail, whose face was suffused by unfeigned fury.

For it was Thripp who had spoken, his head low, his eyes wandering, and his voice weak; but Thripp all the same.

'Elder Senior Brother Thripp?' began Quail, trying to bite back his anger, though his voice shook with it.

'Oh, I do not intercede *lightly*,' said Thripp quickly, and rather more robustly than before, 'but you see, Elder Brethren, it is said that Rooster is a Master of the Delve.'

'That is a lie and a blasphemy!' cried out Skua.

'Can you prove that?' said Thripp, turning his gaze quietly on Skua.

It is a gift of moles with natural authority that they do not need to raise their voices and shout, or wave their paws about, or use strong or threatening words, to make others listen. Indeed, they need do almost nothing to command attention and obedience, to inspire fear even. Such rare moles need only enter a chamber, or raise their head, or merely speak, and others listen . . .

So Thripp spoke now and Skua listened, and an awesome hush fell upon the moles gathered at Wildenhope. Thripp's body might be weak, he might even be old, but after those four words to Skua – Can you prove that? – not a mole could doubt that his spirit and purposefulness were as strong as ever, and though he spoke to one, all listened.

'I . . . I . . .' faltered Skua.

'You cannot, and nomole could without seeing the delvings of this mole. And even then, whatmoles are we, who have never known a living Master before, to judge a Master's work? Certainly not I, Brother Skua! Can *you?*'

'I . . . am not sure, Elder Senior Brother Thripp,' said Skua feebly.

'And you, Brother Quail?' said Thripp, removing his remorseless gaze from the thankful Skua and fixing it on Quail instead.

Quail shook his head, easier before Thripp's authority than Skua, but clearly respectful and wary of it.

'Elder Senior Brother,' he said, 'if it is your wish that the mole Rooster should go unpunished—'

'It is my wish that one mole here at least begs liberty for Rooster, if only because he *might* be Master of the Delve. It is unlikely, that is true, but possible, and I would not wish to be witness to or part of a judgement of such a mole, when nomole lives who may truly judge him. I do not say he is guiltless, or that he has never sinned, but I believe he should have liberty. If he should cause trouble to mole again then I for one will not stance up for him . . . but this one time I will. And I believe that if he is the Master some believe him to be he will not cause hurt or injury to anymole again. Such is the tradition of delvers. Let us forgive and forget what he has done.'

Quail shrugged. 'There is not an Elder Brother here would speak against *your* words. But what of the other, the mole Whillan?'

'What of him?' said Thripp coldly. 'The sentence has been passed, and nomole has begged his liberty. What must be will be—'

'NOOO!' roared Rooster suddenly, his cry as bleak as a rockfall into the sunless depths of Charnel Clough. 'No!' His second cry was the wretched plea of one who values not his own life, and would give it a thousand times to save another mole he places higher than himself. 'Tell them, Privet, tell them what Whillan is!'

Privet raised her head and looked at Rooster, and then at Whillan. She did not speak, for her vow bound her to silence; but she did shed tears, and they spoke of the helpless grief of a whole generation of mothers, even though Whillan was not her true son.

Worse, Whillan saw that even for him she would not speak. Whatever her talk of Silence had meant – and he had barely comprehended its real meaning – he knew only that the mole who had nurtured him as a pup, whose paws had held him close when he was afraid, whose quiet voice had told him the first tales he heard, and shared with him his first ideas – that mole had now abandoned him. And now all he seemed to see was a dark place, wet and cold, the cross-under of Duncton Wood, where his mother had died as he was born and all his siblings been lost as well. There now he was again, a pup alone, raising his head to bleat out his loss and fear to a world he did not understand. So Whillan now, only just an adult, alone, lost, abandoned except for the struggles and shouts of Rooster, began to cry; tears of fear and rejection, tears of a mole already in retreat from forces too great for him to withstand without help.

'Tell them what, mole?' said Quail ruthlessly to Rooster, looking pitilessly on Whillan.

'*He* is Master,' said Rooster. 'I was, but I lost it. He is Master of the Delve. He is our future.'

Quail sighed. 'The Elder Senior Brother Thripp has interceded on your behalf, mole, and for better or for worse you shall have liberty. But this mole,' he pointed a talon at Whillan, 'he shall be punished now for what you all have done!'

He turned finally to Chervil and nodded, and if what had happened so far had been the ruthless justice of a corrupted sect, what followed was brutality made flesh.

Chervil nodded in turn to Feldspar and his two sons Tarn and Fallow, and the four tough moles went to Whillan and displaced the guards surrounding him. Without a word of warning or even a second glance, Chervil raised his right paw and powered a talon-thrust deep into Whillan's flank. Whillan gasped in terrible pain as he collapsed, and blood flowed freely down his fur to his back paws.

'Now,' said Chervil harshly, 'shut up and stance up, for you're coming with us.'

Without more ado Whillan was pulled roughly to his paws and in a state of shock, bewilderment and fear, blood streaming from his left flank, he was hustled from the watching moles and down the slope of the Bluff towards the river-bank.

A hush of horror and shock fell on the assembled moles, and, it must be said, a perverted and sadistic delight appeared in the eyes of Skua and Quail to see their morning's murderous efforts reach, after a few setbacks, so satisfactory a conclusion.

Feldspar and his sons, with Chervil in the lead, took poor Whillan out across the path through the flooded meadows. So far as he was able to support himself he did, though his left hind paw dragged from the wound he had sustained. But nomole thought of that with the final terror of the river coming near. Out beyond the bank's high edge it flowed, driven by the floods from the north, rushing away to the south, as angry and sullen as ever.

'No, no, no . . .' cried Rooster weakly, his guards restraining him close lest in these last moments of his son's short life he tried to break free and rescue him, or simply turn to try to harm his captors, or, worse, the Elder Brothers. But all he did was raise his head and stare at where Whillan had been taken and cry his weak protests.

For her part Privet stared too, eyes bleak, face pinched in disbelief and horror, talons clenched to the grass and soil, whispering a prayer.

131

Then suddenly, as the sorry group reached the very edge of the bank, Whillan was seen to try to break free, and Privet screamed, a terrible scream of hopelessness out of her Silence, for what could an injured mole hope to do against those as resolute as Chervil and his guardmoles? Nothing at all, it seemed. There was a moment's pause, a sudden movement by all four moles and Whillan was thrown over the bank and out of sight, down into the river below.

The watchers were still and silent as death, but for the broken sobs of Privet and the deep groans of Rooster, as they saw Whillan's body disappear, and waited those sickening moments for the river to take it up, swirl it round, and surge with it back into sight in the midst of where the wild waters of river and tributary formed their confluence.

Then a mole muttered, 'There, there he is!' and all saw the limp form of Whillan, head submerged, turning a paw in the air, surely beyond help now of anymole, punished for merely being what he was. A sigh passed over the watchers as Whillan's limp body went under for a moment, and then shot up wildly once more, limbs seeming lifeless now as they were pushed and pulled by the waves and turbulence.

At that moment of shock, the deed almost done, Rooster, always unpredictable – which his guards should have remembered – rose up massively in their midst. With a roar mightier than thunder he picked up the nearest to him and hurled him savagely into two more; he buffeted a fourth into a fifth and sixth, and as for the rest they simply froze.

Then, with a last cry of 'NO!' he was rushing out of their midst, down the Bluff and out across the fields towards where Chervil and the others, all unawares, watched Whillan's limp form being swirled round and round in the turbulence before it was rushed on downstream by the torrent.

The guards on the Bluff picked themselves up, collected their scattered wits, cried out for Rooster to stop, and set off after him. But Rooster's lead was too great, and for so massive a mole he moved with surprising grace and speed. Only as he seemed about to bear down on Chervil and the others, as if to flatten them into the ground, did they hear his roars, or the cries of his pursuing guards, and turn round and see his monstrous approach. To Chervil's credit, if a mole who had committed so vile an act *can* be called creditable, he tried to stop Rooster. Indeed Feldspar and the others did too, but Rooster was a father trying to save his son that day, and was unstoppable. For a moment they all teetered on the bank, but then Rooster broke free, stared out at Whillan's body being sucked below the water once more, and dived in after him. He disappeared from sight over the edge as all the others had done, but the running of Chervil and Feldspar along the high bank told those watching from the Bluff where he was and how powerfully the torrent carried him along.

Then the moles could follow the bank no more, and Rooster reappeared and shot out into sight amidst the turbulence as all the others had done. Even now he seemed huge, tossed and turned by the water though he was, and it was plain what he was trying to do as he swam and rose in the water and flailed his paws and looked desperately about for Whillan.

But the watchers could see it was too late, and that Whillan's body seemed to have gone down for a final time. Yet Rooster struggled on, the turbulence turning him as well, round and round as he tried, and mainly succeeded, to keep his head above the water. Then the full power of the river's current caught him, pulled him down, shot him up, and took him out of the mayhem of the confluence and on towards the bend.

As he reached it he seemed to realize that he would not, could not, save Whillan's life, for he was gone now and unreachable. He turned in the water, seemed to look back at all the moles on the surface of Wildenhope, and let out a roar so loud that they heard it above the river's raging; and then the water surged and he was gone beyond their view, surely beyond anymole's help. Gone as Whillan had gone, from sight and hope, gone at last into violent waters like those of Charnel Clough, whose horrors had haunted his life, and seemed to have claimed him at last.

'From the blood and the waters of their mothers' wombs they came, guilty of sin in the original, from which the Stone offered its full and eternal salvation,' cried out Quail in a sonorous, portentous voice, as if he imagined himself to be some Holy Mole from the days of Uffington. 'They betrayed the Stone's trust beyond redemption, and are returned now unto the blood and the waters of moledom itself. Let this mole remain a living example to their guilt and shame.' Here he pointed a talon at Privet.

'Let my fellow Elder Brothers do the same . . .' and one by one the other Elders raised their talons, some shiny and pointed, some gnarled and old, and pointed them at Privet. 'This mole has her liberty, but of the Newborn, and of redemption, and of the salvation of truth and the love of the brethren and the sisterhood of all her kind, she is made excommunicate.'

Only two Elders did not raise their paws. One was Squelch, who wept and crooned to comfort himself. The other was Thripp, who stared in a way only one mole dared afterwards bear witness to: he stared with love, and infinite sadness.

Then Quail turned, and one by one the brethren left, and the witnesses and the guards as well, until only Privet remained upon the Bluff. Then desultorily, in ones and twos, the guards who had chased Rooster came back, and after them Feldspar and his sons. They stared at Privet and passed her by, until only Chervil remained near her. Even now he did not show pity or remorse for what he had done, but at least he showed respect.

Privet stared at him, and then past him at the river which had taken first Whillan and then Rooster. How long she stared, and how much she seemed to contemplate. Then she went to Chervil and reached out a thin paw to his and touched him.

And had he been a foolish mole, or given to fancies, he would have sworn that she looked at him not with hatred, or contempt, or even fear; but with love.

'Mole . . .' he began.

But she shook her head to silence him, and turning north left him, going slowly from Wildenhope back the long, long way she had come only a few days before – when Madoc was her friend, and Whillan and Rooster still lived. Until she was gone from sight, and Chervil was alone.

'What mole are you?' he whispered after her in awe.

But the wind across Wildenhope Bluff, and the distant river's roar, gave him no answer he could yet understand; and all he knew was that something of the truth of Silence had been taught him that day and it was as dark as it was light, and the journey it foretold frightened him. A journey upon which only one mole had courage and faith to venture, and her name was Privet.

As Chervil watched after her there was the same sadness in his eyes as there had been in his father Thripp's; and this was not the mole of cruel resolution, and frightening purpose, who had shown himself so willing to support Quail earlier.

Dusk began to fall, and still he stanced staring at the way she had gone, only moving when with a quick scurry and a surreptitious glance about to see he was not observed, Brother Rolt suddenly appeared.

'Tell him it was done as he ordered, Stone help us all,' said Chervil heavily. 'Tell him that seeing the mole Privet afterwards and saying nothing was the hardest thing of all.'

134

'She is gone?'

'Gone north, Stone help her.'

'Oh, the Stone will help *her*,' said Rolt ruefully, 'it's the rest of us you should be worrying about.'

Chervil allowed a small smile to play across his face in the half-light. 'I am, I do. But as my father is wont to say, "There is a way if only we can find it."'

'He thinks he *has* found it!' said Rolt.

'Hmmph!' growled Chervil. 'Now go, Rolt, lest others see us talking.'

'Master Chervil,' whispered Rolt gently, and the two moles looked at each other with an affection of moles where one has known the other from birth, and cared for him always, and the other knows it.

'You were staring after her, weren't you?' said Rolt, peering into the darkness.

'Yes,' said Chervil, 'and praying for her as you taught me to pray for moles who are brave and full of faith. But Rolt . . .'

'Chervil?'

'You're staring into the darkness too. What is it you and my father know about this Duncton mole? You know something, that's for sure.'

'Nothing, I know nothing, and if I do you know better than to ask.'

'It's true that you never reveal my father's secrets, so I won't ask. But you know something. And that mole makes me feel . . .'

'What does she make you feel, Chervil?' asked Rolt quietly. Dusk was advancing rapidly into night, and off to their right flank the river's roar seemed louder.

'I . . . don't . . . quite know. Tell me!'

'One day, mole, I shall.'

'A promise from the loyal and circumspect Brother Rolt?'

'I shall tell you when your father needs me to, and may the Stone see that I am right! For what it's worth I suppose it *is* a promise.' The grass rustled about them, darkness was all around, and when Chervil looked again, Rolt had gone.

'What mole are you?' he asked again into the depths of the night into which Privet had long since disappeared. He frowned, he muttered, he scratched himself, he sighed, and again and again he shook his head. Until at last, and suddenly, he laughed aloud.

'Well,' he said to himself, 'at least one mole has finally got the better of Quail, which shows the way forward for the rest of us!' and he went down into the deceitful tunnels of Wildenhope once more.

PART II

Strivings

Chapter Twelve

Of the many mysteries that frustrate historical enquiry few are more puzzling than the way in which rumour and truth travel moledom faster than the swiftest journeymole. Indeed, in happier days before the Newborns became so destructive a force, and Chater was still alive, the Duncton journeymole had often remarked to his beloved Fieldfare that he could not understand how it was that matters only just occurring in Duncton Wood when he left were common currency in the system he was destined for *before he arrived.*

'And I don't dawdle lass, nor do I talk overmuch!' he would add in an aggrieved kind of way.

'Well, I don't know I'm sure, my dearest,' Fieldfare would reply, 'I expect it's the birds.'

'Birds be buggered, it's a bloody mystery, that's what it is!'

'Chater! You know you don't use language like that in Duncton Wood . . .'

Now Chater was gone, but the truths he spoke and the mysteries he observed lived on, and the speed rumours travel was one of them.

So it was that whispers of the killings at Wildenhope seemed to travel across moledom in April and May faster than a single mole could journey; and failing immediate confirmation or denial by any harder evidence, they had time to breed and multiply in the atmosphere of uncertainty and fear which the Newborn Crusades from the major systems had deliberately begun to create. There were several aspects of the Wildenhope killings that caught moles' imaginations and caused them to talk of them in pity, in anger, and, most underminingly of all from the point of view of Quail's ambitions, in hope.

One was the fact, so the stories went, that most of the moles arraigned at Wildenhope were Newborns of long service, *who did not deserve to die.* Quail's and Skua's cynical exercise in exemplary punishment was seen by others far distant as simple brutality, and provoked a sense of the betrayal of natural justice which overrode any fear and abject obedience Quail might have hoped the events at Wildenhope would instil.

Another was the nature of their deaths, by drowning, which to moles is a frightening and foul way to die. It is true there had been drownings enough before as a punishment – the very fear of it was the whole point – but somehow moles throughout the land perceived those particular drownings as excessive and unnecessarily cruel.

Further, there was the matter of the three Duncton moles involved in the killings, and here Quail's insensitivity and historic stupidity were on display for all to discuss, whether the version of events heard by moles in distant systems was correct or not.

The facts were (as moles heard it, in hushed whispers and in the context of outrage earlier described) than an innocent youngster of Duncton Wood, Whillan by name, had been publicly drowned by Quail's guardmoles. Worse, his mother (as they heard) had been forced to witness it. And, just as bad and *most* ominous, Rooster, famous rebel and Master of the Delve, had died in a vain attempt to save the youngster's life. It was this double connection with Duncton and Rooster, both of which held a very special place in so many moles' hearts, that made the story so terrible – and unforgivable. Quail and Skua, though they did not then know it, had, as it were, been seen to talon themselves with their own evil; the wound might possibly heal, but it would leave a scar across their reputations that would seem revolting to any who saw them, or were asked to act on their behalf.

If Maple was looking for allies to strengthen his so-far minute force, he found a great one in these rumours. Or, put another way, if the more intelligent and competent commanders on the Newborn side were wondering if they would find serious challenges to their Crusade, they knew, when they heard of Wildenhope, that Quail had created one and made their task more difficult.

Yet on the Newborn side perhaps only two moles immediately understood the full implications of what had happened, and these were Thripp himself, and the recently side-tracked Brother Commander Thorne. Thripp saw, even as events at Wildenhope unfolded that day, what they might mean, and he had hoped that matters might fall out as they did. He saw with his own eyes the looks of horror, and heard with his own ears the muted cries of dismay amongst the witnesses Quail and Skua had reluctantly summoned for the occasion.

Unlike them, Thripp guessed that their response of sympathy towards the victims would surely be repeated by many like them across moledom – *if they were told.*

But here we come to the point where historical evidence helps diminish a little the mystery of how rumours travel and thrive. For we know now that within hours of the killings, Thripp had contrived to obtain from Snyde the one thing which, he suspected, would be needed to transform rumours into an idea, and then a hope, and finally an astonishing triumph of spirit, against which Quail might find it very hard to fight.

Thripp had fully expected the opportunity to arise, but had been unable to guess what form it would take. But in his own inspired way he had communed with the Stone, and the Stone had answered him: *another mole will show the way; listen to that mole, trust that mole, and act for that mole* . . . and even as Privet, the only female Thripp had ever known happiness with, the only mole he had instinctively felt was his equal, even as she declared herself for Silence, he saw that Quail's ambitions and the corruption of spirit he had wrought might *thereby* be laid waste.

When the rituals were over, and even as elsewhere in Wildenhope Quail and his fellow Senior Brother Inquisitors agreed that the time had come to close-confine Thripp for good so that (in his senility, as it was argued) he could cause no more trouble, Thripp succeeded in achieving one last mischief; and it was the greatest of all.

Snyde was summoned to Thripp by Rolt, Snyde 'permitted' Thripp to ken from his record the precise words Privet had spoken about Silence out on the Bluff, and Snyde fatally left that remarkable text with Thripp while he scurried off to record the very meeting of Senior Brothers whose decision would by that same evening have prevented Thripp doing what he did.

For the Elder Senior Brother was not quite as senile or ill as he pretended; as, indeed, his intervention at Wildenhope had already made clear to Quail himself; which is why, without saying so, Quail wished Thripp to be close-confined, and his few remaining loyal aides like Brother Rolt denied access to him.

Meanwhile, in the short time left that early evening, Thripp and Rolt hurried to perform a task which more than any other would fan the rebellious flames lit by the rumours of the Wildenhope Killings, of the Duncton moles' unhappy involvement with them and, most significant of all, of the extraordinary act of Privet of Duncton in defying Quail's ordinance with a vow of Silence. Using Snyde's most accurate report, a verbatim record of all that had been said, Thripp and Rolt hurriedly and secretly scribed six copies of a text that told what had happened, and quoted Privet's exact words, including these: 'There comes a time when we moles must stop seeking the Silence

141

of the Stone as if it is beyond ourselves, or beyond the present moment, or beyond the present place. We must choose to simply . . . stop.'

Privet had gone on to tell Quail, 'I choose Silence. I pray that one day, when the Light of the Stone is manifest to moledom, and your little puny darkness is gone into the past, I pray I may be able to talk again.'

Such were the words that Thripp now chose to quote from Snyde's record, adding his own description of the killings, and explaining to all who later kenned or heard what he scribed, that Privet's journey into Silence was more difficult, more courageous, more important for moledom than they might at first realize. She was journeying now on their behalf, and if moles were to resist the curse of Quail's Crusades they might find inspiration from knowing what one solitary female scribemole from Duncton was already doing on their behalf . . .

The task of scribing all this down was completed by failing light and with a loyal guard posted nearby to watch out for the expected arrival of Quail's minions, and another in the chamber itself whose task it was to hurry off with each text as it was finished to place it in the safe paws of one of the three moles whose role would be to slip away from Wildenhope that same night to deliver the precious texts to certain of Thripp's most trusted aides in far-off systems, mainly old retired moles whose loyalty and willingness to help he had maintained through the years against just such an eventuality as this.

Those who have seen the three surviving originals of these extraordinary and historic texts will testify to the untidy and inconsistent way they are scribed, as was only to be expected with two moles working under such pressure of time and fear of discovery. Of these three the one that best conveys the circumstances of the scribing – scholars call it the 'Rollright Version' since that is the system in whose library it is now to be found – is but half completed in Thripp's own paw, the final illegible scoring of his talon no doubt indicating the moment when the look-out gave warning that Quail's guards were fast approaching. A mole may well imagine how Thripp's text was taken hastily from him by Rolt, passed to the fleet-pawed guard and, incomplete though it was, sent out from Wildenhope to be finished by another paw in safety, copying from a completed version, and then distributed to do its work.

We know now which three moles so bravely took those subversive texts from under the very snouts of Quail and his kind, and sped with them for the sake of truth and liberty: Sugran of Stratford was one;

Lloyd of Threburrough was another, and Knill of Radnor the last. Their names should never be forgotten, and their kin should ever be proud that having witnessed the killings of Wildenhope they begged Thripp freedom from the Newborn way, and he offered them something more than freedom: he gave them pride. Ordinary moles they were, in extraordinary times, who slipped out from Wildenhope with their precious burdens, and conveyed them to moles far, far away, who had them copied, and distributed them yet more widely.

'Moles,' began that famous text, 'know that at Wildenhope-next-Caradoc of an April morning on the day when Senior Brother Inquisitor Quail assumed the responsibility, awesome and profound, of Elder Senior Brother, the following event took place whereof all moles, whether Newborn or what some call follower, should take pause to ponder upon . . .'

So begins the indictment Thripp scribed but to which he did not put his name, or any name, but told instead the story of twenty-two moles dead or missing, and a mole called Privet, female, past middle age, who sacrificed herself to Silence, for the sake of allmole.

It is said that when Thorne reached Caradoc, and saw a copy of what came to be known as the Wildenhope Indictment he observed, 'The Newborn Crusaders can fight and defeat any foe but this – an idea that is just and inspiring, and a mole who offers no defence, nor any attack, but the talons of Silence.'

By the end of May the tragedy of Wildenhope was too well known in moledom for the Newborns ever to hope they might expunge it from collective consciousness, and the hope inspired by the knowledge that a lonely female had turned her snout towards a living Silence was buried too deep in the hearts of moles for Inquisitors, however skilled, to destroy.

Which meant that Quail's and Skua's declaration at Wildenhope that Privet, though made excommunicate, was not to be harried by anymole, was not a command that zealot Newborns could accept, or even believe. Here, in the flesh, was a mole by herself made anathema. How *dare* anymole defy the Elder Senior Brother and turn to Silence? The declaration *said* to have been made by him about not harming her could not be true. No, no . . . it was a coded command meaning the precise opposite – *she must die!*

How many Newborns said *that* to themselves when they heard about Wildenhope. And yet . . . *She must live!*

Aye, and how many moles, followers and Newborns alike, said this too, moved as they were by her story, and aware of the danger of zealot assassins eager to prove their allegiance to the Stone by killing one whom they were not worthy even to touch!

All over moledom that early summer as the rumours abounded, Thripp's Wildenhope text was kenned ever more widely, and the Newborns and their opponents began to commit themselves to coming Crusades and conflict, a great many moles were asking the same question: 'Where is Privet of Duncton Wood?'

Some wished to know so that they might find her and kill her on Quail's behalf, driven by the insensitivity and arrogance of their fundamentalist Newborn beliefs, thinking that was what the Elder Senior Brother really wanted; others that they might protect her from the moles who wished her dead.

But a few, a very few for now, were moved by something deeper and more mysterious than a desire to punish or protect: the sense that in turning from the busy-ness and madness of the daily world towards Silence, Privet was doing something they themselves would like to do, but knew not how. If they found Privet, such moles thought, they might find an answer to a question that is asked at some time in the heart of everymole. The history of those times, and perhaps of any other, might well be scribed in terms of these three groups of moles: punishers who wish to destroy what they most fear, protectors who in being busy for another may avoid being still for themselves; and pilgrims, who alone and generally unguided turn their snouts to a journey with no clear end but the discovery of truth.

In our history now, which tells of the discovery of the lost Book of Silence, we have punishers aplenty in the form of Newborn moles, and protectors enough (we hope!) in the form of Maple, his supporters, and all their kind. But pilgrims? They are still somewhat thin on the ground, with only Privet, her whereabouts unknown, treading that lonely path.

Therefore let us redress the balance in a symbolic way by choosing one mole, one ordinary and unremarkable mole, from out of the annals and records of those times. Let us name him, locate him, and trace the progress of his life from the moment (he would have said) it truly began, to the moment (he would surely have agreed) when it found a kind of culmination. By this we may learn much about our response to the spiritual history of Privet, for are we not all ordinary moles who, when all is said and done, are seeking answers to questions only the Stone itself seems able to help us with?

We need not detain ourselves for long now with this new-found 'ordinary' companion along our way – it is enough to, as it were, greet

144

him, acknowledge what he is about, and, from time to time, discover where he has got to, in the hope that on that great day we find (or do not find) the Book of Silence, he is there alongflank us, to share what moledom shares.

The mole we arbitrarily choose is Hibbott of Ashbourne Chase, a small, unremarkable system not far from Beechenhill. His modest story is known only to a few scholars, yet it deserves a wider hearing just because it *is* ordinary, and thus representative of those times. We can tell it because when he was old, and grey, and those historic years were done, and all things resolved (as one day they were), Hibbott of Ashbourne Chase scribed his story down, and the text, until now all but forgotten, was lodged in the library of Beechenhill.*

For now we need only concern ourselves with the opening words of his delightful account: 'I, Hibbott of Ashbourne Chase, lately a pilgrim mole in search of peace, recently returned to this my home system after many years away, hereby declare my wish to tell my tale that others may know that if ever they have the impulse to say, "I can't abide this humdrum life any more and will venture forth to find something new!", they would be well advised to do so.

'It did me no harm, indeed it would have done me some harm to stay at home chafing; I believe it will do them no harm either! Therefore, let them ken my tale, and decide for themselves whether or not to follow the impulse to become a pilgrim.

'It was on a May day that there came to the Chase a travelling mole who told us that Privet of Duncton, now too well known for me to describe but then unknown to the likes of North Country moles, had turned to the Silence following the murder of her son Whillan and companion Rooster by the Newborns at Wildenhope. I was strangely affected by this story, as if it pointed me in a direction I had been seeking all my life. I therefore resolved to leave the Chase, and all my kin and friends, and go forth to seek out this Privet and ask her about the Silence.

'Naturally my friends sought to dissuade me, saying, "You've been a sensible mole all your life, Hibbott, why do something so wild and foolish as to go where you're not known and loved?" To which I could find no easy reply except to say that a mole had best do *something* wild and foolish at least once before he dies.

'Since nothing they could say would dissuade me from the course

* Copies of Hibbott's *My Pilgrimage* are now in all the major libraries of moledom.

145

of action I had decided on, my many kin and my good friends decided to accompany me for the first part of my way, my five dearest and closest friends coming with me as far as the Ashley Brook, which marks the end of Ashbourne Dale, and is as far south as most moles from the Chase ever dare venture.

'Here they embraced me, and prayed for me, and tears flowed amongst us almost as noisily, and fulsomely, as water in the Brook itself. Only when I promised to come back one day if ever I met this mole of Duncton called Privet, and discovered the answers to my questions about Silence, would they let me go – which at last, these promises ringing in their ears, they did.

'It was a warm, sunny day, a true May day, and the worms were astir below and the white blossom in the hedges above as I began my journey. I was then somewhat past my middle years, and plump, and I had never raised a talon in anger, in envy or in bitterness in all my life, and I knew I never would. No, I was a contented mole with a discontented mind, who had discovered in Privet of Duncton's search for Silence a calling to my first, and last, and only pilgrimage . . .'

Let us leave Hibbott there for now, and resume our wider history, though never forgetting that that same history would be nothing, nothing at all, but for brave good moles like him!

146

Chapter Thirteen

It was not until some days after Midsummer that word of the Wilden-hope outrage and Privet's retreat reached Fieldfare, Spurling and the other refugees who had stayed hidden up by Seven Barrows beyond Uffington Hill since the previous winter. The news was brought by a party of moles led up from the Vale of Uffington by young Noakes, the mole who had shown such enterprise and bravery on the initial trek to Uffington, and many times since.

Already aware of the violent Crusades that were now taking place in many systems, perpetrated by zealots out of Avebury and Buckland, Noakes and one or two others had made journeys down from the safety of Seven Barrows in the hope of finding moles they might help, and to co-ordinate some kind of local resistance to the Newborns. There had been some close calls, and Noakes had been wounded in one affray with guards, but all had turned out well, and the cautious Spurling's concern over the young mole's dangerous enterprise had been appeased by the results: fourteen more recruits to the refugees at Seven Barrows, many of them strong young males.

The redoubtable Spurling had remained the fugitives' leading elder, with Noakes as the mole now in charge of day-by-day affairs; but it was about Fieldfare that the community really centred. As the numbers had grown, relatively few remembered Chater, and most knew Fieldfare only as the strong dependable Duncton female, versed in the old stories and little rhymes, in whose cheerful face and nurtur-ing nature was refuge indeed for moles who had fled kin and home, and seemed to have nothing new to hope for.

It happens that the growth and development of the Seven Barrows community is exceptionally well recorded, since among its members were several scribes from Avebury, and former library aides. With time on their paws through that long winter it is no wonder that they scribed down their experiences, and frequent reference is made to Fieldfare, 'the first one among us whom all respect and love'.* What

* From Prudele of Yenton's text A Winter Chronicle.

emerges is that after her experience amongst the Stones on the surface near Seven Barrows Fieldfare seems to have become rather more than simply a kind, nurturing mole. The light of destiny had touched her and put a fire into her spirit which warmed the hope of all that community.

As the account by Balyf of Ock puts it, 'In those dark days of doubt and despair, when most of us had times of gloom, there was one mole to whom all could turn and did so: our beloved Fieldfare. She was a mole a little past her prime, whose body showed the signs of a busy life and a well-pupped one, softened by her liking for the fat worm and juicy mushroom. But there was something in her spirit so young, so alive, so full of faith that all would turn out right, that she was the very heart of our hope. Beyond which she knew much of tales and communal pleasures, and all the history of Duncton Wood from where she came, and a howling winter night was not the same if a part of it was not filled by her gentle and confident voice talking to one or other of us.'*

It is quite clear that the moles in Seven Barrows were well informed of the intentions of the Newborns, and the real purpose of the Convocation at Caer Caradoc. At what point Fieldfare and the others began to consider what their role might be once winter had fled and the Newborns began their Crusade no mole can say, but they must early on have decided to improve their defences, for by spring a sophisticated system of redoubts and interlocking tunnels was in place. Moles interested in such matters who have surveyed the site since report that the dispositions of tunnels and trenches were similar to those used at Duncton against the moles of the Word, and it may be that Fieldfare knew these well enough to pass on information to the delvers at Seven Barrows.

At the same time Noakes appears to have gathered about him a number of young, trusty and venturesome moles in the expectation that they would be useful as spies and watchers of Newborn activity. In short, the fugitives at Seven Barrows were not idle, but readied themselves as best they could for the coming struggle.

Then, as March came, they found they had something more than their own lives and liberty to fight for. Among their number were three females who found a mate and wished to get with pup.

* The scribemole Balyf was responsible not only for *Fugitive to Silence*, the autobiography from which this quotation comes, but also for *Fieldfare's Book of Duncton*, his verbatim record of her conversation and tales.

'Best possible thing!' declared Fieldfare. 'There's nothing like having pups to make a group of moles become a community, and to strengthen their resolve to defend what's right!'

Until now the only source of interest and gossip apart from this were the doings of Noakes, always up and off on some foray or another; Spurling was perhaps too ready to grumble and advise caution.

'Anyway, my dear,' said Fieldfare wisely, 'you're never going to stop a mole like Noakes from doing what he wants to. He's a brave mole and does all followers credit!'

'You are right, of course,' responded the elderly Spurling warmly, 'but I've never been one to take risks if I can avoid it, nor encourage others to do so!'

'Take risks! Why, Spurling, since the Newborns forced you out of Avebury you've done nothing but take risks. You take a risk being here!'

There was more than warmth in exchanges such as these – there was respect, and liking, and fond familiarity too. So much so that few at Seven Barrows doubted that now a decent interval had elapsed since the death of Spurling's mate Peach, these two friends would soon get together and inhabit adjacent burrows, if not the same one.

Spurling was far too discreet a mole even to mention such thoughts to anymole-else, but from the look in his eyes when Fieldfare was about (a look which lingered after she had gone off on other business) there was little doubt that he had hopes. However, it must be said that Fieldfare herself had given him no encouragement, having said from time to time that there could never be another mole like Chater, and he could not be replaced.

'And in any case, my dear,' said Spurling to Fieldfare, to whom he had in his gallant and proper way made quite clear his feelings about how good and sensible it would be if they shared a life together, 'we cannot be entirely sure—'

'Oh – he's dead,' she replied clearly and calmly, 'I know it as sure as I know I'm alive. I would like to know how he died, and that he had fulfilled his task of warning Privet, and that he was with friends when he went to the Silence. I do not like to think he was alone, or in pain, though I would prefer to know than not know, whatever the truth is.'

'For your sake I hope you are mistaken.'

'I know you do, Spurling, and I know that though you have affection for me—'

'More than affection, Fieldfare, far more than that!' he rejoined passionately, his wrinkled eyes and thin gaunt face lighting up with the emotion he felt.

'Well then, *more* than affection. I know that if Chater did come back you would be happy for me.'

'Of course, my love for you—'

'No, Spurling, don't use that word. Not yet . . . No!' replied Fieldfare, her snout turning quite red, and her kind eyes moist, as she stopped Spurling going too far too fast – though she was happy, and reassured, that such a mole as he might love her in *that* way. 'Not yet,' she breathed, thinking too that flattered though she was, and distantly tempted, perhaps after all Spurling was not *quite* her type.

'Oh Chater,' she would whisper later in the privacy of her burrow, 'how I miss you! There'll never be another like you, and though I know you'd not want me to be alone, because you know I'm not happy if there's not a mole to love, and nurture and fret about, well those days are done, and I'm content to live on memories.' And if, at such moments, tears came to her eyes, they were not truly unhappy tears, for she never forgot for a moment that it was a blessing to have been loved as she had been, and to have lived as she had.

'Yet I miss another's touch, my dear . . .' she dared to whisper to herself, sniffing and snuffling and easing her comely body into sleep.

Now Noakes had returned yet again, and this time with news of a massacre at a place called Wildenhope, and rumours that the lives of Whillan and Rooster had been lost, and Privet's as well perhaps.

There are some moments in a community's life, of received news, of crisis, of individual triumph or tragedy, which catch the season's mood, and serve to crystallize it, and transmute it into action. The return of Noakes that June with news of the Wildenhope outrage was one such for Seven Barrows, as it was for so many systems in moledom at that time. Just as in far off and unknown Ashbourne Chase, Hibbott had stanced up and declared himself ready to be counted, and set off on his pilgrimage, so now the refugees of Seven Barrows searched out a way to do the same.

Collecting together as a community, with Spurling and Fieldfare in charge, they heard an account of all that was known of the Wildenhope massacre yet again, and then debated the many courses of action that suggested themselves – from attacking the Newborns in a body, to doing absolutely nothing. How that debate raged! How angry and distressed some moles became! But all listened and many spoke, until, it seemed, the ideas were all exhausted.

'What about you, then, eh Fieldfare? What do you think?' called

150

out one of the younger moles at this juncture.

Fieldfare smiled and shook her head. She never minded expressing an opinion if she thought it might help, but on this subject she wasn't sure what to think. In a few short sentences she said as much, suggesting she could see that several different points of view had their strengths, though she would not want to harm anymole, including Newborns, if there was a better way of protecting freedom – a comment that drew a consensual mutter from many of her listeners.

'Be that as it may,' she concluded, 'there is one among us who's seen and heard a lot more change and strife than most of us, and in his own time has used his paws to good effect, if all I've heard is true.' She was thinking of one of the oldest moles at Seven Barrows, named Raistow, who had bravely followed other refugees from the system of Buckland, aged though he was. He was rarely seen these days, being ill and infirm, but had roused himself from his burrow for this great debate, and had so far listened to all the arguments in silence.

'Aye,' continued Fieldfare, 'I'm thinking about Raistow of Buckland who's come up here today despite the fact his paws aren't what they were. There's a lot of us would like to hear what you've got to say, Raistow.'

This was greeted with a murmur of approval, especially among the older moles, who nodded at each other and peered round to where old Raistow was stanced. Some of the youngsters were less respectful, feeling that they did not want another mole rabbiting on and getting into arguments and they continued to chatter, until some 'Sshh's' quietened them. But it was the grave and dignified manner in which Raistow spoke that silenced them completely.

'I'll say my piece,' he began, 'because that's what a mole should do if he feels he's got something worth saying. "Stance up, speak up and then shut up!" That's what my mother used to say. Mind, I was *going* to speak, but there was so much chattering, so much wrangling, that I was beginning to think it wasn't worth it!'

He said this with good humour, though in a gently reproving tone, and several moles grinned ruefully, thinking it was they who were being admonished.

'But then, moles have got to express themselves and I don't think there's been a single mole's spoken today who hasn't had something useful to say!'

'Hear, hear!' cried out one.

'Now I don't suppose an old mole like me will be around to see the outcome of this business with the Newborns, much as I'd like to. One

151

thing's sure though: moles can't force others to their will for ever. Might for a bit, might even for a long time in some places, but sooner or later decent moles will not tolerate it any more! So the first thing to say is this: the Newborns are doomed.'

'Well said, mole!' said two or three voices as a stir of excitement and approval went among the listeners.

'In my young days I would have agreed with those brave moles here who want to be up and at 'em! Quite right too! So I'm not saying they're wrong in what they want, only in how they go about it. It's no good starting a fight, or anything else, if you can't finish it properly – which means successfully. When I got a bit of experience I found it best to plan things – find out as much as possible about a problem and only then try to sort it out. The fact is we don't know much about what's going on in moledom beyond these reports we've had about Newborn Crusades, and Wildenhope. We need to know more. Now that's the first thing.

'The second is this. If my memory serves me right, and I know moles here like the learned Spurling of Avebury who worked in the library, and Fieldfare here who came from Duncton and has a head full of knowledge and history and all sorts of lore, will correct me . . . Like I say, if memory serves, one of the problems in the days of the evil Word was that the followers in different systems weren't in touch with each other. Did not think to be, I suppose. So the disciples of the Word picked off one community after another without difficulty. Well now, we in our time better not make the same mistake. We best band together and find out what's going on, and we better *act* together. That's no easy thing, but it's got to be done.'

'Aye, he's right, what he says is true!' somemole said.

'Sshh! Hear him out,' said others.

'I'm not saying I've got the right answer,' continued Raistow, 'nor an easy one, but let's say it may be a good possibility. I'm saying to myself, "What will other moles like us be deciding now? What action will *they* take?"'

'You reckon there are other groups who want to resist like us?' asked one of the younger moles, one indeed who had initially been among the chatterers.

'Bound to be,' said Raistow reassuringly. 'I'd wager my life on it that there's a *lot* of others like us. And some will be asking the same question I've just asked, "What will the others be deciding?" Well, I'll tell you my answer. They'll be thinking of the old days of the Word, and the mistakes made then, and they'll be remembering that at that time, when things were as dark as they've ever been, and darker than now, there was a system stanced its ground and produced moles who led us back to light again. I'm referring to Duncton Wood.

'We're honoured to have a Duncton mole in our company in the comely shape of Fieldfare here . . .' Raistow allowed himself a wry and wrinkled grin as if to say, 'the times may be past when I can go wooing a young female like her, but I've my own memories!'. Fieldfare's snout glowed a pleasant shade of pink at the compliment. Then Raistow was serious once more.

'All I can say is that if she's typical of Duncton moles today then that's a system we can still rely on. I'll not be the only mole saying that up and down moledom. No, there'll be others who'll be thinking, "If we're going to find inspiration and support it's to Duncton we should turn our snouts."

'Now, Fieldfare has told me that there's still a few moles in Duncton we can rely on, and the one she's mentioned goes by the name of Pumpkin. I reckon we should send a couple of moles – reliable, brave moles – off to Duncton to make contact with Pumpkin, first to find out what's apaw, because he's likely to know, and secondly to say that when the call goes out there's moles up here on the Seven Barrows will move against the Newborns!'

This last remark caused a ragged cheer to break out amongst Raistow's now rapt listeners.

'I may not have been able to take an active part in things of late, seeing as my paws are giving out, but I keep my eyes and ears open and I say that if he's willing he's certainly able! The mole we should send to Duncton is young Noakes over there, who's an example to us all. Well now, that's for him to consider and others to decide, but before I stance down and shut up I'd like to say a couple more things.'

'We're listening!' said many a mole, whispering among themselves that all he had said so far made a lot of sense.

'It may surprise some of you to know that I myself have been to Duncton Wood! It's a long time ago, and a long story I'm not going to waste your time with now. I was young, and so were my mates, and come the summer, off we went to see that famous place for ourselves. Fieldfare here would have been a very young mole then I suppose and I can't say I remember meeting her. But we were given a good welcome, we shared a few tales down in what they call Barrow Vale, and we had the honour of meeting the Elder Drubbins, whom Fieldfare here has mentioned from time to time.

'But what I remember most, and why I mention it, and the thing I'd like you youngsters upon whom we older moles are going to be relying in the hard times ahead to pay special attention to, was the Duncton Stone. I visited it twice – once with my mates, and once alone. It rises out of the ground like nothing I've ever seen, and there's a light about it a mole never forgets. It's humbling, but it doesn't make a mole feel small; it's awesome, but it doesn't make a mole feel it's unattainable; it's holy, but in its presence a mole doesn't feel separate from it.

'The time I was alone before it I did what I daresay most moles do when they go into its presence – I tried to pray, but couldn't! I muttered a few words, I stared at it, and eventually I stumbled back towards the edge of the clearing among the trees where it stands. Just as I was leaving, feeling a bit foolish, an austere, formidable kind of mole comes along and says in the old traditional way, "Whatmole are you, and whither are you bound?"

'I replied in the proper manner and before I knew what I was doing I told him my story, and how we had come up from Buckland without telling anymole. As we spoke he kind of eased me towards the Stone until at the end I was right under it, almost touching it in fact.

'"You looked as if you were running away from it when I stopped you just now!" says he.

'So I told him I was in a manner of speaking, explaining I had tried to pray but couldn't find the words. He said to me, "That's all right, it just shows you were trying. All you have to do is look up at the Stone and open your heart and it will know what's in it, and what you need."

'"Is that all?" I faltered. He nodded and said, "You could do it now if you wanted. After all, you might never get another chance!"

'So I did, and I didn't mind him being there. If anything it made it easier. After a time of silence I said aloud, "I think I know what I want now, although I would never have thought it before." He asked me what it was, and I didn't mind telling him, silly though it seemed then, and often has since. Silly until this very day . . .'

Raistow paused once more and glanced about him, and not one of his listeners spoke, or fidgeted. They saw before them a mole who must once have been strong and large, with a solid sort of head and sound paws. Now he was frail and shrunken, and one of his paws trembled and the others were weak, but such was the quiet dignity of his tale-telling, and the serious import of all that he said, it seemed that the elderly mole who had begun to talk to them had somehow

154

given way once more to the strong mole he had been in his prime, one worthy to face anymole among them.

'Aye,' he said ruminatively, 'I had a fancy come to me all right, and I told that mole what it was, just as I'll tell you now. Says I, "What I would like is for my youngsters to come across the vales as I have done, and return to this ancient wood, and stance before the Duncton Stone as I do now. A mole needs to see it only once, and touch it perhaps, to remember always that it's here as it was, as it is, as it always will be. I'd like my young to know that."

'"It's as good an ambition as any," said the Duncton mole to me. "Now tell me why you'd like them to come to the Duncton Stone."

'"To the Duncton Stone?" I repeated, thinking what these words meant. "It's because a mole who can say he's off to do that, and knows he'll not be troubled on the way, but rather will be helped and guided by those he meets, is a mole who lives in a peaceful Stone-fearing world!"

'That's what I said, those very words, and I surprised myself by saying them. I was only a youngster and not inclined to spiritual things, or to contemplate what I might say one day to my young. Why, I had never thought to have any! But there I was saying I would tell them to be off to the Duncton Stone!'

'Did you ask the name of the mole you were talking to?' asked one of the youngsters.

'Of course I did!' said Raistow. 'And you know what? It was none other than Master Librarian Stour I had been talking to, the most learned mole in moledom!'

'And did you tell them, your own youngsters, what you told him, about going to the Duncton Stone?' asked Fieldfare quietly. 'And did they go?'

Raistow slowly shook his head, and for a moment the shadows of age and regret came to his face and eyes.

'As I say, I've not thought to repeat those words since that day long ago when I was young. You see, I never did have young. That fortune was never mine, though other blessings came my way. But not young. No, not young to call my own.'

He paused again, and a sensitive mole could see that this lack of youngsters of his own was the great sadness of Raistow's life. But then a touching and vulnerable look of shyness went across his face, a kind of diffidence, and it was plain he was struggling to find the right words for what he wished to say. It is at such moments that the true strength of a community may be revealed. When a mole's listeners, sensitive to his needs and forgetting their own selfish whims and desires, give a mole space to express his feelings. Not a mole spoke, not a mole stirred, unless it was in some small and gentle gesture of empathy, as if to say to Raistow, 'You take your time, old mole, for it's clear enough you've been patient with moles aplenty in *your* day. We don't mind waiting, because what's a community for if not to give a mole the chance to speak his mind, or cry, or be silent, or make a suggestion when he wants to?'

'Well anyway,' he continued at last, 'seeing as I never did have young, but seeing as we've been blessed by a few youngsters being born up here in Seven Barrows, I would take it kindly if their parents wouldn't mind if a foolish old mole who's got little time left said to them something that matters to him, and may help them. Go to the Duncton Stone, pray before it if you've a mind to, touch it if the mood takes you, and think of Raistow of Buckland when you do. You'll not regret it, because the journey there and back will see changes that will make a better mole of you; and by going to the Duncton Stone you'll be telling yourself, and allmole, that you live in a Stone-fearing time and place, and amongst moles who respect liberty.

'You keep that before you in the difficult times ahead, and you do it one day come what may, and the Stone will protect you in the going, and it will see you come home safeguarded, as it saw me all those years ago. You've a right to that only if you assert it in the true spirit of a follower, which is what our discussion here today has been about!'

To most of the moles listening he seemed to have finished. The effort of talking had wearied him and his gaze dropped to the ground as all about him stamped their paws and called out their appreciation of his words. Finally Noakes came forward and said, 'I want Raistow to know that I am ready and willing to make the trek to Duncton if this meeting wants me to, and I'll do it all the more readily because I'll have *your* approval.' He said the last with a courteous nod towards Raistow. 'As for you being too old yourself, Raistow, to go to Duncton when times get better, well, I'm not sure about that. You may be a bit tottery of paw, but after what you've said, and the inspiration you've given, I'd like to offer my help to get you back to the Duncton Stone, so you can see for yourself these youngsters here following your advice!'

'Well said, Noakes!' cried out several moles, pleased he had risen to the occasion so well.

'Have you got a last thought for us, Raistow of Buckland?' asked

Spurling at Fieldfare's prompting. She had been to meetings like this in Duncton Wood many times and knew well that wise but diffident moles often saved the best till last.

'I don't want to take up more time, or outstay my welcome as a speaker,' said Raistow quietly, barely raising his eyes. 'But it does seem to me that what I've said about Duncton is all the more to the point because of the action of Privet, formerly of Crowden but now of Duncton. It's no light or simple thing that she's done, choosing to retreat into Silence. In fact I've never in all my years even *heard* of it being done, except by the holy moles who lived up near here on Uffington Hill in times gone by. But they did it in private, so to speak, in special cells and that according to the Chronicles. She's gone and done it publicly, and that's an awesome thing. She's the one to watch, hers is the example we should all pay attention to, follower and New-born alike. That's it you see, she's done something *beyond* us all, which will show us a way to get out of conflict and come together again. Privet's the one, and what she's done is . . . is *everything*.'

Kenning these words of Raistow's now a mole might feel disappointed that so famous a speech as that which he made on that morning at Seven Barrows should seem so ordinary. No histrionics! No overly dramatic pauses! No recourse to insult or invective! Just an elderly mole speaking out his heart in a time of trouble to a community of moles amongst whom he felt safe.

This speech concluded, the debate was over and Spurling was able to propose and carry the consensus view that Noakes and two others of his choosing should set off for Duncton just as Raistow had advised – to make contact with other followers, to seek more news, and to say that there were moles atop Uffington who, if and when the time came, would not hesitate to give their help, and their lives if need be, in the service of the followers of the Stone.

With what burden of advice Noakes left with his companions we may imagine, and with what hopes for better days and the Stone's good guidance amongst those who thronged the grassy slopes of the Seven Barrows to bid them Stone's speed, and wish them well!

There too, we may reasonably guess, that for the first time was heard the clarion cry, 'To the Stone, moles! To the Duncton Stone!'

Chapter Fourteen

It must be said that when Maple and Weeth left Privet and the others in what they thought was complete safety, high on the Wenlock Edge, and began their journey north to Cannock, the feeling that dominated the minds of both was relief, pure and simple.

Maple had devoted all his thought and studies to the idea of leadership and war, driven by an instinctive belief that one day moledom would need his services. He had fully discharged his duties regarding Privet, though had he known, or even suspected, the disaster that would so soon befall her, he would have stayed with her. But he did not, and could not, and would not learn of it for some time yet. Meanwhile, sensing now that his destiny was not far ahead of him, he went forth to Cannock with vigour and purpose, in the best traditions of a Duncton warrior mole, to discover what the Newborns intended for the system, and the strength of local opposition to them, that he might know all the better how the Newborns were likely to organize themselves militarily elsewhere in moledom, so that he could see the best way to co-ordinate resistance to them.

As for Weeth, all his cunning and devious life he had searched for opportunity, and from the moment he had set eyes upon Maple, he had known he had found it. Though much the same age, he looked a little older, and in some ways, especially Newborn ways, he was wiser. He saw in Maple a mole of strength and shining virtues who would surely one day inspire others in what might, perhaps, be as great a war fought for the Stone as ever had been.

'I shall assist and serve!' Weeth had told himself. 'This mole I shall defend to death, though I trust it won't come to that. And, er, Stone, I'd be grateful if you would take *that* as a prayer!'

Now they were off to Cannock, and Weeth felt relief at having found the task he desired more than any other, having served a successful apprenticeship, and now being trusted to get on with it. Added to which, the two moles liked each other very much – the silence of Maple complemented by the loquacity of Weeth; and the sound common sense and wise judgement of Maple complementing Weeth's excitable enthusiasms, and impulsive passions; and, to take this thought to its ultimate conclusion, the strategy of Maple ably complemented by the daily tactics, not to say antics, of cunning Weeth.

So, little knowing the tragedy that had begun on the Edge behind them, the two moles pursued their way to Cannock. When the first spatter of rain came, and the skies lowered over, Maple stopped for a time to put out his paw as if to feel the weather, and the way the wind, until then light, sent occasional flurries through nearby trees.

'It's just a spot of rain,' said Weeth, ever optimistic.

'Let's hope it's not just a spot,' said Maple, slowly surveying the sky. 'Rain now could be greatly to our advantage.'

'It slows us down,' said Weeth.

'No, it slows *everymole* down. But more to the point, if this weather sets in as heavily as I think it may, it will bring floods. Didn't you see how full the streams and rivers in the Vale below the Edge were? That's thaw water, and if it's supplemented by rain we'll have the kind of floods that bring confusion to even the best-ordered systems. All of which will help us to do our work unmolested.'

'Obvious, when *you* think of it,' observed Weeth wryly.

'We'll stay as high above the coming floods as we can,' decreed Maple. 'And we'll travel fast, for there's nothing like heavy rain and turbulent rivers to confuse moles, and make guards less wary. Our story can be that we've been flooded out of our system, and forced to travel north.'

'And we are Newborn?' suggested Weeth.

'Without question, mole,' said Maple, setting his snout northwards. 'At least the wind's behind us, the better to get us there! A mole might almost dare to think the Stone is on our side!'

In a sense it was, and one cannot have shadows, especially long and dark ones, without some concomitant light. In this case the light, the advantage, came from the fact that Privet's tragedy was Maple's gain, for it meant that Thorne and his well-trained guards were many days delayed on their journey to Cannock.

Maple's and Weeth's own trek was a hard slog north through the driving rain; the most dangerous passage was dropping down to the Severn Valley, and crossing the river to gain the higher ground on the far side that would take them finally to the sandstone heights of Cannock Chase. It was a crossing not without incident, for the river was rising fast and by the time they reached it two days after leaving Privet, they were tired out after many hours fatiguing negotiation of

159

rushing brooks and streams. To make matters worse night was falling fast and Maple was determined to cross the river before it rose further. Guided by the doleful yellow glare of the eyes of roaring owls they made their way upstream to a two-foot crossing high and safe over the water.

Nor were they the only ones, for in the shadows below it, just off the way itself, they came across a pathetic huddle of five moles who almost jumped out of their skins with fright when Maple and Weeth loomed out of the darkness behind them.

'Don't hurt *us*, sir,' cried out one of the two males among them, 'we're Newborn through and through! We're on your side.'

When Maple replied, 'I've no intention of hurting anymole, Newborn or otherwise!' their relief was tangible.

'We were just waiting for a good moment to risk the passage over the two-foot way but, well, we're not used to this sort of thing and the roaring owls' gazes frighten and confuse us.'

'They frighten and confuse *me*,' said Maple affably, shaking himself so that muddy water from his underbelly flew in all directions. 'Why do you want to cross anyway?'

'To get away,' said their spokesmole darkly, adding, unconvincingly, 'from the floods.'

'Mmm . . .' mused Maple. Then turning to Weeth, he said, 'Grub about and find some food, Weeth, for all of us. A bit of nourishment is what these moles need.'

'Right away!' said Weeth, his own tiredness leaving him at the sudden change on the faces that had looked so defeated and frightened only a moment before. Now there was a look of gratitude and hope, and the fugitives gazed up at Maple and seemed to absorb something of his confidence and purpose.

'We—' began the mole.

'No, don't speak yet,' said Maple, raising a paw. 'Get some food down first . . . Weeth! Where is it then?'

Up came Weeth with some fat, dark red worms, of the kind that flourish in those parts.

'There's plenty where these came from,' he said. 'The rain's brought them out.'

'Now,' said Maple in a measured way, once the moles had eaten, and dried out a little in a spot of shelter he had found for them, 'I'd guess this is the first time you've ever tried to cross the river this way. Moles like you don't flee their territory because of a bit of flooding.'

'You're right, sir. What I was going to say, since you seem a decent

160

sort of mole, was that, begging your pardon but not *all* Newborns are good, or do right by the Stone.'

'True,' said Maple. 'Have another worm, my friend.'

'Go on, tell him!' said one of the females suddenly. 'Report what happened. *He* could do something about it.'

'He could also have us arraigned!' whispered another. 'Best forget.'

Maple sighed and grinned. 'Out with it, one of you . . .'

One of them? *All* of them more like. As eager as ferrets at a corpse they were to tell him of how a patrol of Newborns, hurrying back to Cannock, had come across several moles of their system making for higher ground to avoid the floods.

'Coming from Broseley as we do, we're used to a spot of water, as you say. So at this season, and sometimes when the autumn years are wet, we head upslope towards the Edge until the danger's past . . .'

'. . . And *I* said we should have gone earlier, and so we should and none of this would . . .'

'. . . have happened? No, it wouldn't, would it Myrtle! You're always so bloody clever you are! Well it *has* happened and we've got to make the best of it!'

The story came out bit by bit. It seemed that the Newborn patrol had picked on the advance party of the Broseley moles, while they waited for others to join them. There was an altercation and a fight ensued, though a one-sided one. Two of the Broseley youngsters had got into difficulties in the water, and while one of the adults went to their aid, the Newborn guards attacked the remainder, mainly older moles.

'Three dead, two died later, four lost in fleeing,' was the final bleak tally. 'And then they just upped and left, no comment, no explanation, nothing. Came, killed, destroyed our community, and left. When the Newborns first came to us and persuaded us to adopt their ways they said we'd get protection! Instead we get harried, bullied, and finally gratuitously attacked because we're not "true" Newborns, whatever that may mean.'

The sorry group stared in righteous outrage at Maple and Weeth.

'Did you get their names?' asked Weeth.

'Names! That's a joke! Brothers Barmy, Bastard and Backward, I should think. If we'd asked their names none of us'd be here to tell the tale. Now we're getting out of it as quick as we can.'

'Where are you heading for?'

'Where we can get some *real* protection, that's where!'

'Where's that?'

'Ssh, Furrow! You've said enough as it is. He *is* Newborn,' hissed the sharp-eyed female.

'You shouldn't believe everymole you meet is Newborn,' said Maple.

'Not Newborn? One thing's sure, you don't come from these parts with an accent like that!'

'Like what?' laughed Maple.

'Sort of, well, clear. Like a scribemole.'

'Aye, well,' said Maple. 'I'm no more Newborn than you are, and nor's my friend. Now, where are you going to?'

'The one place round here that's resisted the Newborns so far,' said the mole promptly, as the others eyed Maple and Weeth with a new friendliness: 'Rowton. That's where.'

Maple looked at Weeth and then back at their new friends. 'Well, then, if that's where you want to get to we'll see you there safely.'

'Even across the river *here*, sir?' said the female.

'There's no time like the present! Come on – Weeth, you take up the rear.'

'But the roaring owls, sir,' said Furrow. 'They'll—'

'They'll do nothing to you if you keep your eyes down and away from their gazes, and avoid breathing their fumes.'

'No, sir! It's no good! You'll not get me going that way!'

'Mole,' said Maple slowly, 'there's far worse trials coming in the molemonths and years ahead. The Stone's got you this far because it needs every true follower it can get, and it needs *you*. *All* of you. As I said before, I'm wary of the roaring owls myself, and so is my timid friend Weeth. But we've got a task ahead of us and that's more important than our fears. So have you.'

'*We*'ve got a task? But we're just ordinary moles.'

'You show me a true follower of the Stone who is anything more than "just an ordinary mole"!' declared Maple, eyes seeming almost alight in the dark, as he stanced up boldly towards the cross-over, the yellow gazes of the passing roaring owls shining in his fur.

'Well, *you*'re not for one,' muttered Weeth to himself as he saw how Maple's words inspired the others; casting their fears aside, they stanced up to follow him.

'Oh yes, you've got a task all right. You're followers of the Stone, aren't you? Well then, the time's coming when moles like you and I are going to have to defend it.'

'Against . . . I mean . . . you don't mean . . .' faltered the older of the moles.

'Of *course* he means the Newborns,' cried out the female Myrtle, eyes ablaze and a new vigour about her. 'And about time too, just like I've been saying!'

'*Do* you mean them, sir?'

'I do. Now, mole, what's your name?'

'Furrow, sir!'

'And this mole, Myrtle?'

'My mate, sir, for better or for worse.'

'Better, like I've always told you,' said Myrtle unexpectedly.

'Well then, Furrow, you come forward over this cross-over with me, and you know what you leave behind you?'

'Floods, sir.'

'Floods and the fear that the Stone's not at your flank always.'

'Yes, *sir*!' said Furrow grinning.

'And you know what you'll find on the far side, the moment you put your paw on the good ground again?'

'Well, I *think* I do,' said Furrow uncertainly.

'You tell him, sir!' said Myrtle.

'No, I think he can tell us,' said Maple.

Furrow ventured a little past Maple towards the two-foot way and peered into the darkness across the river, from which and to which the roaring owls came and went. He was by no means a big mole, nor a strong-looking one. Weeth could not but reflect he was very ordinary indeed. Yet somehow Maple had inspired him to stance up boldly and face his uncertain future so that he looked almost heroic, the brave protector of those with him, and most specially the sharp-tongued Myrtle.

'I can't say as I see much in this darkness, sir, but what I feel is that over that side, if me and my kin can only make our way there and beyond to Rowton, we'll find a way of . . . a way we might . . .'

'You tell him, Furrow, like I've told *you*.'

'. . . a way to *fight* the Newborns.' His body almost shook when he said the word 'fight', as if he had never dared say it before and was surprised he had now. But he *had* said it, and everymole there, including Maple, now looked at him expectantly.

'Well, then,' he said finally, 'I suppose I better lead you all across. No looking at the gazes, no breathing in the fumes, just keep your snouts down and follow the mole in front. And I'd be much obliged if you'd keep up the rear,' he added to Weeth.

'With pleasure, with alacrity,' said Weeth, much moved by Furrow's new-found courage.

163

'Come on then!' gulped Furrow, and turning from them he led them forth.

'I always *said* he had it in him!' said Myrtle with admiration in her voice. 'Didn't I say that? I did, you know.'

'Stop talking, Myrtle, and start moving,' said Furrow over his shoulder, and across the river they went, eyes down, snouts averted from the roaring owls, scurrying one after another to safety.

The following afternoon the party reached Rowton, pawsore and weary, with Maple in the lead finally, to keep them going. Not that Furrow had faltered, but as Maple said to Weeth as they went along, moles find their strengths in fits and starts, and it is best not to push them too hard at the beginning.

'The important thing is to make them realize they can do it by themselves,' he said. 'After that they've got the feel of success. That's our task, Weeth, to make what followers we meet and those who turn to us *know* that they've got the strength to confront the Newborns. *We* can't win the war for them, but if we can make them believe they can fight then we'll win the war with their help!'

Looking at Maple, witnessing the wise way he led even so small a group of 'ordinary' moles, and how he put the new fire and purpose into their paws, Weeth knew he saw a great leader in the making. But it was not just the way he inspired those about him, but also that he seemed never to stop thinking about the landscapes and different sites they travelled through, pondering their military possibilities and pitfalls.

'I can remember no reference in the texts to Rowton,' he said, 'so I shall be interested to survey it – most successful resistance begins with a defensible site, or moles who know how to turn disadvantage to advantage.'

Yet when they came to Rowton, late the following afternoon, the rain now a depressing drizzle, they found it occupied a nondescript north-eastern slope, with woodland above, and a valley, half obscured by the lie of the land, below. It did not look particularly defensible to Weeth.

'Quite so,' said Maple, 'that's why we'll already have been observed.'

'I've seen nomole at all,' said Furrow.

'I've seen two,' said Maple, 'and a possible third. It's a question of knowing where look-outs might be placed.'

He was soon proved right, for two moles were waiting for them as

164

they climbed a steep little rise, sloshing through runnels of water. The guards were bright-eyed and firm, and their interrogation of the party was thorough. They looked a little weary when they heard Furrow's sorry tale, and said they had heard it too many times before. But their interest increased when Maple declined to identify himself or which system he was from unless he knew more about them first.

'You've got a nerve, chum, marching up here anonymously and expecting special treatment.'

'Whatmole's in command here?' asked Maple with a stern authority Weeth had not seen before.

'The elders are . . . sir,' said the guard. 'We'll take you to them.'

'Oh no you won't, mole. How do you know I'm not spying out your ground? Eh? You don't! But these moles'll vouch for me as far as they can. Leave my colleague and me here under guard.'

The guardmole grinned. 'Stone the crows! You'd think there was a war on!'

'There is,' said Maple sharply.

'But anymole can see you're not Newborn . . .' the guardmole's voice faded away at Maple's stare. 'I'll go and get somemole senior, sir,' he said hastily.

'About time,' said Maple heavily, stancing down in the rain: 'we'll wait.'

Furrow and the others went ahead reluctantly, not liking to leave their new-found companions behind. But when they were gone Maple was not the least despondent, rather the opposite as he began to talk cheerfully to the remaining guard, extracting from him in no time at all, and without his realizing it, all kind of information about Rowton. So much so indeed that by the time a rough-furred but determined mole came huffing and puffing to see who these strangers at the system's western portal were, Maple was able in a few short incisive sentences to describe all the main military strengths and weaknesses of the system he had not yet put a paw in.

'Blow me!' exclaimed the Rowton mole, whose name was Whindrell, 'you seem to know a lot about such things. Whatmole are you, then, and whither are you bound?'

An authoritative glance from Maple had the guards retreating discreetly, so that Weeth and he could talk to Whindrell confidentially.

'I am Maple of Duncton Wood, and this is Weeth of no fixed abode, my companion and assistant, and a mole I can vouch for.'

'So, you're a Duncton mole. Then you'll be on business against the Newborns?'

'You guess aright,' said Maple.

'Oh, it's no guess, mole, it's a certainty. Duncton has not failed moledom in the past, and those with a sense of history surely know it will not fail them now that a crisis of faith is upon us again. You are welcome to Rowton, and your advice will be valued. What little I have learned from the moles you brought with you suggests you have the kind of qualities we'll need . . . and sooner rather than later. I'm in charge here since my brother died, but I can't say I know much yet about military matters. But we always believed that with the coming of spring, the Newborn Crusade would begin in earnest . . .'

'Tell me all you know,' said Maple.

'Not here, mole, but in the comfort of the system. Come, there's others you should speak to as well as me since we're all in this together, and between us all we'll answer your questions. As for your concern for secrecy, it is well-founded – the Newborns have spies everywhere these days, though I doubt there are any left in Rowton.' From the firm way he spoke, and the resolution in his eyes, it was obvious the moles of these parts took unkindly to betrayal. By the same token, thought Maple, they'll be loyal and steadfast in times of trial and crisis, and though Whindrell might be a bit rough around the edges he can soon be sorted out!

Maple and Weeth stayed for three days in Rowton, during which time they learnt much about the Newborns of both Caer Caradoc and Cannock Chase, the system being on the borderland between the two, and so escaping from the full attentions of either. It was a discovery that made Maple realize that resistance would be easiest in areas peripheral to the Newborns' different spheres of influence, and communication safest along such borders.

As for Rowton itself, the early impressions he received were broadly correct – the system was well defended on all sides but the open, flatter northern flank was a weakness. But that said, morale was high, not so much because of any successful sustained resistance to the Newborns in the recent past, but because Whindrell inspired confidence and the system had not yet been put to a proper test. Quite how Rowton had gained the reputation of being a safe sanctuary Maple did not know, but moles like Furrow and Myrtle had flocked to it in recent molemonths, and Maple's view was that it might be wise to make a virtue of necessity and train up the willing moles, and give the system better defences.

But at least the elders had had the sense to realize the danger they were in if any Crusade got underway once spring advanced – hence the guards, and Whindrell's quick arrival to investigate Maple and Weeth.

So impressed were the Rowton moles by Maple's rapid understanding of their position, and the warnings he gave as to their vulnerability, and his advice to develop defences on the northern flank, that they offered him there and then a place on their Elder council, and the role of commander of their willing, spirited, but so far undisciplined and untested forces.

He declined, explaining that his mission with Weeth was to make a reconnaissance of Cannock itself – but he promised on his return that way to try to stay a little longer. Meanwhile he had every confidence in Whindrell, provided he was willing to listen to a bit of advice.

'You'll not find stouter-hearted moles hereabout nor ones more willing to learn,' declared Whindrell proudly. 'Why, thanks to the leadership of my late brother we're an island of nonconformity in a sea of Newborn dogma that stretches from Caradoc to Cannock. Moles know it too, for many refugees like Furrow, Myrtle and the others who came up with you, come to us now.' Which was true, for even since they had been there Maple and Weeth had noticed other bedraggled arrivals, and seen how welcome they were made, and how soon they were found quarters and given tasks.

'I'll think about your system before I get back,' said Maple, 'for you could have an important role to play. Moledom is going to need systems that stance firm and uphold their liberty, and the example of one that does so successfully may save ten more from giving in. Aye, you'll hear from me again, Whindrell! Meanwhile double your guard, train them, build your defences on the lines I'll show you before I leave, and always remember that against a strong, organized foe flexibility is what winning is about.'

When they finally set off on their way once more the numbers who came to see them off suggested that their secret was out, and Maple's origin known.

'No matter!' declared Weeth. 'For doesn't it show how a strong mole and the name of Duncton can inspire others?'

'It'll be victories that inspire moles, Weeth,' said Maple grimly, 'and the extent to which moles like these can keep faith with the Stone and each other in times of hardship.'

It was Furrow, already much improved in strength and health since their first meeting, who accompanied them to the last, and said a final farewell: 'There's no escaping the fact, Maple, sir, that you and Weeth here saved our lives. If you ever need *my* help you ask for it, and Myrtle's too, and it won't be wanting.'

There was pride in his voice, and a new light in his eyes, and Weeth knew that Maple meant it when he replied, 'For that I'm grateful, mole, and I'll not forget it. The day is rapidly approaching when it will be upon moles like you that all moledom's liberty will depend! May the Stone be with you!'

'And you, sir, and with Weeth as well!'

Chapter Fifteen

Maple and Weeth pressed on to Cannock without a break; the rain still fell heavily and the spell of storms continued, and the going was as hard as before. But at least that meant, just as Maple had predicted, that when they crossed the last vale towards the heights of Cannock itself, they were not the only travellers, for many moles were escaping the floods lower down.

In consequence the light and airy tunnels of Cannock were besieged by moles like themselves, and after only a cursory check by a harassed guard they were able to enter; and taking advantage of the temporary chaos in the system, they wandered almost at will and surveyed both the physical defences and the morale of the guards, as well as gathering what evidence they could of the nature and strength of opposition to the Newborns. It greatly helped in all of this that Maple was well kenned regarding the scribings of the several moles who had described events at Cannock during the great War of the Word a century before.

'The defence lines are little different to those established by moles of the Word when they realized that the followers might overrun the system,' explained Maple to Weeth. 'But the place is high, and its defences are well constructed and would be hard to take, and only fell originally because by the time followers got here discipline among the disciples of the Word had all but broken down.'

Weeth might know little about military history, but he was good at wheedling information out of moles and soon established that a new commander named Thorne, who was expected daily, had been appointed to the system by Quail, to lead the Crusades out of Cannock into the surrounding systems.

But, interestingly, this process had been partly pre-empted during the milder winter weather by Newborn zealots led by a young Acting Commander named Squilver who had risen through the ranks and had some hopes, it seemed, of making sufficient mark to be appointed Brother Commander himself.

'Bit of an ambitious, ruthless bastard by all accounts,' said Weeth, 'and annoyed not to have got the Brother Commander's position.'

169

'Mmm . . . that's normal enough, and means little if Thorne's competent. Indeed, ambitious subordinates only enhance a leader's abilities if they are properly controlled. Have you learned anything about Thorne?'

'Only that moles say he must be out of favour with Caer Caradoc to be sent here,' replied Weeth. 'Cannock is regarded as a dead-end – the systems most prized by the commanders are ones like Rollright, Duncton and Avebury, the last of which was once Quail's own.'

'The moles I've talked to say there'll be a Brother Adviser with each commander.'

'That's right, meaning a spiritual adviser. The Brother Commander fights and the Brother Adviser prays!' Weeth's eyes twinkled at this and they both understood why: divided leadership could mean less effective campaigns.

'But we shouldn't linger too long here, Maple,' said Weeth, who when they were alone dropped the 'sir', 'for the Brother Commander is already on the way.'

'Aye, but we've not made contact with any moles in opposition to the Newborns and I'm confident there'll be some.'

Their chance came two days later when they heard that Squilver had decided that some miscreants should be punished, though for what crimes nomole knew.

'He's probably just making examples of them to calm things down a bit,' said Weeth.

'And it seems to be working, judging by how quiet the tunnels have suddenly become, and how earnest everymole is trying to look. But I'll warrant the kind of mole we want to meet will be there, so we'll go along,' said Maple.

The following day, as they approached the great communal chamber where the arraignment was to take place, to which a general invitation for males in the system to attend had gone out, they felt that same sickening excitement among the Newborns they had experienced during the strettening at Ludlow. On the way they were stopped and questioned more than once and while their claims to be Newborn seemed as accepted as ever, it was becoming obvious that soon they would be assigned a group and a task, and then might find it hard to escape from Cannock.

Weeth was too busy fulminating against the air of excitement that accompanied the coming punishment to notice anything else, but Maple was in watchful and cautious mood, the more so when they were stopped a third time and a senior mole, an Inquisitor by the look of him, nodded them past but told them to follow others ahead down one way and not another which different moles were taking.

'Why *that* way, Brother?' asked Maple amiably, but watching carefully.

'We have to spread you brothers to different parts of the chamber,' he replied, his stance hard and his response a little too smooth for Maple's liking.

'Right!' Maple said urgently as they went the way they were told. 'You stay close to me, Weeth, and keep your eyes open. There's trickery apaw here . . .'

Behind them more moles pushed forward, forcing them into those in front, invoking a feeling of crushing crowds which added to their unease. If Maple said there was likely to be trickery, Weeth was not going to doubt it, and they went cheek by jowl, and did not separate when the tunnel led them out into a communal chamber only half full of moles. Its lay-out was grimly familiar to both of them, for it had the same raised dais and guarded entrances as the much larger version they had seen in Caer Caradoc.

'Keep close, Weeth, and make for a place near that portal at the back,' said Maple, indicating a particular one. Yet even as they pressed across the chamber towards it, the crowd thickened rapidly, making their progress increasingly difficult, and the problem of keeping together ever greater. Despite the struggle they experienced at the end, when they had to shove their way through a group of moles who took none too kindly to their efforts, the mood in the chamber was still jocular and excited. It was maintained by some cheerful moles up on the dais who were singing rhythmic and jolly songs, though Maple soon pointed out that behind them, peeping out from the shadows, were the pointed snouts and sharp eyes of what looked like more guardmoles.

The crowd about them was now shoulder to shoulder, flank to flank, and Weeth felt the first trickle of sweat at his neck and face as the chamber warmed up, and they struggled to maintain their position by the guarded portal.

'This is dangerous, Weeth, and we must not allow ourselves to be moved out of reach of this portal. Meanwhile, let us remember why we came and talk to some moles and find where their sympathies really lie.'

It was hard, hot work in such a milling, excitable crowd, especially one in the heart of a Newborn system awaiting an event, and Maple, formidable as he looked, made little headway. But Weeth, well used

171

to Newborns and practised in subterfuge, found two moles together who, he whispered to Maple, were probably not the devotees they claimed.

'Sure?'

'Sure-ish,' said Weeth. 'They're not enjoying themselves; their claim to be Newborn was a little too eager.'

'I'll talk to them.'

'You'll scare them!' said Weeth, and he meant it.

Maple pushed past him, looked over the two moles, and fixed them with a stare.

'Hello, Brothers,' he said menacingly.

They stole a hurried glance at each other and mumbled a greeting in return. They looked a little frightened, and they were sweating a lot. They seemed jumpy, as moles all around sang and jostled, and complained that it was about time something happened. The noise level in the chamber had risen and when Maple made up his mind to risk confronting them directly he had to lean close and raise his voice to be heard.

'Listen, you two,' he said, 'and listen well, for your lives and mine may depend on it . . .'

'Maple!' hissed Weeth in his ear.

Maple ignored him: 'I am a mole of Duncton Wood and a follower of the Stone. There's going to be trouble here and danger, so stay close by me.'

'We're followers too,' they said with relief.

'Maple!' whispered Weeth urgently.

'In a moment,' said Maple over his shoulder, 'Go on.'

'We only came because . . .'

The crowd was almost a crush now and the mole's next words could not be heard.

'Stay close by me, whatever else you do!' ordered Maple, turning round with some difficulty to hear what Weeth had to say.

But Weeth had gone, and not a hair of him was visible in the crowd.

'Weeth?' growled Maple, annoyed, as he stanced up as high as he could to see where his companion had got to, and why he had disobeyed instructions. What was he doing?

Maple's two new comrades at least were doing as he said and sticking close, but if they wished to say their piece there was no more time. The singing moles on the dais fell silent, the hidden guards came out in force and as a self-confident-looking brother appeared before them, an expectant hush fell.

172

'That's Brother Squilver,' a mole nearby told another, and an appreciative chanting of his name went up. Squilver was a tough-looking mole with a humourless expression, and dead eyes that scanned the crowd menacingly.

'Where's the sinners, sir?' cried out somemole up front.

'Aye, that's what I'd like to know, Brothers,' roared out Squilver powerfully, glancing round the edge of the chamber and giving what was surely a signal to the guards at the portals, 'that is *indeed* what I'd like to know.' Maple looked behind him at the portal he had tried so hard to stay near and saw issuing forth from it more guards, and then, as his eyes travelled round the chamber, he saw others gathering at each portal.

'This is a massing . . . aye, that's what *this* is,' said Maple to himself grimly. '*Where's Weeth?*'

The Newborns' intention was now increasingly plain, and the crowd began to look about with growing confusion and concern as from the left side of the chamber and that part of the rear furthest from Maple the guards began an ominous, deep-throated chant, quite horrible to hear. It had no words that made sense, but was a guttural noise accompanied by the rhythmic stamp of paws on the ground as very slowly but irresistibly they began to advance upon the crowd of moles.

Suddenly, but only for a few moments, the guards stopped and fell silent, in which time Brother Squilver roared out again, 'There's traitors among you – spies and reprobates – and we will not have it. Let those among you who are untainted, and free of the snake of doubt point the talon of guilt at the culprits and punish them here and now . . .'

His voice was drowned out by the guards' resumption of their stamping chant, accompanying it now with an action which Maple had never seen or heard of before: as the guards advanced they reared up alternately, talon-thrusting violently into the space ahead of them; if a mole got in the way, it was just too bad. Some did, and fell injured, which made the others fight all the harder to get away, and the screams of the first combined with the flailing paws of the second tipped the mass of moles into panic. Over the desperate hubbub of cries, shouts and death-screams the deep and ominous chant continued inexorably.

The crowd pushed and swayed and fought this way and that, while the guards advanced on only two fronts, leaving Maple stanced in a quieter part protecting himself from the worst crush by dint of keeping his two recruits close by, paws and shoulders set firmly. And still he

173

looked for Weeth, whilst kenning the disposition of guards and observing that their advance had ceased now that its objective of causing panic had been achieved. Maple could see all too clearly what its effect was: that the crowd – the massing – was simply killing itself as mole crushed into mole, the weak unable to breathe, the strong climbing over them to get air, and all so far as they were able striking out at any nearby. But Weeth . . .

'Mole!' The voice was a deep guttural roar: 'MOLE!'

Maple turned, the crowd parted, and there was Weeth, some way towards the centre of the chamber; looming over him was a huge, dark, rough-furred mole whom Maple recognized, but could not place. Around him, solid and determined, were others maintaining their position in safety as Maple had been with his two new-found friends. Even as Weeth grinned apologetically, and shrugged, the crowd began to close in again.

Maple's response was instinctive and immediate, as he realized that if three were stronger than one in such a panicking mass and perilous situation, eight or nine would be stronger still than three: he ordered the two with him to follow with all their strength and began to push through towards Weeth. As Weeth disappeared behind a struggling crowd Maple had the satisfaction of seeing that the great mole with him, and his companions, had also begun to press forward to make contact.

Only as Maple pushed, and heaved, and struggled to keep his paws on the ground did it dawn on him who the moles with Weeth were; the name of the big one, his name was . . .Ystwelyn, the mole they had first seen at Caradoc! That's who he was! Maple shouted this out to himself, heaving and thrusting moles out of the way for the final short distance until he found himself snout to snout with Ystwelyn who had been doing the same thing; Weeth emerged gasping from the mass of paws beneath.

'Sorry about that,' he panted, digging some poor mole adjacent to them in the ribs to be rid of him, 'but I spied Ystwelyn here in the crowd and since we were looking for like-minded moles—'

'SILENCE!' roared Maple powerfully, glowering around. Weeth thought at first this command was directed at himself. It had but little effect on others, though a few moles nearby stilled and turned to see whatmole dared cry out so in such a situation.

'Heave me up, lads!' commanded Maple to the two so-far anonymous moles who had valiantly followed him. 'Aye, get me aloft so we can get some order in here.'

174

'Come on!' Ystwelyn said to his followers, putting a huge scarred paw under Maple's belly. 'Do as he says!'

Suddenly Maple was raised above the crowd and precarious though his position felt – for his companions had not only to hold him up but keep themselves steady too – his second cry of 'SILENCE!' had more effect.

'Silence and be still! You're killing yourselves! Order there. Be still . . .'

A sudden wave of quietness and calm went over the crowd, rippling out from the still centre where Maple was, and spread by Weeth, Ystwelyn and the others, themselves calling for silence calmly, and shushing moles nearby.

Maple knew that he had but moments to act before the Newborn guards gathered their senses and Squilver, whom he could see now was still lurking at the portal beyond the dais, protected by guards, came forward to give orders and regain the initiative. It was a moment in which a lesser mole might have hesitated, or a more foolhardy one wasted the opportunity by saying the wrong things. But for Maple it was a moment of decision and commitment, and if moledom's movement to resist the Newborns can be said to have found order and direction at a particular time, a movement that might transform secret criticisms and unstated outrage into an organized spirit of open revolt and action, that time was now.

'If you're looking for a culprit, moles, you see one here! Aye, a mole who resists the Newborn ways, and who scents evil and dark doings in this chamber today! I'm a follower of the Stone!'

'What's your name, mole?' cried out one of those who had fallen silent.

'Maple of Duncton Wood.'

The hush deepened into a profound silence at mention of that famous place from which so many great and worthy moles had come. Duncton, home of liberty and moles of virtue. If they had dreamed of a Duncton warrior mole, then this mole matched their dreams: large, powerful, confident and commanding.

'I'll not be confined a moment longer in this vile chamber!' cried out Maple, 'and I'll warrant there's many a mole here who agrees with me. Therefore any followers who are here today – or "reprobates" as the Newborns call us – stance with me now, and let's fight our way out. Follow me!'

There was a great roar of approval, though a few seemed, by their fearful looks, to doubt the wisdom of this defiance. Ystwelyn and the

175

others let Maple down and with a raised paw he pointed to the portals at the rear of the chamber and cried out boldly, 'Follow us!'

With Ystwelyn at his right flank and Weeth to his left, and the others roaring and shouting close behind, Maple led the moles against the guards at the back. The size of the crowd, which had been the cause of all the danger earlier, now proved an obstruction to the Newborn reinforcements reaching the rear, while a raging Squilver, seeing his career crumbling before his eyes, screamed at the other guards to go and help.

Cut off from their colleagues, the rear guards had to face Maple and the others alone, and soon broke down before the assault, so that after only a few moments of struggle, they were bloodily overrun. Maple crashed his way between them and led the rebels through the portal and up to the surface. Then, making sure that all who wished to escape were helped out of the tunnels, he led them rapidly off to the south-west to a wood where they were able to rest and recuperate.

Here for the first time they had an opportunity to look at each other – and a motley lot they were, all shapes and sizes, some strong in body, a few strong only in spirit, all puffing and panting and with the fire of resistance in their eyes.

'Now listen,' said Maple, 'except for Weeth here, who is a trusted companion and a dependable mole, you don't know me any better than I know you. Except that is for Ystwelyn of Siabod here and, if my memory serves, Arvon, who's something of a route-finder, who I met in Caradoc, and later.'

The two Siabod moles nodded their acknowledgement and muttered their greetings to one and all before turning their attention back to Maple.

'If you heard what I said down in that Newborn chamber of death you'll know what I'm about: resistance and restoration. Resistance to the Newborn ways of repression and punishment of moles that disagree with them; restoration of the liberties of thought, of travel, of worship which our ancestors fought for a century ago when the Word threatened them.'

'Hear, hear!' cried out somemole at the back of the group.

'This is not the time or place for long speeches, but I'm not going a step further without making as plain as I can what's likely to come our way in the moleweeks and months ahead. Hardship, that's for sure. Tiredness, that's sure too. Doubt and uncertainty, they'll be our companions, and along with them will be fear and even pain. No, it won't be easy, the Newborns are well entrenched in all the major systems, and if my intelligence is right, by now all effective opposition will have been suppressed. This spring they're beginning what they call crusades *out* of the main systems, including this one, I dare say.

'So if you follow me it'll be hard going. And it will be harder because I'll make it so. It's no good fighting for liberty if we don't uphold the rights of others in all we do – and that includes the rights of Newborns.'

There was a muttering when he said this which quietened when Ystwelyn growled, 'Hear the Duncton mole out.'

'Aye, the Newborns have rights as have all moles, just so long as what they do doesn't infringe on the liberty of others. I'll not have moles fight alongflank me who are in it for revenge, however justified it may be, or for power over others, however attractive that might seem. I'm a Duncton mole and I'll fight for the freedoms I mentioned because that's the way I was raised. But never let me see a mole in my command raise a talon to another who's weaker, or defeated, or simply disagrees. But fight honestly and honourably, and I'll stance by you to the bitter end.'

'Well said, mole, for that's the old Siabod way as well!' cried out Ystwelyn. 'Though it's easier said than done.'

'I've made plain the way I feel so there's no doubt in your minds what we're about,' Maple continued. 'If you agree with me then come with me today and begin a war which we *will* win, and win justly, however small our force may seem now, for the Stone will have it no other way!'

There was a cheer at this, and a good deal of talk, at the end of which Maple said, 'We'll bide our time for proper introductions and agreement about whatmole does what.'

'We'll obey your command for now, Maple, won't we moles?' cried out Ystwelyn, with Arvon vigorously nodding his agreement.

There was a murmur of general assent.

'Well then,' said Maple decisively, 'is there a mole here knows the routes out of Cannock well enough to guide us to a place we can hide nearby for a day or two? There may be others who'll want to join our cause, or some who failed to get out of that chamber when we did.' Two moles called Warren and Pottle came forward and after a quick conference offered to lead the party to a place called Shoal Hill, a little to the south.

'Ystwelyn, you'll be in second-in-command for now, and stay with me. I want to tell you my plans. Arvon, you could go with a couple of strong moles and Warren here – we'll only need one guide to take up to Shoal Hill, and you'll do that, Pottle . . .'

'Yes *sir!*' said Pottle smartly.

'. . . and pick up what stragglers you can find. But take no risks. Don't be back later than dusk tonight.'

And so the first plans were laid and orders given before the two groups went their different ways.

The hours that followed were anxious ones, but even before dusk Arvon's party returned intact, with seven more moles who wanted to join Maple's force.

'When do we leave, and for where?' asked Arvon stoutly, when he had recovered his breath and eaten.

'We leave now,' said Maple resolutely, 'for the Newborns will be after us tomorrow dawn if they're not already.'

'Now is always the best time!' said Arvon with sudden passion. 'And we Siabod moles won't let you down!'

'I know that, mole, I know it well,' said Maple, 'so let us begin our march for liberty. Tonight we'll disappear into darkness. Tomorrow we'll begin a trek to a system that needs our support . . . no need to name it yet, for the less is said, the less the Newborns can find out.'

'Rowton?' suggested Weeth quietly as they set off.

Maple nodded, his eyes gleaming with purpose and excitement in the gathering twilight. He looked at the moles who followed him, quiet and generally disciplined.

'It's a beginning, Weeth,' he said.

'It's *the* beginning,' replied Weeth with certainty.

Chapter Sixteen

The Newborn Crusades, which had effectively been initiated by Quail the Longest Night before the Wildenhope Killings, began in earnest immediately after them. Indeed, as we have seen, that same evening the first step in their consolidation was taken with the confinement of Thripp of Blagrove Slide and the formal creation of the infamous Crusade Council.

The emergence of the Council, with Quail as its spiritual head and Skua as its inquisitorial leader and second-in-command, seemed to mark the end of the long struggle between Quail and Thripp for effective leadership of the Newborns. With Quail now openly willing to exclude Thripp and deny him access to other moles, and with an Order already issued for his death later that summer,* the second and more brutal generation of Newborns were now in a position to prosecute the Crusades to which the subverted Convocation of Caer Caradoc had been the evil preparation and preface.

The Crusades were naturally disguised by the Newborns as spiritual campaigns aimed to lead the feeble, fainthearted and misguided *peaceably* back to the true way of worship of the Stone. Nominally the Brother Advisers attached to each company of guards were in charge of matters locally, the guards themselves being there only to enforce the 'Stone's will' upon those in whose hearts the twin evils of sin and doubt were too deeply entwined. But, of course, it was often the Brother Commanders and their guards who took charge and set the murderous tone of the Crusades.

In fact, as allmole has long known – and as those who did not will already have deduced from what has been scribed in this history – the Crusades were nothing more or less than the systematic corruption or murder of males of middle age or less, and the seduction or rape of females of pup-rearing age.

It is unfortunately true that if an army of moles is appointed divine

---

* See the chilling twelfth Secret Order in 'Secret Orders in Council' edited by Bunnicle of Witney, based on Snyde's contemporaneous records.

agents of the Stone, and given permission to murder males on one paw and rape females on the other, it will happily do so. The ground had been well prepared over the winter years by well-placed Inquisitors in all the major systems, who had 'cleansed' the libraries and the inhabitants in the way Pumpkin witnessed in Duncton Wood; it was not difficult for the zealots fired and trained at Caradoc to set forth and bring terror and tragedy to any system unfortunate enough to resist them. Immediately after the Wildenhope Killings the Crusade Council began to issue its Orders and commands to all parts of moledom in what seemed for a time like a never-ending succession of instructions to the Brother Advisers and Brother Commanders in the field.

Like all moles who rise to the top through cabals and terror, Quail believed himself capable of running everything and until the various flaws in Newborn organization began to show it must certainly have seemed he was right. The stream of reports that began now to come from the major systems pointed to phenomenal success. On Avebury, for example, the system where Quail had first sharpened his inquisitorial talons, 'all surrounding systems as far as Fyfield' were 'cleansed' by early May – but then that area had the advantage of milder weather and so an earlier start. But only shortly afterwards Brother Inquisitor Fetter was able to report similar success from Duncton Wood, and nearby Rollright was not far behind.

So, through May, the litany of apparent success continued, with Blagrove cleansing the eastern reaches of moledom by the end of the month, and astonishing progress reported from Ashbourne, the system that was the central focus of the Crusades in the north-east, the more historic Beechenhill being too high and obscure for such a role.

Cannock was rather slower to report, and when it did Quail and his minions were unwilling to ken between the lines of what was said and appreciate the significance of Brother Commander Thorne's account of resistance shown to Squilver's guards, prior to his arrival, 'led by one Maple of Duncton Wood'. Yet in his report, more honest and to the point than most others, we begin to see signs of the trouble that was building up for the Newborns, and can glimpse the true tragedy of much that was suffered in those early days.

'We must bring to the attention of the Council that although resistance to the Crusade has in all other cases* been ultimately ineffectual,

* The exception implied is Maple's escape from Cannock and his subsequent flight to Rowton and successful exodus to the Wolds. See below.

180

it has nevertheless been spirited, courageous, and persistent. The moles of Stafford fought us to the death of *every mole* in the system; those of Penkridge caused us considerable problems by dispersing in the surrounding countryside and then attacking us intermittently; while those of Rugeley killed their females rather than let us take them for correction and education . . .'

It would seem that this report, with its implications of serious resistance, was ignored by Quail, and the lessons it might have taught remained ominously unheeded. Worse, from the Newborn point of view, few other of Quail's Brother Commanders in the field appear to have been as honest or perspicacious as Thorne, preferring to ignore the evidence of resistance they must have seen.

Thus, there is no record of the moles led by Spurling and Fieldfare up on Seven Barrows near Uffington, nor of those who escaped to join them from the systems around Avebury; then, too, Brother Fetter was economical with the truth when it came to giving a proper account of Pumpkin's brave retreat with twenty or so moles into the Ancient System of Duncton Wood back in February, and the failure of subsequent attempts to flush them out.

The Ashbourne brothers gave no hint, in the reports they sent the Council, that they had met successful resistance just to the north of their system among the idiosyncratic moles of the Dark Peak; nor, finally, did the Brother Inquisitors of Rollright do anything other than suggest that the cleansing Crusade of their system and those surrounding it was complete and successful, whereas, in fact, the redoubtable Hodder, whom Hamble had met, and his kin and friends had already laid plans for resistance and counter-attack.

But perhaps, after all, these points of opposition seemed as nothing compared to the overwhelming successes the Crusades were showing, and the piecemeal capitulation of system after system to the zealous and reforming brothers. Why muddy the pool with a mere gobbet of soil?

However it really was, through May and into early June all seemed well with the Crusades that Quail inspired and led from Caradoc and Wildenhope. It was simply a matter now of waiting a little longer before all corners and crannies of moledom were finally cleansed.

Meanwhile, as Snyde's reports show, females all over the crusading areas were beginning to give birth to pups sired by their Newborn masters, and the chilling process of killing female pups and educating the males, which had begun first at Blagrove Slide and been perfected

181

at Bowdler near Caradoc, was already well advanced in many systems.*

By the beginning of June, indeed, Quail and Skua were so confident of the success of the Crusades that they were already planning a triumphal tour of four of the major systems, which was to start with Cannock and end, in the autumn, in Duncton Wood itself, where many of the leading Avebury brothers and others from outlying systems would join them. The purpose was partly punitive – we know the Cannock visit was to be made with the intention of arraigning and punishing Thorne – but mainly to consolidate successes ahead of the winter years; Quail had a taste for sudden promotion of some and demotion of others, which he used to create a permanent sense of unease and competition (not to say a culture of deceit and disloyalty towards all but himself) among his subordinates.

Yet by early June, in the time of greatest success and self-congratulation, the first signs of the difficulties about to beset the Newborns began to show themselves. Try as they might, the unctuous and self-serving Brother Advisers in system after system could no longer disguise the fact that there *was* continuing resistance, though its source and strength remained mysterious.

Then, unexpectedly and quite shockingly for Quail and the Crusade Council, came news of something more than resistance. First came reports from the Wolds, until then disregarded, that a force of Brother Crusaders, based at Broadway, had been attacked and virtually massacred by a band of miscellaneous moles from the Cotswold heights. Worse followed two days later when a travel-weary and still-shocked guardmole from the major system of Evesham arrived in Wildenhope reporting that his Brother Commander, Finial of Bromsgrove, had been taken prisoner, and several guardmoles killed in a well-organized attack, the culprits being unknown though believed to be led by the same mole responsible for the Broadway 'outrage' – as the Crusade Council naturally perceived it.

'Name a name, I want a name!' roared Quail, when he heard of this.

---

* Snyde's records show two Brother Advisers to have been especially ruthless in this regard. One was the unpleasant Brother Sapient of Avebury, who maintained the tradition of rigorous cruelty first established by Quail himself in that system; the other was the self-styled Brother Zeon, judged by most to have been insane, whose brief but foul reign at Cannock after Thorne's and Fagg's departure was brought to a precipitate end by his last victim, the Confessed Sister Suede of Cirencester.

The name was forthcoming soon enough, for but a few days later, Wildenhope having been abuzz with rumour, confusion and dismay, who should appear but the 'lost' Brother Commander Finial himself, and with a story to tell of stark and shocking humiliation.

Yes, he had been taken. No, he had not been ill-treated. Yes, he had been released by his captors, he had not escaped from them.

'But you tried, Brother Commander?' demanded Quail.

Finial, who was tired from his journey and recent experience, and humiliated by all that had happened, was perhaps less patient with the Council than he might have been.

'There was no point in "trying" to escape since my captors told me from the first that they intended to let me go.'

'Why then did they take you in the first place?' demanded Skua.

'They told me they wished to educate me,' said Finial, with little sign that he appreciated the irony of being so publicly educated by moles it was *his* job to educate. 'They told me they wished to remind me of what worshipping the Stone was all about. They were wrong and misguided and I am glad to be clear of them.'

'And their leader? Did they have one?' asked Quail, his eyes glinting dangerously.

'Oh yes, I met *him*,' said Finial. 'His name is Maple. A large mole, impressive in his way.'

'Have I heard of him?' asked Quail, the skin of his bald head wrinkling, his eyes flicking about the members of the Council, seeking information, and perhaps explanation. There was a murderous mood about: at the very least Finial might not survive the day. Quail did not like failure or defeat, nor moles who brought news of it.

'I know of this mole,' said an unctuous voice at Quail's right ear.

'Well, Brother Snyde? *Well?*'

Snyde nodded to one of his minions to continue record-keeping and eased his crooked body near Quail, the better to address him discreetly.

'Maple is of Duncton, I regret to say. He has military pretensions. He was the sinning mole who was observed helping the reprobate Rooster escape.'

'Duncton! Rooster!' repeated Quail, spitting out the words as if they were worms gone bad. 'Again! Come closer still, Snyde, and tell me more . . . Mmm . . . I see . . . Quite so . . . The one who made a fool of Brother Commander Thorne in Cannock, eh?'

Snyde whispered his lies and calumnies, only speaking louder when he wanted Finial to hear, for he knew well how the right words to

183

one mole could gain the favour of another. 'The mole Maple is well-kenned in war, and more than likely he had spies to help him at Evesham. Against such evil advantage it might have been hard for any Brother Commander to do better than Brother Finial did.'

The tension eased, Quail nodded, Finial looked less apprehensive: Maple, it seemed, had gained his petty victory unfairly.

'There can be no second chance, Brother Finial. Maple of Duncton shall be caught and made eliminate. See to it.'

'I shall need reinforcements,' said Finial resolutely, 'but it can be done.'

'You shall have more help,' concurred Quail. 'Our will *must* be done. Maple, or the mole that fails to arraign him, must die.'

'Yes, Elder Senior Brother!' said Finial, who had achieved the best he could in difficult circumstances: Maple's life or his own.

Quail nodded to him to dismiss and he went, though reluctantly. He had hoped for discussion of the matter that most concerned him – the rebels' obvious strength and discipline under Maple. But now was not the moment for more controversy, and biting back his desire to warn the Crusade Council that the moles in the Wolds were not merely a disorganized rabble, he tried at least to get support worthy of the name.

'Forgive me, Elder Senior Brother . . .'

'Mole?' said Quail indifferently.

'I wonder if I might request that Brother Commander Thorne be deputed to come to Evesham. He is—'

'He is in Cannock, mole.'

'He is able, Elder Senior Brother.'

'No abler surely than any other Brother Commander?' whispered Quail. 'And not so able as you might think. He let Maple of Duncton escape from Cannock!'

'I heard that was Squilver's doing,' offered Finial bravely – but after that his nerve failed and truth took second place to prudence. Finial sighed. The Crusade Council were fools to think that Crusades could be so easily won against moles of the kind he had met up in the Wolds. It could only be hoped that the Stone had not permitted other such rebels to thrive elsewhere in moledom.

Quail nodded his dismissal, and Finial left, the only mole there who truly knew how uncertain his future was. Make Maple eliminate! Finial remembered the mole he had met – strong, in command, confident, and backed by moles as impressive in their training and disci-

pline as any guardmoles he had under his command. Finial sighed
again and left.

The Maple that Brother Commander Finial had met up in the Wolds
was an altogether maturer and tougher mole than the one who, with
Weeth, had led a 'rabble' of moles out of Cannock back in April.

The word 'rabble' was the one used by Squilver in his self-saving
reports to the Crusade Council concerning Maple's brilliant escape
from Cannock. The force he led with Weeth, Ystwelyn and Arvon
was anything but a rabble after but a few days under his command.
Disciplined and well motivated, they arrived in Rowton only two days
before Thorne reached the same system after the diversion back to
Wildenhope with Privet. Learning of the Newborns' approach, Maple
organized the defence of Rowton, little knowing that the mole he was
engaging was, without question, the ablest of the Newborn Brother
Commanders. Equally, Thorne did not know, nor could he have done,
that the inconspicuous system of Rowton was under the temporary
command of probably the only follower capable of successfully defending it against a determined Newborn force.

So he arrived, and was astonished to find effective resistance by
followers for the first time since leaving active service in Siabod and
North Wales. There were skirmishes, there was a clever ambush by
followers on one of Thorne's patrols. There was retreat, attack and
capture on either side; and there was an exchange of prisoners, at
which Thorne and Maple saw each other from afar, each intrigued
enough to eye the other up and down with interest and respect.

'He's a very different kind of commander from Squilver,' observed
Maple to Weeth.

'His name's Thorne, and he's a military mole first and a Newborn
second,' said Weeth.

Meanwhile . . .

'That's the mole Maple, sir, the big one on the right. We've heard
he's of Duncton.'

Thorne stared impassively at Maple. 'He knows how to lead, and
he knows how to fight,' was all he said.

And, too, he knew how to surprise, for that night Maple led the
Rowton moles secretly out of the system, honours even with the
Newborns.

'We'll fight again, and on better ground,' he said. 'We'll head for
the Wolds.'

And when morning came, and Thorne saw he had been outwitted, and his enemy gone, he said sharply to a Newborn guard who described the followers as cowards, 'Cowards, mole! No! They did as I would have done in their place. We shall hear of this Maple again!' And so he did, but a few days later, when he discovered what a fool Maple had already made of Squilver in Cannock Chase.

The journey south to the Wolds after the triumph of the retreat from Rowton gave Maple the confidence of successful command; while the band of supporters he had inspired at Cannock was now swelled by the addition of the Rowton moles, with moles like Whindrell, Furrow and Myrtle now making a veritable army of moles with a mission.

Before Rowton, Maple had been a mole driven by a dream, now he had real responsibility and purpose, and impressed all those who met him that he had the knowledge and means to make the dream a reality. By the time he reached the Wolds he had already begun to gather a formidable team of moles able to advise him, and to execute his orders. Ystwelyn of Siabod was his impressive second-in-command, a formidable leader in his own right whose willing subordination to Maple added to the Duncton mole's authority and prestige. Arvon, another Siabod mole, was one of those who liked to work independently in the field with a few tough and trusted colleagues, brave, dependable, intelligent – and Maple quickly learned he could rely on him for the most difficult of assignments.

Then there was Weeth, with no fixed position, but recognized as Maple's confidant and friend, adviser and occasional butt, the mole others could rely on to say the difficult thing to their leader, or to protect him when others were too demanding of his time and energy.

Added to these were the considerable skills of Stow, older than the others, wise in the ways of the Wolds, a redoubtable and wily campaigner of moleyears past against the Newborns. A mole sensible enough to recognize his limitations, yet one well able to stance against his younger colleagues' impetuosity and excess, while willing always to support Maple in the one thing he, before all others, never forgot: that their struggle against the Newborns was neither for revenge or retribution, but to uphold the liberty of worship for allmole, and the rights of all to live and let live whatever their beliefs.

Perhaps one reason for Maple's success was that he had a clear and single-minded vision of what was wanted and how it might be achieved. His army would be mobile, never resting in one place for too long, and never stubbornly defending a central position if defeat would mean their heart had been destroyed.

'We are,' as he put it, adapting a felicitous phrase that Weeth had used of himself some time in the past, 'moles of no fixed abode. We shall not pause for long, nor rest, nor cease to fight, until liberty is moledom's once again!'

How inspiring such speeches and sentiments were! How inspiring the Duncton mole who uttered them – large and powerful as he was, his face benign yet etched now with the lines that growing responsibility brings, his manner thoughtful and caring, and his eyes bright, observant, intelligent. To those who met him and served with him he was the personification of Duncton's fabled fighting spirit.

When Maple had come to the Wolds he was well aware that an early success against the Newborns would unite the disparate moles now under his command, and consolidate his authority over them. But he was in no haste, preferring to find the proper target for his nascent army's attentions, one which was achievable, and yet would demonstrate its skills.

The Newborns at Broadway seemed the ideal objective, the more so after Maple was approached by two brave moles who had escaped from a system near Broadway, whose population had been subjected to harsh and especially cruel reprisals following resistance to the Newborn way. With Ystwelyn in charge, but with a force made up more of moles from Stow's group than his own, the attack was made largely to a plan of Maple's devising. Diversion, ambush, and a ruthless follow-through, for Maple understood that this was likely to be the first time moles successfully resisted the Newborns in strength, and wished the Brother Commanders to understand that the resistance was not weak.

But when it was realized that several senior Newborns were fleeing to Evesham to raise the alarm, Maple deputed the enterprising Arvon to take a force in watchful pursuit, and reap what advantage he could. He did so brilliantly – capturing Brother Commander Finial of Evesham as he foolishly came hurrying out towards Broadway with insufficient forces to protect him.

But Finial was kept alive – and in this Arvon was following Maple's strict instructions – since having killed Newborns in Broadway and shown their strength, it seemed prudent to spare others, and show the quality of their mercy. Finial was better alive than dead – better as an emissary from Maple to the very Crusade Council itself, where his effect might be lasting and demoralizing, than as a dead Newborn, swiftly forgotten.

'Tell them we have no wish for war,' said Maple when he met

187

Finial, 'no wish to kill anymole, no wish for strife. But we must defend our right to be free. Tell Quail this, and impress upon him that moles will fight for that right all over moledom until they are sure it is theirs once again.'

So it was that with such reasonable warnings ringing in his ears the humiliated Finial was set free with several of his colleagues, and the first true account of Maple and his army in the Wolds – disciplined, formidable, and enterprising – was heard by the Newborn high command: though with what scant effect we have already seen.

While Finial was away in Wildenhope, and the Newborns were regrouping after a successful breakout of moles from Evesham to join those in the Wolds in the wake of Maple's first successes, a rumour was picked up by Weeth that led to a very different kind of expedition, but one whose results were even more significant.

Maple had long since made clear his views about the Wildenhope outrage, but they were to all but Weeth barely credible. For from the first Maple had refused to believe that so great a mole as Rooster could possibly be dead, and, more controversially still in view of the evidence, he did not really think that Whillan could be dead either. As for Privet and her retreat to Silence, that, to him, was entirely credible, for he had foreseen something of the sort ever since the journey westward out of Duncton Wood with Whillan and Privet so long before.

'The Stone is in all she thinks and does, and I duly pray for her safe deliverance from the journey she has undertaken,' he told his growing number of followers and friends. 'We will *never* forget that the hard physical trials and struggles we must suffer for success will be as nothing compared to the mental and spiritual journey she has undertaken on behalf of allmole. She will return to Duncton Wood safeguarded, and on that day victory will be ours!'

Such were Maple's sincere if controversial views, and it was soon after the success against Finial that partially at least they had startling and inspiring confirmation.

For the rumour – the intelligence – that Weeth had gained from moles of Evesham was this:

'You're telling me *what*?' said Maple when he first heard it.

'I am telling you, sir, most perspicacious mole, that regarding Rooster you may well be right,' said Weeth. 'Whillan, sadly, is another and less cheerful story and I now doubt that he can be alive, but I *do* have reason to believe that a mole who sounds to me very like Rooster is now alive and well and delving in a system some way west of Evesham and more or less under the snouts of the Newborns.'

'Tell me all you know,' growled Maple with a delighted grin – the delight was for the discovery that Rooster might really be alive, the grin was in rueful appreciation of the indirect way in which Weeth sometimes liked to reveal the most important news – infuriating to some of Maple's colleagues, but indulged by Maple, who understood Weeth's subtleties, and knew that he often revealed more indirectly, and reached deeper into moles' hearts, than he would have if he told things simply and starkly.

'Permission to disappear for a few days!' said Weeth, in a tone that suggested that even if Maple did not grant it, he would still go. This was a task he wanted for himself.

'We need you, mole, and there may be others better suited. Tell me what you know that a sensible decision can be made.'

Weeth shook his head, suddenly very serious. 'Must go,' he said, 'only me, all alone. I found Rooster before and helped him be free, and I will again. Other moles don't understand Rooster and why he matters. Don't know how to talk to him.'

Maple frowned, concerned for Weeth's safety. 'Won't you let me send just a couple of moles with you? Arvon's discreet, and—'

'No, sir. But don't worry! Weeth will come back sooner than you think.'

'Go then, mole, go where you must. But remember . . .'

'Yes?'

'This mole cares for you. Many care for you. Now, go!' And Maple's voice was gruff as he said this, and a worried look crossed his face as he watched Weeth leave.

'Maple?'

It was Ystwelyn come to discuss several pressing matters.

'Yes?' muttered Maple vacantly.

'You look concerned, mole. What ails you? Eh?' Ystwelyn had never seen the vulnerable side of Maple before.

'What do you know of Rooster of Charnel Clough?' asked Maple.

'A brave mole, but a strange one. Might have been a Master of the Delve, but was drowned at Wildenhope. Why?' Ystwelyn spoke quickly, his deep Welsh voice betraying his impatience to get on with urgent matters; yet he was puzzled at Maple's mood, and by the question he had asked.

'It could just be,' said Maple, 'that Rooster is alive.'

'Alive?' repeated the Welsh mole, surprised. His gaze sharpened and he asked, 'And free? Available to us?'

189

Maple nodded and stared at Ystwelyn. Both were suddenly calculating what this might mean.

'Aye,' said Maple giving no more away, 'he may be alive and, as you put it, "available to us". And if he is . . .'

'And if he is,' continued Ystwelyn, 'there's not a free mole in moledom will not be cheered and inspired to hear it. Why, if he is . . .'

'*If* he is,' concluded Maple, 'and we can keep him alive, there's no Newborn force, however large, will be able to stop us. Ideas are impossible to defeat. Indeed, the Newborns may already have lost, just when they must be thinking they have won.'

Ystwelyn stared at the Duncton mole, thinking, as often in recent days, that anymole would want to follow one so confident of success and convinced of the justice of their cause.

'Mind you,' said Maple a little ruefully, 'if Rooster *is* alive and joins us you'll not find him an easy mole to know, nor one who's comfortable to live with. As for letting us protect him . . .'

'Let's worry about that when he's with us, Maple! Now we're going to have to move on.'

'Not for a few days. We must wait, it's the least we can do.'

'Wait for Rooster to show his snout? That could be a long wait!'

'It has been already,' said Maple. 'But having waited for centuries for the coming of the Master of the Delve, moledom and ourselves can surely wait patiently for a few more days!'

But a 'few more days' turned into ten long ones before Weeth returned, and when he did it was in a Weeth-like way – quietly, unexpectedly, with few even detecting that he had come back.

Down into the great chamber where Maple and some others were discussing their next move he came, hardly noticed by anymole before his mischievous eyes and much-loved snout appeared at Maple's flank.

'Mission accomplished, sir!' said Weeth with a grin.

'Weeth!' roared Maple, taking the smaller mole in his paws in a great hug, a gesture that delighted his fellow rebels who liked to see their leader relaxed and content once in a while.

'Well, you secretive mole? Well?'

'Well! A bit of a to-do it was, but he's here safe and sound, along with his friend. He's up on the surface, contemplating the stars. He does a lot of that these days.'

'Whatmole's he talking about?' cried out one of the Siabod moles.

'Rooster, Master of the Delve,' said Weeth with mock self-importance.

'*Here*?' said Ystwelyvn, scarcely able to believe his ears. A rush of excited chatter went among the assembled moles, and it seemed that others outside had already heard the extraordinary news, for they came crowding in at various entrances.

'There!' announced Weeth with a flourish, pointing at one of the portals.

And there was Rooster, as massive as ever, making those about him seem smaller than they were. At his flank was a young mole, muddy from journeying. Rooster's eyes were bright, the shaggy fur of his face and shoulders was glossy with health, and he seemed somehow trimmer, or leaner, and thereby even more powerful-looking than ever before. But older, too.

'Rooster!' cried out Maple, rising from his stance and meeting him in the centre of the chamber.

'Have come!' said Rooster unnecessarily. 'Saw all clearly: past, present, and future. Saw all could be well. Saw how it could be.'

'When?' asked Maple; 'and where?'

'In water, looking back at Wildenhope. Saw it all and understood. Now have come, with Weeth, and with a friend. Will tell you about *him* later.' Rooster laughed and suddenly grabbed Maple in the kind of hug that mole gave Weeth moments before. 'Have missed you, Maple, like Weeth. Have missed all I love. But future's coming and we must delve it. We must make all right, so that Privet can bring the Book of Silence to Duncton Wood.'

The watching moles listened in amazement to this, staring at him, for none but those who already knew him could ever have imagined a mole quite like Rooster of Charnel Clough. And many felt then what they were only able to articulate later, that with Rooster's coming to join Maple's rebels it was as if some element of the Stone itself, some aspect of its Silence, had found physical form among them, and the mood of faith and confidence was palpable in the chamber.

'There's a tale in this,' cried out Ystwelyn. 'Give them food, stance them down, and let's hear it from beginning to end!'

'Aye, every bit of it!' cried out many a mole, as food was found, and places too, for Rooster and the quiet youngster he had brought with him.

'Weeth can begin,' said Rooster, as Maple introduced mole after mole to him. 'Weeth knows most of it, if not all!'

Weeth grinned and held up a paw for silence.

'It will be my pleasure, fellow rebels with a cause,' he said, 'with a little bit of help from my new-found friends, to whom you will be introduced in the proper manner. But I fancy this is only the beginning

191

of the tale you'll all tell your grandpups when you're old and grey!'

'Hope you don't mind answering questions, Weeth, 'cos knowing you you're not likely to tell us the whole tale just like that!' cried out one of the moles.

'There's only one question I won't answer,' responded Weeth, 'and that's because I don't know what the answer is.'

'Which is?' asked Ystwelyn jocularly.

Weeth exchanged a glance with Maple. It was serious, and concerned.

'If you ask me where Privet of Duncton is, then I can't tell you.'

A hush fell over the moles, for all of them knew of Privet's retreat, and all wondered how a solitary female, of more than middle age and not especially strong by all accounts, could possibly survive in a moledom dominated by Newborns who were so hostile to her, and unlikely to abide by any edict Quail might have issued that she should be allowed to live. Yet on her, as on Rooster, so much seemed to depend.

'No . . .' sighed Maple, 'no, we know you don't know *that.*'

'Privet?' said Rooster suddenly, rising and looking around the assembled moles, and then almost benignly on Weeth. 'Privet's where nomole can reach her. Journeying. Nomole can help her. Travelling. Nomole can hurt her there. Privet's in darkness now. Must pray for her every day. Privet's journeying for all of us.'

There was absolute silence at this strange and disturbing utterance. Rooster's presence now, his words, his very thoughts and feelings perhaps inhibited the speech of others. He grinned suddenly and lopsidedly at Weeth.

'Not so bad for us though! Tell them how the Stone helped *me*! Tell them the tale they're silent to hear. Told *you*, now you tell *them*.'

'I will, strange delving mole,' said Weeth.

There was a collective sigh and the expectant moles relaxed; Rooster grinned and stanced down again: for Privet, the Privet who was on a journey for all of them, could not, it seemed, be so easily harmed.

'Well then,' began Weeth, 'I'll tell you how I found our friend here, and how he came to be where he was when I found him, and what he was doing there.'

'Delving, presumably,' said one of his audience.

'. . . and I'll tell it, if I may,' continued Weeth with cheerful firmness, 'without *too* many more interruptions . . .'

Chapter Seventeen

Quail and his minions, isolated that spring and early summer in the self-congratulatory world of Caradoc and Wildenhope, might have been slow to react to the damaging effect of Privet's stance of Silence against them, but they were swift to respond to its consequences, and the growing evidence of resistance of the kind Brother Commander Finial had so starkly reported. Orders were quickly sent out to all Brother Commanders to deal harshly and publicly with any sign of rebellion and by mid-June many lesser systems were already suffering the consequences. Public snoutings of the kind used by moles of the Word in the 'bad old days' became all too common once more, as did the murder of young moles by the brothers in front of grieving parents, always an effective tactic to subdue opposition.

Again and again there were the most violent responses to the most innocent of resistance – a careless joke, an attempt to help some confused old mole, an answer back – all could and did result in the deaths of harmless moles. Fear now began to spread out from the major systems in the wake of the Crusades, and these punitive measures, and deceit and treachery among moles who had only recently been friends, became the order of the day once the Brother Crusaders appeared in a system.

Other historians may dwell upon the tragedies of these times, and describe in detail the many incidents of torture, cruelty and deprivation perpetrated by the Newborns. But here we are more concerned with the triumph that faith in the Stone inspires in the face of such tragedy. Yet even the least scholarly of moles is aware of the vile deaths at Bicester that June, when sixty moles from surrounding systems died; and the valiant defence of the moles of Shepton Mallet, down in the south-west, against their age-old rivals of Frome, spurred on by the brothers, when all but three moles died after an eight-day siege; though perhaps it is the treachery of Fiddick of Shefford, which led to the tragic deaths at the Winstow Massing, that moles remember with most horror.

But only now, as a product of recent scholarship and analysis of the

Secret Orders of the Crusade Council, is the true nature of the foul hypocrisy of the sect under Quail's leadership emerging. No better example being the fourteenth Secret Order, calling upon all Brother Commanders *as a matter of priority* to locate and arrest 'the mole Privet, originally of Crowden, latterly of Duncton Wood' whom it describes as a 'dangerous blasphemer and sexual minion of the dead reprobate Rooster, perverter of morals, traducer of the young' and so forth. In short, Quail had reneged on the freedom of passage and the pardon granted to Privet at Wildenhope, and was now calling for her capture, and, by implication, her death.

The language of that Secret Order was, incidentally, a lot less foul than that which accompanied its dictation by Quail. According to Snyde's records Quail was beside himself with fury, his mouth frothing, his eyes bulging, his demeanour nearly insane, when he realized that he had let escape his talons a mole so capable of damaging the Newborn cause.

'I want her,' he screamed, 'and I shall personally drown her, and take time about it, the thin hag-like bitch. To mock us all! To raise the spectre of Silence before our snouts! Having killed her son we shall kill her, for she *is* the Snake, she *is* the doubt that entwines our hearts and endangers us. She shall be found . . .'

Kenning this now a mole shudders to contemplate what Quail had yet to say when he discovered that Rooster was in fact alive . . .

No matter, by mid-June every Newborn in moledom was on the look-out for Privet and most of these would regard it as their duty and privilege to kill her themselves, or deliver her personally to Quail himself.

But, as we have seen, Newborns were not the only ones who sought Privet. Others did too, many of them harmless moles, not given to bravery or bold doings, but who would certainly have lain down their lives for the Duncton scribe and done all they could to see that she came to no harm.

Among them was the delightful and innocent Hibbott of Ashbourne Chase, whose pilgrimage in search of Privet was well underway by that mid-June when Brother Commanders all over moledom were wondering what more they could do to find the elusive Privet – and hoping, no doubt, that time would not prove that she had crossed *their* territory, and that they were culpable of having missed her.

'I had then,' Hibbott tells us with charming understatement in his

194

Pilgrimage, 'taken somewhat of a wrong turning upon my journey, and arrived at a *most* inhospitable place. My mistake had been to follow what I thought to be but a modest roaring owl way, from which I found it increasingly difficult to escape as it grew bigger and ever more hostile.

'The dangers were many and varied – hunting kestrel, scavenging rook, malevolent fox, not to mention the heat, the fumes and the roaring owls themselves. The way became unpleasantly elevated, far from soil, or trees, or natural running water. In consequence, to survive I found it necessary to eat what scraps of rotting carrion I could find, and drink the tainted water which I found in the crevices, cracks and conduits of the way itself. But I was not despondent! Not I! Did I not have the glorious prospect of meeting Privet of Duncton Wood somewhere on the path before me! Did I not have the Light and Silence of the Stone to comfort me! Did I not have memories of friends and home to divert me, and to encourage me, the prospect of returning to them one day with much to tell? I did! And did I not have my health? I did!

'But when these encouragements failed and I felt myself slipping towards the slough of self-pity and despond, I said to myself "Hibbott, what is this? How can you call yourself a pilgrim and let yourself be beset by these trivial problems? Do you imagine that Privet of Duncton Wood, whose path is so much harder than yours, would allow herself to be diverted from her course by such concerns? Of course she would not! Then again, think of those good friends, and your kin, who said goodbye to you when you left Ashbourne Chase, think how downhearted they would be to know you failed them. Therefore Hibbott, put your best paw forward and press on, for what is a pilgrimage without a little local difficulty!"

'With words such as these I encouraged myself to continue on my chosen path, having faith that before too long my journey would become more pleasant.'

In fact, without realizing it, Hibbott had taken a route right towards the very heart of the Midland Wen, a dangerous and sterile two-foot system almost as big as that which lies east of Duncton Wood and is simply called The Wen. For many days he was lost in this great artificial wilderness, supported only by his deep faith in the Stone, and the hope of better things to come, the chief of which was a meeting with Privet of Duncton.

The days passed by; he lost weight, and often he could not find strength to travel on, but he rested patiently, trusted in the Stone, and fought his way forward – past what dangers, and through what fears, a mole shudders to imagine.

Then one day, one glorious day, the walled and elevated way he took dropped down nearer the real ground and taking a kind of steep slipway off it he found himself on soil once more. To learn of his many trials and tribulations in that wasteland in which he found himself, and of how he had to take to the elevated way once more to escape it, a mole must ken Hibbott's own story. But finally the roaring owl way turned south, countryside appeared distantly ahead, and with the two-foot system now largely behind, or to right and left flank, he felt his trials were nearly over. Yet he now recorded a strange reaction.

'There were many opportunities now to leave the roaring owl way and resume my journey through the fields which lay adjacent to it, even if the two-foot places were nearby as well. Yet I had grown accustomed to the narrow life of the way, and its dangers had become my friends; its limitations, my security. I had, in fact, grown afraid of the reality which lay awaiting me in the fields below – and I made various excuses not to join it, but to stay in the sterile world to which I had grown used.

'Then suddenly, one day, peering down to the fields below from my elevated position, with the roaring owls rushing past, I saw something I had not seen for many a long molemonth – the earthy delvings of mole stretching across the grass I surveyed. Added to this I felt a strange conviction that my way to find Privet of Duncton was now on real land again. She was, I thought, near at paw, though perhaps only in spirit. I had rediscovered the impulse that first drove me on my pilgrimage, and feeling myself saved at last from the long journey on the roaring owl way, I took a slipway off it again, and never joined it more.

'I then made my way to the mole system I had seen and in faltering language – for I had not spoken Mole in a long time – I introduced myself and told those I met of my quest. I was ill for many a day after, but they looked after me.

'The "system" I had fallen among was no system in the ordinary sense. Its members called themselves a "community" – the "Community of Rose". Their spiritual leader was the remarkable Sister Caldey, a large robust female about whom, it seemed, various "waifs and strays", as they cheerfully called themselves, had grouped. They had named themselves after Rose, the Healer of Duncton Wood, known to allmole for her dedicated work a century before.* Sister

* See Volume I of *The Duncton Chronicles*.

196

Caldey was large and ungainly, with paws more masculine than feminine and a habit of frowning ferociously when she was thinking or striving for a cure. However, like many before me, and more since no doubt, I found her to be the kindest and gentlest of moles, even if at times she could be brusque and dictatorial!

'Her story seemed to me remarkable, though she herself rarely mentioned it, and what I learned came from certain of the more talkative brothers and sisters in the Community. It seemed she was born into a group of nomadic moles whose territory was in the hills to the south of the Midland Wen. Though she was robust as a pup, she was taken ill as a youngster and finally abandoned to the care of the Redditch Stone, she being by then frail and a liability for wandering moles.

'When she was near death she prayed to the Stone, promising that if it would cure her she would dedicate herself to healing others, and to giving a home to those who had been abandoned, until such time as they were capable of stancing on their own four paws again. The night of that prayer a mole came to her, a cheerful female, who laid paws upon her the long night through, and in the morning she knew she had been cured. When Sister Caldey asked the mole's name she would only say, "Thank Rose of Duncton Wood, and thereby thank the Stone." Soon after the mole left her; remembering her promise, Sister Caldey decided to dedicate her life to helping others. Convinced that it was Rose the Healer who had come to her in time of need, she travelled, seeking out healing moles wherever she could find them to learn all she could of the healing arts. In time she became a recognized healer herself, returning to live for a long time near the Redditch Stone where she had received her visitation.

'Many moles came for her ministrations, and some to learn from her, until she felt the need of a rest from the demands made upon her, and a period of peace. She found a place to be alone, but she was taken ill, as severely as she had been when a youngster. She discovered in that dark time that there are no healers for healers – that it is a solitary life indeed. With great difficulty, she made her way back to the Redditch Stone, and there she was cured a second time by a visitation from the mole she took to be Rose the Healer. Her recovery was slow, but the day came when "Rose" said she must depart.

'"Why have I been ill?" asked Sister Caldey. "Tell me that before you leave." For she guessed there had been a reason for it – to learn something more of healing no doubt, but what?

197

'"You must leave things to take their course more than you do," replied Rose, "and listen more. It is not you who heals, but the Stone through you. You can only help moles know the Stone's healing grace more clearly, you can do no more. Therefore listen, trust, and let things be."

'"Where shall I go?" asked Caldey.

'"Where the next mole tells you!" laughed Rose, and Sister Caldey knew that in those words were truth and wisdom.

'She therefore resolved to wait by the Stone for the next mole that came, and go where he or she told her to. The first mole that she met was one sent to her, she suspected, by Rose herself. His name was Meddick, after the healing herb, and he came to beg her to come north with him to the southern edge of the Midland Wen, where his two surviving kin lived a frugal life. Both were ill.

'Sister Caldey did not hesitate and together the two moles journeyed to where I found them so many years later, along with other moles who had, so to speak, drifted to their simple tunnels and stayed awhile. What they had started became the Community of Rose. The Community was celibate, and the males and females called themselves brothers and sisters, many adopting names of healing herbs as a token of their changed life – for many were ill when they came, and found a cure in that inspiring fellowship. But I cannot say I myself was eager to change my name, since "Hibbott" had served me perfectly well all my life, and so I did not.

'There were some fourteen moles there, of whom five had taken a vow of Silence and spoke not at all. They were a peaceful lot, and numbers at home on any one day varied since it was their practice to journey forth to nearby systems, mainly to the south since the Wen itself lay in all other directions, and there offer their healing services.

'It was only at the end of my sojourn that I discovered to my great surprise that Brother Meddick was still alive, though since he was one of those who was "in the Silence", as they put it, unfortunately I could not converse with him. He was very frail, and constantly attended by two silent sisters, themselves not much stronger than he was!

'Sister Caldey was, as I have said, a somewhat large female, getting on in years. She embodied a sort of practical holiness, and was nothing at all like a mole might imagine a spiritual leader to be. But the sensible, and I may say *sensitive*, pilgrim must keep an open mind if he is to learn from the experiences which the Stone puts in his way.

'I did consider stopping with the Community permanently, for there is something very alluring about finding oneself amidst a group of moles who accept one unreservedly, and do not ask too many questions of the irritating kind. However, it was my habit night and day to remind myself of the task at paw, for I had come to see that there are many temptations waiting to lead a pilgrim off his path, and the feeling that something else is more worthwhile is one of them.

'One evening, therefore, I prostrated myself before the Stone – I did this in my imagination, for the Community held no Stone in the physical sense – and in fact I was at the time lying snug in my burrow. I said, "Hibbott, what is the purpose of your pilgrimage? It is first and foremost to find Privet of Duncton Wood – anything else is a diversion!" I therefore resolved to leave the next day, which I did, though not without a final interview with Sister Caldey in which she sensibly refrained from giving me any advice. Indeed, she spent most of the time asking me what I knew of the mole Privet whom I sought, which was not much beyond what allmole had heard of regarding the Wildenhope Killings. But even this she seemed not to know, and appeared inordinately interested in it, like a mole starved of food from the world beyond.

'She was very anxious to discover if I had talked to other members of the Community about my quest, but for some reason I had not done so, except briefly when I had first arrived. In such a society as that the "outside world", as I have called it, is not allowed to impinge overmuch. There is a sense that it is almost *irrelevant*, which is one good reason why I had said nothing of my quest, and now felt inclined to move on. Peace is all very well, solitude is pleasant in small doses, but to cut oneself off seems to me to be going too far. A small community is after all part of the larger one and each must give to the other if both are to remain healthy.

'Finally Sister Caldey asked to be commended to Privet of Duncton Wood on the day I found her, which she felt sure I would do, and I in my turn asked to be commended to Privet should Caldey get there first, as it were. This she kindly agreed to do.

'She said that I would be in the community's prayers, which I took to be a comfort and honour. Then the Community of Rose, or such as were then in residence the day I left, said farewell to me and wished me well on my way, begging me to visit them should I pass nearby again.

'Such was my meeting with Sister Caldey, whose community would I am sure have offered me much more had I been willing to dedicate myself to it. But a mole must decide where his task and destiny truly lie, and be single-minded in pursuit of them.'

So did Hibbott of Ashbourne Chase, as good-natured yet determined a pilgrim as ever was, journey on in his trusting and ingenuous way, little imagining what impact his news of Privet would have on the Community of Rose, and what changes it would bring. During his stay there Sister Caldey had seemed her normal self, but the moment he had gone she fell into a restless contemplation such that had her companions not known her better they might have fancied her lovesick!

For two days she refused to see anymole and then suddenly she asked if Brother Meddick might visit her. This was not possible as he was unwell and so, in some ill humour, she visited him.

'It would be easier,' she shouted (for Meddick was a little deaf), 'if we were to converse alone!' She was referring to the silent sisters who attended him. Meddick waved them away.

'Now Brother Meddick, Silence is all very well, but there are times when a mole should talk and this is one of them. I presume you have not lost the power of speech?'

Poor Meddick blinked a little and said in a frail and faltering voice, 'I have taken a *vow*, Sister Caldey, I really cannot—'

'Vow? What vow? That was yesterday. Today things are different.'

Meddick sighed – he had seen Sister Caldey like this before, and it was wearing on others, especially when they were old and hoping for a peaceful end, as he was. Even a mole as worthy, even holy he supposed, as Sister Caldey, could be very annoying indeed. And yet . . . in his wise and gentle heart he was not displeased. He remembered that strange visitation so long before by the mole he liked to believe was Rose the Healer, and how she had given him the feeling that he must watch over Caldey, for even a true leader needs support and guidance. He had heard of her restlessness in the days since their visitor Hibbott of Ashbourne Chase had left – a mole who had true humility in his eyes, and an infectious if ingenuous curiosity about life. A mole who sought another, one Privet of Duncton Wood.

'Privet . . .' he muttered, pleased that Sister Caldey had finally come to him. His vow of Silence had become irksome of late and she was quite right, there comes a moment when a mole must have faith enough to move on from vows and discipline, which are but external aids intended only to strengthen the will to journey on towards the Light, and should not be confused with the Light itself.

'Privet?' repeated Caldey sharply. 'What of her?'

The two old friends stared at each other warily until by slow degrees their cautious frowns eased into smiles.

Meddick said at last, 'You know she is *here*, then?'

'I thought it must be her when Hibbott first told me of the mole he is seeking. She is the new one serving you?'

'One of those you asked to leave a few moments ago.'

The two looked at each other in silence once again, each pondering the arrival at the beginning of June of the strange silent, middle-aged female to whom they referred: worn out, pathetically thin, beset by Stone knew what distress . . . and yet . . . all in the Community had recognized a quality in her beyond anything they had ever seen in a mole.

She had been led to Sister Caldey, who with her normal brusqueness and efficiency had ascertained that she chose to be silent and intended to remain that way, and had deputed her to help with Meddick's care. There is no better healing for some moles than the reminder that they are needed by those who are worse off than themselves.

'Well, Brother Meddick. You have been closest to her. Is she the mole Privet of Duncton Wood?'

'I'm sure of it,' said Meddick. 'She is . . . remarkable. And I thought so from the first, before I heard the tale about her that Hibbott told.'

'Yes . . .' sighed Caldey, who had no need to say that she too had recognized the special qualities of the silent mole.

'What will it mean for us? Eh, Sister Caldey? What shall we do?'

'She means change, Brother Meddick. That is what she means. But first she needs time and healing. She is on a journey, one that will go far beyond us before she returns. But here, for a time, she may replenish herself. Perhaps it was for her coming that our Community was formed.'

'When she goes . . .' whispered Meddick ruminatively.

'. . . our work here is done and we shall disperse,' said Sister Caldey very firmly. 'Some north, some south, some . . .'

'. . . some to the Stone itself,' said Meddick, matter-of-factly, his head trembling, his paws a little fretful, his poor body so frail it seemed transparent in the day's light. 'I would have her continue to tend me, Sister Caldey,' he resumed, 'for in her touch I feel a pathway towards peace. Call her back, tell her she is safe with us, call her now . . .'

'Sister!' called Caldey from the sunny entrance of Meddick's tunnels. 'Sister . . .'

The mole came. She stared into Caldey's eyes.

'Sister . . . we have reason to believe you are Privet of Duncton Wood.'

Privet said nothing, and her face betrayed no emotion.

'Our Community has waited for your coming for many a moleyear,' continued Sister Caldey gently, 'and perhaps all moledom has. You will need strength to go forth again, and we will help as best we can. Your silence is respected. By ourselves we're all unfortunate moles, but together we are strong, stronger than the sum of our parts. Learn from us what you will, for surely we can teach you nothing you do not want to learn; such has always been our way. Learn from us as a whole. Then take what you have learned on into your task with the Stone.'

Privet stared at her, utterly silent.

'Sister,' whispered Caldey, for Meddick had slipped into restless sleep, 'Brother Meddick has asked that you continue to tend him. He has taught me so much without once seeking to, and I think . . . I think he will teach you much that you need to know.'

The mole nodded and for the first time to Caldey's knowledge since she had arrived she smiled, then turned towards Meddick to continue her task.

Sister Caldey watched her for a little longer and then, feeling at once contented and excited, she left Meddick's tunnels, returned to her own, and began to ponder what the coming changes would mean for all of them.

Chapter Eighteen

There is no great mystery about why it was that despite Quail's edict that Privet must be found, she so successfully eluded the best efforts of moledom's Brother Commanders and reached the Community of Rose. For one thing, from the night she left Wildenhope and ever afterwards, it seemed that the Stone understood how great was her need for protection and provided her with moles who could give it. We are not talking of strong young moles given to fighting and using their strength to save her life – no, the dangers she faced were more matters of the spirit than the body, and the moles who could help her along the way were not generally the fighting sort.

There was for example the mole (a mild male subordinate helper in Wildenhope) who had been one of the witnesses of the killings, and had seen all that happened. Until that day he had been a loyal Newborn, and had never in his life put a paw out of place where authority was concerned. But late that afternoon he overheard a conversation between two senior guards, the gist of which was that if nomole-else was going to do it, *they* were; which was, to follow the scribemole Privet and throw her into the river like the others, just as she deserved.

Incredibly, considering the risk to himself involved, that same mild minion took it into his head that such a thing was certainly not right, and throwing caution to the winds, set off at once to follow Privet and warn her. Which he duly did, staying hidden with her all that night and the following day, and making sure she was not found by the two self-righteous Newborns who would certainly have killed her with no questions asked.

Throughout this Privet said nothing, but was compliant with her helper, following him to the little scrape he made for her safety, lying low as he bid her, and setting forth once more when he said it was safe to do so.

It was the first of Privet's many such strange encounters and escapes in the dangerous days that followed the killings, until at last she was well clear of Wildenhope, and the vale beyond Wenlock Edge, and had become just a solitary vagrant female, who seemed mute and half stupid to those that met her. The kind of mole who has no place of her own, adrift from whatever community spawned her, and with no hope of anything much ahead but a violent, lonely, or miserable end.

The kind of mole, indeed, that is harmed and harassed by some when she crosses their systems, but upon whom others take pity, and give a place to rest, and a little food. To all of which – and the occasional violence offered her, or aggressive questions, or total indifference – Privet responded in the same way, with a kind of dazed, bruised vacancy, as if unaware of her surroundings, or of anymole she met.

This was the state she was in during the long days and molemonths of April into May following what happened to Wildenhope. For it is a fallacy to think that a mole in retreat is a mole at peace with herself, and in harmony with her surroundings. Perhaps in time such a pleasant state may sometimes be achieved, but never quickly, and not for long, and certainly not at the beginning of such a journey. Rooster had been right to think that where Privet was could not be easily reached by other moles. That day on Wildenhope Bluff she had chosen to begin the loneliest journey anymole ever makes, and it had at once taken her to an alien and most frightening place; only moles who have been there themselves can begin to understand, or sympathize.

If she looked dazed, if she did not respond, if she seemed without a future or hope, it was because that was how she felt. She was lost, alone, and afraid, without help or hope of help; and if there were mountains and voids in the landscape in which she found herself, they were mountains of grief and confusion, and voids of terror and despair.

She could function, just about, but it was an automatic kind of living. One paw in front of another meant moving; a worm was for eating; a scrape in the ground was for resting, not sleeping – there was little sleep in this world.

Trees? They were for going round. Rain? It was for sheltering from. Roaring owls? They were for watching as they rushed by. Moles? They were . . . they were beings she had once known, who now loomed darkly in and out of her life, day by day, some noisy, some silent, some to move away, and a few to stop still near, for they did not impose.

And the tears. They were for shedding. Tears for a whole life that was a burden for memory and feeling in whose huge tunnels and chasms the least thing might suddenly loom up as an unexpected and unwelcome portal to tumble her headlong in.

A puddle of water after a storm of rain; seeing her own reflection she remembered a day when she was a pup and had looked at herself in just such a puddle, and had smiled; a smile at life which did not smile back, but brought her misery in the form of Shire, her cold mother. The tears she shed were like rain upon that puddle, and the tunnels she entered then were dark and long and she did not escape from them for many a day.

The root of a tree at night, and she remembered being stanced down by one with her sister Lime, who had been civil for once and shared dreams of a future that never came to be.

Where did the grief come from which the memory provoked?

An old mole, male, big, his face-fur rough, who showed her kindness – giving her a place to sleep, worms to eat, and made her aware he was nearby but that he'd let her be. He understood. No need for words.

Tears again, terrible tears for Rooster whom she had loved and lost, and loved and lost again. Rooster . . .

Yes, the first part of the landscape Privet began to cross was one of tears, and terrible unspoken griefs for lost things she could not name, and moles she had once seen so clearly but who now . . . where were they now?

To talk to her mother Shire now! To have her paws about her as she had always wanted but never had – not as her sister Lime had. How she cried, how she ached with loss; how she was tormented by the suffering itself, which was like a great torrent inside her – worse than the river that took Rooster and Whillan, worse even than that – and flowing and flowing out of her, full of the detritus and grief of a whole life, overwhelming, and she at once its source and its victim, the torrent and the mole drowning in the torrent.

'Mole!'

A voice spoke to her. Enemy or friend, it did not matter.

'Mole, you can't do that here!' A paw flew out of the air and hit her, and she stumbled on. Do what here?

Weep, it seemed.

'Stone, help me, I have troubles but do not know their name. Stone, help me, I am lost, but do not know where I may be found. Stone, help me, I have life but cannot bear to live it.'

The silent Privet heard her voice crying out across the wilderness

205

in which she was lost, cries and shouts of torment which she wanted another to hear, but which none could, for nomole was there. None to understand, none to bring respite.

'Stone, hear me,' she cried, but even the Stone seemed not to hear, even that comfort was gone.

Gaunt, thin, the fur of her flanks and breast cut and bloodied where she had torn and pulled at it in her grief, Privet of Duncton now stumbled eastward across moledom towards the westernmost reaches of the great and terrifying two-foot system of Midland Wen which, at much the same time, Hibbott of Ashbourne Chase was unwittingly entering from the north.

But whereas the Stone guided him in relative safety by the elevated two-foot way that kept him clear of the dangers below, Privet, unguided, without help, desolate in her silent loneliness and torment, took a more dangerous way. Flooding underground conduits, the greasy stink of rats, unnatural lights at night, foul-smelling murk by day, these were her company and all she knew. Weakened by poisoned water, cut by she knew not what upon and within the ground, cuts which turned septic, her eyes sore and half blinded by Stone knows what afflictions, Privet was truly lost.

'Stone . . .'

But what prayers can a mole utter who feels as forsaken as she did then? What can she hope for? What dream can alleviate the sufferings of restless sleep?

'Stone . . .'

There was no Stone; there never was a Stone; nor could there ever be a Stone in so bereft a place . . . and yet *still* Privet prayed.

'Stone, guide me . . .' For even here, where the Stone's lowliest creature found herself crawling, she made room in her heart to believe the Stone must be . . .

'Even here.'

Day by day, night by night, Privet continued on her dreadful journey, the external place she was in growing progressively more like the internal place she knew in terms of its sterility, confusion and meaninglessness. Gone was the springtime babbling of brooks, gone the call of woodland bird, gone the good scent of fresh earth, or the balmy sweetness of unsullied wind.

Here the water was foul, and ran in concrete conduits in which half-submerged dead creatures lay; here the birds were gone, but for the filthy sparrow and the faded starling; and here the wind seemed dead and fetid most of the time, or if it was not it swirled up into violent eddies that shocked her, and threw odours and detritus in her face.

And all views were gone, but for the harsh and shining angles of two-foot places high above against the distant sky, rising from the fissures and shadows where she was lost like great mockeries of Stones.

For long molemonths in May Privet was utterly lost, and knew herself to be physically and mentally ailing when, for brief periods of stillness, she could see the world into which she had wandered for what it was, and herself as well. Aye, she saw herself down there in an oil-coated puddle, the two-foot structures rising so far above. Her face was that of an old, sick mole, her eyes those of a dead one, her shoulders and neck pitifully thin. Ailing, then, but not yet dying.

That began towards the end of May.

She had slept, and dreamed a dream of Whillan as he once was in Duncton Wood, running from her up into life . . . up into the moors, where he never was.

'Not there, my love, never there . . .'

But when she reached him it was Wildenhope they had come to and he was laughing, but with terrified eyes, for Chervil had hit him and he wanted to tell her he was not hurt, he . . .

But she saw his blood and pain and saw the river, and how it took him powerless in its rushing grip: 'Whillan!'

When she woke she knew he was lost to her for ever and it was then she began to die, which is to say began to give up hope.

How strange the things a mole says and does when she begins to feel forsaken.

'He is not dead, not him, not my Whillan, no no, no . . .' she sang, her voice cracked and crooning among the shadows, 'he cannot be.'

'Chervil killed him,' her own voice replied.

'Chervil is no son of mine; Whillan is, and that pup I knew is not dead, no, oh no . . .'

No, of course he could not be. He was waiting for her in Duncton Wood, up there among the great trees, where on a summer's day the sun came filtering down and lit the dappled path that lay ahead. The same sun which shone that day on the structures far above, and the elevated way along which, day and night, the roaring owls ran eternally unseen, but for their starting, slipping, shooting yellow gazes in the night, and reflection of red lights, receding.

Down in the shadows, unlit by the sun, Privet, too ill and desolate now to recover without help, floundering towards death, sang of lost Whillan's life and began to let him go.

207

'You didn't, Chervil. Not *him*. He was your brother in a way, he was your kin at least. You didn't do what I saw you do on Wildenhope Bluff.'

So Privet turned a corner in her new world and began to face death itself, knowing that in facing the death of Whillan she faced something of her own.

'Stone, guide me,' and now her prayer was uttered in the voice of one in mortal pain who saw that it was not only Whillan who had died, not only part of herself as well, but all the moles she ever loved and knew, all dying from her, all gone, and all leaving her. And if she was to know Silence, she knew she must finally let them die.

Shire.

Stour.

Rooster.

Fieldfare.

Chater.

Pumpkin, even him.

One, by one, by one they were leaving . . . No!

'I am leaving them,' she whispered, 'I, the Privet they knew and perhaps thought they loved, I . . . am . . . leaving . . . them.'

Why did she find comfort in saying that? She did not know. Why did she sleep deeply then, and wake to see the night-time gazes of the roaring owls and think to herself, amazed, there was a kind of beauty in them?

'I am leaving them . . .' and she saw, beyond the two-foot things, the bright stars at deep of night, and the sky in which they were set; not quite black, not quite dark blue, but so beautiful.

'Has it always been there, Stone?' she wondered aloud, breaking the Silence she rarely broke and never with other moles.

'Was it always there?'

When she woke again it was day, and though still ill and in pain from sores that seemed to emanate from her very heart, she was not so ailing that she could not see the beauty in the untidy ragwort, its rich yellow reaching for the summer sky, which clung to the walls of the ruined place where she lay.

She was still alive, that could be said, and there was a beauty in the flowers above her, as great as in the night sky she had seen. She looked at her paws. Grubby, thin and torn; but hers.

Privet wept for something different than before, something simpler; something which had always been and of which, weak though she was, and lowly, she was still a part.

208

'Stone,' she prayed, 'you know which way I must turn; lead me there now. Lead me on.'

So simple a prayer as that had taken all her life to journey to, and she lay her head along her front paws and thought of all those moles she had left behind. Would they be waiting for her already along the way – was that the mystery of community? Or would she one day pause, as now, and wait for them? Was that a choice she had?

'Stone,' she said. 'Stone,' she whispered.

'I will lead you on, mole, for I am here.'

And though aware that the voice was hers she knew it as another's too, the voice of all she had left, and all she would find, before and here and all ahead of her, and she felt the mystery of the Stone, and was touched for a moment by its healing joy.

'Whillan . . .'

'Gone.'

'But I loved him so much . . .'

'Gone.'

'Rooster . . .'

'Gone, now, mole.'

'Yes, he has gone. And Fieldfare . . .'

'Gone.'

'Chater.'

'Gone.'

'I felt him die; I held him as he died.'

'Gone.'

As the leaves of a tree blow and scatter away before the autumn winds of change, Privet let go so much she needed no more. Gone, all of it gone, and she feeling light and frail where she lay.

'The wind might take me up as well, and to where would it carry me? Where leave me be?'

'The Stone has taken you up, mole, and here you are, now.'

'Now . . .' repeated Privet, with a sigh, for it was time to find the energy to move on once more. But she did not need to pray, for now she felt the Stone guiding her paws, and they were light, and the going easy, and she did not need to wonder where she went for she would get there whether she wondered or not. So she left, with a last glance at the yellow ragwort against the sky, knowing that when night came again, there would be the stars.

But there did come a night when there were no stars, for she was lost for days after that in rank, dark tunnels made by two-foots; and she found places where flowers grew pale and deformed, and the only sign of the birds she could no longer hear were their grey and rotting defecations amidst whose foul piles and pools she had to find a way.

'But there are stars at night above, and there are the yellow flowers of ragwort,' she could whisper now, for she had passed beyond the vale of tears to somewhere where hope had been reborn and present trials could be accepted for exactly what they were: reality. Now this moment, without the need to cling to hope, or strive for changes. Now!

Noise. Places of dripping water. Sudden lights. Hiding from the fetid rats, and the black-pawed dog, and Stone knows what fat greasy thing that moved nearby in the dark. Then risking the stagnant orange water whose liquids clung to her fur and made her know she would die if she could not wash them off in a clean brook such as once . . .

Rain did it instead. Sudden, thunderous from the square of grey-black sky high above, pounding, flooding all about her and she out in it to clean herself.

'Thank you, Stone,' she said ironically, grateful for small mercies.

She journeyed on, and on, each day, each hour melting into the struggle and vileness that was the previous one, and that into the one before, until the day of the rain seemed long ago; it had happened to another mole, and would not happen to this one ever again.

A running brook; first the scent, then the sound, then the clambering over broken confused two-foot things and then . . . grass, reeds, and above her, swaying, the delicate yellow petals not of ragwort, but of yellow flag. Real water in a real brook and the scent it carried of real life, and somewhere far away, the countryside.

She bathed, and for days she gloried in the place, especially when the sun shone, a little natural world hemmed in by structures and the noise and lights of roaring owls. Then, recovered a little, the sores healing, the throat less tight, she journeyed upstream, hopeful.

A huge, arcing portal whence the stream issued, and suddenly no way through, none at all. No strength. All suddenly gone. Back, back to depression, back the way she came, back to the sores, to the drifting, back towards the place she thought she had escaped from: back along the way she had come with such difficulty. Back to the beginning again, and she dying now.

'The final test, Stone? One I shall fail? Are you disappointed in your Privet now? Stone? Stone!'

The Stone loomed over her, out of the darkness of her fevers and distress. The Stone moved. The Stone was living after all.

'Mole? Mole!'

It was mole, come to help her after so long.

'Mole?' she wanted to whisper, but must not from out of her great Silence. She reached a paw and touched the mole.

'Try to follow me. It's not far. Not too far. Try to follow . . .'

Privet had followed into a void of tiredness, letting go her frail strength, letting go any strength she ever had.

When she woke from that last stumbling part of her great journey through the Midland Wen, Privet found herself in the Community of Rose. Its moles talked to her, fed her, tended her with touch and healing herbs; but most of all they let her be; they simply let her be. There was no yesterday nor any tomorrow where she was, only now and today. A today which had a night with stars, and a day with nodding flowers, and a night again, and another slow day, an eternal now in which she found her health and mind again. A time of respite, not escape, from the journey she was on.

Sister Caldey, the community's leader, put her to help with an elderly male called Meddick, who understood her silence. To Privet, Caldey felt like a mother, and Meddick seemed a little like a father who had helped her in the past, but who now needed her care. Privet knew that in one way these were only imaginings, but that in another they were much more. As pups, everymole takes what they can, or as much as they are given; as a parent a mole should give freely, expecting no return. But as a mature *adult*, a mole is free to receive and to give, and as such is the medium through which the Light and Silence of the Stone may flow, from one to another, a never-ending cycle of life, belonging and apart, individual and apart . . . giving and receiving, the true sacraments of life.

So now, in this time of respite and renewal, Privet understood that she needed Sister Caldey for a time, just as Brother Meddick needed her.

'He is ailing now, Sister,' said Caldey quietly, 'he is approaching Silence.'

Privet nodded, her paw on Meddick's flank as it trembled and fluttered with his breathing; his throat rasped sometimes, and his eyes opened a little while he slept.

'Midsummer is almost on us, Sister,' continued Caldey, 'but I did not think he would reach it.'

'No,' Privet's look seemed to say, 'Midsummer is the time to celebrate the new, and Meddick whispered to me days ago he did not want to stay until then. And anyway, your Community has no young to give meaning to the speaking of the Midsummer rituals.'

211

'I would like, just once, to have heard you talk, Privet of Duncton Wood. I believe that apart from Meddick here, none in the Community has guessed who you are.'

Privet sighed. She did not know herself any more, or much care! It was a burden being who she was – the retreat into Silence was far harder than she had expected, though she had guessed it would be difficult. It was the hardest way she had ever been on. Oh, she was glad the Stone had guided her to Sister Caldey and Brother Meddick. With them she could express her fears and doubts, not by speaking but by being.

'You will soon need to journey on, Sister,' said Caldey. 'I feel it coming.'

Both knew when it would be, and so perhaps did Meddick, for he stirred, and woke, and coughed in a frail and wheezing way.

'Let her stay,' he muttered, pushing a paw fretfully towards Privet. 'Not long, thank the blessed Stone. Know that now. You will go then, eh, my dears? *Both* of you.'

Privet moved a little to one side as Caldey reached out her paws and held her old friend close.

'You're weeping, Caldey. Unlike you!'

'It's not,' said Caldey, almost aggrieved, 'and I do. You can't know everything about a mole.'

'Where did you find her, eh?' whispered Meddick, perhaps thinking Privet could not hear, or wasn't there.

'Where you found me, I think,' said Caldey. 'Nomole brought her here. She came across the Midland Wen all by herself, except for the Stone that is.'

Privet heard this, and wondered at it. A mole *had* brought her here, of that she was sure.

'Rose!' muttered Meddick matter-of-factly, eyes closing.

'Rose?' whispered Privet to herself. Such strange things happened in the world of Silence, but they *were* real, more real than anything she knew. Rose had been her guide in the last part of her journey.

Two nights later Meddick died, with Caldey and Privet holding his paws and other members of the Community nearby – all of whom had come close in the hours before and touched him, and whispered their names, for he was of them, and their own. Three deep breaths, a pause, and a frail sigh, and Brother Meddick left his old worn body and journeyed on. All in their gentle way seemed to accept it as entirely appropriate that the two with Meddick when he died were Caldey, with whom their Community had started, and the new sister, with whom they were beginning to sense it might end in its present form. It was as if there was a consensus that change was now of the essence, and they must all accept new challenges ahead.

Two days later it was Midsummer and members who had been out and about visiting other communities all came back for the occasion, and brought with them much news. The story of Wildenhope first brought to them by Hibbott on his way through was now confirmed, and some of the brothers and sisters surely guessed who Privet really was. Certainly she herself felt they did, though nothing was said, and most treated her as they had before. A few did not, but their curious glances or outright questions she found did not much worry her: or, if they did, it was only briefly, for that world of Silence, so wild and desolate in places, once so full of tears, now provided her with certain vales of peace, and glades of sunlight into which she could retreat, to be still, to pray, to work at the Silence, and glory that it was available to mole.

'She's so peaceful, that one! So graced by the Stone!'

'She's gifted with a wisdom altogether different from Sister Caldey's, but quite evident all the same. I'm sure she is.'

'She's . . .'

'Privet.'

Privet heard their whispers, and supposed it might be true. If only they knew the turmoil she still often felt, and how the dark voids suddenly seemed to suck her in. Silence was not, could never be, vales of peace and glades of sunlight all the time. Their comments, entirely well meant, made her feel alone, the more so now that Brother Meddick had gone and she realized how deep and gentle his unspoken guidance had been.

'I must leave them soon, just as he said, just as Sister Caldey said. After today, after Midsummer . . . Oh Stone, grant me this last day of rest.'

And restful it was in some ways, that Midsummer Day. The Community of Rose all complete for once – and for one last time. Until dusk came and Sister Caldey addressed them, saying, 'On the morrow some of you will leave us, and in the days that follow more will go. Until, at last, all of us will be gone, for as our Community here had its beginning, so now it has its ending. Brothers, Sisters, be of good heart, be of good cheer for the glories to come, even if we shall grieve at our parting, as we grieve already for beloved Brother Meddick.'

Here she was responding to the tears and sighs of many of the

213

Community, who, as was their way, cried openly, or held each other for comfort.

'Those who have recently returned tell us that great changes are apaw in moledom. I believe we must be part of them, and give our help where we can. You know a little now of the Order of Caradoc, and the Newborn moles led formerly by Thripp of Blagrove Slide, but latterly by Brother Quail. Against him great resistance has begun, and there is a mole called Maple of Duncton Wood . . .'

Here she paused involuntarily, and glanced at Privet, as well she might. Though Privet's face was impassive, how her heart had leapt at mention of Maple's name! The Stone *had* guided him, he was doing what he had long been destined for, but . . . 'Wisely Stone, I pray it is wisely!' she whispered to herself.

'. . . who is leading the resistance against the Newborns. It is not our task as healers to side with any faction or sect. The healing arts we have learnt together here are for allmole, without fear or favour. Therefore we shall go out as I have said, and the Stone will guide each of us to whatever task or tasks is best. I fear there will be fighting, and suffering; I fear we shall be greatly needed. I pray the day will come when peace returns.'

'When it does, Sister Caldey, can we not form our Community here again?' called out one of the brothers.

Speaking slowly now, Caldey said, 'I have thought of this, and prayed about it, asking for Rose the Healer's guidance on the matter. I believe we will form a community of moles again . . . but time must pass, and we must learn new things separately to bring back to teach each other. Perhaps we have become inward-looking . . . perhaps. Therefore let those of us who are still alive next spring, almost a full cycle of seasons away, make our way to the Redditch Stone, where Brother Meddick and I first met, and form whatever community then seems appropriate. Meanwhile . . . oh, do not weep, my good friends . . . or, at least, not for too long! This evening the sun sets on Midsummer, and we celebrate what is new. And *we* are new, all of us. *We* shall go forth, all of us. To serve, to heal, to love our brothers and sisters across moledom, as they may need us . . .'

The following dawn Privet and Caldey embraced, and Caldey wept.

'Sister, dear Sister, I wish I could have talked with you with words, though in spirit we have been, and will remain, closer than words could make us. I wish you well, my dear. Your task is a heavy one, and more than I guessed until I talked with the Brothers and Sisters fresh-returned from communities nearby. There is talk that you are

214

taking the Book of Silence itself to Duncton Wood. Rumour no doubt, wishful thinking at a time of strife. After all, I see no Book. But Sister . . . I feel it may be true that you are seeking it, and will find it!

'So go carefully, know that my prayers and thoughts will be daily with you until I hear you are returned home safeguarded. I would send a Brother or two with you, but the Stone is your protector and is more powerful than any mole!'

They embraced one last time, and by the soft June dawn light Privet slipped away southward, her period of respite over, and the way ahead again unclear, uncertain, and without companionship.

'Stone, guide me,' she whispered to herself, and was gone.

Chapter Nineteen

'Rooster's no ordinary mole, and this is no ordinary tale,' was how Weeth began his account of Rooster's survival of the Wildenhope Killings, 'so don't expect the beginning, middle and end of your average story! In fact, come to think of it, the end is really the beginning, the middle is all the way through and the end is where you start from!'

'Get on with it, Weeth!' said Maple with a frown, and then a half-smile at Rooster, and the young mole he had brought with him who Weeth had seemed in no hurry to introduce. Young, thin, with inquisitive eyes, and a way of constantly checking where Rooster was and if he wanted anything.

'"Get on with it!" he says,' continued Weeth unabashed, 'as if so extraordinary and dramatic a tale as the one I am about to relate can simply be "got on with" like eating a worm or, or . . .'

'Having a crap?' called out one anonymous mole from the Wolds, evoking general laughter. But they all appreciated Weeth's eccentric ways, and those who had already enjoyed the privilege of hearing him tell a tale knew that his preambles and brief diversions were just his way of getting attention, and leading them to settle down to the kind of appreciative silence he liked.

Then, with a friendly grin, and a wink in the direction of Rooster's anonymous young friend, Weeth quickly *did* get on with it . . .

As Rooster broke free from his guards on Wildenhope Bluff that April morning when so many moles were killed, it seemed to him that all the dark and terrible forces that had beset his life had in those moments of Whillan's punishment gathered as one and burst out in his mind.

Perhaps nothing could have prepared anymole for the dreadful sight of his son – his newly-discovered son – being so cruelly taloned and then dragged to so sudden, so horrible, and so public a death; nothing could have forewarned him of the overpowering rage and grief he felt as Whillan was thrown over the edge of the river-bank, to disappear from sight for long and sickening seconds before reappearing as a body

216

already caught and dragged along like inconsequential flotsam in a torrent of water.

All the grief that Rooster had ever felt, all the rage, all the bleak confusions and loneliness of the years, and the belief that he had failed to honour his task as Master of the Delve – all this was in that explosion of darkness and red light that his mind became.

So he had hurled his guards aside, and with only the mad and surely impossible hope to sustain him that he might somehow save Whillan, he bore down upon Chervil, Feldspar and his two sons. And yet . . .

Aye, and yet . . .

Even as he did, even at such a moment, even when he was over and into and lost in the dark void to which his life had brought him, the Stone, which seemed to have been so silent for so long, spoke to him. Not with words, but with a feeling, one whose origin he knew without knowing; it came from a moment long, long before when his mother Samphire held him again after his father Red Ratcher, having so nearly thrown him down into the torrential Reap in the Charnel Clough, brought him back alive to her; and she told him with whispers and caresses that she loved him more than anything and would never let him die.

When a mole is touched by such parental love it is as if he or she has been given a power that lies dormant within heart and body, ready one day, when most it is needed, to emerge once more. It is the power to love another, if only briefly, as we were once loved. This is the gift a good parent gives, and the salvation he or she can deny. This was the gift Samphire had given Rooster, and which had lain dormant in his heart, since before ever he became so troubled and confused.

So then, as Rooster approached Chervil with rage and hatred in his heart, wanting and willing to kill him, if not with a talon-blow then by tumbling him into the river, he felt that power of love. Not as some vague and vapid sentiment, but as a force more powerful by far than the very torrent towards which he rushed.

Chervil finally turned, Rooster bore down on him, and the great mole knew that he could no more harm Chervil, or the guardmoles with him, than harm Privet or Hamble or . . . or any of the moles who had loved him so well and so long. With a sob of relief to know that he could feel so potent and so total a love for the life of another – and ones who in the circumstances seemed the very last moles in moledom to deserve to be the beneficiaries of such a feeling – Rooster veered one way to avoid Chervil, and another to avoid his henchmoles,

217

and plunged over the bank, out into the void, down towards the grey and angry rush of the water.

What he felt in that poised moment of fall was as unexpected and ultimately important as the surge of love for molekind he had just experienced. Indeed it was part of the same continuum or gyring of emotion which stirs a mole with the courage to feel and move on from security to risk.

So now for Rooster love was followed by bleak, black, all-consuming fear. This was not the false fear of what might be if such and such occurred. This was the real fear, which is darkness in all directions, in which breathing constricts and paws are clenched tight and motionless, and the stomach contracts into a knot of terminal pain, as hope, all hope, is gone. This was the fear of death itself, of being made nothing – the fear all warriors, whether of the mind or body or spirit, must in some way conquer.

For Rooster, the river he now fell towards was not that into which Whillan had been thrown just before and from which he had vainly hoped to save him. This river was now the Reap in the Charnel Clough from which his father saved him, and he was falling back through time to the moments before his father thought again.

Now he hung above the torrent, now he knew the ultimate rejection – to be destroyed by the parent who made him – but now, now as he fell, he knew his father had never changed his mind; no, no, his father let him go after all, and fear of death and rejection was as real as the waters of the Reap which roared up towards him, to engulf him and take him for its own.

The fear from which Rooster had been trying to escape all his life was made real, and waited for him now in the Reap. And, he thought, with the wonderous clarity of such infinitesimal moments, he deserved this. Had not his father spared his life? He had. And had Rooster not later taken Red Ratcher's life? Aye, he had. So, of course, he deserved to die, and for his guilt to be assuaged in being made nothing. But the fear was more terrible than he could ever have imagined, as the torrent reached up its grey, remorseless, uncontrollable mass and embraced him to its raging heart. He did not want to die.

Rooster plunged into the water and felt each of his limbs taken by it, and heard a roaring in his ears; there were violent pressures at his eyes and mouth and snout, and all about him, like a tunnel caving in and crushing him, a cold, chill, freezing force such as he had never known. Does a mole scream and roar with shock and fear beneath the water? Rooster did.

And he struggled, desperate to rise towards air again, desperate to reach out a paw to Whillan. But for what? *So that his own son could save him.* In Rooster's wild and terrible fear, lost as he now was in the waters he had sought to avoid all his life, saviour had become victim, and victim sought saviour. It was only that hope that he might be found that kept him struggling for life.

He surfaced, looked desperately about, and was dimly aware of moles on the receding river bank chasing and shouting after him. He turned, saw a glimpse of a paw, Whillan's paw, before it disappeared under water ahead of him, and he cried out for help. He lunged forward in the water to try to reach it, and as he saw that ahead of where it had gone the water turned white-yellow, racing and impossible for mole to control, he felt a surging current at his rear, and then at his front, sucking him forward and down, down beneath the water, down and turning him so that direction had no meaning, and a strength ten thousand times greater than his own gripped his body.

For a moment Rooster wanted to submit to his fear and the power of the river, but mortal terror generates its own strength and fighting against these feelings he struggled and forced his way towards the surging light he could dimly see through the water, now above, now to the side, now below.

Below! Light, life and air was . . . below. Utterly disorientated, he swam what felt downwards to save his life and was thrust suddenly out – and up! – bursting into the air and light. Whillan . . . and Rooster felt his left paw touch something soft and moving – soft, but horrible. His saviour felt foul. Fear ate him and he it, and he was fear palpable.

And for a second time he felt himself pushed down, and that urge to give up returning, because he was tired now and his paws were beginning to ache and nomole could fight such forces as these; and anyway, to give up was to be free of all the darkness he had ever known, free of . . .

He felt his body turned and pushed against another in the drowning darkness of the water. Whillan again. The Stone had delivered him up. A chance to save or be saved.

Rooster grasped his son, his personal fear subsumed by parental love, and struggled up and up and desperately up now to the light and air and life once more. Up through the downward force of that water trying to obliterate them, but against which Rooster knew he must fight for both.

Up and out once more, one paw holding on to Whillan and the

other flailing, pushing, powering against the water to keep them both afloat. Whillan . . .

Rooster, in control again, carried along but still at the surface, looked for the first time at Whillan, pulled his head out of the water, struggled to keep them both upright, looked for signs of life, and saw . . .

'Not!' roared out Rooster. 'Not him!'

Nor was it Whillan, but some other mole; fatter, thinner; darker, lighter; older, younger, he did not know. But bloated and decayed, the eyes staring, the mouth flopping open and foul, the paws heavy and clinging, wrapping around him, climbing on top of him, trying to drown him . . . the odorous mouth trying to embrace him; but not Whillan, not his son. Relief mixed with strange self-mockery to think that all his huge effort and struggle, a journey of a lifetime's striving it seemed, had as its result the embrace of a rotting unknown corpse that was now (as it seemed) doing its dead best to drown him.

He let the sodden, stinking body slide off into the torrent and cried out, 'Where?' For where was Whillan if that thing that flopped and twisted away was not him?

He trod against the water, turned to look back, and saw something that explained everything, and it was then he understood all of the events of the morning. *Then* it was he laughed the roaring laugh which even those up on Wildenhope Bluff heard above the river's clamour. They heard, and saw the great mole turned and turning in the water, before, seeming to give up the unequal struggle, he was taken down by the river again and disappeared for ever from their sight beyond the river-banks.

But Rooster himself was now anything but afraid. Twice he had fought the torrent and reached the surface to breathe again, but this third time he did not. He gave himself up to its power – no, to its care – and happily abandoned that long lifetime's struggle against all he feared. The Stone had shown him he could love, and now what he had seen briefly on the bank meant that the Stone had shown him he could give up and just let go.

'Might drown, but won't!' was his light and easy thought as he felt himself turned head over heels in the water, like a leaf in autumn wind.

'Can't die!' he thought as, needing breath, the Stone surged the river beneath him and brought him to the surface so he might take it.

'Can't if I wanted to!' Rooster almost sang as he was pulled down again, and this time felt not panic and fear but the chill cleansing of the water at every part of his body – at crease and orifice, at face and haunch, at eyes and belly, at curve and cranny. Rooster outstretched his paws into the waters of the river, extended his head and snout back into its great currents, and when he felt his haunches pushed and turned by the crush of the water he relaxed the rest of his body, and let it be pushed and turned also.

He was at one with the torrent, unafraid, its waters his purification as he was rushed along, overturned, thrust up to breathe and pulled down to drown. Now he could only let go the dark confusions that he had grasped at so long, beginning with that first elemental fear of what the Reap in Charnel Clough would do to him if he fell into it. He *was* in it now, and he was alive, never more so, and all the dirt and filth of life, inside him and outside him, was being pulled from him and washed away.

No wonder that he laughed and felt such joy, for no experience he had ever had came near to what he felt now, unless it be that night in Crowden on the Moors so long ago when Privet's sister Lime first embraced him, and taking him, led him to a new world of freedom and release. But that was more physical than spiritual and could not last for long beyond the chamber where he and Lime had snatched love.

But here, now, in the baptismal flow of the river to which he gave himself up, he was enabled to let go all his past – the killing of his father Red Ratcher, the failure to honour his love for Privet, his loss of Hamble, and much else beside; but more than all that was his letting go of a sense of having failed as Master of the Delve. The task as it was set for him had been too great, too onerous, and now, with the freedom that purification brought he saw something which was both simple and startling: it did not matter that he had so far failed – if he wanted he could start again, if he did not want then he did not need to. The Stone is love, it never demands of moles what they cannot give; the Stone is love, it forgives moles their failings if they truly desire forgiveness; the Stone is love, it will show moles the way to what they seek if they only look. The Stone is love . . .

So was Rooster tossed and turned by the river, and cleansed of his confusions, and made new-born.

'New-born!' he growled, aware of the irony, the torrent slowing and easing as the river widened far, far downstream where it had taken him. 'New-born, and will begin again!'

He stared at the passing trees upon the far bank, and felt his

221

strength now was less than a new-born pup's; he hoped that if the Stone willed it he might be allowed somehow or other to reach the far shore, to begin to live again.

His paws touched bottom, he drifted on, they touched again, and stumblingly, like a pilgrim mole who has reached the end of his path but has barely strength left to take the last few steps, he staggered up through one of the eddies of the river, and clambered on to land once more.

Trees rising above him. Mud. Drifting stormclouds. His paws and flanks shivering with cold, he tried to keep awake and reach somewhere less exposed, but sleep overcame him. The river's diminishing roar. A voice. A mole coming out of dusk. The drift back into sleep and the murmuring of the water. A paw touching his head, the gentlest touch he had ever felt. And the voice again.

'Mole! Mole . . .'

Rooster opened his eyes from a great sea of tiredness and found himself staring into the eyes of an elderly mole.

'Whatmole are you? Whither . . . ?' The eyes were kind and clear.

And Rooster dared say at last what mole he was, and what he always had been, and must always be.

'Am Rooster.'

'Rooster?'

'Am Master of the Delve.'

The mole who found him was Dint, beloved elder of the system of Great Stoke, upon whose western periphery the river had delivered him up.

'Though, I must explain,' said Dint a little later, as Rooster consumed the third succulent worm he had been offered, and stretched his aching limbs, 'that we are here in *Nether* Stoke, which as its name implies is lower than the main system, which is on the river terrace some way above us, east of here.'

It seemed that the Stoke moles re-occupied Nether Stoke at the end of each spring when the floods subsided and the tunnels in the water-meadows could be repaired after the depredations of the winter years, when flood and frost routinely ruined many of them, and silted them up.

'I was on the investigative visit one of us elders makes each May,' said Dint, 'and the Stone guided me to the edge of the river bank from where I saw your not inconsiderable bulk stretched out in the mud.'

'May?' said Rooster, for when he hurled himself into the river at Wildenhope it had been April.

'No good doing it earlier,' said Dint, 'too dangerous. We lost an elder that way years ago when I was young.'

'Not April now?'

'You seem confused, if I may say so,' said Dint sympathetically.

'Am,' said Rooster with a comfortable sigh. 'Confused but content. Will talk.'

'Nothing like it,' said Dint, 'to ease the troubled mind. I presume you somehow fell into the river, but that the Stone, wanting you to live, sent you here.'

'Not Newborn here?'

'Trying hard not to be, but with Evesham so close by it isn't easy. We have what they call a Brother Assistant Inquisitor up in Great Stoke, but he has been made comfortable and ineffective – food and a female is all *he* seems to want. He's a mole of the spirit all right, but it's a greedy and lustful one!'

Rooster appeared to contemplate the twin evils of gluttony and lust and finally said, 'Lies are worse. Denying Stone bad. Lust? I had it for a mole called Lime. Gone now. Greed? Eat when I can, don't I? This Newborn Inquisitor, he needs love.'

Dint grinned and Rooster laughed.

'Not from us!' he said.

'So . . .' said Dint judiciously, after studying Rooster in silence for a little and then staring at the slow muddy eddies of the Severn as if for inspiration, 'you're the Master of the Delve. The one we've heard talk of for many a moleyear past.'

'Am,' said Rooster.

'The Master who comes from the Moors up north somewhere where the giant Ratchers roam, and the water tumbles in great torrents off the mountain-tops.'

'Do, sort of,' said Rooster.

'And you've killed more Newborns single-pawed than anymole in moledom.'

'Might have. Shouldn't have. Have been punished, have lived, and now can atone for what I did.'

'"Atone" is something the moles of the Word used to say,' said Dint. 'It's not a word that's pleasing to my ears.'

Rooster shrugged. 'Atone is righting wrong the best way a mole can. I'm not good with words. Words are awkward in my mouth. Words argue with each other in me and make dark. Privet knows

223

words. One day she will speak and scribe for me and I will delve for her and between us in the centre where we are, where there's no speech, no scribing, no delving, there will be our Silence which is our love. Couldn't die because of Privet; she won't die because of me. But Whillan . . .'

'That's her lad,' said Dint. 'That's what moles say. Killed at Wildenhope, along with you. *They* say.'

'He didn't die. *I* didn't die. Whillan's not Privet's son.'

Dint looked both sympathetic and unbelieving. Some rumours take deep root and sprout into great errant trees of whispered tales which moles are reluctant to alter. They like them as they are and they become part of their internal landscape. The idea that Whillan was not Privet's son somehow spoiled the inherent tragedy of the story of the Wildenhope killings, as *he* had heard it. He did not want to let the idea go. But there was something compellingly true in all Rooster said, so much so that Dint, an experienced elder and so a good listener was asking himself, even as Rooster talked, 'Why has the Stone made *me* find this mole? Assuredly he is the Master he says he is. Assuredly he is Rooster. And it is certain that if the Newborns learn he is here then there'll be a whole horde of them on their way from Evesham before they can say "Quail"!'

It said much for Dint that he did not also immediately conclude that the best thing for Stoke was to get Rooster as far away as possible as quickly as he could. No, he saw it only as an honour and opportunity that Rooster had so mysteriously, if unceremoniously, been delivered to Stoke, and that upon his modest and nearly forgotten system had fallen the responsibility of watching over a Master of the Delve.

'Not Privet's son?' repeated Dint automatically. He was playing for time as he pondered what to suggest that Rooster now did, for there was something about the delver that was ungovernable and wild. It had been a relief, for example, that he had said he would not try to 'love' the Newborn Inquisitor, for it would not have surprised him in the least if he had said he *would*. And then, Dint thought worriedly, how could I stop him. This is not a mole anymole *stops*. So, naturally, Dint was paying little attention to Rooster's words, so involved was he in the thorny problem of how to cope with him.

'No,' said Rooster, 'Whillan's *my* son.'

'Your son,' said Dint faintly. *His* son, he repeated to himself. Oh dear, this is all quite beyond me. He was trying to save his son at Wildenhope. One great branch of the errant tree of rumour concerning the killings had cracked and fallen, but now another, bigger one was thrusting forth in its place.

'Do Masters of the Delves have sons?' said Dint, genuinely astonished by the thought. 'After all, Masters are sort of . . . well, surely . . . I mean . . .'

Celibate was the word he was seeking. Holy as well. Not ordinary. Not prone to that sort of thing.

'Do,' said Rooster. 'You look worried. You think I'm in danger. But wrong, very. Am safe here and will stay. Nomole knows I'm here. Will help you. What are you doing here?'

'Ah!' said Dint, unsure what answer to make. He had hoped it was a question he would not be asked. Nomole likes to be asked what he's doing when what he's doing is to find the solution to a problem that has no solution. Though perhaps the solution was Rooster! Of course, the Stone *does* provide.

'Delving,' said Dint, wishing immediately he had said anything else but that.

Rooster grinned and dug one of his huge front paws into the ground. It seemed to Dint that soil and vegetation flew slowly into the air. The ground appeared to tremble. The earth shuddered.

'Er, I'm just delving tunnels,' continued Dint apologetically. 'Clearing them out, repairing them after winter, that sort of thing. Boring, dull, mundane, not your sort of thing I should think.'

'Life's "just" tunnels,' said Rooster with an ominous seriousness. Worse, he stanced up and loomed so large above Dint that it appeared that the sky had suddenly clouded over. He raised his paws and clashed them together with terrible relish, and Dint thought the last moments of his life had come.

Perhaps Rooster saw the effect he was having, which was why he made a doomed attempt to ease Dint's mind.

'Ratcher moles aren't giants,' he said. '*I'm* a Ratcher mole.'

'Ah!' said Dint, trying to creep out from under the shaggy shadow of Rooster. 'You are?'

'Am. And now . . .' said Rooster, his paws still huge and dangerous against the spring sky as he peered down at poor Dint.

'Yes?' squeaked Dint.

'I feel the delving need.'

'The delving need,' panted Dint, scrabbling out of Rooster's shadow and into the sunlight again. 'You feel it?'

'Do,' said Rooster, '*very* much.' Then frowning ferociously (as it seemed to Dint) he said softly, 'Wouldn't harm you, Elder Dint, wouldn't harm anymole. Anger's gone, been washed all away.'

Dint stared into Rooster's eyes and saw concern, love, and genuine sorrow that he should have frightened the old mole. More than that – and perhaps, after all, *this* was why the Stone had chosen him of all moles in moledom to be the one to find Rooster – he suddenly became aware of the profound gentleness and vulnerability that was Rooster; and he saw in Rooster's concern some shadow from the past life that the river had 'washed away' that made him wonder for a moment if he was now, after all, free of what he had hoped was left behind.

Dint smiled, as one who has seen a way forward and is suddenly at ease. He knew what to say, and what to do.

'Mole, we need your skills here. You asked me what I was doing here but I did not really tell you the truth. Rooster . . . er, Master, I was praying for a miracle. I was hoping . . . but I just can't seem to find . . . I just don't . . .'

Then Dint, who until then had seemed such a solid and certain sort of mole, even if he *had* looked a little nervous when Rooster stanced over him so suddenly and waved his paws about, now looked very *un*certain, and very *un*solid. His mouth wobbled, his eyes searched desperately here and there, one of his flanks actually trembled and he cried out, 'I don't know what to do!'

'Tell me,' said Rooster, putting one of those great and terrifying paws upon Dint's shoulder, 'tell me your pain. I will understand.'

'But you won't be able to help. Nomole can help us. We are doomed here in Stoke, all of us, doomed. The Newborns . . .'

'*Tell* me,' said Rooster again; and Dint told him.

Indeed, it did seem that he had not revealed the whole truth about matters at Great Stoke. While it was true that the Assistant Brother Inquisitor he had mentioned had been neutralized by a timely satisfaction of his 'gluttony and lust', it was also true that at the beginning of May some self-righteous and zealous Stoke moles, persuaded of the Newborn way, had gone off to Evesham to report what was going on.

That this might create real danger for the Stoke moles had not occurred to any of them until they received ominous reports of Newborn advances into systems adjacent to Great Stoke. Investigation showed that the Stoke moles had been quietly surrounded, nearby systems had been turned against them, and any hope of escape was gone.

'We can't get out, and can't cross the River Severn. But even if we could we wouldn't want to until the present crop of youngsters are a bit older and less vulnerable,' explained Dint. 'A few of us, and I'm one of them, believe rumours we've heard from a few friendly neighbours that the Newborns are going to make an example of us all. There'll be a massacre here just like there was down at Shepton Mallet back in March.

'Yesterday we heard that the advance on us is imminent and I decided prayer was not enough. The reason I came down to Nether Stoke wasn't to delve at all – what's the use of that now? – but to see for myself if there was any way we might escape across the river. I got *that* idea from what happened at Duncton years ago at the time of the war of Word and Stone, when moles were led to freedom an unexpected way.

'So I came, but I soon saw there's no way to do it, and I was just about to give up and go back upslope to Great Stoke and say to everymole that the only way now is to fight it out, when I saw you down there looking as good as dead. Now I know you're the Master of the Delve, I'm thinking you might be able to help. You might have an idea – but then it may well be there's no idea anymole could have that would save us!'

'May be a way, maybe not,' said Rooster, cutting Dint short. 'You can't escape with young and old, females and male. A few, but not many.'

'No,' said Dint, 'but—'

'But you can be lost, lost to Newborns, lost to neighbour murderers, lost to violence for a time.'

'Lost?' whispered Dint.

'Could delve tunnels to hide good and innocent moles in. Could delve tunnels so that Newborns couldn't get into them without knowing how. Could make tunnels of innocence, with help. Did it in Chieveley Dale when I was younger. Worked then against the Ratcher moles; could work now.'

Dint looked both puzzled and hopeful.

Rooster nodded and said, 'It can be done, to make tunnels, chambers, nooks, places, where mole is at peace. Goes back to where we started. Beginning, when young. Even then was darkness, but where innocence is hurt is less. Can do that, I can, because Gaunt mentioned it. Told me others have done it. You have touched old history in my heart; Dint, you are a *clever* mole. You weren't led by the Stone to me, I was led to you.'

Still Dint did not understand.

'Will show you,' said Rooster. 'Will *teach* you. Your system's young, your females, and the old moles will be safe. Well, safe until river floods again.'

Rooster nodded sombrely towards the great river.

'Am clever but not *that* clever. Can't delve tunnels here that will stop the waters coming back, but . . .'

'Yes?' said Dint eagerly.

'But maybe can nearly do it. Nearly is better than nothing. Now, you show me the ground, show me all, show me where Great Stoke is, and we are, show me everything and all. Can't delve until then, and then will as best the Stone allows me. Will help your system. Being Master is to serve.'

Poor Dint! Cast down by the worst apprehensions for his system, staring out at the grim waters of the Severn and knowing that his last hope of bringing friends and kin to safety was but a dream; astonished to discover a mole, a Master of the Delve no less, muddy and half drowned; in turns amazed and terrified by said Master; and now . . . now falling over himself to show Rooster the dull and empty land-scapes of Nether Stoke, eager to find some feature on which to rest his still distant hopes, or some small landmark where a mole might, as it were, *begin* . . .

'It's all very much the same you see, all, well, nothing much at all,' he said despairingly once they had inspected the surface between river and terrace. How impassive Rooster's face had been, how devoid of even the flicker of interest or possibility that Dint had hoped he might see there. Even a Master of the Delve, it seemed . . .

'Where's Stone?' said Rooster suddenly. 'Nearby, long-lost, found and lost, where, where, where?'

'What Stone? We have no . . . we . . .'

'Said was holy place of Stoke moles once. Long time ago. Said that's why when summer comes you elders come here.'

'But that's a story, that's . . . that's a *tale*, that's . . .'

'Yes?' said Rooster eagerly, surveying the flat meadows where the grass was greening fast. There were a few old water-ruined fences, and clogged-up dykes that had been cut by two-foots centuries before and now forgotten. Rooster was thinking of the Stone in Hobsley Coppice. That was risen now, but the Stone lost here at Nether Stoke was fallen; probably all over moledom there were fallen Stones, rem-nants of a faith that had almost died, but which could still recover if only moles believed again.

'Is Stone here. *Is!*' said Rooster.

The strangest of looks came to Dint's face and he creased his brow as if trying to resurrect a memory.

'Didn't even think of it,' he said at last, light dawning on his face. 'Well, damn my old bones, but I didn't—'

'What? Think what?' said Rooster urgently. 'No time, see. No time now. Your dark nightmare coming over that rise!' He pointed a huge talon to the very top of the terrace, beyond which lay Evesham and danger.

'Old days,' said Dint urgently, almost hopping from one paw to another in excitement. 'In the old days of my grandfather's time a Stone was found, or part of one. They didn't delve it all. Buried under the mud. Silted over. Grass grown on top. Lost and then found.'

'You saw it?'

'Taken to where it had been before I was born. They delved around it, the lost Stone of Stoke. Centre of the old system, *here*, where my ancestors lived long, long ago before the river moved and took their ground. When they found the Stone they tried to raise it before the winter floods. The whole system tried, day by day, working against time, trying to raise it from where it had fallen.'

'Many Stones fallen, few raised,' said Rooster, his eyes narrowing as he seemed to peer towards past and future both at once. 'Raising Stones again is a Master's skill. Not easy.'

'No, no, it wasn't and they didn't succeed. But the winter came early and the Stone was still half buried when the floods rose, and it was lost under mud again.'

'Found too soon,' said Rooster matter-of-factly.

'Nomole could find it again afterwards. Maybe the waters moved it.'

'River changes things,' said Rooster, 'back and forth, back and forth again.'

'Does the Stone mean something?'

Rooster laughed aloud. 'Mean everything here, there and everywhere. Listen. You go and fetch five moles, good moles, to help; I'll find your lost Stone.'

'But . . .' began Dint.

Rooster nodded, his paws fretting to get at the ground.

'You bring five moles, not six, not four, but five. We are two, they are five and together make seven which is best. The moles will tell you they're the ones. They'll know without knowing. Bring them soon. From the Stone we'll make a tunnel, and from that tunnel we'll make

229

two and from those two we'll make four and from those four we'll make seven and so sublime confusion!'

Rooster laughed again.

'But where will you find the Stone?' asked Dint.

Rooster shrugged and said blithely, 'Stone's problem, not mine. Go, go, go, no time. Five moles only, no more nor less.'

'I will!' said Dint, scurrying off across the meadows.

When he looked back Rooster was already half underground.

'Delving,' muttered Dint with excitement and awe. 'And now . . . five moles. Where will I find them? Who shall I choose?'

He heard a shout, turned round again, and saw Rooster far from where he had been, calling something. He heard Rooster laugh. And Rooster's words seemed with him as he turned once more to run as fast as he could: where to find five moles?

'That's the Stone's problem, not mine!' Dint panted to himself.

Chapter Twenty

Dint re-appeared half a day later, but with something more than five helpers.

'Who's the sixth?' growled Rooster, glowering at the youngster whom Dint had vainly tried to make inconspicuous behind himself.

'He's hardly a mole at all,' said Dint apologetically. 'He's only small; he won't say anything, you won't notice him.'

'Have noticed him,' said Rooster irritably, taking a step nearer and staring down at the thin face and wide eyes of the mole at Dint's flank.

'He's kin. He's harmless. He's—'

'Not staying,' said Rooster, reaching down a rough talon and, as it were, prising the youngster from Dint's protection. He prodded him in the chest, and none too gently. 'Why bring him? Five and two make a Seven Stancing, six and two makes nothing. We have work to do. He goes.'

'He . . . well, you see, he has . . .' but Rooster stared blankly at Dint, whose defence of the youngster withered in his mouth.

'You better go,' sighed Dint, turning to him. 'Maybe you'll be allowed to help later, maybe . . .'

'He only wanted to *help*, sir,' said one of the other moles, evidently disappointed at the stance Rooster was taking.

'Am Master of the Delve,' roared Rooster suddenly, so loudly that all of the moles jumped back. All but one. The youngster stolidly stanced his ground, staring at Rooster all the while.

'Why you bring him?' asked Rooster again, but this time more gently.

'Parents dead,' muttered Dint. 'In our system the elders care for orphaned young. His siblings are with other families but this one I care for. He was waiting for me when I went back to Great Stoke this morning. Had waited all the day before and all the night. He wanted to come yesterday.'

'Why?' asked Rooster, turning to the youngster.

'Want to delve,' said the mole, blinking, as it seemed, for the first time. 'Want to delve away the Newborns. Want to make the wind-sound clear.'

'He speaks like that, when he speaks at all,' said one of the others apologetically. 'He means no harm.'

Rooster seemed about to roar again, but somehow the roar transmuted itself into a great chuckle, so warm, so friendly, that the atmosphere within the group was transformed in a moment from uncertainty and disappointment to an easy unity.

'What's your name?' asked Rooster.

'Frogbit,' muttered the young mole, 'unfortunately.'

'That's what his mother named him before she died. Bit hard to change now.'

'It grows in water,' said Rooster gently, his great paw resting on Frogbit's narrow shoulder. 'It floats on water. Good for a delver. It's got three petals. Better for a delver. It's white like the Stone's Light. That's *best* for a delver.'

The others were silent, and a little awestruck. They all knew and liked Frogbit, and felt sympathy for him too. They knew how of all the siblings he had been most affected by his parents' deaths, and how good old Dint had taken him in against his better judgement, because he was the only one with whom the young mole seemed at peace. And they knew how impossible it had been for Dint to refuse to let the youngster come with them that day.

All this they knew. But now, as Rooster spoke, they realized that in some mysterious way Rooster was aware of it too. As the strange mole spoke, not laughing at Frogbit's name as others did but making something important of it, they saw on the youngster's face the look of one who dares think he might be coming out of darkness.

'That's good,' said Rooster. 'The bad is this: you watch and say nothing; you listen and say nothing; you obey and say nothing. And you learn. All you have now is your name, Frogbit. Good name, but is all; that and obedience. Only that.'

'Yes,' said Frogbit.

'You stay near me, or near Dint when I get mad. I do when delving. Watch out!'

'Yes,' said Frogbit. 'What'll I learn?'

'How to delve the Newborns away!' said Rooster vehemently. 'And how to make the wind-sound clear. Like you said. Can only learn what you want.'

'Yes, *sir*,' whispered Frogbit.

'Saying nothing,' growled Rooster.

Frogbit opened his mouth to agree, thought better of it and made his way to a spot a little behind Rooster's left flank, while the others grinned.

'Maybe Frogbit won't count,' grumbled Rooster, half to himself. 'Maybe he's not important, so Seven Stancing not affected. Wish I believed it!'

'So, what do you want us to do?' asked Dint. 'These five are all good workers, and all can be relied on to get on and not talk of what we're about. Tell us what to do and where to begin and we'll get on with it!'

Rooster nodded, looking suddenly very serious.

'Have found lost Stone,' he said, pausing only briefly as the others gasped in amazement. 'Have found the first line to delve and will show you. We work hard and fast, and you do as I say and *you*,' he added, turning to Frogbit, 'you'll find us food, and help clear soil, and keep out of everymole's way.'

Frogbit nodded, eyes shining with excitement.

'Now, follow me,' said Rooster, and he led them across the meadows, far from where he had summoned them when they had come down from Great Stoke. Under two old fences, across a muddy field, above a dyke and out on to a drier meadow which felt as exposed and as indefensible a place as any Dint had ever been to.

'But the Stone can't be here,' said one of the older moles. 'It was found those decades ago *downstream* of there so it must be way down yonder somewhere. At least, that's where we've always looked.'

'It's down there,' said Rooster, pointing to a stretch of unbroken grassland.

'But you've not delved there yet to find out!' said one of the moles.

'Stones speak louder than delves,' Rooster replied. 'Let's start!'

Today, when allmole recognizes Rooster's greatness, those simple words, 'Let's start', are said sometimes as a jest, as moles begin some great and challenging task, so awesome, so intimidating, that repeating the words that Rooster spoke all those years ago on the meadowlands of Nether Stoke somehow gives them courage to begin. If he began so great a delving as that which saved the Stoke moles with such simple words, so might they begin their own task as well.

As for the Stoke delving itself, in all its wonder and subtlety, others have scribed of it much better than a mere historian, concerned with

233

the facts and events of a spiritual history, can ever hope to do.*

It is enough to say here that the lost Stone was found, precisely where Rooster said it would be, and that using it as a centre-point for his tunnel line (though for a true delver 'lines' are rarely straight) he created the tunnel and chamber complex into which the Stoke moles were successfully evacuated over the following days, and only just in time. For within half a day of the last moles being brought down from Great Stoke, and the deliberately debauched and inebriated Brother Inquisitor discovering that he was all alone in the system he had been sent to cleanse, the Newborns from Evesham closed in.

Their bafflement at the disappearance of an entire population was almost as great as their absolute conviction that somewhere across the flat meadows of Nether Stoke moles lay hidden; which in turn was only marginally less than their frustration at discovering that however much they dug and delved across the meadows, and however many tunnels they found – strange tunnels, curiously convoluted, turning back on themselves and yet never conjoined again, mysterious passages and weird chambers where one could swear moles had just been yet where nomole was ever found – they did not find any moles.

Worse, their own guardmoles, trained and hardened through the years, frequently disappeared for days on end, only to reappear with beatific smiles on their faces, talking of love and the Stone, and utterly unable to remember where they had been or what they had done, but certain that they would like to go there and do it again, and saying followers weren't so bad after all.

Little wonder that the 'Miracle' of Stoke was out and abroad as a rumour by late June, and that Weeth, ever a mole to probe and enquire, should ponder on it, and through covert means and by devious methods ascertain, or perhaps deduce, that only one mole could have created such sublime confusion amongst the Newborns: Rooster. So he had gone to Stoke as Maple had finally bid him do, and there, with a little bit of luck, and some considerable courage, he had infiltrated the extraordinary and beautiful tunnels that Rooster had created.

'Thought I would be found,' said Rooster gloomily.

'Yes,' replied Weeth matter-of-factly, saying no more than that.

---

* See in particular the scholarly *The Lost Delvings of Nether Stoke* by Bartolf of Evesham; and, for a more personal account of the dramatic Newborn siege of the delvings, Bryony of Rollright's *The Miracle of Stoke* has not been bettered.

'Will only last until winter floods come,' said Rooster, 'and only right they should. Delving not for war.'

'This is saving lives,' said Weeth, basking in the strange light and ease of the tunnels and chambers centred about the lost Stone in which the Stoke moles now withstood these summer days of siege.

'Humph!' declared Rooster. 'Worms, Frogbit, get some!'

'You're hard on that mole,' observed Weeth.

'He's learning,' said Rooster, 'hard is best.'

'Learning what?'

'Rooster can't live for ever. Once peace won, delvers will be needed to help keep it. Must be trained. Am training *him*. Why've you come?'

'Tell you in my own time,' said Weeth, who understood Rooster better than most.

'Why?' repeated Rooster day by day, frowning and disturbed.

Finally, four days after he had arrived, Weeth confessed. 'I hate to say this, Rooster, but you're needed. Maple sent me.'

'No,' said Rooster, 'you sent you. Maple wouldn't.'

Weeth grinned. 'Yes, I did send me. I think you're going to be needed now. Things are changing fast.'

'Tell me,' said Rooster, and Weeth did.

'Will come,' said Rooster at last. 'Stoke moles can protect themselves now, until winter. By then maybe all right. Maybe not.' He shrugged, not indifferently so much as philosophically: the Stone would see right done.

As soon as it was known that Rooster was to leave, all kinds of moles asked if they might come with him: to protect him, to be with him, to watch over him.

'Can only take one,' declared Rooster.

'Then take the strongest of us,' cried out Dint, pointing out many a strong and powerful mole among them.

Rooster shook his head. 'Will take one who has a lot to learn, but is learning; lot to give, is giving; lot to discover, is discovering. Will take you, Frogbit. Come here, mole!'

Trembling from head to foot, scarcely believing his good fortune, terrified even then that Rooster was going to say he could not go after all, Frogbit went to Rooster, his snout low, his eyes down.

'Need a helper,' said Rooster. 'Need a mole knows that soil is soil and rock is rock, and stones are stones. Have tried all ways to stop you even beginning to be a delver, but your spirit won't be stopped. Once was young myself. Once had the delving need like you –

unformed, untrained, undisciplined. Didn't even know its name. You know what I mean.'

Frogbit nodded, not saying a word.

'Look at me, mole,' said Rooster.

Frogbit raised his head and with the greatest difficulty looked into Rooster's eyes.

'Will be hard, the journey you make. Harder than you ever dreamed. You may not complete it, or you may, only the Stone will decide. If Dint says you can come with me, you can come.'

''Course he can, Rooster, sir, and there's none more proud than me to see it. You've saved our moles and our system, and given us a chance. We view it as an honour that you're taking one of our own with you on your travels. We're a bit off the beaten track down here, we know that, but we're not ignorant moles, and we're faithful to the Stone. You've given us back our heritage and our pride, and if young Frogbit there reminds you from time to time of his home, and you never forget there's moles here will always honour you, we'll be satisfied!'

It was well said, and overwhelming for Frogbit, who could not think of a suitable speech for the occasion, and said so in a faltering voice.

'Wish I could, but I can't. I'll miss you. I'll do my best. I'll not forget where I come from. Like my Master says, "If a delver doesn't know where he's come from, he'll not be able to get where he's going to."'

'Did I say that?' chuckled Rooster. 'Am clever to have said it, and you're clever to remember it! So . . . when to leave, Weeth?'

'Today. Now. Yesterday,' said Weeth, 'or, er, tomorrow? At the latest!'

And, indeed, by the time the farewells were done and the last tales told, and Rooster had entertained his friends with memories of his days on the Moors, the night had passed into dawn, and the morrow had come.

It was in the convoluted tunnels and chambers around the lost Stone of Stoke that Rooster chose to say his final goodbyes.

'Stone will protect you until the waters come. Then you go out by this tunnel – all of you,' he said, indicating a strange narrow passage that few used, which twisted and turned under the base of the Stone itself.

'Down there, go there, Dint. You'll know when. Others must be ahead of you. Tell all to be calm, whatever happens. Stone will protect you! Don't try to go out by any other way. This way, only this!'

236

Dint nodded his understanding. Goodness knows Rooster had told him and others enough times about it: don't be seen on the surface; don't be afraid if the waters are rising, or the Newborns approaching. But be prepared to run!

'Best I can do, very hard delving, might not work. Now Weeth, now Frogbit, we must go! 'Bye!'

Then to the cheers and embraces of their many friends the three moles were gone by routes secret and hidden, which eluded the Newborn guardmoles, and took them south of Evesham and in safety on towards the Wolds.

'So there you are, moles,' declared Weeth, 'that's how Rooster, Master of the Delve, made his way from Wildenhope to join us tonight. And, come to that, it's how his most able, and willing, and obedient helper, Frogbit of Stoke, comes to be among us too!'

'What I'd like to know is what Rooster was on about regarding the lost Stone of Stoke. All that about only using one tunnel, and waiting until the last moment—'

Weeth raised a paw to the questioner, and to others eager to hear more.

'Now, before you ask your questions there's three moles here could do with some food! And as soon as possible!'

The addition of Rooster to the forces of resistance was of considerable importance, as Maple instantly understood. He already had warriors of substance under his command, among them Ystwelyn and Arvon and Stow, and they were helping him to mould the disparate mass of refugees and moles of the Wolds into a united and disciplined force.

The Wildenhope outrage had elevated Privet to an almost mythical status, and certainly a mystical one, for what follower could not empathize with her, and feel that if a thin, middle-aged female could stance up against the Newborns then they themselves could, and to the very death. Now Rooster had come along, and he was not a disappointment. The extraordinary tale of escape and survival Weeth had first recounted to the followers was soon known all across the Wolds, and if it was a little exaggerated here and overstated there, well, nomole was going to gainsay it. But, in fact, such propaganda was unnecessary, for Rooster was so over-sized and extraordinary a mole, and one who in the course of his escape seemed to have found an inner calm and contentment evident to all who met him, that he was now his own best advocate.

237

Somewhat against Rooster's own wishes Maple assigned two of Ystwelyn's best moles to guard him, for there was little doubt that he would be a target of the Newborn forces when they heard of his survival.

Three things helped increase the effect his presence made on the followers: first, the fact that he was, or had been, Privet's companion – 'mate' was not a word moles liked to use; second, his delving, an art he now practised as he felt inclined; those who were able to see his work talked about it in tones both hushed and reverential.

Lastly, regarding the impact Rooster had on others, was the warmth and simplicity of his manner: he said little, but what he said he meant; his furrowed and lop-sided smile was always welcoming, yet when he wished to be alone he made no pretence that he wanted anything else, but said, matter-of-factly, 'Leave me, must think, must try to delve.' Then only Frogbit dared go near him, providing him with food, with delving help, and sometimes with silent company.

So that those who watched over him – and as Maple knew well, there was some truth in the notion that *all* the followers now massing in the Wolds watched over Rooster, just as they daily prayed for Privet on her difficult and mysterious journey – made sure that Rooster had peace and privacy. When he ambled in among his new-found friends, his fur awry, his paws clogged with soil, his brow furrowed in thought, if he did not wish to talk they did not disturb him, sensing that for one who had journeyed through the dark places he had there were often times when all he demanded of others was that they let him be.

One of the reassuring things about Maple's command was the sense he gave those who followed him that he knew what he was doing, and that he did nothing that had not been carefully planned; often what he did seemed obvious and inevitable only when it was achieved.

A few days after Rooster's coming he had ordered the followers to disperse into four groups, explaining that to concentrate so many moles at one point was dangerous, and presented practical difficulties with food, water and grooming.

'As a community disperses itself over its territory to the best advantage,' he said, 'so the followers will now do the same, only coming together when its separate commanders under myself decree that it must be so.'

These commanders, four in number, were not the moles others might have expected him to choose. Ystwelyn, and Arvon, for example, he kept as his immediate subordinates, saying that he needed the former for his excellent advice, and the latter because there was always need of a brilliant independent leader of smaller groups, and, anyway, 'you're not a mole likes the tedium of day-to-day command, Arvon!' – which the Siabod mole acknowledged was indeed true.

Stow took overall command of the two groups of Wold moles, with Runnel, his long-term second-in-command, as the leader of the smaller of the two. Stow was the acknowledged expert on how a large number of moles could keep a low snout in a concentrated area, and in the time they had all been together he had willingly imparted his knowledge to those who had been led to the Wolds from Rowton.

Of these, Whindrell had emerged as a doughty leader, and one others trusted, and though he could not boast the experience of Stow, nor claimed to, he was much liked, and could be severe on those who were lax and ill-disciplined.

The last of the four commanders was the female Malla, or Maella as some more accurately call her, a mole from the deep south-west who spoke with a burr to her voice; though not large, she was fierce, not to say ferocious, and, as many said, 'worth three males at least'. That might or might not have been true, but certainly the band of moles she led up from her own territory at the end of May would have accepted no other leader, and nor, once they were used to the idea, would those whom Maple put under her command, which included his early travelling companions, Furrow and Myrtle.

Myrtle was no slouch herself when it came to being fierce, but in Maella she found more than her match, and was soon happy to serve as her assistant, in much the same way as Weeth served Maple – a role in which she took great pride yet appeared meek as a lamb. Furrow her mate, having found his confidence under Maple in the crossing of the two-foot bridge, soon made himself something of a specialist with the ins and outs of roaring owl ways and the territory of two-foots, who now held no fear for him.

Stow's and Runnel's groups stayed up in the Wolds; Whindrell and his motley of moles moved northwards into the lower slopes towards the Midland plain; while Maella's force was sent eastward to the dangerous and busy vales across which many routes lay; their role was to spy upon the Newborns' movements, and provoke confusion and incident, from which they disappeared into the night, often along the two-foot ways by which Furrow, and those who trained under him, had led them.

While between them all went the moles who in some ways, as Maple often said, were the bravest and most unsung of all – young males and females, swift of paw and quick of mind, who acted as messengers and journeymoles and kept communication between the groups alive. Maple himself, Ystwelyn and the others, moved between these four main groups, appearing and disappearing without warning, always seeming to know when and where they were needed, keeping morale high, watching their moment, and slowly and steadily, almost without the Newborns realizing it, expanding their territory.

And what of Rooster, Master of the Delve? At the suggestion of Maple, and with some gentle persuasion by Weeth, he was put into the care of the moles under Stow, who undertook to hide him high in the Wolds in some place only those closest to Stow could locate.

'I've talked it through with him,' Stow told Maple before the forces went their separate ways, 'and I've an idea of the sort of place he's looking for. Mind, how long he'll agree to stay with us is another matter, but I think he's got it into his head at last that there'll be Newborns sent out to kill him once Quail knows he's alive. Don't you worry, Maple, the moles of the Wold won't let you or Rooster down. It's an honour to watch over that mole.' For so matter-of-fact and stolid a mole, Stow sounded almost fervent.

So the forces under Maple were divided for safety's sake, and the better to confuse and extend the Newborns, and make them wonder quite where the followers were, and when their next assault on a major Newborn-held system would be.

'Do *you* know, Maple?' asked Ystwelyn in the quiet days that followed the departure of Stow and all the others.

Maple smiled enigmatically.

'Do you, sir?' asked Weeth, when he and Maple were alone.

'Aye, I do,' said Maple, 'I know the place, but I don't know when. Now listen, Weeth, there's a task I have for you and it will be dangerous, but you're the mole to do it.'

'A task!' declared Weeth, with just a little less than his usual enthusiasm. There was an air about the way Maple said this that was even more serious than usual.

'And this time it's one for which I'm going to insist that Arvon and a few tough moles accompany you.'

'Arvon!' repeated Weeth. Oh dear, this sounded like a dangerous task rather than an enjoyable venture. 'Will he not be needed here? I'm so much better working alone.'

'He'll be needed rather more where you'll be going, if only to get you in and out alive. He'll be the military muscle and enterprise, you'll be the negotiator.'

240

Weeth grinned feebly. It sounded as if real responsibility was coming his way, and he did not like it.

'To where,' he said carefully, 'do you wish me to go?'

'I have discussed the matter at length with Ystwelyn,' said Maple, 'and we are agreed that it is time a visit was paid to Duncton Wood.'

'Ah!' said Weeth in a thin voice, and with a thinner grin. 'When do I start?' His voice and his grin were both fading fast.

'Today.'

PART III

Dissenters

Chapter Twenty-One

As Weeth set off on one of the most perilous assignments of his event-
ful life, another mole was coming to the end of the most dangerous
of his: Noakes and his two companions from Seven Barrows had not
only reached Duncton, but had infiltrated the High Wood, and now
he was wondering what to do next.

Not that it had been easy reaching Duncton Wood, or sneaking
past the Newborn guardmoles posted in well-organized positions by
the cross-under at the bottom of the south-east slopes. But that done,
and with Fieldfare's detailed description of the topography of Duncton
in mind, they took a direct route up to the High Wood, and hid
themselves in one of its obscurer corners, impressed by the ancient,
soaring beech trees, and the awesome quiet they imposed on the floor
of the Wood beneath them.

Noakes' leadership throughout the journey had been exemplary –
bold, resourceful, and energetic, and his companions, both as young
as he, had until now regarded their task as adventure rather than risk.
But now they were in the hushed High Wood of moledom's most
renowned system, with Newborn patrols no doubt nearby, a certain
sobriety descended upon them, and they wondered quite where they
went from here.

Noakes himself had long since dismissed any notion of bold pretence, such as arriving at the Library with some concocted story that
he was a visiting mole seeking guidance on scribing and scholarship;
bright and clever he might be, but he did not know the first folio of
a text from its last, nor its bottom from its top, and *that* ruse would
not work. Nor was he prepared to risk his life or that of his companions
pretending to be Newborn. This trick had worked for them several
times, but in a system long since in the thrall of Brother Inquisitors
it was unlikely to succeed. No, the strategy he decided to adopt was
one demanding nerve, and a degree of perspicacity, not to mention
patience.

'We know where the Duncton Stone is because Fieldfare told us,'
he said, peering through the soaring trees in a westward direction

and thinking that he had never in his life felt himself to be in such a holy kind of place. 'Well, my plan is this: I'm going to find the Stone this evening under cover of half-light, and there I'll wait until a mole appears to pray before it, as surely somemole will. I shall watch him, and I shall decide whether or not he's a follower. For one thing we do know is that the Newborns are afraid of the Stone and see it as a force they've got to appease, rather than a grace that's on their side. So, I shall wait, and trust that a mole will come along who can guide me to this great mole Pumpkin, wherever he may be.'

'It's risky, Noakes,' said one of his friends.

Noakes shrugged and grinned, scratching his glossy flank.

'Life's risky, but I say to myself, if a mole's not safe by the Duncton Stone, where is he safe! As for you two, you stay here and you don't move until I get back. Dig yourselves in; use this deep litter of beech leaves to cover your tracks. Resist the temptation to burrow deep, for somewhere beneath here, as Fieldfare has warned us, are the tunnels of the Ancient System of Duncton Wood and they are protected by Dark Sound. Nomole knows we're here, and nomole's going to find you. As for me, if I'm not back within three days – though I *will* be, I assure you of that! – then you must decide on a course of action for yourselves.'

'Can't we come with you?'

'You could do, and maybe you should do, but instinct says that this is a task for one mole alone. Trust me, it'll be all right.'

Which they willingly did, not because they were themselves afraid to accompany him, but because so far he had been proved right in most of the decisions he had made, and where he was wrong he had shown the quickness of thought and the resourcefulness to escape and survive. But even moles like Noakes, upon whom the stars usually seem to shine, could be wrong, and he was wrong this time. As he set off towards the Stone, a grey and grizzled shadow with sharp eyes and a doubting snout separated itself from the roots of an imposing beech tree nearby, and followed him silently.

Meanwhile, as his companions dug in so they would not be observed, they were being carefully watched by another shadow, this one grey-black and younger than the first: a shadow so close that it could hear their every word; a shadow that was trying to decide if these infiltrators were followers or very clever Newborns.

In normal circumstances Noakes' plan would have been a reasonable one, but these were abnormal times and he could not know that a secret and extraordinary battle was being fought across the deserted spaces of the High Wood. The aggressors were a group of well-trained Newborn guardmoles, operating out of the system's Library under the direct leadership of Brother Inquisitor Fetter. Their quarry were the moles who had escaped Barrow Vale under Pumpkin's leadership back in December, who, bolstered by the timely arrival of Hamble, now eked out a dangerous existence in the Ancient System itself, harried by Newborns above and Dark Sound below.

Twenty moles had originally escaped, including Pumpkin himself and these along with Hamble made twenty-one. But of these five had since died – four elderly moles had succumbed to the privations of their new life, and a younger one had been killed in a fight with Newborn guards near the Stone. Two more had been caught and were believed to be alive down in the Marsh End, where after a period of torture both had been broken and given away the numbers and general position of their besieged friends up in the High Wood.

One other mole deserves mention: Sturne, still Acting Master of the Library and the only Duncton follower successfully fooling the Newborns into thinking he was one of them. Not that Brother Inquisitor Fetter did not have his suspicions – but then, they were suspicious of everymole. The worms of suspicion were their daily food. But Sturne's bibliographical expertise was so great, and his manner so convincingly hostile towards the followers, that he had survived with the Inquisitors' confidence in him intact.

Not that he had done so without enormous cost to himself. Desperately alone, publicly subscribing to views he detested, forced to be involved in Newborn rituals whose words and symbolism were an affront to his very being and beliefs, Acting Master Sturne had suffered during his lonely struggle for the Stone – a Task Master Librarian Stour had set for him, which now only Pumpkin in all the world knew of though Cluniac had guessed much of the truth.

But nothing had caused him more anguish and suffering than being forced to witness the torturing of the two followers caught by Newborns after their escape to the Ancient System. One was young, the other middle-aged, both with a life ahead; it might have been easier had the two been old; they might perhaps have not survived their ill-treatment so long. Being made to watch their torture in the blood-stained chambers of the Marsh End was a test, and a terrible one, for however much a mole may be justified in hiding his true affiliations he cannot but feel guilt when he is unable to intervene to prevent deliberate cruelty to an innocent mole.

In truth, had Sturne believed his intervention would have had even

247

the smallest chance of success he would have tried it, but he knew otherwise; and it was no comfort to him to know that his brave actions since the Newborn takeover had saved lives, including all those presently hiding with Pumpkin in the Ancient System.

He had to watch as the two moles were harried and hurt in turn; after being cruelly beaten they were blinded and their snouts slowly crushed. Finally, the agony too great, they had betrayed their own kin and friends. It was then that Sturne, for the first time in his life, had allowed a tear to trickle down his face.

'So you feel sympathy, Acting Master Sturne?' whispered the ever-watchful Fetter.

Sturne had long since decided that where the Brother Inquisitors were concerned attack was the best defence: 'Sympathy?' he cried out, wiping the tear away. 'I feel rage that such scum as these are allowed to live. What is Newborn justice if the Snake is allowed to survive in a body, however broken? Do you think that Snake is dead because these two foul moles have finally told the truth about their fellow conspirators against the Stone in the High Wood? Yes, I weep to see such sinfulness still living in the world!'

'Well, Acting Master! Well! Passion at last, from the least passionate mole I have ever met!' said Fetter. 'You have feelings after all, it seems. But if that is a plea for these moles to be executed in the name of the Stone then you do not understand the subtleties of punishment. They will suffer more if they live, and that is good, for it may mean the Snake in their hearts will die and we will have saved two more moles for the Stone. And, by confessing as they have, they have won the right to live. So your plea must be ignored – but it is appreciated.'

All this Sturne knew well enough, just as he knew too that the tortured moles both wished to die. Had they not both screamed out for death? And yet . . . but moments later they were past all thresholds of pain and into the saving grace of numbness, of confusion, or near-madness, and their agony was less. Time would diminish it further.

In that world they had no protectors but the one who was forced to watch their distress; Sturne himself. And he, suffering with them, prayed to the Stone that it alone would decide their fate, and no mole.

'Stone, if they live, grant that I may be allowed to watch over them. Stone . . .' Then another tear had come, more painful to Sturne than a whole flood of tears to any other mole.

No wonder his chill eyes were colder now, no wonder the icy etchings of his face were deeper; no wonder the severe furrows of his brow and the hard downturn of his mouth were ever more intimidating. After the torture, even Brother Inquisitors Fetter and Law were half-afraid of him, and let him alone in the vast and echoing chambers of the Library, once so busy and productive, empty now except for the guardmoles who lingered there, hoping to catch sight or sound of the rebels they knew were hiding in the Ancient System nearby.

Spring had come across Duncton as elsewhere, and there in the Library, among its texts and shelves, vast walls and deep tunnels hushing the joyful sound of bird and mammal from the surface above, Sturne had begun the most dangerous and most important part of his work: liaising with the hidden force that Pumpkin and Hamble now led in the long-lost tunnels beneath the High Wood.

Never for a moment had the Inquisitors suspected that Sturne of all moles was working with the followers hiding in the Ancient System, rather than against them. Never for a moment had anymole questioned the advice Sturne gave about the tunnels, or doubted that the map of them he had forged, claiming it as Mayweed's own original, was anything but genuine.* It is a measure of Sturne's extraordinary courage that he knew what would happen to him, slowly, down in that bloodstained chamber in the Marsh End, if his collusion with the followers was ever discovered.

Meanwhile, despite these enormous pressures, it was Sturne who brilliantly misdirected the campaign of Fetter's guardmoles to bring out into the open the moles they sought. Against the few disasters – the death of the young mole in a skirmish at the Stone, the capture and torture of the two already mentioned, must be set the success with which the rest of the rebels eluded capture and detection. The revelations of the tortured moles proved worthless, for the rebels had already flown from the tunnels where they were reported to be hiding and all the guardmoles' best efforts produced nothing.

Where then *were* the rebels? And how did they achieve their success? Most accounts have made their exploits heroic, and have much romanticized their bravery, the more so that many were elderly, and all knew the fate that awaited them if they were captured.

The truth is that from the time of their going to ground until the coming of Noakes that June, they lived a scurrying, fearful kind of life, with no contact with the outside world (except briefly with Sturne through Pumpkin, who had to keep his source of help secret), with little food (the Ancient System's tunnels are notoriously wormless)

---

* See *The Duncton Chronicles* for mention of the possible existence of this map, made by Mayweed, one of the greatest route-finders moledom has ever known.

and, most seriously, without sufficient water for most of May (when Duncton suffered an unseasonable drought).

All this in tunnels beset by the Dark Sound and other horrors that past Masters of the Delve had carved and etched into the dark and gloomy walls and chambers, leaving traps and devices whose insidious tensions could turn moles half-mad with fear and desolation. These delvings seemed designed primarily to protect the Stone itself, and only the truly innocent and pure in heart, or morally powerful, or profoundly faithful, could long survive them. But the longer the rebels were forced to live among them the more they came to see that as well as the Stone, which lay on the west side of the Ancient System, the Dark Sound seemed also to protect the very centre of the High Wood. Several of the more venturesome rebels did their best to enter that forbidding place, but none got far and all reported that so far as they could tell the tunnels there were now ruinous and root-filled, and surely beyond the ken of mole.

Pumpkin had early on decided against saying anything to anymole, excepting Sturne himself, about the strange and frightening experience he and Cluniac had suffered in early spring when they had tried to venture through immediate dangers to whatever lay beyond.

That something did lie beyond he had no doubt, and it filled him with awe and disquiet. That the tunnels there were the source of much of the Dark Sound that echoed almost continuously through the Ancient System, he was sure, and so were his rebel colleagues. But more than that, and what suspicions he had, he did not say, and nor did anymole-else ask him. As the molemonths of summer passed by the rebels ceased talking about the Dark Sound, or its source, and a conspiracy of silence about it developed; only tearful glances, or the occasional muttered reference about 'not going *that* way' betrayed their unease. Certain tunnels, certain filled-in portals, were avoided, and the rebels created routes that minimized their exposure to these disturbing places, and the sound they seemed to provoke.

Often the sense of this unknown and unexplained place, lost now to mole, was oppressive, and many was the time one or other of the rebels sought to escape the gloom and doom of their refuge, or refused to travel even into those tunnels that *had* been explored, riddled as they constantly were by the sounds of danger.

Meanwhile Pumpkin and Hamble inspired them to control their fears and to survive, the former feeding their collective memory of what Duncton had once been and might be again if only they could show the will to survive, while the latter's stories of the mounting

250

danger of the Newborns in the outside world left them in no doubt where their duty lay. Cold, starvation, boredom, fear, hopelessness, despair – such were the enemies these brave moles faced in that nightmare time of isolation and exclusion.

Brave Pumpkin! What a leader he proved to be. Cheerful, resolute, modest and able to inspire or shame them into never forgetting what a Duncton mole should be. How many times did he conquer his own fear to lead others on and out of danger? Countless times! But at least he was aided and abetted in these acts of courage by the two moles who had first shown such willingness to help him, Elynor and her son Cluniac.

And brave Hamble too, who had finally rejected violence and turned his back on Rooster; he lived with his new-found pacifism, applying all his skills of fieldcraft and warfare, not against the Newborns (who might have suffered heavily at his paws in so secret a war as that which could have been waged in the High Wood), but to help the rebels survive.

So it was that by June, when Noakes arrived, rebel watchers trained by Hamble and posted across the High Wood had spotted the coming of the strangers and spied on them. For molemonths past Hamble had forecast that sooner or later moles would come in from the outside world, to bring news of what was happening and, more important still, to give Hamble and Pumpkin some guidance as to how best to continue their occupation of the High Wood.

'They'll need help reaching the safety of these tunnels when they come,' Hamble had warned, and sure enough, when Noakes arrived, if the rebel watchers down by the cross-under had not diverted the guardmoles the newcomers would certainly have been spotted before they reached the High Wood.

We may imagine the excitement in the rebels' tunnels that greeted the news that after so long, and so many disappointments, three moles had arrived from the outside world of moledom. But there was some consternation that two of them had lain low, while the other set off westward across the wood.

'What's he about then?' growled Hamble.

'As far as I could work it out,' the watcher said, still breathless from running to report, 'he's off to the Stone in the hope that he'll find a follower.'

'Strange they were able to get through so many defences, even if in the end it was our watchers made it possible for them to reach the High Wood undetected,' said Hamble. 'It could be one of the New-

251

borns' little tricks. They send in a few moles from "outside" and wait for us to make contact. Then in come their forces . . .'

'On the other paw,' observed Pumpkin, who always took a positive view of moles, 'if they *are* genuine then one or other of them will run straight into a Newborn patrol before the day's out, and we know what that'll mean for them. We had better reinforce the watchers already with them and take them in for questioning somewhere neutral where we'll give nothing away of ourselves.'

It was in this context, then unknown to him, that there followed a day Noakes never forgot, and an evening he would never wish to repeat. The High Wood through which he travelled seemed to be populated with moles he could not quite hear, and not quite see. Skilled in fieldcraft as he had become, he had the sense that moles were following him who were more experienced than he – at least in that strange and largely silent environment of high and ancient trees, fallen rotting branches, whose mosses and coloured lichens showed they had been undisturbed for many a year, and massive grey beech roots whose shadows could hide a thousand secrets, and many a watching mole. As for moving silently, it was nearly impossible, for the Wood's floor was covered by a deep layer of golden-brown leaf-litter which rustled and crackled as soon as a mole looked at it.

By the time the trees thinned towards what he felt sure was the Stone Clearing he was tired out with the stress of it all, and sweat trickled down his back, though it was not that warm. Then, through the trees, not quite fully visible, he saw for the first time a gathering of light about a rising, soaring form, grey-green, powerful beyond the branches. He sensed that he was about to enter the presence of something living and potent, awesome beyond anything he had ever dreamed.

'The Duncton Stone,' he whispered, putting one faltering paw ahead of the next, his hear thumping, his breathing quickening.

'Aye, mole, so it is!' said a rough voice behind him as four great paws descended, crushed him down to the ground and held him motionless.

'Well, and what are you doing here?' the voice whispered heavily in his ear as he struggled in vain to turn around to see the faces of his captors, rather than merely their solid and determined paws which ranged the ground around him.

Should he say Newborn or follower? He did not know and could not guess. Say the wrong thing and he was done for – though come

252

to think of it, it would be better to claim to be Newborn. If they were Newborn he could perhaps fool them; and if they were not he could seek to convince them of his true identity once . . . they . . . had . . . let . . . him . . . go!

'Stop struggling, Brother,' said the voice harshly, 'and answer our question.'

Newborn, they were Newborn! 'Brother' had given them away.

'I'm just a . . .' But as he began to speak he caught a second glimpse of the Stone between their paws, rising to the sky, solid, glistening with light, so powerful, so true that the lie he was in the act of telling turned and nearly choked him. He could not deny the Stone, or pretend to be what he was not so near its presence. How many times had moles like Fieldfare and Spurling said that there always comes a time when a mole must stance up on all fours and say clearly who he is and what he believes in, come what may. That moment came for Noakes now.

'Follower!' he cried out, struggling. 'I'm a follower and proud of it. Come as a solitary pilgrim to Duncton to worship before the most famous Stone in moledom.'

But they seemed not to believe him.

'Follower, eh!' said one of those holding him, thumping his head into the ground.

'A pilgrim?' Thump.

'Worship?' Thump, thump.

'Famous?' Thump.

There was a ringing in his ears, and stars in his eyes as he was dragged up to his paws; his head reeled and he found himself staring into the eyes of a large, fight-scarred mole of middle age with dark grey eyes. As solid a guardmole as he had ever seen, though he carried himself more like one of the Brother Commanders Noakes had heard of.

'Yes!' said Noakes, his head painful, 'I'm a follower and proud of it.'

'Oh, aye?' said the mole dubiously, with a cynical glance at the two younger moles with him which suggested he did not believe a word. The others smiled bleakly, and looking at them Noakes could not help thinking that they looked mean, thin and hungry, and that he would not like to meet them in a narrow tunnel on a dark night.

'Yes, I *am* a follower,' he said firmly.

The leader seemed about to speak when from behind them, beyond the bole of the tree he had just passed and from which, he guessed, his captors had so silently and effectively emerged, came the cry, 'Newborns! Go west!'

He was summarily grabbed again, and desperately trying to work out what this new turn of events meant – Newborns fleeing from Newborns? Very strange! – he found himself hurried towards the Stone, then past it, across the Clearing and out on the other side before he could catch his breath.

Then, as he breathed in at last and he began to think that these moles might just be followers after all, the ground seemed to open up beneath him, he was rushed down into a huge tunnel and pushed bodily along it for what seemed a long time. His limbs and head banged against walls, roots, as well as the edges of portals and goodness knows what, until suddenly he was thrust into an echoing chamber and told, 'Shut up. Don't move. Don't speak.'

The paws gripping him relaxed; he saw that only one of the thin, mean-looking moles remained with him, and as his eyes adjusted to the gloom he found himself in as ancient and strangely delved a chamber as any he had ever seen.

But if its carvings and convoluted walls, with all their shadows and glimmering light, at first diverted him, it was the strange sounds that soon took up his attention: pawsteps, thousand of them; distant cries, horrible; straining roots of a tree above that seemed about to fall and crush them both; and shadows, that might be more than shadows for all he knew, so dangerous did they feel, so threatening. He looked at the mole who had stayed with him and found sharp, intelligent, weary eyes looking into his.

'Welcome to the Ancient System of Duncton Wood,' whispered the mole, his words gyring away into echoes about him, 'don't move, don't speak. We'll have to wait until they bring your friends.'

'My . . . ?' began Noakes, appalled that they even knew he had come with other moles. He had thought he had done so well. But the mole put a talon to his mouth to shush him, and then glanced meaningfully around the chamber into whose dark crevices that single word 'My' had been sucked, and was now spewed forth back at him, filthy, foul, fragmented and dangerous.

'Dark Sound?' mouthed Noakes, at once frightened and astonished, yet fascinated too.

The mole nodded, brought his head close and whispered, 'Just in case you're wondering, you *never* get used to it!'

The two moles looked at each other and exchanged a wry, conspiratorial grin, and as evening approached and the light dimmed, and the

254

sounds grew worse, all Noakes could think to do to stem the rampant tide of fears that the Dark Sound put in his mind was to remember his brief glimpse of the Duncton Stone. He now understood what he had vaguely sensed as he passed it so swiftly; that in coming to it, he was a mole who had come home.

He remembered old Raistow's account of his journey to the Duncton Stone so many years before, and the speech at the debate in Seven Barrows that had sent him on his way here. Well, he supposed he was here now, and trusted that his friends were somewhere and with someone as safe as he was.

Chapter Twenty-Two

It was not until the next day, after a terrifying night of Dark Sound followed by a trek through echoing tunnels lit only by the dimmest of dawn light, that Noakes was reunited with his friends. It had been 'too dangerous', he had been told, to meet up earlier; the Dark Sound in the tunnels had been stirring malevolently since the previous evening and the rebels had lain low, Noakes and his watcher at one end of the Ancient System, his friends and the rebels who had found them at the other.

The big mole who had treated him so roughly on the surface was Hamble, and he had taken the opportunity to interrogate Noakes' companions, and heard their story. All was now friendly and jocular, though apologies for the head-thumping and battering Noakes had received were perfunctory: that, it seemed, was a risk moles took who dared venture into the High Wood.

The position regarding the Newborns was swiftly explained to the visitors, before they were taken into a chamber mercifully free from Dark Sound, wind-sound or any sound at all, except for the excited chatter of an ill-fed, mostly old, yet strangely inspiring group of moles led, 'Not by *me*,' as the warrior mole Hamble mysteriously explained to Noakes and the other two, 'but by Pumpkin – who will be with us shortly.'

Pumpkin! The mole Noakes had most wanted to meet, and for whom he had many messages from Fieldfare, whose friend he had been in the days before the Newborns. What a leader he must be to be in charge of such moles as these, with a formidable character like Hamble deferring to him! He had never really believed Fieldfare's description of the 'library aide' as thin, old and mild. How could he be?

Hamble had asked Noakes and his companions to postpone more detailed telling of their story until Pumpkin joined them, but it was not easy with so many moles clustering about, as eager for news as for sun at the end of winter.

Suddenly there was a cheer, ragged at first as the moles only slowly realized that Pumpkin had slipped in amongst them, then louder as he was seen, grabbed, and raised on high. Relief in the chamber was palpable. Noakes had never seen so many moles so happy all at once.

But he they cheered was lowered back to the ground, struggling to be let down sooner than he was, blinking with embarrassment, frowning with the dismay of a modest mole upon whom attention has centred, and Noakes realized with a shock that *this* was Pumpkin.

His snout was thin and scholarly, his eyes gentle, his fur so patchy about his face that the skin was creased and crinkly, his paws pale, his manner diffident.

'I must apologize for my friends,' were his first words, 'but they are somewhat over-excited by your arrival here, and attribute it to me, though of course it is the Stone's doing, not mine. Now . . .'

But Noakes, bold mole that he was, and with an instinctive sense of the right thing to do in an assembly of moles such as this, raised a paw and said, 'Pumpkin, sir, before anything else is said there is something I must do!'

There was an immediate and expectant hush.

'I won't say it's an easy thing to do, seeing as I hardly know you, but I did promise that I would do it, as my friends here will confirm.'

The two moles nodded their heads and grinned.

'Yes,' he continued, approaching nearer to Pumpkin and looking somewhat embarrassed, 'I am not a mole to promise to do something and not deliver. Fieldfare's last words to me before we left . . .'

There was a sigh amongst the Duncton followers at this mention of the much-loved Fieldfare, and Pumpkin, always an emotional mole, blinked once or twice.

'. . . her last words were, and she's not a mole easily denied in matters of the heart . . .'

'That's true,' said Pumpkin quietly.

'. . . her last words were, "Noakes! The first thing you do when you see Pumpkin is to tell him Fieldfare loves him through and through and that he's as brave a mole as ever was, and give him a hug from me!"'

There was a great cheer at these words and the sincere way Noakes said them, and an even greater cheer when, without more ado, he took Pumpkin in his paws and gave him such a hug as lifted him right off the ground for a second or two.

'Well!' said Pumpkin, wiping away a tear and straightening the ruffles on his meagre fur. 'Nothing gives me greater pleasure than to know Fieldfare is safe and well and unchanged! Always warm-hearted, always thinking of others!

'But there's news to impart and we all want to hear it, for we've been besieged here without sight or sound of other moles for far too long. Therefore Noakes of the Seven Barrows and your good friends, welcome! If you have slept and eaten and are refreshed then we would be glad if you'll tell us all you know!'

As Noakes began to report the many things that Fieldfare and Spurling had instructed him to impart, beginning with the Wildenhope killings and what was known of Newborn advances in the south, the mood in the chamber changed. Pumpkin and his doughty friends had already been prepared for some of it by Hamble, who had been the first to bring confirmation of Chater's death, a grim fact that Noakes had only so far heard as a surmise by Fieldfare herself.

But this was altogether different: that Whillan had apparently been killed, and Rooster had died trying to save him; and Privet had wandered off alone and had by now probably been done to death by the Newborns. How dark did the feelings run! How sombre the moles, their silence interspersed with tears and cries of grief. Were they then alone now, without hope of being saved?

'No, moles, we are not!' cried out Pumpkin. 'The Stone is with us, and it will be with those we love, who I do not believe for one minute have died! We shall fight on!'

This did something to cheer up the beleaguered moles, as did Hamble's affirmation of faith that all would be well – now was the hour when they must keep their nerve, and plan for victory . . .

There then took place the kind of debate which Noakes had already been part of in Seven Barrows, in which moles cut off from others, and feeling the threat of the enemy, discuss the options open to them and must strike a balance in the end between those eager to rush off and do *anything* just to feel they are doing *something*, and those made passive by events and unwilling to act at all.

Naturally, much was said of Privet's retreat into Silence and its possible meaning, and Pumpkin was able to add something to the ideas expressed that Noakes for one had not heard before.

'You must understand that Keeper Privet is first and foremost a mole of the heart, before ever she was a scholar. Driven by a love of Rooster, Master of the Delve, a love she lost on the Moors as she believed, she journeyed to Beechenhill, and then by slow and tragic degrees to our own system here, in search of the very thing that my Master Stour begged her to set forth and seek once more: the Book of Silence. Be in no doubt that this great Book exists, awaiting a mole worthy enough to find it for the moledom that awaits its coming.'

Pumpkin spoke quietly, and though he never for a moment let moles forget that he regarded himself as no more than an aide to others greater, yet the moleyears of Newborn repression that had forced reluctant leadership upon him had given him a strange and benevolent authority. Few leaders in moledom's modern history have been as gentle, mild, self-effacing, and yet as effective as Pumpkin, library aide.

Now, as he spoke of the Book of Silence in the context of Privet's courageous and historic retreat the moles began to understand for the first time what the goal and purpose of that retreat might be, and it seemed, when it was explained, so obvious: 'To find the Book of Silence, *that*'s Privet's hope and deepest desire,' as Pumpkin put it.

'But moles must understand the paradox in what she does. She seeks what cannot be sought; she desires what cannot be desired; she journeys that she may find a way back to the still centre of her heart. It is a journey others have set out upon, from which none have returned to this life.'

'Will she be successful?' asked Noakes, speaking for them all.

Pumpkin shrugged; 'I do not know. It has been my privilege to serve some of the greatest scholars of moledom – beginning of course with Master Stour himself. Many a student I have seen come to Duncton Wood and emerge years later as a scholar, able to ken the most abstruse texts, able to explicate the difficult, and gloss the obscure, and make associations which others have missed. Yet few of these moles have had what I call heart, or love, for fellow moles: not the deep and abiding love that comes from suffering, from humility, from turning the scholarly snout from text and argument to life and emotion.

'Of them all Privet was the only one I felt had courage and intellect to go beyond. When she left Duncton Wood in those fateful days of the Newborn takeover I sensed she was a mole who was aware that the task ahead might be more onerous than she could ever imagine, and that she needed time and courage to turn her snout towards it.

'Today we have heard only a little of what is happening out in moledom now, and most of that surmise. But more news will come, and it will be better news! Meanwhile somewhere, somehow, Privet saw what she must do, and at Wildenhope she began that journey into Silence – or perhaps, more accurately, I should say she resumed her journey to find the Book of Silence, which started a long time ago

259

at holy Beechenhill. Moles, these are critical times, in which the threat of the Newborns is but a part of a whole, and important though it is to us we should see beyond them to the coming of the Book itself.'

'You believe it will be brought back to Duncton Wood?'

Pumpkin nodded his head slowly. 'The other Books are here, and the Master Stour himself placed them beneath the Stone. That's something I witnessed with my own eyes.'

There was an awed whispering among the moles at this, for though many believed this was what Pumpkin had done he had never before publicly admitted it.

'Aye,' said Pumpkin, 'and the Stillstone of Silence, why, that was returned to Duncton in readiness many decades ago, brought by Woodruff of Arbor Low, grandson of Tryfan of Duncton. And from whence did he bring the Stillstone?'

There was silence, and though many knew the answer only now did they see the significance of Noakes' coming that day, and why Pumpkin should invoke memories of the past of the Stillstone of Silence, and predictions of the future concerning the coming of the Book.

'It came from Seven Barrows, like you and your friends, good Noakes. Such connections are the Stone's way of telling us that its work is being done, its tasks fulfilled. The holy circle is closing, the spirit that deserted Duncton over the centuries during which these tunnels have been lost and desolate of mole, that spirit is returning. With it will come, must come, the holy Book of Silence. The circle gapes still but we of faith wait on, we pray, we trust, we do what we can.'

The community of rebels was hushed as Pumpkin's voice faded, and Noakes, to whom his words had been addressed, had never felt so inspired in his life. This then was the spirit of the Duncton moles of which he had heard so much – not a spirit of battle and war as he had thought, but one of faith and trust, as unstoppable as the seasons. A spirit all the more impressive coming from such as Pumpkin, and having in its service warrior moles like Hamble, who had, it seemed, eschewed force in favour of peaceful persuasion.

'Not that my head isn't still sore!' thought Noakes to himself wryly – force still had its uses for some it seemed!

'It seems to me likely that Noakes here won't be the only mole on his way to Duncton Wood,' said Hamble. 'I've listened well to all he's said, and am appalled by the events of Wildenhope. But there's nomole here can convince me that Rooster's dead. Rooster doesn't die, not until his delving task is done. As for Whillan . . .' But there was something about the Noakes' report that made it more difficult to see how Whillan could have escaped his drowning. '. . . well, words fail me. I only hope it's not true!'

'As you have faith in Rooster's survival, I have faith in Whillan's,' said Pumpkin. 'I can't believe the mole I first saw as a gasping, dying pup, whom I taught scribing to, whose adoptive mother was Privet herself . . . no, no! The Stone wouldn't let him die! Wouldn't . . .'

Pumpkin's voice faded suddenly, and a most strange look came to his face: he seemed puzzled, curious, surprised, even astonished, as if a startling possibility had just occurred to him.

'What is it, mole?' asked Hamble, and they all shifted forward a little, thinking perhaps that Pumpkin had been taken ill.

'You look as if you missed a heartbeat, Pumpkin! You all right?' called out one of the old ones.

'There's more than one way of dying,' whispered Pumpkin, almost to himself. 'A mole said that once . . . no, a mole scribed it. Oh dear, if I was a scholar I'd remember the text but there's so many folios have passed before my eyes and through my paws I get them jumbled up. Sturne would know.'

'You can't trust *him*,' said one of the moles.

'No, no, of course I can't. But there was a mole scribed about death and how moles must die to be new-born, I—'

'Newborn?' called out another mole. 'They've not got you on their side, have they, Pumpkin?'

There was a general laugh, but it was not one Hamble, Elynor or Cluniac joined in, for they could see that Pumpkin was much troubled by some distant memory he could not quite place, which had been prompted by the grim account of Whillan's fate.

'Not just Whillan, don't you see?' said Pumpkin later to these three, when the tale-telling was over and moles had dispersed somewhat. 'All three of them, a trinity of moles: and all so strangely connected! Privet in retreat in search of the Book of Silence; Rooster surely having to "die" if he is to find his way back to his task as Master of the Delve; and Whillan, who came here so young, so innocent, and may have "died" too, aye, died in a way a mere body never can. Died to be new-born.'

'It's time we tried to tell moles outside there's moles in Duncton Wood have survived the Newborn inquisition here!' interrupted the practical Hamble. 'These musings are all very well, but there's work

261

to be done! Now listen, when I came through Rollright on my way here I met some followers who agreed to lie low until they heard from me. It's not been worth the risk contacting them until now, but with Noakes coming here, and the growing sense that the hour of rebellion is approaching, as what you say seems to imply, Pumpkin, we should send moles out to find Hodder, and tell him to . . .'

'We'll go!' cried out Noakes when it was put to him, his friends nodding their agreement. 'And we'll go today!'

'Aye, I know you want to, lads,' said Hamble, 'and I can think of no moles better. You got here in one piece, and the Stone seems to have chosen you for such tasks as these. But not today! You'll need to rest up a bit here, and I'll tell you the safest route, though Rollright's not that far.'

'It isn't!' said Pumpkin. 'Chater the journeymole once did it in a matter of two or three days, as I remember.'

Hamble nodded. 'Meanwhile, we'll send more watchers down to the cross-under, for I've a feeling what Pumpkin said earlier is true: now Noakes has reached Duncton, soon others will follow, and they'll need help as well if they're to get through safely.'

'So they will – for now,' said Pumpkin softly. 'But there'll come a day when the cross-under of Duncton is free again, and moles do not have to cross the roaring owl way to gain access to what should be a place of liberty. And then . . .' and here Pumpkin's face assumed a wistful look, '. . . this mole, for one, will be happy to retreat from the stresses and strains of secret rebellion, and return to helping scholars with their texts, and pursuing his own quiet interests in the matter of Duncton's local history! Not all this . . . this . . . this fuss! This bother! It's so tiresome, so off the point of what the Stone's about!'

The moles laughed in sympathy with Pumpkin, and went about their tasks with a sense of faith and purpose they had not dared feel for many a long moleyear.

Chapter Twenty-Three

But where Duncton was concerned, matters were moving even faster than Pumpkin and Hamble could have predicted.

Two days after Noakes' arrival, and but hours before he set off on his quest to find Hodder in Rollright, a watcher from the cross-under came racing up the slopes to find Pumpkin and the others.

'There's moles come!' he declared. 'And such moles too! Fierce-looking, silent, warriors all of them! They were spotted on the far side of the way, trying to cross, and whilst the other watchers stayed behind to receive them – for it's plain they're not Newborns – I was sent up here to alert you.'

'Hamble! Noakes! If you'll be so kind, come with me!' said Pumpkin, at his most assertive. 'No, not you, Cluniac. You can gather the others under the eye of Elynor and make sure nomole goes off for a wander. We've been lucky these days past not to have Newborn attention, but with more moles on the way to the High Wood you never can tell.'

'It's all right, Cluniac,' growled Hamble, 'you can go with Pumpkin if you like, for my bones are aching this afternoon. I'll gather our moles together with Elynor.'

'Thank you!' said the youngster, who had earlier been denied permission to travel with Noakes and was feeling frustrated.

Noakes' coming had been the cause of excitement; the arrival now of 'warrior moles' gave rise to much eager speculation. Who were they? What did they want? And what did it mean for the rebels? One thing seemed certain: all was changing now, the long-awaited time of conflict and resolution was at paw.

How the time dragged up in the High Wood as Hamble and Elynor waited with the older moles to see whatmoles had arrived. Then another watcher came racing in, from the edge of the High Wood itself.

'They're followers all right, and quite a few of them, and they're coming now!'

A patter of paws above, deep voices, echoing tunnels, the rumble and roar of Dark Sound responding from the depths of the Ancient

System, as if it knew change was apaw, and suddenly the communal chamber was filling with strangers who stopped and peered for a time into the gloom as their eyes grew accustomed to the change of light.

Big moles, strong moles, fierce-looking moles, unkempt from travelling, scenting of sweat and mud and the fumes of the roaring owl way; mutters and occasional laughter until, emerging from their midst came thin Pumpkin saying, 'If you'll come this way please, yes, follow me, Hamble's over here.'

'Hamble!' cried out a familiar voice from the crowding strangers, and for a moment Hamble did not recognize the grinning, sharp features of Weeth; which was barely surprising, for down the left side of his face, beginning dangerously near his eye and ending only at the corner of his mouth, was a jagged and barely-healed wound.

'Yes, it's me, remember?'

Hamble laughed in his warm deep way, and with a buffet to Weeth's shoulders said, 'Nomole is more welcome here than you. But you've been in the wars, my friend!' He quickly confirmed to Pumpkin and the others that this was the cunning Weeth he had often mentioned to them.

'I wish there were more of us,' said Weeth at last, the grin fading. 'Maple sent us from the Wolds to find out what was apaw in Duncton and give you what news we had, but things are changing fast in moledom now, and dangerously so.'

'How come?' said Hamble, suddenly alert.

'First, let me introduce my companions,' said Weeth. 'I'm the talker, they're the doers! First there's Arvon of Siabod . . .'

'Siabod!' went the whisper throughout the chamber, for allmole knew that from Bracken's day more than a century before there had been connections between Duncton and dark Siabod, original home of Mandrake, whose takeover of Duncton had marked the beginning of its modern history, and perhaps that of all moledom. They looked at Arvon in awe – at his black wiry fur, his stolid muscular body, his sharp fierce eyes, and they felt his natural authority.

'Good-day,' he said nodding at them with the briefest of smiles. 'I'll not labour over the rest of the introductions as Weeth would, liking the graceful word as he does. There's no time for that now, and you'll get to know us well enough in the days ahead.' His voice was lilting and accented, and nothing brought home to the Duncton moles better than his coming that there was a great world beyond their system, and its dangers and possibilities would soon be more a part of their lives than ever before. Their isolation was over.

264

But Arvon had said 'There's no time for that now,' and referred ominously to 'the days ahead'. Matters sounded serious indeed, and this inference was confirmed when Weeth spoke again.

'Matters are very serious. We came, as I say, to make contact, expecting to exchange news and plans for contingencies. Maple likes doing things thoroughly. But, well . . .'

'Well, Weeth? Get on with it, mole!' said Hamble.

'All my life moles have been telling me to get on with it! One day . . .' sighed Weeth, with mock self-pity.

'One day, Weeth, a mole's going to throttle you,' muttered Arvon, though not without evident affection, 'and it will probably be me.'

'Well then,' said Weeth, suddenly becoming grave. 'We had been hoping to come direct to Duncton from the Wolds by the south-eastern route of the River Evenlode, but Newborns were thick on the ground in the vales and we were forced into northerly diversions by way of systems like Norton and Banbury. I am not exactly a fighting mole, but there were skirmishes enough to last a lifetime before I received this present injury at nearby Rollright; fortunately I had Arvon and his band of merry moles with me.'

The 'merry' moles looked on grimly as Weeth ran briefly through what had in fact been a hard and dangerous journey in which his own role had been conspicuous and courageous.

'But at least the diversions meant we saw more of the Newborn Crusades than we might otherwise have done, and took the opportunity of having a quiet little chat to a few Newborn guardmoles who wandered across our path.' Weeth grinned amiably, but none was left in doubt that a 'little chat' with Arvon and the others might not be a pleasant experience.

'It seems that things are not going quite the way the Newborns would have wanted. The solid occupation of the Wolds by Maple has taken up the time and energy of more Newborns than Quail would wish, and he is not pleased. At the same time there are reports of resistance in many systems across moledom, for which Privet's heroic stance at Wildenhope, and the subsequent dissemination from an anonymous source of a very accurate text describing the killings may be thanked, or blamed, depending on your point of view.*

'Putting it bluntly, it seems that the Newborns are just beginning to realize that their Crusades may not succeed. Now, we've just come

---

* It was not yet known that Thripp himself had been the author of the text concerning the Wildenhope Killings which did so much damage to Quail's cause.

265

from Rollright after a little altercation with some of their guardmoles, and finally with their Brother Commander no less, from which I gained this facial memento. We learned that Quail, the Elder Senior Brother Quail, is coming to Duncton Wood in the hope that he might be able to direct his war upon moledom better from here than from obscure Caradoc. You should expect no mercy at all from Quail, since he is showing none to his hapless Brother Commanders. To be recalled to Caradoc by Quail is as likely to end with a sentence of death as with promotion; all, naturally, in the name of the glorious Stone!'

'Quail's coming here?' gasped his listeners.

'So it seems. Now, I suggest that Hamble and Arvon, who know about such things, advise you how best to defend yourselves, while the worthy Pumpkin and I – and I have many a message for *you*, sir, from Maple and Rooster—'

'Rooster?' cried out several moles. 'The Master of the Delve?' The news was coming almost too thick and fast for moles to take in.

'The same,' cried out Weeth dramatically. 'Safe and sound, if a little wet, after his ordeal in a certain river east of Wildenhope Bluff . . .'

But his voice was drowned by cheering, and a chattering excitement that told its own story: their time of isolation was truly over. Relief had come, but with it new danger and new challenges. But Rooster, Master of the Delve, was *alive*, and in that news was the best indication they had yet received that the Stone's purpose was being served by the followers, amongst whom they so proudly numbered themselves.

'Yes, he's alive. And he says Whillan's alive too . . .' (which provoked still louder cheers) '. . . though how he knows I have no idea. Masters of the Delve are *most* mysterious! But, as I was trying to say, the defence will be in the capable paws of Hamble and Arvon, whilst Pumpkin and myself have several matters to discuss, and possibilities to consider!'

It was as much as Weeth could say before a mêlée of talk, excited exclamations and greetings drowned the rest of his words. Food, rest, talk, news, and plans, all were needed now, and the rebels of the High Wood rushed about servicing the needs of the weary guests, and listening to the stories and tales that they told; while moles like Hamble and Pumpkin, Arvon and Weeth, with Noakes available to do whatever task they set him, and young Cluniac hoping for an assignment of some sort, talked on and on in low voices and with furrowed brows: Quail coming; defence needed; and the Newborns no longer in the ascendant in moledom.

266

'But danger, danger, everywhere,' said Weeth, much later, 'and much to decide.'

Later again, when sleep was creeping up on many a mole but before any quite succumbed to it, Pumpkin said this prayer in the communal chamber for them all: 'Stone, grant that the troubled days ahead of moledom may be resolved without loss of life to follower or Newborn. Grant that a way may be found that leads to reconciliation. Grant that those who seek to fulfil the tasks they pursue in your name may be guided by your Light. We are troubled, Stone, and wander still in the tunnels of darkness: give us comfort, give us hope, give us life again.'

'Some hope,' muttered more than one mole to himself as sleep overtook him; yet there was comfort in Pumpkin's simple plea.

Much later still, when deep night had come and all moles but the watchers slept, Pumpkin stirred and crept out and up through the whispering tunnels to the surface.

'Can't sleep, sir?' asked a look-out softly.

'Not too well, no,' said Pumpkin, the stars of the night shining on his tired and worried face.

'Going to the Stone as usual, sir?'

'To pray, yes,' said Pumpkin.

'Let one of us accompany you. For Stone's sake, one of these nights—'

Pumpkin shook his head and said quietly, 'No, no, I need to be alone sometimes. Now, I must be off.'

But it was not to the Stone that he went; nor towards the Stone that he hurried through the night-still Wood; nor to the Stone he went to pray – but to Sturne's austere quarters on the Eastside slopes just beyond the Library, to report and to warn. Of the coming of Weeth and the others sent by Maple, Sturne naturally knew nothing, but of Quail . . .

'I know, I know, Pumpkin, I heard it from Brother Fetter this afternoon. I have been much concerned about how to tell you: Quail will be here before two days are out. He has Thripp with him. There are to be trials and arraignments, and from Duncton a new wave of terror is to be prosecuted across moledom. Pumpkin, what is to come will be worse than what has gone before, unless there is some way to stop it.'

'There *will* be a way, there *must* be a way,' said Pumpkin earnestly, 'but I don't know where to turn to find it. The coming of moles like Weeth and Arvon is all to the good I'm sure, but I do not want to see

Duncton itself riven by a bloody war, and nor does Hamble. There has got to be another way forward.'

'You're tired, mole,' said Sturne with unaccustomed gentleness. 'Here, stance yourself down and rest. Dawn will not be with us for a while yet.'

Pumpkin did as he was asked, and Sturne found him a thin worm from his meagre stock, which the library aide dabbed at in a dilatory sort of way.

'I wasn't trained for this kind of thing, Sturne,' he muttered. 'I'm no good at it at all, full of doubts, not a strong leader . . .'

Sturne admitted a bleak smile to his lined face.

'You are a leader, Pumpkin, and a good one, whether you like it or not.'

'Humph!' said Pumpkin, finally chewing the worm and relaxing. 'Humph! What other news did you get from Fetter?'

'Rumours, stories, nothing factual. Nothing certain, nothing you would wish to scribe into a text.'

'Like what?' said Pumpkin, who could see Sturne had something more to say, but was reluctant to do so. He either doesn't believe it, Pumpkin thought to himself, or it's not 'factually substantiated' enough for his academic mind!

'Tittle-tattle. Idle dreams of moles with nothing better to talk about. I dislike peddling rumours – they become accepted fact and then scholars like me have to spend the years disproving them.'

'Like *what*?' said Pumpkin again, the familiar exasperation with Sturne returning. If only the Acting Master Librarian would let himself go for once! Rumour arose from emotion, and that was why he did not like it.

'Well then,' said Sturne, reluctant, his mouth pursing with distaste, 'I'll tell you what I'm told is being said, and it's the main reason Quail is so anxious to get to Duncton fast. He wants to be here before it comes.'

'*What* comes?' poor Pumpkin almost shouted.

'The Book of Silence.'

The Book of Silence . . .

'The Book itself?' gasped Pumpkin.

'They're saying the Book of Silence has been found.'

Pumpkin could only stare into the enshadowed eyes of Sturne. His own eyes were wide with excitement, all weariness gone.

'But it's not true, you see, it can't be true,' said Sturne.

'Why not?'

268

'The Book's here, it has always been here.'

'*Here?*'

'That's what our Master Stour always believed, that it was deep and safe in the Ancient System.'

'Here in the Ancient System?' said Pumpkin incredulously.

Sturne nodded. 'That's why he went into retreat into the Ancient System not once but twice, and it killed him in the end. He was seeking the Book of Silence.'

'How do you know?'

'He told me.' The two moles looked at each other and Pumpkin knew that Sturne would never lie, and had never lied. He spoke the truth.

'But he never found it?' said Pumpkin.

'Oh, but he did, you see, he did – or more accurately, he found out where it must be. It was just that he did not have the strength to go on into that Dark Sound. You saw what the other Books involved, you shared the burden of them with me in the Chamber of Roots at Longest Night when we helped Master Stour take them at last to the Stone.'

'Why did he not tell me? I was . . . I mean I would have . . . I . . .'

For the first time in his long life Pumpkin felt he had been betrayed by Master Stour, or not trusted at any rate. *That* felt like betrayal, and Sturne saw how deeply hurt he was.

'My dear friend,' said Sturne, 'Master Stour wanted to tell you so much and he knew how hurt you would be when you found out you had not been told. But you see, he was sure that if you knew, you would, as you were about to say, have wished to help him. More than that, that you would have done anything to help him, for you were and remain a library aide whose sense of service goes far beyond the bounds of duty. He knew it, and he valued it, but he also wished to protect you from it.'

'But why? If he had found the Book, then it was only a matter—'

'"Only a matter"!' cried out Sturne. 'Mole, it would have killed you as it so nearly killed him. He knew where the Book could be found – deep in the Ancient System, through those tunnels nomole can venture through, nor emerge from alive. The ones, my dear friend, *you* know something about . . .'

They looked at each other, remembering that grim night when Pumpkin and Cluniac had barely escaped with their lives from their foolhardy attempt to explore the central section of the Ancient System.

'I now think that but one mole can lead the way right into the centre and find what it is that the mediaeval Masters of the Delve sought so successfully to hide away, and protect with Dark Sound.'

'You think the Book of Silence is hidden there, don't you?'

'I do.'

'And that Privet's the one to fetch it?'

'Aye, I do,' said Sturne quietly.

A tawny owl hooted and then was gone from a nearby tree on the surface above them; the first light of dawn touched the portal of Sturne's tunnels, grey-violet and dim.

'I want to think the same, but if it's so why did Stour send her from Duncton?' demanded Pumpkin, angry now, and confused. 'If he knew the Book was here . . . did he see the Book? Are you sure he could have known?'

'He knew or guessed,' said Sturne firmly. 'Why did he send Privet forth? I think because he understood that she was not yet ready to take up the challenge of the Book of Silence, and find a way, or the strength, to take it up from the centre of the Ancient System and then through the Chamber of Roots to the base of the Stone and so complete the circle of Books and Stillstones. Her present retreat into Silence is the last part of a journey that will bring her back in readiness to Duncton Wood.'

'And to the Newborns, and Quail, and danger,' said Pumpkin regretfully.

'You will help her,' said Sturne softly. 'Stour believed you would be the one she would need.'

'Me?' said Pumpkin faintly. Oh yes, he remembered the Books, and the near-impossibility of holding them and the terrible toll they took of a mole. He thought too of the Dark Sound of the Ancient System, delved so many centuries before by Masters unknown, as he guessed too, to protect the Book of Silence until a great mole came. It was all waiting for them! As, in some way, he had always felt it must be.

'I will do whatever I can, Keeper Sturne, you know that.'

'I know it, mole, and the Master Stour knew it. Above all moles he ever worked with or ever knew, you were the one he trusted for the task of aiding Privet of Crowden.'

'A mole can only do his best,' whispered Pumpkin.

'And *your* best, Library Aide Pumpkin, is the very best there is!'

Weeth's description of the panic and recriminations that had swept across moledom through the molemonths of June and the beginning of July was accurate, and it had been into this very wave of danger, bloody and terrible, that Hibbott of Ashbourne Chase had unknowingly set off after his stay in the Community of Rose at the southern edge of the Midland Wen. Let us join him on his pilgrimage once more . . .

His cause had not been helped by his bold, if ingenuous, insistence that there was no virtue in going on a pilgrimage in search of Privet of Duncton Wood if he did not honestly tell others whatmole it was he sought.

'I was surprised,' he later scribed in the account of his great pilgrimage, 'that mere mention of Privet's name should send moles scurrying for cover, or disappearing into their portals, or hotpaw (as it finally turned out) to report my presence to a group of Newborn guardmoles who, unhappily, were ensconced nearby.

'Before I knew what was happening I was surrounded by large and brutal moles who demanded my name, and asked where I had come from. It seemed plain to me that the Stone must have sent me into their path because in some way as yet unknown to me they would help lead me nearer the object of my quest. I therefore bade them welcome, and told them they really had no need to buffet me to the ground, stamp on my head and abuse me, as we had common cause. Were we not all seeking peace and harmony? However, these words appeared to incense them further and I found myself being dragged along into unwholesome tunnels and cast into a chamber with other moles, who, I came to realize, were their captives.

'Only later did I know that I had unwittingly arrived at the notorious place of containment called Leamington, whose moles were generally elderly and infirm, and disinclined to support the Newborn cause. This being so they had been massed into a great and unwholesome chamber and there I now joined them, after some unpleasant questioning from which the Newborns deduced that I was a fool and knew nothing about Privet.

'Surrounded as I now was by the groans of the injured and dying, not to mention sights and odours about which I have no wish to scribe, I told myself, "Hibbott, you are on the edge of a void. Gloom and depression beckons, hopelessness and desolation calls, and you must now use all your strength and faith not to be lured towards them, and so into the depth of black despair like these other moles. Therefore, your progress temporarily halted, and the fulfilment of your task in abeyance, you must keep yourself busy and occupied by creating a task for yourself. The Stone will guide you . . ."

271

'With such words as these the positive pilgrim can remind himself of his responsibilities, and avoid the sloughs of despond into which he will be in danger of floundering from time to time on his long journey. Certainly it worked on that occasion for me and I raised my snout, took a good look around, and decided that my task must be to help those poor moles of Leamington as I myself had been helped by the healers of the Community of Rose.

'I am not a healer, and know little of such matters as herbs, and touch, and prayer, as healers need to know. However, it is my observation that moles know more about helping others than they realize, and they may draw upon it, as a honeybee draws upon the nectar of a flower, much more easily if they forget their own little trials and tribulations. A self-absorbed mole is not much help to others, justified though his self-absorption might be! And it is a strange paradox of life, which I will not try to explain here or anywhere else, that a mole often finds that the quickest way to help himself is to help another. I resolved therefore to give what aid I could, and bring what healing to the injured and comfort to the dying I was able.

'Ah, but little did I know how dire was our situation at Leamington, nor how onerous and long would be the time I was forced to spend there!'

Hibbott, as unwittingly as ever, had journeyed straight into one of the most notorious massings of those times, in which some two-thirds of Leamington's followers died in circumstances of much horror and suffering. Deprived of food and water, unable to relieve themselves but where they lay, and with the heat of summer adding to their discomforts, disease and death was their slow lot.

It was Hibbott's fortune, if such a word can apply to such a circumstance, that he was captured towards the end of the massing when the Newborns were growing unwilling to impose the harshest disciplines in the chambers where moles were held, because the conditions had become so foul that guardmoles would no longer venture in. For this reason he had considerable freedom of movement, and as he was in good health, and elicited the sympathy of one or two of the guards, he was able to secure at least a little food and water for those he tried to help. For himself he took the minimum, sensing that he had longer to die than the others, and that if he might keep a few moles alive a few more days then the decline of his own health and strength would be worthwhile.

Never once in his account of those terrible times does he complain of his own grim lot, nor does he make much of his own great contribution. Indeed it has only been through the recent scholarship of Bunnicle the Second (of Witney), that we have come to realize that the shadowy mole mentioned in many of the contemporaneous accounts of the Massing of Leamington as having been a source of comfort and healing to many a mole, was in fact good Hibbott himself.

Yet his is not the only mystery attached to that terrible incident, though it has taken many years for scholars to make sense of the clues; for it is now known that Privet herself was involved, and even more anonymously than she was in the Community of Rose.

This later passage in Hibbott's until now obscure *Pilgrimage*, both explains his anonymity in relation to Leamington, and provides the missing clues which connect Privet with the same affair, and indeed with Hibbott himself.

'I believe,' says Hibbott, 'that after some two molemonths of these conditions, and doing all I could for my fellow moles to keep my own spirit up, I succumbed to fatigue and illness. Certainly I grew gaunt and thin, as one of my charges constantly told me, and my mind began to wander.*

'For this reason I can remember little of Leamington's now famous relief at the paws not of followers but of a new contingent of Newborns led by Brother Commander Thorne of Cannock. Starved and ill as I was, I remember days of wandering, though I now believe that this was largely in my fevered mind. But I woke to reason, and the beginnings of health once more at the gentle paws of a healing mole, a middle-aged female of greying fur, and thin face. She did not speak then, nor did I ever hear her speak, yet to her many found themselves talking, as if in her silence they found a release for their own doubts and fears, hopes and joys.

'I found myself among many others who had barely survived the massing, and in need of time and respite while we recovered ourselves, much as wounded moles from a battle might recover together in some safe place. I remember only that dear, silent mole who came and tended me day and night, as others did, and it was to her visits that I most looked forward.

* This was the redoubtable Spire of Leamington, one-time elder, whose *Out of Disaster came Triumph*, though occasionally inaccurate, offers a personal and moving account of the most notorious Newborn massing of those times. His reference to the mole we know to be Hibbott graphically describes how he ministered to others despite the slow decline of his health, how towards the end he refused several opportunities to escape, and how his faith and prayers sustained the lives of so many until the massing was finally ended.

'I talked little, and nor did I desire to when others asked me what-mole I was and whither I was bound. Certainly I did not dare at first say that it was Privet of Duncton Wood I sought, for what trouble had that got me in already! Yet one night I found myself whispering Privet's name to that silent mole, feeling it was safe to do so, for she never spoke and would not give my secret away!

'Soon I found myself speaking less of Privet than of the many feelings and experiences that had so far arisen in the course of my pilgrimage. It may seem strange that I should have asked her questions knowing she would not answer, but there is something about silence in another that encourages a mole to seek answers to questions he has not dared even ask before. So then I began to do what I had not yet done, which was to wonder why I was upon a pilgrimage, and what it was I hoped to discover.

' "It isn't Privet herself I seek," I told my confidante, "but something about the idea she represents. Yes, I'm sure it's that. Her stance at Wildenhope, of which no doubt you've heard, made me realize that there comes a moment in a mole's life, perhaps many moments, when he must take stock and ask himself truly whither he is bound. I believe with my whole heart that the Stone will guide me to Privet when the time is right, but to discover that moment I must journey trustfully, trying not to strive for what I seek, trying not to seek at all! I feel *you* understand, I feel sure you do!"

'How her clear eyes seemed to bore into me with love and under-standing, how careless I was of her and concerned with my own thoughts and desires! How free I felt to talk of things I had never thought of before. To journey without hope! To seek without desire! To find without searching! What strange ideas were these? What per-plexing paradoxes! Yet such are the questions a pilgrim begins to ask himself along the way, shedding hope and desire, ceasing striving, letting his hungry spirit be as free and vagrant as his roaming body and errant mind!

'Such were the ideas I expressed to that silent healer that long night! And the most abiding impression of all? The sense she gave me that I was free to say what I most feared to say and she would not judge or admonish me. I was free, free to speak what darkness or silliness or nonsense came to my mind, and had time to do so, for she was there like the Silence of the Stone itself.

'I must have fallen asleep, for the next thing I remember was that it was dawn, she had gone, and that I was well, if weak, and ready to resume my pilgrimage. I felt stronger in my mind than I ever had, and all because of a conversation with a mole who never said a word. There is something to be learned from that!

'I knew my time of respite was over and I resolved therefore to slip away from Leamington as anonymously as my silent mentor had slipped away from me. I rose, went quietly and without interruption up to the surface, surveyed the unfamiliar landscape and said to myself, "Well, Hibbott, and in which direction will you point your snout?"

'The sun was rising, there was a morning hush across the distant trees, and I swear I heard a voice, a voice out of Silence, a female voice, and, yes, *her* voice, say, "Mole, you surely know that your way now is south, south to Duncton Wood".

'So, as simply as that, the decision was made. And what did it matter if I knew already that Duncton was occupied by the Newborns, as all the major systems were? It did not. It was there the Stone wished me to go, and if I was captured again, so be it. If I found Privet there, well and good! If not, at least I had followed my pilgrim heart to where instinct and trust had told me I should go. I turned and said a silent farewell to Leamington, I whispered a prayer for the many moles I had come close to in the molemonths past and whom I was now leaving behind, and, shaking the dust from my paws, and whiffling my snout at the cool morning air, I was off and away, and free once more!'

Certainly, then, this passage shows that Hibbott had not then realized that the mole who had helped care for him after the Leamington massing, and to whom through that night of self-confession he had confided the purpose of his pilgrimage, was Privet herself.

But had anymole identified her?

They had, and that a Newborn, and arguably the one with most to gain from her capture and deliverance to the enraged paws of Elder Senior Brother Quail: Brother Commander Thorne, scourge of Cannock, most able of the Newborn Commanders, and the one Newborn capable of cutting through the panic and incompetence of Quail's military leadership, and put his Crusade back on course to a crushing victory over the followers.

Few things are so strange in the long course of moledom's modern history, nor so significant, as how it was that Thorne discovered Privet at Leamington, and let her go.

Chapter Twenty-Four

The vital importance of Thorne's coming to Leamington, not only in his actions when he discovered Privet but also regarding his attitude towards the Crusade Council and his transfer of loyalty elsewhere, is most easily understood in the context of events at Wildenhope.

By the third part of July even the over-confident Crusade Council could not deny that the reports coming back were not quite as convincing in their claims of victory as they would have liked, and that in some places the Newborns had even been a little on the retreat.

Two events towards the end of June had tipped Quail over the edge into what Snyde, the greatest of the contemporary chroniclers, and the closest to Quail himself, privately called 'a madness of rage, retribution and misjudgement'.

'He,' continues Snyde's startlingly honest private record – created with the help of the now alienated Squelch who had access to (and was the butt of) Quail's worst excesses of mindless anger and cruel punishment of aides he believed had been disloyal or transgressed Newborn dogma – 'became increasingly unbalanced and deranged as the mole-months of June passed by into July, and it became all too plain that the Crusades were not proceeding as smoothly as we had hoped.

'The first time I saw him kill an aide with his own paws – or rather with his teeth, for he bit the mole to death – was when a messenger brought the news from Evesham that Finial's attempts to subdue Maple in the Wolds had ended in failure and the capitulation of the important system of Broadway to the rebels, which meant that they thereafter controlled the north-eastern approaches into the Wolds.

'When he heard that Finial was killed in that engagement, along with many of his best commanders and guardmoles, Quail's face suddenly became suffused with a kind of swelling anger, in which the blood vessels about his eyes and snout distended and engorged, his eyes took on a strange, fixed, bulging look and his snout turned a violet-red colour which would have been comic had not his murderous and arbitrary rage been so terrifying to those about him.

'The snout of the messenger, whose name I was unfortunately

276

unable to obtain, turned as white as Quail's turned puce, and his eyes widened in abject fear. Then, with a snarl of rage, Quail lunged forward into a ghastly embrace, his teeth about the other's throat. He stanced up, twisted and ripped at the mole and hurled him bodily towards the Council chamber's portal. Blood was everywhere, not least about the mouth of Quail, who, no sooner was the deed done, assumed a benign smile, wiping the blood from his face before ordering that the dying victim be dragged away by guards so that the Council could resume its debate.

'I noted a curious odour in the chamber afterwards, a rotten odour, as of decaying flesh whose fumes of putrefaction have been only partly disguised by some herb or other. It was faint, but quite nauseating, and I reluctantly concluded that its source was in some way Quail himself. Others seemed not to notice it at the time, and certainly none later admitted to doing so, though I and my minions questioned them several times.

'As for the murder of the messenger, it seemed afterwards almost as if it had not occurred. Not one Brother Inquisitor who was witness to it ever mentioned it to me again, and nor, later, when my enquiries were beginning to concentrate upon Quail's growing insanity and its source, was it ever referred to.

'The second occasion on which Quail's rage over-reached itself was rather more public, yet the culture of pretence that nothing untoward had taken place again obtained. This was that afternoon at the beginning of July when news reached Wildenhope that the mole Rooster, supposed Master of the Delve, had survived, and was alive somewhere high in the Wolds.

'This news was brought to us by the informer Kritch of Norton, aide to Stow, and one of the few followers ever to betray his cause. Kritch's absence from the rebels' ranks went unnoticed because of his clever stratagem of pretending to have been mortally wounded at the engagement in Broadway in which Finial was killed.

'He would have reached Wildenhope with his information earlier but that he was incarcerated by the Newborns at Evesham pending confirmation of his identity as informer and spy.* Having survived

---

* Justice demands an extended note here to revise the reputation of a much-maligned mole. This reference in Snyde's record is the source of the notorious reputation that Kritch of Norton so unfairly gained with the succeeding generation of followers. His true heroism, as a mole who dared infiltrate the Newborn ranks on behalf of the followers and risk his life many times in the service of Maple has only emerged in recent years. *This* history is recounted (*continued overleaf*)

that, he eventually made his way to Wildenhope and brought the unwelcome news of Rooster's survival, and much other information concerning the disposition of the rebel forces in the Wolds. My own view is that it was this news of Rooster which pushed Quail over into the dark void of insanity, though its full effects were not to be seen for many a molemonth yet.

'The news was imparted at a full meeting of the Crusade Council at which a number of Brother Commanders who had been recalled for further consultation and orders were also present. On hearing the news Quail's rage was absolute. Indeed, I myself, stanced immediately behind him, believed that he had been taken acutely ill.

'He spoke in a strange, gasping voice, words that few could have heard clearly, apart from myself and one or two close to him: "Had him. Here. Could have crushed him. Here. Had him in Caer Caradoc. There. Kill him. Rip him. Eat him, the Rooster mole. Devour him for he is Snake. He is doubt. Had him here and did not gorge on him, his blood to drink his entrails to chew, his beating heart to swallow into me."

'I scribed down these extraordinary words, which he spat out in staccato style like bad food, even as he shook and gesticulated in his maddened fury at having let Rooster escape his grasp, not once but twice. And as he spoke of eating his enemy, of gorging on his flesh, of making Rooster become a part of him, I was aware once more of that vile and retch-making odour, as rotten as putrid flesh, and as cloying in the gullet. It was a stench so horrid and so heavy that I nearly disgraced myself by vomiting, but a scribe must expect to continue to report in all circumstances and conditions, and I did so. Only later did I learn to enjoy that stench.

'Stanced next to Quail on this occasion was his son Squelch, who, as I have reported elsewhere, was by now disenchanted with and alienated from his father and so an especially useful source of knowledge to me on those occasions when I was unable to elicit information from the Elder Senior Brother Quail himself. I glanced at Squelch to observe his response to the odour and was surprised to see a look of

in the follower tradition, which generally, for the sake of clarity, preserves Kritch's disguise as the traitor he was not; and certainly, though it was true he was an aide to Stow, as Snyde suggests, to his follower contemporaries he appeared only as a lowly one and is never mentioned in the memoirs of Maple or Stow. It was, in fact, in the text concerning those times left by Chervil of Blagrove Slide that Kritch's true identity, and therefore his true greatness, was first publicly acknowledged and the startling claim made that he was 'probably' kin of Weeth.

peace and pleasure on his face, as if he did not notice it or (a thought that did not then occur to me) as if he was actually enjoying it.

'The moment of rage, and odour, passed, and Quail reverted to a cold and calculated anger, which I felt certain would result in the death of the spy Kritch, who had brought the bad news. To that mole's great good fortune, at this significant moment Brother Commander Bale, then in command of Stratford and unused to the imperative rule that no brother spoke without Quail's permission, turned to the Welsh Brother Commander Caerwys and said something which made Caerwys smile and glance at Quail.

'I saw Quail's anger mount again; he opened his mouth to admonish the Welsh mole when, to my great surprise, Kritch dared step forward and say in a clear low voice, "A privy word with you Elder Senior Brother, if I may."

'It was boldly done, confidently, but with due deference, and Quail, floundering perhaps in his sea of rage, turned to this island of calm and nodded his head, gesturing Kritch to come very near. He did so, and I eased myself forward as so often in the past to hear what was said and record it, and was astounded to find myself scribing down these words: "Beware the Brother Commanders Bale and Caerwys, for they are in collusion with the Snake that is in Rooster's heart."

'"You have evidence?" whispered Quail.

'"Proof positive," said Kritch, "and there are the others."

'"Others?" whispered my Master Quail.

'"The others in the plot are Brother Commanders Fenney and Blinke and the Brother Adviser Kilvert. The snakes are entwined about their hearts, the worms of evil devour their brains, the poisons of corruption imbue their talons." Kritch spoke like the true Newborn he was, and a mole could not doubt that he pointed the talon of accusation justly.

'"Snakes . . . worms . . . poisons," hissed Quail, his eyes beginning to bulge once more as he turned his terrible gaze upon the accused, from whom other Inquisitors and commanders alike backed away.

'"Kill them," Quail ordered peremptorily, and mole looked at mole to see who would carry out the deed. "All of us will kill them, for we share the guilt of their crimes and must cleanse our talons with their blood and offer it up to the sacred Stone."

'In this private record I have nothing of significance to add to the official report on the deaths of those five miscreants who had crept into the very heart of our Council. They attempted to resist in a cowardly fashion. The Inquisitor Ranke, assistant to Skua himself, was

279

mortally injured in the struggle, and all five were killed by the Council itself. The spy Kritch was well rewarded by Quail, but pride soon overcame him, as it often does with minions who do not know their place, and he was banished to some minor assignment far from the pleasures of power at Wildenhope.

'This was one of the first occasions my Master Quail specifically rewarded me, pointing at the five corpses as the Council adjourned and saying, "Do with them as you will. I do not wish to see them again." My colleague Squelch asked if he might "stay and watch", which I permitted to some degree.*

'My own view of the killing of the brothers in Council was that it suggested that Quail was insane, in the sense that the needs of the Newborn masses (which surely dictated that these five competent moles be kept alive and useful even if they were guilty as indicted) were taking second place to his zeal for the Stone. Quail was now in thrall to faith, dogma, and his own passions, rather than acting with reason and clear purpose as he had before.

'Thus my own task as record-keeper and scribemole for the most powerful mole in moledom assumed an even greater importance. I therefore resolved to keep my accounts even more assiduously than before so that history might know the truth, whilst, at the same time, using my position of trust and confidence to try to keep Quail's darker passions in check. In this way I sought to guide him in his leadership back towards the resolute Crusade against the followers, which was in danger of faltering.'

This extended extract from Snyde's secret record expresses well the reign of intrigue, arbitrary terror and sycophancy that now began to infect Quail's high command. Snyde and Squelch, in spite of the

* Scholars of those times will be uncomfortably aware of the deformed Snyde's perverse interest in the dead, though mercifully, reference to his necrophilia need be but passing in this history, which is concerned with better things. This ambiguous reference to the way his foul and usually secret lusts were on occasion rewarded by the grateful Quail, leaves little doubt of the nature of the concourse that he had with those five dead moles before he had guards remove them. The fact that he allowed the reference to remain in this record suggests that this filthy performance, in the chamber of the Crusade Council, and before an audience consisting solely of Squelch, his partner in the exploration of deviance and pornography, was possibly the highlight of his sexual life *to that date*. Snyde, like his 'Master Quail', still had a way to travel, and the Stone, in its wisdom (and to use the liturgy of one of Skua's own sentencings for crimes committed), had yet to find the 'just and exquisitely fitting final punishment' his life, and that of Quail, deserved.

280

latter's known dislike of his own father, both now began to gain his fullest confidence, above all others, and their will, especially Snyde's, began to prevail.

The plan that Snyde now tried to persuade Quail to follow may be simply and brutally stated: Chervil, who had prudently journeyed to the north-east of moledom in early June, was to be recalled (no doubt to assume command over Quail, and set the Crusades back on course). Brother Commander Thorne, in Cannock, rightly recognized by Snyde as the only leader capable of successfully countering the followers' advances, was to be given supreme military power; and former Elder Senior Brother Thripp, now dubbed 'Emeritus Brother Thripp' to mark his retirement from power, was to be further isolated, and later secretly assassinated, and those who did the deed to be themselves eliminated.

This was now Snyde's agenda, and whilst being impressed by his acuity in identifying the three moles most capable of furthering the Newborn cause if they wished to, we may be grateful that he failed to achieve most of it. Had Chervil come to Wildenhope – as under Snyde's and Squelch's influence Quail soon ordered him to do – he would undoubtedly have been killed despite Snyde's intentions. Quail would not have tolerated him for long. The same may be said of Thorne.

As for Thripp – already in Quail's control and presently immured in a comfortable but impregnable suite of cells in Wildenhope – this was one act of murder Quail was as yet unwilling to commit.

However, Snyde's plotting succeeded in ensuring that Thripp was completely isolated from loyal supporters, for soon after the murders in Council, a formal charge of conspiring against Quail was raised against Thripp's one remaining aide, the faithful Brother Rolt. But it was too late, for Rolt, always well-informed, had bade his reluctant and tearful farewell to Thripp the night before the guardmoles came to take him into custody, and fled Wildenhope. This was no easy thing to do, but Rolt had not survived the long years of the rise of the Caradocian Order for nothing, and knew better than most which guardmoles would turn a blind eye on his departure, the best tunnels to take to avoid the Wildenhope patrols, and where he might lie low in safe retreat if guards were sent out after him. It should be added that the ever-faithful Rolt also knew which of the guards and minions still remaining in Wildenhope might be relied on to watch over their Master Thripp as best as they were able. It is not only among the followers that courage is to be found.

Nor did Rolt go before Thripp had given him clear and detailed instructions. The former Elder Senior Brother might still choose to appear frail and weak-headed to the rest of moledom, but Rolt knew him to be physically fitter than he had been for years. It helped his pretence that his face was now thin and lined, and his fur pale and patchy; but his mind was clear, and his spirit had discovered a new kind of peace ever since Privet's coming and subsequent escape from Wildenhope. He, if nomole else as yet, had seen a clear way forward.

'So, there you are, Rolt, you know what you must do, and we must pray that the others will play their parts as well as Quail is unconsciously playing his. Once you have gone I doubt that I shall be able to learn much of what is going on, and it may be that Quail will have me made eliminate.'

Poor Rolt was close to tears to hear this, which was, after all, his worst fear. What would he do if he could not serve Thripp?

'I do not want to leave, Master,' he said.

'I know it, but you must. You have important tasks to fulfil, and moles to motivate, and none in moledom apart from you can do these things. But Chervil . . .'

Only at mention of his son did the cool, calm eyes of Thripp seem to falter, and his gaze become unsteady.

'Why, mole, I cannot think the Stone will take both myself and Chervil's mother to its Silence before the Book has come. Therefore, if I am gone by then, bring Chervil to his mother, ensure that they talk and know each other.'

'And his sisters, Master, remember them.'

For a moment Thripp's face clouded again, but then he looked away with seeming indifference.

'I did what I had to for them, and it is better their names are mentioned to nomole, least of all myself. Some things are best left alone.'

'Master . . .'

Thripp essayed a brief smile. 'You are a sentimentalist, Rolt, you—'

'They are the nearest to pups of my own I ever had, Elder Senior Brother, and you must forgive me. I saw them at birth; I made sure they were nurtured when Privet left Blagrove Slide; and when they were old enough I accompanied them to Mallerstang in the north, not a pleasant journey.'

'I do not wish to know,' said Thripp sharply. This was the one remaining subject which called up his old chilly dogmatic self. He forbade all mention of his daughters, and Chervil had never been told

282

the full story even when some vestigial memory of his puphood days spurred him to wonder if he had not once had siblings, for he remembered, he remembered . . . But the loyal Rolt, despite his better judgement, had never told him the truth.

'I accompanied them to that place,' Rolt persevered, feeling perhaps that he would never have another chance to speak his mind or draw from Thripp some hint of paternal love for his and Privet's daughters, the value of whose very life the early Caradocian creed, as propounded by Thripp himself, all but denied. 'I saw them there in safety, and they embraced me—'

'Mole, I do not wish to hear!' cried out Thripp.

'But they did, they did!' said Rolt, surprising himself at his boldness. How sharp the pain was of that distant, secret farewell! 'The two surviving females embraced me, as they would you, if you had ever let them. First Loosestrife and then Sampion. Master, you would have been proud of them! And Privet, she would as well! It is my regret that I did not tell her the full truth of how they survived, and where they are, when I had the chance at Caer Caradoc.'

'It would not have been fitting or possible for them to stay in Blagrove Slide,' insisted Thripp, 'and anyway, when I am gone to the Silence you may do and tell what you will!' His voice held a trace of bitterness; it had been a long, long time since it sounded so.

Rolt stared at him with affection and understanding.

'I never sullied your name to their ears, Master, nor that of their mother.'

'They do not know her name?' asked Thripp quickly.

Rolt looked ambiguous. 'They know little of her, though I could never quite bring myself to say she was dead, as you wished me to,' he said carefully. '"Gone away" is a poor substitute for a mother, but "dead" is surely worse. But you they honour, Master, and they know you did what you had to for their safety.'

'Rolt, I am not a perfect mole as well you know. Perhaps only you know it truly. I do not mean to be harsh, but these memories remain as painful to me now as ever they were. Do you think I did not suffer to see my pups reach out to me and I unable to put my paws to them? Do you not think I wept to see you leave Blagrove with them?

'But with moles like Brother Quail in the ascendant, what would their lives have been worth if they had stayed? To be attached to some Brother Confessor or Inquisitor, to be used, to be made to breed, to be made as nothing before the Stone. To be so forced by a creed I had myself created, but which was becoming a monster.'

Thripp spoke from out of a despair he rarely expressed, and his voice took on a terrible intensity: 'It was all my hypocrisy, my weakness, the lie I told, and a day does not go by but that I ask the Stone's forgiveness for it. But I promised Privet, she made me promise it, and you took them where they would be safe. And you were as much a father to them as I ever was.'

'Master . . .' began Rolt, beginning to regret his outburst.

But then there came that brief smile again, and the searching gaze of those clear eyes; Thripp's punishment in life had always been that he did not, could not, turn from the searing truth about himself, when the Stone's Light made him see it.

'No, Rolt, you were right to speak as you did. You may not get another chance. Tell moles only the truth about me, only that. And if I am made eliminate and you see me no more before the day of the coming of the Book, whisper a prayer for me for the many sins I committed, and the little good that I did. Now, you must go. You have great tasks to perform. Moledom depends upon you now, and no doubt it will be grateful one day. Trust Thorne, he will do right. Tell Chervil that I always loved him. Ask Privet for my forgiveness for the sacrifice we had to ask Whillan to make.'

'Master—'

'Be gone, Brother Rolt, and know that I love thee. It is my privilege that the last act I accomplish before the Crusade Council robs me of my final freedoms, but sees you, whom I hold so dear, escape to safety. Now go!'

How Rolt would have liked to stay! How he would have liked to say more! How he would have liked to embrace the mole in whose service he had spent all his adult life. But there were heavy pawsteps in the tunnels, and Wildenhope was becoming more menacing and dangerous by the hour. With one last anguished look into Thripp's eyes, which were already retreating into that place of meditation and Silence wherein the likes of Quail could never hurt him, Rolt turned, and was gone.

So it was that Rolt escaped Wildenhope and began the long and dangerous journey northwards that would bring him to Cannock, and into the councils of Brother Commander Thorne . . .

Rolt and Thorne were friends of a sort, the one a political mole, the other a military one. But it was a fact that Thorne's rise under Thripp had been due not only to his remarkable abilities shown in dealing with strife along the Welsh Borderland; Rolt had spoken highly of him to Thripp and helped bring him out of obscurity.

Thripp's own judgement of moles was always acute, even if, early during his emergence as leader, he had misjudged Quail and under-estimated Privet. But generally he knew ability when he saw it, and was quick to spot a mole who had something more than ability, which is the flair, the boldness and the resolution to carry through schemes where risk must be finely judged, and faltering and doubt invite failure.

In Thorne he saw these rare qualities, and even as Quail inexorably gained the ascendancy he had made sure that the Brother Commander held offices and was given postings which extended his experience, and kept him far enough away from Quail to be unharmed. Indeed, it was as if he was grooming Thorne for some future task; a preparation which one might almost call nurturing, for when Thorne was banished by Quail to Cannock, it was Thripp who suggested that it would be prudent to banish his closest aides and most loyal guardmoles with him – 'Lest they breed dissension elsewhere'. In short, Thripp, who knew how important loyal subordinates were, made certain that Thorne went into isolation with the best of his supporters, ready for the day . . .

For what day? Perhaps only one mole, Rolt, knew the full truth of Thripp's subtle scheme. While in only one mind, that of the acute and brilliant Snyde, was the suspicion beginning to grow that Thripp's apparent acquiescence to Quail in recent moleyears had, in fact, been a clever disengagement from the worst excesses that Quail's policies might have inflicted. Snyde was beginning to believe, and history has proved him correct, that Thripp himself was the greatest traitor to the Newborn cause, and that by assuming the guise of age and infirmity he had deliberately let Quail gain power, believing he would finally destroy himself. If this were so it makes more sense that Thripp encouraged Quail to banish the one Brother Commander who had the ability to lead the Crusades successfully.

Not that Thorne himself was yet aware of such arcane manipulations – but the subtle Rolt was, and his flight to Cannock, not only to save his own life but as agent for Thripp, was the beginning of the delicate and dangerous endeavour by the former Elder Senior Brother to begin a more overt attempt to hasten Quail's process of self-destruction.

Rolt reached Cannock in July, and its ordered, disciplined, yet relaxed atmosphere, its clean tunnels, polite guardmoles and comfort-able visitors' quarters could hardly have been in greater contrast to all that he had left behind at Wildenhope. Thorne was away on a venture to the north and would not be back for several

285

days, but Rolt already knew several of Thorne's subordinates, and in particular Adkin, who was to Thorne what Rolt had always been to Thripp.

'Brother Rolt, this is an honour!' declared Adkin, once Rolt was settled in and recovered somewhat from the ordeal of his flight from Wildenhope. 'The Brother Commander isn't here, as you've heard, but if there's anything . . . ?'

Rolt looked instinctively over his shoulder, and round at the portal of the chamber, which made Adkin grin.

'This isn't Wildenhope, you know! There's not a spy at every corner! There used to be, mind you, but Thorne's got a way of winkling out spies and sneaks and those kinds of moles, and they don't last long with him. Not that we shouldn't be careful. These are dangerous times.'

'They are, Adkin, they are,' said Rolt. 'Now listen. There *is* something you can do. It is likely that before long, perhaps within days, the Crusade Council will send an order to have a certain mole arraigned as a miscreant.'

'Would that mole be yourself by any chance, Brother Rolt?'

'It might well be,' said Rolt, who had lived in the twisted atmosphere of Caer Caradoc and Wildenhope so long that he found it hard, even in friendly company, to say a simple 'Yes'.

'No problem,' said Adkin, 'and if orders do come I am sure that in the absence of the Commander, and knowing his high regard for you, and since you are more experienced in such things than almost any mole in moledom, we would be much obliged if you would advise us on how to deal with them! I mean, we wouldn't want to do wrong, would we?'

The two moles grinned mischievously at each other before Adkin said, 'Things are bad then, sir? I mean, really bad?'

Rolt nodded grimly.

'And the Elder Senior Brother Thripp, sir, how is he?'

Adkin looked at Rolt, guessing how the good brother must feel, for did he not also serve a mole he loved and would do anything for? Did he himself not fret when Thorne was too long out of his sight?

'The only thing protecting my master now,' said Rolt quietly, 'is the Stone itself.'

'Then I'll pray to the Stone for his life,' said Adkin fervently, 'and there'll be many another in Cannock will do the same. It's *him* they serve in their hearts, not that Qu . . .' He began to look ferocious.

'Guardmole Adkin!' admonished Rolt. 'It is best not to say such things, not even amongst friends. But, still, I'm glad to hear you nearly say it.'

'There's not many moles round here *wouldn't* say it!' muttered Adkin.

Rolt was proved right – three days after his arrival at Cannock two tough guardmoles from Wildenhope brought new orders from the Crusade Council, among them the very demand to arraign himself that he had expected; but in addition was one demanding that Thorne travel to Wildenhope immediately, with the guardmoles who had brought the orders, and report for a new command.

'It might be better that he didn't,' said Rolt, whose presence at Cannock had been kept well hidden from the messengers. 'Quail will probably promote him to supreme field command on his arrival, and have him arraigned and executed the day after that.'

'More than likely, Brother Rolt! But I'll tell you a bit of gossip the guardmoles gave me – not that they're the gossiping kind, those two, but they opened up with a bit of food inside them. It seems that our old friend Brother Commander Squilver, who made such a cock-up of that massing here in Cannock before Brother Commander Thorne came, has now wheedled his way into seniority at Wildenhope.'

'Well, I doubt if he'll survive for long! Nomole can, for their lives depend upon the rages and the whims of Quail,' said Rolt. 'Now, what are we going to do about the guardmoles?'

'Oh, them!' said Adkin innocently. 'We've told 'em that the Brother Commander is south of here and the quickest way to get him back to Wildenhope is to go and find him and take him on from where he is. Well, how was I to know he's still some way north?'

But Thorne, like all great commanders, had an instinct for where he should be and when, and had cut short his current expedition to return to Cannock, where he arrived that same evening.

Rolt had known Thorne for moleyears, and though the two had never been close there was a mutual respect and liking born of the knowledge that each in his own way more than fulfilled his task, and that that task was, broadly, to seek to make real the great spiritual dream for moledom, in worship of the Stone, that Thripp had created in the minds of many of his followers. Perhaps this liking was all the greater, and more likely to turn into a mutually beneficial friendship, now that so many of Thripp's close supporters had felt it wise to subordinate themselves to Quail and his fellow Inquisitors, or, worse, had been eliminated.

Each mole could see the changes that time and recent pressures had wrought in the other. Thorne saw immediately that Rolt, older than he, now looked older than he remembered. He was thinner, his fur had greyed, his snout had wrinkled, his paws bore the fresh scars of travel such as the paws of scribemoles and sedentary moles often bear.

'But his eyes are as bright and kind and wise as they were when he first summoned me from oblivion!' said Thorne to himself.

Rolt *was* wise, and his years in the service of Thripp had taught him to sum up moles quickly and accurately. It seemed a long time since he had seen Thorne and he was well pleased with what he found. The Brother Commander's natural authority had developed, his face grown more lined, the set of his eyes deeper, his voice more assured in its commands to subordinates.

'He is the mole we need!' thought Rolt to himself, pleased at having thought to bring Thorne to Thripp's attention so long ago; pleased, too, that Thripp had given Thorne such support and sound advice.

'So . . .' began Thorne carefully, after listening to Rolt's version of the events at Wildenhope about which he had already heard so much from so many different sources, '. . . so that's what's really happening at Wildenhope and Caradoc. Quail is losing his grip and going the way leaders often do in such circumstances, which is towards vengeful and erratic decisions which will lose Newborn lives needlessly. It will not help him, or anymole, if he gives power to those like Squilver who made a mess of things here before I came.

'Naturally, I knew already of the Wildenhope killings. For a time it was all that anymole, whether Newborn or not, could talk about. The Crusade Council's actions that morning, sanctioned I presume by Quail, did more damage to the Crusades than any other single act. Nevertheless,' he continued grimly, 'I do not think our cause is lost. With the right leadership, discipline and determination all round, it will be possible for the Crusades to be saved, and proper order imposed in moledom. But it will not now be as straightforward as it would have been.'

Rolt nodded silently, contemplating the implications of what Thorne said. It was good to be in the presence of a mole who knew his mind, and had the ability to carry through his ideas. It was just a pity, Rolt said wryly to himself, that this most able of moles was not likely to be ready yet to be part of the radical policy that Thripp now had in mind for the Newborns.

'But you don't look very upset about what's happening, Brother Rolt! If I did not know that whatever your feelings about Quail you

288

are still at heart a Newborn I might almost think you were pleased that Quail has made such a bad error of judgement.'

'You are a perspicacious mole, Thorne,' said Rolt, wondering quite how to continue. 'When in doubt, say nowt and ask questions' his old father had once told him in distant and better days. It was good advice which he had often followed, and he followed it now. 'You are confident then that the rebels can be subdued?' he murmured.

'Of course I am,' said Thorne a little impatiently. 'Only one rebel has emerged across the whole of moledom who shows any signs of real leadership and a sense of strategy. I am referring to Maple of Duncton Wood.'

'Of course,' said Rolt, thinking of how he had met the great Duncton mole up by the Stones of Caer Caradoc before Longest Night. A mole of integrity, and one who, like Thorne himself, had destiny scribed all over his face. It was a pity, as Thripp himself had said when giving Rolt his final secret instructions, that these two were ranged against each other.

'It happens that I crossed talons with him on my way to assume command here,' said Thorne. 'I didn't actually meet him though I saw him at a distance. I must say that he effected a disciplined, orderly and effective retreat from a system south of here in a manner that made pursuit very dangerous if not quite impossible . . . He pawdled it quite brilliantly.'

Thorne quickly told Rolt of the engagement at Rowton, when Maple had so impressed him.

'In addition to all that, he did something few of my fellow Brother Commanders would have done – he sent emissaries to negotiate for the safety of the injured and infirm who could not travel with him, which not only gained his retreat time, but probably saved the lives of those moles as well. It is what I myself would have done. It was a tactic that Gareg of Merthyr himself once used, though it is too much to suppose that this Maple and I have kenned the same texts!'

'Is it?' said Rolt with a twinkle to his eye.

'Why, mole, you know more than you're saying. You . . . I believe you know this mole!' There was astonishment mixed with admiration in his voice at how Rolt contrived to know, or know something about, almost anymole of importance in moledom.

But still Rolt said nothing, and to encourage him Thorne went on, 'Allmole knows of how the rebel Maple has consolidated his forces in the Wolds, and turned what was a place of no consequence into what may be the crux of the struggle against the rebels. He has made fools of several Brother Commanders, and been responsible for the deaths of at least one of them at the paws of Quail.'

'Four, as a matter of fact,' said Rolt.

'So what do you know?'

'I have met him,' admitted Rolt. 'He is, I would say, impressive, which means well-kenned in military history, fair-minded, brave, and an inspiration to those he leads. Worthy to be counted among the best of the long line of Duncton warriors.'

'But inexperienced.'

Rolt shrugged and said, 'I can think of moles who have been good in war without much prior experience. It is, I presume, spirit that matters as much as experience. In any case he knows how to appoint subordinates who complement his strengths with their own.'

'Aye, I've heard as much. I am told he relies on the Siabodian warrior Ystwelyn, whom of course I know from my days along the north Welsh borderland. A formidable mole, who would not second himself to just anymole. Then there is Arvon, who is a brilliant leader of small forces and the kind of risk-taker I would like to have on my own side.'

'You are well informed, Brother Commander.'

'I need to be with so few friends in the Crusade Council. I have spies of my own. Yes, Maple's force has proved impressive so far, but he has not really been tested. But Brother Rolt, you have drawn me out enough. What task is it that the Elder Senior Brother asks of me? You know I will do it if I can.'

'He knows that, and is sure you will. First, he asks that you trust me as you would him.'

'Of course I do, Brother, of course. I can say the same of no other mole.'

'Well then, listen to me. You must not go to Wildenhope, or obey any command to do so.'

'I have received no command to that effect,' said Thorne with a blank stare, 'or none that has been passed on to me. Nor would I go if I did. I value my life too well.'

'Nor must you appear to ignore Quail's orders, for that will provoke him to send moles to pursue which would be . . . tedious, and complicating. No, you must be in the wrong place at the right time: you must travel east towards Ashbourne.'

'Will you give me a reason, or must I trust you blindly?'

'I will give you a name: Chervil. He has been in the north, conveniently out of the way, sent by Quail who thought thereby to neutralize a potential rival.'

Thorne's eyes darkened. 'But Chervil it was personally killed the Duncton mole Whillan and by that proved he was loyal to Quail. I did not think . . .'

His voice faded as he gazed into the subtle eyes of Rolt. Did they twinkle, or did they glitter? Thorne could not say.

'Chervil,' muttered Thorne, pondering, calculating, wondering: 'they say he was as much your son as Thripp's.'

'If he was the mole killed Whillan he is no son of mine, nor Thripp's.'

'If it was not him then who was it?'

Rolt did not reply, and seeing he would give nothing of that away Thorne moved on to something else: 'And what do you want me to do at Ashbourne?'

'Not be here, of course. And to wait.'

'Wait until the right time comes to move against the rebels and set right this disarray Quail has brought to the Caradocian Order?'

'Perhaps,' said Rolt judiciously. 'It is all Thripp asks of you.'

'For now!'

Rolt grinned faintly. 'It will be enough.'

'Well then, let it be so. I shall leave guardmoles enough at Cannock to watch over it well. We must prepare against the possibility of some kind of move from Wildenhope against us here. This system has seen war before, and a bloody one, and it has a modicum of good defences. I would not have minded defending it against the incompetents that Quail might send. But I must not talk treason. I am, after all, simply making myself scarce, along with my best guardmoles, and then . . . waiting!'

'Have you a Brother Adviser here who may be difficult?'

Thorne laughed. 'We had, Brother Rolt, until this evening. The treacherous Fagg, one of Quail's worst. But I understand that when he heard, which guardmole Adkin made sure he did, that messengers with orders from the Crusade Council have come in my absence, and now mistakenly gone south to find me, he went hurrying after them. In any case he has been in collusion with Squilver and I have no doubt he will follow him to Wildenhope. We shall leave tomorrow, and if he does follow us it may take him time to catch up with us by the time he has gone south, come north, and chased around in the wrong direction. No, Fagg is a fool and as great an example of Quail's misjudgement as we need.'

'I understand that your predecessor here, Brother Commander

291

Squilver, has gained some advantage at Wildenhope.'

Thorne's eyes glittered with distaste. 'A dangerous mole, who can make others follow him but allows his judgement to be clouded by a desire for personal gain. Now, Brother Rolt, if you'll forgive me, we have things to do which cannot wait. I assume you will be travelling with us now, for you'll not be safe anywhere else. Expect to leave for Ashbourne on the morrow. Meanwhile, get some sleep, for the coming days will be long.'

'And not just for us!' said Rolt. 'May the Stone protect the Elder Senior Brother!'

'Aye,' growled Thorne, pausing in prayer for only a moment before he summoned Adkin, and began the complex process of selecting which of his guardmole forces were to stay behind at Cannock, and which to go with him.

Chapter Twenty-Five

So it was that the balance of power in moledom began to shift away from Quail as Thorne, having effectively secured Cannock, and the systems north and north-east of it, journeyed eastward with Rolt, imposing his benign discipline and influence as he went.

System after system he reached, assessed, and quickly won the confidence of the demoralized Newborn forces he found there, pausing only as long as it took to put one of his own supporters in control, taking with him any that might have proved troublesome had they been left behind. It was as plain as the trunk of a silver birch at twilight that confidence in Quail was seeping away, even amongst those brothers who had attended the Convocation of Caer Caradoc. No doubt those who had gained places in the more important systems like Rollright and Avebury were satisfied with the power they had acquired, and glad to give their support to Quail; but there was much unrest in the small peripheral systems to which less able or less well connected brothers had been sent, and here Thorne made easy headway.

Not that he represented himself as in opposition to Quail in any way. Rather, as he seemed strong-minded and competent, with a solid and well-disciplined force of guardmoles at his flanks, those systems he visited were happy to accept his claim that he was 'expanding the Crusade Council's powers from Cannock', and willing to yield authority to him.

His ruse of absorbing troublesome brothers into his own ranks was a clever one, for it would have taken a powerful and resourceful mole to resist Thorne's authority once he was in the midst of Thorne's ablest guardmoles; and a fit one too, for Thorne worked the newcomers hard, and gave them little space for causing trouble. In this way he gained useful extra guardmoles and commanders, while reducing the chances of leaving hostages to fortune behind him in territory he had gained.

By the end of June Thorne had reached Ashbourne, and was able to approach it in the knowledge that the systems to its west were already his. Its proximity to the fabled Beechenhill, where the holy Beechen had died at the paws of Eldrene Wort, which lay a little to the north, meant that he proceeded cautiously.

Advance reconnaissance, and contact with a couple of disgruntled guardmoles from Ashbourne who had been deputed to watch over the grubby and rebellious little system of Ellastone, was reassuring. The Brother Commander of Ashbourne was the ageing Dunmow, once a rising star among the Inquisitors and assistant to Skua himself; but he had offended his superior in some way and been relegated to the outpost of Ashbourne. For a time, however, Dunmow had redeemed himself with a brutal campaign of violence against sundry systems round and about his new domain. His ill-disciplined and unkempt guardmoles, finding little opposition amongst the small settlements of those parts, had raped, plundered and tortured their way over hill, down dale, and across valley. But they had no grasp of strategy, and easy success bred indolence and indifference to the task at paw, so that the advantages that might have been reaped from their early progress by a leader such as Thorne were let slip.

Local communities rallied, leading followers escaped, and soon all that Dunmow controlled was an empty landscape of deserted systems from which moles had fled to the north and east, beyond the reach of his lazy guardmoles. Meanwhile the reports that reached the Crusade Council in Wildenhope continued to sound good, and Quail concentrated his efforts on areas further south, where his intelligence was better. Ashbourne and the north seemed of little consequence – and in any case, Senior Brother Chervil was out that way, and if problems arose, no doubt he could deal with them . . .

'The Crusade Council makes a mistake in thinking that because it is isolated in these northern parts, Beechenhill lacks importance,' observed Brother Rolt sagely, with that special glint in his eye that Thorne now recognized as prefacing some little scheme or subtle plot. 'It is not isolated in moledom's heart, and nor in the hearts of the rebel followers. Fancy visiting it, Brother Commander?'

'But it is on high ground, and some way off our destination, which is Ashbourne itself,' said Thorne.

'But supposing you were to find Beechenhill ill-guarded, which against the forces you command will likely be the case. If it is, then you have the perfect excuse to dispossess your incompetent fellow Brother Commander Dunmow of his power at Ashbourne. You might charge him with, let us say, dereliction of duty. You military moles probably have a word for it. Whatever, he is unlikely to get much

294

support from a Crusade Council in which Skua is so powerful.'

Thorne smiled broadly. He liked travelling with Brother Rolt, for in addition to the subtlety of his thought there was his ironic sense of humour, unusual in a highly-placed Newborn.

'I shall send a small force under Adkin, who is good at that kind of work; that will be swifter than if all of us go. It need only take a matter of days.'

It took four days, and Adkin came back with the news that not only was Beechenhill ill-guarded but the library had been virtually destroyed by marauding guardmoles from Ashbourne. *Dunmow's* guardmoles. It was enough to allow Thorne to approach Ashbourne with equanimity. In a quick and effective operation he imposed his authority on a soon-terrified Dunmow, isolated him in a cell, and gained ascendancy over his large, ill-led force of guardmoles, who were too craven to do anything other than welcome Thorne.

'It is a beginning,' said Thorne with satisfaction some days later, 'and a good one. We have a secure base from which we can begin to impose some order on the Crusade Council's thinking. It is time we made an effort to contact Chervil, for surely the future lies with the son of Thripp. Yet he has been strangely silent for so important a mole, and when moles talk of him being "in the north" I'm not sure what that means.'

But discovering whatever it did mean would have to wait a while, for but a short time later first news of the terror and shame of the Leamington massing reached Thorne, in the shape of two brave young Newborns. Frightened witnesses of some of the worst of the early brutality, probably saved from death only by being young, male, and having good potential as guardmoles, they had been isolated for education in a small colony of similar moles, and all but forgotten.

As Leamington declined into starvation, disease and hopelessness, and the guardmoles under the leadership of Assistant Brother Commander Sickle became brutalized and satiated with violence, the two moles tried to help certain of the victims. What they saw and heard, and the privations to which they themselves were subject, had rendered one of them mute, and the other as gaunt as death itself. Yet, somehow, they found the strength and inspiration to escape, believing that what was happening must be stopped. Then, learning that only days before Brother Commander Thorne of Cannock had taken over Ashbourne, they had fled north to appeal to his known sense of justice.

Having heard their story Thorne did not hesitate – recognizing, it must be said, not only the need to eradicate a blot on Newborn's reputation, but also a further opportunity to annex territory and demonstrate that Quail was unfit to lead the Crusade Council. He took a force of experienced moles and set off for Leamington at once, leaving Rolt behind at Ashbourne to discover the whereabouts of Chervil.

Nothing in Thorne's experience prepared him for the chaos and horror of the foul and odorous chambers of Leamington. Not only had the elderly and female population of the system been crammed into them, with little food and no access to water, but prisoners from adjacent systems had been driven down into them, day after day, molemonth after molemonth. No wonder that it was not long before the guardmoles refused to go down into the main tunnels and chambers, staying instead at or near the surface, to prevent those poor moles who had gone in from coming out again.

The smell of the place was evident to Thorne and his force even some way out of Leamington – a heavy, sweet, sickly odour of death, so foul it made a mole retch. But Thorne went on, his progress unchallenged by the fat and diseased guards, and ventured down into the tunnels, and saw for himself the shame that was Leamington.

Mole had eaten mole to survive; the air was fetid and hot, and it was impossible to breathe without sucking in myriad of the tiny flies that flew and crawled in the darkness, hatched in the summer heat from the maggots that infested the dead. Yet when the bodies themselves became too rotten to eat, many moles, half mad with starvation and fear, had taken to eating the maggots instead. Others, eyes sunken, silent, lay trembling or deathly still, staring at nothing, dying. Yet more, maddened by it all, had turned violent, and killed the weak and sick where they lay, or maimed them out of some inner rage at what life had done to them.

While away from it all, on higher ground and upwind of the stench, Thorne's guardmoles found Sickle, and the bullying, debauched subordinates he favoured, in wormful tunnels, near clean running water, enjoying the company of laughing and hysterical consorts who, it seemed, were the pick of the female prisoners.

Thorne did not waste much time on Sickle, the more because he seemed unable to understand what he was or what he had done, but only laughed, and railed at never having been promoted beyond the rank of Assistant Brother Commander.

'That old fool Dunmow told me to cleanse Leamington of blasphemy and that is what I am doing. Let the bastards and the bitches who call themselves followers die in their own excrement. Let them suffer in life as they will in death when the Stone takes them into eternal punishment. Let them—'

Thorne turned to his aides. 'Arraign him and his colleagues and bring Dunmow from Ashbourne to stand trial as well; scribe down the proceedings fully; call witnesses; leave no possibility of doubt about what has occurred here. Do it swiftly and thoroughly.'

'And the punishment, sir?'

Thorne's eyes were at their coldest. 'Let seven moles decide and I will sanction their decision.'

'It may be death, sir, and the execution of such senior brothers as these surely needs the sanction of the Crusade Council itself; perhaps even Elder Senior Brother Quail.'

'We are at war, and I am in command here,' said Thorne. 'If death is the sentence, death it will be, and I will take responsibility for it. Now take these scum out of my sight and deal with them as I have instructed. If the sentence is death I myself will act as executioner, that none other may be accused of doing so.'

Death it was, quick, brutal, despite the pleas, squeals and weeping of those senior Newborn brothers.

Nine times Thorne raised his right paw above their heads; nine times he plunged his talons down and killed a mole. Before witnesses, with a scribemole in attendance, that none could ever say it was done privily, or shamefully, or without good cause.

'I was only doing what I was told to do!' sobbed Sickle at the end, shaking and sweating before his awesome executioner.

'A brother takes responsibility for himself, just as he should for those in his care. It has been adjudged that you have done neither, and so, culpable thereby of murder, and of undermining the justice of the Newborn cause, you must be punished.' And so Sickle died, and much more swiftly and less painfully than many of his victims. Accounts of the outrage and Thorne's resolute response to it filtered out into moledom, and few things did more to undermine the position of Quail and enhance the reputation of Thorne.

It was now, in the aftermath of the relief of Leamington, when the survivors were taken to clean quarters on higher ground, and the worst of the chambers where the massing occurred were sealed, that Thorne came upon Privet.

She was among those who had appeared at Leamington soon after Thorne's coming, emerging from the surrounding countryside as life emerges after winter, some to help, some to trace missing kin and friends, many just to mourn. No doubt Privet's wanderings had brought her into contact with followers who had kin at Leamington, and when the system was relieved she journeyed with them to serve as silent healer and helpmeet to those who needed her.

In those sombre days when the summer sun beat down on moles with shadowed hearts and clouded minds, Newborn and follower freely mixed, their mutual fear and antipathy subsumed by the horror of what had taken place, and the peace preserved by the character and discipline of Thorne's forces. It was an extraordinary achievement, and gave the lie to the conflict and distrust between two systems of belief which had given rise to this situation.

It was in those strange days that Adkin, accompanying his Brother Commander in a review of the system and what had been achieved, passed by one of the healing chambers and caught sight of something that stopped him in his tracks.

'Come on Adkin, stop dawdling!' called out Thorne ahead of him. 'We've much to see, and other work to do. Why, mole, what is it?'

Silently Adkin pointed a talon through a portal and down the length of the busy chamber. Thorne retraced his steps, looked, and was at once astonished and appalled. The two moles simply stared. Privet was much changed since they had known her on the fraught journey from Wenlock Edge to her captivity in Wildenhope: thinner, shrivelled, lost in a silent world of her own. But both knew her at once, less by her appearance than by the spirit of faith and truth she projected.

'By the Stone, sir, but that's the mole Privet, the one—'

'Adkin, you better get her out of there at once and without fuss,' said Thorne calmly. 'Bring her to my chamber. No, that will attract attention. Bring her to those derelict tunnels we passed through a while back; it is best we talk to her unseen by others.'

'Yes, sir,' said Adkin, still shaking his head in amazement. 'Leave it to me, sir. But here? It's unbelievable.'

'Get on with it, mole,' said Thorne with unusual sharpness. 'If anymole-else realizes who she is . . .'

Whatever was in Thorne's mind at the beginning of his meeting with Privet – a meeting held in dusty tunnels watched over by Adkin, to which Privet had been brought on the pretext of a mole needing urgent healing – by the end of it he had decided to let her go. Once before he had held her captive against his better judgement, and that had nearly resulted in her death, not to mention the death it seemed of Whillan, if not of Rooster. No, Thorne would not take that responsibility again.

But what to do with her? It would have helped if she had talked, but she did not. She remained silent, mostly with her eyes cast down peacefully, though occasionally and disconcertingly she raised them and looked into his eyes. Her gaze was pale and clear, dispassionate, and Thorne felt when he looked on her that he was floundering into a sea of truth from which he might not have strength to emerge alive.

'Mole, mole . . . what are we to do with you?' he whispered.

But he knew that the real question her presence posed him was what he was to do with himself. He wished Rolt was there . . . and he found himself talking about how they had journeyed to Ashbourne, and how he had come on to Leamington. He felt he was talking to the Stone itself, and that it heard and understood his evasions, his half-truths, his hesitations.

'Mole, finding you puts me in an impossible position.'

He wondered aloud what he was going to do after Leamington: how to bring the rebels to order with a minimum loss of life on both sides; how to address the problem of Quail. He spoke of his hope that Chervil would be found, and a way become clear, but . . . but . . .

'But, mole! Where am I to put you where you'll be safe and yet do no harm?'

The Stone . . . the Stone knows all, and he felt that in her presence he was before the Silence of the Stone. He must think, he must try. He could not, he would not, he . . .

'Adkin!'

Thorne summoned his aide, and knew that long hours had passed. Time with this mole was not its normal self.

'Sir?'

'The Stone will decide what happens to her, not I. It has probably decided already! Now listen. If she would speak she would probably tell me simply to let her go. But it is too great a risk. Anarchy looms over moledom now, and moles such as she, even unrecognized, are vulnerable. No, she needs protection.'

'So what do you want me to do?'

Quickly Thorne told him to go to where a large number of followers had been confined pending Thorne's decision about what to do with them.

'You've an eye for a resourceful mole, and the Stone will surely guide you—' He stopped, for a look of amazement appeared on Adkin's face.

'Not like you to invoke the Stone, sir, I must say!' he said, glancing at Privet and winking at her in a familiar way. She smiled.

'Well, that's how it is!' said Thorne, for once defensive. 'Now,

299

Adkin, go and find a follower or two you like the look of and you think can look after Privet here, whether she wants them to or not.'

Adkin grinned. It was the kind of assignment he liked. 'As a matter of fact there's a couple of moles who might just be suitable, if they're still deigning to be with us. They have a habit of scarpering, and very good at it they are. Yes, they could be the ones!'

While he was gone Thorne found himself facing the void of Privet's silence once more. He tried to stay silent also, and could not, but when he spoke, what he said seemed foolish and wild. It was the lack of response he could not cope with, the peaceful indifference to anything he said. Until he mentioned how it was being said that Rooster had survived the torrent at Wildenhope, and for the first time Privet responded, though still mutely. Her head came back, her eyes widened and a look of pure joy came to her face. Thorne realized she had not known: until that moment her Rooster, as allmole knew him to be, had been dead to her.

'Privet,' said Thorne, 'I'm sorry, I would have told you earlier. But he did survive, it seems, and is now somewhere in the Wolds.'

She sighed, the nearest she came to speech, and it seemed to Thorne that it was a sigh from a far and distant place, a terrible, fearful place, which he himself would never have strength to reach.

'Mole, we're going to get you away to safety, with those you can trust. I'm a Brother Commander, not the keeper of spiritual moles who've more to teach us by far than we have them!'

Adkin returned with two wily, fit-looking moles in tow, a male and a female. They looked wary, a little fearful, but also bold.

'So you're what they call the Brother Commander of this place, are you?' said the male at once. 'How you've got the nerve to tell moles how to run their lives when all you lot can do is murder innocent moles, and then keep us captive for no reason—'

'Mole,' roared Thorne, his usual composure disturbed by the frustrations of his strange meeting with Privet, 'be quiet and listen. Now, what are your names?'

'We'll tell you that but not much more,' said the male grudgingly. 'My name's Hodder of Rollright, and this is my sister Arliss, and you've no right—'

Thorne raised a paw and with a fierce glance silenced Hodder. He looked at Privet, and Hodder and Arliss did the same.

'Now listen very carefully, for I'll say it once, and then Adkin here, and a couple of other guardmoles, are going to accompany you in safety as far as a day-and-night journey will take you.'

Hodder and Arliss exchanged a wary glance.

'This is not a trick, but instinct,' said Thorne. 'The more I think about it the less I'm likely to do it, so let's get on with it. In exchange for your freedom I'm going to give you a task. Some would think it an important task, others a dangerous one.'

'Try us,' said Hodder resolutely.

'Do you know this mole?'

They looked at Privet and shook their heads.

'Is she a follower or Newborn?' asked Hodder unenthusiastically.

'I would suggest you ask her, but she won't tell you. She's not a talkative mole,' said Thorne ironically. Privet smiled very slightly. 'I want you to look after her, see her through to safety, watch over her in the coming troubles. Take her far from where Newborns can find her.'

'Who is she?' asked Hodder again.

'When she used to speak,' said Adkin suddenly, sensing that Thorne would not mind his intervention, 'she called herself Privet; once of Crowden, now of Duncton Wood.'

'But it can't be!' gasped Hodder and Arliss together, staring at Privet as if she had fallen out of the sky; which in a sense she had.

'Well she is, and nomole but Adkin here and myself knows it – yet. Once they do there'll be problems that will complicate the military task I have ahead of me. I'm not much of a religious mole, and no doubt I should be, but my heart tells me I'm doing the right thing entrusting her to followers. You're two resourceful moles, even if you landed up here, but Adkin says you keep trying to get away. Now's your chance to do so, and perform a service for a mole all moledom has been searching for, for ill and for good.

'And if I know Privet – and I do, just a little – then I've no doubt that even without words she'll help you find out what needs to be done. There, that's it said and almost done. Take them all off my paws right now, Adkin, for if you don't I swear I'll change my mind.'

'Yes, *sir*! Now, sir!' cried out his assistant, beginning to herd them out and away.

For a moment Privet and Thorne stared at each other. Then she came to him and reached out a paw to touch his face. It was a strange and moving gesture which brought a broken smile from the Brother Commander; her love was palpable, and in her touch, and in her eyes, was an acceptance of a depth he felt nomole had ever given him.

'May you return home safeguarded,' he found himself saying, but he knew it was what she was saying to him. Home to where a mole is loved; home to where the search is over, and the restless spirit can be still.

She turned, joined the two followers, and they were gone, and he was left staring after them and whispering to himself, 'What is it I must do, mole? What is it I must do?'

Why had he let her go? Why did he feel utterly bereft now she was gone? Whatmole was she after all, to him and to all of moledom? Privet of Duncton, formerly of Crowden. He felt her touch upon his face and understood how through the power of her chosen Silence she was surely going to touch all moledom.

Evening. Night. Stars, and for a time Brother Commander Thorne abandoned his command to subordinates, to wander among the tragedy and emerging triumph that was the aftermath of Leamington. Sometimes he met mole, and they stared at him and fell away from him whispering.

'Sir!'

Not now mole, not this long night.

'Sir!'

Newborn or follower? He could not tell them apart now, for there was no difference, none at all.

'But sir!'

It was dawn, and he turned at last to attend to yet another guardmole who had come to him. An old campaigner, one of Adkin's friends.

'Brought you some food, sir. Here, sir. Yes, you lay down there, sir.'

'Mole, there's been others asking for me.'

'It's no matter, sir, if Adkin was here he'd tell them to wait. They'll wait all right. You eat this, sir, and you sleep.'

'What is it, mole?'

'Nothing, sir, you sleep now, you . . . It's all right, sir, it's been a long few days here, days we want to forget. I'll watch over you, sir; it's all right . . .'

Thorne was in a vale of tears. Those chambers, all those moles, all dead and dying, all lost. And Privet's touch upon his face, and now, now, sleep, dark and troubled; sleep, slipping into it at last. Lost, and a paw reaching out to him, yes, oh yes.

Thorne woke to the afternoon sun. The kindly paternal guardmole, Adkin's friend, was at his flank, tired but at the ready.

Thorne smiled.

302

'Better now, sir? Food here, drink over there.'

Thorne attended to his needs, and felt better than he had for mole-months past.

'Adkin's coming, sir.'

Thorne's assistant came hurrying – concern and then relief on his face.

'Thought we'd lost you, Thorne, sir, but . . . but you were looked after.'

'I was, Adkin,' said Thorne, smiling appreciatively at the guard who had watched over him.

'Well, now there's moles come, sir, important moles,' said Adkin mysteriously and with some awe in his voice.

'Send them to me.'

'Yes, sir,' said Adkin with obvious pleasure and relief. His Brother Commander was himself again. He hurried off. Thorne stretched himself again in the sun; shadows fell, and he turned.

'Greetings, Brother Commander! I trust you slept well, for there's work to do.'

Thorne found himself staring into the hard, glittering eyes of Chervil; with him was Brother Rolt. Behind them were ranged Chervil's bodyguards – Feldspar, and his powerful sons Fallow and Tarn. Instinctively three of Thorne's own guardmoles came to his flank along with Adkin, including the one who had watched over him with such sympathy and care through the night – and who would not mention his commander's tears and strange distress to anymole, until he was old, and scribemoles tracked him down and persuaded him to talk of those times.

'Greetings,' replied Thorne, his mind as clear and purposeful as it had ever been. 'Yes, there is much work to do now, and we shall do it.'

'Aye,' said Chervil, dismissing all but Feldspar, as Thorne dismissed his own guardmoles, 'I believe that with your help, Brother Commander, and Brother Rolt's here, if we act swiftly and with resolution, all is not lost. Now, listen . . .'

Across the surface of Leamington, and through its newly ordered tunnels, the word went out that Brother Commander Thorne, and Chervil, son of Thripp, and that important Brother Rolt, assistant to Elder Senior Brother Thripp himself, were deep in conference, and the future was being planned.

'It's all happening now,' said the guardmole who had watched over Thorne to Tarn. 'I tell you, this is where it's at now. There'll be things happening soon we'll be telling our pups about one day.'

Tarn nodded his head grimly: 'If we're not pushing up daisies first!'

'Not with the Brother Commander in charge, mate. Talk about being Newborn – he looked *reborn* when he woke up this afternoon.'

'He'll need to be if Senior Brother Chervil's involved!' said Fallow. 'Now, let's get some food ourselves, for they'll be talking till dusk or beyond.'

Which they did – far beyond, and into another night.

Chapter Twenty-Six

The Leamington Massing was but one of many excesses that had afflicted moledom since Quail's assumption of power at Wildenhope the previous Longest Night.

There were certainly many more such 'excesses' – some well known, others that were only discovered or revealed in the years and decades following, and many that will remain ever unrecorded, unless the shadows and ill-winds that lurk still in the tunnels and vales where they took place be taken as evidence.

Certainly, few moles now venture through the broken portals and into the crumbling tunnels of such systems as Swindon, south-west of Duncton. There is every reason to believe that the complete disappearance of moles from that formerly populous system in Newborn times was accompanied by an appalling orgy of violence and extended suffering. Only screams on a wild winter's day, and untraceable whimperings in the night, heard by frightened travellers who hurry quickly on, now tell of what once happened. All else is lost.

But evidence of an even larger and viler massing than Leamington has recently emerged at Malvern, in the Welsh Borderland, possibly involving the infamous dark-furred moles of the Forest of Dean. Many local moles, and even some visiting researchers, have said that the curious red stains on the tunnel walls, and up the lower trunks and trees of Malvern, were made by followers' blood. Others, less superstitious, have said the cause is simply a local variety of the poisonous death-scent lichen. No matter: there is truth in fancy as well as fact, and both speak with equal force of those harsh times.

Yet morbidly fascinating though such local tragedies may be, a historian is aware that they were but symptoms of the deep and vile malaise that had overtaken moledom after Quail had supplanted Thripp as Newborn leader. Some historians have said that Quail was already suffering from a growing dementia by that fateful Longest Night at Caer Caradoc when Thripp lost power, but 'dementia' is only a convenient label for a vile and evil condition of the spirit.

Much of our evidence concerning Quail at that time comes from

Snyde, whose meticulous records of the high councils of the Newborns are especially detailed where Quail was concerned, indeed, obsessively so. It would seem that having weaselled his way into Quail's confidence, Snyde did everything he could to exploit and extend the power of his position.

What makes Snyde's scribings so horrible for those who ken them now is his evident pleasure in Quail's insane energy and his gradual surrender to seemingly uncontrollable rages and evil lusts. It is all too plain that Snyde saw Quail not only as master, but as an object of study as well, observing his progress into madness as dispassionately as an adder might watch the death struggles of a vole. Not only that, but Snyde and one or two others who contrived to gain Quail's trust learned how to encourage and connive at his madness, and use it to their own advantage.

Thus, for example, did the mole Squilver, whom Thorne had demoted in Cannock, who had fled to Wildenhope in the hope of gaining advantage, have his rivals for command eliminated. This with the help of Snyde, who was aware that he himself did not have the qualities needed to take military command and was always eager to help those who did, and so gain their favour. The emergence in the third part of July of Squilver as Supreme Commander of the Newborns says as much about Snyde's cunning and Quail's clouded judgement as it does about the deviousness of Squilver himself.

The title 'Supreme Commander' was a new one, but it was almost meaningless from the beginning since the few competent Brother Commanders in the field had taken local matters into their own paws and were openly ignoring the Crusade Council's orders. It may seem odd that Quail should permit another to bear so exalted a title, especially a mole as relatively unknown as Squilver, when allmole knew only too well that if anymole was 'Supreme Commander', it was Quail himself. But perhaps Quail enjoyed the unctuous flattery of Squilver, and liked even more the knowledge, shared by many at Wildenhope, that one so easily raised to 'supreme' command might as easily be reduced to supreme humiliation.

Yet while Squilver's methods can never be condoned, killing to gain position seems somehow less shocking than murder for sexual gratification, which was Snyde's predilection. We have seen already that his secret pleasures were taken with corpses, and we know now through the evidence of his own scribings that he was well aware that the decline of his master's reason gave him the opportunity, frequently taken, of having innocent moles done to death that he might be

306

rewarded with their cadavers. For Quail was dominated by evil lusts; in plain language, he took a sadistic delight in perverting and destroying the lives of young moles – whether male or female mattered not to him. It was now the province of the crooked and deformed Snyde, acting as his pimp, to bring these unfortunates to his private chambers, night after night.

These murderous nocturnal atrocities were an open secret in Wildenhope; allmole knew of them, though they were never discussed. Brother Advisers like the wretched Fagg, so despised by Thorne, knew well that it was part of their task to provide what were euphemistically called 'Assistants to the Crusade Council' – usually young, appealing, malleable moles abducted from systems under their control. These victims (there is no better word for it) were then taken to Wildenhope and conducted into its cells by an entrance to the south-east of the system used for no other purpose.

These young moles, often deluded into thinking opportunity had come their way (though many were no doubt stricken by growing fears that only made worse the tortures to come), were then selected for use by the hierarchy of Wildenhope, beginning with Quail himself, who, towards the end of his time there, allowed the choosing to be done by Snyde. We may all too easily imagine that bent and twisted mole scurrying down the secret tunnels of Wildenhope to view the latest arrivals, eyeing them with Stone knows what filthy criterion of shape, colour, size, and raising his stunted talon to point out one or the other; no doubt too, with his perverted predilections, while he thought of them alive for Quail, he imagined them dead for himself.

From that moment of special selection on they were better dead than alive; or, if alive, better off if they came into Quail's private chamber to find him in a killing mood. Most lived but a few hours once his brutal attentions began. But some survived for three days in that place; a few four; and one, a male from Wantage, endured eight nights of pain and terror at Quail's malodorous paws, though he was quite mad by the end. We know all this because Snyde, utilizing his peepholes, and occasionally permitted to witness the final killing of these victims, recorded every loathsome detail.

Yes, 'malodorous' is by now the correct word. The curious odour which Snyde had recorded Quail as giving out when he was enraged, increased in frequency and duration through that July, and like many other things, was an unspoken fact of life in Wildenhope. Nomole dared speak of it and Quail himself seemed not to notice. But he was fetid now, the stench connected perhaps with the foul and oily sweat that seeped from his furless skin when he grew excited or angered.

Snyde himself, who especially delighted to record in detail such obscene matters, blamed it on some unnamed illness or malignant disease. Certainly something dire was now physically wrong with Quail, of which his baldness had been but the first sign. Throughout July, in addition to the bodily odour he emitted, it became undeniably clear that slowly and inexorably swellings or growths were beginning to disfigure him.

The first noticeable one was on the left side of his face, at his jawbone; he began to look as if he held some foreign object in his mouth. This growth increased slowly and the skin covering it grew taut and shiny, in contrast to that on the rest of his head which was criss-crossed by a thousand tiny creases, like ancient bark.

The second swelling, and this less subtle, was a distended and twisted growth at his rear end which, from some angles, and in certain lights, gave the foul impression of a stool that had not been quite evacuated from his body. Whether or not he knew of its existence nomole can say: Snyde recorded its onset and its development – for it grew as Quail's malady worsened – but it seems none ever dared mention it to Quail himself, nor heard him refer to it.

Another excrescence emerged upon his body at this time – a growth above his left eye which caused the eyelid to droop, and sometimes to close involuntarily for a moment or so.

Lastly, in this catalogue of bodily decay, so lovingly detailed in Snyde's records, we might note that it was during that same summer that Quail's teeth, once so white and sharp, began to discolour and fall out. Perhaps they were rotting, and certainly those moles unfortunate enough to come within range of his breath could not avoid its moist and clinging stench.

Yet, for all this, Quail had not entirely lost his power to lead, and to describe him as merely 'demented' is to do him a disservice. When he was calm, and before his evening lusts overtook him, his mind was clear enough. If there was a sign of madness, it was that his decisions, always harsh and cruel, grew more so.

He revelled in his power as head of the Crusade Council, convening it at strange and arbitrary times, listening to the reports it received and waiting for the councillors' responses in an intimidating and mal-evolent way, as if to say, 'You tell us what *you* think, but get it wrong and I'll have you killed, or kill you myself.' And how he grew to enjoy summoning moles that reports had maligned or praised, to accord them punishment or promotion.

It is natural to wonder how a mole so grotesque and increasingly unbalanced could hold sway over so many moles more healthy, more competent, and no doubt more intelligent than he. But this is to forget the fear that any brutal tyrant can inspire in all around him; jostling and struggling for survival and promotion, they become so corrupted by fear, so self-serving in all they do, that maintaining their position becomes all-important to them. When this finally depends on the tyrant who gave it to them, then, sadly, it is with his continuing survival that their own is linked and so they must support him.

By that July and August all competent Newborns had learned to keep their mouths shut, and all intelligent ones had found sinecures as far as possible from Wildenhope itself. The most talented of all – like Thorne and Chervil – were already alienated and now waited to find some way to wrest power from Quail. The least talented but most ambitious were, in the main, the ones who remained at Wildenhope, unwilling and afraid to express the truth that was surely all too plain to see: that bit by bit their bald, odoriferous, insatiable, decaying leader was losing touch with the Newborn Crusade he himself had planned. Whether he was yet aware that the Crusade was losing pace, and that the dominance of the Newborns had begun to wane, is impossible to say. But probably not, for Snyde, so accurate on all else, says nothing of it.

But what Quail did finally come to understand was that moles trained as Inquisitors did not make the best commanders in the field. No wonder then that realizing that many of his Brother Commanders were ill-suited to the power and responsibilities given them, he had them killed or demoted. In this he was helped by Snyde, often more perspicacious than Quail in assessing the qualities of others.

At times, however, Quail was capable of recognizing competence where it existed. The diatribes against Thorne decreased as that mole's regular reports through the earlier part of the summer came to make more and more sense of what was really going on, especially after Maple's emergence in the Wolds as leader of the followers. Thorne's reports analysing the threat of growing resistance, and the order and expansion he established at Cannock, had increasingly exemplified to the Wildenhope leadership how affairs should be conducted more widely.

So it was that Quail promoted two junior brothers, Sapient and Turling, to commands in Avebury and nearby Buckland respectively. Although we know them to have been murderous tyrants in their locales, they were at least efficient in what they did. But it was, rather, in the peripheral ground, Blagrove Slide and Ashbourne, where the Brother Commanders were fatally weak, and frequently replaced; and in northern and western territories, where too little attention was given.

In the key system of Duncton Wood no Brother Commander had been appointed – partly because Brother Inquisitor Fetter appeared to have everything under control (the insurgents in the Ancient System, led by Pumpkin, had gone unreported) – but also because Duncton occupied a special place in Quail's imagination. Like most other moles, he held it in awe for its history and the existence of its famous Stone, and wished to preserve for himself the right to be its Brother Commander.

'Whichever mole controls Duncton, controls the hearts of allmole,' Quail was inclined to say, making clear that the day would come when he would move his entourage and court from Wildenhope to Duncton Wood.

This opinion was not original, for moleyears before, when Thripp had been dominant and Quail a striving assistant Inquisitor, the Elder Senior Brother had confided that his greatest wish was to enter Duncton Wood as a spiritual conqueror, and by some new ritual or other be acknowledged master of moledom. Thripp had long since forgotten such youthful ambitions, and in any case if he had used the words 'master of moledom' he had quite specifically meant a conqueror of the spirit rather than the body. But how that phrase had stayed with Quail, its spiritual resonances long since replaced by a simple lust for power. That, to him, was what 'master of moledom' would mean, and it was what he intended to achieve.

This being so, it becomes easier to understand why Quail had so long permitted Thripp to live, albeit in complete isolation, down one of the deeper tunnels, and in one of the darker cells, of Wildenhope.

'Kill him? *Kill* him, mole?' Quail had rasped one night when Snyde had whispered the proposition in his ear. 'You're a fool, Snyde, and not always a clever one. Kill Thripp and I might as well kill myself. Indeed, I make sure he does not die, though by all these talons of mine I wish that he would . . . Aye, I wish it. But he does not, he will not, he must not. For . . . he . . . is . . . *loved*.'

Quail spat out the last word like some rotting piece of wormflesh that had caught between his broken, crumbling teeth and come suddenly free and loose in his stenchy mouth.

'Loved?' whispered Snyde, who was not a fool. He chose his moments well for such questions, using them to gain information, or provoke action, as the occasion demanded.

310

Quail turned, impatiently pushing aside the torn and broken body of the youngster upon whom he had just satiated his lusts.

'Yours,' he mumbled, suddenly tired.

Snyde eyed the dying body in the gloom, listening to its shocked and painful breathing appraisingly. Death was near, but not so near that he had not this exquisite time of lingering before taking his own pleasures in Stone knows what dark places his master had been before him.

'I am a fool, no doubt,' he purred, his right paw reaching out to caress the near-corpse, 'and so I do not understand your hesit—, your *decision*, to keep Thripp alive.'

'I shall be master of moledom and I wish him to live to see it. No!'

This last word was a sudden shout, like one of pain, and since his mouth was opened wide in making it and close to Snyde's twisted snout, the librarian took the full blast of Quail's foul and heavy breath. For a moment he almost vomited, but then, submitting to the odour as an unwilling female might to a dominant male, with a shudder of horrid release, he inhaled Quail's breath, and sighed it out again.

'No,' snarled Quail, 'I keep him alive not only that he may live to see my triumph at Duncton Stone, but so that he shall die to see it too.'

'Die, Master?' simpered Snyde, joyous in the contemplation of such evil at the Stone he knew so well; he much looked forward to returning there in triumph as Quail's Recorder and the new Master Librarian of Duncton Wood.

'The last thing Thripp shall see is my confirmation as mole Paramount and Prime, and the true way established corporeally through me across all moledom. We shall establish this ancient position once more and it is most fitting that it should end in the contemplation of the spiritual triumph of whose beginning he was the inspiration.'

'Most fitting,' murmured Snyde, repeating Quail's words over to himself that he might the more accurately scribe them down later, for the notion of serving he who was Paramount and Prime appealed to him and he revelled in his use of the word 'corporeally'.

Of the body; of the body as symbol of all else; of the body we do come, into which we went to procreate, and out of which we flee when its work is done and the Silence calls us.

'Yes, yes, yes,' said Snyde, ecstatic now, for Quail had turned from him towards the slumber that followed the nightly gratification of his

311

lusts; all the hours that lay ahead could be measured and enjoyed in the satisfaction of his own.

'Guardmole!' called out Snyde.

They came running, and supporting the dying youngster on either side they dragged and pushed him out into the tunnels, and thence to Snyde's own cell, a trail of blood behind.

'Corporeally,' repeated Snyde slowly, sniffing Quail's smells before he left, that they might linger like ethereal scent in his snout, and carry him forth to the dark necrophilism of the night.

'Leave us,' smiled Snyde, in his cell at last, the body almost dead.

'Yes, sir,' winked the guardmole, 'and have a good night.'

'I will,' said Snyde, eyes alight across the haunches of the cadaver-to-be.

'I don't doubt you will,' said the guard, whose companionable impudence Snyde rather liked, even encouraged, the more because it *was* impudence, and one day, or night, rather, that plump guard would be well checked. It was one of Snyde's perverted and disgusting pleasures to be especially nice to those he fancied . . . dead. One day this cheeky guardmole, and the next? Whatmole knows? Quail himself, perhaps.

Snyde's haunches trembled at admitting so forbidden a thought to the consciousness of his imagination. Quail, dead. Quail, his own at last. Quail become his plaything. Oh, oh, oh, sighed Snyde, *that* was worth waiting for. Meanwhile . . .

'Corporeally,' murmured Snyde again, enjoying the sensuousness of the word. His paw shivered with anticipation as it reached towards the body, the reward his master gave for his loyalty.

Peepholes in the night.

Snyde shifted, and darted a dark glance towards a shadowed place high in the wall of the cell. He smiled conspiratorially, and then stalked around the corpse as if it were living prey.

'Are you there?' he whispered towards that little hole through which Squelch was allowed to watch. He knew not, but it was not the knowledge of being watched so much as the possibility that he might be that gave Snyde his extra pleasure.

Beyond the cell's wall Squelch giggled and sighed, and heaved his obese body about excitedly, as below him, Snyde snouted at the body he had power over, which could not mock his deformities or threaten him, then savagely began his pleasures.

*

312

Such dark goings-on as these were the nightly norm at Wildenhope that corrupted summer. And corruption was the word, for even the most innocent and naïve of visiting brothers – come to Wildenhope to give the latest news of his part in the Crusade -- might find himself rewarded with some offer or other he found hard to refuse.

A scurry at the portal of his cell, the laugh of a guardmole melding with the whimper of some forsaken youngster who had offended the Newborns in some way, and was now offered up as temporary amusement to the visitor.

'What am I to do with her?' the brother might call out to the retreating guard.

'As you will, sir, as you will,' came the reply, 'but you'd be advised to do something, know what I mean?'

A brother who had reached as far as to be entertained at Wildenhope knew at least what *that* meant: he must do something, or be considered to have insulted his host, Quail himself. Such a brother might also be aware that he was being watched, as happened elsewhere in Newborn visitor and pleasure cells, usually through peepholes reached by secret galleries.

The sin was not in failing, so much as not trying at all. And so the brother, tired from his journey perhaps, beset by the deep fears that the tunnels of Wildenhope instilled in a mole, terrified and awed by the Elder Senior Brother Quail and the impassive cold eyes of the Crusade Council, would stare at the waiting victim, and then perform. Often these inhibited brothers, reared in a culture of hatred and contempt for followers, deprived of love from the very beginning of their lives, presented with such sudden and unexpected opportunity, discovered in themselves strange and terrible depravities.

Quail watched. Squelch watched and giggled. Snyde watched and recorded. The guardmoles watched. Everymole in the place seemed to do, or to watch, or a bit of both.

When so many knew so much, and all were implicated, no wonder nomole dared speak, or tried to explain the cries and sobs in the night; and it is not surprising that, from time to time, some brother or other, visibly distressed by what he had found himself capable of when given permission or threatened, would wander over the bluff of Wildenhope and hurl himself into that great river of blood whose deeps were a punishment for others, but now an escape for him.

Another daybreak, and the business of directing the Crusade could continue once more.

'Or can it?' rasped Quail, tired from his night's activities.

'Elder Senior Brother?' one of the Councillors dared ask.

'The Crusade, mole. Directing it from here? Eh?'

Quail expectorated, turned the yellow-green phlegm about his stinking mouth, and spat it out against the nearby wall, down which it slowly slid as if alive.

'It is becoming . . . difficult,' opined another Councillor, and one but recently elevated to his office. 'The intelligence comes later by the day as the crusades reach further north, and east and south. We need . . .'

He paused and faltered. Something in Quail's look warned him. Some fractional change in the Elder Senior Brother's stance, some brief flare of his powerful snout; something . . .

'. . . we need,' he continued in a placatory and servile way, 'your advice, Master, your *guidance*.'

He who dared speak was none other than Fagg, former Brother Adviser to Thorne, and now well ensconced and thriving at Wildenhope. It helped that Squilver was a friend of his, their mutual admiration and interests going back to the days when they were in training as brothers, the one for military tasks, the other for a spying and inquisitorial role.

Quail's face softened as he looked at Fagg, his bald head glowed rather than glowered in the morning light, and he smiled briefly before staring around at the Crusade Council, and even at Snyde tucked away in the shadows behind him, with a look authoritative yet paternal.

'We have indeed considered the point that Brother Fagg makes, and rightly makes,' he began. The Council visibly relaxed around him, especially Fagg, though he was careful not to let the smugness he felt show upon his face. 'Supreme Commander Squilver will apprise you of our future plans. They will involve changes, new resolution, perhaps even some sacrifice.'

His knotted and bulging left eyelid dropped, blinked, and slowly opened up again, his head jerked very briefly to the right and a look suggestive of pain came to his face, though the moment it was gone the paternal smile returned. But probably nomole but Snyde noticed it, for Quail's words were greeted with a sudden buzz of excitement, which died down swiftly into an apprehensive hush as Squilver came forward to speak.

'Let us pause only briefly over our successes,' he began, his voice sharply aggressive, his manner clipped and efficient, his nod towards Quail confident as the Elder Senior Brother beamed and shone, his

314

eyes twinkling to show what great confidence he had in the new young commander.

'Wales is all but won, and may by now be completely Newborn. The north-east is purified, and the north-west will give us no further trouble. As for the south and south-west, an area close to our Elder Senior Brother's heart, we need fear no resistance now. It is ours – Sapient and Turling have done their work well.'

There was a ripple of applause, a few excited shouts, and many smiles and the muttering of mutual praise.

'Yet,' continued Squilver quickly, his voice cutting through the self-congratulations, 'there are still places of resistance to which we must direct our resolve. The treachery of Brother Thorne, of whom I myself warned this Council, is now amply confirmed. Beechenhill, though strategically unimportant, is now in followers' paws thanks to Thorne's support. The glorious victory at Leamington, in which a few brave brothers routed the follower hordes, has now been blighted by Thorne's deviant and malicious intervention.

'The Duncton reprobate Maple remains at large in the Wolds, though surely not for long, for his support has dwindled before the truth and might of our Crusade, and many of his followers have come over to our side and found redemption through confession and abjection. Whilst at Seven Barrows, near notorious Uffington, a force of followers survives, claiming the sanctuary of the pagan Stones that rise there.'

Squilver, an impressive orator, paused and looked about the Council, his eyes dark and narrowing.

Mole glanced at mole, serious and expectant, and excited too. Although to those who ken his speech for the first time today he said little that was new, to his listeners at the time the very admission that some resistance was persisting and successful was like a breath of fresh air in the fetid, self-deluding atmosphere of Wildenhope.

Thorne alive and successful! The Wolds still under the control of the mole Maple! Followers holding on near Uffington!

'And Duncton Wood,' rasped Squilver dramatically. His eyes widened, his black glossy coat caught the light, and he frowned with puzzled disappointment as he continued. 'Aye, fabled Duncton Wood is still infected. The worm feeds in its heart, the snakes of doubt and uncertainty seek still to entwine about its mind. We have heard that a few followers, not many, but one is enough, have fled into the Ancient System there and mock our Inquisitors' great work. Worse, these same followers sneak out at night and attack our brave brothers

315

when they can find them by themselves, and torture them. Some of our good brothers have been snouted, some blinded, by these so-called followers of the Stone!'

He had begun slowly and quietly, but the pace of his speech had quickened, and his voice grew powerful and accusatory as he piled up these calumnies against the followers.

'But now their time has come!' he thundered. 'The worm shall be crushed, the snake taloned, the—'

He got no further in his oratory, for Quail, not enjoying the spectacle of another mole holding sway over the Council, nor wishing his young protégé to overstep the fine line between humility and pride, interrupted him with a peremptory grunt and wave of his paw.

Squilver had the sense to fall silent immediately, lowering his snout to his mentor, and casting a glance at his friends Snyde and Fagg which seemed to say, 'I was perhaps going a bit too far, but the Elder Senior Brother surely appreciates a mole who dares!'

Perhaps this was true, for the moment Squilver had stanced down Quail's face assumed its former look of arrogant condescension.

'The Supreme Commander speaks clearly and well, but he has no need to be inspiration with us!' he said.

It was a cheerful admonition, accepted with good grace by Squilver, who grinned ruefully when the Councillors laughed in a brotherly way.

'Be inspirational with your forces, Commander, and leave us to inspire each other.'

It was hardly funny, but since it was the nearest Quail had approached to a joke for a long time the assembly felt obliged to laugh at it, which they did rather too long and rather too loudly, as if vying with each other to show their leader how appreciative each was.

'We have resolved,' continued Quail quietly, his voice silencing everymole with the gravity of the morning's real message, 'to leave these hallowed tunnels and chambers of Wildenhope and Caer Caradoc and journey forth upon a final Crusade to moledom's heart!'

There was a gasp and then a ragged cheer – the gasp expressing amazement at so radical a step, the cheer because it seemed appropriate to welcome it; but the voices died away as Quail continued.

'The early work has been done by our fellow brothers who have long since gone forth to cleanse moledom of the worm and snake. But their strength and their will, though great, is not yet enough. We must now commit our spirits and our bodies to the final struggle. We must forsake our spiritual home and discover ourselves anew on the

316

crusading pilgrimage to take up our rightful place in those tunnels, and chambers, and across those surface runs, to which allmole looks for leadership and support.

'In a few days time we shall set forth for Duncton Wood and end the great Crusade to establish the only true way to worship the Stone! My fellow brothers, fellow Caradocians, are you ready to forsake your past and set forth to the future?'

'We are!' cried out the Council.

'Are you ready to forsake those friends who have faltered on the way, and falter still, and so threaten the Crusade's passage to the Stone?'

'Oh, we are, Elder Senior Brother, yes, we are!'

'I am ready to sacrifice my own life in this last struggle for our great cause,' said Quail quietly, bowing his swollen, shiny head, dropping his bulging, bloodshot eyes, and lowering his excrescence of a snout.

'And so are we,' cried his fellow Councillors, echoing his foul and hypocritical servility towards the Stone they could not see, even if it had appeared amongst them, so clouded by dogma was their vision.

Quail panted with the effort of his speech, his stomach palpitating, his odour wafting all about like the stench of death, the strange projecting growth at his rear end stiff and quivering like some pus-filled swollen talon pointing backwards towards fate.

'Brother Squilver, you shall order the military exodus to protect our front, rear, and flanks. Your best guardmoles will range ahead, ready to bring back news of infidel followers. See to it!'

'I will, Elder Senior Brother.'

'You, Brother Fagg, will bring to me a list of those brothers and anymole else adjudged by the Council, after due consultation this day, to be unfit for the final Crusade. Know neither fear nor favour in your work. See to it!'

'I shall, Elder Senior Brother,' whispered Fagg, betraying no surprise at this sudden elevation to a position that would inspire fear in allmole at Wildenhope.

'And you, good Brother Snyde, shall stay close by me, recording our words and deeds in the days following, that in time to come moledom shall know of these great events.'

'Indeed I will,' purred Snyde, breathing in Quail's stench with pleasure.

'Go to it, Brothers, go to it! Plan and prepare; prepare, and be ready for the glory of the Crusade into spiritual triumph! For the worm shall turn no more, nor the snake entwine, but they shall be

317

crushed and taloned, and laid waste before the accusing Light of the Stone, and its judgement!'

Quail ended with a laugh, now deep, now falsetto, and tears rolled down his furless face, and his distended eyelid blinked by itself as if he was winking grotesquely at some image of the Stone that was all his own.

Of the terrible days that followed we need barely speak. Fagg did his work well and thoroughly. Those poor youngsters who remained untouched and unsullied in the cells were subject to peremptory and final abuse, or cast into the river and drowned, or both. Various of the older brothers, mainly those once made venerable by early association with Thripp, but tainted now by the very fact of survival, were catalogued and listed, and after a brief nod of agreement by Quail, made eliminate. Most were taloned to death and left where they fell, others were drowned. A very few, who guessed their likely fate and sought to flee, were picked up by guardmoles posted out by Squilver for just such an eventuality. These few were kept alive by Quail's command until the last moments of the exodus.

'We shall need them. Hurt them not.'

'Which leaves one mole more, sir, one I did not put on the list.'

It was a hot afternoon, their last at Wildenhope, and Fagg whispered these words to Quail as sweat trickled down both their faces.

'Hmmph!' said Quail. 'And which would that be?'

'Thripp,' said Fagg softly, hardly daring to speak the name without the title of Elder Senior Brother before it.

'Thripp is coming with us, isn't he, Brother Snyde?'

Snyde smiled, familiar yet obsequious. 'You have said so, Master, and I have no reason to doubt that it will be so. Most sensible, most wise.'

'There you are, Fagg, Brother Snyde says I am sensible and wise. As for Thripp, a mole I once loved and respected as my own father – *he* has not been sensible or wise. He has betrayed the cause. Yet none must know of that, or that he travels with us. No, no, it is better not. He . . . is . . . still . . . *loved*. He would be a focus of discontent.'

Nomole dared respond to this, not even Snyde. It was certainly true that Thripp was loved by Newborns who did not know better all across moledom. It was also plain that the fact – the injustice of it, the unfairness too – caused Quail pain.

'But what of it?' he rasped. 'What are we, when all is said and done? Servants of the Stone, that is all. As is Thripp. He shall make sacrifice before the Duncton Stone and his blood – whether that of a holy mole or a hypocrite matters not – shall be seen to anoint the mole who must lead us to the future. Anointing of the head and body, imbibing of the blood. The old shall give way to the new; the ill to the whole; the then to the now. I *shall* be Prime.'

Quail mumbled and muttered these words as if for him they embodied a ritual, and perhaps this was so, for he waved his paw suddenly in Snyde's direction and barked, 'Get them down, scribe them down, for a liturgy must be prepared.'

'I have, Elder Senior Brother, I am,' said Snyde soothingly, nodding at Fagg to wait awhile.

'I am in pain,' whispered Quail quietly, 'caress me.'

His voice seemed suddenly that of a pup.

Snyde ran his deformed paws over Quail's back and flanks, over his haunches, over his oily face, down his spine, and then, slowly, over that thing that grew from him and was so foul, kneading it like a well-filled teat.

'Master, you do too much for us, too much. You must rest.'

'Fagg,' said Quail, his eyes closed, 'let nomole see Thripp. Let him be kept from my sight, but never let him far from me. Arrange it with Squilver.'

'I will, Elder Senior Brother. He shall ever be near you, none but his guards will know it, and you will not be troubled by the sight of his vile form.'

'Not vile,' whispered Quail as Fagg left, 'never vile. He was my *master*, Snyde, as I am yours. Do you understand? He was most beautiful, his eyes most bright. I . . . miss him, Snyde.'

'I know it, Master, and how he has caused you suffering. Yet still you shall honour him before the Duncton Stone and immortalize his memory with his own blood.'

'Yesssss . . .' sighed Quail.

'Do you wish to see . . . ?'

'No, no,' said Quail weakly, a look almost of pleading in his eyes. 'It is such pain to me to see him as he has become. A betrayer now, the very harbourer of worm and snake. No, no, I shall not see him again until he atones with his life at the Duncton Stone, and through my supping of his blood he may be purified in me once more, and I made whole again with he who was once so much to me.'

If Snyde realized that at moments such as this Quail was approaching the borderlands of his sanity, he did not show it. In his sympathetic smiles and grunts, his gentle caresses and empathic winks and nods, he seemed the very image of care and concern, though an image made grotesque by his own deformities, and the unmistakable evidence of Quail's bodily decay.

'Shall I myself go and oversee Fagg's administration of his departure, that nomole but trusted guardmoles know that it is Thripp himself who journeys forth?'

'I would be grateful if you would,' said Quail softly. 'Meanwhile, my dear Snyde, night approaches and I fear it. The last at Wildenhope. Shall I get through it, do you think?'

Though Quail's voice was weak, he was playing now, foreplaying. It was true that he dreaded the night *alone*, and could no longer fall into sleep until he had satisfied his lusts. But since he was not alone, and had no intention of being so, fear was not what he now felt so much as pleasant expectation. It was a game that Snyde, his pimp, counterpointed to perfection by hesitating, titillating, and then, at the right moment, providing.

'Master,' he said smoothly, 'do you not wish simply to sleep on your last night, without interruption?'

Quail laughed loudly at the absurdity of it. Then, when Snyde held back just a moment too long his eyes hardened and his voice found its usual edge. The games were over.

'Snyde, what have you for me?'

'Female, master. Untouched. Welsh. Young.'

'Frightened?'

'Very.'

Quail smiled once more, a cruel, sadistic smile.

'She awaits your pleasure,' said Snyde.

'Send her to me.'

'And after?'

'Yours, yours this night. Services well rendered. But see about that other matter first.'

Snyde left him, and signalled to the guardmoles nearby to bring the female, who approached him as if it was he whom she had been sent to pleasure. Which though it might later be true, was not yet so. She was shaking, and as she reached Snyde her eyes widened in horror at the sight of the distended fur across his twisted knobbly back, and his skewed snout.

'Take her in to him,' said Snyde.

'Come to me, my dear,' said a voice behind them both.

Impatient, Quail had come to welcome her through his portal, and stanced now staring, his mouth open in a ghastly smile, his eyes like bloody holes in his shining head, his eyelid drooping, his few discoloured teeth glistening with spit.

The female gasped and began to cry and struggle.

'Come, my dear,' said Quail, and his talons were sharp and vicious at her back and haunch as he hauled her into the darkness of his den; her fearful cry echoed down the tunnels ahead, as Snyde, chuckling, went on his busy way.

Dawn, and a glow of rising sun lit the summer grasses of Wildenhope.

An old mole surfaced, preceded by two guards, flanked by two more, and followed by a fifth and a sixth. He paused momentarily and breathed in the clear air. It was Thripp.

'Where are we going?' His eyes narrowed against the unfamiliar light, but they were pale and clear, and filled with calm resignation. 'Has my time come on such a day as this?' he mused, staring across the water-meadows to where the river, the place of punishment, waited. He had been confined so long below he had forgotten the glory of a summer dawn. 'Have they fattened me up for this?

'Where?' he asked again, his voice gentle yet compelling.

'A long way, sir,' muttered one of the guards, glancing at the others as if to say, 'we must tell him *something*.'

Thripp frowned for a moment, thinking. A long way, and they were turning from the meadowlands to go north along the bluff, which led, he knew, to the two-foot crossing-place.

A long way . . .

Newborn code for death? Was he to be finally disappeared? The sun grew warmer with every moment and the nightmare of his mole-years of confinement in Wildenhope receded with each step on the springy turf, each glistening of light in grass and thistle, each shimmer of the river that flowed slowly southwards in the vale to his right.

A long way . . .

'We're going to Duncton Wood, sir,' whispered the guardmole, 'think you can make it?'

'Duncton . . .' whispered Thripp, his snout lowering with emotion before he nodded almost imperceptibly to the friendly guard.

Duncton . . . and the sun rose in the east, bright and clear, warm and good, and its rays troubled the portals of Wildenhope, and harried at the last screams and tears, and drove them away, and half-blinded Snyde as he watched Thripp's departure, with Fagg at his flank.

'Going to his death, isn't he?' said Fagg.

321

'He should have been killed moleyears ago,' snarled Snyde. 'As long as he's alive he's a rallying-point.'

Fagg grinned. 'As I say, he's going to his death. Squilver's arranged it all. Watch him go, for when he's out of sight of here he's history.'

'I'd have preferred to have seen him dead with my own eyes,' said Snyde with a twisted smile, 'but the master would not have it so, or any other way but this.'

'The master . . .' began Fagg.

'. . . is weak where Thripp is concerned,' said Snyde. 'How else would he be? He *said* he wanted Thripp at Duncton Wood, but he is too kind, too generous. Our duty lies in thinking and doing for him what he cannot for himself.'

'Aye,' purred Fagg, his eyes bright with the power of it all.

'Aye,' whispered Snyde, thinking that here, this dawn, on Wildenhope Bluff, the rising sun found him as powerful as a mole could be.

'Aye,' said Snyde again, as Thripp was lost from view, 'all shall be well.'

Chapter Twenty-Seven

'She seems so *sad*,' Hodder whispered to Arliss on the second evening of their departure from Leamington, casting a worried glance at Privet who, ever silent, stared now across a darkening vale. 'Are we doing right to take her this way?'

Arliss stared at their charge, no more certain than her brother.

'If only she would just say *something*,' she said, 'something to show we are doing the right thing.'

But to where can moles lead one whose journey is inward, whose voice is silent, and whose face betrays nothing but a wistful longing to reach a goal which has no name?

'I feel we're . . . we're intruding.'

'We may be,' said Arliss frowning, 'but she seems grateful when we do things for her, like finding her food when we stopped this evening. She seems almost lost somewhere, lost and trying to find where to go.'

'I don't even know whether to talk to her or not.'

They fell silent, watching Privet, and then looking beyond her to the mauve sky in which stars began to prick out one by one as the valley below lost its form and colour in the gathering gloom. So deep was the silence of the twilight, so immense the starlit sky above them, that they hardly noticed when Privet turned back towards them from the spot to which she had retreated for a time.

When they did, she was already coming slowly towards them, her thin body struck with strange light, her eyes as bright as the reflection of stars in deep water. They were transfixed, breathless, hushed by her coming. Her face-fur shone with tears and never had they been looked on so gently in their lives. She reached a paw to each of them, though whether to seek reassurance, or to give it, they were not sure.

'We don't know what to do,' whispered Hodder, his normally confident Rollright voice faltering and quiet.

Privet stared at him.

'We don't know what you want,' added Arliss. 'We want to help, we want to know . . . to know we're doing the right thing. We don't even know where you want to go or what you need.'

'If only you could speak, just for a moment, to tell us, to help us,' said Hodder, his voice suddenly hopeful. It seemed such a simple thing, such a harmless thing, just a word of . . .

Reassurance; it was Privet who was giving it to them.

'You don't even know who we are, or where we're from.'

'We could tell you that . . .'

Their words, their explanations, tumbled out, and all their story too; the horrors they had seen, the fears they had felt, the courage and faith that had kept them together and alive; and the miracle of their freedom now, and the task they had been given, for which they felt so inadequate.

Then, when they had said what they must, and the night had darkened and deepened still more, and Privet had not withdrawn her touch from them, they fell slowly into silence for a time.

'Feel better,' said Hodder, ruminatively.

'Feel more certain now,' said Arliss.

'We thought it was a trick or something by that Thorne to let us go, but it wasn't.'

'I didn't think you were really Privet of Duncton when they first said your name,' said Arliss with the incredulous laugh of a mole who wonders how she could have been so silly as to doubt something that now seemed so evidently true. 'Of course you're Privet. You couldn't be anymole-else.'

'We've got to decide where to take you, haven't we?' said Hodder rhetorically. 'Well, I think—'

'*I* think we should go by way of whatever Stones we can find.'

'That's what I was going . . .'

Arliss grinned in the night. Hodder laughed lightly, easy with his sister.

'*Eventually*,' he said heavily, daring her to interrupt him again, 'we'll go to Duncton, like Thorne said. But slowly, safely, beyond the ken of anymole. We're good at that. It was only by chance we were caught. If you'll only trust us . . .'

'If you'll believe in us we'll see you home to Duncton safeguarded. We will!'

They sensed that Privet did not doubt it, and she took her paws from theirs at last, and turned back to look at the sky.

'There is somewhere you want us to go, isn't there?' said Hodder. 'There *is*,' he added for the benefit of Arliss.

'Yes,' she said matter-of-factly, 'and we'll find it, we *will*.'

But Privet had gone below ground to sleep.

Those summer months of late June and early July, when Privet travelled south in the protection of Hodder and Arliss of Rollright, and they learned in the bleak wilderness of her silence to begin to trust themselves, was a time that moles all across the land remembered as oppressive and full of perils.

Yet, in fact, the weather was fine and warm, though enough rain fell to green the trees and fill out the hedges with leaf and blossom. But when oppression and peril are in moles' hearts, it is hard to see the light of the sun, or feel the warmth of its rays. All the more so as the moles whom the early success of the Newborns had elevated to power began to surrender to the brutal demands of ambition and warped self-righteousness, and fell victim to the inner decay that comes when inspirational leadership gives way to bullying and contempt by the oppressor for his victims' weakening struggles against his greater force.

So Hodder and Arliss might well wonder where to go and what to do, across a landscape of systems where the Newborns seemed to them increasingly to hold all power, and the voice of protest and revolt to be muted and fading. Well might they be uncertain when they knew that one false turn, one mistake, could put them back into the power of moles from whom their escape, and their new-found task, seemed but a lucky chance that would not be repeated.

It did not occur to them that in its wisdom the Stone had known how to find just the right two moles for the task of protecting Privet in those perilous months. Though they came from Rollright, a system that like Duncton Wood itself had always provided its share of courageous moles to stance up boldly without fear or favour, and fight for the rights of the Stone's traditional followers, they did not pause to consider that they were part of a great tradition. They had a task, perhaps the greatest of their lives, and they would fulfil it as best they could.

It cannot be said that before they met Privet, Hodder and Arliss were deeply spiritual. Their faith was simple, their observance of the rituals of worship straightforward, and their spirit that of moles who have been reared to be loyal to their system and their kin, and to trust the Stone boldly, and with good hearts. Yet as the days went by in Privet's silent company both found themselves drawn to thoughts of the spirit they had never had before, let alone expressed, as they understood with increasing depth and awe the lonely striving and journey that their ward was making. They discovered too that her silence was not mere wordlessness, but many things, and at many levels. And though it was her struggling sadness they had noticed at first, now they saw that she experienced strange joys and ecstasies as well, and times of utter indifference to the normal dangers and pleasures of daily life.

Rain? Often she ignored it until she was led to shelter.

Food? Usually she did not seek it unless it was placed before her.

Heat and dust? What were such trivial discomforts to a mole whose journey seemed to have been greater than a thousand lifetimes, and still had more than a lifetime to go?

'She's old enough to be our mother,' observed Arliss some days after their fugitive journey had begun, 'and yet I feel we're mothering her.'

'And fathering,' said Hodder drily. 'I don't think I've ever felt so protective towards a mole in my whole life, except you.'

He looked at his sister with bright clear eyes, and if she knew that he had never been moved to speak so to her, or express his love for her so directly, she did not say so. As she hugged him close she thought to herself with gratitude that while Privet's silence might be strange, and hard to live with day by day, it was a powerful force that brought forth good, and stripped away pretensions and embarrassments that got in the way in ordinary life, even for such close siblings as she and Hodder. Faced with such discoveries, how could Arliss and Hodder not begin to love Privet, and feel a burning and passionate need to keep her safe from threat and danger while she pursued the task she had taken upon herself?

So far as the two had different roles, Hodder's was to route-find and scout ahead, while Arliss stayed close by Privet, observant of her needs, and not just for food and shelter, but for companionship as well. For sometimes, and once for more than a day and a night, Privet was struck still and weeping, seemingly beset by fears and horrors she found in the lonely place that she was in. Then would Arliss gently lead her to a snug, safe scrape, and Hodder be watchful for danger thereabouts.

Perhaps the Stone, aware of the siblings' need to learn to understand Privet and come to terms with their own personal discoveries in her company, had at first directed their paws by safe and peaceful ways, for in those initial days and weeks they met with little trouble.

They led Privet south by way of routes overlooking the Cherwell valley, whose soft green ways and water-meadows are the natural route from the midlands to Duncton Wood. But higher up the valley sides, on tracks Hodder had heard of from his father, and explored on their journey north from Rollright, they met only a few over-curious vagrants, a patrol they easily evaded, and the Newborn system of Upper Gaydon, into which they made their way by mistake, and found it hard to leave without causing untoward interest.

It was mid-June before they experienced real difficulty, and that was when, with some misgiving, they dropped downslope near muddy Wardington, where they ran straight into a rapacious rabble of Newborns. Fresh from making massacre and mayhem at nearby Banbury, and led by Jugly, a minor Inquisitor of the cruel and brutal kind then beginning to take local control, these fearsome moles were on the way north for the easy pickings they believed they would find there.

Hodder, realizing his mistake too late, found himself prevented by the wet and muddy ground from leading Privet and Arliss away from the danger. Overtaken by an advance group, herded up with some other strays and vagrants much as ants herd maggots for their later exploitation, it was all too plain that their position was serious.

The usual claims that they were good Newborns on their way to 'serve in Duncton Wood' did not cut much ice with moles whose pastime was murder, and whose pleasure was rape. It was as well for Arliss that Jugly was already satiated with another wretched victim, who having been used and abused now lay half dead, too weak to scream, her eyes deadened with shock and the realization that she could not survive much longer.

'Aye, you can take *her*, lads, if you want,' declared Jugly brutally, as he eyed Arliss with lascivious interest, 'but *this* one I'll have later.'

The vile leader watched with weary amusement as two of his colleagues, great tough moles with scarred faces and the arrogant ease of bullies surrounded by others of their kind, beat Hodder into the ground because he protested too much.

Yet, most oddly, Privet they ignored. Indeed it was almost as if, as a recovered Hodder later observed, they were afraid of something about her. It would have been hard then to say quite what it was, for she looked thin and insignificant, just a dried-up pupless female with lowered snout who could do with a bit of flesh on her body. The kind, in fact, that such ravaging Newborns frequently abused for a moment or two and then left to wander bereft, often badly injured, and die, forlorn and forgotten.

But this was not to be Privet's lot it seemed, not among these

327

Newborns. When the quick-thinking Arliss, ignoring her own mortal danger, asked if 'her old mother' might stay with her, a ruse which served not only to keep Privet nearby but also to take the moles' attention away from Hodder, Jugly nodded indifferently. He called his guardmoles off, leaving a couple to watch over Arliss and the others, along with some poor moles who had been rounded up, and moved on. Except that . . .

'But don't think I won't be back, for *you*,' he rasped at Arliss, 'so you lot keep your frigging paws off of her.'

Shoved and harried, they found themselves in a little dell along with ten or twelve other captives, with just three guards to keep an eye on them all. Escape seemed unlikely – some of the moles were too shocked to talk or even move, several were bruised and injured like Hodder; only a couple showed defiance, and all were very apprehensive indeed. Nor did the site help, for it was a steep-sided little place, with muddy slopes to three sides and a turbulent stream rushing noisily along the fourth, giving the air a cold, dank feel.

The guards watched them idly, quite evidently irritable and bored, eager no doubt to join their colleagues in whatever savage pillaging of the local system they were undertaking. One of the stronger moles tried arguing with them and was severely taloned for his pains. Hodder meanwhile, his wounds bloody but superficial and his natural fortitude soon overcoming any shock he felt at the battering he suffered while trying to protect the other two, assumed an abject and miserable stance while using his sharp eyes to reconnoitre the ground. Arliss, understanding what he was about, tended Privet, or simply looked afraid, wandering here and there among the group to assess their strengths and weaknesses, and the possibilities for escape.

'One thing's certain,' whispered Hodder when the guards weren't looking, 'we're not going to hang about here waiting for that foul leader of theirs to come back and . . . and . . .'

'No,' said Arliss firmly, 'we're not. I've already told Privet that, and though she didn't say anything of course, there was a determined look in her eyes.'

'What about the others here, have you had a chance to talk to any of them?'

''Ere you two, shut up your talking!' cried out one of the guards.

'He's not well and needs tending,' responded Arliss boldly, partly because it was her nature to be bold rather than meek, but also because experience told her that a resolute mole is often a mole who survives.

'He'll need a sight more than tending, he will, if you don't . . .'

The guardmole started towards her, Hodder prepared to defend her yet again, but one of the others pulled his friend back.

'Leave her be, mate; she's the one Jugly's got his beady eye on. She won't give trouble after that!'

The guardmole retreated and he and his friends laughed knowingly and winked at each other. The sky suddenly seemed a little gloomier, and the day colder.

'Yes,' whispered Arliss later when the guards were preoccupied once more with their own talk and things had settled down, 'those two over there are game for a fight, and that one . . .' (she pointed to a large male who had been injured as Hodder had and stanced now scowling at the ground), '. . . he's ready to have a go, he told me. We could—'

'We could indeed,' said Hodder resolutely, 'and we will. I'll have a word with him myself. Get Privet near you so you're ready to help her make a dash for it when the moment comes. The sooner the better, I reckon.'

Arliss grinned conspiratorially. She and Hodder had been in many a scrape together, and when that fierce and determined look came into his eyes, and his voice lowered to its present subdued snarl, she rather pitied the moles he was up against. As for being 'ready when the moment comes', it was one of the great strengths of the two of them that they understood each other so well that they acted together in moments of crisis, almost telepathically. It had been like that when they were pups, and remained so now.

Arliss drifted as inconspicuously as she could over to Privet's flank, while Hodder, staggering and dragging one paw lamely behind him, went up to the guards and begged them to allow him to go down to the stream to get drink.

'Get on with it then, and no funny business,' one said, and Hodder limped slowly back, his route taking him past the moles Arliss had pointed out, to whom he simply whispered, 'It's now or never, so you wait for the signal and go for them. Otherwise we're all dead.'

He did not dally, sensing that once the warnings had been given it was best not to let the moles he was about to lead have time for doubts.

He got his drink, washed his wounds, staggered about a bit more, and then meandered back, seemingly half dazed. Arliss watched his every move, and she saw others doing the same. She had warned Privet to be ready and had seen a flicker of response.

'Just follow me!' Arliss had told her, hoping she would.

At such moments surprise is a potent force, especially when an attack by one brave mole is followed by the charge of a mass of angry and aggrieved moles, ailing and injured though they may be.

Hodder chose his moment well, suddenly rising up from his abject stance and crying out, 'Here, you!' in a loud voice. This served not only to bring the guardmole swinging round nicely into taloning range, but acted as a rallying cry to those hardy moles already alert and willing to follow. No doubt fear as well as anger put power into their paws, for no sooner had the hapless guardmole turned and been taloned hard in the face by Hodder than those behind him charged to his flanks, and those that remained soon found courage to do the same. What might have been an untidy tussle turned into a bloody rout of the remaining guardmoles, and three of their companions who came running.

Arliss did not dally. With a firm, 'You're coming with me!' she took a hold of Privet and hustled her upslope away from the now triumphant prisoners, over a ridge and out of sight amongst the undergrowth alongside the stream beyond.

She had no need to worry that Hodder would not know what she was about – and nor did she fear for his safety. He would send their fellow prisoners on their way and, returning after the two of them, soon catch up with them. Such was the trust and understanding between the siblings that when Arliss at last saw what she was looking for she felt no need to mark the place.

The stream tumbled over a waterfall above them, and after a slippery scramble through vegetation and between wet rocks the two females reached the edge of the pool from which the water flowed. Here, after a further struggle over loose stones, and a short swim across the pool itself, they reached the far side of the stream and greater safety.

'We'll wait here,' said Arliss, pulling Privet down into lush grass, 'he'll be with us soon enough.'

He was too, appearing suddenly on the far side from where they had just come, bloodied but seemingly not seriously hurt. Arliss called softly to him and Hodder made his way across and sank down into the grass facing them, his fur dripping, the congealed blood of the guardmole he had taloned still red across his face, and a look of excitement and triumph in his eyes.

'Well? All got away?' said Arliss.

Hodder nodded, too breathless to talk for a few moments until, calming down a little, he described how the guardmole he had struck fell down, the other prisoners charged, and the escape was achieved.

'We've given the others their chance,' he said, 'and we can't do more. I knew you'd come this way so I just followed as soon as I could.'

They were suddenly aware of Privet, staring silently into Hodder's eyes. Her own were dark and still as the deep pool they had crossed and before her gaze Hodder fell silent, his own eyes a little furtive, his breathing still heavy, and oddly troubled. He frowned.

'Had to do it that way,' he said. 'Had to be decisive!'

His voice was defensive, and Arliss looked from him to Privet and back again, aware that some unspoken interrogation was taking place between them. Privet might be silent, but sometimes her silence was loud, and questioning.

'If I hadn't taloned him the way I did,' began Hodder again. 'I mean . . . he . . .'

Hodder's snout lowered, and he looked distressed.

'Did you kill him?' asked Arliss quietly.

Hodder was silent; Privet stared; Arliss waited.

'Might have been better if I had,' muttered her unhappy brother. Then, after a pause, and as if sharing a guilty secret, he added, 'I think I blinded him. His fellow guardmoles fled, and so did the other prisoners and I was left. It was just him and me. He asked me, he said . . .' And now Hodder looked up at them, real anguish in his face.

'What did he ask you?' whispered Arliss.

'He asked me to kill him. He was crying out in pain and shock, and he said if I didn't his mates would, now he was no use to them. "Better you do it", was what he said. I couldn't say anything, but just came here and left him where he was.'

Hodder looked filled with guilt and distress.

Then, as he and Arliss stared at each other mutely, Privet suddenly rose up out of the grass, and began to make her way back towards the pool. So quick and determined was her movement that she had reached the water's edge and was preparing to re-enter it before Arliss could get to her flank and restrain her.

'It's all right,' called out Hodder with sudden decision. 'I'll go back for him.'

Relief and purpose was in his face as he brushed Arliss's half-protest aside and went back into the water and re-crossed to the far side of the stream. Then he was gone back downslope and out of sight the

331

way he had come with such alacrity but a short time before and, as it had seemed, such triumph.

Privet retreated into the longer grass, and settled down in a peaceful, meditative way, quite unconcerned that they were so close to the Newborn position, or that Hodder might now be recaptured. Wrong deeds, she seemed to have said, made moles go backwards, not forwards. Right deeds were the only way.

As the time dragged by and the morning gave way to afternoon, the normal equanimity that Arliss felt about her brother gave way to concern, and all kinds of doubts and wonderings troubled her. On the one paw she felt inclined to go back over the stream herself; on the other her duty lay with Privet.

'And what if Hodder had *not* taloned that guardmole?' she debated with herself. 'It's all very well for Privet to be high and mighty but if he hadn't done what he did we might all be dead by now, or . . . or worse!' She glanced, as often in recent days, at Privet, and wondered again at the nature of her silence.

'The fact is she hasn't *said* anything,' continued Arliss to herself. 'That's the strange thing about it – she says nothing but Hodder and I keep being provoked into thinking and doing things we mightn't have before! If she had . . .'

If Privet had tried with words to persuade Hodder to go back to the guardmole's aid, Arliss had been about to say to herself, then it was very unlikely that he would have done so. But *silence*, that was a very different and more powerful thing.

'Hmmph!' was the thought that Arliss was finally reduced to, as she waited with great unease and growing despair for Hodder's return.

Then, as suddenly as he had gone, he was back in view again, and this time accompanied by a mole. There was no doubt which mole, for he was large, and dark, and his face was covered in blood as Hodder helped him slowly on. Their passage across the stream was an awkward one, marked by a dreadful cry of pain from the guardmole as cold water splashed for a moment into his torn eyes.

Then, with a final shove from Hodder, the great mole emerged from the water and fell amidst the gravelly mud of the river-bank, his breathing heavy and painful, his head poking and peering about sightlessly in a frightened way. More pathetic still was the way his left paw went out behind him to seek Hodder's again, for in getting out of the water the two moles had lost contact.

'Come on, mate,' said Hodder, giving him support once more,

'there's just a short climb and then we'll be in grass. There's friends here.'

The guardmole tensed, half rearing up as if in expectation of attack, but whether from Hodder's reassuring touch, or from loss of blood, his resolve lasted but moments and, head lowering, his limbs dragging, he struggled up the bank and into the grass near where Arliss and Privet lay.

Since Privet did not move, Arliss left her flank and went to the injured mole, whispering words of reassurance to him before she reached out a paw to touch him, and examine the terrible wound that her brother had inflicted. As for Hodder himself, with a final comforting pat on the guardmole's shoulder, he muttered, 'This is my sister, she'll do what she can for you,' and slumped down nearby, eyes closing with exhaustion.

Arliss had seen plenty of wounds before, and more gruesome ones too. Yet it seemed hard to believe that a single blow, however powerful and well aimed, could have caused such extensive damage to eyes and snout. Both eyes seemed punctured, and the lower part of the snout was crushed and open; the loss of blood was considerable, and continuing. It dribbled now from eyes and snout, deep red and beyond the power of all congealing and pressure to stop.

For a time indeed it flowed faster, for Arliss, who knew a little of the healing arts, took the mole back to the water's edge and bathed his face and removed from the wounds the clogging of earth and filth that had collected there on his journey to their hiding-place. This procedure was not easy, for the mole was in constant pain, and the chill of the water only increased it.

To make matters worse for Arliss, the guardmole cried out in his suffering, cries that combined a most distressing hiss and bubbling of broken breathing where his snout was damaged and its structure exposed. As for the eyes themselves, once the congealed blood was cleared a little, and the yellow nasal phlegm removed, it could be seen all too well that they had whitened in parts, and seemed sightless; but when, occasionally, they moved a little, light seemed to reach into them like jagged thorns.

It was evening before Arliss felt she had done all she could, and she was aware that the guardmole was weakening still. He had not spoken since his coming, and now his cries and whimpers were fainter and more despairing, as if he felt life leaving him and he was unsure whether, after all, it was best to let it go. Once or twice he reared up his head towards the sky as if seeking some help he felt might be there, greater than anymole could give. Then down he slumped once more, his laboured, noisy breathing and the bubbling of phlegm and blood like heralds of a painful blinded death.

Throughout all this Privet only watched, her eyes small and bright, but full of concern. Sometimes she glanced at the sleeping Hodder, occasionally at Arliss, but for the most part she watched the guardmole. Arliss wished she might have helped, and felt annoyed when she did not.

'You'll be all right,' Arliss whispered helplessly, 'mole, you'll find a way again.'

It was only as dusk came that he spoke intelligibly at last.

'Whatmoles are you?'

'Arliss,' she replied. 'It was my brother Hodder came for you.'

'He was the one . . . ?'

'Yes,' Arliss replied bleakly.

'Why did he come back for me? Better to have left me to die.'

Arliss shook her head and held him. A touch, a hug, speak louder than words to a mole in such a plight.

'What's your name?' she asked.

'Guardmole Rees,' he said, and for the briefest of moments his voice held no pain and he sounded normal. He had the burrish accent of the southern Welsh border country.

But then quite suddenly, as if in speaking his name he had been reminded of what he had been a short time before, and now might never be again, he began to shake and sob, his rasping breathing horrible to hear, and blood flowing once more from one of his damaged eyes like terrible tears.

Nothing Arliss could do or say could still or comfort him, and though the shaking slowed, and the cries quietened, it was plain that he was beginning to fail rapidly. Arliss looked at the sleeping Hodder and then at Privet in utter despair, her own tears shining bright upon her face.

Then, as suddenly as he had started shaking he stopped, his breathing slowed, and he was still and almost quiet. He did not answer to his name but seemed unconscious, or lost in some place of his own.

'Is he dying?' whispered Arliss almost to herself, her paws tightening about him. She looked up at the darkening sky that Rees could no longer see and said, 'Stone, help him. He is but mole and no real enemy of ours or yours. Just a mole in distress, so help him.'

She held him for a moment, and then, quite satisfied that there was no more she could do for him until he woke, and hoping that he

334

would, for that seemed rather uncertain now, she moved a little from him amongst the grass, as exhausted as Hodder, and slept. Yet, later, before night quite came, troubled and turning in her sleep, she reached out a paw unknowingly to Rees, and put it to one of his.

Privet stared unblinking at the stars, apparently unaware of the sighs and grunts and troubled pain of the three sleeping moles about her.

Arliss had said, 'He is just a mole in distress, so help him,' and they were words which seemed scribed in light across the great night sky.

A strange, disturbing clattering broke into the other sounds and though few moles would have known what it was, Privet knew. She had heard it sometimes at the Community of Rose in ill and feverish moles, or those near death. It was the sound of a mole's teeth as he went into a rigor of shaking and despair before the tide of pain and injury that engulfed him, and threatened now to sweep him off for ever into the eternal darkness that death seemed to be. Privet moved, but not yet towards Rees.

She rose and shivered her thin flanks in a stretch. She stared at the stars again, and let her eyes wander their vast course. She shook her head, almost as a mole might shake off some troubling wraith of cobweb, or skein of cleaver-weed, that had clung on too long after a rough passage through tunnels and undergrowth whose difficulties were all past.

Then, these short moments of farewell to another life over, for that is what they were, she turned to Rees, went to him, gently removed Arliss's paw from his, and reached out her paws to his wounded face. Starlight was on them, or in them perhaps, and slowly he stilled beneath her touch.

'Mole,' she whispered, 'listen now to me. The Stone is with thee, by thee, in thee, and your long night will become day once more. Be still now, be still.'

How long Privet offered her healing paws and words to him nomole could ever say, certainly not Guardmole Rees, who woke to the gentlest touch he had ever felt, and thought he saw the most beautiful stars where before there had only been the pain of eternal darkness.

Nor Hodder, who stirred and thought he dreamt, and afterwards was almost sure he had: for he saw in the night the mole Privet, stanced up before the injured Newborn, her paws to his face, and her voice like the very sky itself.

Nor Arliss, who woke and knew she did not dream, and saw paws filled with light upon the face of Rees, and a mole she had never seen or heard before, talking to him, praying for him, guiding him out of the darkness of the vales into which he had slipped, back towards the light of dawn and life.

'Yes, yes, there was a mole,' she sometimes said later, her voice always hushed, 'but I cannot say it was Privet, not in any form of her that I knew. Before I turned to sleep that night, having done all I could for Rees, I prayed for the Stone. At dawn I woke, and knew the Stone had come. The Stone was there, and Rees was being healed, and we were all safe. But Privet? I think . . . she was asleep. She was . . .'

Privet *was* asleep, when the others woke to morning sun, and the sounds of the guardmole grumbling and splashing at the water, grunting sometimes with pain.

'Come back up here where you can't be seen,' said Hodder, going to him.

'Throat like bloody oak-bark, mole,' said Rees, 'and can't see except for shadows. Shit!'

A shaft of sunlight had caught his face and he turned from it. Hodder helped him back into the shade.

'I didn't mean . . .' began Hodder, wishing to apologize for something too big for sorrow.

'Don't be bloody stupid, mole, you did well. Caught us unawares. Did what any fighting mole would have done. I'm hungry as a stoat, but if I try to scent worms it feels like talons up my snout.'

He swore once more, turned, and blundered into Arliss.

'You!' he said, feeling her touch.

'You're improved!' she said in astonishment.

Rees laughed ironically. 'Never been better,' he grunted. 'Was it you in the night who talked to me? Didn't think it was, but was it you?'

'Me?' said Arliss, wondering, and half remembering.

'Not you,' said Rees, not taking his paw from hers. 'Different voice. Like a gentle brook. Beautiful. Knew I'd be all right.'

'You will be,' said Arliss, glancing round to where, oblivious to all this, Privet slept.

'Wasn't *her*,' said Hodder, 'she never talks.'

'It was somemole,' said Rees quietly, all his strength suddenly deserting him. 'Now, you better leave me, for they'll come searching.' He sighed and his breathing deepened.

'We're staying here,' said Arliss fiercely, never more certain in her life. 'Till you're better. Till . . .'

'He's asleep,' said Hodder, grinning weakly, a sense of relief flooding into him. 'I think he'll see again.'

He looked at the drying wounds on Rees' face, where only one eye still seeped, and he said slowly, 'As long as I live I swear I'll never strike a mole again. It isn't the right way, Arliss, it can't be right, not this . . .'

Rees' protests continued in the days that followed, but all three moles ignored him, and each helped him in different ways: Hodder by finding food, and keeping a watch out for the Newborn patrols, one of which it was necessary for him to divert and lead off when they came too close; Arliss with words of comfort when the guardmole suffered an occasional relapse into pain and doubt that his sight would ever recover; and Privet by an occasional touch, a silent prayer.

Only slowly it seemed did Rees become aware of Privet's presence, but when he did he did not doubt that in some way he did not understand it was really to her that he owed his recovery. Not that he spoke to her at all, for it was with Arliss and Hodder that he communicated in his wild, swearing way. To him, it seemed, Privet was hardly there at all as a mole, but rather as something much more substantial, of which he was in increasing awe.

'Who is she?' he whispered to Arliss one night.

'Just a mole,' she replied, a little too quickly.

'Just a mole my arse!' said Rees in a growly kind of voice. 'She's the one, isn't she?'

'Which one? I don't know what you mean!' said Arliss too quickly again, her voice high and strained with the effort of lying.

Rees grinned, the better of his eyes blinking with sudden pain where his face creased and caught his healing wounds. He almost winked, and Arliss allowed herself a quick smile.

'You know which one,' he said quietly.

Arliss looked at him, familiar now with his torn face and strong, scarred body, and the different ranges of his voice, which was presently in its reverential mode. She would not concede for one moment who Privet was, yet she knew that he knew, though not how. She turned away.

'You fancy him, Arliss,' teased her brother later.

'No, I don't; of course I don't,' responded Arliss, her snout turning pink. Hodder enjoyed seeing his sister discomfited in this way, and

337

knew he was right. As for Rees, Hodder was beginning to feel a bond with him which was almost brotherly.

'Can you see more clearly?' he would ask him each day. Rees would nod, and grumble, and peer, and all of them could see his eyes were becoming less cloudy; the better one was almost clear.

'Aye, I can see shapes now as well as light and dark, but I'll never see the same way as before.'

'Yes, you will,' Arliss would earnestly reply, 'your sight will come back completely.'

'I don't mean seeing with my eyes, mole. Don't mean that.'

Suddenly, they woke up one morning and there was the sense of parting in the air. Privet, who often slept longer than the others, was already up and about, and when they surfaced she went off through the grass to peer upslope to the east.

'She's saying it's time to leave,' said Hodder matter-of-factly.

They looked at Rees, the so-far unmentioned question in both their minds.

If he was aware of it he did not show it but instead he said, 'She's right, that one, it's time you went.'

In his rough direct way he quelled their protests with a rasping, 'No, I'll not come with you. Too dangerous. I'll be slow as yet, and I probably look what I am, a Newborn. And you probably look what you are: followers.'

'But . . .' said Arliss, fully aware for the first time of what she might have found in Rees, and what she did not want to let go.

'Better not say it,' he said, reaching a big paw for hers and, after a moment's fumbling, for his sight was not yet clear, finding her. 'Better not even think it. You saved my life, and my sight and—'

'You *could* come with us,' said Arliss.

'Tell her,' said Rees gruffly to Hodder.

'You tell her,' replied Hodder wisely.

'I would come, for I've no stomach for the Newborn way now. It's gone from me. But I know whatmole it is travels with you, and one night I felt her paws on my face, and I heard her voice, or thought I did. The Stone made me see something then, Stone help me. I was touched by the future. Heard the voice of Silence. Know it's true. Won't deny I feel something for you, Arliss, and even for that brother of yours. But she's . . . more important. I won't help her cause travelling with you. But she needs you two, 'cos she's not with us half the time but in that place where I briefly went. You don't know the strength needed for her to stay there, but I do. I saw that darkness.

338

I wouldn't have the strength to journey on into it hoping there's light far beyond.

'Heard of Privet and how she escaped from Wildenhope. Know it's her here, *know* it, so don't let's end on a lie that she isn't. I wouldn't betray that mole, or you, *ever*, so you can rest easy.'

'I didn't think . . .' began Arliss, who felt a wild rush of emotions through her heart at Rees' fierce declaration of faith and loyalty to things that were so new to him; and strange comfort too that he could so openly put her second to Privet's needs, as if, thereby, he was telling her how much he really cared but dared not say.

'We better go,' said Hodder. 'Rees and I talked about it last night. Best this way. There'll be other times when the troubles are over and we can follow our hearts and faith again.'

He turned from the two of them to give them a moment together, and heard Arliss sob as she reached out to put her paws about Rees one last time.

Then, finding Privet a little way off, he said, 'We're going, aren't we? Not that you'll say yes!'

Privet smiled and turned back to the other two. She parted them gently, and somehow, as she stanced between them, her left paw to Rees and her right to Arliss, the two knew that somewhere, somehow, the Stone would bring them back together once more.

'Watch her well, mole,' said Rees, peering down at Privet. 'I wish you'd stayed long enough for me to see you as you are, and not just as a thin grey shape, which is all I can make out now. But it was your voice I heard, from out of your silence. Wasn't it?'

Privet reached a gentle paw to his scarred eyes, and he became still, and nodded, and felt at peace.

'You watch over each other!' he called after them. 'And don't worry about me! If I can survive so many days in the company of followers I expect I'll survive back in the company of my brother Newborns!'

There was an uneasy edge to his wry laughter, but it was Arliss's final wish that the Stone be with him that he afterwards remembered; and the touch of a mole he had never seen clearly, but who had entered into his suffering heart deeper than anymole before.

'Stone, protect them all.' he whispered when they were quite gone; and his tears were clear now, clear as the water of the stream by which he had learned to begin to see again.

PART IV

Quail Paramount

Chapter Twenty-Eight

It is with the deepest regret that I must interrupt this tale . . . just as Privet has set forth on the final stages of her historic return to Duncton Wood, and Thorne and Chervil seem bent on a powerful alliance whose objective is to displace Quail!

Just as, indeed, Maple is set fair to expand his power from the Wolds, whilst the rebels in Duncton Wood, led by bold Pumpkin, are readying themselves for a confrontation with Quail himself . . .

In short, this tale seems interrupted at its very crux, when all things are poised to turn and change in readiness for the discovery of the truth of the Book of Silence. Yet interrupt it I must, for I have no wish to delude you, who have been so loyal and steadfast a companion on this long journey towards Silence, and have shared with me these discoveries, which together constitute the last tale of Duncton Wood.

For I would not have you think that the voice that takes up the tale from now until its end, is the same you heard before. Sadly, it is not so, it cannot be so . . .

You will recall that at the start of the text now called Duncton Tales, *which is the first part of what historians know as* The Book of Silence, *I came to Duncton Wood. I was a young mole then in search of life and knowledge, and the answer to a question: 'What is the truth of the Book of Silence?' Up by the Duncton Stone I found the aged mole who began to tell me the answer – which telling, with his permission, I scribed down, first as 'Duncton Tales', then as 'Duncton Rising' and latterly as 'Duncton Stone' – upon the journey of whose telling we are currently embarked.*

In the course of time, and the many days and months, and the moleyears of that memorable summer that I spent in the wise company of that good mole, he became my master. I know not when that happened, but it did.

I served him as best I could – fetching him food, helping him to places where he might drink, finding new quarters for him when (as it often did) the mood took him to move on. I did what I could for the wisest mole I ever knew, whom only myself ever called 'Master'.

I was much distressed when, for a long time, between the scribing down of 'Duncton Rising' and the commencement of 'Duncton Stone', he chose to separate himself from me, saying he needed time to think and to contemplate what he knew (though I did not) would be the final part of his journey to the Stone's Silence. More than that, he understood that through a period of separation and estrangement I might mature and so be ready to scribe down the last part of the tale. That, at least, was how I reconciled myself to the fact of separation from him.

In that difficult time when he refused to see me, summer gave way to autumn, and the leaves of the great beech trees of the High Wood turned to gold and began to tumble to the ground before the winds of September and October. Then it was that my master permitted me to serve him once more, saying that he was ready now to tell me the last part of the story of the Book of Silence, and confessing to me that he was afraid to tell it. The Silence awaited him now, the Stone rose before his gaze, and he was afraid, and needed company.

So he began the tale that I have faithfully scribed down, which, until now, you have kenned in the confidence that as it began in his voice, so surely would it end. Is not that normally the way with tales?

I do not now believe that so far as the tale of the Book of Silence is concerned my master ever thought that his would be the voice that would end it. Not so much because he knew he was growing weaker as he drew nearer to the Silence, but because he understood something profound about this particular tale, which is this: the last part of the journey to the truth of the Book of Silence cannot be made for one mole by another. The journeyer, the pilgrim, must make it for himself, and draw what conclusion from it best suits his need and purpose.

I have said that my master withdrew himself from me between his telling of 'Duncton Rising' and that of 'Duncton Stone'. When he began again he did so more diffidently, almost fearfully. Then as he told the tale autumn advanced towards winter, and the crisp and golden leaves across the High Wood's floor grew dark and limp as the cold winds came, and the rains drove down through the leafless trees. My master grew ever weaker, and sometimes, though he summoned me to his flank and bade me scribe down what he said, I could not understand the words he spoke. His voice became weak and indistinct, his pauses seemed to grow longer, his mouth moved in the semblance of speech about moles and incidents that I swear his staring eyes seemed to see, but words there came none.

'Have you got that, mole? Have you scribed that down?'

'Master . . . I . . . I . . .' But I could not lie to him. 'Master, I cannot hear the words you speak, I have scribed nothing all morning.'

'But I told you so much, mole, I took you to pl . . . places . . . mole . . .' And he would grasp my paw as if he were a frightened pup, and weep for something he had rediscovered for a moment and now believed was irretrievably lost, for want of my scribing it down.

'I spoke, yet no words came,' he whispered later, and in wonder. 'We are approaching Silence now, mole, do you see? Do you see?'

'Master . . . I . . .' was all I could whisper, which was not much.

'You will, mole, one day you will, and then you'll be ready to complete the journey of the Book of Silence which I set you off on so long ago.'

'Master, I cannot journey on through this tale without your help. Your words, your memories, are the tale, and without them I can never reach the end. I cannot journey on alone.'

'Privet journeyed on alone, didn't she? Eh, mole? Didn't she?'

'But she was Privet, and I . . . I am . . .'

'And what are you?'

'An ordinary mole.'

'We are all of us ordinary moles, and it was for us she journeyed, not to show us the way, for that is for us each to find, but to show us how to journey, and that it could be done by any one of us. That is by far the greater gift.'

'But Privet was strong of purpose.'

'No stronger than any other mole can be.'

'She was courageous.'

'Yet not with a courage others cannot seek and find.'

'Oh, but she was wise!'

'Her wisdom was to trust the Stone, and that we all can do. She showed us how, mole, she showed us how.'

'Master, did you know Privet?'

I must confess at once that I knew the answer to this question, for others in Duncton Wood had often told me the story of the mole I simply call, and call still, my master. Yet he had never told me the story in his own words. Now, as winter seemed to have overtaken him, and he seemed less and less willing to proceed with the great tale he had begun, I sensed I might have no other chance to hear him talk about himself.

'Yes, mole, I knew her,' he answered, nodding his lined head, and blinking his crinkled rheumy eyes into the gentlest softest smile I ever saw upon his face.

345

'Master . . .' I began again, with the remorselessness of a scholar-scribe, scenting the end of a quest long since begun.

He raised his paw in sweet admonishment and I stopped and smiled in return, ruefully.

'Mole,' he whispered, 'come near to me. Now listen, for soon I must leave you. Yes, yes, it must be so. I am tired now, and have lived far beyond my years, sustained only by your ministrations and my need to tell you of the coming of the Book of Silence. Now I hear the Silence ever louder in my old ears, and see the Stone's Light ever brighter, and I do not wish to turn from it more. I am ready to go to the Silence now and have told you almost all I need to.

'The rest you will understand better without my intercession, and your final steps towards the truth of the lost and last Book must be taken alone. Yet, one final thing I shall tell you before I leave, for I doubt that what they've said about me in Duncton, and down in the communal tunnels and chambers of Barrow Vale, and what they have told you about my own part in the coming of the Book, is quite as it was . . .'

'They said you were brave, Master, and that without you—'

He waved his paw impatiently for me to be silent and I obeyed.

'Brave? I was not brave. The Stone was always with me, and Privet and Rooster, and all those moles. No, no, I was not brave. I fulfilled the task ordained me by the Stone, no more, no less, and so I was a part of the coming of the Book. That is all, a part. By ourselves we are nothing; together we are life itself. That is what Privet had to discover, and it is what she taught us all.

'Now, listen, and let me tell you while I am still able the one thing nomole-else knows, for I have never spoken of it until now. What you have heard are guesses, what I shall tell you is the truth. Of the rest, and the parts played by so many others after those terrible summer years when Quail seemed in the ascendant, and a bitter anarchy spread across moledom, you must discover for yourself.

'But of the days when I met Privet, and understood the nature of the Book of Silence, I shall tell you now. Therefore, mole, listen . . . and touch me if I seem to slip away, keep me with you until I have done and then, when the sound of Silence overwhelms me, and the Light of the Stone becomes too bright for me to resist it, lead my old body to the Stone, settle me there, and stay with me until I have gone, for I shall be afraid and will need you near.

'Now, mole, listen, and listen well . . .'

Then did my master speak to me one last time, his paw to mine,

346

his voice growing weaker, but his eyes brightening with the light he saw. He told me what he had told no other, how he saw the lost Book's truth. He told me of the part he played, which some have said was nearly the greatest of all, but which he said was but a part of something far greater than himself.

'Understand that!' he said again and again. 'Understand!'

It was as he said it would be. He told me what he needed to and then he turned towards the Silence, his paw to mine, and I led my dear master up through the trees of the High Wood and back to the Stone itself. I think others joined us, to witness his passing, but I do not really remember them. Only him, and the sound of Silence about him, and the Light of the Stone, and my tears that he was leaving me and I would hear his beloved voice no more.

'Journey as they did, mole; go to the holy places; listen to the winds that whispered and roared where they went; sound the delvings that they knew. Then come back to Duncton Wood and finish for me the tale that I began here by our Stone so long ago. You will be ready then.'

Did he speak these words? I think he did. I think I heard them from out of the Silence to which he had finally turned. I felt his paw in mine, I saw him stare up at the Stone with eyes that saw mortal things no more, and then I knew he had gone on ahead of me, into the truth of the tale he told.

'Master,' I whispered after him, 'you never let me speak my name, never once in all the moleyears I was with you.'

Nor had he. To him I was always 'mole'. No more, no less.

'Master, my name is . . .' and I told him then, or told it to the Stone.

Then I turned from where he lay and I think that others came and said prayers of celebration and farewell to the last mole who remembered Privet, and knew the truth of what she had done for all of us.

I turned and I did not look back, but set off as he had bid me do, to the holy places, to where the wind blew, to where great delvings had been made. To Caer Caradoc I went, to Blagrove Slide; to Cannock and to Hobsley Coppice, to see the risen Stone; to Beechenhill and on to Whern; and, yes, to Mallerstang, even to there I went. To Sedlescombe, where I myself began . . .

Then back through the years I came by ways strange and dark, back to the Light of Duncton's Stone, to fulfil the task my master set me, which was to end the tale that he began.

347

Only as I did so did I come to understand why for this last part of the tale I had needed to journey alone; and why my master always said he had no need to know my name.

As for whatmole he was, where he came from, what he did, we must journey some way yet to find.

Through darkness must we go, through danger, to that place far beyond where we may hope the Book of Silence awaits our coming . . .

Stone, guide us, for darkness comes upon us now, the Worm turns, and the Snake entwines . . .

The progress of Quail and his entourage to Duncton Wood that late July is too well chronicled for us to record it here in detail – not only because the indefatigable Snyde has already done the job for us in repugnant detail, but also because the impact of Quail's passing is etched like acid across the face of innocence in the communal memories of system after system unlucky enough to be upon his route. We are striving to reach Silence, not to explore every unwashed and odorous cranny of the Newborn's ailing body. Let us, then, be as brief as possible . . .

Quail chose to take his time, and in each place he came to it was his pleasure to mete out exemplary punishment to whatever hapless moles were presented to him by the Brother Commander in charge. Whether these victims were followers or Newborns mattered not, provided there *were* victims; *that* much successive Brother Commanders and the Brother Advisers working with them came to understand very quickly.

Which was not surprising after news reached them of Quail's treatment of Shap and Bunting, Brother Commander and Adviser respectively of Stanton Long, the Newborn stronghold that lay on the east side of the River Corve beyond Shipton. Shap was one of the older Commanders who had first gained ascendancy under Thripp, and perhaps as a result was not likely to be much favoured by Quail and his acolytes. Bunting was not one of the brightest of the Advisers but should have known better than to have no victims at all in readiness for the Elder Senior Brother Quail's arrival; or to have rustled some up when it became clear that Quail was displeased.

'No tainted moles, Brother Commander?'

'None, Elder Senior Brother,' declared Shap with fatal smugness, feeling that to have none meant he was doing his job well, which normally it would. Such 'tainted moles' as had come his way had long since been confined, re-educated, or done to death.

'None at all, Adviser Bunting?' hissed Quail, his bulging head growing more shiny and threatening by the moment.

'Not of late, Elder Senior Brother, no, we have cleansed the tunnels and chambers of the system hereabout long since and are confident—'

'Confident! He said confident, my good Brother Snyde!' said Quail softly over his shoulder. 'Scribe it down: "confident". A happy word.'

'Happy indeed, Master, were it true.'

'Ah, yessss . . . Scribe it, Snyde!'

The chamber where they stanced was silent but for the scratching of Snyde's scribing talon.

'"Confident",' the distorted mole said lightly, permitting himself a little laugh.

Quail stared at Shap and Bunting in turn, his black eyes impenetrable. Perhaps they knew then they stared into the eyes of their own death.

'So, Brothers, you are both *confident* that the snakes of doubt, and the worms of treachery, are not here in these pure cleansed tunnels of – where did you say we were, Snyde?'

'Stanton Long, Master.'

'Just so. Stanton Long.'

'I did not say . . .' gabbled Bunting, aware suddenly of his danger.

'We did not mean . . .' faltered Shap.

'The Snake never *says*, the worms never *mean*,' said Quail, expelling a sigh that sent a wave of foul air into the shaking snouts of Shap and Bunting. Bunting retched; Shap's eyes watered with the strain of trying not to look as if the stench of Quail's breath made him feel sick. Snyde, Fagg and Squilver almost quivered with the pleasure of coming punishments; Skua's eyes were icily enraged at such palpable evidence of incompetence.

'Well, then, Senior Brother Inquisitor, what shall we do with them?' purred Quail.

'Arraign them, and let them be judged,' began Skua in his inquisitorial way.

'No time for that!' said Quail sharply, frowning. He stared for a moment more and then his eyes wandered, a sign that he was growing bored.

'Snout them at this system's eastern edge,' he continued, 'that other such brothers in responsible positions should be warned to be always vigilant, lest the snakes and worms creep into their own hearts. Aye, snout them!'

This last he said so savagely that Shap fainted on the spot, and

Bunting began to whimper and shake and beg forgiveness, saying he could find reprobates and miscreants aplenty but had not wished to besmirch the Elder Senior Brother's day with such things as that.

'Lies,' said Skua rightly, knowing a fabrication when he heard one.

'Lies,' said Snyde, scribing the word down.

'Lies,' repeated Fagg gleefully and encouraging others in the chamber to do the same so that before a mole could blink the place was filled with shouts of 'Lies!' repeated over and over until they were all almost exhausted.

Then the system's guards and many others assembled on the eastern boundary, and Shap and Bunting were snouted on the spikes of a wire fence that ran there, their screams ignored but their ignominy not forgotten.

After that there was a positive plague of victims found and kept at the ready in each system that Quail and the others came to, though whatmoles, or how many, or whether any at all were used and abused depended entirely on Quail's mood of the day. To those like Fagg and Squilver and others near to Quail, who were able to observe and discuss such matters, it soon became clear that increasingly Quail's mood could be manipulated by others, up to a point.

A well-timed word in his ear, the withholding of news good (or bad) from the outreaches of the Newborn territories, dark insinuations, even intimations that the weather might soon improve (or worsen) – all these were techniques used by his minions to try to swing him one way or another. In this way old scores might be settled – as with Fagg's well-timed revelation of some minor losses in the Wolds to Maple's forces just as Quail had settled down one morning for a consultation with the unlucky Brother Adviser Sturrick of Burwarton. Sturrick was an old enemy of Fagg, and earlier in his career had outshone him, gaining a promotion that the vengeful Fagg felt he had deserved more.

When Quail arrived at Burwarton, whose cleansing Sturrick had organized with exemplary efficiency, and whose indigenous moles had over recent moleyears provided useful guards for training at Bowdler and Caradoc, and some memorable fodder for the lusts of Wildenhope, Sturrick might have seemed in a strong enough position to resist mere 'moods'. Not so. Quail listened to Burwarton's report on a day when his ailments were giving him some pain, and to those who knew him well it was plain he was irritable, and in danger of swinging from mere irritation towards rage.

Fagg whispered his bad news at just the right moment to touch off

350

Quail's anger, knowing that it would be visited upon Sturrick – and it was.

'Eh? What did you say? Speak up, mole,' rasped Quail, the skin at the back of his neck creasing and bulging, his diseased eye swelling dangerously, the eyelid drooping; the protuberance at his rear developing a stiff little tremor, which was a sure sign of approaching fury.

'I said nothing, Elder Senior Brother, I mean to say . . .' whimpered Sturrick, helplessly borne into the maelstrom of rage and anger from which he did not escape with his life.

'Take him; he bores me, he wriggles, he whines . . .' snarled Quail at the end.

'What would you have me do with him, Elder Senior Brother?' wondered the foul Fagg, smiling evilly.

'What you will, what you will,' said Quail, dismissing them both, along with the guardmoles who were always at the ready for such moments.

'Make him excommunicate?' hissed Fagg, delighting in the widening into fear of Sturrick's eyes, and the squeaky way his voice vainly implored their master for mercy, and the cold sweat that prickled at his flanks as witness to his terror.

'Yes, yes, yes, good Fagg, you are right. Take him, I wish to know him no more.'

Sturrick was taken to the surface of the system he had commanded so effectively and faultlessly for so long. He was maimed in the front right paw and the left hind paw, so that he could only crawl; he was mutilated so that his maleness was all gone; his snout was sheered off at its tip, to cause him agony.

'And finally,' scribed Snyde in his relentless record of those evil days and nights, 'the screaming Sturrick was pushed and dragged beyond any territory that he knew and there, despite his pleas, Fagg blinded him and left him to wander, if so maimed a mole could wander, to his death, an excommunicant.'

Two moles surpassed all others in their skill at manipulating Quail, and by the time of the exodus from Wildenhope and the passage to Duncton Wood, they were in conflict. One was Skua, so long Quail's ally and inquisitorial helpmeet, but now a falling star; the other was Snyde, Quail's deformed shadow, observer, recorder, conniver, and, increasingly, sole adviser. It was Quail's delight to remind each of these moles of their vulnerability by choosing, at times, to favour the other – and though few doubted that Snyde would now finally win

351

the struggle for their master's favour, Skua was given sufficient encouragement for a significant proportion of the Senior Brothers to believe he might still be the victor, and so they continued to give him tacit support.

Thus, even as Brother Adviser Sturrick was dragged away from Quail's presence, Skua, very aware that he was a worthy Newborn and not one to be easily replaced, strove to change Quail's mind. On some days he might well have succeeded but on that day he was out of favour, and Snyde was very much in Quail's warm thoughts.

'Well, Brother Snyde, you have heard your esteemed colleague plead for the wretched Sturrick's life, and a commutation of his sentence. Haven't you, haven't you?'

Snyde inclined his pointed head and opened his shining eyes a little wider to indicate that he had indeed heard.

'So what do you think? Give us the benefit of your judgement.'

'I think,' said Snyde in his weaselly but measured way, 'that our master has been wise, even tolerant.'

'Tolerant always,' interjected Skua carefully, 'but perhaps—'

'Not wise?' said Snyde quickly.

'Always wise of course, but . . .'

'Well then,' said Snyde with a benign shrug, 'what more can a mole say? Let alone a Senior Brother? *Least* of all the Senior Brother Inquisitor?'

Skua wisely said nothing more, and so Sturrick, his last chance gone, had been punished in the manner described, and wandered for three days and three nights east of Burwarton, until the rooks of Chatmore Wood harried him into death.

But let nomole think that Quail was merely clay in the paws of those about him. Had he been he would not have lasted so long, nor made such diabolic impact. On his good days, which were then still the majority, his mind was clear, and his energy and decisiveness almost as potent as they always had been.

He certainly arranged the secret passage of Thripp well enough, with Fagg in charge of the exercise, and Snyde given a watching brief over it. Nomole but those directly involved and some senior members of the Crusade Council seems to have guessed that throughout the journey Thripp was always near, though always hidden. In this Quail certainly calculated right, for had others known what mole it was, so privily conducted by night from place to place in the shadow of the main group of moles with Quail, there would have been much interest in him, and real danger of defection from Quail's ranks back to the kinder and more benign influence of the former Elder Senior Brother.

Nor was Quail slow to ken the information gleaned from the systems through which they passed concerning growing divisions in Newborn ranks. As yet he said little of it, but he saw it, he almost smelt it, and he had his thoughts and bided his time. The journey to Duncton Wood, with all its attendant dangers and discomforts, was not the best time to reassert his authority. That, he believed, could wait, and in this his judgement was probably sound.

Indeed, had Quail not been a mole concerned so much with power and the domination of others, and with the perverted pleasures of imposing the extreme dogmas and doubts of the sect he had taken over, he might have been the very mole needed to carry on the best of the work first begun by Thripp at Blagrove Slide.

But he was not; and in addition to his basic malevolence towards life and the living was the dreadful fact that he was dominated almost hourly by the need to satisfy his sadistic lusts, or the planning for the prospect of doing so. Which made for poor judgement, and the appointment of self-serving subordinates more interested in maintaining their positions by servicing his weaknesses, than promoting a noble cause and being willing to stance up to a leader who seemed in the process of betraying it. *Such* excellent subordinates – Brother Rolt, for example – it had been Thripp's gift to be able to find and appoint, though with Quail himself, Thripp seemed to have fatally failed.

Yet even had Quail, by some miracle of transmutation imposed upon him by the Stone, become a reformed mole, it seems unlikely that by the time the journey from Wildenhope to Duncton took place he could have done much to improve the situation. Not only because the process of civil strife within the Newborn movement seemed already irreversible, but also because his own illness, for that was plainly what it was, was beyond curing, and whatever caused the swellings, and the odours, and increasingly the rages, was beginning to overtake his sanity as surely as black ivy can cover and choke a healthy tree.

Quail's progress to Duncton was not rapid, but it was steady, for he preferred not to stay in one place for too long, and by mid-August he had reached Banbury, which lies in the vale of the River Cherwell, a good way north of Duncton Wood. Their route had been chosen with some care – if they had gone further south as they might have wished then there would have been the possibility of a clash with the forces of the followers led by Maple from the Wolds, while a more northerly route would have risked bringing to a head the tacit but as yet unresolved conflict with Brother Commander Thorne, late of Cannock.

As it was they had reached Banbury with no opposition at all, the only violence being that which Quail himself had inflicted as 'just punishment' upon whatever victims successive Commanders and Advisers were pleased to offer up to him. Indeed, Squilver, Supreme Commander and executant of Quail's occasional military orders, congratulated himself on the safe and successful passage of the entourage to Banbury.

'From here,' he was able to predict confidently to a special meeting of the Crusade Council (special, because it was graced by the presence of a whole collection of Brother Commanders summoned from near and far), 'it is merely a matter of following the vale of the River Cherwell down to Duncton itself, a journey that the Elder Senior Brother has chosen to make a triumph to express the glorious achievements of his personal crusade thus far.'

If Squilver sounded a little relieved as he made this announcement, it was because he had been greatly concerned that they had been obliged to take a route between two forces whose strengths and inclinations he was uncertain of. He was less sanguine than Quail, and indeed Snyde, about the potential threat of the followers under Maple. He tended rather to agree with Skua, who had thoughtfully observed that whilst no large force of followers had ever emerged out of the Wolds, yet whenever and wherever the Newborns attempted a foray into that higher ground, whether up some vale whose lower reaches they controlled, or over some fell which seemed devoid of mole, followers were always quickly to paw in just sufficient numbers, and just the right dispositions, to make further progress difficult and dangerous.

'Chance,' was how Snyde, not a military mole, dismissively put it, but this was rather too simplistic an explanation. No, Squilver, for all his arrogance and strategic inexperience, could recognize well-organized opposition when he saw it, and rightly guessed that Maple's force was much more formidable than it had yet bothered to show itself to be.

As for the potential threat from Thorne to the north, that was a more difficult problem to analyse, and one of the reasons for the calling of the Council at Banbury – rather than later at Duncton Wood itself as Quail had originally intended – was to discuss it. The difficulty was that nomole yet knew Thorne's intentions, since despite several

354

direct and indirect efforts to communicate with him, he had refused to attend the Crusade Council, or send emissaries to it. Mysteriously, the messengers sent to him had simply not returned, leaving Quail's informants generally in the dark.

Two attempts had been made, one involving Squilver's paw-picked guardmoles, the other utilizing Fagg's supposed contacts within Thorne's camp, to force contact with Thorne. The first was a crude plan to abduct three of his guards, which ended in complete failure when all fourteen of Squilver's team died in the attempt, with nothing but silent corpses left behind to tell what happened. Squilver barely survived this humiliation.

The second, of which historians have few details, involved certain of the forces once supposed to be loyal to the disgraced Brother Commander Dunmow of Ashbourne and by then under the influence of Thorne, and trusted by him. These were reached by one of Fagg's minions, the slithery Purde, and they appear to have agreed to carry out a bold but doomed attempt to kill Thorne himself. Again all the Newborns implicated died, though Fagg's original contact, Purde, withdrew before the coup was attempted and reached the safety of the Council.

This Purde was thus the only useful source of information the Council had of what went on within Thorne's ranks. From him the Crusade Council first learnt of the arraignment and execution of the foul Sickle and his colleagues, instigators of the Leamington Massing. If this was not bad enough, and sufficient evidence to Quail of Thorne's perfidy, worse was the news Purde brought that Thorne had moved to consolidate his hold on the territories east and west of Leamington, the region further north, and the north itself, as yet unreported on.

All this was unwelcome news, but it is often the way with tyrants to dismiss bad news and concentrate on the good, and discourage those around them who would like to breathe upon discussions the fresh air of truth and reality.

In this respect, despite his inexperience, Squilver did his best to guide deliberations at Banbury towards what was achievable, and might build upon the Newborn strengths.

'And what are these?' he asked rhetorically of one small private gathering of moles, which did not include Quail or Snyde, though Fagg and Skua were present – the record being kept privily by one of Snyde's minions whose task was to spy on such occasions, and report back.

'What are our strengths? First, that we hold Duncton Wood and the territories like this one immediately around it, and have consolidated our position in the south at Buckland and Avebury,' said Squilver. 'Next, that we hold all the territory to the west as far as Siabod, so that the Welsh Marches are ours. Recently, too, we have heard that Cannock is ours once more, Thorne having fled from it.* Our weakness is in allowing the followers in the Wolds under Maple to go unchecked, and I would prefer to see a resolute campaign against them before any decisive move is made against Thorne. In any case, that mole is plainly prevaricating, and I cannot believe he would openly defy the Elder Senior Brother.'

It seems that the powerful and independent Brother Commanders Sapient and Turling of Avebury and Buckland respectively, who were present at this secret meeting, agreed with Squilver, both giving their support to the plan that if he invaded the Wolds from the north they would move in from the south.

'But this should not be done until the Elder Senior Brother is secure in Duncton Wood,' stressed Squilver.

It is hard now to know quite what to make of such a report. Did Snyde immediately reveal its contents to Quail when he learned of it? Were Sapient and Turling preparing a takeover of power from Quail once they had secured the Wolds, perhaps with the intention of getting rid of Squilver also? Did Quail himself set up this 'secret' meeting, perhaps with the connivance of Snyde, so that he might have reason later to rid himself of one or other of Squilver, Sapient and Turling (or all three), at some future date?

Not unnaturally, historians of that period have had to ask such questions, though we, whose eyes are on the coming of the Book of Silence, need concern ourselves only with the fact that they need to be asked, revealing as this does the internecine double-dealing of Quail and all around him, and the treachery and feuding that ultimately made him and his entourage all but impotent.

One thing is plain enough about the discussion at Banbury that August – the position of Chervil, and his decision to side with Thorne, was not yet known to Quail. We know this not only because there

* This was the period when the cruel Brother Zeon had taken power in Cannock, though Squilver was not to know that it was at Thorne's initiative. Far from 'having fled' Thorne decided to withdraw his own guardmoles from Cannock for use in the battles he was then planning, and allowed Zeon to take over, whom he knew to be corrupted. Zeon was, of course, assassinated by the Confessed Sister Suede the following October, creating precisely the kind of anarchy that Thorne had expected, and which later he might exploit.

would have been mention of it in Snyde's records, but also because the Crusade Council, at Quail's suggestion, sent emissaries north to Whern, to make contact with the elusive Chervil, the hope being that he might journey southwards and apply pressure on Thorne.

The fact was that Chervil had deliberately led the Crusade Council to think he was still active on their behalf – sending occasional missives to them, always (so he said) when he was on the move and prosecuting some new local Crusade against the snakes and worms of doubt and faithlessness up there in the north in Whern. So Quail, with Thripp under secret and close guard and Chervil now apparently an active Crusader, out of harm's way, naturally felt a certain confidence, a view shared by most moles at the Banbury discussions.

Then, one sultry August night, all suddenly changed when a curious incident turned into a bloody skirmish, which led inexorably to a series of engagements, and those to a winter of war. The incident, which took Squilver and his guardmoles completely by surprise, occurred deep in the night, which was the hot humid kind in which sweat trickles uncomfortably down a mole's flanks, and sleep remains elusive for hours on end, yet he has not quite energy enough to rise up and do other things.

Quail's headquarters were on the bluff of ground local moles call Calthorpe, which looks north-eastward down to the River Cherwell. The surface is mainly grassland pasture, though here and there an isolated tree rises up towards the sky. The place was well guarded, though after so long without incident the guards had become complacent, and the close night air did not help their concentration.

Yet, even had they been fully alert, it is doubtful whether they would have spotted the four moles, no more than shifting shadows, who expertly moved up from the softly-flowing Cherwell to reach the bluff, and then shifted from clump to tree, from tree to sparse bush, and then on to shadowed clump again.

Nor would they have heard them as they snouted down entrances, sent out as signals soft whistles that seemed no more than some day-bird waking into night and calling out of dreams and back again. Finally, turning back to each other, they whispered of what they had seen and surmised, and what they must do.

'Quail's west of an entrance just over there,' said one. His voice was calm, his eyes steady, his body powerful.

'Three guardmoles above him; two to east, and three more to north,' said another tersely.

'Wind north-westerly,' said the third, needing to say no more. Such a wind, over a bluff with a north-east aspect, made things more difficult.

'But the route out's clear, and the escape route too.'

'Aye, by tunnel and only two guards.'

'You stay, both of you. Ready to warn, ready to guide, and we'll fetch Arvon,' said the mole who had first spoken.

'Aye, sir. Watch out for the youngsters . . . but they should be all right. I'll deploy Cluniac to the rear, so you'll likely see him first if there's a retreat.'

'Noakes'll be all right. Unorthodox bugger.'

'Right! We're off. Be ready, but I'll not expect to see you.'

Sly grins in the night. These were moles who prided themselves on their skills, and on their co-operation with each other. These were well-trained moles. These were Maple's moles and . . .

Cluniac? Aye, none other than the one who had led Pumpkin out of danger in the Marsh End back on Longest Night, and so helped make possible the escape of the Duncton followers into the Ancient System below the High Wood. The Cluniac who had pleaded through spring and summer to be allowed to do something more adventurous to help the followers against the Newborns.

And Noakes? That same intrepid Noakes who had led a small party out of Seven Barrows in July and then on all the way to Duncton, to make contact with Pumpkin? The very same, ready now to . . . And Arvon. He, who . . .

But no time for explanations this summer night, as a heaving of shadows rises up along the Calthorpe Bluff and follows the two guidemoles who were here a little before.

'Where's the watchers and guides in case we have trouble?' rasped the deep Welsh voice of Arvon.

'Ready and hidden, sir.'

'Hmmph!' growled Arvon, satisfied. He always checked and double-checked, that was his way; and treble-checked. That was why he was the best. But even for the best not everything always goes right, and those hidden guides might be needed.

'Post another here, mole, the line is a little too long.'

'Aye, sir. You!'

And a shadow detached itself from the party; after swift instructions about where to lead others if the need arose, the shadow was left behind.

Eight moles crept on, reached the first obstacle, moved with deadly swiftness in the night, and only two sighs marked the passing into

358

death of two Newborn guards. Then six went on, two remaining behind to act the part of those who had died.

'It's going well, sir.'

'Never say that, mole, until you're away and all are alive!'

Yet it was true.

'We'll go on for a short time more . . .'

They went, down into the tunnels, past a sleeping guard; had he not been so deeply asleep, he would certainly not have survived that night. And then . . .

'By the Stone, he's almost unprotected!'

And indeed Quail *was* almost unprotected, and had Arvon been able to abduct him out of Banbury, matters in moledom might have been brought to a head rather more swiftly. But, unfortunately for the followers, and luckily for Quail, who lay obscenely exposed in post-coital stupor, with the youthful object of his lusts huddled bleeding and near death in a corner of the chamber where she slept, another awoke.

Snyde, his thin snout twitching at the scent of danger, his ugly hump vibrating with the pleasures of discovered danger and incompetence in the night, opened his eyes, and saw the followers.

Oh, yes, he knew what they were! He could almost smell their worthiness, their zeal, and whereas Quail's stenches once made him retch, now it was the sight and smell of faith and courage that made him want to be sick.

'Halt there!' he cried out, and stepped out of the shadows where he habitually lurked about his master, and stanced in the intruders' way.

Quail woke blearily, raising himself up behind Snyde to stare, open-mouthed. His victim began to scream in fear, little knowing that a chance beyond imagining offered her, alone of all Quail's victims since the days of Wildenhope, an opportunity of escape from what had been until then certain death.

'Shut up!' growled Quail, waking as fast as he could, his head throbbing, his left paw reaching out to squeeze silence into his unwilling companion of the night.

'How dare you!' snarled Snyde, rearing up towards Arvon, his twisted talons playing in the dark light, sharp as thorns.

Arvon stopped and stared at the ghastly sight. A deformed mole, quite unafraid. Beyond him a bald mole whose head shone in the dark, whose left eye drooped, and from whose cell and body emanated vile smells. And, to one side, two bulging eyes now white with terror

– a female the bald mole was throttling to death.

'Leave her be!' roared Arvon, his companions silent and threatening behind him.

Quail let the female drop choking to the ground and said in his softest voice, 'Who are they, Brother Snyde, and whoever they are, how dare they?'

'Evils, Elder Senior Brother; sins; snakes; doubts; the followers incarnate. Names unknown.'

His eyes flicked to the tunnel roof above where the welcome, but none-too-early pawsteps of guardmoles came running. Moles would die for this.

'Quail,' said Arvon, and never had Snyde and Quail come so near death. It stared at them through Arvon's eyes; it glinted out of the eyes of those behind him. It would have taken almost nothing to cast Snyde aside and reach into that odorous chamber to kill Quail. But . . .

'Retreat,' ordered Arvon as the first of the guards came tumbling down into a tunnel behind Quail's chamber.

There was a collective sigh from the followers, but they understood why. This had not been the aim, the death of Quail, not that. Abduction if possible, that would have been good. But not death. Martyrs would not help.

'Retreat, now!' repeated Arvon, needing all his enormous discipline not to push forward past this *thing* that stared so fearlessly up at him.

He looked beyond to Quail again, at his round, shining, dead black eyes, as certain of himself as a mole could be; then at the female retching on the floor, and then back at Brother Snyde. Arvon shivered with the evil of the scene.

'Help us,' whispered the female crawling round and looking up from her hell towards him.

Arvon's eyes darkened and he turned, and his great paw held fast to young Cluniac who had come up behind him, and should not have done.

'No,' he whispered, 'no . . .' and the orderly retreat began over the protests of Cluniac, who wanted to try to save the female who had said, so strangely, 'Help *us* . . .'

Who? All of them? Others like her?

'NO!' ordered Arvon again, and his powerful grip brought tears to Cluniac's eyes and the young mole found his paws pattering ahead of him as he retreated as ordered. But something of his heart was left behind as he strained round for one last look at the female. Then the

360

followers were gone, almost as mysteriously and swiftly as they had come, up to the surface, past the dead guards, to the guides that waited and led them rapidly away into the night. Using the shadows of tree and bush, of clump and tree, of clump again, and then the tunnels earlier surveyed, they melted away into the night. Behind them, from that den of filth they had briefly entered, came the sound of orders and guardmoles running, and the last scream of a female whom chance and bravado might have saved, but who finally found no respite. Ringing darkness descended upon her, and released her from the malodorous paws that reached out for her one final time.

Down near the River Cherwell, all pursuit eluded, but with watchers posted all around, Arvon and some others immersed themselves in a stream's clear water. As one, and without a word, they felt they needed the water's flow to wash away not only the dust and grime of the night's operation, but also the filth that had been deposited within by what they had seen.

'*That* was Quail,' whispered Arvon at last, stancing down on the stream's bank as dawn light rose about them.

'And *that* was the notorious Snyde,' said Weeth.

'We have done more than we could have hoped,' said Arvon.

'We didn't save that female,' said Cluniac.

'Nor could we have done without risking more lives. Discretion is the better part of valour, mole, remember that. There will be other chances to put right the wrong you witnessed.'

'Not for her.' The others nodded grimly, sighing, muttering, staring at the coming light, as their mood took them.

'What did she mean, "Help us"?'

'She meant help all victims like her,' said Weeth. 'Had she said something different she might have saved herself.'

Cluniac looked puzzled.

'Had she said "Help *me*" I would probably have done so,' said Arvon, 'but at what cost? Some of us would not now be here. But had she done so . . . well!' He shook his head as if surprised at his own fallibility, and sighed. 'We had a task and we have fulfilled it. Now it is time for us to go. Some to Duncton, some to the Wolds. You know what to do.'

He rose and shook the last of the stream's water from his fur and for a moment there was a halo of morning light about him. Cluniac glanced westward upslope towards Calthorpe, the horror of what he had witnessed already receding, but the pain remaining.

Arvon clapped Weeth roughly on the shoulder. 'Give Ystwelyn my greetings, mole, and tell Maple all you can. We'll not be many days behind you. As for you, Noakes, you've proved yourself with us. We'll be proud to keep you in our forces for a time – along with Cluniac.'

Noakes grinned and nodded his thanks to several other moles' grunts of appreciation.

Weeth and two others set off downvale while Arvon and his party turned upstream and northward, one moment there and the next all but gone into the shadows which they knew how to exploit so well.

'Snyde, who were they?'

'Traitors, Master.'

'Names?'

Snyde shrugged. 'I think I knew one of them.'

'Think?'

'One of them – but possibly not. A glimpse of a profile behind; something in the eyes; the echo of a voice . . .'

'Whatmole is it you think you saw? Name the traitor in our ranks.'

Snyde paused, revelling. He loved it all, even the danger. Especially the danger. Oh, yes, when he had looked up into that great mole's fierce eyes and seen such courage, such nobility! He had almost quivered with the pleasure of seeing what he was not, could never be, never wished now to be. Oh, oh, he would not have minded death at those paws. Fear? No, he had not felt it. Yet Quail had called him brave for what he did.

Or, as he would scribe the moment he had opportunity, as Quail had put it, 'I was impressed, Brother Snyde. You did not turn a hair. I thought that in such circumstances you might have been . . . shall we say, unwilling. Even cowardly. Until now I had not kept you close by me for your courage so much as for your mind.'

'Master,' Snyde had replied, 'I love you, and love knows no fear. My life is ever yours.'

Quail had stared at him, his skin taut and gleaming with the excitements of the night. He too had nearly known ecstasy to be so close to death, and with only the distorted form of Snyde between it and himself. It was a reminder of how thin the line between glory and inconsequence really is. Naturally, the Stone had protected him. He felt a new mole for the night's doings yet revelled in the prospect of punishing the incompetence that had allowed intruders so near his cell. But who was the traitor that permitted followers to get past his guards? Squilver?

'No, Master, not Squilver I think, he was not the mole I heard and saw.'

'Who then?' pleaded Quail in the game they played.

Snyde looked sad. 'The Senior Brother Inquisitor, I fear it was he.'

'Skua . . .' sighed Quail, his voice breaking, his eyes watering. 'Then must I let him go?'

'I wish it were anymole but he.'

'You lie, Brother Snyde,' said Quail, the excitement of it all too much for him. He grabbed Snyde and pushed his ugly body to the wall and then raised it up.

'Then make me excommunicate,' said Snyde coolly.

Quail let him go, and sobbed.

'Must I then let him go. Skua? Who has been my friend? My helpmeet?'

'It shall be so,' said Snyde, looking away from Quail to where the light of day cast the shadows of the guards across the portal of the council chamber where they talked. Now Snyde's voice held new authority. 'And you shall punish him yourself, for what other mole can bring the judgement of the Stone upon a Senior Brother Inquisitor?'

'None other,' whispered Quail.

Snyde turned from him without another word, the skewed angles of his paws and back, snout and ungraced shoulder blocking out the light of the portal as he passed through it, and was gone, Master of the Newborns now in all but name.

'But you love me?' whispered Quail after Snyde had gone, and he sobbed again, not for Skua whom he must kill, nor even because Skua, whom he had favoured for so long, had betrayed him, though Stone knows there were tears enough in that. Quail sobbed because the pains he felt in his body were increasing and they were deep and sharp, and he was afraid they would get worse, still far worse. And because he felt alone.

'Yet *you* love me?' he whispered again after Snyde. Then Quail did the thing that gave Snyde reason for the first time to record in his account of Quail's slow decline those terrible words: '. . . and then my Master screamed.'

Chapter Twenty-Nine

'Sir, we must stop awhile and rest, we must,' said one of Weeth's two companions the second evening out from Banbury on the way back to the Wolds.

'Rest?' snapped Weeth. 'We have no time to rest, mole. Don't you see? Can't you feel it coming across moledom now? We shall have our whole lives to rest if we can only do what's right now. But if not we shall be overwhelmed. It's coming, and it's coming now!'

'Er . . . Sir . . .' repeated the mole as Weeth headed on towards the setting sun, 'we . . .' But he and his friend fell silent and after a glance at each other, and a puzzled shrug, they followed on after the mole they thought they had got to know so well; suddenly they felt they did not know him at all.

'What's up with him, then?'

'Stone knows. It was seeing that bloody Quail, I think. He muttered about it earlier, and then hurried on.'

Weeth was not himself, and nor had he been since the grotesque sight of Quail and Snyde in the tunnels near Banbury. But since they had started their journey a wild kind of mood had overtaken him, born only partly of the excitement he felt to be returning at last to serve Maple directly. But if it had only been pleasurable excitement that drove him on, he would have been better company than he was. Mixed with it, however, was the feeling that he was near finding an answer to that extra task which Maple had given him when he originally left the Wolds for Duncton Wood.

'Find out that *special thing*, that sense of what moles in moledom are about, which military moles need to know if their decisions are to be of the best, and win greatest power and control for the least lives lost. I know you can find things out that others can't, Weeth. It's all I ask.'

'Hmmph!' muttered Weeth to himself now, stomping his paws into the dusty ground, '"It's all I ask" indeed! Well, I know nothing more than a thousand other moles, and that's what I'll tell Maple.'

But this was not quite true. Most of Arvon's force had wondered why their leader had let Quail live, but only to Weeth had he confided the reason, knowing that he would pass the knowledge on to Maple and Ystwelyn when he reached the Wolds.

Arvon had explained that he had let Quail live because it seemed to him that if so debauched a mole was in control of the Newborns the followers had less to fear than if a strong mole was in charge. Arvon was subtler in his thinking than he seemed.

'But you better get back to Maple fast, mole, for believe me, Quail won't last long. Well, long enough to harm a lot of moles, but maybe not quite long enough to lose a war to us. No, some other mole will take over from him, and I'll warrant it will be Thorne. So get back to Maple while we seek further information, and tell him we'll cause as much confusion and delay in the Newborns' forces as we can, and then head south back towards Duncton Wood, but not enter it again. Tell him Arvon will be at paw and ready to do his bidding when it comes to it.'

All of which Weeth could have coped with happily enough had he not had the nasty feeling that events were building up too fast, stormclouds were looming, danger threatened on all sides and . . .

'. . . and I'm sure there's something I *should* be reporting to Maple which will help him make the right decisions. But what is it?'

He looked about the gentle vales across which they were travelling with barely a pause, well aware that his two companions wanted to stop, but unwilling to do so until he had found an answer to a question he could not quite articulate; trying, too, to escape from quite other questions which loomed up before him most unexpectedly, and left him in a very irritable mood indeed. Why did the Stone allow such moles as Quail and Snyde to live, to exist at all?

'Yes, why?' repeated Weeth much later as the first stars began to shine in a blue-black sky. But he had no answer to his question.

'We'll stop here,' he told the other two shortly, 'but not for long. Eat, rest, watch in turn and then we'll press on. We must get to Maple now and tell him all we know and what we saw.'

'Saw something we should have killed,' muttered one.

'Saw something that made me sick,' said the other.

Weeth turned from them and surprised himself by muttering aloud, 'Saw ourselves! Saw a darkness I've only known as a name until now. Saw the far side of the Stone. Saw the tunnel that does not lead to light. We . . . must . . . get . . . to . . . Maple.'

They heard him muttering, exhausted; they saw him fall asleep. Disturbed by his words, they argued about who should take the watch, for neither could face sleep, tired though they were.

Later, in the dead of night, Weeth woke suddenly, and lay staring at the stars above the entrance to the simple scrape he occupied. He had an overwhelming sense that Maple needed him again, and his usefulness anywhere else was over. Yet what more could he tell him? What was that 'special thing'? The failure to identify it nagged at him, the more so because he began to feel it might exist.

Tossing and turning, restless, unable to work things out yet unwilling to stop trying, Weeth suddenly decided they must leave. He almost burst out of the scrape into the night, and immediately one of the followers was at his flank with, 'What is it, sir?'

'We've got to go. We must get to Maple.'

The follower, one of Arvon's most experienced guards, put a restraining paw on Weeth's shoulder and slowly shook his head.

'Better rest up a bit more, sir. More haste . . . you know what the chief says. You're overwrought, sir, which is not something I've seen in you before. Was it that Quail? Did you see something more than I did?'

All the energy fled from Weeth's body, and he looked into the mole's eyes and saw how they shone with stars. He felt the mole's touch, so like his father's touch so long ago. He inhaled the mole's scent, and it was that of a friend who cared. And he saw a young female dying before his eyes who had called out of her agony, 'Help us.'

Weeth wanted to weep. He turned away, fighting back his tears, but before they had time to flow his sorrow was overwhelmed by questions to which, for once, he could find no ready answers. He had heard the female die and her last scream haunted him.

He had seen the darkness that moles fear, he had smelt the Dark Sound that kept moles out of the deepest parts of the High Wood, and he no longer knew who the female's collective 'us' included. Rather more than just victims like herself, he saw now. A chink of light revealed itself at the end of a very long tunnel in his mind.

'What was her name?' he said aloud.

'Whatmole's that, Weeth, sir?' asked the nearest follower.

'The one he killed. Whatmole was she? One of . . .'

All of us. Yes, everymole of us. Hers was the cry of allmole for allmole. The darkness he had seen was his own. The stench was his; the crippled mind of a distorted mole, his too. The den they had seen, a place that existed somewhere in his own heart.

'You better try to rest, sir.'

'You're right, mole. Thank you, you're right. Get some rest your-self.'

'My watch, sir.'

'And mine?' asked Weeth, for with Arvon's moles it was share and share alike and no exceptions except for the wounded.

'I'll wake you, sir, never fear, but the night's got a way to go yet.'

Yes, Weeth felt solemn and he feared it might be a long time before he laughed again. He knew now what it was they struggled for, and that Maple's reluctance to attack and kill and do the obvious thing was justified. He remembered Pumpkin's quiet expositions of what the Master Stour had argued, that peace was the only way. He remembered those gentle old moles, fugitives all, who lived so meag-rely up in the High Wood, the last followers left in Duncton Wood. Suddenly, as real as if it had risen up before him then and there, he saw the Duncton Stone and round it many moles, Pumpkin among them. Many Pumpkins. And himself, but tired after a journey he had never known he was on.

'Help us,' he whispered to the sky, and to the Stone, and his tears flowed silently and long, and he knew he had much to say to Maple, and they all had much to do now, for all the horizons were dark and threatening, and moledom was vulnerable and weak.

A paw shook his shoulder, and he woke to the warmth of sun on his face, and an ache in his head that would leave him much sooner than the ache in his heart.

'You took my watch for me,' he admonished the mole gratefully.

He grinned. 'You'll be taking mine tonight, sir, and I'm looking forward to it already.' This was typical of the rough and cheerful exchanges of such followers.

'So . . . a few more days and we'll be back with Maple and Ystwelyn.'

'Aye,' growled the other, munching some food and contemplating the vale below them which they had to cross to reach higher ground ahead. 'Bit quiet for my liking.'

They all stared ahead, wary. Always wary. It was how mole survived.

'But not how they succeed,' Arvon had once said in a rare philo-sophical moment. 'Risk is what it's finally about.'

'Hmmph!' muttered Weeth, finishing his food. 'Better be off.'

And off they went, leaving no trace where they had been, nor more than momentary shadows along an empty path.

But if talk about it being 'too quiet' usually signalled trouble, this

367

was an exception. They met nomole for two more days, and when they finally did it was but a solitary traveller, middle-aged, gentle of expression, and singing to himself. Having washed in a stream and had a meal (all observed by Weeth and his two friends for a long time before they revealed themselves), he lay out in the afternoon sun and rested. When their shadows fell across his face he opened his eyes, but it cannot be said he showed much inclination to defend himself.

'Follower or Newborn?' one of them asked, looking about warily, though by then they were sure he was alone.

The mole laughed and said, 'Neither. I'm a pilgrim. Hibbott's my name, and if you want to join me, do. I could do with the conversation. If you want to kill me, do. But if you want to convert me, I'm afraid it's too late. I'm too old to change.'

'Hibbott of . . . ?'

'Ashbourne Chase, a system nomole has ever heard of, unless it be in association with Ashbourne, which lies downstream.'

'And where are you off to, may we ask?'

'You may, good moles. And I'll tell you, for I've quite given up dissemblement.'

'"Dissemblement"?' repeated one of the followers suspiciously. 'Is that a sect?'

Weeth grinned for the first time since leaving Banbury, and said, 'It might seem so to some, perhaps. It means pretence. Being what you're not. This mole is saying he wishes simply to be what he is.'

'Correct, mole. Well put. "Where are you off to?" you ask, as if I were on some little jaunt a mole might begin in the morning confident that he'll be back in his burrow by late afternoon! I'm off to find a mole called Privet, whom I expect eventually to find by the Stone in Duncton Wood – that's where I'm off to.'

Weeth stared at him in astonishment, for he spoke as if Privet might be round the next corner; as if he knew . . .

'Explain yourself, mole,' said Weeth.

Hibbott sighed; 'Well now, it all started rather a long time ago really. A lifetime or three ago, in fact. You see, well . . .'

So Hibbott began to tell them of his journey and his astonishing adventures, of his departure from Ashbourne Chase; of his trek across the Midland Wen; of his sojourn with Sister Caldey in the Community of Rose; of his coming to Leamington and the arrival of Brother Commander Thorne; of a silent female healer who listened to him . . .

'Thin, and grey, and middle-aged, but . . .'

'Thin and grey and middle-aged,' repeated Weeth, remembering a female he knew who fitted that description perfectly.

'And she didn't speak?'

'Not once,' said Hibbott. 'Now, where had I got to . . .'

He told them of his departure from Leamington and how the Newborns under Thorne simply let him go, and how he had begun to realize that finding Privet by way of searching for her directly, as it were, was not the thing at all.

'No, no, my friends, I decided that a pilgrim is more likely to find what he wants by not looking for it, or not looking directly at it – rather as some moles see things better in the dark if they don't look straight at them.'

Somehow or other he had heard the rumour that Rooster, Master of the Delve, had not only survived Wildenhope, but was now safely living up in the Wolds and it was to find him that he was now journeying in the hope he would lead him to Privet.

Such was his story, and it was all the more astonishing that a mole so evidently without the resources of strength, or aggression, or even cunning, had so cheerfully survived the trials of his journey.

'Well, that may be, that may be. But, well, I always say to myself that Privet of Duncton is worse off than I am, seeing as she is on a journey into the interior, as it were, which is a fearfully hard thing, you see. Why, praying in silence – and I mean real silence – for more than a few moments is something I find so very hard to do. But she – it is what she is trying to do all the time.'

'How do you know that, mole? And why so sure she is still alive?'

'I know it because I have thought it. As for her being alive, well!' Hibbott shrugged and smiled, and there was not one tiny shadow of doubt in his eyes.

What he had told them had been extraordinary, though he seemed unaware of its military importance. He had been in and out of Thorne's territory and might even have met Thorne himself. His account made plain as a paw in front of a mole's snout that Thorne was the real danger now, and it was but a matter of time before he took power from Quail, in the way Arvon had predicted but days before.

Weeth had no doubt, from Hibbott's account, that Thorne was likely to be a far more formidable opponent than Quail. Maple was going to have to act quickly and decisively to retain the initiative over the Newborns. Weeth shuddered at the thought, his new seriousness diluting the thrill of excitement he had anticipated for so long when the days of campaigning came.

369

'We're going to have to get back to Maple as quickly as we can,' he muttered to his two friends unnecessarily, when Hibbott had gone back to the stream for a drink.

'Rum mole, that one. Not scared of a bloody thing. You going to tell him you know Privet, sir?'

But Hibbott came back, and Weeth left the question unanswered.

They ate and rested for a time, and talked again only much later.

'You're some way off the path to Duncton Wood,' said Weeth.

'You know it then?'

Weeth smiled. 'We've come from there as a matter of fact.'

'Ah!' observed Hibbott with scant interest. 'Yes, it's certainly no place to stay, from all accounts. Riddled with Newborns.'

'You could say,' said one of the followers heavily.

'But you said . . .' prompted Weeth, continuing his inquisition of the mole.

'I did, I did: that I was going to Duncton and in search of Privet,' rejoined Hibbott, with a faint hint of reproach in his voice. 'I am, I am, but this is a pilgrimage, not an errand. I shall reach Duncton eventually I daresay, and when I stop seeking her I shall find Privet, with the Stone's help. At this moment – and it might change on the morrow, for I am learning to think in the present – but as of now, I am still hoping I might meet the mole Rooster, for he is a friend of Privet and might advise me on how to reach her. But enough of me! I have talked too much! Yourselves, yourselves! Not mere pilgrims, it seems. Very much on an errand I should say!'

Weeth grinned. 'Heading in your direction, you might say. Going up into the Wolds. But we're travelling rather faster than you, I think.'

He gave little away, not because he distrusted Hibbott, but because Hibbott might be caught by Newborns again, Stone help him, and be forced to tell what he knew. Yet Weeth felt uncomfortable . . . dissembling. He would have liked to talk further to Hibbott. His account of Leamington and Thorne had been interesting enough, but his description of the female who had nursed him even more so. Thin, silent, a little more than middle-aged, peaceful . . . *had* she been Privet? Weeth was inclined to think so. Was this the 'special thing' he had been sent to find out?

'There are others like me, you know, quite a few of us I think,' said Hibbott suddenly out of the dark, as if he had lost interest in finding out about Weeth and his friends and wished simply to spend the remaining time sharing thoughts of his own.

370

'Are there?' said Weeth, thinking suddenly of that female, and her cry in Quail's den.

Hibbott's snout, pale in the night, moved up and down as he nodded, and he came a little nearer.

'I think moledom is tired now, and wants peace. It is to Privet we look, not the others. Not the mole Maple and those like him, who perhaps you are going to. Oh, they're needed, very much so. But we who have started our journeys already, *our* thoughts are on the Silence Privet has entered before us. There are many of us, and we travel alone. We have to, it is the only way.'

'Aren't you afraid, mole? Alone, and Newborns about?'

It was one of the follower guards, and Weeth recognized the respect in his voice.

'No. Not in the sense you mean. I was; for a long time I was. But the Stone is ahead of me and I see its Light, and I hear its Silence and I know it protects me. I cannot hide from it, so why hide from the Newborns or anymole-else? I help nomole doing so, least of all myself. Sometimes I meet another like myself and I am comforted and feel less alone. Often such moles have no idea they are pilgrims.' He smiled. Weeth was sure Hibbott's eyes were fixed acutely on his own.

'I'm tired,' said Hibbott quite suddenly, 'and my snout is burning from too much sun. Tomorrow I shall stay in the shade. And by then you will probably be gone, as silently as you came.'

'Aye,' conceded one of them.

'Well then, watch out for Privet for me. And if you reach her before I do, tell her that Hibbott of Ashbourne Chase seeks her. Watch out for me too, for I too am heading for Duncton Stone. We all are, all of us travellers.'

'Mole,' whispered Weeth gruffly, 'will you say a prayer? We would be obliged.'

'Well, I . . . I may be a pilgrim but I am not much of a one for saying prayers with others. I'm not sure I know how. The words, I mean.'

'Try, mole,' said Weeth.

Hibbott stared at the stars for a time as all of them settled down into a comfortable stance.

'It's not just us four, is it, Stone?' he began. 'Therefore, help us all, wherever we may be. Help us . . .'

Weeth heard no more, for ahead, or above in the night sky perhaps, or across the darkened vale, he thought he glimpsed for a moment the Stone's Light, and he fancied he heard the whisper of the Stone's Silence, and he knew that even he, even cunning Weeth, was one of those whom Hibbott had described, who were travellers alone, as that lost female had been.

'Help us . . .' whispered Weeth as dawn came, and he and his companions quietly rose and left Hibbott of Ashbourne Chase soundly asleep behind them; and as they went Weeth glanced back and for the first time had an idea of what that special thing might be that Maple had bid him seek out. It was, as Hibbott had suggested, that there were many more like him, many many more, and together they would be an army more powerful by far than the forces of Newborn and follower combined, and their mission was for peace, and would make the prosecution of war redundant almost before it started.

'Help us . . .' said Weeth again, and he felt he had never spoken two words more fervently.

Chapter Thirty

Maple now held absolute sway in the Wolds, and Newborn fears concerning the followers' true strengths were far more justified than even Supreme Commander Squilver realized. For not only were the Wolds now entirely in Maple's paws, and the many systems there well protected from the excesses of the Newborn Crusades that continued beyond their boundaries, but increasingly through the summer years he had subtly extended the followers' power.

Even a mole as well informed as Squilver could be forgiven for underestimating the followers' strength, for unlike the Newborns, who were concentrated in important systems, and linked by aggressive and visible patrols, the followers were dispersed and rarely seen together in force. The small group of which Arvon was in charge, although an elite, was one of several similar ones which operated more or less secretly throughout that summer, gathering information concerning Newborn strengths and weaknesses, and, increasingly, collecting evidence of their mounting atrocities.

Maple no longer doubted that in the end the followers would triumph over the Newborns, for their cause was right, and such evidence as he had showed that Quail was losing control of the Crusades he had begun. In that case, Maple knew, a strong military leader, with a disciplined but fair force, could establish his authority far more quickly than moles generally realized. Time and circumstance seemed on the followers' side.

'But what concerns me,' said Maple, speaking to his most able and charismatic commander, the Siabodian warrior Ystwelyn, 'is what happens if a powerful leader emerges on the Newborn side who does what I would do: gets rid of Quail, and establishes a more rigorous command, building on their considerable strengths of force and territory, and begins to repair some of the weaknesses.'

'Aye,' answered Ystwelyn, 'it'll make our task a lot harder if that happens. That mole Thorne . . .'

'Exactly – Thorne. You remember when we confronted him across the vale at Rowton? You remember I said that he looked formidable, and not like the usual conniving weak-willed Newborn Brother Commanders we've come to expect?'

'Yes, mole, I do,' responded Ystwelyn.

They were talking out on the eastern slopes of Bourton, the system in the centre of the Wolds of which the inestimable Stow, one of Maple's toughest and most reliable commanders, was the Elder. Nomole knew the Wolds better than he, nor loved its moles and landscape more, and to him had been entrusted the thankless task of watching over Rooster, and hiding him away somewhere in the High Wolds where no Newborn could reach him.

Ystwelyn had toured the followers' various encampments in the past few days and had returned late the night before to brief Maple about the morale and readiness of the followers. Now he and Maple had begun their talk in a shady nook, a river flowing blue and leisurely down the vale below them, and the sun growing warmer by the hour. The Siabod mole eyed Maple expectantly, for he sensed his return had been well-timed, and that in his calm and careful way, Maple was talking generally on familiar themes before getting down to business.

'Yes, I remember Thorne well. As you say, a formidable mole.'

Maple nodded, only half listening, turning from Ystwelyn to a travel-stained journeymole who waited respectfully nearby, one eye on Maple, the other on some food he was hungrily finishing off.

'Take your time, mole,' said Maple cheerfully, 'you've earned it!'

The journeymole gratefully finished his meal, tidied himself up a bit, and then came on over to them.

'I needed that, sir! No food for two days!'

'You've done well and you'll be able to go and get some sleep soon. But before you do . . . you've told me most of what I need to know but it never hurts to hear it twice, and Commander Ystwelyn likes to hear things at first paw.'

'Name's Radish, sir, of Dorchester way,' he said, looking at Ystwelyn. He was a typical journeymole – stocky, big-pawed, scarred from scrapes he had been in, and with an independence in his eyes typical of such moles. He was older than both of them but clearly a disciplined, loyal follower, and one not intimidated by meeting the two most powerful commanders. He barked rather than spoke his words, as if there was no time for full sentences and he might have to dash off somewhere at any moment, so he might as well get on with it. But this curious manner was alleviated by the pleasing soft burr of his southern accent.

'One of Maella's journeymoles, then?' said Ystwelyn, naming the only senior female commander amongst the followers, who had originally led a band of moles up from the south-west, done sterling work on the eastward slopes of the Wolds, and in the high summer years of July had been deputed by Maple to reconnoitre the dangerous area south of the Wolds and west of Duncton – a Newborn stronghold dominated by Avebury and notorious Buckland, both firmly in Newborn paws.

'Aye, sir. Heading here but got diverted. Long story, told Commander Maple here. But a lucky break. Met the mole Weeth, sir.'

Ystwelyn's eyes lit with excitement and he glanced appreciatively at Maple.

'Near entrance to Duncton, just by chance. Joined them on a jaunt to Banbury, sir, at Arvon's suggestion, sir. Tagged along to help, observe and report. This I am now doing.'

He rattled off his story in simple direct terms, passing on all he had learnt about the state of affairs with Pumpkin in Duncton, and Quail in Banbury.

'Didn't see this Quail myself, sir, seeing as I'm not trained in that line of night work. Waited as was ordered, and when Arvon, Weeth and the others came back in one piece, well, I was impressed, sir. Each to his own. Gave me the willies what I heard of Quail and that.

'I was to tell you that Weeth is two or three days behind me, no more. On his way back right now. He guessed you'd be in Bourton by now so he'll not lose time finding you.'

'What's he dallying for, mole?'

Radish grinned. 'Said you'd ask that and told me to reply, quote: "Tell Maple I'm still looking for the special something he was hoping for, he'll understand." End of quote. I think I got that right.'

Maple laughed and said, 'He didn't have to stay away until he found it, but that's Weeth. Three days, you say?'

'No more. Maybe less, though I travel fast and he had a couple of guards with him which slows things up, one being quicker than three.'

Maple nodded. 'Now tell the commander what you heard about Thorne.'

'Yes, sir. Former commander of Cannock is now established at Leamington and has control of the east and north. It's said that a Brother Rolt, Thripp's aide, is with him, and there's rumours of Chervil, Thripp's son, being there too. Just rumours, no more.'

Ystwelyn looked at Maple, serious. Thorne, Rolt, and Chervil . . . a formidable cabal of moles, and one capable of taking power from Quail. Things were moving fast, perhaps too fast, in precisely the direction Maple feared, for such a grouping of Newborns would surely have little difficulty wresting power from Quail if his leadership was as flawed and failing as they thought.

'When did you hear this, mole?'

'Days ago, sir, from Arvon himself.'

'And he got it from Newborns, I suppose?'

'No, sir, not Newborns.'

He looked a little discomfited, as if dealing with something unfamiliar and disliked. This was a military journeymole, and he did not like things he could make no sense of.

'Er, he got it from what are called "pilgrims", sir. Meaning moles of no fixed abode, sir.'

'"No fixed abode"?' repeated Maple, smiling.

'Exactly, sir. Wander around they do, sir, praying and that. But a useful source of information it seems, as Arvon has found. They come from and go to places others don't. Find things out. Not of this world, a pilgrim isn't. Have met some. Don't talk sense. Unreliable. Inclined to wander off, like raw recruits. So I don't place much reliance on these reports from Leamington, speaking personally; but I pass on what I'm told and that's what Arvon and Weeth told me, *sir*.'

Radish talked some more, but he had reported the main points, and once he had rested he could tell what remained – detailed dispositions of forces south of Duncton, and much he had learned about Buckland and Avebury – to one of Ystwelyn's subordinates, trained to scribe down such things.

'Well done, mole. Now, take that rest you've earned, and be easy for a day or two. But after that . . .'

'Yes, sir?'

Despite his tiredness Radish spoke eagerly. Allmole at Bourton guessed that matters were moving apace and soon decisions would be made and campaign orders given.

'I'll be ready, sir!'

'Oh! Radish?'

'Sir?' said the journeymole, turning back to Maple. Ystwelyn listened carefully, recognizing the sharp and alert tone in Maple's voice, and the attention in his eyes. Maple had spotted something he had not.

'These pilgrims. You say you have met a few of them?'

'Quite a few. In odd places. They're growing in numbers if you ask me, like fleas on a warm day. It's Duncton Wood they talk of, it's the mole Privet they think about. But why or what for, Stone only knows, 'cos they don't. It's my belief they've lost their home systems, sir, and don't know what to do with themselves. It's all nonsense they talk, that's what I think. Is that all, sir?'

Radish suddenly looked tired and with another word of thanks Maple let him go.

'Pilgrims,' repeated Ystwelyn dubiously. He evidently shared some of Radish's doubts about such moles.

'Hmmph!' said Maple, frowning, and thinking for a time.

'I'd feel happier if Weeth was back with us already,' said Maple finally, 'though at least we know he's on his way. I'm a patient mole, Ystwelyn, but sometimes . . .'

His strong clear face cracked into a grim smile, and it was one his friend returned. Radish had given them much to think about, but at the very least there was now the sense in both of them that the long wait was almost over, and the real struggle against the Newborns could begin.

'He had no need to risk his life on some venture into Quail's stronghold,' grumbled Maple, for he missed Weeth sorely, the more so now that he was so nearly back again.

'He's not one to take risks he doesn't calculate,' said Ystwelyn reassuringly, 'and nor is Arvon. Don't know why he's not returning with Weeth, but he'll have reason enough, and Weeth'll know what it is. Maybe Arvon just wants to get the very latest information. I'll warrant that part of Arvon's purpose in going to Banbury was to disconcert the Newborns and show them that they're not as invulnerable as they think. It's a trick we used to play on the Newborns around Siabod before we came to Caer Caradoc and got caught up with you.'

'Well . . .' growled Maple, unconvinced.

'Anyway, you've been telling us to be patient these molemonths past, so I don't see why you can't be patient for a couple more days. Weeth won't be far behind. And he's a survivor.'

'Aye,' sighed Maple, 'so he is, so he is. And maybe there are a few things we can do. Yes, I think maybe the time's come . . .'

A flash of excitement went across Ystwelyn's eyes and he moved closer to Maple, to hear what he was suggesting, and to offer his thoughts as well, which it was his trusted role to do.

Finally the meeting was over and Ystwelyn went off to issue new orders to the fittest and fastest messengers he could find, and to oversee deployment, training and checking of the forces that in recent days had begun to arrive at Bourton in expectation of imminent action. In fact, Maple had begun to concentrate the followers in and around

Bourton since the beginning of August in preparation for mounting an autumn offensive against the Newborns in the cooler, mistier weather of September and October. Excitement was mounting daily.

Now, as messenger after messenger left Bourton, in pairs for extra safety and support, a new buzz of excitement went around the tunnels and surface, and rumours, ever present when an army of moles gathers for coming action, began to multiply, and tunnel-talk increased.

Morale among the followers was high, for there was a general belief that they were lucky to be led by such a mole as Maple, one who cared and thought. They respected his unwillingness ever to pass comment on others, and the way he always took final responsibility for the sometimes hard decisions he had to make.

There *had* been hard decisions, and some appalling moments, when all Maple's resolve had been needed to keep the followers together and abiding by the strict code of conduct he imposed. Had he not acted swiftly over that group of senior followers who had been about to kill eight Newborn guardmoles in late May when it had been discovered they had tortured and massacred at least thirty moles in the harmless Woldian system at Cheltenham? He had: all were demoted, and the guardmoles set free and told to return to their Brother Commander, Maple personally chastising the senior follower who by turning a blind eye had permitted the attempted reprisal.

Had he not personally intervened when twenty angry followers tried to do to two Newborn captives what had been done to some followers a few days before? Which was, to hang them by their paws from the barbs of wire and taunt and torture them for three days before drowning them in the mud of a ditch.

Oh yes, Maple had stopped *that* in short order, charging in among the followers, roaring down their protest, fighting off their assault upon his person, and by himself rescuing the Newborns.

'If only one of you does such things you reduce all of us to no better than our enemy. It is for truth and justice we fight, not to seek revenge.'

And when, as happened, revenge was taken, his treatment of those guilty was arraignment, and severe punishment, and execution if need be. The followers who fought with him came to fear him, but respect him too, and to accept his strict treatment where other commanders in other wars might have been far more tolerant.

As when he had been angry when news of Quail's exodus from Wildenhope was late reaching him because the follower patrol that should have spotted it were off and away fornicating with some over-friendly females down Willersey way, where the females were known to be on the loose side. Could anymole really blame them – and who could say that if they had reported Quail's move sooner it would have made any difference?

'There's nothing wrong with a little dalliance,' Maple admonished them, 'but not while you're on duty. Because you took your pleasures others may in time lose their lives.' And when reports of the outrages committed by Quail's entourage were heard, he called back the grumbling followers who had been caught out and let them hear for themselves a first-paw account of one of Quail's atrocities so that they might know what dereliction of duty by one mole could lead to for another.

Yet when the guilty moles, hearing the foul reports, offered to lead the attack on Quail's forces, Maple would have none of it.

'I shall decide when and where we attack,' was all he had said to them. 'Now back to your posts . . .'

How sleepless his nights had been in the times that followed, as report after report of atrocities came in, and his commanders, Ystwelyn among them, urged him to let them descend upon Quail and his foul forces while he was still within reach in territory where the followers were strong. How great was the pressure on him to do what almost all the followers wanted. They had had enough of skulking about the Wolds and watching, and never taking action. Now, surely . . .

But now it was that Maple showed his greatest leadership in holding back his force, in biding his time, in not taking the obvious easier course.

'We are not strong enough. Though moles will die, and die horribly at his paws, the time is not yet right. Had we known sooner of his coming we might have got some systems cleared, but that was our failure. Now he's on his way and going to Duncton Wood no doubt. Well, then, let him go, and may the Stone forgive me, but each step of the way that he commits more violence I swear will build up opposition and hatred for him of which in time we will reap the benefit.'

'But are we not here to save lives?' demanded commander after commander.

Maple shook his head. 'We are here to defeat Quail, and rid moledom of the Newborns. We will not do that by rushing in because we are angry. His greatest enemy for now is himself. Let his actions prepare the ground for us. We will go in when we must, and not too soon.'

379

Sensing disagreement and disaffection in the follower ranks, Maple had exhausted himself for moleweeks on end travelling all around the Wolds, explaining, persuading, threatening, and holding his forces in check. Few moles knew better than Ystwelyn what stamina and resolve this had needed, who saw at first paw the determination and wisdom that underlay all that Maple said.

'He is a great mole . . .'

'Even though he's never won a major battle? Eh? Come off it Ystwelyn!'

'And whatmole's to say he has not? Which of us can deny that without him we would not now be in the strong position we are, with so few lives lost, with our pride intact, and without reducing ourselves – as some want us to – to the filth and slime against which we are fighting. Aye, Maple's day will come, and when it does he will choose it for himself and not when others do. And I, Ystwelyn of Siabod, will be at his flank, and if he says to me, "Lie down mole and don't defend yourself!" or "Jump and touch the moon!" I shall do so, because I believe in him.'

It said much for Maple that so strong and purposeful a mole as Ystwelyn was his subordinate, and it is a mark of Maple's skills as a commander that he should have known how to find and inspire such a mole. When Ystwelyn doubted his leader, and sometimes he did, he was in the habit of reminding himself that it had been a Duncton mole who a century before had trekked to Siabod, and brought that ancient and backward-looking system into the modern age.

Weeth and his two companions finally reached Bourton two evenings later, just a little sooner than Radish had predicted, and they found a system busy with activity. Maple had rarely been so glad to see a mole and once they were established in his simple quarters, the two did not waste time with many preliminaries.

'The journeymole Radish got here all right then?' said Weeth.

'Aye, he did, and told us all he could: of the disposition of Newborn forces south of Duncton as he saw it; of Duncton itself; and of your expedition to Banbury.'

A cloud crossed Weeth's face. 'Not good, Maple, not good at all; that Quail . . .'

Weeth began to talk of his experiences and would have continued had not Maple stopped him, told him it was best Ystwelyn heard it all as well, and ordered him to eat and rest.

'We're not rushing out of Bourton after Newborns tonight. We can wait a little on your report.'

'But you'll not be hanging about?'

Maple shook his head grimly. 'We'll be going either on the morrow, or the day after that, depending on what you report of Arvon's movements.'

'He's going south to wait near Duncton.'

'Ah, then it's as I thought.'

Weeth nodded, glad to be with Maple again.

'You've aged, if I may say so,' he said. 'Your face is more lined; your snout's a shade thinner; but . . .'

'But what?' No other mole spoke to Maple like this and he rather liked it. 'I've missed you, mole!' he said impulsively. 'Now . . . but what . . . ?'

'You're more angry.'

'I've had the reports of what Quail and his underlings have been doing to moles that cross his path.'

'I've *seen* him recently,' said Weeth. 'He's changed since we saw him in Caer Caradoc. He's grown . . . foul.'

Maple held up a paw. 'Keep it until Ystwelyn's here.'

'Where is he?'

'Attending to followers nearby. And seeing if he can get Stow to persuade Rooster to show his snout in so busy a place as this.'

Weeth yawned. 'Too hungry to eat. Sleep . . .'

'Sleep and eat and *then* talk.'

Weeth grinned suddenly, impishly. 'Good to be back, sir,' he said quietly, his eyes tired but wrinkling with contentment. 'I've things to say, things which will take time to say. But not so long they'll delay our campaigning.'

'Sleep now, mole,' said Maple gently, nodding towards the portal that led into the tiny chamber that was his own sleeping place. 'Like when we were travelling to Cannock from the Wenlock Edge.'

Weeth remembered those harried days, which seemed so long ago now. Maple was referring to the way that when they needed rest they made a single shallow scrape and one watched while the other slept, the second lying in the warmth left by the first.

'Ystwelyn will be coming, and others with him, and we'll be conferring. Listen in if you're awake, but don't worry if you sleep on.'

Weeth nodded, wearily.

'Go on, sleep now,' Maple ordered; and with darkness falling, Weeth ducked through the portal and stretched out into the comfortable space, and slept.

Night, and the growl of voices, sometimes singly, sometimes

together in debate. Weeth shifted to hear the better though still half asleep. A series of reports, of the kind Maple liked moles to make before he made up his own mind. A listener was Maple, and after that a decider.

A Welsh voice spoke, deep and authoritative: Ystwelyn. Then a female's: unknown to Weeth, who drifted back to sleep. He woke once more to the sharper, thinner accents of a mole from the northern Welsh Marches . . . Furrow, he decided. He shifted again and peered out from the blackness of the sleeping cell on to the murkily-lit scene in the bigger chamber which Maple was using for a council of commanders.

Suddenly he felt fully awake and popped his head through the portal, Weeth-like, and said, 'Greetings friends, colleagues, and fellow enemies of the Newborn!'

Those who had not known Weeth before, knew him now. He grinned and grimaced, went to those he knew and greeted them, winked at Maple and Ystwelyn, put his paws briefly round Furrow, and expressed enormous surprise to see Myrtle, Furrow's mate.

'Didn't recognize your voice!' he said. 'I must be weakening for something!'

After a quick glance at Maple to be sure that laughter *was* in order, those who had not meet Weeth before joined in the welcome, and for some moments more the gathering was all talk and good cheer.

Then Maple shifted and coughed, Weeth fell in dutifully at his left flank, and the meeting came to order once more; a little lighter in mood, yet somehow more purposeful, as if Weeth's return confirmed once and for all that matters in moledom had reached a head.

'We were reporting, Weeth, on how we see things; where we're at.'

'I heard,' he said. 'Action imminent, it seems.'

'Imminent indeed,' said Maple, turning to one of the commanders and nodding at him to continue. There were perhaps eight or nine there, including the senior commanders Whindrell, and Runnel, Stow's second-in-command; along with a few more like Furrow, and the atmosphere was close and warm. The contributions continued, one after another so that all had their say. They were varied: some long and complex, others short and to the point, but all tended the same way, wherever the moles came from, whatever their recent experience. As a day of close hot weather leads towards a storm, so matters in moledom were leading that way too.

At last all had spoken but for Weeth, to whom all now turned expectantly. Maple signalled for him to speak, which he did in his rapid graphic way, dwelling only briefly on the ground he sensed had been covered already by journeymole Radish, and concentrating instead on those areas where he had information Arvon had revealed to him alone for just such a council as this.

'Arvon's view is that the most important discovery we made from our little chats with the Newborns who came our way is this: most senior Brother Commanders have been summoned for council at Banbury with Quail. We know that Taunt of Rollright was there, for example, though that we might expect, considering Rollright's so close. Much more interesting is the fact that Brother Commanders Sapient and Turling were there.'

'Of Avebury and Buckland? *Both* of them?'

It was one of the junior commanders who spoke, but he expressed the surprise and excitement of them all.

Weeth nodded slowly, looking round with narrowing eyes as he made sure that what he said was understood by all, and its significance sinking in.

'Yes, Avebury and Buckland are – or were when I left – without their proper leaders. No doubt both Sapient and Turling have left capable deputies in charge, but they can't be greatly experienced since we understood that all senior commanders from the systems south of Duncton were summoned to Banbury.'

There was a feeling of exultant disbelief in the chamber.

'It agrees with those other reports,' said Ystwelyn.

'And my own observations near Nuneham,' said a younger commander, who had reported the northern movement of Newborn forces at about the time Quail must have been arriving in Banbury.

Allmole turned expectantly to Maple, but he chose to say nothing more than, 'Anymole with questions for our friend Weeth?'

There were a few, mainly to clarify what little was known of Thorne, and to find out anything more Weeth might know about the strength of Quail's forces and of the southern commanders' presence.

'I can't say much more than I have,' said Weeth finally, 'but I will add that Arvon was impressed by some of the patrols and encampments of Newborns that Squilver commands. We know little of him, but for what we saw at Cannock, and stories of his subsequent ousting by Thorne, but the mole seems to know how to command forces, and position them. And they seem loyal to him. He is not the tyrannical type like Sapient, but a mole would not expect Quail to have such as Squilver as Supreme Commander.'

They all nodded.

'And Thripp?' asked one of them finally. 'Any news of him?'

Weeth shrugged. 'Nothing. I know nothing, and nor does anymole that we of Arvon's force interrogated. That was one of the things he went on to discover, that and information of Thorne.'

'And to delay him, perhaps,' said Ystwelyn quietly.

There was silence at this new thought until Maple looked expectantly at the Siabod mole and indicated that he might continue.

'Well,' said Ystwelyn slowly, 'Arvon does nothing without careful thought. I've been wondering why he did not confide in Weeth here what his further intentions were after they parted, except to say that he would eventually make his way back to be on paw near Duncton.

'We all know Weeth can be relied on, so it was not lack of trust. No, I think it was because he saw no reason to burden Weeth with secrets which might come out if he was caught and interrogated. Secrets which were well worth the keeping. We can only guess at what they were. Well, now, nomole is better than Arvon at using small forces to good effect: one of his moles is worth twenty of any other commander's. Even my own.' He grinned ruefully at this blunt admission of his brother's superiority in that kind of campaigning. 'He'll have an eye out for news of Thripp, that's certain. But, no doubt, Quail has *him* well under guard – assuming he's still alive. No, what I think Arvon's about is making a strike of some kind against Thorne, enough to hold him back. He'll be aware of the dangers of Thorne taking over from Quail, just as we are. He's gaining us time, and he'll know that's how I'll interpret it.'

After another moment's silence Maple said, 'You have all spoken well and to the point, and I think we see the way things must go.'

He paused and looked about, the decision finally made. The chamber was in absolute silence, the moles' faces lit only by the faintest of light from the night sky that came in at its two surface entrances.

'We shall advance on southern moledom. We shall, subject only to intelligence that indicates that Avebury and Buckland are better protected than we think, occupy those systems in force. Avebury, as you all know, is one of the Ancient Systems, and its place in followers' hearts is secure. We cannot say how many followers are still alive there, but we do know that some of them at least have survived up near Seven Barrows where Duncton's own Fieldfare is a refugee.

'I would be surprised if, when we take Avebury, we do not find followers ready to emerge from hiding or from the pretence that they are Newborn. We shall therefore treat that system gently. No bloody campaigning until we are sure it is Newborns we fight. No kill first and ask questions after. You know my views on that. We shall be liberating Avebury, no more, no less, and with news of its liberation a great wave of sympathy will go before us and we shall advance upon Duncton in its wake.'

Maple spoke slowly, looking from one to another as he did so, his eyes growing more serious.

'But Buckland – that is a different thing. The system is accursed. It was a place of torture and death in the distant days of moles of the Word, as we know from the grim record of the Duncton Chronicles. Well, the Newborns chose to take the place over and make it their own, and we have reports enough of the horrors committed there, second only, I suspect, to what in time may emerge from the evil that I believe is Wildenhope.*

'We shall destroy Buckland and we shall do it in the name of the Stone. Aye, in vengeful and dark spirit shall we do it. For there shall be an example set, *that* one. But hear me well, each one of you. Only in Buckland shall we destroy all we see, only there. For we wish to end these wars, not renew them. We shall crush the Newborn spirit, if so foul a thing can be called by so positive a name. We shall crush it, and lay its filthy body bare, and allmole shall know what we have done. As our liberation of Avebury shall lift the hearts of those who believe in freedom and tolerance, so shall our annihilation of Buckland cast down for ever the Newborn spectre, down into the darkness from where it came, down into the muck and filth across which moles must sometimes go, but in which they do not wish to rest and wallow if they are to reach the Stone's Light.'

Maple's voice had risen just a little, and he himself had reared up in the dark and seemed to look down upon them all. They had never known him so fearsome, and perhaps only Weeth and Ystwelyn had ever even guessed that it was this power of controlled anger, of purpose, and of ruthless intent, that made Maple the great warrior he was. Like a storm that only hints at its powers by roaring and shifting in the topmost branches of the highest trees in a wood, Maple was

* At this point, nomole was yet aware of the full truth of Wildenhope, and the foul use made of its tunnels by the Newborn Inquisitors and the hierarchy. Snyde's records were yet to be issued, and few Newborns had spoken out. Maple, right though he proved to be, was speaking on the basis of rumours then current. The truth, when it emerged, was far worse.

now showing what would happen when he came down to earth, and it seemed that already its surface trembled before his coming.

'We shall leave tomorrow, in the afternoon,' he said, and the others were barely able to refrain from cheering. 'In the morning Ystwelyn and I shall wish to speak to all other commanders and their immediate subordinates, to tell them what our decisions are, and what the dispositions of our campaign will be. I would hope that by then our good friend Rooster will be with us, for many of us, myself especially, would like to feel that he approves of what we are doing. Such an affirmation will start us off well. So somemole here please send out for Stow, who has been trying to track him down. Aye, Runnel, you do it, Rooster has a liking for you, though Stone knows why!'

There was general laughter, deep and generous, but dangerous too. It would have made a Newborn tremble through and through.

'You others, assemble those who need to be briefed and have them ready hereabout by mid-morning.'

'Aye, sir!' cried out many a voice as the Council began to break up, and its members to go out into the night.

'No, Ystwelyn, you stay with me a moment more . . . and you Weeth, you stay as well. Good, yes, so . . . you others, thank you all.'

386

Chapter Thirty-One

The others left, their pawsteps fading away along with their excited and purposeful voices. The chamber felt suddenly empty, and Maple, Ystwelyn and Weeth stanced without a word until the others' pawsteps retreated finally on to the surface and were heard no more.

'Well then,' muttered Maple, almost to himself, 'decision made. And yet . . .'

Ystwelyn laughed and said, 'Don't try and tell me you have doubts, Maple. Not after *that* speech.'

Maple grinned. 'Doubts? None at all. We shall take Avebury and free it; we shall crush Buckland; and then we shall advance on Duncton. And we shall do it all before Longest Night. Which is all very well, but I feel something's missing in all of this and I think that you, good Weeth, know what it is.'

'I? Weeth?' said Weeth conspiratorially, as if talking about some other mole.

'That "special thing",' reminded Maple. 'Remember?'

'Ah, yes. So the journeymole Radish reported my comment to you. Never trust a journeymole!' He laughed, a little uneasily.

'I would have reminded you anyway, mole,' said Maple.

'I know, I know,' said Weeth, suddenly serious. 'Let's move to the surface. It's too hot and close for comfort in here and I would see the stars . . .'

The two bigger moles followed him, all climbing up through tunnels in silence, glad to breathe in the cooler night air, and see the spread of shining stars above their heads.

Three of Ystwelyn's Siabod guardmoles moved protectively about, acknowledging the presence of their most senior commanders with a guttural 'Sir!' in the night, watchful, caring, proud. They were moles who had been with Ystwelyn from the beginning, and though they acknowledged Maple as their ultimate superior, it was Ystwelyn they served, and Siabodian, his home language, they spoke amongst themselves.

To them Ystwelyn was their greatest leader, come out of the fastness of dark Siabod to serve the greater cause. One day, and it was one they often dreamed of, he would lead them all back, their task in moledom fulfilled, the Stone's demands of them met, and they would feel the rough grass of Moel Siabod beneath their paws once more, and tell the greatest tale of their lives, and hear once more the deep rhythmic songs of their homeland, ancient in origin, ever changing in melody and word to meet the need of moment and occasion, and express the passions of their Siabodian hearts.

'You promised to teach me some Siabodian one day,' said Maple softly, when they had found a place to stance down and talk once more.

'He's no teacher, mole!' said the rasping voice of one of the guards from out of the darkness. He brought some food and placed it near them. 'Ystwelyn's a commander, a warrior, and not much of a one for talk. If you want to learn Siabodian, sir, I'll teach you!'

Maple laughed. He knew the mole well, had often stanced down in some dangerous place with Newborns nearby and felt the security the guardmole's presence gave him.

'I'll remember that, Curig,' he said.

'And I'll not forget, sir. It is true . . . ?'

He glanced at Ystwelyn in the darkness, uncertain perhaps whether he had taken his familiarity too far.

'Aye, it's true, Curig: we're off on the morrow, Buckland way. We'll be giving a briefing in the morning. Now . . .'

'Aye, sir!' said Curig, smiling briefly and retreating to a respectful distance.

'Make me feel safe, your moles do. Always have.'

'They'd die for you,' said Ystwelyn.

'For you first, mole,' said Weeth matter-of-factly.

'No mole, not for me. For Maple. It's me they love, but the one I serve whom they serve first.'

Maple sighed and they all ate the food, thinking sombre thoughts of the morrow, and the coming campaign, and fearing that some moles would not see the Wolds again.

'Now,' said Maple at last, 'What's on your mind, Weeth?'

'I do not want to be apart from you again, sir, *that's* on my mind. I did not enjoy it. I fretted. I worried for you.'

'And I missed you, mole, as Ystwelyn will testify. You have been at my flank from the beginning, and you will be there at the end. You shall not leave it again. But I needed you to go to Duncton, to see what you saw and bring back the reports you have. But there's more, isn't there?' He stared down at Weeth, his face troubled, his eyes attentive. 'You have not told everything – but everything is what I need to know.'

'There is more,' admitted Weeth, 'but I can't put a name to it.'

'Try.'

'The mole I told you we met . . .'

'The traveller, Hyssop?'

'Hibbott, he said his name was, but I don't think his name matters much. Nor was he merely a traveller, and that may be the point. He wasn't afraid of anything. Really, not a thing! My doughty companions couldn't believe it, thought it was a show. But it wasn't. He said there were more like him, many more.'

'Travellers?'

'No, pilgrims.'

'Pilgrims,' whispered Maple, wondering, remembering Radish's dismissive mention of them.

'Yes, pilgrims, like we've heard of in medieval times. Hibbott said he was looking for Privet. Simple as that. He had seen too much, suffered too much perhaps, to care any more for Quail and the New-borns, or you, Maple, and the followers. He was somehow beyond us, and made me realize that Privet must be too. He was simply looking for her.'

'He thinks she's travelled this way, does he?'

'On the contrary. He's confident that he's going to find her in Duncton Wood. He's come this way to find Rooster. He's hoping he'll tell him how best to find Privet. Not where – he's expecting her to be at the Duncton Stone – but *how*.'

'How?' repeated Maple, puzzled.

'And that poor female with Quail, the one I . . .'

Maple and Ystwelyn nodded, dark looks on their faces. They had no need to have that part of Weeth's account repeated. Downslope behind them some guardmoles broke into a soft Siabodian song of the kind such moles sing when they are preparing to set off on a march of destiny.

'She was like Hibbott,' went on Weeth quietly, 'and he made me think I was one of them too. All of us. There's no time left, Maple, or hardly any at all.'

'More like Hibbott, eh? More like the female? It's what Radish put in my mind as well. And this is the final part of your report, the "special thing"?'

389

Weeth nodded, a little unhappily; said like this it did not seem much.

Maple stared at the stars and said, 'A long time ago, in Duncton Wood, it was my privilege to guard Master Librarian Stour as he climbed the slopes up into the tunnels of the High Wood, away from the Newborns. I wanted to hurry him, but he took his own time, which taught me something of patience. He showed me an old dead treetrunk and told me that it was where a party of moles sheltered from the fire that beset the System in Bracken's day. Too tired to flee further they prayed for deliverance. The fire stopped but a pace or two from where they sheltered, and they survived.

'Upslope, beyond that tree, the shady reaches of the High Wood stretch, and through them a mole may make his way to the Stone. We warriors are the flames, and the campaign we are just beginning is the fire: fire and flames which must know when to stop. So far, no further. We *must* know when to stop, remember that, for others may not. War is too often a fire that consumes the cause on whose behalf it is waged. Remember and be warned.'

Maple fell silent again, frowning and thinking. Around them, in the night, on the slopes below where they stanced, moles were gathering under the stars, but Maple and Ystwelyn and Weeth saw them not. Nor did they hear any longer the singing, nor see the mole that came upslope towards them from out of the crowd.

For Maple's words had been more than his own, more than himself, more . . .

'And the pilgrims?' he whispered, trying to reach back to himself again; trying to pull himself down from the soaring night sky.

'Are allmole,' cried out a deep voice. 'Are you, Maple. You, Weeth. You, Ystwelyn. Won't forget, not any of us. Is delved into our heart, this time coming.'

It was Rooster's voice rising up out of the darkness; he had come among the followers, and learning that Maple and the other two were conferring out in the open, had led the commanders, and their subordinates, and many more beside up after him. Hardly leading at all, but just being followed, in silence, slowly, up into the night to where Maple was.

When he was level with Weeth he turned, the light of the risen moon across the fur of his back, like the rough grass of a high moor at night. Stow was a little behind him, and many others crowded up to be near.

'Stow came to find me, but had been found already. Was coming,

390

have come, and soon will go. Time now for us all. Some by low ways, some by high, all turning their snout to the same place in the end. Maple said "pilgrim". Small word, big thing. One of us and all of us. Like river flowing. Maple said "flames" and he said "fire". You and the flames and together you are the fire. Must burn bright and hot; must do your great work.

'Then river will flow on, like always, mostly forgotten. Pilgrims are the river. See? Drops of water, nothing by themselves. But together!'

Rooster raised his paws into the sky and his huge twisted talons glinted and seemed like moving stars.

'Most times that river of faith flows unheard, unseen, silent, deep. But sometimes it rises, deepens, flooding, pushing to change course. Now is happening, is that. Now! Fire. Water. And rock. Can run from fire. Can swim for a time in water. But rock! Can't avoid it, we can't. Fire will go over rock but won't hurt it. Rock will be there when fire gone. Rock is there where river flows. Rock will force it a new way. Rock will show that way. Then river will flow on and rock will be forgotten or submerged.'

He laughed suddenly, deeply, wildly, the sound huge and mysterious as the night sky itself.

'Privet is that rock. She stances waiting for the river to flow her way. She will force it a new way. She will not be hurt by fire and flames. Today, a mole came. One of many. Hibbott, but name unimportant. He doesn't care. Privet sent him.'

There was a mutter of surprise among the awestruck moles who listened to Rooster's words.

'He didn't know she sent him but she did. He thought I would tell him how to find her, but he told me. He came and I knew time had come. Time in Wolds over for us all. Privet needs us, is ready for us, and we will go our ways until we come together as we should. She will be there and us she will need. Each one of us; the pilgrims, the warriors, even delvers like me. Follow Maple. He knows the way back to the Duncton Stone. Only way, his way. Follow him.'

'But you're coming with us, Rooster,' cried out one of the listeners from the darkness below.

Rooster shook his head. 'Delvers delve, don't fight. Now Privet needs me. Privet beginning to die. Time beginning to be short. That mole Hibbott who came has set off already, gone into the dark night, not waiting till day comes. I will follow.'

'But Rooster . . .' It was Weeth, trying to talk quietly, but so still and silent was the night that all heard his words and understood the plea in them. For molemonths past Stow and his guardmoles had watched over Rooster precisely to keep him alive until the day when the campaign against the Newborns could begin. And now . . .

Rooster shook his head. 'Jumped in a river once. Got out alive. Am jumping in a greater river now and will get out alive again!'

There was a ripple of laughter at his good humour, and his unassailable courage.

'No, no, Weeth. Will go my way. You will go yours. All the same.'

'But you should have moles to protect you—'

'Have!' declared Rooster and produced at his left flank, almost by magic it seemed, for nomole had noticed him before, a mole.

Young, but not as young as he once was; small, but not as small as he had been; diffident, but not as diffident as before.

'Is Frogbit,' said Rooster with a grin. 'Have trained him well. He's a delver. He's all I need! Now, I go!'

Which Rooster did, without another word, his assistant Frogbit silent at his flank, down among the followers, who parted to let them through.

Maple stared after them – still as stone, Weeth wanted to say, but dared not. Very still indeed.

'When do *we* begin, sir?' called out a voice, breaking the silence.

'On the morrow, mole; on the morrow. But for now let's hear that song we heard before, a song of campaigning I think it was, Ystwelyn?'

'Aye, a Siabod song, but one for all of us.'

It was better than a speech, better perhaps than a prayer, and as one by one the followers on Bourton Hill began that song, loud and long enough for Rooster and Frogbit to hear it far along their nightbound way, allmole knew that here was the beginning of a long march into history that would not, could not, *must* not, end until it reached the Duncton Stone. But of those that so boldly set off, how many would be there at the end?

Ystwelyn's forecast of Arvon's intentions following the raid on Banbury was so near the mark that historians have subsequently argued that he must have known of them, and that Weeth's reported ignorance of Arvon's plans must be a mistake. But such moles, more used to the solitary life of script and scholarship, unused to the deep dependence and understanding of each other that kin and comrades discover in the trials and stress of war, cannot imagine how close such moles as Ystwelyn and Arvon had long been, nor how each might learn to think as the other did.

Nor do such historians, looking too often for the glamour of action to dramatize their tale, quite recognize the depth of foresight and genius that Maple of Duncton displayed in those difficult and dangerous days. It is, in fact, more than likely that he had already conceived an outline of the strategy that Arvon in one place, and he and Ystwelyn in another, now began to put into action.

Certainly there had been some prior agreement that when Arvon's work was done, and if events dictated it, he should not slow things down or make himself unavailable to the followers by rushing back to the Wolds in the hope of catching up with Maple and the others there.

No, it seems likely that Maple had long since understood that if there was to be a military climax or turning-point in the struggle between followers and Newborn it would be at or near Duncton Wood. From there the followers' inspiration had always come, to there, surely, the Newborns must finally go and triumph if they were to crush for ever the followers' spirit across moledom.

Aye, a ruined Duncton, its ways and moles destroyed for ever whilst its Stone's shelter and support were subverted to dogmatic rituals and bloody rites – such must now be the Newborn aim, the final dreadful outcome of the process begun so many years before with such brilliance and mistaken idealistic zeal by Thripp of Blagrove Slide.

Maple, then, had long since predicted that Duncton would be where all finally came to a head, and the last battle between the forces of dogma and of tolerance be fought, and had left no doubt in the doughty Arvon's mind that this would be so.

Thus it was not so difficult as historians have seemed to think to explain Ystwelyn's accurate prediction of what Arvon would do.

In one respect only was he wrong . . .

After Arvon had parted from Weeth, and sent him hurrying back to the Wolds, he and his band of paw-picked warriors headed north. They travelled fast, for the intelligence they had gained from their recent rough interrogations of Newborn guards who had been unfortunate enough to cross their path, indicated that as senior a pack of Newborn commanders was gathered in Council at Banbury as had likely sullied the slopes of moledom before.

'They'll not stay together longer than they have to!' Arvon had told his friends. 'Such moles as Brother Commander Sapient are always looking over their own shoulder to see whatmole is trying to usurp them, and he'll not want to stay long from his power-base at Avebury. If he's the mole I think he is he'll have taken one look at Quail and decided the best place to be is as far as possible from him, with as large a force of loyal moles as he can muster: which means Avebury. That being so, our task now is to keep him and his like hereabout.'

'But doesn't that make Quail stronger? Sapient brought a large force of his own when he came to Banbury.'

It was Noakes who spoke, for Arvon had been so impressed by his fieldcraft that he had taken him in as part of his force, though a somewhat independent part. Noakes was nobody's mole but his own, and in that he was more in the Duncton tradition than Siabodian, from where most of Arvon's group came.

'Well, maybe it does, in a way. But I'm asking myself what Maple and Ystwelyn will decide to do when Weeth gets to the Wolds and tells them all he knows. And I think, in fact I'm as certain as I can be, that they'll see the presence of Brother Commanders like Sapient and Turling in Banbury as the perfect opportunity to travel south and wreak what havoc they can.'

'But if that's what is going to happen,' said Noakes boldly, 'the south is where I want to be. It's my home territory, I've travelled it, I know it—'

'I am well aware of that,' growled Arvon, silencing Noakes with a frown. He liked Noakes – secretly he envied him his spirit – but he did not have quite the taciturn discipline of a Siabod mole. 'You'll be needed, mole, needed badly. But we'll not be dallying in these parts long – just long enough to set Thorne and Quail against each other and keep the Newborn Brother Commanders so busy chasing their tails here that they do not return south quite yet, or further occupy Duncton Wood immediately and make things even harder for Maple when he turns back towards there.'

'Set Thorne against Quail . . .' pondered Noakes, unused to such strategies.

'It's an old trick,' said a Siabod mole, almost dismissively. A lesser mole than Noakes might have thought from their silences, and their monosyllabic conversation, that they resented his presence, but he had confidence in himself, and had proved his worth again and again. The difference between him and them was that he did not look Siabodian, being smaller and more delicate of snout, and so did not look alien in those parts.

His willingness to go forth alone and lure some unsuspecting Newborn guard into conversation, and lead him astray to where others could take him, or to distract his attention long enough so that they all might pass, greatly impressed. So did his enthusiastic accounts of

394

Duncton's lore and history, and Avebury's too, gained in the long winter years when Fieldfare and Spurling had made the nights seem short with their tales of the systems and moles they loved.

It was a different world he showed to Arvon and his friends, and a gentler one, and he was sensitive enough to understand that their gruff ways and silences were not malevolent or dismissive but the shy and diffident behaviour of brave warriors, led out of their own land for the cause of liberty and worship of the Stone in the old ways for which they were willing to lay down their lives.

As for roughness, and their sometimes brutal behaviour with each other, Noakes did not confuse it with lack of thought or sensitivity. He heard their talk of Moel Siabod, and their deep songs, and their longing to be home. He envied them in his own turn, for the community he came from in the south had no such powerful sense of communion and support as they showed each other.

So each learned from the other, and if, on occasion, as now, Noakes displayed a certain innocence about tactics that were second nature to Arvon and the others, nomole really minded. Each to his own, and Noakes would come into his own once more.

So Arvon's intention was to set Thorne's forces against Quail's, and to do that he needed information, and fast. Within two days of parting from Weeth he had led his force north to Gaydon, which lies roughly halfway between Leamington and Banbury. Here he established a headquarters in the murky shadows of a derelict piece of ground that lies beneath the huge raised roaring owl way that dominates those parts: the same indeed which, were a mole foolish or brave enough to risk the fumes and constant blinding gazes of the roaring owls for so long, leads southwards to the very edge of Duncton Wood itself.

It was the kind of location favoured by Arvon, who thought nothing of the danger and noisome fumes of such a place if it gave him advantage of both communication and defence.

'Here we shall not easily be found, or, if we are, not easily caught. Four of you . . .' – and here he paw-picked four of his most reliable guardmoles – 'shall go north and discover what you can of Thorne's strength and intentions. Cluniac, you will go with them, but be obedient and subordinate. Help them as far as you are able, follow orders, act as messenger if need be, and learn what you can.'

Cluniac nodded silently, his eyes grim, but grateful for such an opportunity.

'Four more of you shall go back south, using the roaring owl way, as far as Banbury. I want information on all the places where we may quickly gain access to it and so escape the fields and two-foot places below. Others of you . . .'

He issued his orders quickly and clearly, and not a mole there had not a task to do, all important, all of potential value to the rest.

'Be back before night falls three days from now, there is no more time than that. Noakes, you will stay here with me. I wish to learn what I can from you of southern moledom, and to teach you something in return – for I have noticed that your roaring owl way skills are lacking.'

Arvon raised a solid paw towards the way that towered above them, and from which ominous roars and rattles, flashes and yellow gazes of light came forth over their heads.

Noakes had always avoided such places, preferring quieter, more natural ways as far from two-foots and roaring owls as possible, and now he looked reluctantly above.

'You must learn all you can, for in times of need such routes can provide a mole with the advantage of surprise and speed, unpleasant and debilitating though we all know them to be. You mole . . .' Here he pointed to one of their number who had been wounded in an encounter with Newborns a few days before. 'Stay here with us and wait. You others without an immediate task, explore hereabout for a day or two in twos and see what information you can find. Anything may be useful. Now, go to it, and good luck!'

'Arvon! Mole!'

Two days had passed and some of those who had gone to reconnoitre were back and had discovered the presence and strength of Newborns to the north and south.

Arvon heard their reports one by one, asked questions as he needed to, waited for the sleepers to awake, and ascertained that only four moles were missing – the group that had gone north into what was believed to be Thorne's territory.

'Wake me when they get back,' said Arvon finally, it now being past midnight. It was plain enough that he had absolute confidence that they *would* get back safely.

'*Those* moles don't get taken by surprise,' said one of the Siabod guards, and Noakes did not doubt it.

Nor were they. At some grey pre-dawn hour Noakes was woken from deep slumber in the communal chamber they all shared by the sound of moles arriving. It was the northern group, and one was wounded, or at least limping.

'It's nothing that some sleep and rest won't cure,' Noakes heard him say. 'We had a little argument with some Newborns.'

The next day Arvon's forces gathered together again, as rough-looking but comradely a group of moles as Noakes ever remembered being in company with. Arvon did not waste time on niceties. The reports were all in and the position was alarmingly clear: Thorne's forces were far larger and more disciplined than they had expected, and the rumours of Chervil's involvement were true. How the four moles had gained their information Noakes dreaded to think, but he pitied the Newborns who had crossed the followers' path.

'You're talking big, powerful and well led,' said one of the four. 'They're impressive, and they're only a day or two from moving south. Our understanding is that they intend to bypass Quail and get to Duncton before he does. They want to make him fight for it so they're not seen as the aggressors.'

Thorne, it seemed, was well informed, for the story that the moles who had gone south had gathered was that Quail too was imminently moving – also to Duncton Wood.

'Vicious lot of bastards, they really are,' came the report. 'I wouldn't call them disciplined, and from the account we've heard, Thorne would have no trouble with them in a location like Banbury. Well, I mean, the defences aren't bloody well there, are they?'

There was a general deprecating murmur and shaking of heads.

'Anything else?' asked Arvon, looking about.

More shaking of heads, and a general sense that everymole knew what needed to be done.

'Well, then, lads, it's going to be risky but I think we know what we've got to do.'

And as Noakes listened, and heard what Arvon proposed, he wondered if wars had always been like this – not great armies of moles moving as one, but smaller groups, working together, knowing what their objectives were and how to achieve them.

'. . . the point is that nomole on either side must ever know who we are, or even that *we* were there at all. We go in where we've got to, and we come out; go in again and come out again. Get caught and you're on the other side, and Stone help you! Don't get caught!'

Noakes looked about and thought that it would take twenty Newborns to catch any one of the moles stanced about him.

'And you, Noakes, you go with . . .' and suddenly Noakes' heart was pounding. He was part of it. He was one of them . . . no, one of *these*!

397

'You, Cluniac, you'll stay with me, mole, for you're not up to much fighting yet, and I'm not sure you should be.'

Noakes exchanged a glance with Cluniac, a mole he had got to know and like. He was surprised at the gentleness in Arvon's deep voice, and his obvious concern for the Duncton mole.

'So you all know what you've to do. Any questions?'

'The meeting place afterwards, sir . . .'

'Aye, we'll have the usual arrangement: one central place at the end of operations, and a secondary location for stragglers. Here will do – say the second night from now. We'll leave a couple of moles behind to pick up stragglers. The rest of us will travel south to a location not far from Duncton called Cuddesdon – Noakes here knows of it, and Cluniac, though neither have been to it. But it's well enough known to be easy to find, even for anymole that gets separated. It's from there that we'll be mounting any operation we may have to make into Duncton Wood itself. It's to the south-east and useful for the cross-under into the Wood, which you all know.'

'Aye, sir,' they said, nodding their heads and beginning to break up into the groups they would be working in.

'And lads . . .' growled Arvon right at the end, his voice commanding instant attention, 'I swear to you by the Holy Stones of Tryfan that after we've set paw in Duncton Wood once more, and seen that all is as it should be – *and* we shall, *and* it will be – then those of you who long as I do for the clean air of Siabod will set paw for home.'

There was a cheer, but a quiet one of moles who sensed that a time of destiny was upon them and that for some of them perhaps it would be their last chance to serve the Stone, for theirs would be a final sacrifice. But for others – and whatmole could say who they would be? – there would be life beyond the coming conflicts, and a chance to return to Siabod and see their kin and their home system once more, and remember the days when they were led by a great mole to do great things. Somemole began singing, and soon all joined in . . .

> *Moles of Siabod,*
> *At the break of dawn*
> *Arise . . .*
> *Siabod arise,*
> *Spawner of warriors.*
> *I have watched over you,*
> *Though I am not only yours . . .*

'Though you are not only watching over me . . .' whispered Hibbott that same dawn, far to the west, high in the Wolds.

He invoked, he prayed and he hoped, and though his words may finally have been different from those of Arvon and his friends caught now so perilously between the Newborn forces of Thorne and Quail, yet their intention was similar: to invoke the Stone's help for deeds yet to be done. For Arvon and the others it concerned war, for Hibbott a pilgrimage to peace.

'Though you are not only watching over me, Stone, give me the sense that you are with me. Yesterday I was witness to a dreadful thing, and now my heart is heavy. What can I, a solitary pilgrim, usefully do at such a time as this?'

The 'dreadful thing' Hibbott had seen, and of which his is the only eye-witness account, was the followers' exodus from Bourton at the start of their great Crusade against the Newborns. From this we may reasonably surmise that his own departure from the Wolds the follow-ing morning coincided with that secret and dramatic scene near Ban-bury when Arvon briefed his force for an operation designed to bring Thorne against Quail, and so make time for the followers in the south. Let us repeat part of Hibbott's account of the followers' departure from the Wolds.

'Tired from my exertions over the days past to find the Master of the Delve, more familiarly known as Rooster of Charnel Clough, and strangely affected by my conversation with him when I did so, I began to weaken in my resolve to get a good start on my onward journey. Then, my paws already heavy, and my eyes unable to stare long at the stars to gain inspiration from them without closing towards sleep, I heard a deep chanting of moles from Bourton, the system at whose edge I had found Rooster.

'I stopped and turned to look back, and over Bourton Hill, from where the chant came, and where I imagined many moles to have assembled, a great spread of stars seemed to hang, like a huge tree of hawthorn blossom caught by a bright sun. I knew I could travel no further and, for prudence's sake, as was my habit, I climbed upslope above my path and made a scrape in some obscure spot overlooking it. I listened to the chant for but a short time more before I fell asleep, Rooster's mysterious words in my mind: "You show way to Privet, not me. Master of Delve is Master of Delve only; servant otherwise! You lead now! Go, go, go, mole! Flames come, fire burns, go to river now. Needs you too."

'"Well! And what is a mole to make of that?" I wondered! Still, his words must mean something, and I had done his bidding to "Go" as best I could. But now sleep overtook me, and his words and the moles' chanting mingled into some heavy awe-inspiring dream which carried me along through night and late into the morning, though when I woke all details of it fled before I could grasp them to my memory. I was left feeling lonely and afraid, and therefore lethargic, a condition I had known often enough before to have faith that it would pass.

'I stayed where I was and let the sun rise higher before I even moved to find a little food. My limbs were heavy, my mind slow, and I decided to rest for a time. I am glad I did, for from my secret place I saw what few others can have seen, the departure of the forces of the followers out of Bourton, to begin what allmole now knows to be their campaign across southern moledom.

'I saw them all, as if in place of the dream I had lost, except they seemed still a part of it: mole after mole, large and small, warriors all. I did not know their names, or that among them great moles went. Later I learnt that Maple was there, but I did not know him; the great Siabodian leader Ystwelyn went by, so I have been told, but I did not know him either.

'Yet my eyes scanned them all, hoping to see the two moles I knew – Weeth and Rooster. Weeth I did see, and glimpsed as well one of those moles who had been his companions on the way back to the Wolds when we had briefly met. Rooster I did not see, and since once seen he is not a mole one forgets, I concluded he was not of the Crusade that day.

'One by one, dark-furred and fair, famous and less so, but to me all one, I watched them go, their eyes fixed on the glories they hoped to find on the westward horizon, and thus not seeing me, Hibbott of Ashbourne Chase, a mole getting older, dustier each day, and troubled. Why *should* they see me?

'They left behind them a haze of dust stirred up by the tramp of their paws. I prayed then to the Stone, for their sakes as well as my own, concluding with these words, for I felt very alone: "Though you are not only watching over me, Stone, give me the sense that you are with me."

'The dust was still in the air when I slipped into sleep again. I woke to find dusk had come, and with it a clear cool sky. I slept into night and another dawn came, the first day of October, a time of change that brings in autumn and the falling of the leaves. I knew that now my long pilgrimage had taken another turn, into new tunnels and strange ways, and they seemed bleak and long and without end.

'"Hibbott," I told myself, "they have gone their way, and now you must go yours." And where was that? Surely, to the Duncton Stone . . .

'Though I rose then, and journeyed on, never had I done so with such a sense of foreboding, nor felt that my journey's destination, and moledom's, was so far away, and reaching it so fraught with difficulty.'

Chapter Thirty-Two

'Where are they?'

'Just over there, sir, just beyond the rise.'

The guardmole moved smartly out of the way as Brother Commander Thorne and no less a mole than Chervil, formidable son of Thripp, moved past him to view the corpses for themselves. A little behind, puffing from the exertion of climbing the steep slope, came old Brother Rolt, frowning, a little reluctant, concerned.

The three dead guardmoles lay where they had been attacked, paws outstretched, mouths open to the blue October sky, red-brown blood like excrement smeared on grass and fur, in one case in a trail where the mole had crawled a little way before dying.

'You heard nothing, mole?'

The guardmole came hurrying over to Thorne and gave what account he could, which was not much. He himself, along with several others, had been in the nearby guard-chamber. The patrol of watchers – doubled in number for safety after three other recent murderous night-time attacks – had simply been patrolling. When they did not come in for the change of watch the next guards on duty had gone to investigate and found all but one dead. It had all been done with ruthless efficiency.

The fourth guardmole in the patrol, to whom Thorne and the others had spoken a short time before where he was being tended below ground, was alive, though wounded. He had played dead and got away with it, and in doing so he had gained useful information about his attackers.

'They were of Squilver's force, sir, no doubt of it. I heard them refer to yourself and our forces, and how the Elder Senior Brother would have a report of *this* operation, and it would serve their promotions well. They talked of another successful "softening-up operation" for the assaults yet to come.'

The mole winced with pain, the wound in his flank still seeping a watery blood.

'You have done well, mole,' Thorne had said, pleased that even under such pressure the mole had kept his ears open and his eyes shut.

'I hardly dared breathe, sir, they were that close. Five of them.'

'But you got a glimpse of them before they wounded you?'

'Not much of one. They tricked us into giving them our attention – made a whistling kind of noise as if it was one of our own – and then reared up out of the dark and went for us. We'll have a chance to go after them, won't we, sir? They were my friends Quail's lot killed.'

Now Thorne stanced looking at the dead, Chervil and Rolt at his flank. Near them a strong force of guardmoles, brought in at dawn in case of further trouble, waited patiently, staring downslope to the south, towards the territory they knew to be in Quail's control. Where they stanced was the boundary between the two, so far as one could be defined. A good way off to their left flank a huge roaring owl way rose into the sky.

'The system over there's called Gaydon,' said Rolt, 'so I am told. Nomole about there any more, it seems.'

'Hmmph!' grunted Thorne, glancing at Chervil. None of them were at all pleased at what had happened. 'We know there aren't any other Caradocians about, at least not in force, otherwise patrols would have spotted them long since. This is obviously a small force working under cover, and I must say I am impressed. I didn't think Squilver had it in him to organize such a thing. Six killed three days ago, two yesterday and now three more, nearly four.'

'You have the forces to retaliate in the same way,' said Chervil. 'It's just that you haven't chosen to use them.'

'Well, I think that time is now coming,' said Thorne. For Chervil was right, Thorne had long since had a force of well-trained moles for just such work as this – tough, efficient, disciplined moles able to work in small groups.

'But Brother Commander, I thought you had decided to avoid conflict with Quail's force and reach Duncton as quickly as possible and so cut it off to him!'

'I *said*, Brother Rolt, that I would *like* to do that, but we must pay heed to what is happening on the ground. If we had been able to muster our forces from the north, and consolidate the eastern territories sooner, then we might have been able to set off for Duncton earlier, but only now have we come to full strength, and it seems it is too late for what I had in mind. In any case, a little show of force by us here and now might well serve to delay Quail, and if he proves as weak as I think, make it easier for us finally to make the break-through to Duncton. My wish is to contain the violence. I do not want civil war. But . . .' He frowned, thinking, his eyes dark. 'My moles demand retaliation, and they may well be right – they have been very disciplined so far, but there are limits. I am as concerned for your father Thripp as you are, Chervil, of course I am. But we do not know where he is, and I think Rolt is right to believe that Quail will not allow harm to come to him because he still needs him. Frankly, if he had wanted to kill him he would have done so long since. Perhaps he has . . .'

Rolt shook his head slowly, his eyes full of care for the master he loved so much but of whom nomole had heard a thing. That much Quail – or Snyde, perhaps – had done well.

'I remain dubious about the wisdom of attacking Quail's force,' Chervil said. 'But perhaps we cannot show weakness, especially at a time when the followers are gaining support.'

The others nodded, thinking no doubt of the growing number of pilgrims who had begun to appear from out of nowhere, as it seemed. Ever since mid-July such fearless moles had begun to trek southwards, and they all told the same story: they were heading for Duncton Wood, they came in peace, they were showing their support for the mole Privet. Some of them even refused to speak, seeming to have chosen to adopt a vow of silence in sympathy with a mole who had become both heroine and martyr to them. One group of moles brought into Leamington had all chosen silence, but for one who acted as their spokesmole.

'Praise be, brothers,' he told them, 'but we're on our way in silence to mark our respect, and show our faith in the virtues of holy Privet, whose blessed words we hope to hear when her vow of silence is complete.'

'And when might that be, pilgrim?' wondered Thorne.

'When the lost and last Book, which is of Silence, is brought back to Duncton Wood.'

Thorne and Chervil had decreed that such moles should be unharmed, given shelter, and sent on their way – or he had for a time. Then, when two of them were found snouted some way south of Leamington, the outrage perpetrated by Quail's moles, the pilgrims had been told to return to the north.

Not that this policy had been very effective: they came back again, or they were found detouring to the east and then moving south, despite all the warnings Thorne's moles gave them about what

404

would happen to them if the Caradocians caught them.

'Brother! Have faith in the Stone!' the pilgrims hectored him. 'Free yourselves of fear as Privet has done! Feel the healing power of fear-lessness!'

Throughout the summer years Thorne had made every effort to track down Privet, having greatly regretted letting her slip away from Leamington. Now he had a use for her, and in any case he feared for her safety. The only positive lead he had came from one of a rough group of moles his own forces had captured who had been in the thrall of one of the independent Newborns who had begun to flourish at that time. The mole was called Rees; he was badly scarred about the eyes and had only limited vision, and told a strange story of having been attacked by some followers, temporarily blinded, and then healed by the touch of a female who sounded very like the Privet Thorne had known up on Wenlock Edge. Rees confessed he had been transformed by the experience, and had even been tempted to join the pilgrims, but Thorne had persuaded him he might serve Privet's cause better by staying with him. He had the natural instinct good leaders have for moles who have qualities which may prove useful.

Clouds had begun to mount in the sky, and a late afternoon chill came to the air, as often happens in October. The days were drawing in . . .

'The decision's made, then,' said Thorne forcefully, bringing to an end further discussion about the slain patrol. 'We'll attack the positions to the south-west on which we have had our eyes for a long time. We'll do it in a limited way, and then seek to parley with Squilver. I prefer to persuade him to make Quail stance down, than to take Quail himself by force – it will be easier to contain things afterwards if we take power quietly.'

'Quail will *never* go quietly,' said Chervil darkly, glancing at Rolt who shrugged unhappily and nodded his agreement.

'He would rather die,' said Rolt.

'He will die, then,' said Thorne grimly. 'Meanwhile, tonight he will get a clear message that we mean business, and not before time. Now, we have moles to brief and plans to implement.'

Rolt turned to leave, Chervil also, feeling perhaps that military matters were best left to Thorne, but the Brother Commander suggested they stay some moments more.

'It's not one of my senior commanders I'm going to speak to first, as a matter of fact, nor even the moles who will be mounting the night's attack. No, it's a mole we all have an interest in, and perhaps the time is right for him to succeed in a task at which so many have failed.'

He summoned Rees, he who claimed to have been healed by Privet.

'Sir? They said you wanted to see me.'

Rees peered round at Chervil and Rolt, his poor sight making him seem over-inquisitive. But for all that he had a strong look about him, and a solid stance.

'Aye, mole, we do,' said Thorne. 'You've wanted a task, and in the past you've expressed a willingness to undertake a dangerous one.'

'Aye, sir! But as you see, I'm past my fighting days, though I'm not a fool and could give a good account of myself if I chose my own ground, like a tunnel or chamber where I knew nomole was behind me. So just give the order and if it does not offend against the Stone—'

'I'll be the judge of that,' said Thorne sharply. Give a mole a mite of worm and he'll take the whole lot!

'Yes, sir,' said Rees, chastened.

'I want you to slip away from Leamington with the next pilgrims that come by.'

'Sir?' said Rees, astonished.

'Aye, that's what I said. Become a pilgrim mole, just as you've wanted to. But a pilgrim with a task. I want you to find Privet, if you can.'

'The whole of moledom's been looking for her, sir.'

'The whole of moledom does not know what she looks like. You do.'

'I never actually saw her clearly, sir, for my eyes had been injured and what sight I have now returned only after she had gone. I just heard her voice, but I'd know that anywhere. At the end of my time with her and her two friends I did succeed in glimpsing her dimly. She seemed not to be a big mole.'

'Quite right, she's not,' said Thorne impulsively.

'And how would you know that, sir?' said Rees, astonished.

Thorne repeated for all their benefits the story of how he had arrested Privet on the Wenlock Edge, and how he had talked to her before delivering her up to Wildenhope, now much to his regret. He admitted too how much Privet had impressed him.

'So you see, mole, I happen to recognize the mole you describe, and so do Senior Brother Chervil and Brother Rolt here, for reasons we have no need to go into.'

The two moles nodded, Rolt with a look of concern and care in his eyes for the mole he had first met in Blagrove Slide so many years before as a Confessed Sister. Chervil, thus far, knew her only as a mole who had spoken so compellingly to him on the trek up towards Caer Caradoc for the ill-fated Convocation before the last Longest Night.

'You see, Rees, I am sympathetic to her,' said Thorne. 'Don't ask me why, for she's not Newborn. But . . .'

'Exactly, sir.' There was surely more goodness and real faith in Privet than in a decade of Newborn 'education'!

Neither had to speak blasphemy against the Newborn way to think it, though whether Rees realized that Rolt and Chervil were thinking it too nomole can say.

'You said she had two companions,' said Chervil. Ever since Wildenhope he had harboured suspicions about Privet that he scarcely dared believe, which Rolt had refused to assuage. 'Describe them both.'

Rees' loyalties were divided; he felt he should obey the commands of senior moles he had come to respect, in whom he saw the only chance of recovering something of the idealism of the Crusades he had once believed in, yet he wished to protect the memory of two moles, Hodder and Arliss. He greatly respected Hodder, who had saved his life, and he had fallen in love with Arliss. One day, he dared hope, he might meet her again.

'Well, sir, it's hard, for both were good to me.' He repeated his story, and told how Hodder had come back to save his life, and how Arliss had helped heal him, before Privet — if it had been her — completed the process.

'You sound like a mole in love,' said Chervil slowly, his dark eyes as warm as they ever were.

Rees looked uncomfortable, scuffing his paws at the ground and smiling uncertainly.

'What exactly do you want me to do, sir?' he said at last, turning back to Thorne.

'Try to find her. Warn her that civil war is breaking out, and worse, if my guess about the follower Maple is right, for he'll be active this autumn, bound to be. Find her, warn her, and tell her that it was I who sent you. Tell her . . . tell her to go home now, to Duncton Wood. Tell her that I don't know why, but she'll be needed there. And soon — before Quail gets there.'

He fell silent, a little surprised by his own words. If she went, pilgrims would follow, and that might make things very hard for Quail, and easier for his own force to bring order back to moledom.

407

'Well, now, that's all very well,' exclaimed Rolt. '*If* he found her he would find a mole not easy to persuade to do anything. Why, Privet's the most formidable mole I've ever met, along with Elder Senior Brother Thripp—'

'Ah, so you know her, Rolt!' exclaimed Chervil.

Rolt looked annoyed with himself and muttered, 'I suppose I do. I suppose I did.'

'Any questions, Rees?' asked Thorne, sensing there was more to this exchange between Rolt and Chervil than Rees needed to know about.

Rees grinned and said, 'Pilgrims prefer silence to questions, sir!'

He grinned again, a curious look of relief in his scarred eyes and face.

'You say she healed you, mole?' said Chervil, suddenly gentle.

'Gave me back the faith that I'd see again, sir. I'd travel a lifetime to hear *her* voice again.'

'Then get started, mole!' said Thorne. 'You'll be more useful in the coming days doing that, than fighting here with impaired sight.'

'Yes, sir,' said Rees quietly. Then he added, gently, 'And good luck, sir, with what's coming and that! Good luck to all of you!'

They smiled and watched him go, envying him suddenly. A pilgrim's life might, after all, have more to offer a mole than the responsibilities they had.

'Guardmole!' roared Thorne.

Several came at double time.

'Send for the following senior commanders,' he said, detailing a list of names, 'and fast! No, no, I'll come with you; I think these two moles have matters to discuss.'

Then he too was gone, and Rolt and Chervil were left facing each other alone.

'Well?' said Chervil quietly. 'Well, Brother Rolt? Isn't it time you told me the truth about Privet?'

Rolt looked at the mole he had known ever since the day he was born. Thripp's son, to whom he had been surrogate father. Chervil, of whom, if only at second paw, he felt so proud, the more so these summer moleyears past as he had seen his ward struggle to cast off the training and dogma of his past and make sense of a world that was changing so quickly. Chervil was now a formidable and worthy mole. Perhaps all he needed was a mother's love . . .

All of which was the more moving because nomole knew better than Rolt the nature of the quest Thripp himself had set off on so many years before, which had gone so wrong and yet which still might turn out right.

'She was the best thing in my life, the Stone speaking through her to me,' Thripp had said of Privet, and Rolt remembered how Thripp and Privet, both hurt so much by the past, had dared to discover love in each other.

Nomole could yet guess Thripp's true greatness, and how he had set out to remind moles of the nature of the Stone's Light and Silence, feeling that though the distant war of Stone on Word had been won by the followers, its spiritual message had been all but lost. Charismatic and compelling, Thripp had persuaded a generation of moles to follow his lead back to a new austerity and purity, only to see ideals turned to nightmares as the dream was corrupted, and the dark side of moles' nature emerged through the Brother Inquisitors.

These things Rolt thought of in those moments of pondering how to reply to Chervil's question about Privet, and who she was to him. Did he really not know? Could he not have guessed?

The evening was drawing in; the summer years were over now, and the chill in the air and the distant cold mists might almost have been winter beckoning.

'Mole,' said Brother Rolt gently, 'there are many, many things I have to tell you and the time has come to do so, now that we are on the eve of violence that may escalate into war, though Stone knows none of us wants it. But, yes, there are things you should know, the knowledge of which I alone have been entrusted with these many years. Why do you think your father ordered me to leave him at Wildenhope and join Thorne?'

'My father never had a simple reason for doing anything!' exclaimed Chervil ruefully.

They laughed in the way moles who love and respect each other laugh when they are alone, talking of a mole they both love.

'Well, that's true enough! One of the reasons was because he knew you would join forces with Thorne sooner or later, and when you did I would be able to talk to you, as we talk now. He knew the right moment would come, and trusted me to know when it did. It has come today.'

'You said you had many things to tell me, many things.'

Rolt nodded, and began to talk, telling Chervil of what his father was like when he was young.

'He preached like nomole I have ever heard, his eyes shining with the Light and truth of the Stone, his belief in a simpler way of contemplation and worship impossible to resist. Love, chastity, truth, compassion, discipline, all these things he spoke of, and some he practised.'

'Some!' exclaimed Chervil.

'"Nomole is born perfect, and he must struggle along the hard way towards perfection, ever mindful that he needs the Stone's Light to guide him, and its Silence to still him." Those were your father's words, which have stayed with me since the first time I heard him preach beside the stream at Blagrove Slide. In its clear waters I, and many like me, committed ourselves to follow him: a stream which became muddy, whose currents became too strong, and whose power turned to corruption in the drownings at Wildenhope. You were there, mole, you were there.'

'I was there,' whispered Chervil, remembering. 'Why did my father let that be?'

Rolt almost shuddered with distress as he shook his old head, and stared into Chervil's troubled eyes.

'It went wrong, it all went wrong. Yet did he not see a way of making it right, of containing it, of turning it back towards light, as the seasons turn at Longest Night?'

'How contain something so grotesque as Quail? And what light?'

'Quail? Snyde? Do you think if they had not come along there would not have been others to take their place? Do you think when they go there will not be others? There have always been such moles lurking in the shadows at the Stone's base. But Thripp saw something others perhaps had not, though I do not think his vision of how such moles might be contained came suddenly. But I know *when* it began to be clear to him – when Privet came into his over-disciplined life as his Confessed Sister.'

'Privet?' whispered Chervil, his eyes widening in surprise and his face deepening into thought and the beginning of insight into what it might be that Rolt was going to tell him.

'Oh, yes, it was Privet all right who changed him as no other could.'

Rolt talked then of Privet's coming to Blagrove Slide and how of all the Confessed Sisters she was the only one who had strength of mind to resist the 'education' such moles received.

'Your father noticed her, perhaps seeing in her an intelligence and spirit something like his own. But more than that, he recognized in her the same loveless austerity of his upbringing, or something very like it. He was, I believe, frightened of the intimacy implicit in a

410

brother's work with a Confessed Sister and had until then resisted the very thing that most brothers, less pure in purpose than he, looked forward to as a reward for seniority.

'I watched as a struggle of spirit and flesh, truth and falsehood, honesty and hypocrisy took place between them, though neither seemed to know it. I watched as she fought to retain her independence, and he strove not to lose his. I watched as the Stone led them both out of darkness through the passions of love and beyond.'

'Privet . . . ?' whispered Chervil again, remembering the mole who had talked to him just once, and disturbed him so much. A thin, middle-aged kind of mole, though with eyes as bright as stars – as he remembered it. But with his father?

'Aye,' said Rolt, a shade tartly. 'You may only see them as getting old, but I saw them when they were younger. I knew their passion, and it was a blessed thing, precious as life, which is why it made life.'

Chervil's eyes widened a little in surprise, and then he stared in astonishment.

'Yes, mole, yes. I watched as Privet got with pup by your father, and discovered a different purpose to life, and new strengths; he tried to make sense of it, and he strove to find a way forward for the great dream he had through the narrow and confining prejudices of his birth and rearing. I watched, Chervil, and I suffered and rejoiced for them both.'

'It was *Privet* who was my . . . ?'

There was more than surprise in his voice: there was a kind of wonder.

'Aye, mole, Privet was your mother. And in your birth she found her salvation, and, though the years have been long, Thripp found his. A mole who had been taught all but love, which is the most important thing; yet he found it, and dared reach out to it. A mole who knew the vocabulary of all things spiritual, dared try to speak words for something nomole had ever taught him. A great mole who was flawed by life did that most difficult and fearful thing – he looked at himself and saw what he was and tried to change.'

'And you, Rolt, what were you?'

'I?' faltered Rolt, staring into Chervil's eyes, and seeing the tears upon his face. 'I was *there*. I loved them both. I tried to make them see what they were together. And when you and your siblings came . . .'

'How many were there, mole?' asked Chervil huskily.

'Four; three females and you.'

'Three?'

411

'One died; her name was Brimmel. But two survived, Loosestrife and Sampion.'

'Loosestrife and Sampion? Striking names, not very Newborn.' His voice had become blank, as if he did not dare react to what he heard.

'Privet chose them,' said Rolt, not without irony. If he felt lighter of spirit it was because Chervil did too, but then his eyes clouded again.

'What happened to them?' asked Chervil. 'Killed, I suppose.' His voice was bleak now, and he seemed afraid.

'Oh, no, mole, no,' said Rolt gently, understanding Chervil's fear, and his sudden tears at what he had not lost and yet not ever had. 'Your mother, your brave and formidable mother, made Thripp promise to let them live. Which promise he kept, devolving their early rearing, along with your own, on me, who was but a Brother Assistant. When Loosestrife and Sampion were of an age to travel Thripp decreed that they went to a system out of harm's way; the place chosen was Mallerstang – a system with a history of isolation and independence, in the far north-east. I know they got there because I took them myself.'

'You! So, that was when you went missing!' said Chervil in wonder, beginning to make connections with events he had never quite understood. 'And that was why at Wildenhope it was Mallerstang I had to say . . . Whillan . . . ' His eyes clouded at the memory.

'Aye,' said Rolt. 'Mallerstang was where the two females were taken. Your mother had already had to leave – again, it was I who got her out of Blagrove Slide. It would not have been wise for her to stay, not wise at all. When I came back from taking the two females north, which was the longest until now I had ever been away from Thripp, I found that Quail had gained power and influence and even become involved with your education.'

'He tried,' said Chervil grimly, 'but with me he did not get far.'

'I came back, regained my influence over you, and finally your father arranged for you to be sent to Duncton Wood to protect you from Quail and certain of the other Brother Inquisitors.'

'To protect me! I thought I had been banished by you! I missed you, Rolt.'

'I know it, Chervil, I know it well.'

There was a long silence as each thought about the troubled past.

Then Rolt continued, 'Your father saw greatness in Privet. I spoke of him seeing the Stone's Light, and a way forward. Well, it was to come through her. When she spoke to him of a quest for the Book of

Silence, which I personally thought was the wild talk of a mole too educated for her own good, he understood that *she* might be on the only way that would free moledom of the dark shadows of strife, and the renewal in a different form of the war of Stone and Word. He saw it, though she herself didn't.'

'And I? And my sisters?'

Rolt shrugged, feeling suddenly rather tired. He had told Chervil the main things, the rest could come later. No longer was he burdened by secrets he had no wish to keep.

'I cannot speak of your sisters since those days. I asked the moles who were to rear them to tell them of their father and mother when they were old enough to understand. Such things should not be secret. But of you I can say this: yours is a great heritage, and a troublesome one. You have been born of two of the most remarkable moles of an age of remarkable moles. As your parents were united for a time by passion and love, so yours may be the task of uniting moledom, as he always wanted. To see peace come, and trust return; to see the Stone worshipped as it should be; to know the lost and last book has finally "come to ground", as the old teaching goes.

'These are great times, Chervil, and if your past is shadowed and strange, well, it may make you all the more able to deal with the shadow and light that successively beset and inspire moledom.'

Chervil frowned and said, not without regret, 'And meanwhile. My mother? My father? My sisters? I discover them now, and I do not know if a single one of them is alive.'

'You shall rediscover them, mole.'

'Hmmph!' said Chervil, and it was all he said for a very long time.

Chapter Thirty-Three

Quail, Snyde, and Supreme Commander Squilver were not in the least surprised when news of the assault by Thorne's forces came through to their Banbury headquarters the following evening. After all, had not moles from Thorne's force already been responsible for several outrages in recent days past, including the killing of four moles at Ratley, and the massacre of all but one of a patrol of five near Wellesbourne? It seemed so.

They knew, for example, that Thorne's guardmoles were responsible for the killings at Ratley because the sole surviving member of the patrol – wounded and mistakenly left for dead – had overheard his assailants talk of how pleased Brother Commander Thorne would be.

That this might be the work of followers rather than Newborns, and, worse, designed to put the blame on Thorne, does not seem to have occurred to Quail or Squilver; nor even to Snyde, who might perhaps have been expected to suspect such a thing. Yet his meticulous records give no clue that he did. On the contrary, the 'evidence' that the outrages were the work of Thorne's moles caused him to revise his belief that it had been followers who had so rudely invaded the Banbury headquarters, and so nearly – but for his brave intervention! – caused harm to the Elder Senior Brother himself. Mistrusting his own instincts he now believed that the moles who infiltrated Banbury, aided as he still maintained by the now disgraced Skua, were traitorous Newborns, spawned by Thorne.

'It is a pity we did not ourselves make the first assault,' observed Quail accusingly. 'Is it not, Squilver?'

It was another Crusade Council meeting, in another chamber, and once more the atmosphere was heavy with fear – and also with the now undeniable odours of Quail himself, which were like the vomit of fox, or the sweet-sick stench of a cadaver rotting in a dark pool on a summer's day.

Experienced members of the Council took positions near the portals in the hope that a fresh breeze might blow the smell away from them.

Snyde, as usual, crouched at Quail's flank, positively revelling in the nauseous perfume of his master's body. They were there to debate a sudden and unexpected opening of hostilities by Thorne's forces.

Quail's eyes were dark and impassive; there were drops of sweat on his bald head, and his mouth was open in a grotesque and cruel smile, wide enough to reveal the few rotten teeth he still had.

'*Well?*' he rasped, sticking his snout forward and peering at Squilver, angry not to have had a reply to his question.

Squilver hesitated, and understandably so. His advice *had* been to mount an assault, but Snyde himself had counselled against it, saying that they would be better advised to let Thorne be seen to be the aggressor so that he might the easier be arraigned, tried, and executed when he was caught, as he surely would be. So Squilver smiled uneasily, reluctant to risk reminding them of what they all knew had been the basis for inaction; instead he attempted to divert Quail.

'Eight of ours are dead, to ten of theirs, Master; a good result in the difficult circumstances in which they fought – taken by surprise as they were, and against superior numbers.'

Snyde nodded approvingly, Quail winced from some internal pain or other, Squilver waited. In fact what he had just reported was not true. The losses had been ten Caradocians to only three of Thorne's force, and the numbers fighting had been roughly equal. Nor was there any surprise that could not have been guarded against had Squilver not advised his moles to concentrate their forces in another area than that which Thorne attacked.

'We took one of their moles prisoner, Master.'

'Ah,' sighed Quail. 'And?'

'Under pressure of the Stone's correction, the mole confessed freely. More assaults are coming, as we expected. That he knew, and much else.'

Squilver glanced at Snyde, who had been present at the 'Stone's correction', the euphemism the Caradocians used for torture.

'Master, the mole revealed much of interest, some of which is distressing,' began Snyde. 'If I may refer to my memorandum of the interview . . .'

Snyde's report was short and accurate. The reluctant informant had revealed that Thorne's forces were now strong and well-placed; that many systems to the east had been made subjugate to Thorne; that the northern territories were under the sway of Chervil himself, who was now in alliance with Thorne; that Brother Commanders had been sent as far west as Cannock, and had taken a large number

415

of systems, including, it was thought, Cannock itself; that—

'Yes, yes, *yes!*' snarled Quail; his carbuncled snout turned puce, his eyes bulged; the veins distended above his eyes and down his thick neck, and the protuberance at his rear wobbled and shook like the body of a dead worm bloated with filthy floodwater. 'Enough, mole, we have heard enough . . .'

For once, it seemed, Snyde had gone too far, perhaps allowing himself to sound a little too smug in this reporting of Thorne's successes.

Quail turned to Squilver and asked, 'What do you advise?'

It was an interesting moment, for Squilver could not easily prevaricate, though he could try. But if he agreed with what Snyde had said at the previous Council, and Snyde now changed his mind, well . . . he would have lost too much face to survive if Snyde chose to put the talons in. If he advocated an assault, and Snyde resisted, then the ensuing struggle might be bloody; it was not an easy . . .

'We should attack them, Master,' said Squilver suddenly, his words cutting short whatever private calculations the Council was making. 'We should freely admit our mistakes as a Council in advocating tolerance and peace, and prosecute war forthwith against the worms and snakes of the evil that is Thorne. We should arraign him, and punish Brother Rolt, who is also amongst his allies.'

It was neatly done, this reference to Rolt, whom Snyde had indeed omitted to mention.

'Rolt?' whispered Quail, eyes cold as ice. 'He?'

'Aye, my Lord,' said Squilver who had now committed himself and clearly felt he might as well go for everything, 'Brother Rolt, the former Elder Senior Brother's aide, is part of Thorne's cabal.'

'Even Rolt, even he?' sighed Quail, looking at Snyde in a hurt and puzzled way as if disappointed this information had not been divulged earlier, and hoping there was a good reason.

'My Master,' said Snyde softly, discomfited not one bit by Squilver's taking of the initiative, 'I did not wish to distress you more on a day when I know that you feel weak and are in pain. I did not wish—'

Quail waved him into silence, suddenly amiable and expansive. 'Supreme Commander Squilver, your frankness does you credit, and Brother Snyde's concern for me, though mistaken, touches my heart. Rolt was once dear to me – he is so no more. Such must be the buffets and bruises that come with responsibility, but they must not deter a mole from making the right decision. Personal feelings must be put

416

to one side in favour of what is right for moledom, in the Stone's name!'

'Amen!'

'Praise be!'

'Stone be with our Master!'

Quail permitted a momentary expression of modesty to cross his hideous face. A fragment of a smile struggled at his mouth and his eyelid drooped down as it did when he relaxed, or was tired.

'Let me ask Brother Commanders Sapient and Turling for their view.'

Sapient, whose brutal face and cruel eyes rarely looked anything but malevolent and displeased, replied immediately: 'Elder Senior Brother, I confess that I am anxious to get back to Avebury, but this you know. Autumn is a time of change and the followers are likely to get as restive at this season as the rest of us. I am therefore not anxious to express a view that might lead you to feel that my presence—'

'Yes, yes, Brother Commander, but what do you think we should do?' said Quail, interrupting him.

'Attack, in numbers, and forcefully. Kill as many of Thorne's forces as we can lay our talons on. Hang them up by their snouts for others to see. Make an example of them that will show on this earth the terrors that the Stone has waiting for them in the place of non-Silence to which such moles shall be sent at the moment of their final breath.'

There was a growl of approval around the chamber.

'It seems your policy of appeasement pleases nomole now, Brother Snyde,' commented Quail unpleasantly.

'Kill, yes. Example, yes. Be forceful, yes,' said Snyde. 'But linger, no! We must get to Duncton Wood. That is the crux of everything, Master, and the only place where you can be seen in a setting that will be fitting for assumption of supreme spiritual leadership over moledom as the mole who is Paramount and Prime. To see that glorious day is my only desire, and what advice I have given is directed towards achieving it. If I risk unpopularity by advising caution against becoming embroiled in open civil war here in Banbury, where even the most war-minded of my colleagues admits defence is not easy . . .'

Snyde looked about the Council, smiling slightly. He was impressive, and as usual never short of the right word at the right time; many moles nodded their agreement, including even Squilver.

'If I risk disapproval, so be it. I must advise as my heart and mind tell me to. But yes, perhaps the Supreme Commander's instincts were better than my own. We have allowed Thorne's followers too much latitude. They must be shown how they might be crushed and then . . . then we must make our way to Duncton. Once safely established there, and with the Elder Senior Brother honoured before the Stone that none may deny him his peerlessness in body and in spirit, we must show moledom whither it shall now be bound.'

The Council sighed. Nomole was to be blamed, all were to have their chance, the way forward was clear. Snyde had not actually said that the sooner they got Quail to Duncton the better, for the safer he would be, but that was the gist of it all. Seeing his deteriorating condition, whatmole could doubt that if they were to retain their power and control over events the best place for their master was somewhere safe and secure, like Duncton Wood.

Quail looked suddenly tired, as he often did now: councils were fatiguing, decisions difficult, moles argumentative, and authority heavy upon his shoulders.

'The details I shall leave to you, Supreme Commander. Let the attack be bold and total. Let Sapient's forces be brought up from the south of Banbury, and yours too, Turling.'

'Forgive me, Master,' said Squilver, 'but it would be sensible to decree that the Brother Commanders' forces be interspersed with my own – to gain from their mutual strengths.' He was hoping thereby to get more control over those forces, and prevent their premature withdrawal by Sapient and Turling.

Indeed, a look of alarm and dislike passed over Sapient's face, and then resolute refusal, but Quail was not interested, and ignored Squilver's plea.

'Brother Inquisitor Fagg,' he continued, 'I have instructions for you, and for you, Brother Inquisitor Taunt of Rollright. Yes, yes, pause awhile. For the rest, good luck. Let me hear good reports; let me know the Stone triumphs over its enemies; let me know I can sleep easy.'

'Bless thee, Elder Senior Brother, bless thee,' they murmured as they left, their blessings a new feature of Quail's court, an unspoken acknowledgement that Quail was beginning in some way to slip away from them towards a holier place, his present physical trials a penance perhaps that he must suffer before the glorification of his greatness that was soon to come at Duncton Wood.

'Good Brothers,' he whispered to Taunt and Fagg, when they came near, 'only you and Brother Snyde know where Thripp is. He has been well hidden in Rollright. Prepare now to have him taken privily into Brother Inquisitor Fetter's care in Duncton Wood. Take the disgraced Skua with him, for he may serve us yet and so redeem himself; and my son, my dear son Squelch, estranged from me these hard summer years past, get him to Duncton too. But tell him not of Chervil's treachery, it would distress him.'

'Yes, Master,' they murmured, 'it shall be done.'

Snyde nodded them away.

'I miss my Squelch,' said Quail, 'I miss him singing me to sleep. I miss his caress and love. I miss my son.'

'You are tired, Elder Senior Brother.'

'And you are . . .' But Quail's anger or irritation was that of an old mole, or a pup's, petulant, puppish, weak. 'The pains, Snyde, they are deep today, deep as sin.' He shook his head low and wept silently as Snyde touched him. Quail's voice was that of a mole who knows he is slipping into a void of helpless pain.

'Sleep, Master; forgetting. I shall find another healer for thee.'

'A healer!' protested Quail. 'Oils and embrocation, massage and the useless word. The last healer, the last . . .'

The last healer Quail had crippled and then killed, for he had caused too much pain. Quail's eyes wandered as his voice faded; he could not remember what he had done with the last healer.

'Privet,' he said suddenly, and without apparent relevance, 'she escaped.'

'Probably dead.'

'*She* might have healed me,' said Quail, and laughed a strange, hysterical, almost silent laugh.

Snyde stared at him coldly. He must get him to Duncton Wood. They must not dally too long fighting Thorne. Time was running away ahead of them, and they were being left behind.

'You knew Privet, Snyde.'

'Yes, Master, so I did. She was a scholar and a scribemole, not a healer.'

'No?' said Quail, almost mockingly, almost smiling. 'Yet she escaped?'

Snyde frowned, not liking the turn that Quail's thoughts were taking.

'Master, I shall find you comfort for the night.'

'Not a healer, mole, not one of those.'

'Not that kind of comfort, no.'

'Some little mole whose dalliance will help me forget the pain.'

'Just so, Elder Senior Brother, just such a mole.'

'When Fagg sends for Squelch to go to Duncton Wood, let him say that his father loves him.'

Quail turned slowly and painfully towards the portal, his left paw dragging now as he went, the protuberances on his head and neck and rear swaying and pulling at themselves as night approached.

The Caradocian attack on Thorne's forward positions took place next dawn, suddenly and with brutal effect. Across a field of dew the first moles led, and many followed and the autumn cobwebs were rent by the screams and spattered with the blood of Caradocian and Thorne guardmole alike. All that day they fought there; and the next elsewhere; and the day after that somewhere else again, and so began a bloody campaign along an east-west front that would have no easy end.

October advanced into interminable days of struggle and war as from south of Banbury, around Rollright, Brother Commander Sapient brought forces northward which he had been hoping he would not have to commit. But his hopes of returning to Avebury soon were dashed as the war with Thorne dragged on and slowed. The hope he and Squilver had of a quick end to the fighting blew away to nothing, like leaves on the autumn winds; while their enemy, Thorne, began to accept that the struggle would be longer than he wished as he watched it settle upon them all like steady autumn rain.

Yet there *was* one small group of moles most satisfied with the way matters were turning out, and that was Arvon's force. Having so successfully provoked the fighting between the two sides, first by killing some moles on Thorne's side and making conversation that would be overheard by survivors who would identify them as Quail's guardmoles, then by covertly attacking Squilver's moles, they slipped away back to their secret headquarters at Gaydon. From there Arvon led them southwards, to take up their position near the entrance to Duncton Wood, and await news of Maple and all those who fought with him, and to offer what further help they could to the followers' cause.

It was during one of the violent gales that swept across eastern moledom that October that Rees cast off for ever the Newborn bonds that had restrained him for so long, and began a far greater journey than the simpler one he had set out upon – he became a pilgrim journeying south to find not just Privet, but the Stone in himself.

When the rain pelted down, he had not minded; when the way had

420

been all mud, he had plodded on; when the wind had driven the dead leaves far ahead of him, he retained his faith that he would get there in the end.

'Where do you hail from, Brother?' fellow travellers sometimes asked him, but he only shrugged. His past was lost somewhere behind him now.

'Do you need help across this stream, friend?' others might suggest, seeing him trying to focus his poor eyes upon the water's flow, to find a pawhold and a safe way across.

'Aye, and thank you!' he would say, no longer proud nor always striving to be independent, understanding that in accepting help he gave something in return.

'Come on then . . . hold my paw . . . no, not there with the right paw, a little to the left . . . that's it, mole, nearly there . . .'

Nearly there! He had almost given up thinking he might be nearly anywhere, preferring now to journey as his heart led him, pausing awhile in places, being alone, or sharing a worm or two with fellow travellers like himself.

Then, when one day he plodded on and the wind turned to a gale and he felt his heart fill with hope and purpose and he heard a mole say who sheltered out of the bad weather, 'That's another of them, those pilgrims, trekking on in some bloody silly hope of finding that Privet mole,' he knew it was so: he was a pilgrim now and a Newborn no more. But he was different from the others he met. He heard their excited talk of what *she* would be like, what she would or would not say to them. But *he* had felt her paw upon his hurt face; he had heard her voice.

When moles asked where he hailed from, and whither he was bound, he could no longer satisfactorily answer the first question, and was uncertain about the second. She had touched him, she had spoken to him, and when she had left him and gone off in the safe company of the followers Hodder and Arliss, she had taken something of his spirit with her, as Arliss had taken something of his heart.

Now, each step he took, each stumble he suffered, each dim dawn that alighted on his scarred face and peering eyes, brought him nearer to the place towards which his life would always be directed. But if that *was* whither he was now bound, he had no name for it. It left him wordless, passive yet purposeful, and others watched him pass silently by and shook their heads. There were plenty of such moles about, disturbed by the anarchy of the times and pursuing a search for new faith, and there would be more.

So, mostly alone, he journeyed on, believing that when the Stone willed it, it would lead him to her. And then he would know what to say and what to do. Sometimes he thought of Arliss, Privet's helper, and wondered at the way the love he had felt for her when they had met and then parted had become subdued, passive, dormant, like a plant that dies away to nothing as autumn turns to winter, and needs the coming of the spring to wake to life again.

Arliss. Sister of Hodder. Helper of Privet. Mole of Rollright. Yet passive though it seemed Rees wondered at the simple certainty of the love he felt, which awaited so patiently their reunion. Her last touch upon his paw he felt still, and he now began to think of it not as last, but first, and to believe there would be many more.

Meanwhile . . . he would find Privet as pilgrim and not as Newborn. He would tell her what Brother Commander Thorne had said about going to Duncton Wood, though he doubted if such words from him would make the slightest difference to anything. And he would meet Arliss again and see if his thoughts of her, wild and compulsive when they had first parted, but now subdued and confusing, were anything at all like her thoughts of him.

Such were Rees' feelings and musings through the first two thirds of October, when, choosing a route along the High Chilterns, he made his way among isolated systems asking after Privet. When that had no result, he simply wandered watchful and with his ears open. Many others were doing the same, some genuine and some spies, but after Ivinghoe, where the route dropped away towards the vale of Thame, many turned south, believing their best hope of finding Privet lay Dunctonwards.

The fact that it might be dangerous, being territory under the control of the Crusades, mattered not to most moles, though their internecine feuds had been such that up in the Chilterns the Newborns' control was now but nominal. Yet Rees chose not to go that way, not for fear of the dangers, but because he believed that had Privet gone that way she would long since have been captured, and he would have heard of it. No, if he had been Hodder and Arliss, he would have taken her further south and east, perhaps even down into the grim periphery of the Great Wen which, from the vantage of the Chiltern Ridge, could be seen stretching away in a grey-blue haze by daytime and as an awesome spread of lights at night, above which the clouds loomed lurid and threatening. Between Ridge and Wen a strip of mucky landscape ran and it was here, Rees believed, that Privet must be hidden and where he began to search for her.

The storms he had endured earlier came again and now, though the sun shone once in a while, trees were leafless and bleak, dykes filled with water, and even the most sheltered scrapes and hides felt draughty and uncomfortable. Such systems as there were seemed hopeless places, with moles who cared not for the Stone, and had not heard of wars, civil or otherwise. Newborns, followers, darkness, light, all seemed the same to them. Oppressed by the proximity of two-foots, their territories crossed by roaring owl ways, sick with the pollution and fumes that beset such areas, the moles Rees met were haggard and thin.

Yet despite their ignorance of almost everything else, many of them had heard of Privet of Duncton Wood, and their narrow eyes would light up at the mention of her name, and their gaunt faces smile for a moment at the thought of her.

'Lost her whole family, she did, at a westward place called Wildenhope, and went into the Silence to search for them.' Such was their version of events. No matter, they had heard of her, and some from even these communities had gone in search of her.

'Heard she was going to Duncton Wood. But has she been *this* way? No, not her, though you hear things from time to time, you know?'

'What things?'

'Things.'

It was enough to keep Rees plodding on, the escarpment to his right paw, the Wen to his left, the south ahead, and a slim chance of finding out something about Privet in between.

There were sometimes more than rumours. At Tebworth he met a mole who claimed to have met a party of three moles some molemonths before trekking by themselves near Leighton, which lay westward. One of them was a female and silent, and, 'I didn't put two and two together until later I had a friend who met a mole who cured her of ague by touch alone. "Silent as death" she said she was and I thought, "That's Privet, that is." But I said nothing.'

'Why not? And why tell me?'

The mole shrugged and said, 'Some you speak to, some you don't. She was heading south-east, Totternhoe way.'

Reed found nothing there, but in nearby Eaton, to the south-west, the story of three moles was confirmed, and the other two were a female and a male, *from Rollright*.

And so it went on, day by day, better than rumours but not quite fact, enough to keep Rees in an area which others rejected as being marginal, a place to pass through, and in any case not near enough to Duncton Wood, to where, allmole said, she would eventually have to go.

Then suddenly he learned quite positively where she was. Indeed, the moles who had heard of it were in such a hurry getting there that they had no time to do more than shout, 'It's true! We've heard! Privet's in Amersham! Everymole in the vicinity is going there!'

'But how do you—'

'No time to stop and talk about it, mate! There's times you've got to go for it and this is one.'

'How far's Amersham?'

'Four days, no more. Come with us, we're all strangers to each other and making a party of it. But don't dawdle.'

'Where have you come from?'

'Thame way,' they said, slowing only momentarily as he caught up with them. They went faster than he customarily did and their conversation was as breathless as their pace, their minds being set on the way ahead and not on any talk for long.

He soon worked out that they had no facts at all on which to base the idea that Privet was at Amersham. It was merely a rumour, yet one which had more force than most since as they travelled along others joined them and they heard that moles from all directions were converging on a system that until then had been but a name to him. But as for where the rumour had come from, nomole knew nor even cared. Like moles fleeing a flood because others have told them of its coming, they seemed caught up in a journey with which they would not be satisfied until they reached its destination.

Their numbers increased as they drew closer to Amersham, and they overtook moles along the way, for many had grown tired, or were ill, or lame, or simply old and slow.

'She's there all right,' moles said, 'give us a paw and help us along the way. The Stone'll bless you if you will.'

But there was no time to linger and help such moles: if they could not get there on their own four paws then it was a pity, but they must fend for themselves! So Rees found himself caught up in the same panic – there was no better word for it – as come a new dawn, they were off again.

It was near Chesham that he called a halt to his mad march with the mob to Amersham, as suddenly and impulsively as he had begun it. It was something to do with the scrabble to get on along the way, and the indifference shown to those who fell by the wayside. They had passed a couple of sick old males who had stanced down to rest, and had watched with something dangerously close to amusement as two younger moles, the old moles' kin, had grown angry with their relatives and finally after much shouting and cursing had abandoned them, saying that they would find them on the way back.

'But it's for us and our illness that we set off in the first place,' one of them cried out pathetically, his voice shaking, half with anger, half with tears.

Rees had gone on some way after that with growing self-disgust, thinking of those poor moles left behind, and reflecting on the fact that Hodder had turned back and helped *him* and perhaps he ought to do the same. But worthy thoughts are one thing, worthy action another, and Rees tramped on until dusk, his conscience wrestling with the sense that if he did not go on he might miss the only opportunity he would ever have to see Privet and the others again.

At dusk, when the company stopped to rest, he was silent and refused all food, his new-found friends wondering what was wrong. Then, peremptorily, he told them he had had enough, that they were all wrong to go on as they were, that there were better things in life than . . . than . . . Then, only feeling worse for his outburst, he turned back to retrace his steps and see if he could find the moles who had been left behind.

He never did. Sleep overcame him and he lay his head upon a grassy bank and took his rest where he was.

'Mole, mole!' a voice said waking him. 'Are you ill? Can I help?'

It was an old female, one they had also passed earlier that day for she went but slowly, pausing frequently to catch her breath, which was raspy and troubled.

'*You* help *me*?' he exclaimed, feeling light and refreshed from his sleep, and thinking that the morning air felt good for the first time in days, 'I should help you.'

He found her food; and he talked, and confessed to her his discomfort with himself.

She laughed in a wheezy, patient kind of way. 'And what do they expect to gain when they find Privet? If she's silent, as they say, she'll not tell them anything at all. If she speaks, why, they'll be disappointed in her!'

'So where are you going then, if not to Amersham as well?' he said.

'Me? I'm bound for Comfrey's Stone, which lies some way east of here.'

He had heard of it – it was where Comfrey of Duncton Wood had

425

died decades before, and for a time had been a place of pilgrimage.

'No more, of course, for moles soon forget such things. Whatmole remembers Comfrey now, but as a mole in a story of long ago?'

'Why are you going there, mole?'

'To touch it. To find a healing for my breathlessness. All the summer years I promised myself I would, but what with one thing and another, well, time's slipped away. Autumn came, and the wind and rain, and I knew in my heart that I would not survive the winter unless I did something like this. So here I am, overtaken every day by moles bound for Amersham to find Privet.'

'I'll come with you!' said Rees impulsively.

'Sleep on it, mole,' she said gently, and he thought that perhaps she preferred to travel alone.

He slept well and deeply the rest of that day and following night, and was only woken occasionally by the sound of travellers on the way, jostling and pushing and giving him the same looks of pity and contempt that *he* (he now realized) had given others who had stopped. The female was still there.

'I'd still like to help you on,' he said, 'at least part of the way.'

'You don't want to go with them?'

He shook his head and the decision was made: 'No, I'm coming with you,' he said.

Chapter Thirty-Four

It was late October when Maple and the followers finally got within striking distance of Avebury. They had assembled their forces a little to the north-east on Barbury Hill, to regroup and recuperate from their arduous journey, and form a plan of attack.

Having travelled in three groups, partly to confuse the Newborns, but also to gather as much information and support along the way as they could, they were more powerful and better prepared than Maple and Ystwelyn had dared hope. Mole after mole had joined them, and here and there groups of Newborns had given up without a struggle. But in the main the Newborns they met had either offered immediate resistance, and very bloody some of the fighting had been, or they had retreated for a time only to return later in greater numbers. So the going had been tough, and the setbacks many. Both sides had lost moles, and certainly Maple had wounded followers to think about now as well – which was one reason why he had ordered the rest on Barbury Hill.

'When we go on,' he said confidently, 'at least we can be sure those moles who cannot go with us will be safely out of the way, ready to join us when we press over the vales to Buckland. Meanwhile we shall wait for a few more to join us, and some of us can reconnoitre Avebury and decide on the best approach.'

In the days that followed a good many more moles joined them and proper plans were made.

'We have, I'm afraid, lost all chance of surprise,' observed Maple at a final council of war, 'but our numbers are increasing and our spirits high, and in the hard molemonths of journeying past, and especially the past few days, we have shown that we are a match for the Newborns.'

There was a grim nodding of heads, but little more, for the Newborns had proved to be rough and dogged fighters who gave little quarter, and showed no mercy to those they caught. But if they hoped that torturing and killing prisoners, or snouting them along barbed fences where they knew the followers would find them, would deter

Maple's forces, they were badly mistaken. Such tactics might terrorize and subdue small isolated communities, but the followers under Maple were made of sterner stuff, and these crude devices served only to harden their resolve. Of more concern was that some elements amongst the followers became vengeful once more towards the Newborns, so much so that Maple had to discipline them harshly, and warn what he would do if he found any further retaliation.

'We are for freedom and tolerance, and if we do to the Newborns what they do to us we do not help our cause. We fight only as hard as we need to, to win, and after that we think of the peace to come.'

They were noble words, and none doubted that Maple would stance by them, but it was hard for moles *not* to want revenge in kind, who heard the screams of their friends as they died in agony across the vales, and later found their corpses hanging along the way in postures so twisted and distorted, and with mutilations so vile, that none could doubt the suffering they had endured before they died.

Maple did not underestimate the difficulties of taking a system such as Avebury, which had by now been so long occupied by the Newborns that its defences were well developed. But his knowledge of past wars and battles was great, and the experience of moles like Ystwelyn considerable, and he had the inestimable advantage of disciplined and motivated moles who would do as they were ordered, and fight to the end.

'Also, moles who have been in occupation of a system so long become lax, and forget how it might be if they were attacked,' he said the night before the assault. One other advantage he had, and it was one he had planned for carefully, and fully prepared. He had four moles who knew Avebury well. Two were Newborn guards, captured in recent days, who had been 'turned' to inform to save their lives. These had been caught and interrogated separately, and the information they gave was consistent. Areas of doubt remained, but broadly Maple and his subordinates had as good an idea of the disposition of Avebury's tunnels and defences as anymole then alive.

The other two moles were followers who had lived in Avebury and escaped from the Newborns. One had made his way to the Wolds, and had long since told Maple and the others all he knew, and been ready to guide them as best he was able when it came to an attack.

The second was none other than Spurling, the brave refugee from Avebury and later Buckland, and latterly leader, along with Fieldfare, of the rebels hiding out at Seven Barrows. It had been Weeth's idea to make his way to Uffington and find some former Avebury moles, having heard from Noakes before the two had gone their separate ways after the raid on Banbury that there were moles aplenty at Seven Barrows just waiting to get their talons on the Newborns.

Weeth had wanted to take a younger mole than Spurling, who was old and slow, but for one thing it was plain that he had clear memories of Avebury and particularly of the complex tunnels about its library, and for another he was determined to go. Most touchingly, Fieldfare wanted to go with him, but that Weeth would not allow. He knew from what he saw, and from what Noakes had told him, that she was effectively joint leader with Spurling of the rebels, and Maple had made clear to him that her greatest usefulness would be helping with any future relief of Duncton Wood, not in bloody campaigns across the southern vales for which she was ill-fitted.

Weeth had witnessed few things so touching as Spurling's farewell from Fieldfare, and the way that, a little reluctantly perhaps, she agreed that when he came back – 'as surely I will, madam, for I love you like no other mole I have ever known!' – she would be his mate till death did them part!

'Tears, madam, are in my eyes,' said Weeth as he made his own farewell to Fieldfare, who was every bit as remarkable and doughty a female, and worthy to have been Chater's mate, as he had expected. 'I see that Spurling loves you, even if your own love is less passionate than his!'

'There'll only ever be one Chater for me!' said Fieldfare. 'But if it helps Spurling keep on going I'll welcome him into my burrow on his return, for I've never known a truer, or nobler, or braver mole than him, and that's a fact!'

So Weeth was the agent of their parting, and had some explaining to do when it was but an elderly mole, and one somewhat slow of paw, whom he brought to Barbury Hill to add what extra information he could to that already collected by Maple through the other three informers.

But Spurling soon proved his worth, filling in details of tunnels and old ways about Avebury that the two Newborns did not seem to know, and even more important, as it proved, giving a full account of the disposition of the famous ring of Stones that lies on one side of the system. More than this, he knew a good deal about Buckland as well.

'You wait till I get my paws on those . . . those . . . those *wicked* moles!' he exclaimed excitedly, his ascetic face animated for once as he waved his thin front paws aggressively about in front of him.

'We want no heroics, Spurling!' Maple warned sternly. 'You leave the fighting to moles younger than yourself. In fact, you'll stay close behind me, with Weeth to keep his eyes on you, and when we need your help we'll ask for it!'

Of the brilliance of Maple's attack on Avebury, which began the following day in rain, and came in waves from three different directions, many moles have since scribed. Though the Newborns must have long expected it, yet they were taken by surprise – not just by the swiftness of it, and by the resolution of the followers, but by the way in which the attack came first on one side of the system, then another, and then a third, with no indication until too late that the main assault was a surface one, through the maze of Stones the Newborns feared so much, which brought the followers rushing headlong down into the very heart of Avebury.

The system was in follower paws by mid-afternoon, and though in two or three places the fighting had been fierce, the loss of life was not nearly as great as Maple had feared, for panic seemed to have overtaken the Newborns as they rushed hither and thither trying to decide where the real attack was coming from, and then, as often happens where forces are ill-disciplined, a general flight had ensued.

But not quite so 'general' that it was not well managed; the followers were delayed, their attention was successfully diverted by small counter-attacks, and a great many Newborns got clean away, before Avebury was over-run.

'It's almost as if they planned not to fight to the last,' observed Maple with concern. 'Are they saving their strength for Buckland?'

Maple's triumph was further muddied by the grim discovery that the Newborns had had time enough to maim or kill a good many moles within the system – some being their own guardmoles who must have incurred their displeasure, others being followers for whom, presumably, they had no further use. The sight of these dead and dying moles was not one that anymole wished to see, and Weeth hoped that Spurling might be spared it and the dead moles cleared away or sealed up before he was allowed into the heart of the system.

But that was not his wish and Maple respected it. Spurling went about the tunnels in which he had been raised, dry-eyed and white of snout, keeping his feelings to himself. Only when he came across the bodies of two former friends, moles who might well have collaborated but with whom he had run and played in happier puppish days, did his emotions betray themselves in anger, tears, and grief.

430

'Not just for them, but for allmole, for a generation lost, for what might have been . . .'

Then as dusk fell a worse horror came upon them, and one that turned the partial triumph of Avebury into a kind of tragedy. The wounded had been treated and the dead disposed of as seemed fitting, and the few prisoners made safe, when a mole stumbled into the system from the west. He was badly cut about the face and shoulders, and his paws were torn by briars and caked with mud and grime, and he was so exhausted he could hardly speak. His eyes spoke of the horror he had witnessed far more plainly than any words he said.

'It is Barbury Hill,' he said. 'Newborns came. Dozens of 'em. We were overwhelmed. All gone, all dead, and I, I ran and somehow got away. There were too many for us guards, too many. I heard their cries as I ran . . .'

He broke down, unable to say more, but already Ystwelyn was issuing orders for volunteers to go back the long way to Barbury Hill and investigate. If it were true it meant . . . well, a mole dreaded to think what it meant – that the Newborns had planned such an attack, for those who had fled Avebury could not have perpetrated such an outrage. It meant that the defences left by Maple had not been good enough. It meant failure of a kind . . .

'It means,' said Maple a day later, when a large contingent of the followers made their way back to Barbury Hill, Ystwelyn having been left behind to conclude matters at Avebury and establish a garrison that would not be so easily over-run, 'that it will be almost impossible to prevent our forces from retaliating against the Newborns in kind.'

The hill was littered with the slain, moles hacked down where they had vainly tried to defend themselves against a force superior in number, and vengeful in spirit. The victims had been the old, the wounded, the harmless ones, and those left behind to defend them. Two or three were found alive, though seriously wounded, left not out of mercy but omission: the Newborns had simply missed them in the litter of bodies across the ground, and in the temporary tunnels. Such reports as these were able to corroborate the account of the one who had reached Avebury to raise the alarm, adding only what had happened after he had escaped, which was the systematic killing, sometimes most cruelly, of those who were wounded.

'But they never came into the tunnel where I lay,' explained one, 'not after their first visit there.' He was the only survivor of thirty recuperating moles.

'I watched 'em at it, and they were methodical, believe you me,' said another. 'Stone knows why they didn't come for me. I 'spect they couldn't see I was alive in that heap of dead. But I was, I was . . .'

'Let's go and get the bastards, sir. Let's *do* it!' cried out a rough young follower from the Wolds.

He was speaking to Stow, the veteran Woldian leader, but Maple overheard the remark, and saw how it fuelled an ugly flame of rage and hatred amongst the followers, as sudden and dangerous as a spontaneous fire through sun-dried moorland grass.

Indeed, there was nothing he or Stow could do to stop the shouting and surge of moles about them, asking, no, demanding revenge for the cowardly killings of Barbury Hill. It was the very thing that Maple and his fellow commanders had struggled to avoid through all the moleyears of summer, for it might destroy all credibility for the followers' cause.

Not that the followers would lose the war against the Newborns, of that Maple was certain, but they would lose a greater war, which was being fought not *against* anymole at all, however sectarian and cruel they might be, but *for* liberty and tolerance and for the Stone, which is to say for allmoles' hearts and spirits.

'No, no, no!' roared Maple, cuffing one mole to shut him up, buffeting another who was becoming hysterical, and felling a third who had actually raised his paws to him, so deep were his anger and need to see the Newborns punished for the suffering they had caused.

He talked to them, and so did Stow, but they did not want to listen, and he knew for the first time how it felt to be disliked by his own force.

'If you'll not lead us against them now there's many a mole will know what to do,' moles growled and threatened, though with some misgivings, for the sight of Maple angry, and ready to settle accounts with anymole who so openly challenged his authority was formidable, even frightening.

'But the disgruntlement remains,' he told Ystwelyn and other commanders a day or two later, when their forces had regrouped, and some of the outward anger at the Barbury massacre had subsided. 'They will be hard to contain, and I greatly fear there will be incidents of revenge which we will not know about unless we keep a close eye upon our forces. Therefore, we will not advance upon Buckland as we had planned.'

'But sir . . . !'

'You can't . . . !'

'I can't answer for my . . .'

And even Ystwelyn's voice was joined to all the others in protest at Maple's decision. Worse, to Maple, was that Ystwelyn finally counselled that it would be sensible to let some of the followers go after Newborns to 'mete out to them what they did to us! It helps calm things down a bit, and we should turn a blind eye to it.'

Maple listened to them all in silence, and for the first time in his generalship understood the isolation a leader sometimes feels, and the strength of will he must have if he is to pursue the course of action he judges right. He could only be grateful for small mercies, for dependable Stow, who alone among the senior commanders remembered well how Privet had talked to them of the true nature of peace and Silence on her passage through the Wolds on the way to Caer Caradoc. He stanced solidly by Maple in his opposition to revenge attacks; and Weeth, he was always there.

Many historians have said, and rightly so, that it was in those dark hours and days, when almost singlepawedly Maple held back the followers from setting forth to hunt down and kill any Newborn they could find, that his greatness began to show itself. As he had in the Wolds when similar demands for revenge had surfaced, he went tirelessly now from troop to troop of followers, persuading, ordering, warning.

Weeth was at his flank, Stow nearby, and Ystwelyn was temporarily sanctioned for failing to be clearer in his condemnation of those who wanted to satisfy their need for revenge. This was done indirectly, so that Ystwelyn did not lose face, for while Maple took personal control of the Siabod moles, the Welsh leader was sent forth with followers absolutely loyal to Stow, ostensibly to round up any Newborns around Avebury and to check out the positions of the main body that had escaped.

Nor did Maple hesitate to include with Ystwelyn's force two moles who had been with him from the beginning, and whose common sense and faith in the Stone he trusted absolutely: Furrow and his mate Myrtle. These went along partly to advise on any crossing of two-foot ways the followers came upon, but also to report back to Maple any indiscretions.

'They're spies!' roared Ystwelyn, when he learned of Maple's intentions.

'Aye, they may be,' said Maple, 'and if one hair of a Newborn's fur is touched gratuitously, and without proper arraignment and trial, I shall know of it. You failed me at Barbury Hill, Ystwelyn, and I must know I can trust thee again.'

Perhaps he used the traditional 'thee' to indicate how much he cared for Ystwelyn, and how hard he found it that the two comrades were in disagreement.

'I warn you, Maple of Duncton, you will not be able to contain the anger of the followers for ever. It is better that you let them loose on a few Newborns now than try to stop them doing what such moles have done from time immemorial.'

'Enough, Ystwelyn of Siabod.'

'No, Maple, hear me, for I am your friend.'

'A friend who has disappointed.'

'Mole,' said Ystwelyn more reasonably, 'let me stay with you now. Accept my apology. You cannot hold back my forces—'

'They are the Stone's forces!'

'Aye, and the Newborns would say the same! By the Stone, Maple, you know as well as I that the Newborns they are likely to catch and, yes, rough up and hurt a bit, deserve that and more for what they have done.'

'There is a greater principle involved, my friend,' said Maple quietly, 'and one taught by Master Librarian Stour, and by Privet as well: finally we must meet talons with peace and love. Finally, we must stance down before our enemies and let *them* decide to cease the war. If we allow our moles to take revenge now we put back the day when strife stops because both sides will it; not out of weakness and surrender, but out of strength and desire.

'Now, mole, go as I have bid you, take prisoner what Newborns you find. Let them be brought back to Barbury Hill unmolested and in safety. They shall be arraigned and judged in truth and justice. If any be guilty of massacre they shall be punished; but those that are guiltless of that shall not be punished for it. Our followers will witness this, and see the worth of it.'

'And what of Buckland, to which we should long since have gone if we were to have taken advantage of the initiative we gained?' asked Ystwelyn. 'Don't you think the Newborns will have retreated there and made it impregnable? They're not fools, Maple: they will have learned from their complaisance at Avebury.'

Maple shrugged indifferently. 'No doubt they will have done so. But then our followers should have shown themselves more worthy and ready to continue the campaign in a proper spirit. They did not, and you did not, and others like you. Stow alone among the commanders, along with Weeth, stanced loyally at my flank! Why, there were more just moles among the ordinary warriors than among my so-called senior command!'

'Like Furrow? Like Myrtle?' said Ystwelyn ironically.

'Aye, mole, like them. Do not mock them, learn from them, for if you do then all the Siabod moles will follow your example. So go to it, mole! And meanwhile, I shall take what risks I must among moles who seem dangerously close to putting their loyalty to you before their loyalty to the Stone!'

Ystwelyn left him, muttering, irritable, yet chastened and prepared to do as he had been bid; though a wave of bitter anger and humiliation spread through the Siabodian moles at news of the dressing-down Maple had given him.

It was a testing time, and Maple did not scruple to stance up to Ystwelyn's loyal followers, challenging them, talking to them, daring them to defy him; but not one did.

So it was that though Maple gained Avebury, he gave away the initiative to the Newborns on a point of principle and risked a heavy toll of life in the future if he was to regain it.

Several Newborns *were* brought back unmolested to Barbury Hill to be tried for the crimes committed there, and two of them were found guilty and sentenced to death, the execution carried out by four moles, each from different commands, so that no individual could be described as executioner. The moles acquitted were led away, and at Maple's orders removed back to Avebury, partly for their own protection, partly to demonstrate that the followers under Maple could dispense justice fairly and without favour, however much disliked the accused might be. They were grim times, and dangerous ones, when at any moment the seething discontent and anger that Maple had worked so hard to control and redirect could have surfaced like a foul boil on the face of an ailing mole, and despoiled everything.

But it did not happen, and Maple found his position immeasurably strengthened, along with the followers' pride and discipline, for now they knew that if anymole erred towards undisciplined revenge, or cruelty towards Newborns rather than simple force of talons to win the war, there would be trouble for them all.

'Yet I still fear it will happen, Maple!' warned Ystwelyn a little later, reinstated in his position as Maple's deputy, his respect for the mole he served greater than ever before.

'Aye, it will I suppose. But at least our followers know how extreme the penalty will be for any who tries to mete out unjust punishments. But enough of that! We have dallied long enough, and lost much ground. Now we make trek for Buckland, and for what I fear will be the hardest struggle of our lives!'

Buckland! The name of that loathed system went through the ranks of the followers like a sharp talon in a mole's flank, and if they had once felt excitement at the prospect it was muted now, and they were cautious, for none doubted that the struggle would be difficult and bloody, and that the mole who led them would expect the highest standards of discipline and conduct – and woe betide the mole who, however great the provocation, disobeyed orders and yielded to impulses of hatred and revenge.

But troubled as those last October days were for most, at least Rees and the elderly female whose companion he had become travelled eastward towards Comfrey's Stone in relative peace. Rees went some-what reluctantly, for the way they took no other mole followed, and, indeed, a fair number of searchers for Privet were going in the oppo-site direction.

The pace was slow, and became slower, for the female was not a well mole, with her laboured breathing and enforced stops while she struggled for breath at the top of the slightest climb.

'Is it far?' she would ask, leaning against him. 'Will I *ever* get there?'

But gradually Rees put what he believed he was leaving behind to the back of his mind and abandoned any immediate hope of finding Privet. At least the female's talk of the Stone they were seeking, and her loving and graphic account, drawn from the Duncton Chronicles, of how Comfrey had come to die there, moved him deeply.

The ground rose higher and a little wilder, and the slope up which they were gradually climbing was exposed to a wind that seemed more cold and wintry each day. There were few communities, and such moles as they came across wanted little to do with two strangers, one of whom was plainly ill, whilst the other had a strange and peering look to his scarred face.

Once in a while Rees found a mole willing to point a talon in the general direction of 'the Stone', as they called it in those parts, though moles thereabouts seemed to regard it with little interest or honour. A clue to this lay in one old mole's recollection that he had been told that Tryfan's and Comfrey's passage through those parts had brought moles of the dread Word in their wake, and that had led to oppression and massacre.

As for any history to do with Beechen and Boswell, whose transfor-mations at Comfrey's Stone remain one of the holy mysteries in the Duncton Chronicles, nomole thereabouts seemed in the slightest bit interested. And then, as for Privet . . .

'Well! They don't seem to want to know round here!' Rees told his friend.

'Expect they want to forget such things: too much trouble and strife in recent years, and when there's memories in a place it's sometimes the darker ones that linger, not the good ones. Moles'll take decades to forget the coming of the Newborns into their systems, just as they've not forgotten the grikes and moles of the Word, if their systems were cursed for a time by their presence. Such moles shut up and keep their snouts low.'

She broke off into a fit of wheezy coughing and mutely shook her head when Rees offered her food.

'Well, then, mole, come below into the scrape I've made and rest. Maybe tomorrow we'll get to the Stone you seek.'

She did so, and weary and dispirited he stanced down near her and drifted into sleep. He woke but once that night, with the strange feeling that his name had been called, and paws touched lightly to his face.

'Mole, mole!' he whispered.

He heard only her breathing, rasping and slow, and the hollow echo of his own voice. But the touch of paws lingered on, and a voice he could not quite place drifted about in his mind, calling his name as he went back to sleep.

He woke only when cold dawn light came upon his face, but he had no need to open his eyes to know the old female had died. The little scrape was deathly still and cold and she, when he looked at her, was grey of snout, and her eyes, half open, were rheumy and yellow.

He was not afraid of death, nor even sorry that she had died, for he had sensed that she had not long to live. But he would have liked her to have reached the Stone she sought, and in the prayers he said before he left he vowed he would touch it on her behalf if he found it. He whispered too of his gratitude that she had not been alone when she died, but that the Stone had put him near her, to help her, to comfort her.

'But I never knew her name, Stone,' he said finally, and in wonder, surprised that he had never thought to ask it. But perhaps the pilgrim travels best who travels with no name.

He looked at her one last time before he sealed up the little scrape, as anonymous a last resting-place as a mole could find, and he thought to himself that her name did not matter: whatmole she had been until he knew her he did not know, and nor did she know what he had been. But for a time they had journeyed together, their past behind them and the Stone ahead, and they had been a help and comfort to each other.

Rees wept a little, and hoped that she found peace in the great Silence to which she had gone. He left her then, the day grey and chill, and suddenly, like a shaft of sun illuminating a patch of stormy sky, he knew with absolute certainty that he would reach Comfrey's Stone that day.

Slowly he journeyed on, at peace and without expectation of what was to come, feeling as strongly as he had ever felt that he was of the earth his paws touched, and the grey sky above, and of life, and death, and the Stone that waited ahead.

Then, when in late afternoon he came to a rise and peering off to his right saw the form of a Stone along the edge of the escarpment he had reached, he felt it was a destination to which he had been heading all his life.

He felt no surprise – except perhaps at the simplicity of it all. He paused awhile and thought again of the old female he had left behind, as if he had a last goodbye to make. But then, thinking more, it seemed to him that she was not left behind at all, but with him, and in some way she always would be: nameless, a journeyer, a mole of faith, a mole who accepted what help life gave and complained not at all of the difficulties it put in her way.

'Come on, then,' he said aloud, unaccustomed tears wetting his face again, 'let's trek this last part of our journey to Comfrey's Stone together.'

But when he came closer and saw three moles waiting for him by the Stone he stopped again, snout low, barely able to put one paw in front of another, so moved and in awe did he feel. Two of them came to meet and greet him, a male and a female, with gentle laughs, and an embrace.

'I . . . I . . .' But what could he say before such wonder, and what words could there ever be to explain what power had directed his paws the way he had come.

'Though I felt sure somemole was coming, I never imagined it might be you,' whispered Arliss through her tears, her paws caressing his scarred eyes with a touch he seemed to have felt the night before.

'Rees, Privet wanted to wait for somemole, but of course she couldn't say . . .'

Rees, she had said, but that was not the voice that had called his name. He turned to Hodder and knew again what he had known

438

before, that he was a friend for life, though so strangely made and found again.

'Arliss is right, we've been waiting for you,' said Hodder. 'Stone knows why, and you might too.'

Rees broke free of them both and went forward to where Privet waited by the Stone.

'I heard you call my name,' he said.

Her eyes were grey as the sky, and light in parts as the Stone that soared away above her.

'I was sent by three moles to find you,' he said as Hodder and Arliss joined him.

'What moles were they?' asked Hodder.

'Brother Commander Thorne was one. Brother Rolt another. And Senior Brother Chervil was the third.'

'What did they want?' asked Arliss.

Rees' eyes were still lost in Privet's, and the light and depth in them seemed to increase at mention of the names of Rolt and Chervil.

'They think it is time you returned to Duncton Wood,' said Rees.

And Privet smiled just for a moment, and glanced at Hodder and then Arliss, and nodded her head.

'Time to go home,' she seemed to say, though it was not she who spoke the words but moledom all about, or the rough grass, or the clouds, or the dark and leafless hedges that stretched away further than the eyes could see.

'It's time at last,' said Arliss.

And later, when night was come and they had stanced down in nearby tunnels to rest before beginning their journey 'home', Arliss whispered to Rees, whose paws were about her, 'Since insisting in that silent way she has, far more powerful than any words she might speak, she has been waiting here for days. None knew we were here, or who we were, though many passed us by. They seem unable to see the very mole they're searching for. But how did she know you were coming? How?'

Rees chuckled and said he had no idea. He had come and now they were all together once again. His was not to reason why. He knew only that now they would travel on together and it would take every Newborn and follower in moledom to part them again.

'I didn't know what I would feel when I saw you,' he whispered.

'Nor I,' she said.

'Well, you do now,' growled Hodder out of the darkness. 'Go to sleep.'

Rees started up and said, 'I haven't touched the Stone. There was a mole . . . I promised her . . . I . . .'

He went to the surface, Arliss with him, Hodder grumbling as they went and Privet sleeping deeply.

The Stone rose above them, now black against the night sky.

'Was this where Comfrey died? And Boswell was . . . ?'

Arliss nodded, holding his paw.

He reached out and touched the Stone and said, 'I don't know her name, but she's here, very close, and she's in pain no more.'

'Rees,' whispered Arliss, 'I feel I've known you all my life, long before we really met.'

'I feel I've been coming here all my life. But what's ahead? I can't even begin to think.'

'How did she know you were coming? How did she know?' repeated Arliss in wonder.

Rees shook his head and said nothing, as silent as the Stone he touched. They stanced down where they were, and when they woke it was dawn; the sky was pale and a watery sun was rising in the east.

'Remember us?' called Hodder cheerfully. He was stanced with Privet by some grass nearby, and they had finished eating some food he had collected. Privet was already looking westward across the high bleak landscape.

'Time to go,' said Hodder, coming closer. 'She's been up since before dawn, and I think she wants to go.'

Arliss and Rees hurriedly prepared themselves, Rees rubbing cold dew in his face to wake himself up, an old guardmole habit.

'Let's be off then,' said Hodder impatiently.

'To Duncton Wood,' said Arliss, trying to make it the most natural thing in moledom. But it did not feel as natural or as light as she sought to be, and though the sun rose slowly behind them, the sky ahead remained dark, and full of foreboding.

Chapter Thirty-Five

The astonishing speed with which even the strongest and most entrenched of leaders can lose support and power, and be forced into flight or a final confrontation with their enemies, is always a surprise – especially to the moles who suffer it.

To the historian however, who can take the longer view, and has an accumulation of evidence not available to moles bound up with the events at the time they occurred, the rapid demise of the great and the good – or the great and the bad, as is fortunately more often the case – is no surprise at all. Indeed, the surprise lies only in how long the vilest and most evil of moles can sometimes cling on to power.

Which brings us now to Quail, and Snyde, and Squilver, and all their minions from Wildenhope, who had shared in the planning and execution of the Crusades since the previous Longest Night, and in the privileges and perquisites that had resulted. It was as if the black looming clouds that Rees and the others had observed towards Duncton from their vantage-point of Comfrey's Stone, and towards which they set forth without demur, now hung over Quail and his fellow malefactors, and a storm seemed about to break.

Yet had they not arrived at Banbury, and had not Brother Commanders like Sapient of Avebury hurried north to confer with them, in a mood of sublime confidence? They had. It had seemed then but a matter of deciding a final strategy by which moledom would be cleansed for all time of the followers, and its territories divided up between moles who could govern them easily in the name of the Caradocian Order. All so simple, all so plain . . .

No doubt Quail, with Snyde's connivance and, before his disgrace and confinement, Skua's as well, had worked out how to spread power about moledom in a way that ensured that local Brother Commanders remained at loggerheads with each other, and the Crusade Council retained the power to promote, and execute. At the same it is beyond dispute that Elder Senior Brother Quail, having gained supreme temporal power, would soon be seeking to move on towards a new spiritual authority, which in the course of time would allow him to confer upon himself an inviolate holiness. A position in which he would need a clever and astute subordinate, whom he had found to perfection in the nauseating form of Snyde.

But then, pride before the fall . . . Despite their instincts and reservations, driven by wounded vanity and over-confidence, without proper information about the nature and strength of their enemy, Quail and his friends had allowed themselves to enter into the struggle with Thorne. Yet not just Thorne, but Chervil and Rolt as well, and all the moles they led.

It must be said, however, that though Quail began this civil war with reluctance, his Council, and in particular Squilver, prosecuted their attacks with considerable vigour. Squilver might have had little experience of strategy and the grand cause, but he acquitted himself passably, aided no doubt by the cunning of Brother Commander Sapient and his very ruthless guardmoles. Perhaps, too, they gained the benefit for a time of the natural reluctance of Thorne to be involved in such a war with fellow Newborns, and his unwillingness to let his own force behave with quite such efficient brutality as the moles under Squilver and Sapient.

Whatever the reason, through mid-October, the moles of which Quail was Elder Senior Brother, who gave him their loyalty out of fear and awe, or for self-aggrandizement, gained some early tactical victories against Thorne. Here and there the loss of life was heavy, though Thorne's skill was such that though initially in retreat he succeeded in reducing his losses to a minimum – the heavier losses being on the initially more successful side.

But wars often drag on which both sides are confident will be short and sweet, and by the last third of October, with Sapient now very anxious to turn back south, for he had long feared that the very disaster that was about to afflict his forces in Avebury *would* occur, the two sides were deeply dug in north of Banbury, neither giving quarter, neither gaining ground for long. The situation was made worse by the series of storms and heavy wet weather that set in about then, creating muddy, cloying conditions that clogged up a mole's paws, and seemed to clog up his mind as well.

This deadlock might have continued for a molemonth or two more but for the arrival in Banbury of a mole who had travelled night and day with news that was to change everything, and directly bring about the downfall of Quail and Squilver, and lead to their headlong flight south into Duncton Wood.

This mole, the tough and unpleasant Newborn commander Dirke

442

of Devizes, deputed by Sapient for precisely this kind of intelligence work, had come hot-paw from Avebury to report that system's devastating capture by the followers under Maple, and the danger that now confronted Buckland.

To be more accurate, Dirke had come from Avebury by way of Barbury Hill where, 'We caught them napping, Sapient, sir, and killed a good few in the Stone's name.' In short, it was Dirke who should have been among those arraigned and executed by the followers for the crimes of Barbury.

But he had got away, and now he was speaking to Sapient privily, for he knew enough not to tell anymole-else what his errand was, though his condition – filthy, tired, and cut and torn along the way – provoked questions aplenty. But Sapient's guardmoles knew him well and acted as his bodyguard when they brought him north of Banbury and into Sapient's presence.

Nothing can describe the raw rage and anger of Sapient as he heard how quickly and totally the system and area he regarded as his personal territory had been taken over.

'Moles will die for this!' he hissed, digging his talons savagely into Dirke's chest and peering at him with so much malevolence that a lesser mole than Dirke might have thought *he* was about to die for it. But Sapient was not Quail, and retained control of both his temper and his talons. And like all successful tyrants and bullies he knew advantage when he saw it, even in what others might consider failure.

'But anyway, mole, this may be just what we were planning for. We did after all make provision for a hasty retreat if need be, for as you know well, I have long believed that Buckland is the real centre of the south, and the system I desire to be in control of. Turling has resisted that, but now an opportunity arises, does it not?'

'It certainly does, sir.'

'Does Turling of Buckland know yet of the Avebury retreat?'

'I doubt it. It may be one of his moles has come north on hearing news of it, but if they have they would not have made the speed I did. Night and day, sir, night and day.'

'It is what I expect of you,' said Sapient coldly. 'Now, this matter of Barbury Hill?'

'We hoped it would slow them down, sir. None were left alive, though in such circumstances one can never be sure. But it will have frightened them, caused them to regroup and slow down, and our main force deliberately headed south for a day or two to lead them

443

away from Buckland when they came in pursuit, just as your contingency plans arranged.'

Sapient nodded, well satisfied. 'Tell only as much to Turling as you need to, and concerning the future of that mole, await my personal instructions. Matters here are not good. The Elder Senior Brother is . . . well, shall we say he is less reliable than he was. It is a matter only of time . . .'

He said no more on that subject: Dirke had no need that he should, for he was a mole who worked best in the shadowy world of the half-spoken word, and the meaningful silence. Dirke could construct a whole series of orders from Sapient out of almost nothing, and he would be right about every one of them. There was no love lost between Sapient and Turling, he knew that. Nor did Sapient any longer feel that Avebury fully satisfied his talents and ambitions. Had not the Elder Senior Brother himself once been Brother Commander of Avebury? He had. And look at how he had had to move away to rise up in the world!

'Aye, look at him now,' muttered Sapient. 'No, we can dally here no longer, Dirke, and I regret not returning south earlier. Quail will not like it, Squilver even less, but needs must, for if we do not get to Buckland fast that system may fall to the followers and the south will be much harder to regain control of.'

'I have to say that they are doughty fighters, sir, and well led too.'

'Hmmph!' said Sapient. 'They will be no match for my guardmoles when I order them to stance their ground. The easy victory we allowed them at Avebury will have made them complacent, you mark my words! Now . . . rest up the night, Dirke, and then be ready to travel back with me, for I shall have need of you; there is work you alone must do. Change is coming now and we must be ready, and act swiftly if we are to secure the future for ourselves, and for moledom.'

There was a glint of excitement in Dirke's eyes, and of ambition and hope of reward.

'I must talk to Turling now,' said Sapient. 'Our withdrawal from here has been long planned, and I fancy Squilver has guessed as much.' Then he continued, almost to himself: 'Well, he can't fight two wars at once against his own side, and will not be able to stop us leaving him. In any case, he should not *need* us to hold the territory here, his own forces should be capable. So rest up, Dirke, for we shall leave on the morrow. Be ready to brief me more fully at dawn on what I might expect in the territory south of here.'

'Loose discipline, that's what you should expect, Crusade Councillor,' said Dirke, using Sapient's grander title. 'That's what I saw wherever I passed through. Newborns in command still, but too much that is lax. Vagrant moles seem all about, calling themselves pilgrims. It is the mole Privet they seek, and they think she's in Duncton, for they are beginning to converge on it.'

'Privet!' exclaimed Sapient in disgust. 'She should have been killed at Wildenhope with the rest of them. When I heard—'

'I was there at your flank when you *heard*, sir,' said Dirke, grinning. 'You were not well pleased.'

'Well pleased! The Elder Senior Brother and his advisers, notably Brother Inquisitor Skua, made a grave mistake in letting her live. They should at the very least have got a confession from her. Stone help us if she is still alive.'

'There's many think so!'

'Quail's problem, not ours. It may have been a fatal mistake, and she may return to cause his downfall if his disease doesn't do it first.'

'He still . . . ?'

'Yes, mole, he stinks. Like rotting flesh, he stinks. I stay upwind of him when we are outside, and by the nearest draughty portal when we are down below. Yet he is our leader, and though he may have many faults as a mole, as our spirit in the Stone he must be seen as faultless.'

'And the former Elder Senior Brother, sir?'

'Thripp lives, but is kept out of sight. They say he is incarcerated in Rollright, though by now, were I Quail, I would have had him removed to Duncton itself. But . . . but . . . enough of talk, Dirke. Rest your head. Say nothing to anymole. Brief me at dawn and then to Buckland we shall go.'

Sapient smiled faintly with relief that circumstances had fallen out so well.

'Dirke!' he called, summoning his subordinate back. 'Do I understand that we lost hardly any moles at Avebury?'

'You do, sir: just the ones you wanted to lose. Old scores well settled there! As for the rest, they got clean away and by now should be waiting, and ready and willing, just as you have wished.'

'Ahhh!' sighed Sapient: and now he smiled broadly, and Dirke grinned in return, darkly.

The departure of Sapient and Turling and all their forces from the ranks of the Newborns beyond Banbury was as sudden as it had been well rehearsed. There was no discussion, nor even time for argument, and both Brother Commanders were too canny to give Quail time or opportunity to arraign them, which he would certainly have done.

There was not even any final scene, for though Sapient (with a strong contingent of his own bodyguards to protect him) offered to visit the Elder Senior Brother, Quail did not deign to see him. Instead, Squilver and Sapient exchanged some angry words and the two former allies parted on the worst of terms.

But the words and anger were ineffectual and too late: whole contingents of moles were already leaving their positions and heading south, and Squilver, who now realized his folly in not integrating the southern-based Newborn guardmoles with his own, could do nothing about it. So that one moment the frontier with Thorne's force, though static, was at least secure, and the next it was as exposed as a starling chick fallen out of a nest in a north-east gale.

Squilver was nothing if not realistic.

'We have a day at most to effect a proper retreat,' he told Snyde, having failed to gain quick audience with Quail. 'After that Thorne's moles, who are for ever testing us, will have found our weakness and taken advantage of it and what might be orderly retreat will turn into a rout. You must tell the Elder Senior Brother—'

'Tell him yourself, Squilver,' a voice whispered. 'Speak your mind, Supreme Commander. Come on, mole, come closer, come close and speak to the mole who loves you so.'

It was Quail, coming out of the shadows of his inner sanctum, his left front paw dragging, his eyes red-rimmed and rheumy. He wheezed a little as he moved, and occasionally he winced in pain. As he spoke the words 'who loves you' he smiled a smile that was a mask to suffering.

Squilver told him, told him all, and made no bones of the danger they were now in.

'We can fool Thorne for a day, perhaps a little more, but only by dint of moving our forces about, and they will soon tire and then begin to become less malleable.'

'Aye, aye, the snake stirs still, close by, ever closer, sliding and sleeking its way towards us,' said Quail in a voice that was sometimes a whisper, sometimes a rasp, and just occasionally became a phlegmy rattle, like some half-broken branch in a tree past its prime.

'Yes, Elder Senior Brother,' intoned Squilver, not sure what else to say. He was in any case fighting to stop himself from gagging, for Quail's odour was so pungent it was almost tangible, and growths and excrescences seemed to be spreading across his body and his head daily now. What had once been simply bald and smooth was ridged and crinkled now, and bulging in places, while from that normally unseen place between body and forepaws peeped sacs of skin, filled with Stone knew what foul bile. As for that excrescence at his rear, sometimes soft and flaccid, sometimes erect and threatening, Squilver could hardly bring himself to look at it – but look at it he must. For Quail turned, slowly, painfully, and there it was, longer, dropping into a knob of yellowness, and seeming about to burst.

'What . . . is . . . he?' Quail asked Snyde, meaning Squilver.

'Your friend, Master, and mine.'

Snyde smiled over Quail's foul, bent head and Squilver did his best to smile back.

'He jokes, Master, he is but jocular today,' said Snyde.

'Are you that, Squilver?' asked Quail, somewhat disconcertingly not turning back to the Supreme Commander, but reaching out a paw to Snyde, whose hump he caressed.

'I am jocular,' said Squilver, 'I joke, I jest.'

'He makes a jape.'

'A pretty jape,' whispered Quail, laughing terribly, and then sobbing softly. Then falling silent, snout low.

Snyde looked intently at Squilver, whose mind raced for something to say, or rather, to find what he was expected to say.

'Elder Senior Brother,' said Squilver with sudden confidence, 'the serpent that is Thorne shall shrivel in defeat. Already he does so. We must not permit him to be an obstacle to your rightful entry into Duncton Wood. Eschew further parleys and parries with him; turn from him; leave him to shrivel up alone.'

'You hear, dear Snyde? He *was* jocular; now he jests not.'

'No, my Lord, he jests not,' said Snyde heavily. 'The Supreme Commander is right, we must be bold and go to Duncton Wood. And you must rest while the preparations are made.'

'Thripp will be there. And my son Squelch. And Privet, she shall come as well to see the Stone honour me. And mine eyes shall be talons into Thripp's heart, who came so near, so near, to the greatness that shall shine upon me instead, and make me whole again. For . . .' And here, most horribly, he swung round, all his appendages with him, to stance snout to snout with Squilver. '. . . for I have been unwell.'

'Have you, Lord?' said Squilver.

Quail nodded his head, his eyes puplike and wide, as if to share some secret nomole-else could know.

'But I am getting better.'

'*Much* better,' said Snyde, jocularly.

'Do I not look it?'

'Elder Senior Brother, I never noticed that you were ill,' lied Squilver with delicacy, 'but now you mention it you look well indeed; never better, never better.' He too smiled with ghastly enthusiasm.

'No, no, I have been ill, I have,' simpered Quail like a flattered female. 'But now I am better, and ready to go to the Duncton Stone in triumph and there be made first among moles, nearest to the Stone, which is no more than I am. For allmole I shall do it, for thee, Squilver. You shall come?'

Quail turned from him before Squilver could find a suitable reply, and has gone into darkness again.

'We leave today,' said Snyde rapidly. 'Depute a strong guard to be with us. Deceive Thorne a while longer, for the Elder Senior Brother cannot travel fast when he is in contemplation. It is not fitting.'

Being 'in contemplation' was an expression new to Squilver, but no matter. He supposed it must mean 'ill'. Retreat it must be, though not to defeat.

'We shall consolidate and we shall overcome Thorne's forces,' said Squilver. 'Here we have been at a disadvantage, and perhaps Sapient has held us back. Now we shall make Duncton our own, and from it send forth the Last Crusade.'

And he meant it, as foolish commanders whose delusions lead moles to their deaths always do.

'So be it,' said Snyde, 'then go to it.'

'I shall!' cried Squilver, and was gone.

'And is he gone?' said Quail, emerging a little later. 'Has that jumped-up little has-been gone?'

'He has.'

'He cannot win against Thorne – he will lose. He is a fool, that's all.'

'Probably.'

'His thoughts, his efforts, the work of those who do his bidding and follow his orders – orders issued in my name, Brother Snyde, my very own – will all be in vain, of course.'

Quail spoke in a clear, cold, dispassionate way, and a mole who did not know him as well as Snyde might have thought him a different mole altogether. Certainly what he said seemed true, and chillingly sane. What hope had Squilver against Thorne without Sapient's and Turling's forces to back him up?

'And so Squilver will fail, and then he will die. I will kill him myself. He is beginning to displease me.'

Quail's gaze slid away to some vacant corner of the chamber. A dusty half-worm turned and twisted in the murk.

'But it does not matter. We have no need of guardmoles finally to keep us in power. The Stone is our army, our force, and it will crush the Worm and the Snake that seek to eat and entwine, to slither and to bite. Do you see, Snyde, do you see that all those things Squilver does – and Thorne, and that treacherous Sapient, the things they do as well – are in vain. The Stone will crush them all. Righteousness is our might. I shall be left, supreme; and you, Snyde, at my flank. Can you not see it coming soon now?'

'Yes, Master,' said Snyde. He sniffed at Quail, he closed his eyes, he thought of nothing but the day when Quail would die and he, Snyde, would have the ultimate pleasure of loving the mole that had been greatest in the land. Snyde eyed the living Quail with expectant lust and said softly, 'Oh, yes, Lord.'

'Then shall the pains I have suffered for allmole,' went on Quail, 'and borne without complaint, then, then, *then* shall they be banished from my body, and peace return once more, and Light, and Silence. Thripp will be there, his blood to anoint me. And Squelch, my son, his love to embrace me, and his song to soothe me; and she will be there, that Privet, that mole I was guided to let free: she shall be there to offer up the Book of Silence to my safe-keeping, and for ever and all time I shall be remembered as the mole who brought the lost last Book to ground. She shall come back to Duncton Wood to love me, Snyde. Forgiveness is the greatest thing. And you . . .'

Unadulterated lust was in Snyde's bent eyes but what he said was this: 'And I shall be Master Librarian of Duncton Wood, successor to Stour. It is all I ask.'

'Yes . . .' said Quail vaguely, utterly uninterested in Snyde's dream, utterly unaware of the nightmare nature of his real desire. 'Can you not see?'

'Yes, Master. I see it all.'

'And Sapient will have Turling killed.'

This last was so unexpected and irrelevant to what had gone before, and spoken so simply and matter-of-factly, that Snyde almost thought he had misheard. But now he considered it, yes, it did seem the most likely thing.

'Master,' said Snyde, 'your mind is the clearest of them all.'

'Pain has not conquered me. Pain has sharpened me. My hour will soon come and I shall be released from it a stronger and more powerful mole, my penance paid.'

449

'Master, you must sleep. Tomorrow your triumphal progress to Duncton shall begin, and you must look your best.'

'It does and it will; and I shall,' laughed Quail crazily, and with sudden and obscene intimacy he tried to get Snyde to join him in a dance.

Snyde declined, smiling most uncomfortably, backing away until Quail let him be.

'You see!' said Quail, as all his energy fled him and he dropped his outstretched paws; he looked old, and ugly, and frightened. 'I too can be jocular.'

Chapter Thirty-Six

No struggle – not a single one from out of the grisly procession of wars in the mediaeval era, nor one from the ghastly catalogue of cruelty perpetrated by moles of the Word in more modern times – can compare for the fierceness of its fighting and the horror of its outcome to the battle of Buckland, waged over eight days that late October, in the period when Privet was returning to Duncton Wood.

The 'failure' of the Newborns at Avebury had been a clever strategy by Sapient, planned long before against the possibility that his sojourn with Quail would be so long that he was unable to return to Avebury before the followers reached it. As we have seen, he did not get back and they *did* reach it, and so trusty moles like Dirke of Devizes oversaw a clever retreat from Avebury, keeping most of the Newborn force intact.

We know now that behind Sapient's strategy was the desire to take over Turling's command in Buckland, thus securing for himself sufficient territory, and moles, to emerge as undisputed master of the south. Sapient appears to have agreed to go up to Banbury partly to gauge Quail's strengths and weaknesses, but also to investigate creating some kind of pact with Squilver. We may only guess at this, for no records remain, and Snyde seems to have been unaware of such possibilities – or, just as likely, was by then too uninterested in such details to bother recording them.

By then *his* narrow vision had narrowed still further to the coming inauguration of Quail by the Duncton Stone as Prime Mole – or some such absurd over-reaching title – legitimized by the presence and blood of Thripp himself. We need not doubt Sapient's assessment of Quail as a spent force, one literally dying; and of Squilver as a mole who did not have quite the ruthlessness to last long once his sponsors, Quail and Snyde, were gone. No, Sapient rightly saw that Thorne was likely to be the greatest obstacle between himself and real power, and his hurried return to the south and determination to take over Buckland and all its appurtenances, reflected the insight that unless he got on with fulfilling his ambition, it might be too late.

451

The matter of the followers concerned him rather less, though he was not so sanguine as Turling, a less cunning and imaginative Brother Commander, about their weaknesses. The followers under Maple had, after all, held the Wolds well against Caradoc and Wildenhope, and Sapient's own forces from the south.

But like all arrogant bullies, success had blunted Sapient's judgement, and he dismissed Maple's Woldian campaigns as trivial and unimportant. Yet Maple's rapid overwhelming of Avebury, achieved far more quickly and with far less loss of life than Sapient expected, caused him to revise his opinion.

'This is a mole who needs a beating,' he told Dirke of Devizes, two days out of Banbury and well on the way to the south, 'and we shall see that he gets it.'

'You shall share the campaign against the followers with Brother Commander Turling, sir?' asked Dirke provocatively.

'Shall I?' said Sapient, eyes chilly, snout thrusting out as if considering a future shared with *anymole* as a most disagreeable prospect.

'Shan't you, sir?' asked Dirke.

'I hope that Turling suffers no accident, mole, that will force me to assume responsibilities I have no wish for,' responded Sapient ambiguously, shifting his yellow eyes from the middle distance down to his sharp and shiny talons.

'Yes, sir,' said Dirke, smiling, 'or do I mean no, sir?'

'You must decide, Dirke, and only you, what you mean by that.'

Dirke made his decision and a few days later, Brother Commander Turling was found dead at dawn in a temporary scrape near Littlemore, to the south-east of Duncton Wood. He had been suffocated, though only after a fierce struggle. His personal bodyguards, six in number, were unable to give a satisfactory explanation why not one of them was at least within shouting distance at the time, though one report states that all six were seen near Dirke's quarters, in dubious female company, enjoying themselves.

Sapient expressed surprise and rage at the loss of so able a Brother Commander, and had all Turling's guards drowned in the river near Sandford. Then, assembling such of Turling's commanders as had travelled north with him, he announced that he must forthwith 'assume responsibilities he had not wished to even consider'. In the circumstances loyalty would be demanded, and to emphasize the point Sapient had one of Turling's commanders (who made the mistake of not declaring himself loyal to Sapient with quite sufficient alacrity) killed as well. So by the time Sapient approached Buckland some days

452

later, he was able to claim to be its Acting Brother Commander.

He did not attempt to enter the infamous tunnels of Buckland until the large and well-trained force that had escaped Avebury had made contact with him, which it duly did at the place, and in the way, he had arranged. Indeed, an observant mole, able to watch the disposition of the Avebury Newborns about Buckland, might well have concluded that this was an invading force rather than one on the same side. But Sapient was not inclined to leave such things to chance, and wished to be sure that the Buckland Newborns would give him fealty.

He need not have worried. He sent Dirke himself in to the misleadingly clean and spacious lower tunnels of Buckland with the sad tidings of Turling's demise, and before long all the junior commanders in Buckland, and four of the five senior commanders, were falling over themselves in rushing out and offering themselves up to Sapient's leadership.

Two exceptions, one a cousin of Turling, and the other his oldest crony, were caught trying to escape, and put to death. A few others whom Sapient decided he could not trust were demoted, and so, with relative ease, Sapient took control of Buckland and, in effect, of southern moledom.

Those moles who have kenned the Duncton Chronicles will be familiar with the position of this most notorious of systems, and the role it played in the war of Word on Stone. Suffice it to say that the system lies on a low bluff of ground some way to the south of the River Thames. The place is wormful, and its tunnels, though generally nondescript, are airy and well suited to supporting a large number of moles. For this reason, and because of its position between Duncton to the east, Uffington and Seven Barrows to the south, and Avebury to the south-west, Buckland is a system suitable as the headquarters for any army of moles that wishes to dominate southern moledom.

Although in itself it has little to commend it, it has a certain appeal to those with a ghoulish or twisted curiosity, since the southern part of the system, named the Slopeside, is where the zealots of the Word perfected their punishment system by which moles were condemned as 'clearers' and forced to cleanse out the Slopeside tunnels, wherein, during an earlier time of plague, countless numbers of moles had been confined to live and die.

It was in this nightmare place that history's greatest route-finder, Mayweed, was born, and there the moles who helped Mayweed free himself from this terrible past – Tryfan, Spindle, Skint and others – were confined for a time.

It is not surprising therefore that when the Newborns began to gain power, Buckland should once again be used as the system from which the new tyranny could be imposed. Nor will anymole who knows anything about the Newborns once they became corrupted by Quail be astonished that Buckland was used both as a place of confinement for recalcitrant moles like Spurling of Avebury, and of reward to Newborn brothers and guardmoles who had earned the thanks of their seniors. For 'reward' ken 'respite' and for 'respite' ken 'food and females' – such were the rewards of service to the noble Newborn cause.

We know from the testimony of moles like Spurling, and Noakes as well, that the Slopeside was used little by the Newborns, extensive and well designed for confinement though its tunnels were. It seems that they were nervous of its reputation as a place of ill-health and ill-fortune: moles who were confined there for any length of time a century before had usually suffered from scalpskin, a debilitating and disfiguring condition of the fur, afflicting particularly the face and flanks, from which, indeed, Mayweed himself had suffered.

The place was said to be infested too by the more lethal talon worms, shiny, carnivorous worms, some black, some white, which invaded a mole's body and fed off him internally until he died – a danger the great Tryfan himself faced in the Slopeside, and against which he was warned.

There was some early attempt by the Newborns to use the Slopeside for their prisoners, but this was stopped by Quail himself who, staying at the system for a time, indulged his debauched interests in such things and explored the Slopeside before declaring it out of bounds. The single entrance into the Slopeside from the main system was well sealed up once more and the few prisoners already living there were left to die, their feeble knocking at the seal and cries of mercy at the ruined and guarded exits to the surface the last thing anymole heard of them.

Such was Buckland when Sapient came to it that October, except that since Quail's days successive Brother Commanders had developed and improved the defences of the place against the day that the followers might gain sufficient strength of numbers and purpose to attack. Although this had seemed less and less likely, Sapient had persuaded Turling to continue such improvements, saying no doubt that it would be a prudent and wise thing to do. In fact, we may guess that he did so knowing that the day would come when he would seize power from Turling, and thus inherit a system which not only

454

dominated the south, but from which it would be extremely difficult for any enemy, follower or Newborn, to dislodge him.

We may imagine too that Sapient was overjoyed to discover that the followers had been unaccountably slow to journey up from Avebury following their victory there, giving time for the defences to be improved still more, first by Turling's subordinates, and then by Sapient himself after he had entered Buckland.

'It may be that Maple is a fool and did not realize that he should have followed on from his assault on Avebury with an attack here,' he was able to say but a day or two after his arrival, and following a tour of the system, 'or it may be that our little diversion at Barbury Hill had more effect than we expected. No matter, the delay has given us time to make ourselves as nearly impregnable as a system can be. But not entirely – no system can be that, for there is always the worm of treachery within. But Maple has left it too late, and now he will lose ten moles to every one of ours if he ever tries to take Buckland, and will run out of moles in the attempt long before we do!'

The wisdom of Maple's delay at Barbury will be argued as long as there are moles to discuss it, and many will say that he should have taken a lower moral stance than he did and charged north-west once Avebury was secure, and taken Buckland before Sapient arrived.

He himself, always a mole who spoke the truth, never believed so, before or afterwards. Certainly, when some two days after Sapient's arrival his main force reached nearby Carswell Copse, which lay to the west and was a Newborn outpost, he did not think so. He took the position with little difficulty, and rapidly deployed his moles in strategic places around the system, effectively surrounding Buckland with sufficient forces under trusted commanders such that no Newborn could easily get in or out. He discovered two tunnels – to north and east – being used by Newborn spies, but these were quickly taken.

'You see, Ystwelyn,' he observed, 'the system may be easy to defend, but it is also a trap and had we taken it I have no doubt that Sapient would have quickly surrounded us, as we have surrounded him. He may think he is hard to get at, and he is; but so are we to him. If he has made any mistake it is to take too much of his force inside, so that he has no relief or reserves outside who might cause us difficulty.'

Ystwelyn, now re-instated in Maple's confidence, had surveyed the position thoroughly, and now they had begun the general debate with their commanders to decide what strategy of attack to adopt.

455

'The fact that there seems little danger from Newborns outside Buckland, or from nearby systems, shows how the Newborns are occupiers, and have not integrated themselves at all,' replied Ystwelyn. 'If it's a matter now of slow attrition, our force will see to it – we have experience from the Wolds of holding up and waiting, but . . .'

'Aye,' grunted Maple.

'Aye, we need to get to Duncton as quickly as possible if all that Noakes here has said of Arvon's warnings is true,' interrupted Weeth. There were general agreement that speed was of the essence and that a long delay at Buckland was not desirable.

'It never is,' said Maple, 'but especially is that so here, and Sapient probably knows it. We have the advantage of Noakes' presence, for he knows the ground well, and of yours, Spurling, for you were confined here.'

'Couldn't have kept me away!' declared the redoubtable Avebury mole, who had been offered the chance of staying in his home system but had declined it. 'And anyway there's a female I'm nearer to here than there.'

'You should be ashamed to think such things at your age, Spurling!' said somemole, and they all laughed, for everymole had heard of Spurling's attachment to Fieldfare, and her promise to accept him as mate on his return from the campaign.

'One day you'll be my age too and if you're not pushing up daisies, as I hope you won't be, then you'll discover a mole is only as old as he feels. Fieldfare's a mole who—'

'Yes, yes, Spurling, we know what Fieldfare means to you – but not now! Not now!' laughed Maple, who was glad of the diversion. He knew what only Noakes knew, that Fieldfare and those other moles at Seven Barrows had already begun a brave trek west back towards Duncton Wood, taking advantage at Maple's suggestion of the concentration of Newborns in Buckland to get back in relative safety to a Duncton that might very soon have need of them.

He guessed how grim matters might become at Duncton, and how grim they were soon going to be in Buckland, and a little lightheartedness hurt nomole. None knew better than he that there was indeed little time, far less perhaps than any of them yet realized. They must take Buckland and destroy the Newborn power, and then move on, Stone help them, to Duncton itself.

But how to take Buckland quickly? There must be a way, but he did not yet see it. What he had seen would, as he had implied, take many long days to resolve, and could drag on for far longer than that.

'What we are going to do is to begin mounting attacks in one place after another, partly to test their strengths and weaknesses, partly to wear them down. We shall get to know the ground ever more thoroughly, and none of our attacks will be half-hearted or weak,' he said, outlining a strategy already agreed with Ystwelyn. 'It will be . . . hard.'

The mood changed the moment he spoke these words, as he intended, and the gathering began to plan their various assaults in detail. Again and again he told them to keep their minds open to a wider view – if there was a way to bring forward the moment of victory by one hour then let the mole who saw it say so. It is not only for commanders to win battles, the ordinary ranks have a role to play too.

'You should say that to all our forces,' Ystwelyn suggested, but Maple shook his head.

'You each must say it to the moles you lead. Each one of us can contribute, each one . . .'

It had long been Maple's habit to let certain trusted moles, experienced fighters all, wander here and there, free agents in an otherwise ordered field, for such small forces often had much to give, or saw opportunities even the most aware commanders did not. This was something of which Arvon was the master, and indeed something he had taught Maple from Siabodian experience.

'Which means *you*, among others, Noakes,' he said, issuing some final instructions after the general debate. 'You have spent more time than anymole recently in Arvon's company and ought to have picked up a trick or two. And anyway, you're not the kind of mole happy to be subordinate and follow orders.'

'I'm not, sir,' said Noakes gratefully.

'Report direct to me, and take Weeth along with you.'

'Me?' protested Weeth. 'You promised I should not be parted from you, not again.'

Maple grinned. 'Hardly parting, Weeth. You're to keep in touch, which is what you're good at doing, and to pass back to me anything which Noakes thinks I should be aware of.'

The followers did not dally in carrying out Maple's orders, and that same night began an attack out of Carswell Copse itself, and the following dawn Maella, the dauntless female commander from the south-west, led one up from Buckland Marsh, and became involved

457

in the first truly heavy fighting, which would lead in the following days to losses on both sides.

The battle was characterized in these initial stages by lowering skies, and day after day, by dull wet air and with grey winds from the east, the fighting moved from one quarter to another, with nomole sure of where the next attack would come, or the next retreat be forced.

Moles grew more tired each day, and the number of dead and wounded steadily increased. Maple designated the little copse of Harrowdown, which lies to the south-east, a place of recovery and respite. The lesson of Barbury Hill had been well learnt, and Maple and Ystwelyn made sure Harrowdown was properly guarded. Indeed, as the days wore dreadfully on and such incursions as were made into the solid defences of Buckland seemed able to get no further, going to Harrowdown seemed blessed relief to many of the fighters. The place was safe and for a few hours at least the fit could rest, and the wounded find comfort and help.

As for the dying, they were tended as best they could be, the followers protecting their own and dragging them off to safety, whilst being generally meticulous about leaving the fallen Newborns unmolested, for all knew Maple's views of *that*.

By the fourth day the position was this: substantial incursions had been made into the tunnels of Buckland from north and east; the outer defences had been breached in both places, but the inner defences on the surface and below ground had proved too difficult to get through, so that Maple had to order nomole to try, eager though many were to make the attempt.

To the west the followers had less success, and indeed had lost many a mole in a complex range of tunnels there in which moles became separated from their fellows, and were easily picked off by Newborns operating out of well-made exits. On the south side the Newborns had very effective surface defences which were serviced from deep tunnels rising out of Buckland's inner parts, near where the sealed tunnel of the Slopeside began. The ground beyond these defences, below which the contaminated tunnels of the Slopeside ran, was open meadow, hard to cross without being seen by the waiting Newborns.

But the same applied in reverse; indeed, when Tryfan and his friends had escaped the Slopeside a century before across this same open ground, they had had to do so at night to avoid the zealots of the Word, and even then had nearly been caught.

One way or another it was a difficult no-go area and it was for this reason that Maple had ordained that Harrowdown, which rises beyond a stream some way to the south-east of the Slopeside, should be the place of refuge.

On the fifth evening after the first assault Maple held a council of war at Harrowdown, summoning all the commanders from the different quarters, and many junior ranks as well. Maella was the only one not there, for Maple felt it wise to leave her in charge of things down at Buckland Marsh, where such ground as they had gained might so easily be lost again.

For the rest only Noakes and Weeth had not arrived, and did not do so until a general review of all the fronts had taken place. Then they came to the little Stone clearing at Harrowdown, where the meeting was taking place in blustery wind, by the sporadic light of stars and a moon lost now and then behind scudding cloud.

Maple summed up what had been said, partly for the new arrivals' benefit, partly because he was a methodical mole who liked everymole to understand what had been said before proceeding to further discussion.

'Well, then, Noakes, and have you seen something the rest of us haven't?'

Noakes glanced at Weeth and said, 'We've got a few ideas, but most of them carry too much risk. Let's wait and see what the discussion brings out.'

It seemed obvious to Maple that Noakes *did* have a useful idea or two, not so much from what Noakes himself said as from the look of excited intent in Weeth's eyes. Weeth was not a mole who found it easy to keep quiet about an idea when he had one, and it seemed he had one now, or he knew that Noakes did.

'Well, then,' said Maple, 'each side knows the other can fight, and will fight, and now we are in deadlock. We have not enough moles to overwhelm them, nor can we find a place weak enough to attack without losing too many of our own, which Sapient knows full well.

'There are various ways of changing the situation – one is to draw them out, but we've tried that and they're not falling for it. Another is to surprise them, but that seems virtually impossible now. A third, which is a variation of the first, is to withdraw and head rapidly to Duncton, which might force them to follow us so that we could fight on different ground.'

This option drew a murmur of assent from some, dismay from others.

459

'Aye,' said Maple, 'it would be seen as defeat by many, and would give the Newborns a new strength of purpose. If Thorne came south to fight us we might easily find ourselves trapped. The fourth option is to continue as we are and hope that they will weaken, but I doubt that they will. I am not a commander who likes to persist with tactics that are producing no change.'

These points were discussed in detail, and the debate began to favour a partial withdrawal, to see if that would draw the Newborns out. At least such a strategy meant saving lives for a while, and had the added advantage of allowing more time for many so far wounded to recover.

'And yet,' said Maple as moles began to grow tired and the meeting to break down, 'I still believe that if we could come up with a strategy involving surprise, that would be the quickest way of resolving a battle whose every day of prolongation is another day when we are not getting ourselves to Duncton Wood, where by now, or very soon, we shall be needed.

'Now, I am mindful of the history of this place, and that all those decades ago those great warriors Tryfan, Spindle, Mayweed, Skint and Smithills – names of which all of you have heard tell – stanced at this very spot. They had escaped from the Slopeside and I am sure had no wish ever to go back there, but if they were stanced here tonight as we are, faced by our dilemma, what would they say?'

'Humbleness wishes to speak! He does, good sirs, he wishes to pop a thrusting thought into the tired brains of our worried warriors!'

The voice came out of the murk, and at first none but Noakes, who was nearest him, saw that it was Weeth who spoke. His eyes were mischievous, his stance a little low and bent, and he had to mutter in that wheedling, persuasive, curiously confident kind of way a few more words of 'Humbleness!' and 'Not wishing to intrude' and even, and rather too daringly perhaps, 'Muddled Maple', before moles realized that he was pretending to be Mayweed.

'Speak, Weeth,' said Maple heavily, causing allmole to laugh.

'Sir, I speak for myself and Noakes and answer the question you have asked. "What would Tryfan and Mayweed and others like them have done?" I believe they would have followed the one line we have not discussed, and which the Newborns would least expect: the tunnels of the Slopeside.'

There was an uneasy murmur among the commanders, for all knew its reputation.

'It is not as bad as it seems,' said Noakes, coming forward, with

460

Weeth at his flank. 'Earlier today Weeth and I went exploring there. I cannot say it is a pleasant place, and we did not get very far; all is now dust, and the white bones of the long-lost dead of the distant plague years.'

'Scalpskin remains virulent for decades, doesn't it?' observed one commander dubiously.

'Maybe it does, maybe it doesn't. Tryfan did not suffer it and nor did many others who lived for molemonths in the Slopeside. We are thinking we might only need to be there two or three days.'

'Tell us your idea, mole,' said Maple.

The plan was as simple as it was startling, but as risky as it was simple: a band of selected warriors, all volunteers, would enter the Slopeside unobserved. They would get as near to the existing Buckland tunnels as possible, preferably finding the seal-up that Quail had made. Then, and here timing would be of the essence, they would wait until two attacks were made. One overhead, across the Slopeside, which would draw out any defenders below ground; the other would be down at Buckland Marsh. The Newborns' attention and resources taken up with these assaults, the Slopeside moles would break the seal and invade the system from within.

'We know the system's lay-out well enough, and those of us who have kenned the Duncton Chronicles know something of the Slopeside too. The Newborns are superstitious of old tunnels, which is why they have left Pumpkin and the rebels up in Duncton's Ancient System where they are,' said Noakes.

'I doubt that they would relish being attacked by a lot of contaminated moles,' said Weeth, 'whatmole would? They're set in their ways are Newborns, which is why they are happy to fight this battle on their terms. These would be our terms.'

The debate resumed and the dangers of the new plan, and its possibilities, were fully aired. Then, as the discussion drifted in its favour, somemole turned to Ystwelyn, for his views were needed on such a risky strategy.

'Yes, I like it. I like it very much!' was his pronouncement when it was put to him – bold words which carried the night and caused moles to cheer. 'But the moles who go into the Slopeside must be volunteers.'

'Aye,' said Maple, 'for there are real though unknown dangers. Quail would not have ordered the place re-sealed without good reason.'

'I'm willing to go, sir!'

'And I am . . .'

'And all *our* group, sir, you count us in. We're experienced in tunnel fighting.'

Maple and Ystwelyn raised their paws to stop the clamour of volunteers, including several who had been wounded in earlier fighting, and were pleased to be leading such moles as these. Both knew that if there was going to be a crux to the battle this was likely to be it, and some of these brave and loyal moles would never get to see the light of more than two or three dawns, let alone the Duncton Stone of which they had long dreamed.

Yet how differently these two most senior commanders felt about it, though none could have guessed it, for both looked assured and in control. Ystwelyn knew now that if this was not to be the greatest battle he was ever likely to fight as a warrior, then the one following it, at Duncton Wood, most certainly would be and he would give his all; while Maple's thought went beyond that, to the very Stone itself, before which he trusted he would one day soon lower his snout, and ask that never again would he need to lead even one mole to his death.

'I will say only this before a final decision is made,' declared Maple at the end of the debate. 'Tomorrow morning I shall enter the Slopeside myself in company with Noakes, and two of you volunteers, in case we run into difficulty with Newborns. We shall assess the tunnels, and how easily we may get from them into the main system of Buckland itself. Only then shall I give the order for this new strategy to be followed through.'

He did as he had promised, following Noakes, in the company of a couple of hefty warriors, to the place where Noakes had broken into the tunnels the day before, and down they went. The air was clear enough at first, though the passages were narrow and ill-made.

'It gets worse, I'm afraid,' said Noakes, 'and you'll see things you'd rather not.'

He was right: the air turned musty and sour, and the tunnels grew narrow and more winding still, and were dusty with death's decay. The deeper they went, and the nearer towards the Newborns' surface lines, the more evidence they came upon of the plague victims for which the place was so notorious. Here whole families and communities of moles had been incarcerated, and those that did not already have the plague when they arrived soon caught it in the fetid, flea-ridden conditions that prevailed. Many weaker groups had been

462

sealed up and starved by stronger, healthier ones, in the vain hope they might escape infection.

It was not to be, and scores died slow and lonely deaths of disfigurement and suffering, until none, or almost none – for Mayweed was a celebrated exception – survived. It was into this hell that the cruel moles of the Word had sent moles like Tryfan to work as 'clearers' of corpses, and some of these moles contracted scalpskin, a less virulent form of plague but one that caused fur to fall out, and a mole's flesh to waste away before madness and death overtook him.

It was evidence of the activities of these long-gone clearers that Maple and Noakes now literally stumbled upon, for the place was murky and the tunnels so deep in the hard soil that they were ill-lit.

'It's best to avoid the corpses, even if they are but skin and bones, for do we not ken in the Duncton Chronicles that even the desiccated remains of moles can be the host of talon worms?' said Maple, stancing near a corpse they came upon so that the others were forced to go a longer way round it.

'Surely not after so many years?' said Noakes. But he gave the corpse a wide berth.

But they all looked concerned, and where they were forced to squeeze amongst the cadaverous debris in some of the larger chambers, or when, as happened twice, they found bones and mole-matter inextricably entwined with roots through and over which they had to clamber, the hardiest of them felt revulsion, and the urge to pull away rapidly. They went slowly on, ever more uneasy, and glad when they emerged out of the maze of small tunnels, with all their fearful adjacent chambers, some sealed and some not, in which corpses had been and might well be still, into a larger communal tunnel that clearly led downslope in the direction they wished to go.

The air so far had been no more than musty, and the sounds no more significant than the whispers of wind-sound prevalent in all ill-kept tunnels. Then things changed. The air grew a little warmer, and certainly more fetid, and they heard the unmistakable sound of moles overhead, and even on occasion the murmur of their voices. They were under the Newborn lines.

Maple had no need to order silence, and they carried on down the tunnel and into a huge collection chamber of some kind as quietly as they could. At least the tunnels and chambers here were clear of old corpses, though dust was everywhere and the air felt heavy. Maple held up a paw to stop them all, and at first Noakes thought it was because of the sounds they heard ahead.

'Aye, I heard them too,' whispered Maple, 'but it's not for that I've stopped.' He snouted at the air and turned to them saying, 'Well, and can you scent it too?'

'An odour,' said one of the warriors.

'Not unpleasant,' observed the other, pushing forward a little until Maple held him back.

'No, mole, I think not.'

'It scents of crushed nettles,' said Noakes slowly, 'now where have I heard . . .'

'I know where *I've* heard,' said Maple grimly. 'In the Duncton Chronicles – I remember it well. Tryfan was warned in this very place that if ever he came upon the scent of nettles in such tunnels as these he should beware of the talon worm.'

Instinctively they all backed away, if only fractionally.

'We will go on, but carefully, and we shall avoid all corpses.'

They did so, aware not only of the potential danger they faced from the rarest but most dangerous worm in moledom, but also that Newborns' sounds were not only overhead now, but straight ahead as well. Noakes, who was now in the lead, turned a bend and his sharp intake of breath told the others that whatever he saw was unusual and perhaps unpleasant.

It was both, for a veil of roots hung across the passage ahead, completely obscuring what lay beyond. There had been a partial roof-fall, admitting a narrow shaft of light. The roots were pale green in places, white in others, but mostly old, dusty and cobwebby. Grotesquely caught up in them, and hanging a little above shoulder height, were the thin whitened bones and bleached translucent talons of a mole's paw. There seemed nothing else attached to it, though it was hard to see for sure, but the impression they received was of some long-departed mole, risen from the dead, coming their way and about to pull aside the roots and peer at them.

Noakes went carefully ahead, reached out to touch the roots as far from the paw as he could and . . .

Whump!

Thump!

Tangle and struggle! The whole lot swung over and round in a shambles of dead roots, body bones and disintegrating fur, on them and around them all. For a moment they thought the roof might cave in altogether to expose them to anymole above, but that did not happen.

In the dust they stanced, unsure which way to look or go; then, from some dreadful nest or fissure above their heads there came tumbling and then pouring shiny forms, some black, some white, dropping as if in slow motion upon them, hitting their upturned faces and snouts, even making way into the mouths of one or two of them.

Worms. Shiny, legged at front, jawed, their heads cruelly pointed. They recoiled in disgust, brushing the foul things off themselves.

'Dead,' gasped Maple, his breath sending several of this long-dead nest rolling along the floor, or back up into the air again. 'Dead husks, no more!'

His voice was unashamedly relieved, as all about them the scent of nettles wafted as if in the dust that had been released, and then drifted away. They looked at each other in mute alarm, brushing away the husky things, and then thankfully pushed on through the screen of roots to the tunnel beyond.

The scent remained, though they found no further sign of worms, coming at last to another chamber, one in which, assuming that the way ahead might be the way an attack might later go, would be useful to muster their force in relative comfort.

They went on, turned a corner, and saw ahead the huge and recent seal-up across the tunnel which had been the object of their search. But a grim obstacle lay before it . . .

'Stone alive!' muttered one of the warrior moles, already thoroughly shaken by the dust and roots and dead worms that had fallen on them, 'Stone . . . !'

'Go no further,' ordered Maple, staring at what looked as much barrier as obstacle across their path.

It was a pile of bodies that they saw, entangled with each other, piled against the seal-up as if they had reached it and died. These were more recent corpses than any others they had seen, the fur of most of them intact, the bones only showing here and there, the postures lifelike, the heads and flanks hardly shrunken into death at all. Yet no odour, just dry still air and this frieze of death.

'We go no further now,' said Maple, though it was plain they had no need to. Clear as if they were just round the next bend, had the tunnel continued, they heard the sound of moles. Moles talking, moles resting, moles eating, moles ordering: Newborn moles.

'That's no tunnel beyond,' whispered Noakes, 'but a great chamber.'

'Perfect for a surprise attack,' said Maple, 'perfect. We needed a chamber and if we stance here long enough we'll be able to deduce what chamber this is.'

'Perfect, but for *them*,' replied Noakes, indicating the dead bodies,

465

evidently those of the moles left incarcerated when Quail sealed up the Slopeside once again.

'We'll have to find a way round, or under, or just pick our way carefully between them and the wall,' whispered one of the warriors, creeping closer. 'They seem just dry, not contaminated.'

They all went closer and stared at the wretched pile of death, and indeed there seemed nothing untoward but the manner of death itself, and the mystery of why these moles had stayed where they were and not tried to escape back up the tunnels the way Noakes had led them in.

For the rest of the day the four moles listened to the sounds of the Newborns coming and going in the chamber beyond, and were able to deduce that it was a resting-place for moles who went on up to the surface and out to fight the followers, or came back down wounded or just tired.

More than that, they were able to work out the numbers in it at any one time, and to conclude that if Maple could muster twice as many in the Slopeside ready to break through, they could easily take the chamber and cause panic and disarray.

'We have done enough,' said Maple finally, 'and now we shall return. Noakes, your plan will work, with the Stone's help and our own courage.'

Chapter Thirty-Seven

Quail's slow and painful southward journey to Duncton Wood over the next few days, though presented to him as a 'triumphal progress', was really a flight, and one for which time was very rapidly running out.

For Squilver had been right. Thorne was quick to spot the weaknesses in the Caradocian front line and to exploit them. Had he known the true extent of the weakening Quail had suffered by Sapient's and Turling's withdrawal, and had not Squilver driven his moles almost to exhaustion in their efforts to hurry from one place to another and give the impression they were more numerous than they were, Thorne would certainly have pushed hard through their ranks, and gone south without bothering to secure territory to either side. And had he done so, Quail would never have reached the sanctuary of Duncton Wood, and . . . but history speaks of what happened, not what might have been.

As it was, Thorne, ever careful and thorough, covered himself as he went and gave Squilver too much opportunity to make his retreat orderly and effective. Indeed, Quail even had time to hold court for a day in Rollright, and suffer such few followers as remained alive and in captivity there to be tried and punished within the holy orbit of Rollright's famous circle of Stones.

Snyde arranged that this spectacle should be at dusk, that Quail be not seen in the full glare of daylight, for now he grew more foul and hideous with each day that passed, and even the loyal and mindless guardmoles who watched closest over him were beginning to avoid being *too* close. They abided him for the prestige and power that he gave them, and the special titbits of food, and the favours sexual and otherwise that they came to expect. And too, which cannot be denied, despite all he had become, Quail retained an awesome power, born perhaps of the unequivocal strength of purpose and decision he had shown in the past, and occasionally showed still, which was attractive and alluring to those who came within his dark ambit.

In Rollright, Brother Adviser Fagg, prompted by Snyde no doubt, offered two pleasing surprises to Quail. One was a final youthful victim who, perhaps mercifully, died of fright on being dragged into Quail's personal chamber, and thereafter became Snyde's dead plaything for the night.

The other was a reunion with his son Squelch, which gave Quail almost pathetic delight. How he burbled and chuckled as at Snyde's suggestion Squelch first revealed himself not visually but aurally, by singing.

'Oh, oh, oh,' cried Quail, panting and sobbing and exclaiming in glee, 'it is my son, my beauty, my beloved Squelch! No other has a voice like his! Show yourself! Become!'

But Squelch, knowing his father liked to look forward to his pleasures and revel in the idea of them before actually enjoying them, let his beautiful and unforgettable falsetto voice play out of the darkness where he hid; whilst other singers there, well rehearsed, counterpointing his high notes with their low ones, provided the perfect accompaniment to the ritual executions of some Rollright followers.

'Oh, my dear!' exalted Quail, watching a mole die, and then another, and then a third, their heads crushed and battered against a Stone, their blood running darkly in the dusk. Squelch's voice soared above their screams, and gave them a kind of sonority.

'Oh, stop torturing me, my love, my son, and *show* yourself!'

Eventually Squelch emerged, larger than when the two had last met, or wider, his paws like the fins of some fat chub stranded on a river-bank, his mouth gobbling at the air with every tiny effort that he made.

'Father!' he exclaimed, his eyes widening in horror at what he saw, and his sensitive snout recoiling in disgust as Quail opened his paws to him.

'Yes, yes, come here and kiss me, Squelch,' simpered Quail, offering up his rotten mouth to Squelch's unwilling embrace.

'Father,' said Squelch, yielding to the kiss with feigned pleasure and delight, 'it is so good to see you. How are you? Have your travels been hard?'

'I must not complain if the Stone puts pain into my body to try my spirit and test my resolve,' replied Quail, 'and nor do I. I am better than I was. I am better.'

Squelch eyed Quail's saccy parts, the drooping eyes whose cornea was now bulging and turning white and blind; he saw the downward fall of the mouth, sign of some internal breaking down, and the black stumps of teeth; he saw the tremor to the flanks, and the hollows and swellings; and he smelled the stench, which was like death itself.

'You look so well,' he said, 'and now . . . now I am to accompany you to Duncton Wood! How nice! What fun we shall have along the way, how much to talk about!'

Squelch's fat eyes flicked ruefully into the shadows behind Quail, from where Snyde watched, and Snyde's cold black eyes blinked back in return, the quick opaque blink that lizards have.

'Fun,' he purred softly, 'is what we all shall have.'

Perhaps they did have fun next day, trekking very slowly, for Quail was overcome with fatigue from the night before, and with excitement at the prospect ahead.

'Will it be soon that we see Duncton? Sooner than soon?'

Squelch giggled at his flank and said that sooner than soon was not soon enough for *him*, but yet they must wait. It was not too far.

'Too far is far too far,' responded Quail, and Squelch began to think he had never known his father in so playful a mood, nor known him to be *light*.

They might have paused more than they did but that Snyde, to whom messengers constantly came and went from the rear of their party of moles, with grim news of how Thorne's forces were pressing ever closer, harried them on whilst trying not to seem to.

'We shall enjoy this final part of the great journey, Snyde, we shall,' said Quail, stopping.

'All the more shall our enjoyment be when we get there,' said Squelch, urging him on an extra pace or two.

'We must . . .' began Snyde.

'What *must* the Elder Senior Brother and his son do, Brother Snyde?' asked Quail sharply.

'We must remember that the Stone grows impatient, Lord, even for the highest, even for you.'

'Does it? I think he's right, son.'

'He usually is, Pa,' said Squelch familiarly.

They dawdled on and Snyde sent orders to Squilver to prepare a final stance that evening, for they would not make Duncton that same day, though Stone knows it was not far, not now . . .

The sky was black as night at times, with great stormclouds looming up, and the jagged, ugly rumble and roar of thunder off to the right and left.

'Soon we shall see it,' insinuated Snyde, urging them on a few steps more, up the muddy slopes of Begbroke Hill. Strangely it was not the way a journeymole would have gone, but Snyde calculated that the sight of Duncton Wood across the Thames Valley might encourage them.

They puffed and panted, moaned and whinged, but finally, eager as weasels but slow as snails, they crested a rise and there before them across the vale, only a little further than it seemed, rose Duncton.

'Bliss,' said Quail, and Squelch sang the most wistful of songs, which spoke of a great journey undertaken and now almost complete, and all the life that had been left behind to get where they were going.

'It is dark and impressive,' said Quail, and well he might. This was no springtime view of a great wood in bud, nor summer scene of trees rising beyond the river vale; nor even wild and colourful autumn, for all the leaves had flown. This was Duncton from the north, with winter all but come, black and leafless, yet not so black now as the huge sky mounting up behind.

'See!' said Quail.

'Listen!' said Squelch.

And a flash of lightning diffused by cloud was followed by the roll of far-off thunder. But no rain fell, and no wind blew and all was ominous.

'All to come, all to come,' said Quail. 'Let's go on!'

'It seems far,' said Squelch, puffing and sweating from the climb, despite the cold.

'We will follow the roaring owl way that runs to our left paw,' explained Snyde, 'and will use the cross-under that lies south-east of the hill. Fetter's guardmoles will be there to welcome us and see us safely in.'

'Not so far as we have come,' said Quail, pressing on.

Squelch sighed and did not sing, but followed on. And somewhere then, along the way, they saw the first of many pilgrims, in ones and twos, in little groups, going the same way as they did, though pushed to one side by the guardmoles so Quail's party could pass.

'And who are they?' asked Quail.

'They have come to see you, Master, in praise and adoration,' said Snyde, eyes filled with hatred, for he knew they came in Privet's name.

'They are in the way,' said Squelch, 'but I suppose there are too many to kill.'

That evening, but an hour or two's fast trek to the north of where the party finally halted from sheer exhaustion, Squilver turned his forces to face north again at Begbroke, just where the main party had paused earlier that day. Thorne's advance guard began the attack as the first rains came, and a close and desperate battle was engaged.

'We need more moles!' cried a commander on Thorne's side, but it might have been Squilver's cry. He had sent his wearier force southward to be with Quail and now he held what ground he could, hoping that darkness and rain would bring respite.

They did, and in that he was lucky. Reviled by Thorne though he had been, sneered at by those on the Crusade Council who had expected the 'Supreme' Brother Commander to fail much earlier on, Squilver's defence of Begbroke was as fine an achievement on a small scale as there has ever been. Outnumbered by far fitter moles, staunch in his defence, Squilver, and a thunderstorm, gained time.

Then with bodies all about, and under cover of night, Squilver gave the order to retreat: silently, carefully, himself among the last, away downslope to the roaring owl way, and then in the pawsteps of the Elder Senior Brother's party.

'Now, away . . .' he said, sliding and slipping in the mud and down towards Yarnton, 'and may the Stone grant this rain stays heavy.'

It did, only stopping at the first glimmer of a bedraggled dawn when Thorne's advance guards saw that the positions they had been watching were occupied now by dead moles, positioned to seem alive. Dead, wet, deserted positions, Squilver's last legacy of a brutal battle.

'Come on!' a commander roared, and the charge down towards Yarnton began.

'Go on!' urged Squilver as he caught up with Snyde. 'We must go on! Only get him to Duncton and they'll not easily get us out again. But if they catch us here we're lost.'

Quail was dragged out of sleep, and Squelch out of somnolence, and both were urged and pushed, chivvied and chased, hurried and harried along.

'The Worm and the Snake come fast behind, even here, even now!' cried Snyde.

'Thorne?'

'Aye, him. And Chervil. And Rolt.'

'Then we must not let them take us at the last!' said Quail, doing his best to hurry his aching limbs.

'Must, Master?' whispered Snyde with a thin smile.

'You are jocular, Brother,' panted Quail, 'you joke.'

'I do, I do,' said Snyde, trotting along as well.

'Squelch!'

'Father?'

471

'Stir and shift, for now our pilgrimage is nearly done and our triumph complete. The Snake is behind, but too far to take us, the Stone ahead.'

'Stir!' muttered Squelch, padding fatly along. 'Shift! I stir and you stink! I shift and still you stink!'

'What?' cried out Quail over his shoulder, for he had not heard clearly.

'I come!' said Squelch, peering at the steep embankment of the roaring owl way on his left-paw side and then ahead for signs of a cross-under, wondering how far it was now.

'We *must* hurry, sir,' said Squilver, coming alongside, and shoving some vagrant moles out of the way, for the path was crowded now and the guardmoles could not contain all the pilgrims who went the way they did.

'We are *flying*,' puffed Squelch. 'Are they far behind?'

'Within sight, sir,' said Squilver, lying only slightly, and marvelling that so grossly fat a mole could move at all. And through all their ranks something almost like panic spread as mighty and minion alike sped or waddled, trotted or tripped, ever more breathless, as behind them the Worm and the Snake loomed, and before them, spread in solid ranks just as Squilver had ordered two days before, stanced lines of guardmole, ready to herd them through the cross-under if only they could reach it, and thence into the safety of Duncton Wood.

It was in the cross-under itself that Brother Inquisitor Fetter waited, his finest hour nigh. A mud-spattered messenger had come racing in a little earlier from the knoll on which Fetter had placed him, to report that the Elder Senior Brother's party was in sight at last.

Now Fetter fretted, moving restlessly back and forth, avoiding the puddles on the concrete of the cross-under's floor; eyeing the rook that perched impatiently on the parapet above, watching over the slopes of the pastures that led up to the High Wood; listening to the sound of the roaring owls that raced by unseen above.

Guards stanced discreetly some way off, for Snyde had ordered that there should be only himself to welcome the Elder Senior Brother: he would be tired, formalities could come later, rituals later still. Meanwhile, at least the pilgrims who had crowded at the cross-under for days past had been cleared back somewhat. Some had died in the struggle, and their bodies had been tidied away at Fetter's insistence.

His restlessness now was that of a mole who has waited a lifetime for what is about to happen and is so confident of its outcome and the

472

praise that will follow that he is eager to get on with it. Not that his bitter face and inquisitorial eyes betrayed these emotions, though if friends who knew him well had been close enough, which they were not, they might have detected some marginal softening in his face, some slight cheerful glistening to his thin snout.

He looked here and there just a mite suspiciously, as if something might still go wrong, though all preparations for the Elder Senior Brother's coming had been double checked, and checked again. He knew if it did what it would be, though . . .

'I have planned for it! I have prepared. I hope they try!'

What he had meant when he had said this the day before to his subordinates, he referred to again now as he repeated it to himself; the 'threat' of the wretched followers led by the miscreant Pumpkin, and incarcerated up in the tunnels of the High Wood.

Incarcerated was the word, since with the help of extra forces sent by Supreme Commander Squilver himself, Fetter had virtually every leaf and surface root in the High Wood, every known tunnel entrance and many that were simply suspected, watched, patrolled, guarded, and overseen.

The rebels were dying anyway, that was plain. Bodies of emaciated moles had been found. Three more caught, too weak even for torture. Should have fattened them up before hauling them down to the Marsh End to face the talons of truth. Hmmph!

'It would be a pleasure if they tried anything,' he had said; and he thought it again now, going forward impatiently and peering round the edge of the far wall of the cross-under to see if Quail's party was in sight at last. There was movement . . . it was but the guardmoles . . . something was happening . . . nearly, now . . .

Fetter allowed himself the final luxury of easing back into the darkest part of the cross-under, sniffing and scenting about, and then wandering over to the Duncton side and peering up towards the High Wood. Always compelling was that great wall of trees, as leafless now as they had been the full cycle of seasons ago when he had come here. The pinnacle of his career as Inquisitor, this posting. Hard work, but now the reward . . .

He had good reason to feel satisfied. Not only was the system in order and the minor matter of the followers absolutely contained, but he had conquered what he now regarded as his greatest challenge: the reception and placing of the former Elder Senior . . . of Thripp.

How his heart had thumped when the guardmoles had brought Thripp into Duncton. How Fetter, as mole-in-charge, had inwardly

trembled as he turned to face the mole who had once been the inspiration for them all, but was now disgraced. How he had been shocked
and then filled with contempt to see how low that mole had fallen:
thin, haggard, grey, his eyes cast down, hardly mole at all.

'You are Thripp?'

'I am.'

'Look at me, mole!' Fetter had dared to say, and sharply too!

Thripp had looked at him and Fetter had found himself, finally,
nearly unafraid.

'My orders are that you shall be kept in the shadow of Duncton
Stone. You are to be fed and watered by the same guards who have
watched over you these molemonths past, and none other. Nomole
shall speak to you.'

Thripp had stared at him and for moment Fetter had felt a tremor
in his heart, for he fancied he saw some strange light in Thripp's pale
eyes. But a fancy was surely all it was.

'Have you anything to say?' asked Fetter, his throat just a little dry.

'What would a mole have to say who is to be taken before Duncton
Stone?' Thripp had said. 'It is hardly punishment.'

'Take him there!' ordered Fetter. For a few moments Fetter allowed
himself to think there had been insolence in Thripp's voice, and a
strength that was belied by the old mole's thin body and lined face.
For a moment more Fetter dared think he felt a kind of elemental
fear.

Then he banished such nonsense from his mind, and watching the
former Elder Senior Brother being led meekly away, had told himself,
'Nonsense!', and thought of such things no more.

Now, days later, the rightful Elder Senior Brother almost there,
Fetter felt he had done well and been much blessed by the Stone.
More than that, he felt a conviction that he would do better yet. Some
new triumph was yet to be his. Capture of the mole Pumpkin, perhaps!
That would be a final bliss. Something . . . he did not know
what, but he had a pleasant premonition of it. So his restlessness was
composed of many things, many, many things . . .

Voices echoing through the cross-under; a patter of guardmole pawsteps; shadows and then silhouettes.

'They are here. He is here. He comes,' said Fetter to himself,
smoothing his face-fur one last time, fixing an expression on his cold
face that he hoped was at once obedient, adoring, masterful, and,
well . . . welcoming.

'Brother Inquisitor Fetter!' purred Snyde, coming first out of the shadows and off the concrete into the light, 'we are pleased to see you once again.'

The loathsome form of Snyde, which Fetter remembered all too well, came forward to greet him. Snyde's fur was glossy, and barely touched with mud at all; his eyes sparkled with confidence; his hobbling gait was spry.

'Welcome, Brother Snyde,' hissed Fetter in his politest voice.

Snyde stanced to one side and turned back to the shadowed cross-under. Fetter readied himself, his paws sweaty despite the cold.

A fat form appeared, puffing, gasping, frowning, and red of snout.

'Squelch,' said Snyde quietly, perhaps thinking that Fetter did not know the mole. But Fetter remembered him all too well from his training days at Bowdler. He proffered up to Squelch the smile he had prepared for the Elder Senior Brother.

'Yes,' said Squelch, going past them both and staring with open curiosity upslope towards the High Wood. 'Awesome, oh my, it is. That's the word, Snyde.'

'It is,' said Snyde lightly, happier than he could ever have believed to be on his own ground once more. They all turned back to the shadows.

A delay. Scurrying in the dark. Silhouettes stancing back. Then out into the light he came, slowly, peering, appalling, Quail.

'Elder Senior Brother,' rasped Fetter, his voice almost failing him when he saw what moledom's greatest had become. Then, summoning up all his self-possession, for he needed every scrap of it, for what had appeared before him was the vilest, foulest mole he had ever seen, he said, 'It is an honour, a great honour, and I am not worthy—'

'Yes, yes, yes,' said Quail, reaching out to Squelch for support and waving a distorted paw in the air to shut Fetter up. 'Where is Thripp?'

'He is in the shadow of Duncton Stone, Elder Sen—'

'Take me there!' ordered Quail, a terrible look of bitter hatred, and then of cruel triumph, in his eyes.

As Fetter led the party upslope towards the High Wood Squilver barked harsh orders behind them. Guardmoles came rushing, ranks formed one after another, four deep; patrols were strengthened along the dykes and conduits at either side of the cross-under. Pilgrims who had pressed forward, staring, were pushed back.

Halfway up the slope Squelch, too tired for a moment to go on, paused and looked back. From here they could see some of the ground on the far side of the cross-under.

'Who are those moles?' he asked. For there were many of them,

475

in groups here and there, tired, and staring longingly at the closely-guarded cross-under, and up to the slopes beyond; the slopes from which Squelch and the others now looked down.

'Pilgrims,' said Fetter, too late.

'Not come for me?' said Quail. 'What do they want?'

'They cause us no trouble. What they want is the mole Privet. They think she's here.'

'And is she?' whispered Quail.

'Why, no, no, of course she is not, Elder Senior Brother,' faltered Fetter.

'She will be; oh, she will be,' said Quail, 'for her time has come.'

Below them, beyond the rumble of the roaring owl way, moles cried out and seemed to surge. Then the cries faded.

'The guardmoles have them under control,' said Fetter dismissively, turning back upslope.

'Doesn't matter if they haven't, Pa says,' said Squelch. 'The Stone is our protector.'

To Fetter it seemed half dream, half nightmare, this trek upslope with these moles and their words; and the smell, so terrible, the odour of a holy mole. The leafless wall of the High Wood swayed towards him, and Squelch and Quail uttered their ecstasies before it, and again on entering. The great beech trees opened their ranks to them, and their shadows took them in, but Quail and Squelch seemed not to see how awesome the High Wood was, or how lost they looked amidst it.

'The Stone, the Stone, where Thripp is, how far now?' said Quail impatiently.

'It is on the far side of the High Wood,' said Fetter, wishing it were nearer.

'Then hasten, hasten.'

'Brother Inquisitor, Brother!'

It was the messenger he had used earlier, come into the High Wood after them, calling out, noisy, and most unseemly.

'Mole . . .' began Fetter with a warning look, but something in the mole's eyes and face silenced him, something extraordinary. 'What is it?' he said faintly.

'A mole, Brother Inquisitor.'

Fetter signalled him to come close and whisper, which he did. Fetter's eyes narrowed, he asked a question or two, his eyes glinted and then softened into what was undeniably a look of pride and triumph.

476

'What is it, mole?' asked Snyde.

Fetter dared ignore him, dared even to call after the Elder Senior Brother and stop him in his tracks with what was almost a command.

'Elder Senior Brother!' he cried out.

What he had to say must be important indeed.

It was.

'Well, Fetter?' said Quail, anxious to reach the Stone and face Thripp in triumph and disdain.

The great dark trees soared up towards a distant shut-off sky; deep silence reigned; green-lichened roots twisted bent and gnarled about them across the shadowed russet surface of the High Wood.

'The mole Privet, Elder Senior Brother.'

'What of her?' said Quail, his voice as sharp as the points of the dead holly tree that leaned nearby.

'My subordinates,' said Fetter, relishing the word, even loving it, 'my subordinates have . . . apprehended her. But a short while ago. She is in our custody.'

Silence deep and blissful, everywhere.

'Where?' wondered Quail dreamily, coming back towards Fetter just a shade.

'Here, now, in Duncton, Elder Senior Brother. Back at the cross-under. This mole—'

'Yes, yes, I do believe she must be. The Worm has found a face; the Snake a name; and the Stone has delivered it to us. Brother Inquisitor Fetter . . . ?'

'Master?' said Fetter, coming close and even braving the stench of Quail's breath for the glory of this most glorious of moments.

'Bring her to me,' whispered Quail, his voice seeming to echo about the trees as if in a holy chamber. 'Bring her to me *personally*.'

'Yes, Elder Senior Brother.'

'You know where you shall find me. I shall be with Thripp and we shall await her together, by the Stone. Snyde, whose home this once was, will guide me there, won't you, Snyde?'

Snyde nodded. 'Privet!' he said, surprised for once.

Quail laughed. Squelch giggled almost silently.

'Bring her to me by the Stone then,' said Quail, as if she was a worm to eat. Then he went on his slow and painful way, full of joy, until he was lost among the ancient trees of the High Wood.

*

477

'And you let her, by herself, without escort, unaccompanied, give herself up to Quail's guardmoles at the cross-under into Duncton Wood?'

If ever a mole sounded incredulous and angry and nearly impotent with rage it was Arvon, interrogating Hodder, Rees and Arliss. He hopped about from paw to paw, stabbing at the air with his talons, shaking his head with disbelief, his eyes wild.

'You don't understand . . .' Hodder tried to explain once more.

'Don't understand?' roared Arvon, the walls of the chamber where they stanced shaking with the sound. 'I understand all right. I understand too bloody well. Oh, I understand! What I can't begin to believe is that you did it!'

'It is what she wanted,' Arliss said.

'What she wanted! Hear that, Cluniac? It's what she wanted!'

'It *was* what she wanted, I'm convinced of it,' said Cluniac quietly. 'Privet is after all not an ordinary mole.'

'Not ordinary! Of course she's not ordinary! Can't even you speak sense to me?'

He stared at them belligerently, his mouth a little open, breathless with rage and frustration. Privet, the mole for whom all moledom had been searching, the mole who . . . the mole who . . . on whom . . . about whom . . . everything whom! *These* three hapless, useless moles, who claimed to have been her protectors, had allowed her to . . . aided and abetted by Cluniac, a mole he thought he had got to know well, who had seemed in all respects sensible and competent. And that other mole, who started it all . . .

'It was what she wanted, you see, what was right for her!'

It was Rees who spoke now, and he did so quietly but firmly, thrusting his snout towards Arvon, and so far as his weakened eyes allowed it, out-staring him.

'What she wanted . . . ?' repeated Arvon faintly, stilled a little by Rees' calmness, and perhaps realizing that outrage was getting him nowhere, and certainly not nearer a solution to the problem posed by Privet's disappearance into Duncton Wood, if there ever could be a solution to such a thing. He was calmed too by the continuing stillness of the others in the chamber, who stared, not with alarm, as he might have expected and perhaps even hoped, but with a kind of sympathy, which he could not abide.

Rees continued: 'She did not speak, but simply looked at us and nodded, as if to say "You've brought me back safely, now it is for me to go on alone once more."'

478

'Hmmph!' said Arvon, frowning but now prepared to listen, if only because he could think of no further protest to make.

'Three days we were here at the cross-under, along with the other pilgrims. None asked who we were, none guessed then who Privet was, though it was to find her that all had come,' explained Rees. 'At first we could not believe it, for *we* knew who she was and thought the others would. But they were looking for somemole more striking perhaps, somemole more grand; somemole who was holy on the outside, as well as inside. Why, I don't think they knew what they were looking for, and so they did not see her. They dismissed Privet as just another pilgrim like themselves.'

'Except *him*,' said Arvon, nodding towards an elderly mole who stanced down in one corner of the chamber looking a little apologetic. He had grey grizzled fur and a pleasantly lined face, and like the others, he had a certain peace about him. He was the one Arvon had thought of as starting it all.

'Yes, him,' said Hodder. 'He came near to us just after the guard-moles pushed and shoved us upslope out of the way, when that great party of moles arrived and were allowed into the cross-under.'

'Aye,' growled Arvon: 'Quail and his gang – Squelch, Snyde, Squilver. The whole lot of them.'

'We wouldn't know,' said Arliss quietly, taking up the story, 'we've been out of touch with such things lately. You see, although she was always silent, yet somehow you knew what she wanted . . . or rather, her silence made you realize what you wanted, or needed to do.'

'Go on,' said Arvon.

'Well, he came over to us, did that mole, just as the parties you've named were arriving and going into Duncton and he said to her, "I know you, I saw you at Leamington, you healed me. My name's Hibbott." That's what he said.'

Hibbott nodded, acknowledging that that was exactly what he had said.

'It was *her*,' he explained, 'the female who made me well after the Leamington Massing.'

'You survived that?' said Arvon, in some awe.

Hibbott nodded, and such was the openness of his gaze, and his simplicity, that none could doubt it was true. Everymole there knew of the shame and tragedy of the Leamington Massing, when so many moles had died in such appalling conditions that a survivor was taken seriously, and Hibbott gained a certain credibility.

'So what happened?'

Hibbott sighed and said, 'I really don't know what came over me because I looked at her and I knew . . . I knew suddenly whatmole she was. Before I could stop myself I said, "You're Privet of Duncton, *you* are . . ."'

'And others nearby heard,' said Rees, reliving the alarm he had felt, 'others knew. And then moles began to say "She's here, she's *that* one. Privet's come among us." And they pressed forward . . .'

'They did,' said Hibbott very quietly, 'and I knew I should not have said it. I should have stayed quiet. It was not what she wanted, or needed.'

'They began to press and shout,' went on Hodder, reliving the nightmare too, 'and we had to crowd round her to protect her, to try to get her away. Well, we couldn't go up, the slope was too steep, and anyway, moles were pressing down. We couldn't go sideways: they were pressing in from right and left. You wouldn't believe how quickly information like that spreads. We could only go down, and down, down towards the guardmoles by the cross-under . . .'

'. . . and I went with them, trying to help, trying to keep moles back, but their shouts were like rage or anger,' whispered Hibbott, upset.

'So we linked paws and pushed and shoved a way downslope to the guardmoles themselves and then he – this mole here – came to our help.'

Cluniac nodded sombrely. 'I couldn't believe my eyes. There I was following your orders, Arvon, to spy out the land, when who should come helter-skelter down towards me almost chased by the crowd but Privet herself, right into my paws. I had only seen her once or twice in Duncton Wood, but I knew it was her. And she said—'

'She didn't *say* anything,' said Arliss.

'No, no, she did not *speak*,' conceded Cluniac. 'She only seemed to. She made me ask her, "What do you want to do, Privet?" She was so thin, so slight, so lined compared to what I remember, as if she had suffered, but Arvon, she . . .'

'What, mole?' Arvon said gruffly, though gently, for he had grown to love Cluniac like a son in the molemonths of campaigning past.

'She looked at me and I was still,' said Cluniac in some bewilderment. 'Then she turned and faced the rabble of pilgrims pursuing her and stared up towards them and they faltered to a stop, speechless. I cannot explain by what power she did it, but she did. Then she turned to us all – these three moles who have travelled with her as we have learnt, and the pilgrim Hibbott here, and myself, and it was

480

as if whilst none of us knew what to do individually, together we did. We turned with her, six in all counting her, and she led us to a guardmole, which made seven.'

'A Seven Stancing,' breathed Hodder, taking up the tale again, 'a safe haven of moles. Seven of us. And the thick ranks of the guardmoles opened up before us and we led her into the shadows of the cross-under and she turned to us again and we knew we must go no further. It was just a grubby, shadowy corner, with puddles on the concrete floor, and a rectangle of light beyond where pasture grass rises up towards the Wood itself.'

'The High Wood,' said Cluniac.

'"You must leave me here, and let me go on alone again. Another mole was here alone once, a long, long time ago, he was here and called out for help, and help came. It will come to me, for the Stone will send it." That's what she seemed to say, and our limbs wouldn't move to go with her, and she left us and went on into Duncton by herself.'

These last were the words of Arliss, but all of them might have uttered them, though none of them had known quite where they came from, or whatmole it was whose memory arose about them, and gave her faith to go on alone.

'The guardmoles let us out as peaceably as they let us in, and that solitary guardmole who made up our seven stayed with us, and saw us to safety,' said Hodder. 'I don't know what his name was, I didn't ask it, but I will remember his face for ever as if he were my brother.'

He looked around at the others, and they nodded in agreement. Silence reigned, but for the drumming of one of Arvon's talons.

Hibbott, in his account of his pilgrimage, tells us what happened next: 'Those moments following our explanation of how Privet had come to enter once more into the tender care and protection of Elder Senior Brother Quail and his guardmoles remain, in memory, some of the longest in my life. Arvon was a big mole and a most powerful personality, and not somemole the average harmless pilgrim like myself either wishes, or expects, to come into close touch with.

'But there we were, faced by a dilemma which, I felt strongly, might not have been so bad if I had kept quiet! However, I consoled myself in those slow passing moments with the thought that thus far when I had given myself up to the Stone, all had turned out well.

'I ventured to share this thought with Commander Arvon, but he told me in no uncertain terms that I had said enough and that I should be silent as he was thinking, or words to that effect.

'His thinking continued, and the silence grew ever more oppressive, and I swear that not only I, but all the company, could hear my heart thumping in my chest, which it does not normally do so loudly. Finally Commander Arvon said, "We're going to have to try to rescue her, though Stone knows how. I would have preferred to remain where we are, for we may be needed here when Maple comes north from Avebury and Buckland as he undoubtedly will. What is more, there is the matter of Noakes."

'Commander Arvon appeared to be in a discursive mood, perhaps because we were all moles who had, one way or another, spent time in Leamington, a dubious but powerful experience to have shared. So when Hodder asked who Noakes was Arvon told him, explaining that that great and enterprising mole had been sent south by him to make what contact he could with Maple, and with the rebels from Seven Barrows.

'I cannot say,' Hibbott continues in his engaging narrative of those events, 'that such matters should concern a pilgrim, whose eyes ought surely to be solely upon the Stone and the Silence, and the object of his quest, which had until then been the mole Privet. I confess that my discovery that I had unknowingly met her already, and indeed that she had helped heal me in Leamington, came as something of a surprise, for it meant I had been no more able than any other of the many moles seeking her to recognize who she was. Having met her once and not known her, to meet her again and know her, and to have misguidedly shared that knowledge with others, thus causing her having to flee into the paws of Quail, the mole most dangerous to her, did not raise my self-esteem.

'However, I have tried in this account to be honest, and I would be less than honest if I did not say that as Arvon and the others discussed military matters, which were of little concern to me, I offered up a quiet and humble prayer to the Stone asking that I might be granted a third and final meeting with Privet, and a chance of redressing the balance of mistakes, if opportunity arose.

'I mentioned just now that the military matters under discussion were "of little concern to me", but this is ambiguous. How hard and treacherous the way of the pilgrim! To be frank, I was fascinated by them, though I knew I should not be. How heady to be in the company of a commander such as Arvon, how exciting to breathe the air of decision and coming action. How . . .

'Alas, I got carried away with myself, for I ventured the remark that I did not think the notion of trying to rescue Privet was a good idea – moles might get killed, I suggested, and anyway, did Privet wish to be rescued? I am proud to say that the moles Arliss and Rees agreed with me, though Cluniac and Hodder did not.

'Before my well-intentioned suggestion Commander Arvon had been silent for some time, and though clearly not in a cheerful mood he had at least allowed the debate to continue. On hearing my voice he rudely told me that he would throw me down the nearest slopes if I was not silent "like pilgrims ought to be".

'He calmed down a little and then continued, "This is not a matter for discussion. Until Maple himself arrives here from the south I am in command. Unfortunately you civilian moles seem unaware that Brother Commander Thorne is but a short time from arriving at the cross-under from the north, and he will have a formidable army of moles with him. Until this happened my own small force had intended simply to infiltrate with the wanderers and vagrants hereabout who grandly call themselves pilgrims, and see if we could find a way into the Duncton system itself. Not an easy thing when the only point of access is so heavily guarded, but we have been in and out of the system before and there are ways of doing it, if a mole is willing to take a risk with roaring owls, and perhaps venture across the dangerous marshes that lie beyond the northern Marsh End of the Wood and extend to the River Thames itself. Well, we shall have to see.

'"But as for *not* trying to rescue her . . . it's all very well for pacifists like yourselves, I suppose, and Privet herself I dare say, to declaim against war and fighting—"

'"Privet never declaimed against anything, Arvon!" said Cluniac quietly.

'"Well, all right then, but you know what I mean. It's all very well, but how do things get achieved? Eh? Where would Duncton have been but for the doughty moles who defended its tunnels and Stone with their lives in the past?"

'Impressive though Arvon was,' continues Hibbott, 'I was not so intimidated by his earlier warnings (for a mole must speak his mind if he thinks himself right) not to boldly say that wherever Duncton had got itself in the past, and however brave and worthy its previous defenders might have been, *today* it was in the paws of evil moles, and that was plain fact. Had the loss of lives previously been worth it, if that was the result? Perhaps the system was better defended by a mole such as Privet than by a whole army of fighting followers! Pacifism might be the better way, and a mole ought to ask another what they want before setting forth to rescue them.

483

'Arvon sighed at this and looked weary. "But we must make the attempt," he said, somewhat illogically in my view. After this I said no more, but decided to slip away from these fearsome debates and coming fights as soon as I was able, and trust that my prayers to the Stone for a peaceful end to matters would be answered.

'Arvon had one more question for us, and I remember it because it was surprising nomole had asked it before, or even thought to do so, including ourselves: "Did she have this fabled last lost Book with her? The Book of Silence? Or any sign of it? I mean, that's what moles say she set forth to discover in the first place, isn't it?"

'I was forced to shake my head and say that there had been no sign of the Book at all.

'"You've travelled with her these molemonths past," he continued, looking at Hodder and Arliss, "so . . . where *is* it?"

'They shrugged, and shook their heads as well, and I am quite sure they had no idea at all where it was. Indeed, I rather think they had forgotten all about it once they were in the presence of Privet herself.

'The meeting with Arvon was now over, and despite the entreaties of Hodder and Arliss to stay with them, which I found flattering, I decided to make my exit from their company, and seek my own way forward once more, just as Privet had done – alone.'

Such is Hibbott's testimony concerning his role in Privet's strange and unexpected return to Duncton Wood, and we have no reason to doubt that matters occurred much as he described. Sensing that fighting and trouble were imminent, and feeling – wrongly as it turned out – that he had nothing to contribute to such a situation and that matters would not resolve themselves for a day or two more at least, he left the area forthwith to visit Cuddesdon and find respite from debates and coming fights, as he had put it. What he found was something very different from respite . . .

Chapter Thirty-Eight

By dusk on the same day that Maple had explored the Slopeside tunnels, the suggestion by Noakes and Weeth that they might be used to mount an attack had been turned into a solid plan of action. A covert route into the Slopeside was established, moles chosen who would brave the Slopeside tunnels, and diversionary thrusts organized in the finest detail. Maple himself solved the problem of communication, utilizing the services of fast-running moles who could cover the ground between different groups in an established time, using moonrise as the starting-point; and the all-important signal for the breakthrough into the main system from the Slopeside itself would be conveyed by the drumming of paws in a given way – a method once used by moles of the Word to intimidate those they were hunting down so that they were panicked into breaking cover.

Ystwelyn was entrusted with leading the surface attack across the Slopeside, whilst to the north, in Buckland Marsh, Commander Maella gathered her forces for the crucial assault she would lead. Stow was given the task of holding reserves at Carswell Copse, ready to attack direct into the system, or to reinforce the assaults down at the Marsh, or up by the Slopeside.

Whilst between them all young fit moles waited in twos, to back each other up, ready to race with the orders for the assaults to begin, or with news after them, as had been preordained.

In all the annals of moledom's wars and battles, few episodes are more dramatic, exciting, and uncertain as that which began with the charge of Ystwelyn's Siabod moles across the Slopeside meadows at moonrise the following night. It is a pity that no scribemole like Snyde was then resident in Buckland to record the sequence of events over the following nights and days, as first one attack and then another savaged the Newborn defences.

As it is we have but fragmentary accounts by survivors on both sides to show how Sapient, directing operations from a chamber deep in the heart of Buckland, though closer to the Slopeside than might have been expected, utilized his own well-trained messengers to keep track of events, and calculate his responses.

There is no doubt that he was well organized, and that his force was so deeply dug in that conventional attacks along the established lines could not have succeeded before too many were killed to continue them. The Newborns' line of communications, their clever use of chambers for reinforcements and respite, their ability to service attacks on all three fronts, and the fanaticism of their warriors, would certainly have defeated their opponents best efforts in the end, though out on open ground advantage might have favoured the followers.

But historians piecing together the evidence from within have now no doubt that by the second night of the attack Sapient's force was just beginning to be over-stretched. On the northern front, above the Marsh, two followers' lives were lost to every one of the Newborns, but the Newborns in that quarter were beginning to tire.

On the Carswell Copse side, Stow's brave moles were an equal match to those within and the fighting was steady, and deadly, with the followers beginning to make ground by the third dawn of the battle. On that flank Sapient could not afford to withdraw one mole, though he was beginning to need more elsewhere; yet even had he had any to add they would not have helped, for the followers had broken through to narrower tunnels where 'more' did not mean 'more effective'. Here it was a matter of one to one, and it was beginning to be plain that the followers were courageous beyond mere bravery, and disciplined in a way the fanatical Newborns never were.

But it was across the Slopeside that the most interesting, and in the early and middle stages of the battle, the most decisive fighting raged, for here the Siabod moles finally came into their own. Used to the surface tactics necessary on their own home ground, where the earth is often too wet and acid to tunnel, they understood the flank and the falaise, the redoubt and the hidden bluff, and though attacking across ground whose features they did not know, their expertise put a pressure on the Newborns they had never experienced before.

More than that, Ystwelyn understood well the Siabodian tactic of the false retreat when, his moles pretending to be yielding, Newborns were lured out of secure positions on to open ground, and attacked where they could less easily defend themselves. In this way the followers were able to make effective inroads into the Newborn position and force them to retreat into their deep tunnels. But this meant, as Ystwelyn well knew, that with moles confined below ground it would be too dangerous to signal that the attack out of the Slopeside tunnels

486

begin. Indeed, so concerned was Ystwelyn by the deadlock that was developing that he sent a messenger into the Slopeside requesting Maple to come out and judge matters for himself.

Maple was tired from the tension of his long and secret confinement in dreadful conditions below ground, but he and Ystwelyn sensed that a difficult decision would have to be made. With dawn light rising across the misty fields, and bodies lying where they had fallen, Maple silently reviewed the situation, moving from position to position, asking questions as he needed to, and then moving on.

Nomole, perhaps not even Ystwelyn, could have helped him then in the choices he had to make, and he knew it to be the moment which all great commanders face, when finally hard decisions must be made, risks taken, orders given, and many lives, and perhaps the future of moledom itself, left to what unfolds.

'Well, mole?' growled Ystwelyn, eyes narrowed with concentration and fatigue.

'We wait. I sent Weeth himself across to Stow earlier today, for Weeth is more reliable than a messenger in discussing the situation with a taciturn mole like old Stow. But news should come soon from Buckland Marsh.'

They waited as a cold sun rose; Ystwelyn urged his force to maintain the pressure, giving not one hair's breadth of ground, yet not regaining any. Maple seldom spoke, knowing that if Weeth on one paw or the messenger on the other, or both indeed, did not appear before long, he must make a decision with incomplete knowledge.

It was mid-morning when he rose from the dug-out in which he hid, and sighed, and looked about.

'He's coming, sir, a messenger mole up from the Marsh . . .'

The news was dire. Maella herself had been killed during the night – 'It was chance, sir, and not a sign of our weakness, but matters are critical now and the followers there cannot hold on long before they must retreat and regroup. Such a loss has hit them hard.'

'But you told them . . .'

'I told them you would wish them to fight to the very end and not give up a mite of ground.'

'Aye, mole, and you told them right.'

The youngster seemed about to collapse, so tired was he, his fur flecked with mud, sweat and blood, his eyes wild with the stress and dismay of all he had witnessed.

'How goes it, sir?'

'You have come back in time to see us win,' said Maple, and he said it loud enough that others heard, and the Siabod moles looked at each other, and nodded, and readied themselves to stay their ground and do what their leaders bid.

'Come on, Weeth! Come on!' Maple muttered to himself. 'For I cannot hold out longer. Yet I need to know . . .'

Weeth arrived just after that, as surreptitiously as ever, evading even Ystwelyn's tired guards and appearing amongst them as if he were on some summer jaunt. But his words were anything but jaunty.

'Not good. Stow reckons he can hold the morning out, but the Newborns seem to have found a second wind – or a third or fourth – and have begun to gain a little ground. He can hold them, but not for long now unless there is a change.'

'A change,' muttered Maple with sudden resolution, 'aye, there'll be a change. Ystwelyn, bring me ten of the freshest warriors you've got.'

'Ten is too many to take out from here, Maple.'

'Ten it must be, and fear not, Ystwelyn, they will see action before the afternoon comes – and so will you. Weeth, wait here with me. You, mole, what's your name?' Here he beckoned over the mole who had just come up from Buckland Marsh.

'Radley, sir, *of* Radley,' he said as ten grim-faced Siabod moles appeared, and though they may have been fresh it was a relative word, for all looked tired, all bloodied, all caked with mud. But all, to a mole, looked as if they would do all that might be asked of them.

'Now listen, Radley of Radley, and listen well, for much may depend on those tired paws of yours, much. You know the safe way back to the Marsh, for you've just come that way.'

'Yes, sir.'

Maple pointed a paw at the pale, struggling sun which by now had risen some way above the wintry horizon, though not yet as high as it would that day.

'Get back down to the Marsh before the sun is at its highest.'

'But, sir—'

'Can you do it, mole?'

'If these Siabod moles can, a mole of Radley can as well!' said the youngster boldly.

Maple nodded approvingly. 'So, lead them there, and take them to the commander in charge and tell him to strike as hard as ever he can by tunnel with his present force as midday comes and the sun reaches its highest point. Tell whatever mole is in command to direct these ten Siabod warriors to the surface entrance or entrances he

488

thinks most vulnerable. At that kind of attack they are supreme. And tell him to have faith, for as I am Maple of Duncton, before the sun has fallen far from its zenith today, so shall the Newborns begin to retreat. Whatever happens, they must continue pushing on, to the very last mole they must push!'

'But how do you know they'll retreat, sir?' whispered Radley, reasonably enough.

Maple put a rough paw to the youngster's shoulder and smiling, said, 'Yours is not to question why, mole, but since you have I'll tell. Because the Newborns *shall* retreat, and we *shall* advance!'

'Yes, sir!' said Radley, faintly. In such a mood Maple seemed a force as inevitable as time itself.

'As for the rest, it is best you don't know – less known, least told to the enemy. Now, can you make it?'

'If I was alone I could, sir, but together with snail-paced Siabodians, well!'

It was well and boldly said, just as the Siabodians liked, and Radley led them off, suffering a buffet or two for his impudence, and winning approving glances too.

'At midday, sir!' were their final words, and they were gone.

Weeth raised his paws in alarm. 'Don't look at me, if you're looking for a mole to make trek back to Stow. For one thing, I'm not shifting from your flank, and for another I'm too tired to go anywhere else – until midday!'

'No need for that: Stow will hold his own, and he'll know to advance when the Newborns begin to falter. Now listen, Ystwelyn; just before midday, and Stone help us if that sun gets more obscure, you retreat—'

'Retreat?'

'Aye, mole, and I *mean* retreat. Do so after putting up a push that looks like your last and best. Affect disunity and disarray. Retreat up towards Harrowdown, and slow enough for the Newborns to catch you by that stream beyond the meadows – or rather to catch you just as you have crossed it.'

'And as we do you'll . . . ?'

'Aye, we'll attack within at your signal that the Newborns *are* emerging, and *only* then. For Sapient must already believe he's winning on two fronts and we shall make him think he's winning on all three, which, for a time he will be.'

'And what if . . . ?' began Ystwelyn.

'There is no "what if"!' said Maple savagely. 'If the Newborns scent

489

victory, which I believe they already do, they will lose discipline. They will!'

'They must,' said Ystwelyn quietly.

'Well,' growled Maple, 'we shall hope they will, for if they do not we shall all be trapped within, and without we shall be divided. But I can sense in my paws that this is the right way, and this the right hour.'

'Then, mole,' said Ystwelyn with a grin, 'that is enough for me!'

'Go to it then, and may the Stone be with us all.'

Maple and Weeth returned immediately to the Slopeside tunnels where a couple of Siabodians were waiting patiently to guide them back to the others, to lead this most covert and most dangerous part of the operation. They knew already what to expect within the Slopeside, having survived two days in silence down there before emerging to debate strategy with Ystwelyn, and they did not relish going back again.

'You've advanced no further than the point we reached before?' asked Maple worriedly.

'No, sir. We did as you asked and just kept our ears open and our paws still, and we went no further.'

'Well, we're going further now, Stone help us all, but with luck we'll not have to wait so long that we get contaminated by whatever filthy disease is down there. Now, lead us on.' And down into the mazy tunnels of the Slopeside they went, to right and left, past dark dens of long-forgotten death, through the still and fetid air of tunnels whose best future would be that they were destroyed for ever.

It seemed to Maple that they took a long time to reach the chamber before the seal-up, where he had earlier ordained that the Slopeside force would wait, and in such diffused light they had no way of knowing how near to midday it was.

'Have you heard anymole above?' he asked.

'Nothing unusual, sir, just the same comings and goings as before.'

'Well, you'll be hearing some more goings than previously,' he said, drawing the force about him and briefing them thoroughly on what had been agreed. 'The only thing we can do until we get Ystwelyn's signal is to clear the way for the break through the seal-up, not a task I willingly delegate to anymole.'

As usual everymole there volunteered for the grim duty, and Maple selected four as randomly as he could.

'Move as few of the bodies as you need for us to get round them

490

with access to the seal-up, and only you four go down initially . . . and you, Noakes, oversee them.'

It was no sooner said than they went off to get on with it, reporting back a little later that the job had not been too bad – and no sign of infestation, nor any odour of nettles, or anything else.

'Just bodies, sir, and old ones. I've seen worse, though Stone knows why anymole would leave them to starve there and why they didn't try—'

'To escape?' Maple shrugged. Fear? Weakness? Despair?

There was a dragging over the surface above them, and cries, and the patter of pawsteps back and forth, and shouts and orders, and a deep voice, perhaps of Ystwelyn himself. The 'retreat' seemed to have begun. Maple deputed two of the moles back to the seal-up to discover what could be heard in the chamber beyond.

Time, slow time, passed. More sounds above. The rush of pawsteps from the chamber beyond. Silence, stealthy and suspicious. Then: *thump! thump!*

'Not enough,' growled Maple, 'there'll be more to the signal than that.'

But he ordered his force to begin to advance in readiness along the tunnel towards the seal-up – out of the chamber, around the bend beyond it, edging past the filthy debris of the roof-fall that had given them such a shock two days before; then on to the seal-up itself, the clearers' work well done. No mess, no smell, no talon worms, just the corpses to one side, and the seal-up rising beyond.

The tension mounted, the sounds beyond faded.

'They're on the surface, sir, more than before . . . wait . . . more coming . . .'

The drag of moles' flanks along the other side of the seal-up, slow and careful, cautious as squirrels.

THUMP! THUMP! THUMP!

The signal had come, midday must be past, elsewhere the attacks must now be well under way and here . . .

'Can't hear a bloody thing from the other side, sir, or hardly anything,' whispered a mole who had made himself chief listener. 'Most of them seem to have surfaced.'

Maple nodded and signalled through the gloom for more to advance, until the tunnel was full of moles, but for a small circle of space around the pile of bodies.

Silence. A nod. Two moles had long since been deputed for the task, because of their powerful paws and excavating skills, along with

491

a third, a smaller friend of theirs well taught in the art of structures and defences, and good at detecting weakness in a wall. It was perhaps the most quiet and delicate moment in a battle that had now continued for six days, and was about to enter its bloodiest and most desperate phase.

The two bigger moles stanced back while the smaller one ran a paw softly over the seal-up, and then listened at different parts of it. He snouted at it, high and low, first to one side and then the other, and finally with supreme gentleness he touched a place in its upper-right-paw part and nodded at the nearest of his two friends, who came forward, talons raised to strike. Then the small mole touched a second place, lower down and on the far side, and nodded at the other to be prepared.

Finally, as quietly as he could, he scraped at an area in the central part of the seal-up where loose soil fell away and revealed a boulder twice the size of a mole's head.

'Strike twice where I've shown you, and that'll weaken the wall. Then go for this stone, get it out, and the whole bleeding lot will come down, so get clear. Then we can go through.'

His instructions quite clear, he pulled away to let the bigger moles do their destructive work.

'Wait until you hear another mole beyond,' whispered Maple, 'for their surprise will cause more panic. And if they're still there when we break through *let them go*, if they've got a mind to flee. Their panic will be worth more to us than their immediate death. And finally . . .'

'Yes, sir?' said one of the Siabod moles.

'Roar! When you get through, that is.'

'Yes, sir!'

'Right, off you go!'

The big moles struck the wall twice each, just as they had been shown, and then they hauled the boulder out of position. For a moment the seal-up held but then, just as had been predicted, with a great roar, amid clouds of dust and grime, it collapsed towards them. A hole appeared through the murk and beyond the chamber stretched, smaller than they had imagined, and lighter than the tunnel they had been in. Stanced there were two moles transfixed and terrified.

One fled; the other, to his credit, made a vain attempt to fight. He was taloned at once, the first bloody death of the many that followed in the next hour. With a roar Maple's force charged into the chamber and struck down the few moles about the place, meeting resistance

492

only for a moment or two from three guardmoles near a portal.

The chamber taken, the Siabod moles did not delay in striking straight up and out on to the surface to attack and scatter the Newborns there into a panic. Their orders had not been to pursue and nor did they. So surprised were the Newborns, convinced perhaps that the system had been overrun from within, that they fled after their fellow guardmoles, spreading panic and confusion as they went.

Upslope, by the brook, Ystwelyn watched the coming attack turn into a mêlée of moles not knowing if they were in pursuit or pursued, and timed his counter-attack perfectly. Rarely has a force in seeming retreat become so suddenly a force assaulting, and of the two or three Newborns who survived that part of the struggle none ever forgot, or was able to recall without a shudder, the sight of those great followers turning back from flight, to charge them down, and kill their colleagues where they stanced in surprise and disorder.

Meanwhile, in the chamber by the seal-up, Maple established his stronghold with ruthless speed and determination. There was only one surface exit, and this was quickly secured, with moles on the surface above already summoning back those who had gone outside. Of the two portals that led further into the system one was plainly more significant than the other. The smaller was stationed with two guards, but it was through the larger, and down the tunnel beyond that an advance party went, killing several moles either sheltering there, confused, or coming to see what was going on.

Maple did not advance further until he was satisfied that the moles who had gone out on the surface were safely back in – and left some by that exit against the possibility that other Newborns might try to retreat into the chamber, not realizing it had been taken over. Only then did he order the advance, steadily and methodically, through the tunnels towards the centre of Buckland, and hopefully to Sapient himself.

It was now that the heaviest and most critical fighting took place, for the Newborns were not defeated yet, but fell back to well-made positions planned long since by Turling himself, against just such an invasion as this or, perhaps, internal mutiny.

Across the system at Carswell Copse, Stow now sensed a weakening in the opposition, subtle yet significant, and began to push his hard-stretched moles to their utmost, to take precisely the advantage that Maple had guessed he would. Nomole knows quite when this great mole received the injuries that proved fatal to him, but most agree that sometime in that critical struggle old Stow, the greatest warrior that the Wolds ever produced, loyal to the Stone and his leader Maple, saw that his tired force was wavering once more.

'On, and on, and on again!' he is said to have cried out, pulling back the waverers and leading a fresher group through. On and on he fought, despite injury to face and flank; on and on, in the name of the Stone, on beyond duty, on beyond courage, for now he knew he must lead his moles and so help others elsewhere, fighting, as he guessed, for their lives.

'On, on!' he cried, weakening, falling, sinking, fading. 'On . . .'

And on past him the Woldian moles went, forcing passage through, driving the Newborns before them, turning them, putting fear and panic into them, defeating them until the tunnel ahead was clearing, and the last of the opposition fleeing or falling, as the western flank of Buckland became the first to yield to the followers' zeal and force.

While to the north, when the sun reached its zenith, the moles who had been under Maella began their indomitable struggle to make their own way through. Mole after mole fell there, yet still they fought on, as the Siabodians took the surface route as directed by Maple, and fought a local fight such as all great battles know.

All but three of Ystwelyn's best died securing the first turn of the tide in the Buckland Marsh tunnels, but then it was those three who led the others on, wild and terrible, wounded yet unstoppable. Where the followers had died before now the Newborns fell, retreating in a haze of blood and fear, turning from a scourge they could hold back no more, fleeing into the dark tunnels of Buckland behind them, with nowhere else to go.

Did Ystwelyn sense the loss of those seven great warriors to the north of him? Did he sense that now, now, *now* was the time when Maple needed him to advance across the Slopeside? Did he know?

For Maple was in sudden retreat, driven back by a resurgence of the Newborn force, not knowing that the surge came not from courage and good leadership, but from retreat elsewhere which forced the Newborn moles back through the centre, back, back towards the Slopeside, and up against *his* force.

For a moment he must have thought his end had come: retreating, battered, his warriors wounded and grim about him as they struggled to resist the torrent of guardmoles that now raised their talons upon them as the Newborns streamed suddenly back down through the surface exit.

Now were those four followers he had placed there needed, fighting and struggling in a tiring, wearying, dreadful talon-to-talon fight to the very end. Newborn after Newborn fell until they tangled and obstructed each other, trying to rush forth and overwhelm the four moles who stanced their ground, shoulder to shoulder, one for all and all of everymole of them.

In the midst, assaulted as it seemed from all sides, Maple must have thought the battle lost when suddenly Newborns tore in at him from the second smaller portal and he had only two followers to hold it, except . . .

'Mole! Here, miscreant, face us!'

And Maple turned, with only Weeth left at his flank, and there, at the broken seal-up into the Slopeside, having gained access by Stone knows what covert way, stanced the brooding malevolent form of a formidable mole.

'Sapient!' roared Maple.

'Yes,' hissed Sapient. His yellow eyes were venomous, he was smeared with the blood of everymole but himself, flanked by his own evil bodyguards, laughing, mad, filled with the lust for power and for blood. Or death.

'Kill him, my moles, and the battle shall be ours,' he cried.

No warrior could come to great Maple's aid as he stanced facing the mole who would be tyrant of the south, and if not that, would take anymole with him into death. Maple knew then that the critical day had become the critical hour, and the critical hour the moment, and the moment was now. He raised his paws, roaring as he had bid the other followers do, and charged Sapient.

What if two huge guardmoles stanced in his way? They reeled back before the speed and power of his blows as all the rage and tension of the long campaign found its expression in them.

What if from somewhere else another Newborn broke through and charged Maple's flank? Weeth felled him, and did not dally over killing him, nor from raising his bloody talons once more and rushing to his master's flank.

What if there were three more guardmoles between Maple and now fearful Sapient, his eyes widening, his retreat back through the seal-up beginning, and taking him all unknowing not into clear space, but straight into that pile of rotted death? Maple cared not, his bloody intent now only to kill the mole who led the Buckland brood, and whose death would signal the liberation of all the south!

Maple raised his paws, the world still about him, his wounds of no consequence, and first one guardmole and then another fell before his brutal blows. And the third, the foulest and the cruellest of Sapient's guards? What of him?

He knew fear at last, he saw death, and he turned and tried to flee and Maple felled him from behind and wounded him, and he crawled away into the darkness of the Slopeside to die alone.

It was the crux, the moment when all turned. Behind him, inspired by his example, Maple's forces began to make ground once more, ever more swiftly. All fell before them, away into the foul recesses of Buckland, away to the defeat of the Newborns, and the victory of the followers.

While from the surface, Ystwelyn himself was the first to break through the last faltering lines and rush down into the chamber where Maple fought, scattering the last of the Newborns, in time to see Maple raise his paws over the unrepentant form of Sapient, who had slipped into the inert pile of bones and skin and dried-up flesh, from which he struggled to stance upright as Maple's paws bore down upon him.

'No, mole, let *him* live!'

But Maple saw only evil before him, and felt the dread and dangerous power of revenge in his own paws.

'No, sir, leave him,' cried out Weeth, struggling to bring Maple to his senses and being hurled backwards for his pains. It was better that Sapient survived.

'Noooo!'

Perhaps it was Weeth's voice that let out that final cry.

Or Ystwelyn's, too late to stop Maple doing what he should not do.

Or Sapient's own voice, as the talons of revenge and righteousness drove down upon him, into his face and eyes, blinding him and crushing him back down, down into that inert yet not quite lifeless matter they earlier sought so hard to avoid and that was now his final resting-place.

Down into decay and the odour, pungent as death, of nettles amidst the blood. Aye, the fresh scent of nettles.

'Noooo!' And it was Maple's voice at last, staring at the bloodied, torn fur above his right paw where Sapient had tried to fend off his killing blow and where now, foul, wriggling, all opaque white, shiny and with stinging, questing jaws set in pointed, darting heads, talon worms attacked.

'No . . .' whispered Weeth, seeking to brush the vile things out and off, and watching aghast. As he pulled Maple back, Sapient's dead, blood-red head came up, opened its dead mouth, and was alive with the dangerous creatures. While there, in Maple's wound, not deep but perhaps fatal now, the shiny tails of several talon worms wriggled and were gone as they seared their way into his living flesh. They had found a prey in which to incubate; they had found a new and better home.

''Tis nothing,' whispered Maple later, the victory complete. 'I . . . feel . . . nothing.'

Nothing but occasional light, stinging pains inside, and a mortal fear of worms that eat so slowly deep within, like shame, or guilt, or the sense of moral worthlessness.

'I should not have . . . I should not have killed him, Weeth,' he whispered late that night.

'Master, nomole blames you. Sapient deserved to die.'

'But he should have been judged,' said Maple. 'But I killed him myself, and none but me. By the Stone am I judged for killing in revenge. The worms live in me now, inside me, Weeth. I should have let him live and had him publicly arraigned. I should . . !'

Sounds of celebration came into the chamber where they stanced, Ystwelyn silent, sad, grief-stricken for the comrades he had lost.

Yet Weeth was right: it *was* a famous victory. Few Newborns survived, not because, as Maple had feared, they were murdered in cold blood by a vengeful force, but because, more terribly perhaps, in their panic they had fled from west and north, from east and south, into Buckland's communal chamber, fled and panicked, pushed and crushed, and there, too terrible to contemplate, occurred the largest massing of them.

Crushed, suffocated, maddened by panic, the southern Newborn army died, killing itself in its own tunnels in a last frenzy of fear. Yet what mole should care? Once the fighting was finished, and moles investigated, they found horrors beyond imagining inside the Newborn cells – moles nearly starved to death; moles blinded; moles forced to kill and cannibalize their fellow captives to live.

Yet such Newborn prisoners, living and sane, as were taken at Buckland, the wounded Maple ordered be set free, and they wandered off across those bloody fields, and were lost forever to moledom's memory. Lost and known no more.

Whilst on those fields, many followers lay dead and were never identified. Whilst others were dead, and known. Spurling, who would have been Fieldfare's mate, died uttering her beloved name. And brave Furrow, he died, defending Myrtle who lived, proud to tell the tale. And two senior commanders, Whindrell and Runnel, the latter the lifelong friend of Stow, they bled their lives away in the fields of victory.

Aye, and brave Noakes, younger than most, yet a mole who had given a lifetime of bravery and service to the followers' cause. Somewhere in the tunnels he was lost, and fought a final battle on his own, against what odds nomole can know, and died unknown and never found.

Two days passed, and the victors barely moved, but to wander those red fields and search the dykes, to find what friends they could, or listen to the grim, grey wind, and wish they heard more than silence on its breath. They heard no voices that they knew; nor any laughter from friends who would never laugh, or cry, again.

Just the desolation.

They heard the last plaints of lapwings, and the croak of rook and crow; they knew only loss, and wondered why victory caused such pain.

This, they blankly knew, was the Battle of Buckland.

These, they saw, were the rotten fruits of victory.

Those were the days and the hours that Weeth, and Maple, and Ystwelyn and many more, swore nomole must ever glorify, nor praise, nor ever let moledom forget.

Until, on the third day, Maple, his wound sore but healing, the stinging internal pains dying into a new and deeper pain, the guilt of what he had done invisible to all but himself, and Weeth, and Ystwelyn: great Maple, destroyer Maple, triumphant Maple, led them away.

But as he looked back one final time to the fields where the Newborns had been crushed and vanquished, and where now rooks flew and darted down to feed on the dead, Maple said, 'In what we did in Buckland there is no sound of Silence. There is no Light. There will be no Book of Silence found in this war that we fought.'

Then Maple led a silent army of moles away from Buckland, and across the vales towards the south-east, not to seek victory, but to ask forgiveness at the Duncton Stone.

Chapter Thirty-Nine

Hibbott was glad to leave the frenetic atmosphere around the cross-under by Duncton Wood, and head instead for Cuddesdon. Naturally he knew of its venerable past, and how a religious community had been established there a century before.

No doubt, too, he had heard from other travellers that the place was of little account to the Newborns, and it was therefore likely to be a safe, as well as an interesting, sanctuary for a short time. Perhaps, in his innocence, Hibbott believed that he might return to the cross-under after a few days and find, miraculously, entry no longer obstructed by guardmoles.

However it was, off he went. He seems to have made good time for a middle-aged mole, reaching Cuddesdon somewhat before dusk and clambering up its slopes quite openly, so that if anymole was about he might be easily seen.

As it happened a mole was very much about, and that was Purvey, the sole surviving brother of the massacre first reported by Chater a long time before, and the same who had welcomed Hamble on his arrival from Caradoc, before he ventured on into Duncton Wood.

Hibbott introduced himself and explained that he had come simply to see a system that had in its time been a famous centre for study and contemplation, and any relics and texts that might be there, adding, '. . . or old tunnels, and chambers and suchlike, which a pilgrim like me is always curious to see.'

'Old tunnels? Old chambers?' said Purvey dismissively. 'There are a few, I suppose, but hardly worth mentioning. The library chamber is the only thing worth preserving, though even that needs improvement. I had rather thought you had come to see our new tunnels, and new chambers.'

'I was not aware . . .' began Hibbott, eyeing Purvey's weedy stature and very much doubting whether such a mole could even think of creating anything new at all. He looked about the bleak slopes of Cuddesdon and wondered if solitude and isolation had affected the mole's mind, and given him delusions of grandeur.

'But I'm always happy to see anything new, if you want to show me that is,' he said.

Purvey was only too eager to show him, then and there, before Hibbott even had time to get the grit and grime out of his talons and find some food. Which Hibbott, gentle mole that he was, yielded to without complaint.

Delusion it certainly seemed to be, for he was led over a rutted, ruined surface, and past caved-in tunnels and chambers which spoke of the former glories of Cuddesdon of which he had heard, but promised nothing new at all.

'Not here, not here, mole,' said Purvey, hurrying him past part of a tunnel and a glimpse of a subterranean arch which he would have liked to explore further, 'there's nothing worth seeing down there. No, it's all this way, on the south side, here.'

They mounted a slight slope, turned a bend amongst some bedraggled undergrowth, and there came into view a sloping area of ground across which, to Hibbott's astonishment, spread a whole host of recently delved mounds of soil and rock particles. It looked as if an army of moles had been at work.

'This way,' said Purvey, beaming with proprietorial pride.

Hibbott was led underground by way of a subtle slipway, from whose depths he heard the softest and most pleasant of wind-sound, like the running of a distant brook in summer. The lighting was varied and surprising, taking him from light of day into near-darkness and then, almost before he knew it, round a corner into light again to a wide, arched tunnel, of a style and solidity he had never seen before.

'We thought this would be the entrance into the first of the chambers,' said Purvey, hurrying busily forward, talking almost like a mole with a new mate in the process of creating a new burrow ahead of a spring birthing, and not a religious brother whom Hibbott had taken to be celibate.

When Hibbott went through the portal at the far end of the tunnel he found himself in a deeply delved chamber, full of light and shade, whose subtle lines and curves took a mole's eye on and on and then around, and all the way back again. The wind-sound was still gentle, balanced, and whispered of tunnels and chambers beyond, one way and another, and peacefulness. It all made Hibbott want to stance down and contemplate.

'It is remarkable,' said Hibbott stopping, and looking about appreciatively. 'When did you . . . ?'

'Me? I do nothing! I provide them with food and a place to rest, and they delve. Don't *talk* much, mind, which is a shame, even when they're not delving.'

'What moles are they?' asked Hibbott, setting forth again through the chamber to reach the other end, for he fancied he heard the sound of moles that way.

'Oh, you mustn't disturb them, whatever you do. He shouts and roars if you do . . .'

'He's not . . .' began Hibbott, suddenly thinking whatmole it might be that shouted and roared. Not that he had at *him* on the one occasion they met.

'Rooster, that's the one.'

'And his assistant, Frogbit?' said Hibbott with delight.

'You know them!' exclaimed Purvey. 'Then you're a delver yourself?'

Hibbott explained that he was not, and that he was only too happy to pause awhile until the delving was finished. He knew enough about such things not to wish to disturb work in progress.

But he did not have to wait long, for dusk had already begun to fall; the sounds beyond became sporadic, and eventually pawsteps approached and Frogbit appeared, looking dusty and dishevelled.

'Oh,' he said, seeing Hibbott and not seeming to recognize him.

Hibbott reminded him who he was, and how they had met in the Wolds; Frogbit, mute and wide-eyed, stared at him and when he had quite finished, and after a silence, said, 'I know. I remember. He'll be pleased. Said you went ahead of him, now we've caught you up.'

'Er, yes,' said Hibbott, unsure what all this meant.

'No good going to him. Delving's not gone well for days past. Reached a natural end, *I* say. But what am I? Only his assistant!'

'An end!' exclaimed Purvey in alarm. 'But you've only just begun. I mean the grand scheme, the Great Chamber, the—'

'Beginning's the most difficult bit,' said Frogbit matter-of-factly. 'Delvings grow by themselves after that. Others do them. You'll see, I expect. Hibbott's coming's the end for now, I reckon. That's what I think. Could be wrong. Often am with Rooster, but getting better. Know what I mean?' He grinned briefly and said, 'He's coming now. No he's not, he's stopped. Thinking he is, about the northern portal. Difficult, bit of a bodge, that is.'

Whether Rooster had been coming Hibbott did not know, since he did not appear.

Purvey leaned towards Hibbott and whispered, 'He's usually right.

501

'Queer fellows, delvers. Ears like snouts: hear things you and I can't.'

They all fell into a pleasant silence, so relaxing that as the light faded in the chamber Hibbott's eyes began to droop and sleep was beginning to come over him.

Then Rooster appeared, quite suddenly, as if he had been lurking just out of sight and had decided to surprise them all by rushing in. One moment he was not there and the next the chamber seemed full of him.

'Hibbott the pilgrim mole we talked to at Bourton's here,' said Frogbit.

'Hibbott,' said Rooster coming near and peering hard at him. 'Why? Privet?'

Hibbott told him of Privet's coming to Duncton, and, as best he could, the situation around and about Duncton: pilgrims massing, Thorne coming from the north, rumours of Maple and the followers fighting the Newborns in the south, and Quail safely beyond the well-defended cross-under through which Privet had now gone.

'Privet's near end of her beginning, like us here and now, and I should be there,' said Rooster at the end of it all, most mysteriously. 'You've come to get me.'

'Have I?' wondered Hibbott.

Rooster nodded, scratching his face from which the reddish dust of soil came up in clouds and made Purvey sneeze.

Frogbit blinked in surprise and said, 'Bless you.'

'Did she have the Book?' asked Purvey, dabbing at his snout. 'I mean . . .'

'She did not seem to,' said Hibbott.

'No,' said Rooster, 'no, no. Not outside Duncton. Inside. That's what Duncton *is*.'

Hibbott looked uncomprehendingly at Rooster, who frowned as ferociously as ever, though his eyes were warmer and his stance easier than before.

'You tend, if I may say so, to talk oddly,' said Hibbott. 'What do you mean by "Duncton *is*"?'

Rooster ignored this altogether and grumbled to himself instead, finally declaring that he was hungry, at which Purvey bustled off and found some worms.

'Duncton,' said Rooster finally, 'is where we must all go. Is where the Book of Silence must be, which we are, all of us, even . . .'

Rooster cast around for somemole or other who might be generally

502

considered not to be part of 'all of us', or only a very peripheral part, and Frogbit offered up a name.

'Snyde?' he said.

'No,' said Rooster, 'Snyde's important. Can't have Silence without him.'

'Quail?' tried Purvey.

Rooster shook his head and said, 'Like Snyde. Would be nothing, all of us, without him.'

'Then, how about me?' said Hibbott, perfectly happy to be peripheral.

Rooster laughed generously and patted Hibbott on the back with his great right paw, so that Hibbott was nearly flattened on the ground and Frogbit had to come hurrying and help him up and dust him down.'

'No!' said Rooster. 'Like Rowan's descendant.'

'Who's he?' asked Hibbott.

'Long time ago, was Rowan,' said Rooster. 'Spindle and Mayweed knew him in old days, when modern times began, when Book of Silence began to be again. Before I was born. Rowan lived in the Wen.'

Light dawned on Purvey's face and he said, 'My, you have a good memory, Rooster, sir, not many would remember him. He was *very* insignificant.'

'Nomole is insignificant. That's what I meant, not even Rowan's descendant.'

'But who is he?' asked Hibbott.

Rooster shrugged and Frogbit said, 'Who knows? Rooster doesn't know. I don't. You don't. Purvey mole doesn't. Therefore, peripheral. But important all the same, like the delving at the edge is important to the part in the middle.'

Rooster nodded approvingly and said, 'Frogbit's learning. One day Frogbit will have learnt. One day Frogbit will be a delver true, through and through, from snout to talon, from head to heart. That day gets nearer and will suddenly be.'

Frogbit was so surprised and embarrassed by this unexpected eulogy that his snout blushed bright red, and he tried to hide it between his paws.

'So, Purvey mole, we must go,' said Rooster not unkindly. 'Must go to Duncton now that Privet's come to ground. Nomole is alone, though all must travel alone. Now Privet needs all our help.'

'But what about the delving still to be done, the Great Chamber, the southern tunnels, the lower extension, the . . . the . . .' Purvey's voice faded as his dreams seemed to crumble before his eyes.

'Tell him, Frogbit.'

'Did, Master. Said. Others will come, now beginning's been made. Cuddesdon is on the way to fame!'

Rooster laughed. 'Master of the Delve will come again, Purvey,' he said gently, 'so you stay here. You help best here. Be ready and Master will come as I came.'

'But you are the Master of the Delve,' whispered Purvey, thoroughly miserable.

'Another will be. Another is in the making. We made tunnels and chambers new, ready for life to come: another Master will bring life and Rooster and Privet will be made happy.'

Rooster stayed where he was for some hours more, not because he did not want to leave, but because, as Hibbott reported, he sensed that Purvey needed to talk a little, and express his sense of disappointment and loss. More even than that, he sensed that he needed to show Frogbit that being Master of the Delve was more than delving, it was being with those a delver delves for, too.

But finally, deep in the night, with Purvey consoled, Rooster said, 'Must go now, must go to Duncton Wood. All things coming, all moledom waiting, and soon now the Book of Silence will begin. Like a great delving it is, like Cuddesdon, like the Ancient System of Duncton, like Whern, like Hilbert's Top, like Hobsley Coppice . . . one mole's paws make a delving begin, many make it grow, one must complete it. For the Book of Silence Privet is that one, and we must help her.'

Purvey sniffed and snivelled in the darkness but nodded his head.

'I'll come and see you off, like I've seen other moles. If you see Hamble, tell him it would give me much pleasure if he came this way again. Tell him I enjoyed his company and missed him when he left. As I shall miss you. Will you tell him that?'

'Will,' said Rooster and with a last deep chuckle he led Hibbott and Frogbit out of Cuddesdon, and back towards Duncton Wood.

But by now they were not the only moles heading in that direction: all of moledom seemed to be doing so. The word had already spread abroad that Privet had finally been seen at Duncton itself, and though most had merely heard what Hibbott himself had witnessed, that she had delivered herself into the paws of Quail, this did not deter any-mole at all. Just the opposite in fact, for now it was not only pilgrims that were apaw, but anymole with half a spark of life and faith in him, who sensed that now great things were happening, and he should be party to them.

For some it was simple curiosity; for others an opportunity to direct their anger against the Newborns, whose evident growing weakness in those parts gave them courage to come forward now. For many more, however, it was more than that; it was the feeling that a time had come, a time of history, which might have to do with the Book of Silence, or might not. But whatever it was, it was a time when a mole who professed faith in the Stone must stance up and be counted.

Not that all the many travellers Rooster and the others met were followers. Many were Newborns, though these were less willing to profess their particular brand of faith, and perhaps few of them were brothers in the strict sense of the word, but rather moles who had come under the influence of the Newborns and, for now at least, adhered to their belief.

The nearer they came to Duncton, the busier were the routeways. There was a strange mood abroad, part festive, part concerned, part belligerent, part awed. Mole looked at mole suspiciously, or with a welcome, depending what they looked like and who they said they were.

Nomole yet recognized Rooster at all, though he remained what he always had been: the most striking of moles in any company – larger than most, wild of fur and eye, huge and unbalanced of paw, charismatic. Some pilgrims seemed to think he was an idiot mole, for more than one whispered sympathetically to Hibbott, who looked like a pilgrim if ever a mole did, 'Going to be healed, is he? Hoping she might lay paws on him and make him whole?'

'I certainly am hoping!' Hibbott heartily rejoined, once he realized that Rooster did not mind their mistake at all.

'Am fool at heart. Have been always,' he said cheerfully. 'Masters of the Delve must be to delve at all. Can't delve a true line if you worry about beginning, and worry about end. Got to be free with your talons in the middle. See?'

'Er, yes,' said Hibbott, eyeing Rooster's paws warily, for at such moments, even though he spoke in a low voice and was doing his best not to attract attention, he was inclined to let his passions get the better of him and wave his paws about, always frustrated that his words could not convey all he wanted to say. In addition, whenever he spoke of delving, he was inclined to make delving motions in the air, which always seemed to Hibbott very wild indeed. Hibbott had no wish to be flattened again.

Strangely, Rooster did not hurry, and nor did he seem overly concerned with any particular plan to help Privet. He was going to her now and that was enough.

'Pleased, he is,' said Frogbit when they stopped to eat some food – food which had been hard to find along the path since the many who had gone before had found the obvious worms, and driven the rest away. 'Pleased and happy. So am I.'

'What's he going to *do* when he gets to Duncton?'

'What do you do?' asked Frogbit unexpectedly.

'Me? I wander where my heart takes me and as the spirit moves me,' said Hibbott, a little dreamily.

'That's what he'll do,' said Frogbit.

'Talking too much,' growled Rooster, his brow furrowing and his eyes narrowing. 'That's what you are.'

'Sorry,' said Frogbit meekly.

'Don't no more,' said Rooster.

Frogbit did not.

Not having hurried themselves, it was getting towards midday when they came over the last rise before Duncton Wood itself, and for the first time the festive mood shifted towards something more sombre. It was not hard to see why, for groups of very solid-looking moles were posted some way off the path, watching the crowds intently.

'Uh, oh!' muttered Frogbit: 'Newborn guardmoles.'

Others had clearly come to the same conclusion, for the chatter had ceased, and moles were either looking in every direction but the guardmoles, or *only* in their direction, and belligerently.

'Keep your snout low and mind clean,' said Rooster, cuffing Frogbit, who was staring at the guardmoles a little too pointedly. 'Not looking for *them*,' he added grumpily.

Hibbott wondered what they *were* looking for, and might even have asked Rooster had not two of the guardmoles detached themselves from some others and come heading downslope straight towards them.

If Rooster saw them he did not say, but with his head thrust forward, his eyes on the ground, and his shoulders hunched most formidably, he set off at a fast pace down towards the largest group of moles he could see. Frogbit and Hibbott had almost to jog to keep up with him, and the two guardmoles, who were coming at a tangent, began to lose ground; throwing dignity aside, they began to run to catch up, shouting as they came.

506

'Hey, you there!'

'*You*, mole!'

The crowd of moles towards which Rooster hurried them was spread across a terrace of grass on the near side of the vale up whose far side the pasture ground rose to Duncton's High Wood. Along the vale's bottom, and someway below and beyond these moles, the roaring owl way that cut off Duncton Wood so effectively ran from north to south.

Because they were hurrying, and the Newborn guardmoles were catching them up, they had not time or inclination to take in much of the scene, or what was happening in it, but it was clear that the crowd was a restless one, for it was milling about and full of excited chatter, and moles seemed to be craning to see things below them, first on the right flank, and then on the left.

Even in the short time since Hibbott had been there the numbers had increased, but they had fallen back from the cross-under, which lay directly in the vale below.

'Yes, you mole,' said one of the guardmoles finally reaching Rooster as he mingled with the crowd. The guardmole's voice was noticeably less commanding than it had been, and he seemed aware that other moles were watching him, and that they were none too friendly and that he and his companion were out-numbered.

'I've seen you before, Brother,' he said, quite softly now, as if he wished to attract as little attention to himself and his burly colleagues as possible.

Rooster turned slowly and stared at him, and if moles stared even more curiously it was, in truth, less because of the Newborns, than because of Rooster himself. He towered over most of them, and though he answered quietly his voice had a rough resonance and depth that caught others' attention.

'Have seen you,' said Rooster, 'seen you many times.'

'Why, by the Stone, it *is* him,' said the second guardmole to the first, his voice quiet but excited.

Surprisingly, Rooster smiled and went closer and the moles about them relaxed and seemed to lose interest, as if they saw, or thought they did, not an arrest of the kind they had seen so many times before, but merely a meeting of old acquaintances.

'Aye,' said Rooster, 'is him. But don't say it. Don't let others hear my name. Better not.'

'By the Stone!' muttered the first of the guardmoles, peering into Rooster's eyes and then down at his paws. 'It really is. Saw you at

507

Caradoc, mate. Then at Wildenhope. Saw you *drown*. How did you get away with it?'

'Did drown. Lived again. Newborn!' Rooster laughed suddenly, and rather too loudly, at his own joke, and for a moment others looked around at the group again curiously. Then whatever was happening in the vale below took up their attention once more.

'What do you want?' Hibbott ventured.

The guardmole stared at Hibbott vacantly, and then turned his attention back to Rooster.

'You can run but you can't hide,' he said, 'because I'm going to keep an eye on you.'

'Not difficult,' said Frogbit brightly, 'he's very big.'

'Go and inform somemole that our old friend the Master of the Delve has deigned to put in an appearance, will you?' said the guardmole calmly to his friend; and he was off just as fast as he could go.

So now they were four, and an odd lot (as Hibbott was later to put it) they were. His account is not the only one, nor even the best known, of what happened in the following hour or so, but it is the most straightforward, and possibly the most accurate. He was, after all, right there, and his view was more objective and less coloured by the emotions and stresses of the day, than most.

'Surprising as it may seem,' he scribes in his *Pilgrimage*, 'I did not feel worried by this latest turn of events. There was such a strange inevitability about what happened that day that a mole was wise not to think beyond the present moment. I was therefore rather less concerned than I might otherwise have been about what moles were now to be informed of Rooster's presence, and what they might do.

'In any case, such events were unfolding on the ground below us before the cross-under that I doubt if anymole in that crowd, except the guardmole who had said that Rooster could not hide, was interested in much else.

'By dint of talking to those about us, and from what we could see for ourselves, it soon became clear what was apaw, and of all the many strange and exciting sights I had been witness to on my long journey from Ashbourne Chase, this was to be almost the strangest, and almost the most exciting. I say "almost" advisedly, for there was one more to come, of which I shall scribe in due course.

'For now, and in the presence of Rooster on my right flank and Frogbit on my left, with the guardmole clinging on to us like black ivy just behind, we watched as the formidable Newborn army of

508

Thorne gathered in force across the vale, and up the slopes to our right . . .'

What Hibbott was witnessing, along with scores of other moles who had wisely backed away from the likely place of conflict, yet wished to make their presence felt, was the resolution, one way or another, of the terrible conflict between Newborn and follower.

Thorne's army had arrived at the cross-under to Duncton Wood, and its relative quiet, its order, its large number, indicated that it was a formidable and disciplined force. Yet it had been stopped in its tracks by the apparent impossibility of breaching the cross-under by force, for now it was filled, as were the slopes on the Duncton side of it, by the serried ranks of Quail's moles, led by Squilver.

They were considerably outnumbered, but as anymole knows, it is easy for a few moles to hold a narrow defile against an enemy many times its size. On open ground Quail's remaining supporters would have been overwhelmed in moments, and forced to flee before so great a number. Here, Squilver's moles needed only to hold their ground and nomole could get through.

Nor could an easy assault be made by way of a route over the roaring owl way. Apart from the dangers implicit in such a crossing Squilver had so disposed some of his force to make such an attempt likely to be dangerous and costly. An advance guard had long since positioned themselves along the top of the embankment up which attacking moles would need to climb, and if a defile is easily defended by a minimum of moles, so too is the top of a steep and tiring climb.

In short, it was plain to even the most non-military of moles that Squilver had disposed his limited force well, to cause maximum delay and loss to Thorne's. As a result, nomole was moving on either side, except a few here and there whose task seemed to be to keep watch on one flank or another in case an assault was tried to break the deadlock.

These messengers, who were seen hurrying about, were therefore the main point of interest to the watchers from the bluff, and what they might or might not be conveying in the way of information was the subject of much of the chatter and discussion among them. Much, but not all, for as Hibbott and the others rapidly discovered, there were certain persistent rumours abroad as well, and these added greatly to the mounting tension of the day, and the sense that though nothing was happening now something very soon would. One of these concerned Quail, and the notion that he would be making an appearance later that day.

509

This idea, so prevalent and simple that it was taken as certain truth, was said to have originated from one of the guardmoles at the cross-under, and was the cause of periodic flurries of interest and heightened expectation whenever a mole appeared on the stretch of pasture below the High Wood visible to the watchers. Not that much could be seen at all, but in crowds of that kind, intermingled rumour and fact travel with the speed of wind across the face of woodland in full leaf, beginning noisily at one end and traversing to the other in no time at all.

The second of these rumours was that Maple was coming up from the south with an army of followers. Allmole appeared to know long before Hibbott, Rooster and Frogbit arrived that Avebury had fallen and, more recently, Brother Commander Sapient had suffered a crushing defeat at Buckland. The knowledge of this was what appeared to have kept Thorne and his force where they were, for to engage seriously with Squilver and become weakened would have provided Maple with the perfect opportunity to attack Thorne.

Such, at least, was the consensus amongst the moles into whose company Rooster had so carefully led them, and amongst whom they now appeared to be but three more ordinary watchers awaiting the outcome of events that were surely far beyond their capacity to influence in any way.

To add to the day's strange excitement and foreboding, moles seemed to keep arriving from a variety of directions, not in great numbers, but steadily, in ones or twos. Those arriving from the south were directed upslope by the guardmoles lower down, came slogging up to join the others, and were immediately quizzed by the crowd to find out if they had anything to add to what moles already thought they knew.

Usually with such arrivals the interest was brief, and the disappointment great, for they had nothing much to say at all, being more interested in asking questions than in answering them. The day was a mild one, the sky milky blue in parts, and with high pale mauve clouds in others.

Just after midday a mole came upvale from the south and headed straight for the cross-under. He appeared to be Newborn, and part of Squilver's force, for after a brief inquisition he gained access and was lost from sight. But not long after that moles noticed that the force along the roaring owl way was strengthened and some guardmole watchers posted further along the way from where, it seemed, they had a vantage to see *southwards*.

Soon after that a group of bedraggled moles appeared from the south, pilgrims all, and these were directed, as the others had been, upslope away from the cross-under, but only after long talks with the guardmoles lower down, and indeed with some of Thorne's moles.

A few intrepid moles hurried down to meet them and within moments, as it seemed, back upslope came news, simple and exciting, and enough to set the whole crowd abuzz: 'Maple is coming, and with him the followers . . .'

This kept moles chattering for a little while longer before another expectant hush, deeper than any previously, fell upon the crowd. Even Rooster, who had stanced down and dozed off for a while, stanced up once more and peered about, restless, his paws fretting.

'We could go nearer,' said Frogbit, hopefully.

'We could,' said Rooster, not moving a muscle.

'We *could've*,' muttered Frogbit a good bit later, a shade grumpily.

The day grew ominously dark, as if a giant mole had put his paw between the sun and the earth below. Some of the roaring owls' gazes came on, white-yellow as they approached from north or south, then red as they sped by and retreated once more. There was a further flurry of action by Squilver's moles along the top of the roaring owl embankment and a few were moved from their position overlooking Thorne's force above the cross-under to watch the other way, and southwards, as if they saw moles coming.

The crowd, sensing this, surged downslope, looking to the left flank to catch sight of whatever it was.

'Maple's coming!'

'It's him! It's *him*!'

As the crowd moved downslope Rooster reached out a paw to prevent Frogbit moving with it, yet turned to Hibbott, nodded his great head and said, 'You go now. Go and see.'

'I did not want to leave him, or Frogbit,' Hibbott was to scribe later, 'but though there was no command in his voice to go, yet there seemed a plea which I must obey. I sensed he wished now to be alone, and that he was ordinary mole no more, but Master of the Delve. I hesitated, the crowd surged down and round us, and suddenly I was moving with them, straining to see over them and through them and beyond them, through the dim light that seemed to have overtaken all of us – and which overtakes something of my memory now.

'Then I saw them, or it, for it was a single entity, small at first, and unformed, then a little bigger and taking shape, and then, suddenly, like a roll of thunder that begins in the far distance and comes rapidly towards a mole and quite overwhelms him, it was there, there below us, potent and powerful, unforgettable.'

Hibbott was right; what came, came slowly. He was right too that it grew bigger, and bigger still, and was finally huge before them all, spreading up from the southern end of the vale below.

'The followers have come! The followers . . !'

Maple was leading with several others alongflank him, marching slowly but steadily, appearing above a near horizon, the perspective strange at first as he headed the line of moles that was the first contingent of his army.

Slowly, their black heads and pale snouts bobbing or swaying back and forth, they made trek as moles who have marched for a long time make trek: steadily, rhythmically, indomitably.

'Maple! Ma-ple! MA-PLE! MAPLE!'

The chant of his name came up from the vale, perhaps from his own forces at first, and then it overtook him like flames across dry moorland, leaping over water to burn yet more fiercely on the other side.

'MAPLE!' the crowd roared as he came on relentlessly, and the moles with him pressed behind, and more behind them, and more and more and *more* behind even them.

'Maple!' they cried, and even the gentle voice of Hibbott was joined to theirs.

Then, as he crowd surged on down, faster, dangerous, unstoppable, Hibbott sought desperately to turn back, to move against their tide, to reach back upslope and be with Rooster again, where he was, where . . .

'Rooster, mole!' cried Hibbott, pushed and shoved, turned and forced, hurried and harried and taken, 'Rooster!'

And Hibbott had time to see, before he was swallowed up into the crowd that surged down to join the warriors and pilgrims and ordinary moles that were Maple's great army now . . . had time to see Rooster: dark and brooding on the slope, and alone now, but for Frogbit, and the dark forms of several Newborn moles, who had come down from above to surround him, and take him to themselves once more.

'Rooster of the Charnel Clough, in the name of the Stone . . .'

At the sound of the deep, authoritative voice that spoke his name, Rooster turned at last from the extraordinary scene in the vale below, where Newborn and follower armies came snout to snout to confront each other before the cross-under into Duncton Wood, to face the mole who spoke.

'*You*,' growled Rooster, his paw reaching out to Frogbit to reassure him, and indicate that he must be still, and say nothing now. Nothing at all.

The mole was dark, his eyes darker still, his form smaller than Rooster's yet still formidable, his paws impressive.

'Yes, it is I,' said Chervil.

'Didn't know,' said Rooster, 'didn't understand at Wildenhope. Whillan was my son.'

His eyes moved from Chervil to the moles on either flank – his bodyguards Feldspar, and Feldspar's sons Fallow and Tarn; and another mole, older, wiser, sadder than the others. Frogbit stared at all of them and had never felt so small. Yet he could feel from Rooster's gentle touch that there was nothing to fear, nothing at all. These moles, whoever they were, were friends.

'Go to *him*, mole,' said Rooster gently, pushing Frogbit up towards the old greyer mole.

Frogbit scampered upslope and said to the mole who put out a peaceful paw to welcome him, 'What's your name?'

'Brother Rolt,' smiled Rolt. 'I'm a friend of Privet. What's yours?'

'Frogbit.'

'Delver Frogbit,' corrected Rooster, and a look of joy and pride came to Frogbit's face.

Then Chervil went down to where Frogbit had stanced and said, 'Rooster of Charnel Clough, in the name of the Stone, and for the sake of Privet of Duncton Wood, I ask for your help.'

'Whillan . . .' whispered Rooster, troubled.

'It was the only way,' said Chervil, his voice a shade softer. Then glancing at Feldspar and his two sons, who had been party to what had happened to Whillan at Wildenhope, he said, 'It was the only recourse we had. *You* lived . . .'

'Was *cold* in the waters of the river,' said Rooster with the slightest of grins. Then after a pause, he said, 'Have entrusted Whillan to the Stone, as you did. But want him back. Miss him.'

'Yes,' said Chervil non-committally.

'Now,' said Rooster coming closer still. 'What help? What shall Frogbit and I do? Delvers only do what others ask.'

Frogbit looked even more joyful at this, as if his promotion to the status of delver was now not only confirmed, but about to be affirmed as well.

'We don't know what you can do, or anymole,' said Chervil. 'Look . . .'

Chervil put a paw to Rooster's shaggy shoulder and turned him to look downslope.

The only movement across the vale below, and that somewhat above it, was that of the roaring owls passing back and forth along their way – for the armies of followers and Newborn were more than stationary as they faced each other and contemplated what to do: they were deadly still, but that there was something dangerous and imminent of movement and violence about their stance.

Then, as Rooster and Chervil stared down as one, the moles below seemed to begin a curious swaying, almost imperceptible from above, which was accompanied by an ugly ripping sound, which was of different conflicting chants, mocking shouts and jeering, the sound not of armies but of mobs.

'We need your help I think, Rooster, and we need it now,' said Chervil urgently, his grasp on Rooster tightening. 'I cannot speak for Maple, but Thorne desires no conflict and yet cannot give way – his moles would not let him. And judging from the sounds of Maple's force they may feel the same.'

'Am delver,' muttered Rooster, 'am not this, not there, nowhere but here where paws—'

'Mole, we need your help now, we . . .' began Chervil again, his voice rising just a little, his stance more powerful.

There was movement behind him; Frogbit, breaking free of Rolt, came down the slope between them and tugged at Chervil's paw.

'He's thinking. He *makes* time. Leave him.'

And to everymole's surprise and consternation, Frogbit pushed at Chervil, to get him away from Rooster, though he would not have moved him had not Chervil wished it.

'Time?' whispered Rooster to himself. 'Is where paws are!'

'Paws can move,' said Frogbit, raising one paw after another in an exaggerated way.

Suddenly, and to the further consternation of Chervil and the others, Rooster laughed, and slowly, in parody of Frogbit, he raised his own paws one by one.

Then he said to allmole, 'Paws can move. He's delver all right!'

Then he laughed again, short and deep and loud, so that moles on the slopes below, who were stanced in utter silence watching the escalation of the dangerous scene below, turned and looked up at where Rooster and the others stanced.

'Come on!' said Rooster quietly to Frogbit. 'We go! For Privet and for Chervil her son, and for Thripp his father all three.'

Chervil had no time to express his astonishment, for then they did go, slowly and deliberately, downslope, steady and sure.

'And *you*, you *all*,' said Rooster, turning back to where the others watched astonished and uncertain, 'we go now to Privet most of all. Your mother, Chervil and my . . .'

But he could find no words to express what Privet was to him, and had been from the day they first met up on Hilbert's Top, when they were young, so young.

'Time's come, time's come,' said Rooster.

Then down they all followed, straight towards the cross-under, straight into the silent, still, terrible waiting gap that lay between one army and another and seemed about to be filled by violence; down amidst the ugly shouting, and the stamping of paws, and the imminent beginning of something that once started would not end until the winter grass was red with blood.

While far across the vale, beyond the roaring owl way, from the edge of the High Wood, two moles also came, running downslope, unnoticed then by anymole, follower or Newborn, hurrying down towards the cross-under. Black, unidentified, breathless, shocked, running and running, the counterpoint to the coming of Rooster.

Meanwhile, outside Duncton Wood, moles began to notice the approach of Rooster, with Frogbit at his flank, and Chervil and Rolt, and the others with them, like a tiny third force, but one that had purpose and a presence far, far greater than its numbers.

The ugly shouts died away, whispers replaced them, and then the whispers changed to a name, and the name was uttered first by one mole and then another, then four, then eight, then sixteen, then . . .

'Rooster! Rooster! ROOSTER!'

It was a roaring chant, now loud, now soft, and if Rooster heard it he showed no sign. His eyes were on the cross-under, which could be clearly seen now, and the line upon line of Squilver's moles that defended it, five moles deep; and then more beyond on the other side. Impregnable.

But Rooster continued straight at it, the chanting of his name powerful all about him; Thorne to one side and Maple to the other separated from the armies they led to join his march, subordinates at their flanks, watching, astonished, all following. While through the cross-under there was movement amongst Squilver's ranks. Two moles arriving, breathless and with news. Flurries of activity.

Rooster came on and on, ever nearer, unstoppable, Frogbit to his right, almost running now to keep up, and the others all behind.

515

Thorne and Maple were together now; and Ystwelyn and Brother Rolt; follower and Newborn, pilgrim and rebel, strong and weak. Not a mob now, nor even a crowd, but moles behind those that led, and in front of them all, Rooster, Master of the Delve, advancing like the spirit of moledom that had been troubled and uncertain, but is troubled no more.

The bark of an order echoed out of the shadowed recess of the cross-under and the first line of Squilver's force, their talons raised, cold sweat trickling down their faces, fear in their eyes, backed away and parted. Then the second, and then the third: and Rooster advanced in amongst them, certain and unafraid.

Until there, facing him on the grass beyond, the High Wood upslope behind, stanced Supreme Brother Commander Squilver, a look of horrid triumph on his face.

'You're too late, mole,' cried out Squilver dismissively, his voice sharp and a shade smug, the voice of one who cares not what happens from now on, even to himself, for his task is fulfilled and nomole can change things now.

'Where is the mole Privet?' called out Chervil in a commanding voice from behind Rooster.

'Aye, it's she we've come to protect,' said Maple at Thorne's flank.

Fear showed in Squilver's eyes, and not just of moles, but of something that carried these moles towards him, something it seemed he had not ever seen or guessed at before.

'Protect Privet?' replied Squilver, still managing to sound triumphant. 'You're too late. She gave herself up to the protection of the Elder Senior Brother to make obeisance to him, and to offer herself to him, as Thripp has done. You are too late to give her protection now!'

But now Squilver suddenly looked afraid, as a mole might well look who sees the great tide almost upon him that will sweep him aside for ever.

'Too late?' roared Rooster.

Squilver's face showed anger and surprise, dismay and finally bewilderment, for what was advancing on him *was* more than he could ever have imagined; more than anymole could imagine.

'Yes, yes, too late,' he gabbled, his voice rising to a scream that it might be heard, that his message might be known, 'the holy ordination of the Elder Senior Brother Quail by the anointing of the blood and the transmutation of the flesh of others into his has already begun.'

Then Squilver fell away and was lost for ever beneath the marching, taloned paws of time.

Chapter Forty

It had begun, the ritual of anointment had begun . . .

Yet not so late perhaps that Privet might not be saved; nor so late that moles were not already apaw in the tunnels of the Marsh End and High Wood before Rooster, Chervil and the others came into Duncton.

It was but a day and a half since Privet had so strangely come to the cross-under and been admitted as quietly and as easily as if she were a mole making an afternoon visit in answer to an invitation made long before. A lifetime of a day, *ten* lifetimes more of half a day, to Pumpkin and Hamble and the rebels in the High Wood who had heard from Sturne of her coming, and had been wondering since what they might do about it.

As long, too, had that day and a half been to Arvon and his covert group, who, ignoring all the advice of Hibbott that Privet might not wish to be rescued, and the later pleas of Arliss and Rees, who were quite sure that more killing to rescue her was not what she would want, had bravely and brilliantly entered Duncton by way of its marshy north end.

Moles knowing the history of both these groups and their indomitable courage and unswerving purpose in the cause of traditional worship of the Stone, will not doubt that they had done – no, they *were doing* their best to devise some means by which they might bypass the heavy guard that Squilver had placed about the Stone, to reach Privet and anymole else who needed help.

Certainly Arvon, who knew the secrets of Pumpkin's rebels in the High Wood as well as any mole then living, had no doubt at all of what Pumpkin and his friends would be up to.

'If only we can reach them, or let them know we are coming and that they can rely on us, then perhaps something positive may be made of this,' Arvon had said, when the decision to try to infiltrate Duncton had been agreed.

Of the ascent of the embankment north of the cross-under, of the killing and hiding of three guardmoles before they crept into the

dangerous marshy ground that lies beyond the Marsh End, and of
the bloody fight to enter the Marsh End itself, we need not here
relate. We know of what Arvon was capable, and those with him, and
we may be sure that having guessed that time would be against them
they did not hesitate in what they did.

But Brother Inquisitor Fetter was no fool, and he had had time,
plenty of time, in the molemonths of the autumn and since news of
the arrival of Quail in Banbury, to prepare Duncton Wood against
attack and invasion from any flank. More than that, Squilver had long
since deployed some of his force to Duncton, and these guardmoles,
added to those already in residence, were enough to create a ring of
talons about the system's edge, north, south, east and west, if not
quite the marshy ground as well.

There is always a way in, as Arvon was in the habit of saying, but
this time, there might not be a way beyond that.

For there were more than enough guardmoles to go round, which
was why Fetter, determined as he was to be the one who had the
honour of seeing Quail safely ordained and exalted into greatness
before the Stone, had disposed so many moles about the High Wood.

So, bold and brave though Privet's rescuers might be, the chances
of any of them getting through, especially such a small force as Arvon's,
or so debilitated a one as Pumpkin's, were slim.

News of the deaths caused by invaders on the northern end of the
roaring owl embankment reached Fetter and Squilver soon enough
for them to deploy more guardmoles down to that end of the Wood,
so that even as Arvon's party reached the Marsh End it was seen,
ambushed, and decimated.

Yet even so, with half his force dead, and the rest, including himself,
wounded, Arvon broke through and made his escape into the narrow
dank tunnels of the Marsh End; here he was forced to lie low through
the night that followed, as moles hunted for them, quartered the
tunnels where they had gone to ground, and waited for the dawn.

The same dawn which saw the coming of Thorne's army; and dawn
of the same day that saw the arrival of Rooster on the valeside above
the cross-under, and when Maple led his army, and the pilgrim force
that followed it, up out of the south to the cross-under.

Trapped, hunted, desperate, the weakening Arvon led his few
moles on, and as the skies darkened that day he broke out again.
More died, his force was smaller, his hopes decreasing, but out into
the tunnels of the Eastside he went, whilst his pursuers, fooled for a
time, headed for the Westside. Yet what could so few hope to do

against so many, knowing not where Privet was, nor what the New-borns intended?

But Stone help the mole who tried to get in their way . . .

'Talk, bastard. Where would followers be? Eh? Talk!'

The Stone did not help the hapless guardmole who had fallen into Arvon's paws, and now lay helpless in the tunnel he had been patrolling, his companion already dead and he faced by talons not poised to kill him, but to cause him pain.

'Don't know. None left alive in the main system. Honest, honestttttschhh!' His scream would have been heard had it not been muffled by Arvon himself. The dark side of warriorship.

'Only followers are in the High Wood. Rebels, starving. Dead probably.'

'Where's Quail?'

'The Elder . . . ?'

'Quail?'

The guardmole began to cry. All moles will if hurt enough.

'Everymole's up by the Stone. Brother Inquisitor's prepared it. Thripp—'

'Thripp?'

The mole's eyes widened, a talon began to turn and then stopped and was withdrawn; the mole breathed easier, broken now, eager, desperate to say what little he knew.

'Thripp's been kept up there for three days now. Waiting for the coming of the Eld . . .the . . . of Quail. They'll all be *there*.'

They kept the mole alive, and with them: he might be useful. Then, through that day, slowly, silently, secretly, Arvon began the long journey by shadow and by stealth, by the secluded root and the ruined portals of tunnels fit only for diseased stoats and voles, up the Slopes towards the Stone.

'We'll be too late . . .'

'Try going faster and we'll be too dead,' said one of his Siabodian friends, wry and ironic even in this, their most dangerous hour.

Pumpkin and Hamble had no idea that anymole other than themselves might be trying to reach the Stone to help Privet, if she was there. Dreadfully isolated since the departure of Weeth, Arvon and the others, the territory available to them ever more encroached upon and watched over by the Newborns, it had sometimes seemed that it was faith not food that sustained them.

Sometime in October, as the weather grew colder and insect life declined towards winter somnolence, the molemonths of semi-starvation began to take their toll, and some of them began to die. Already by then the twenty or so moles who had originally fled with Pumpkin had dropped to only twelve in all, with three lost to the Newborns and seen no more, and the rest dying from natural causes, if stress and weight-loss, and an abandonment of hope, be deemed 'natural' in a system that ought to be wormful for allmole, and was blessed by the presence of the Stone.

For his part Pumpkin was always the first to do without and to offer what little food he had to others more needful of it than himself. The first, too, to say that but for Hamble's coming, and the advice and training he had given on survival, they would all by now be lost. Now, even Hamble looked gaunt and weak, and sometimes felt listless and unable to summon up the energy to inspire others as he had when he first came.

Yet, such was the inner spirit of this suffering refugee community of Duncton moles, in whom the last vestiges of the Duncton spirit might be said to survive, that when one was down, another found strength to be the source of inspiration. The female Elynor, mother of Cluniac, was one who would raise her spirits and those of others when Hamble or Pumpkin, or both of them, were low.

'Now, now, we're not defeated yet. We'll . . . we'll sing a song! We'll tell a tale!'

'We'll have two worms each this evening!' rasped one old male, grinning toothlessly, and chuckling feebly to himself at the thought of it.

'You shall!' Elynor might say, and that mole did, once at least. For she deputed everymole to search and search again, to take little risks if need be, to find those extra worms, that the old mole's fancy might come true.

'Not two each,' declared Elynor that same evening, 'but two for *you*, mole, and with all our love.'

'For me?' whispered the old mole, staring at the two thin, sour worms that were all that could be found, yet seemed a feast to him. 'No, no, not for me, I couldn't eat so much!'

'You eat 'em, and tell us how good they are!' declared Hamble, who until then had been low for days past, but whose spirit revived to see such real communion.

'Those worms have your name scribed on them!' said Pumpkin.

'Well, you ought to know, seeing as you're a library aide and knows about such things!' said the mole. 'I'll tell you what I'll do. I'll eat them as best I may and what's left can be shared out between you all, for a wise mole accepts a gift in the spirit in which it's given.'

He ate, and truly, not one who watched him felt envy or greed or disappointment when he ate the lot, and slept afterwards as he might have done when a pup after the feast of Longest Night.

'Bless him,' said Elynor.

'Bless us all,' responded Pumpkin, 'and may the Stone continue to give us such blessings, and the strength to do right, to be strong, and to have faith that one day all will be well in Duncton Wood once more. And may the Stone give its protection to all those we love: Maple, who is fighting for us; Weeth, his friend, who so courageously came here to see us – may he be safe; Cluniac, Elynor's son and the mole who saved my life; and that mole Noakes, who came to us from Seven Barrows where Fieldfare helps refugees survive as we are here, Stone be with both of them; and Privet and all the moles she loves.

'And Whillan, her son, in whose life as you all know I have faith. Wherever he is, whether in the Silence as most moles say, or somewhere in moledom, safe and struggling, as I believe . . . Stone, give him strength.'

So Pumpkin had prayed that night when their hard-pressed community found extra food for one of their own; and so he had often prayed before, and since.

In all that time, with the exception of Cluniac, none had guessed the vital role that Sturne had played in giving Pumpkin the information he needed to lead his friends from one peripheral tunnel to another, or to bid them lie low and still for a search would be on for several days yet; or to say that it would be unwise to go worm-hunting after dark out on the pastures, for that area was under special scrutiny.

If any guessed that he had such a source of information, none declared it, and nor did any ever question him when he said, even when much danger was about, 'Well, I think I'll just pop up to the surface to contemplate the stars and have a little time alone.'

'My dear, I wish you wouldn't go,' Elynor might sometimes say.

Pumpkin would only smile at her, as he did at Hamble, or any other mole who tried to stop him. Then he would say, 'This is *our* system, our High Wood, not *theirs*, and I will assert my right to be free in it, if only for a little time, and at night, and in shadows.'

This was the nearest Pumpkin ever came to a lie, and even then it was half true, for he was asserting his right, and he did pause and contemplate the better past, and what he hoped would be the better time to come. But then he would creep away surreptitiously to make

521

a rendezvous with Sturne, and learn what he could that might help towards their continuing survival.

Then, at the end of October, after many previous failures to reach their meeting-place near the library because so many guardmole patrols were about, Pumpkin succeeded in seeing Sturne again, and heard for the first time that Thripp had been 'delivered' to Duncton Wood and was now being kept up in the Slopes nearest to the Stone, and that Elder Senior Brother Quail was expected very soon.

'Keep going, Pumpkin,' urged Sturne, 'for now all must surely change. I have heard that Quail's forces are in disarray since Brother Commander Sapient went hurrying south following Avebury's fall to Maple.'

'Avebury! No longer in Newborns' paws! Blest be! Oh, blest be, Sturne!' cried out Pumpkin, so far unable to contain himself that he threw his paws about the chilly exterior of Sturne and . . . well . . . embraced him.

'Yes, yes, that may be, that may be, Pumpkin!' said Sturne, always most discomfited by such demonstrations of emotion. 'But over-excitement is not going to help.'

'Joy, not excitement!' interjected Pumpkin.

'Well, yes, of course . . . joy . . .' said Sturne, the word so unfamiliar to him that he could hardly get his mouth round its soft and happy sound. 'I had forgotten that it is so long since we were able to meet that you did not know about Avebury. Fetter is naturally very worried indeed. He sees it as a threat to his hope that he will be host to Quail here, and honoured in some way. Having heard that Senior Brother Skua is out of favour with Quail, perhaps Fetter is hoping that he will be promoted.'

'Ah . . .' said Pumpkin, never much interested in such intrigues.

'Suffice it to say, much is changing and we need to keep in touch. Therefore, I shall strive to be . . .' and here they made a further arrangement which, though dangerous, was a feasible way of getting information daily to Pumpkin if something of significance happened. So it was that when at the beginning of November something of the gravest significance happened, Pumpkin knew about it that same day.

'I haven't got long,' whispered Sturne from out of the gloom of the ruined side tunnel that was their meeting-place.

'What's apaw, Sturne? There seem to be more guardmoles about than ever, and though we've tried to get to the Stone since I last saw you, it has been quite impossible. Is Thripp still there?'

'He is. But it's Privet . . .'

Pumpkin's heart sank, and the world began to darken, for it must be bad news.

'Mole, *Pumpkin*,' said Sturne, coming forward to give support to his lifelong friend, 'she's alive. She's *here*. She's—'

'Here in Duncton?' gasped Pumpkin, the tunnel swimming darkly about him once more.

Sturne held on to him, surprised at how thin he was, how old he seemed.

'What have they done to you?' he whispered, as Pumpkin came round for the second time. 'May the Stone bring such evil to an end soon. Yes, mole, she's in Duncton Wood. In the High Wood.'

'Here in the High Wood?' repeated Pumpkin faintly. 'I must go to her!'

'You'll do no such thing, mole. They've taken her to the Stone, and I fear the worst, for Quail now is here as well.'

'Quail . . . ?' whispered Pumpkin; all this news was too much to take in.

'Aye,' said Sturne grimly, 'Quail himself, Stone help us. And Snyde, and all their brood of hangers-on and evil-doers, and guardmoles whose talons drip with the blood of innocents. Now listen. Small and weak though the few moles you lead are, they are all Privet has, along with myself. I do not know what we can hope to achieve against such numbers of malevolent moles as Quail commands, but we must do something. We have a little time, a day or two perhaps, for Quail is ill and was tired from his journey and must rest. Snyde is anxious that he looks his best for his ritual before the Stone.'

'Snyde's here too? It sounds as if every evil mole in moledom has descended upon us. Hmm . . . Well, even if we could, we must try to do nothing by force,' said Pumpkin without hesitation, 'for that is not Privet's way, and nor was it the Master Librarian's.'

'No, mole, it was not,' agreed Sturne. 'But what other means we have at our disposal I do not know.'

'Faith, moral strength, purpose of will, liberty of thought,' whispered Pumpkin, 'these are all that are left to us. But they are everything, I think, if only we had a mole strong enough and wise enough to lead us. But . . .'

'You, Pumpkin, you are that mole.'

'Me?' said Pumpkin, always surprised when anymole dubbed him leader, or even wise, for humility was his second name.

Sturne nodded. 'For myself I can promise only this, Pumpkin. I will not raise my paws in aggression against anymole, not even Quail

523

himself. But I shall get as close to Privet as I can, and if any try to harm her I shall put myself in the way of their talons.'

Pumpkin looked at Sturne, and regretted that nomole-else heard his words, or saw what courage and purpose his friend showed.

'Now, you had better go back to the rebels. I know no more than I have told you – except that it would seem that Quail is planning some ritual or other before the Stone, involving himself, and for this he may need to consult not only Snyde, but me as well. So I may be able to delay things a little.'

'The more time the better, Sturne, that we may have space to find *something* we can do.'

Few communal debates in moledom's long past can have been more touching, nor more significant in its moral history, than that between the hard-pressed and physically weak followers who had hidden so long around the tunnels of the High Wood, about what they might do to help Privet. Let there be no doubt in anymole's mind that old and starved though many of these moles were, there was no lack of desire to be up and away across to the Stone, whatever the consequences.

'There may be only a few of us, and we may not have much fighting experience, but by the Stone we can have a go at saving Privet!' cried out one old female who was so weak she could hardly put one paw in front of another – yet her brave words brought forth a cheer, and a surge towards the nearest exit.

'Moles!' cried out Hamble, the only one among them who could lay claim to any real fighting experience. 'I must remind you that I was sent to Duncton from Caer Caradoc by Privet herself, and she did not send me to kill moles, or even to fight them. I had grown sick and tired of such things, and she sent me to warn against violence. Her journey into Silence is, no doubt, many things, but one of them is a journey into the peaceful way of change.

'By all means set off towards the Stone if you must, but even if you survived – *even* if you achieved your objective of "saving" Privet – she would not thank you for it, and nor would you feel better. No, no . . . that cannot be the way.'

The moles nodded their heads ruefully, even the female who had made the initial call to action, and pondered what they might do. That 'pondering', which lasted all night and into the next day and refused to be hurried, or to move to a quick decision because time was passing, is surely one of the high points of Duncton's history.

Moleyears before, Master Librarian Stour had inspired a few moles to begin a search for peace, a search that might or might not have to do with the Book of Silence; now, here, finally, it came down to this: a few moles, mostly old, asking themselves what power there was that might be greater than force, and if it existed, did they possess it? It was a debate for all moles, and all time, but it was especially mindful of the modern history of Duncton, which had been concerned to protect the idea of tolerance and freedom and peace against the dogmas of the Word, and of the Newborn; but in the course of which violence had too often been used in the name of the Stone.

In the long course of that history, moles recorded, and many more unrecorded no doubt, had stanced up for the non-violent way: Boswell and Beechen; Rose; Mayweed in his special way; Tryfan, who had discovered the path of peace only through suffering and pain; and the Master Librarian of Duncton Wood, wise Stour.

Then, finally, Privet, a wandering female scholar from the north who came in search of a Book that might not even exist, and found in her pursuit of it, at Wildenhope, a violence so absolute and shocking that she had chosen the way of Silence, which is the hardest way of all.

These great names were all invoked in that long dark night when Pumpkin and the others, fearful for Privet and themselves, uncertain, without guidance other than that they could give themselves, harried by the sense that time was running out, debated what they might do.

Dawn came to a chamberful of tired and distressed moles, a dawn they felt that might well be the last for the mole who had set out from Duncton Wood in all their names, and now had come back to it in silence, and in grave jeopardy. Many had been the suggestions, but none had found favour with them all, and now, as grey light lit their tired faces, and uncertainty reigned in their tired minds, there seemed no way forward left to them.

'We must rest and sleep if we can,' said Elynor at last, 'for one thing we have agreed upon, though future generations – if they ever know of our discussion and our plight – may blame us for inaction: we have agreed that we shall act together. Therefore, let us rest our bodies and our minds and hope that in slumber a solution may come to us which has evaded us in waking. It often does.'

'Aye,' said Hamble wearily, 'that's true, it does. Though how I'll sleep knowing the peril that Privet is in . . .' He yawned, and others did the same, and some he saw were already lowering their snouts to their paws, and beginning to close their eyes.

So sleep came to them that morning – the morning of that great day – when busy crowds assembled outside Duncton beyond the cross-under, and Thorne was preparing his army for action. And they slept even as Maple was leading the followers and pilgrim army ever nearer, and Rooster was approaching from the east. Whilst nearer still, unknown to anymole, Arvon and that pawful of warriors still alive at his flanks, were making their hindered bloody way up through the tunnels and byways of the Eastside towards the Slopes.

So the hours passed in the cramped chamber where Pumpkin and his friends lay in fitful rest, until the sky darkened, and they woke to the sound of a far-distant chant, rhythmic and strange, that told them that many moles were nearby, somewhere down on the south-east slopes or beyond.

'Beyond! They're beyond the cross-under – and there's more than a pawful, I tell you.'

It was Hamble, fresh back from a stealthy journey by tunnel and secret shadows beneath fallen treetrunks, smelling of the musty odours of the fungi and rotted leaf-litter in which he had had to crawl.

'I'd tell you if you'd believe me, but you won't.'

'Tell us,' said Pumpkin.

'If my ears did not mistake that chant it sounded first like "Maple" and then, more recently, like "Rooster".'

'Could they really be here, so near?' asked Elynor.

'They could,' said Hamble, 'and I want to believe they are.'

'Well then, friends,' she continued, 'our time for decision has come. We have argued all night, and wisely we have rested. Now there is no more time. If we can agree a course of action we shall follow it. If not we shall do nothing. There is no dishonour in doing nothing.'

There was silence, uneasy and concerned. There might not be dishonour in it, but allmole there felt that there must be a better way than doing nothing.

'"Maple", you said; and "Rooster"?' said Pumpkin.

'Yes, Pumpkin, I am sure it was their names that were spoken. But I could see very little – only the backs of ranks and ranks of Newborn guardmoles down by the cross-under, through which it will be very hard for moles to battle their way.'

'Then it is up to us, isn't it?' said Pumpkin. 'You know, perhaps we have talked so much that we have missed the obvious thing . . .' His voice wandered a little, as did his eyes, and all there recognized that this was Pumpkin thinking, thinking hard and yet trying not to think: this was Pumpkin reaching out for all of them beyond the words they said, for guidance from the spirit of the High Wood and the moles of Duncton past, and present, and future.

'You all know that until October it was my habit to go alone to the Duncton Stone to pray, as it had been all my life. Through good times and bad, through conviction and doubt, when I have been happy, and when I have sometimes been sad, though that affliction has fortunately not often been mine, why, it is to the Stone I have turned.'

'We know it,' they said.

'I have gone to it and bowed my snout down to it and I have said, "Stone, listen to me, for I have lost touch with the Silence that is in my own heart. Stone, help me, for I cannot help myself always. Stone, put your grace into me, for without you I am nothing."

'My dear friends, with a prayer such as that I have often begun a contemplation before the Stone, and the Stone has not failed me. It has listened, and found an answer, though often the answer was not one I expected; it has helped me, though often I did not accept its help with gladness; it has shown me its grace, and I have found meaning.

'We have debated, and we have found no solution. We have agreed to act together, though we do not know how to act. And now I know only that I must turn to the Stone, as so often before, and pray to it, and seek its guidance.'

'But Pumpkin, that's all very well and fine,' said Elynor, 'but we've been through it so many times already . . . *tell* him, Hamble.'

Hamble scratched his head and shrugged a little, perhaps understanding rather better than Elynor what Pumpkin was getting at, and said, 'You wouldn't last long up on the surface before you were caught, Pumpkin, and what good would that do? If they didn't kill you outright, they'd arraign you, or whatever it is they do, and then we'd have to try and rescue you as well.'

Pumpkin sighed and said, 'We've made it all too complicated, like moles generally do, and it isn't complicated at all, and that's what I was trying to say. I want to go to the Stone, just as I always have. That's all. Unfortunately I can't, and do not want to even try to persuade any of you to go with me.

'Perhaps we were right to try and find a solution as a community, one we could all agree on. Well, we haven't, and now I've made up my mind what I want to do, and I don't suppose it is what anymole-else wants to do. You've been good enough to call me your leader since we first came here, and although I felt a little flattered I've never felt it was a task I'm fitted for. I'm a library aide, pure and simple. It's what I've always been since I became adult, and it's how I want to end my life.

'Well, now, so long as Privet was out of Duncton Wood I was happy to try my best to be your leader. Now she's back and she needs help, it's as a library aide I must go to her. I hope she's up by the Stone, because then I can serve it and her at one and the same time.

'I have no speeches to make, or anything much else to say. She's waiting and the Stone's waiting and I must go to them and take what chances with the Newborns I must. These things feel right to me, and if my faith in the Stone is justified, as I think it is, and if my duty as a library aide is worthwhile, which I believe, then there is no other decision I can make, or want to make. So I will leave you now.'

'Pumpkin,' muttered Hamble, at a loss for words.

'You cannot go up to the surface alone,' said Elynor, 'you won't—'

'I must, my dear, and I shall,' said Pumpkin firmly.

How small he seemed, how suddenly frail, as with the gentlest smile of farewell he turned into the light of the slipway up to the exit and began to ascend to the surface.

'But, *Pumpkin . . .*'

But he meant it, and had said his last, and would not be persuaded otherwise.

'We *can't* let him go alone,' cried Elynor to the others, 'and I won't, however foolish it seems.'

'Nor I,' said Hamble, frowning and looking about the astonished group. 'You must each make up your own minds, but I'm with Elynor in following that . . . that . . . that library aide!'

Then they both followed after him, and with sighs, or shrugs, or even the occasional rueful swear-word, the rebels all followed one by one, up into the dangerous light of day, their difficult decision made.

'*Pumpkin!*' Elynor called out after him, for he was already wending his way across the surface between the great beech trees. 'We're coming with you. Wait for us!'

Pumpkin turned and saw that one by one, some irritably (like Elynor), some a little rueful (like Hamble), but all with real trust in their eyes, they were following him.

'Stone,' he grumbled under his breath, 'I didn't *want* them to follow me.'

He turned from them and proceeded on his way, leading as strange a procession of moles as the High Wood ever saw. Until, not so long afterwards, and when through the trees they caught the first glimpse of the Stone and the sound of singing and chanting, there came across their path, and from out behind beech trees to right and left, Newborn guardmoles, many of them.

'Whatmole are *you*?' one of them asked in astonishment.

'My name is Pumpkin, and I am going to the Stone.'

'My name is Elynor of Barrow Vale, and I am going to the Stone.'

'I am Hamble of Crowden in the Moors and I am going to the Stone . . .'

And as each of them spoke, each felt that they were rebels no more, nor skulking moles, nor anything but moles who could hold their heads high, for before them was the Duncton Stone and what lay between them was nothing, nothing at all, compared to the Stone's glory, and the Silence it offered.

'You're going to your bloody deaths, that's where you lot are going,' said one of the guardmoles.

'No,' Pumpkin replied with what he regarded as simple truth, 'we are going to the Stone, as is our right. The Stone is for allmole, whatever and however they believe, not just for a single sect. Therefore, let us pass.' Then, with a twinkle in his wrinkled eyes, Pumpkin dared add, 'Better still, moles, come together with us, but come in peace.'

The Newborns blocked their way, angry but unwilling to bring their talons down on the rebels without proper authority; not sure what to do, eventually they sent one of their number on up the path to the Stone Clearing.

'We can wait, for a little while anyway,' said Pumpkin, stancing down where he was, 'we have waited long enough.'

But only a short time later the mole came back with a couple of others with him, one of them a senior Brother Adviser judging by the dark look to him, and his natural authority.

He looked at them curiously, and then said the following extraordinary words, with evident reluctance and displeasure: 'The Elder Senior Brother will permit these witnesses to his ordination in the Stone. But they are to be quiet, for the ritual of anointment is beginning.'

Pumpkin rose and followed the mole, ignoring the astonished guardmoles altogether. But Hamble, who had seen some strange things in his life, thought this was the strangest of them all, and exchanged a glance with Elynor, who evidently thought the same.

'With Pumpkin,' she whispered to Hamble as they followed on, 'wonders never cease.'

'More's the pity,' muttered Hamble.

Chapter Forty-One

Quail's pains having grown steadily worse all along the long way from Banbury to Duncton Wood, once there he experienced a new depth of agony. For deep and nagging though his pains had been until then, now they became at times mortally profound, so that there was nothing inside and outside his head, but the pain.

This first occurred in that moment in which (at Snyde's insidious prompting) he had hoped to know the first beginning of the absolution of the pain – not the opposite. This was as he passed through the High Wood and thence, at last, into the Clearing on its western side, and there set his eyes upon the Duncton Stone.

'I am nervous, Brother Snyde, I confess it,' he said as the trees thinned and the first partial glimpse of the great and soaring Stone was to be had.

'Your release shall begin soon now, Master, for the Stone is merciful. You have taken upon yourself the sins of allmole, and dared confront the Snake and the Worm, and the Stone shall give you liberty of your pain.'

'Will it?' whispered Quail, racked and shaken by doubt for a moment, and perhaps by a premonition of the new degree of pain to come. 'Will it love me?'

'Lean on me, Master,' said Snyde, and he led him into the light of the clearing about the Stone.

There, ready, waiting, stanced Thripp, aged now but staring as powerfully as ever.

'It has eyes, Snyde, that Stone has eyes and they look upon me,' whispered Quail, unsure what he saw.

'Raise yours to it, Master.'

Then Quail, turning in dismay from Thripp, saw Privet. She was worn and made thin by the journey into Silence upon which she had embarked. Yet from some place she had reached, which lay far far ahead, she seemed to look back now and her eyes were on Quail's, and they were even brighter than Thripp's.

'Its eyes pierce me and sting me and hate me,' cried the stricken

Quail, and the new pain came upon him, and he could not be free of it.

'Reach your paw to the Stone, Master, and your pain shall be taken from you.'

Then Quail dared raise his eyes towards the Stone he feared, which he had always feared, dared reach out to it, and touch it . . . and he screamed and fell back, clutching at himself.

The new pain had seemed to turn and gnash inside him, more terrible than all that had gone before. His face contorted and stiffened, his eyes stared, and his paw reached out for comfort, not from the Stone but from Snyde, that he might know he was not alone.

Oh yes, from Snyde he sought comfort, not from the Stone.

'Take me from it, Brother, for I am not yet ready to be made consecrate . . .'

Back across the High Wood they took him, and the further he was from the Stone the less his pain, until they took him down into the Library, and made a place of rest for him there, where the texts had been cleansed, and the old ways of thought destroyed. There he might find peace for a time.

'Rest, Master, for the journey has been long. We went to the Stone too soon.' In truth, Quail was so slow and ill that the journey from Stone to Library took until nightfall.

'Too soon it was . . . For they were there. Thripp was there and *she* was there and unafraid.'

'They suffer, Master,' Snyde lied.

'Do they?' asked Quail, hope in his horrid voice.

Snyde nodded his thin head.

'I suffer, Snyde, I suffer for all molekind,' Quail said, 'and I am afraid now, afraid that there will come a time when the pain will not abate.'

'Master, only you have strength for this great trial, only you are blessed to suffer it,' Snyde replied. 'Your pains shall be plucked from you before the Stone, as thorns from a mole's paw, and when your pain has gone from you you shall be . . . holy.'

'Holy and divine,' corrected Quail, his body made peaceful at the thought of it, and the pains subsiding away even further. 'Shall I have strength to survive until then?'

'Yes, Master, you shall. Now, sleep, Master.'

'But I am thirsty . . .'

They took him to the surface, to a pool of water caught in the ancient surface roots of a tree.

Quail stared into it and cried out, 'I see their eyes upon me, evil, horrible, turned and twisted like these roots.'

'Drink, Master.'

Closing his eyes he thrust his toothless mouth down and drank at his own ancient image.

'I am hungry.'

'We shall find you worms.'

'Worms shall not be enough. By the blood of Thripp and Privet shall I be anointed, Snyde, and in their flesh shall I not find sustenance? I yearn for it now, I am so tired.'

'Their living flesh you shall have, Master. Now eat these paltry worms as a sign of your humility, accepting them as a token of the flesh that the Stone shall give to you.'

'Newborn shall I be!' cried out Quail hysterically.

'That, Master, and that . . . Now come down below to sleep, come to sleep.'

'With you, Brother, that I do not wake alone in the dark night.'

Snyde submitted to Quail's embrace that night, took pleasure in it, revelled in it, in expectation of the greater pleasures to come. Now Quail held him; soon he would hold Quail. More than hold him, and he would take him, he would have congress with him, he would!

So were Thripp and Privet spared another night before the Stone, waiting, shivering, fed the paltry worm, given no water but that which drizzled down at dawn. He bidden to silence, she continuing to obey it, humiliated in the eyes of the guardmoles who watched over them, yet not by the Stone; nothing now to anymole but themselves.

Quail had been right to suffer when he looked into their eyes, for theirs was an old love, strong as time, and understanding, for each had journeyed far, and each knew there was still a way to go.

Sometime in that night, the nearest guardmoles dozed, the furthest turned away to talk, and Thripp was able to speak to Privet for the first and only time since their separate coming together to the Stone.

'My dear,' he whispered, 'I know you cannot talk, and I wish to less and less. But know this, which none could tell you at Wildenhope, not even our son Chervil, though he it was who made it be. Whillan lives.'

'Whillan my . . . son . . .'

Did she say this? Did the mole of Silence break her vow and speak? If so, the Stone forgave her, for its Light shone more brightly in her eyes. If not, it was the Stone spoke for her.

'He *lives*. He had to seem to die, my dear. He had to seem to drown.'

'I saw the river take him. I saw Rooster try to save him. I saw them drown. I saw no living mole.'

'Rooster saw and Rooster lives. *Whillan* lives.'

Great tears of anguish came to Privet's eyes, for living in the Silence, which must be what he meant, was not enough. Her eyes fell from Thripp's and she knew that the Silence was not yet hers.

'Help me, Stone,' she seemed to say.

'Help her, Stone!' Thripp said.

'Silence, mole!' shouted a guardmole, coming to him and raising his paw to strike him.

'Silence . . .' whispered Thripp, the Stone's Light in his eyes too, and the guardmole fell back, abashed, his paw hurting, his eyes dazzled, his head reeling.

Whillan lives . . . but what Thripp had briefly tried to say, and the hope in it, did not stop the night advancing over all of them.

Dawn came across the High Wood, where Quail woke, screamed because he was in pain, and Snyde soothed him, ordering up the flesh of worm, feeding it him and then letting him sleep alone.

'I have business to attend to,' whispered Snyde to his sleeping, sweating Master, 'but I shall not be far, nor gone long.'

But long enough to meet with Sturne and demote him back to Keeper as he himself assumed his right to be Master Librarian. Master, indeed, of all he surveyed, for Snyde could not resist ascending that slipway up to where once Master Librarian Stour had had his study and his gallery.

'Stay down there, Sturne, where I can see you. And work. Work now for me. Find those texts I have commanded you find and bring them here.'

'Yes, Master Librarian,' Sturne said heavily, and searched among the stacks for the texts of ancient liturgy and rite which Snyde had ordered.

'Bring them here, up here, mole.'

'They are fragile. Master, can you not come down?'

'Bring them here,' snarled Snyde, 'all of them.'

Which Sturne did, grieving to see the dry and brittle things rubbed and worn, falling apart in his paws. Why had he not thought to copy these old texts?

'Good,' said Snyde when the last one was laid before him.

'And now?' asked Sturne.

'We create a liturgy, Keeper Sturne, which shall be most fitting for the elevation of a mole to Paramount and Prime.'

Why did good Sturne feel the first stirring of horror then? Why feel the impulse to strike vile Snyde dead where he was stanced, snouting and sneering, and sliding his talons amongst the folios of texts he was not worthy to touch?

'"Almighty Stone, fill this your servant with the light and power which you gave the white moles who have been your apostles,"' whispered Snyde. 'Do you agree with my kenning, mole? Eh?'

Sturne ran his talons over the mediaeval text twice and said, 'Not quite, Master Librarian. For "light" I would ken "grace" . . .'

'Oh would you, Sturne? Would you!' said Snyde with deadly anger. 'It is enough. Leave me be. Go back to your work. Summon me when Qu . . . when the Elder Senior Brother wakes.'

'Yes, Master Librarian,' said Sturne.

'Sturne?'

'Master Librarian?'

'Once I thought you were a fool, but you are not. You know your mediaeval texts. You are right about light and grace.'

'Thank you, Master Librarian,' said Sturne, surprised.

'Oh, it is nothing. I have missed fellow scholarship. I missed it much. You shall help me with the liturgy, Sturne?'

'I shall do as my Master Librarian bids,' said Sturne, summoning up a brief smile, for he knew it was expected.

At midday he was called back by Snyde, who kenned the beginning of a liturgy to him with proprietorial pride.

Yet the words that Snyde spoke were not his own, but ones he had plagiarized for his liturgy from the texts that Sturne had found for him. Not that he had progressed very far with this onerous task, for it was so long since he had done real scholarship, and he had been involved in so much that was more exciting since, that the truth was he had soon tired of the task, and grown bored with it. So he had summoned Sturne back to help.

'Yes, yes, Keeper Sturne, it shall be called the Liturgy of Paramount and Prime,' he said irritably. Though he needed Sturne's help he did not disguise his contempt for him.

'Prime, Master Librarian?' Sturne said evenly. His voice had been 'even' ever since Snyde's arrival back in the Library the day before, and his peremptory demotion of Sturne from Acting Master Librarian back to *Keeper*. And only Snyde could have managed to impart to the word 'Keeper' so rich a quality of contempt and insignificance.

534

Though 'Keeper' Sturne did not mind, nor feel much surprise, yet as the day had worn on he had begun to think that nothing he had had to endure and suffer in the long moleyears since Snyde had left Duncton Wood compared to the spiritual filth he was now witnessing on his return.

'I said "Prime", Keeper Sturne, and I meant Prime. Does not that ancient and revered word mean anything to you? Eh, mole? Eh?'

Snyde thrust his snout at Sturne's and his eyes narrowed suspiciously.

'In terms of the present day, I cannot say it does,' said Sturne, 'though I believe the word had meaning in mediaeval times, in such texts as you have been . . . kenning.'

Sturne's guard had nearly dropped, for he had almost said 'plagiarizing'.

'Yes, it did have meaning in those glorious days when there was less sin in moledom, and moles knew their place. When scribemoles were revered and Uffington was great. But we must get on, as there is little time before the end of day when we shall begin. Now, was not Balagan the First Mole and Supreme? In other words he was Paramount and Prime.'

'Yes, but it was only an idea, a metaphor, a . . .'

Snyde's eyes glinted over the texts. 'Oh yes, so it was, it was. *But we shall make it flesh, Keeper Sturne, don't you see? Don't you see?*'

'Flesh?' said Sturne, most uneasily. Horror was one thing, but this was sinking to nightmare. Snyde, he began to think, was mad.

'And blood,' added Snyde matter-of-factly. 'The Elder Senior Brother takes to himself the pain of all of us, that we may the more easily know the Stone's Silence in this life. The First Mole, He who was Paramount and Prime, gave allmole life. Now He is returned among us to exemplify for us the Newborn life of the spirit on this earth. His mortal body suffers and is dying and it must be transubstantiated back into the purity of the First by the anointment of the blood and the taking of the flesh. Eh? You see?'

There was a pause, by which Sturne understood he was to make some kind of response to this horrific jumble of insanity. His mind raced, for he remembered his last promise to Pumpkin, that he would find a way of delaying matters, and staying close to Privet. Was she the blood? Was Thripp the flesh? Not much on either of them . . . Some distant light of normality allowed this moment of dark mirth into Sturne's horrified mind.

'Well, mole?' said Snyde with some eagerness.

535

Sturne affected serious thought and said, 'But Master Librarian, forgive me if I am slow in this matter . . .'

'Yes, mole, yes? What is it?'

'The doctrine of transubstantiation was declared a heresy by Dunbar himself. Mole's blood, mole's flesh, could not, he said, be—'

'Dunbar!' said Snyde, waving his paw dismissively. 'Ken the texts, Keeper Sturne, and you will see that Dunbar was the heretic. Scirpus—'

'Forgive me, but he was of the Word.'

'Exactly; of the Word. The Word made.'

'Made?'

'Flesh; everything.'

'Transubstantiation?'

Snyde smiled. 'Good, Sturne, good. You see, we shall make a liturgy for the Elder Senior Brother, which *shall* be the Liturgy of Paramount and Prime, and through its mysteries first and last shall he become exalted, unforgotten. You understand?'

'I understand, Master Librarian.'

'Oh . . .' sighed Snyde, 'but you and I, Sturne, might have been friends.'

'We are, Master Librarian,' lied Sturne, the greatest lie he ever told. Or almost, for he added, 'I learn much from you, Master Librarian. We have missed you.' That was the bigger lie.

Snyde almost purred. 'You have learnt much, Brother Sturne, in your time in the wilderness.'

The wilderness, it seemed, was being separated from Snyde.

'Master, what would you have me do?'

'Good, good. Humility, obedience, silence, these are a trinity you display and we should include. Now, listen, for I must attend to the Elder Senior Brother, if he is to live long enough to be exalted before the Stone.'

Snyde laughed horribly when he said this, and his eyes glistened lustfully at this implication of death.

'I am being jocular,' he said. 'The Elder Senior Brother shall live, of course. You shall help me make up this liturgy, using these texts, and your knowledge.'

They talked technically a little while, Snyde outlining what he wanted, happy it seemed to be with a mole who understood.

'Oh, we could have been such friends, you and I,' he said once more when he had done. 'Now, on with your work, Keeper Sturne, on, on!'

'Yes, Master Librarian.'

And in all his life Sturne had never worked so hard as in the hours of that strange morning when the chambers and stacks of the Library echoed to the muffled screams of Quail, and whispered to the scratch of Sturne's talons as he scribed a most unholy liturgy.

'Paramount and Prime!' muttered Sturne, frowning, and looking about the Library that he loved. 'May you forgive me, Master Librarian Stour, but I sense your paw has guided mine this morning!'

Then, from somewhere deep inside himself, Sturne dared think that it might be possible, if he should ever live through the night to come, that a day would follow when he could talk of this to his friend Pumpkin, and . . . laugh.

Then the hobbling pawsteps of Snyde approached, and he called up from the stacks below.

'Well, Keeper Sturne, well?'

Sturne looked down, down from where the Master Librarian traditionally took his stance, down to where the twisted Snyde looked up, and said: 'Master Librarian, it is finished and I have done my best.'

'Let me see, let me see,' said Snyde, eager and breathless as he clambered up the slipway to snatch the new liturgy from Sturne's paws. 'Let me see how I can improve it, mole.'

'Only you can, Master Librarian, only you know how,' said Sturne, his eyes as cold as death.

Then Sturne had suffered Snyde to maul his work a little, ken it aloud, and pronounce it ready to show Quail.

Quail awoke once more in the early afternoon, pain-free and confident. He ate and he drank and he was so unafraid that he prattled about his coming elevation to the position of First Mole incarnate, whilst Snyde talked him through the liturgy.

'When shall it be, this ceremony? How long shall it be?'

'At dusk shall it begin, with chant and prayers, and into night continue; and then shall be the Vigil of the Dark Night, during which you shall be made exculpate, and thy sins torn out of your heart and your mind and scattered like the dust of the dead. Then into your purified body—'

'Purified,' sighed Quail, expelling an effluvium of malodorous breath which Snyde sucked in greedily and seemed to gulp down, trembling and shivering with the dark pleasure of it.

'Yes, purified thou shalt be . . . ' continued Snyde.

*

Gravely ill though Quail now was, his pains and hallucinations worsening by the hour, he was not yet wholly dependent on others, or incapable of thought or mischief. Sometime that afternoon, as Snyde further busied himself in the Library with 'his' creation and put the finishing touches to it with Sturne's help, Quail signalled one of his guardmoles near and whispered the name, 'Skua'.

'Elder Senior Brother?'

'Send him to me, for I love him.'

The guardmole, well trained, hurried to inform Snyde of this unexpected development. Skua was, after all, disgraced and excommunicate, held alive only that he might be made sacrifice in the coming ritual.

'He said he loved him, Brother Snyde.'

Snyde grinned crookedly and muttered the words 'Love him?' with a disbelief that almost made Sturne smile again, and hurried off once more, no doubt to dissuade Quail from any course other than the sacrifice of Skua. But astonishingly Quail was not to be dissuaded.

'He shall utter the liturgy of Presentation and Declaration, and he shall ask the seven questions.'

Snyde frowned, but remained calm. 'He is our Brother, despite his sins,' he conceded. 'You seem better, Master.'

'We are all brothers, despite our sins, Snyde,' said Quail, for once ignoring the reference to his health, which usually succeeded in provoking a wave of pious self-pity which subsumed all else. 'Forgiveness shall be mine and *is* mine. He shall be forgiven for the space it takes for the Presentation of my body to the Stone, and the Declaration, which is the testing of my mind and spirit thereafter before the Stone. Is it not?'

'Yes, Master,' agreed Snyde.

'After that I shall feast upon the sacrament of his flesh, to sustain me through the Vigil.'

'Ah . . .' sighed Snyde, to himself, content once more. Skua was to be made sacrifice after all.

'There are *eight* questions, Master, not seven, I think,' said Snyde to divert him.

'I think not, Brother,' said Quail firmly, though his sudden rush of energy seemed to be in decline once more, for his eyes had that haunted look that now preceded the onslaught of further pain.

'You think not,' repeated Snyde, knowing how useful delay could be. In any case, he had no wish to change that part of the liturgy now. It was the later parts that excited him more.

'Yes, I think not,' said Quail impatiently, 'for how can the mole who is Prime undertake to be obedient to those in authority? Remove the Fourth Inquisition, Snyde.'

'But obedience is—'

'Shall be an irrelevance. I shall not argue about it, but command you to do it. Now, summon Skua that I may give him the good news that he is forgiven. Then bring to me the final version of the liturgy, that I may study it. Brother!'

Quail's voice had a warning tone, and he cast a glance towards his guardmole as if to say that even now, even at so late a moment in the proceeding towards his elevation, there were other moles could be made sacrifice.

Snyde knew the warning signs well enough to bring his objections to a halt. He could wait. The pains would return. Quail would be his once more, and before long he would be his entirely, for evermore, his to . . .

'. . . to love,' he whispered, mouth moist, eyes on Quail's, challenging him to understand the dreadful ambiguity of what he said.

But Quail did not. Instead he relaxed, he felt his pain, and he waited, grey of snout, yellow of eye, for Skua to come to him. He wanted to forgive: and he wanted to see this part of his sustenance at least, for he could not face Thripp or Privet again until the moment of their sacrifice. But Skua he could look at, knowing he would eat a part of him.

'No, no, no . . .' he crooned when Skua came, looking most uneasy, 'I love you still.'

'And I you, Elder Senior Brother.'

'And I forgive you.'

At which Skua blinked, the only sign his face dared express of the hope he felt. There was yet a chance. The Stone could be merciful in great things, if not always in small.

Skua had suffered since Banbury. Doubt had been his visitor and had not gone away. Despondency had been his friend, and would not leave him be. Despair had been his lover, and had exhausted him. All this Skua knew but now it seemed he was forgiven, and he stared at the declining form of Quail, whom he had once loved, and at Snyde, the victor over him, and welcomed hatred into his heart, most gladly.

'What shall you have me do for you, Elder Senior Brother?' asked Skua.

'See. Here. Look . . .' and Quail waved a paw at the folios that Sturne had prepared and Snyde had amended, 'your part is here.'

'I am to make the Presentation then?' said Skua, kenning the strange text. 'And then the Declaration?'

'Yes,' said Quail, happy to hear Skua's dry clear voice again. He was so much easier than Snyde, who confused him.

'And then?' asked Skua.

'We shall make sacrifice,' said Quail, his eyes never leaving Skua's.

'And after that?' said Skua, indifferently it seemed. 'What mole shall utter the prayers before thy ordination, if not . . .'

Quail winced and said, 'Oh, you, mole, you do it.'

'But, Master, I . . .' hissed Snyde, furious. What of the sacrifice?

'Skua shall do it. The more he does the greater I shall love him, Brother Snyde.'

Which could mean anything.

The two enemies looked venomously at each other over the misshapen, swollen head of Quail.

'And whose paw is this, Elder Senior Brother,' asked Skua, indicating the text of the liturgy, 'for this is not Brother Snyde's, which we all know so very well?'

'A mole called Sturne. A Keeper.'

'He scribes well. He seems to know his texts.'

'He . . .' began Snyde, trying to stop Skua going on. But Skua was not to be stopped now, and nor did Quail wish it.

'And what part shall this Keeper Sturne play in the Holy Rites to honour you?' asked Skua, sensing this might weaken Snyde. 'It is not the tradition that he who utters the Declaration should proceed to the liturgy of ordination. Is that his role?'

'Master, I . . .' snarled Snyde, for the ordination was his role, his glorious role and could not, must not be taken from him.

'Fetter . . . will know Sturne,' gasped Quail, the pains returning. 'Ask him. Summon them both. Skua, do it for me.'

'As I love you, Master,' said Skua smoothly, nodding to one of the guardmoles who had always been an ally, 'they shall be brought to your holy presence now.'

'Not holy yet,' said Quail with false modesty.

'Most holy is he to us,' replied Skua unctuously, 'who the Stone hath chosen to be Paramount and Prime.'

'I like that,' laughed Quail delightedly, 'let it be part of the liturgy! "Most holy is he to us who the Stone hath chosen to be Paramount and Prime".'

He sang the words, so far as his cracked and weakening voice allowed of singing, and then he said, 'Summon my dear Squelch as well. He shall make a song of those words you spoke, Skua, and play his part as well.'

'I am honoured, Master.'

So it was that Sturne was there in Quail's chamber when the final decisions were made about what the liturgy would be, and what the form, and whatmole would play which part.

Snyde got his way over the ordination at least, and that seemed enough to him. But Fetter, being inferior in rank to Skua, must precede him in anything he did, and so to him was allotted the task of the Ministry of the Word, which is to say certain readings from ancient molish texts, and more modern ones, and the singing of a canticle, which Fetter would first speak, and Squelch then sing.

Sturne was left with what seemed the lesser task of uttering the introit to the Vigil of the Dark Night, which preceded the Commendation and Committal of Quail's pain-racked body to the Stone before the ordination. That would occur with the dawn light, when he would be made Prime at last.

'Whatmole shall conduct the Commendation and Committal?' whispered Snyde, hoping that it might be he, thereby bringing him back into the centre of affairs.

'Shall I do it?' said Sturne with due humility, 'for it is meet that a mole who does not know thee personally should conduct you out of the perdition of this life into the mystery of Paramount and Prime.'

'Is it meet?' asked Quail.

'It is most meet,' concurred Skua, pleased to be the cause of a further diminution of Snyde's role.

'It is so,' added Snyde, 'and meet too that one should welcome you into the ordination at dawn who knows you well, for we shall be joyous then.'

'Good, good,' said Quail. 'Keeper Sturne, you are a mole of sense.'

'And the sacraments of blood and flesh, Elder Senior Brother?' said Sturne, suddenly forceful.

'Those! You utter them, for the rest of us will be quite lost by then!'

It was Quail being jocular, and they all laughed, except the guardmoles in the shadows all about. But Snyde frowned once more, for in that last decision he sensed danger, though why he did not know. Perhaps Sturne was more than he seemed.

Quail said, 'I shall sleep a little, and then we shall not delay more. Is all else ready?'

'It is, Master,' Fetter was the first to say. The day was darkening.

'My pains have almost gone,' said Quail. 'I am minded not to sleep at all, but to begin now.'

There was absolute silence. Discussion was one thing, now reality loomed. Snyde glanced at Skua and Skua at Snyde, and Fetter at them both, all assessing, all calculating.

It was Sturne who dared take the initiative once more.

'Why not, Master?' he said gently. 'There is no time like the present, and we are eager to celebrate the coming of Prime.'

'Even I cannot advance the coming of the dawn when the Vigil shall be kept, but you are right, Keeper Sturne, it is a celebration and as such will give me strength for the Commendation and Committal, and the Vigil that follows . . . and I like you. Stay close by me. We shall begin now.'

'Now?' whispered Snyde.

'Yessss,' said Quail, 'for I am weary and I would begin before the pains return, which in sleep they might. Sturne advises well. Now it shall be. Yet, I am nervous.'

He looked about them all, with that fearful look that sometimes crosses the face of a female about to pup who has never pupped before, not unlike the expression that may cross the face of a mole about to suffer punishment or execution.

'Moles, help me through the trial to come.'

They all murmured that they would, but only one there felt a vestige of pity, slight though it was, yet pity all the same.

'We shall,' said Sturne once more, wondering how it might be that after so long living in the Newborn darkness he should feel pity for this most foul and vile of moles. Perhaps it was that he saw the tyrant become his own most pitiful victim.

He followed along in the procession that now left the Library, and headed towards the Stone Clearing through the morning light. He did feel pity and shame, but then he put that all behind him, and hardened his heart as he repeated to himself that part of the liturgy that he was especially to speak, and pondered the coming Vigil of the Dark Hour, which is the vigil unto death. He contemplated some of the words . . .

'Renew in him, most loving Stone, whatsoever hath been decayed by the fraud and malice of the Snake and the Worm, or by his own carnal will and frailty . . .'

Even as Sturne repeated these words to himself in readiness for the rite to come – and there were many more of the same in the liturgy he had put together for Snyde – the sky seemed to darken further and ahead of him Quail cried out in pain, mortal and profound. Then he who would be Paramount and Prime faltered, and staggered, and put his paw out to one he still trusted most of all – Snyde, who stanced firm, though to Sturne, watching from the back of the procession, it seemed that Snyde was only as firm as rock that has been twisted, turned and contorted, and so malformed by the fires of the deep.

Sturne saw how massive was the deployment of guardmoles in the High Wood, for they were everywhere he looked, in every shadow, by every gap. But as the procession wound on in among the larger and more formidable beech trees of the High Wood, he could not but think that with their massive roots and trunks, and leafless branches thrusting up towards the darkened sky, they were surely guardians of something far more ancient and venerable than a mole who sought to be Paramount and Prime.

Chapter Forty-Two

Although Squilver had been among those in the procession to the Stone, moments before the Clearing was reached moles came running up from the south-east slopes with news of the first sighting of Maple and the followers. Thorne's coming he already knew about, and that threat was contained, but the arrival now of Maple, half expected for several days, was not good, and most inconvenient.

We do not know if Squilver seriously expected to long survive the coming of Thorne and Maple, though probably he did. The news of Sapient's death had, perhaps, given him some pleasure, even hope. That mole's departure from Banbury had forced the Elder Senior Brother's retreat and now the Stone had arraigned him, judged him, and found him wanting, and his death was a just punishment.

Possibly Squilver hoped that a war would be fought between Thorne and Maple which would so weaken both of them that if he could stay within the sanctuary of Duncton Wood he might live on as Supreme Commander. We do not know . . .

Nevertheless, Maple had arrived at Duncton inconveniently soon, and we know that Squilver left the High Wood reluctantly, before the ceremony really started, giving very strict instructions that he should be informed when it began so that he might hasten back. Meanwhile – and for this commentators on his conduct as Supreme Commander give him praise – he made sure that the guardmoles about the High Wood were very well deployed indeed.

One other thing we know, which gives a historian no pleasure to relate. At about the time that the procession started off from the Library, Arvon and the few moles he still had under his command made their last brave bid to reach the High Wood and the Stone. They were caught and held only shortly before Squilver's reluctant trek back through the High Wood and so it was before the Supreme Commander himself that they were brought.

He looked at them and wondered whether to spare their lives long enough for them to be used in the sacrificial rites that he knew would soon be part of Quail's elevation. But his mind was on the imminent arrival of Maple, and dealing with three captured rebels was an irritating diversion.

'Kill them,' he said, 'and let them lie where they fall as warning to others who may seek to come this way. No,' he said, turning back for a moment, 'put their bodies out at the edge of the trees above the pasture slopes down to the cross-under. They will be more easily found.'

His words were as brief and brutal as the talon-thrusts which, but moments later, put to their deaths Arvon of Siabod and the last two moles he led. They had lived by the talon, and themselves had killed moles, as they were killed then.

Stolid, silent, with what last memory of Siabod's mountains, or what last sight of the soaring branches above their heads, we know not, they died as such warriors so often die: not in glory, not in light or triumph, but somewhere; anywhere, unremarkable, ordinary, unmemorable, forgotten. Moles who seek that site in the High Wood today look for signs of it in vain. Trees are trees; roots, roots; and the rotting surface litter of the wood always looks the same, though it is always changing.

Before he died, did Arvon think of what the moles Rees and Arliss had told him, that Privet would not have thanked him for rescuing her? Did he wish he had seen Ystwelyn one more time? Or did he, perhaps, think finally of Cluniac, who he had trained in the covert arts he knew so well, but whom, despite every entreaty, he had refused permission to accompany him back into Duncton?

'I was born in Siabod, mole, and I am a warrior through and through. So may the Stone grant that I die. But you, why, mole, you are a Duncton mole and in you, despite your bravery, I see another way. Therefore, though we have need of you, and this is your system, you shall not come with us. Stay here with these . . . pilgrims. Wait for Maple's coming, which cannot be long delayed. If I do not live, tell him that I was loyal to his cause to the very end. Then, mole, pray for me at the Duncton Stone and wish me well.'

Such were his last words to Cluniac. Perhaps in his final moments he remembered his refusal to let the Duncton mole come with him that day with gratitude, and felt that the Stone had been with him then, as he hoped it was with him now.

Perhaps . . . but we do not know.

But there was nothing uncertain about the pomp and circumstance with which Quail was led into the Clearing to take his place near the

545

Stone. Squelch preceded him with a motley choir of younger moles, followed by Brother Inquisitor Fetter, the choir humming while Fetter chanted the first part of the Ministry of the Word – as Sturne and Snyde had redrafted it within the Liturgy of Prime.

> *'Almighty Stone,*
> *With grace you sent Balagan, First Mole*
> *Who was Prime,*
> *Father of White Moles and precursor;*
>
> *With grace you decreed the Blessed Boswell*
> *To be the Father of Beechen, who came to us*
> *And gave his life for us.*
>
> *By the same grace,*
> *Show us obedience, through you . . .*
> *Discipline, through you . . .*
> *Silence, through you . . .*
> *And prepare us for the transformation*
> *Of our blessed Elder Senior Brother,*
> *Quail of Avebury,*
> *Into Prime.'*

These, more or less, were the words Fetter uttered, and it must be said that as he did so and the chant continued, and Squelch moved the choir's humming on into a counterpointing song, a certain sense of awe and majesty came over the proceedings.

Subsequent reports have sought to persuade us that the unholy ceremony that was now beginning, and would not be complete in all its ghastliness until the following dawn, was wholly without true purpose or merit. It was, such commentators argue, merely about the exaltation and elevation of a foul mole, and nothing more at all, and had no virtue.

But they are wrong, and misunderstand not only the subtle and brilliant achievement of Sturne in subversively transforming a vile ceremony to something redemptive, but also that it is in moments of life's greatest darkness that the Stone's Light may shine forth at its most bright. This was the paradox of those crucial hours which were indeed about death and rebirth, of which the elevation of Quail was but a context, and a parody.

However, despite the ceremony's confident beginning all was not quite well. The Stone was larger and more impressive than Snyde remembered it, and the Clearing rather wider, and the trees that

546

formed it rather taller. Which meant that all in all, a mole like Quail, striving as he was to look grand, even holy, despite his hideous swellings and baldness, managed only to appear paltry, foul, and dwarfed. This last impression was strengthened by the fact that though there *was* a crowd of moles, it was of a size to spread along only one part of the Clearing's edge.

Snyde was very displeased by this, and calling a temporary halt to the proceedings, he whispered fiercely to Fetter to put things right. Much annoyed, the Brother Inquisitor had to scurry about and draft in some of the guardmoles from about the High Wood. But this was easier said than done, for though more guardmoles were summoned, to make things look busier, yet the space was vast, and seemed to grow vaster as little by little the light gave way towards dusk, and the Stone grew more massive in the gloom, and the beech trees seemed more towering still.

None of this appeared to affect Quail at all; having been brought before the Stone, he now stanced by it with his swollen eyes shut, muttering incoherently to himself. And dwarfed though he was by the Stone, and the High Wood, there was in fact no denying that he was, in some strange, ghastly way, impressive.

Equally, there was no denying that the moles who would be offered up in sacrifice as blood and flesh, which is to say Thripp and Privet, looked very unimpressive indeed. Though Thripp was stronger-looking than in the Wildenhope days, by virtue of being fattened up for the ceremony, he was old, and his head was low, his eyes downcast.

Privet seemed to have retreated into some inner place, leaving her body grey and slumped, and her face wan.

Though their eyes had pierced Quail to the heart when he had seen them for the first time a day and a half before, now they seemed dull and dim, and tired. Which perhaps he sensed, for at the end of Fetter's chant, and while Snyde was having the crowd augmented and re-arranged, he looked up, searched among the moles, saw them, noted how they did not look at him, and drew himself up somewhat and felt more confident.

The Ministry of the Word was now resumed by Fetter, with Skua beginning to play a part in such a way that it was made quite plain that he was the superior of the two. This effect was achieved by having Fetter utter interminable canticles of obscure mediaeval texts, the last line of which Skua would repeat more loudly, much as one mole might crunch up a worm only to have his superior take up and eat the juiciest morsel.

If there had been any sense earlier that Duncton Wood was besieged by moles beyond the cross-under, whose numbers had steadily increased in recent days and who must surely before long break into the system by persuasion or by force, it was not much felt by the Stone that evening and even less so as the ceremony continued.

For as the liturgy unfolded, interspersed with chant and song, a kind of enchantment fell about the Stone which allowed no concern for what went on beyond it.

The world beyond, indeed, was becoming inconsequential, and all that mattered was the here and now of the ceremony itself. Most fortuitously, it was at this time, and with the lack of numbers still worrying Snyde, who had imagined something more glorious for a ritual whose ending, he secretly hoped, would be with him, that news of the emergence of Pumpkin and the others was brought to him.

Had not Fetter been so heavily engaged, and stanced in the centre of the Clearing before Quail, the news might have reached him first, and the outcome been very different, very peremptory, and very violent. But it did not, and Snyde, hearing that Pumpkin had been caught, and regarding him as of no real consequence but as fodder for the coming ceremony, gave instructions that he and his rebel companions be brought to the Clearing and placed near the other captive moles.

'Tell them they shall be obedient, and silent, and that if they are not they will be killed forthwith,' he said.

Which they did not for one moment doubt, and came along most obediently and silently, surprised to be alive at all, and to be witnesses to what was taking place.

What Snyde could not then tell, nor any other Newborn there, was that their coming, and particularly that of Pumpkin and Hamble, was *part* of what occurred. Chance, or the Stone perhaps, placed both those good moles within sight of Privet, who until then had kept her snout and eyes cast down. She looked up, she saw them, she saw the love and wonder and delight and most of all the support in their eyes and a shudder of relief went through her. She said nothing, but glanced at where Thripp stanced and he, too, looked up, and following her gaze to her dear friends, understood as well that for the first time the trust that each had so long placed in the Stone might be rewarded. Thripp too seemed to shiver with a kind of awed apprehension, and his eyes were beacons of faith shining in the gloom.

'I think *that*'s Thripp,' whispered Hamble, and Pumpkin nodded, sure that it was, but quite unable for more than a moment to take his

548

gaze from Privet, in whom he saw such change; he was now quite sure – as sure as faith itself – that if the Stone would allow him, he would serve her as aide to his dying breath.

Of the participants in the ritual one alone saw these things, and understood their great significance, and that was Sturne. He had seen Pumpkin's coming with wonder, he had gazed on Hamble with curiosity, for he had only seen him once before when he first came to the system, though he knew of him in so many other ways, and he saw that with their arrival a new purpose and intent came to Privet and Thripp. In seeing this he knew that the Stone was with them now, urging them on, and that by communion of their spirit they might together subvert the ceremony that had now begun.

Then, suddenly, like the unexpected cracking of a great branch in an ancient oak, Snyde's voice was heard.

'Those who have authority to do so have chosen Brother Quail, born of Avebury, and a mole of worthy life and sound learning to be Paramount and Prime among the moles of this earth.

Of those present now before the Blessed Stone, who have sight of this venerable and humble mole, and know that he has suffered the trial of Snake and Worm, and that his body bears the marks and pain of that suffering, we ask this question: Is it your will that he should be ordained?'

There could be no denying the power and authority with which Snyde spoke, and as his voice rose at the end of his question the assembly shouted, 'It is! It is our will!' And if, among those shouting, some of the rebel followers found themselves involuntarily joining in, a mole should not be surprised, nor even censorious.

For as they did so, and Pumpkin, Elynor and Hamble heard them, these three began to understand what Sturne had already realized, that the more they entered into the spirit of things, the more in some mysterious way they might succeed in subverting the ceremony.

Nor did these three have to wait long for a chance to join in again, for Snyde followed up the first question with a second.

'Of those here present we now ask in all solemnity, will you uphold Quail, born of Avebury, in his holy ministry?'

'We shall! We shall uphold Quail in his holy ministry!' they all cried out, and Pumpkin and the others loudest of all. Only Thripp and Privet were silent, and they cast down their eyes once more.

The Presentation of Quail having been made, and he having looked

549

up once more at the crowd that proclaimed him worthy by their assent, he turned for the first time to face the Stone. He did so with some difficulty, Fetter and Snyde having to come to his flanks to help him, and all could hear the pain in his rasping breath, and sense the truth in Snyde's reference to his suffering. Several of the Newborns in the crowd, carried away by a genuine sense of awe and occasion, were leaning forward where they stanced and whispering to him, and offering their paws towards him, as if to give him support and encouragement. In him, it seemed, they really did see something of themselves; in him, as well, they believed the power of the Stone might soon be made incarnate.

Skua now moved slowly towards the Stone and took his place between it and the gasping Quail, every bit the Senior Brother Inquisitor. The time for the sevenfold inquisition had come, though had Snyde had his way it would have been eightfold. But there they were, and there Skua was, gaunt in the evening gloom, the Stone rising most impressively above him. Quail, his back to the crowd, snout low, seemed like a supplicant.

Skua paused, no doubt for effect, but in that pause the crowd noticed for the first time, perhaps because there came the slightest of breezes to the branches high above, and then down to the surface below, an odour: *the* odour indeed, which all had heard about but of which few had suffered the full-blown scent. They suffered it now and it was a most wretched and retch-making thing, like the smell of excrement mixed with the bile of a dying mole. So bad was it, so foul, that there was a tremor through the crowd, a sort of group recoil, which was steadied only by the resolution of the guardmoles, and a sudden departure from the rite by Snyde.

Sensitive as he was to danger and attuned to all that was best for his own purpose, he swung round to face the crowd, raising his paws as he did so, and declaimed, 'Blessed are we to suffer the odours of his corporeal decay as now he who shall be Paramount and Prime commences his lonely journey towards the Dark Night, casting off the rottenness of his weak flesh to assume the holy form of the White Mole he shall become.

'Scent his odour, moles! It is thine own! Scent his decay! It is thine own! Scent the beginning of the death he must suffer and the pains he must endure before the Vigil we shall celebrate!'

There was silence at first; then, like fickle reeds blown first one way by the wind, and then another, most of the moles there cried out their approval and delight at Snyde's words. Then, incredibly, horribly, some – not many, thank the Stone – broke through the cordon formed by the guardmoles in front of the crowd and running to Quail's hinderparts, sniffed and snouted the odours therefrom like dogs, and as if intoxicated and a little nearer holiness themselves, wandered ecstatically back in among the crowd.

'Blest be!' the others cried. 'Blest be!'

Skua now began the First Inquisition, which, since Sturne had only scribed it earlier that day, he was not wholly familiar with, and so was forced to peer at a crumpled birch-bark text thrust at him by some minion or other; he then kenned it with the talons of his right paw. Nevertheless, this kenning lent the Inquisition a certain air of learning and seriousness, which added to the rapidly escalating sense of drama and excitement.

> '*Do you believe, so far as you know your own heart, that the Stone has called you to perform the highest and most sacred office of Paramount and Prime?*'

'I do,' rasped Quail in a voice that was beginning to seem to come out of a void of terror and fear, of pain and of suffering, 'oh, I do . . .'

'*Do you believe,*' continued Skua, moving on to the Second Inquisition, as his eyes seemed to catch the light of the first stars that were now beginning to show in the eastern sky, '*the doctrine of the Stone as granted incontrovertibly and exclusively to those moles of the Caradocian Order who are Newborn?*'

'I do believe it,' gasped Quail, reeling to one side and grasping his flank and then pressing at it as if to hold in something that wished to get out.

'He suffers for us . . . he cries out in pain for us . . . his is the perdition of the Snake and the Worm, for all of us,' members of the crowd cried out, as if to urge him on further through the Seven Inquisitions.

By now the odour was thicker still about the Clearing, and moles all about were openly snouting at it and breathing it in, their eyes streaming, some no doubt with tears of ecstasy, and others with the bitter tears of those who feel they are choking to death. Yet still they stanced their ground, Pumpkin and Hamble and Elynor among them, carried along now by the momentum of the liturgy itself; and only Privet and Thripp were still, and silent, and seemingly unmoved.

As the Inquisitions proceeded – and each was longer than the first and padded out somewhat by song and chant, and various interruptions from the increasingly hysterical crowd – it seemed that Quail's

551

agonies began to deepen and increase. What had at first been gasping replies became cries, and then moans, and then sobs and then finally, with the seventh and last Inquisition, a scream.

'Will you then be a faithful witness of the Stone to those among whom you live, and lead them by virtue of your office as Paramount and Prime to make disciples of the Doctrine of allmole, and bring to judgement and perdition those who permit the Snake and the Worm of blasphemy and doubt to live within?'

'I will,' screamed out Quail, his body seeming to spasm so that his back arced down, his paws up, and his bald swollen excrescence of a head rose towards the Stone. The scream came from his open, toothless mouth, and with it, almost palpable in the air, like stinking mist, and accompanied by the untoward sounds of the expulsion of decayed air from his bodily orifices, an odour worse than any yet.

It was as well the Clearing was now so dark, for many in the crowd gasped and retched, and some seemed to vomit, and yet . . . and yet this moment passed and the crowd cried out its jubilation as Skua proclaimed, 'Quail, born of Avebury, you have answered all of the Inquisitions truly, and I pronounce you spiritually clean. Now are we ready for burial and interment into forgetting of thy broken body, whose fragrant decay gives us such witness of thy worthiness.'

'Fragrant decay!' muttered Sturne to himself savagely, and though his stomach was in his throat with Quail's effusions, he did not now delay in coming forward to take up the next part of the ceremony. For Skua had departed fractionally from the proper words, and that fraction might now be everything. He should have said 'Now art *thou* ready . . .' but he had said '*we* . . .' and Sturne recognized in that 'we' an unconscious shifting of attention from the needs of Quail to a concern for the needs of the congregation about him.

There had been a wresting of power from the individual to the community, and through the coming Commendation and Committal of the body he intended to exploit it. As if to bolster and support this intention a whispered voice from out of the congregation repeated, 'Now are we ready . . .' Sturne stared into the murk of faces all about and saw one pair of eyes clear upon him, clearer and more penetrating than any other that then looked at him, and they were Thripp's.

'Now are we ready . . .'

Thripp had said it; Thripp understood what Sturne was about, and was showing the direction in which he might go. Thripp *knew!*

In the brief moment it took Sturne to step into the centre of the

Clearing and coolly displace Skua, as if by right of the ceremony itself and because the imperative of the congregation demanded it, he became aware of several startling implications in Thripp's soft interjection. One was so astonishing that Sturne saw it and put it to one side, for it implied that *all* of this – right back to the elevation of Thripp to power at Caradoc in the first place – was Thripp's doing; that this was ordained indeed . . . right back even beyond Caradoc, back to that first bitter-sweet meeting between a Confessed Sister and an anonymous Brother Confessor in Blagrove Slide so many years before.

Sturne had to glance at the Stone for support at the thought of this . . . and then he could ponder it no more, there was no time.

The second implication was simpler and more immediately important. It was this: he, Sturne, could rely on Thripp for support, and it was support he would need, and need desperately if in the hours ahead the unholy ceremony upon which they were now embarked was to be subverted by the Light and Silence of the Stone.

These thoughts were exciting and exhilarating to Sturne, though not a trace of them showed upon his benighted face, except perhaps an extra gleam and purpose in his eyes. He raised his paws over Quail in what he hoped looked like a gesture of gentleness and sorrow and invited everymole there to pray for Quail as he embarked on a journey that Sturne hoped might be rather more final than intended.

'Before we enter the period of Vigil, when each of us shall journey forth in spirit as companions of our departing Brother Quail, let us together take corporeal leave of him . . .'

Not only was Sturne's look gentle, almost avuncular, but his voice succeeded in sounding sweet and most solicitous.

'Trusting in the Stone we have witnessed our Brother's Inquisition and now we come to a last farewell to his mortal, flawed body before its resurrection before us with the glory of light of coming dawn, when we shall see him become Paramount and Prime and his body, which is the outer form of his inner holiness, will change to that of a blessed White Mole.'

'Blest be!' cried out a mole or two.

'The pains, the pains . . .' whispered Quail, staggering from where he stanced to grasp hold of Sturne, his paws so wet with sweat and inner filth that his grasp slipped, and he had to grip yet tighter to take a hold.

'Help me . . .' whispered Quail, his eyes rolling and wide with pain, his agony real.

For a brief moment Sturne felt a return of pity, but he had only to reflect momentarily on this mole's life to see in him the very embodiment of the forces that had so long striven to destroy the followers; worse, to see a mole that had always and for ever put himself before the Stone. And, *now*, he dared seek to elevate himself through its power to be . . . *Prime*. Sturne could hardly bring himself to even think the word and knew he must feel no pity, none at all.

'See, Brothers and Sisters,' Sturne continued, 'how his inner being struggles and strives to be free of his outward form!'

'We see, we see that struggle!'

'It is the Snake that struggles!' cried out Skua suddenly, quite carried away it seemed.

'It is the Worm that strives!' shouted Snyde, almost as if he had made a great discovery.

With Quail's slippery paws about his own, the pace of Sturne's delivery now increased and he moved rapidly through the Commendation to the Committal, omitting whole words and phrases as if he sensed that Quail, and to some extent all those with him, were now being inexorably borne along towards the darkest hours by the very words of their own liturgy.

'*Mole is born of mole and hath but a short time to live and is most full of misery,*' cried out Sturne, freeing himself from Quail's grip and placing his own paw on Quail's shaking shoulder, as if to direct him once more towards the Stone – as if, in fact, he were a father herding a recalcitrant youngster towards a portal through which he had no wish to go.

Nor did Quail now seem to wish to move, for as he found himself forcibly turned towards the Stone, and felt Sturne's firm grip upon him, a grip that was not friendly, nor sympathetic, nor gentle in any way, he seemed to see some light upon the Stone's dark face he did not like, something he might well fear; something that might not take the pains away, the hope of which had sustained him this far, but instead make them far, far worse.

'No,' he whispered at this sudden realization, struggling but unable to be free.

'Yes, yes!' Snyde shouted ecstatically. 'The Snake struggles, the Worm strives but we shall not let them be free!'

Quail turned briefly to his former ally and saw that he too was part of this nightmare march towards that . . . this . . . those eyes of painful light that stared at him from the Stone.

'No!' he cried out, but the moles about him cried out yes, and Sturne's voice took him on and on towards that void of pain.

'. . . yea, is full of misery. He cometh up but is cast back down, like the flowers of the field. He fleeth as it were a shadow, and never stances at peace. In the midst of life we are in death. Of what may we seek succour but of thee, Stone . . . ?'

Here, despite Quail's screaming protests, Sturne shoved him bodily forward until his snout was thrust against the Stone, which rose sheer above him towards the night sky.

'. . . of thee, Stone, who for our sins art justly displeased.'

'Justly displeased,' came the whisper of Thripp again, a touch louder this time. It was the most perfect timely emphasis.

'Aye, justly displeased,' chanted the crowd, as somewhere in the darkness, quite carried away, Squelch began a falsetto requiem which melded most beautifully, most perfectly, with his father's scream.

'Oh holy and most merciful Stone,' cried out Sturne, his voice sharp, and accusatory of the mole he now pressed so hard against the Stone itself, 'thou most worthy Judge eternal, suffer us not, at our last hour, for any pains of death, to fall from thee, but . . .'

But?

For the first time a look of alarm and suspicion came into Snyde's eyes. But? There was no 'but'. Sturne should have reached the end of that part of the liturgy and be moving now to the committal itself, but he was not . . .

'But,' thundered Sturne, defying anymole to stop him, most of all Snyde who was alone in his doubts as the rest of the congregation roared and cried out for this casting-off of Quail's flesh in expectation of the glories yet to come. 'But this mole, you alone shall judge, Stone, and if the Snake and the Worm struggle and strive in him still, even now, thou shalt cast him out, even if in all else he is worthy to be Paramount and Prime.'

It was cleverly put, using all the arcane language of a dead religion, and Snyde could not quite find fault with it; yet somehow it had put doubt in moles' minds by suggesting the possibility that after all the Stone might find Quail wanting.

'In this wise,' continued Sturne, not letting up for one moment, 'we commit our Brother's body to thee, that his blood be turned to *earth once more, and his flesh to that same earth, in sure and certain hope of his resurrection into wholeness and purity if he is worthy through thy love, Stone; which is the only thing that can transmute our vile body into oneness with thy Silence.'*

The committal was done and Sturne pulled back sharply from Quail and fell silent. Then all were still, waiting for some sign that the Stone had judged Quail favourably, or . . .

Unfavourably. Yes, now that possibility was countenanced. Sturne had put into the congregation's heart the very Snake and Worm against which Quail and his representatives had so long railed: doubt.

The silence deepened for a moment more and then was broken by a rasping, gasping voice which spoke to them from out of a place they barely dared contemplate.

'Brothers . . .' whispered Quail, 'the pains, the p . . . p . . .'

He screamed again and his anguish was all too plain. His paws reached out and as one scrabbled against the Stone the other seemed to seek support from Sturne and then, failing that, from Snyde.

'Br . . . Brother Snyde . . .'

The voice was abject now, horrified, unutterably afraid and it told moles far better than words could that this was a mole who *had* been judged, *and been found wanting*; this was a mole who had not faith that the Stone would help him, or could help him. This was a mole who in the moment that should have been most glorious, not just for him but for all of them, sought comfort not from the Stone but from the contorted form of Snyde.

Yet Snyde seemed blind to the possibility that this might be how others in the congregation saw it. Instead, all unaware, he compounded Quail's failure with his own.

A gentle word might have been enough; a genuine caress; a call for the Stone's mercy and encouragement and further help to a mole who still, most there hoped, might yet be Prime.

But gentleness, simplicity, mercy were not qualities Snyde knew or could even pretend to have. In Quail's decline before the Stone, and his evident descent into a corporeal hell of pain and utter agony, Snyde saw his own ascension.

With arrogant, almost sadistic slowness he approached Quail, and before he reached out to him he turned to Sturne, and then to Skua and the other moles, and dim though the light, and few though the stars, his smugness, his ambition, and his cruelty shone out from his little eyes and glittering teeth as plain as blackthorns against a grey sky in winter.

556

It was now, from some movement of Sturne's towards Thripp, that others there, like Pumpkin and Hamble, saw for the first time the subtle enormity of what Sturne was trying to achieve, which indeed he almost *had* achieved.

But it was Elynor who hissed, and though it was no more at first than the touch of frozen snow blown across ice it was enough to set others at it, and some of the Newborns – some even of the guardmoles. For few liked Snyde, and with his blasphemous ambition so plain to see, most liked him even less. So they hissed, and Snyde retreated a little before it, back towards the Stone, until he was flank to flank with the mole whom he more and more began to see not only as his mentor, but also his victim.

'Good Brother . . .' gasped Quail, his scrabbling desperate paw now finding Snyde's.

'What is it?' said Snyde sharply, looking now at Quail, now at the hissing crowd and lastly up at the fearful Stone.

'The pains . . . the pains have not gone. They are worse.'

There, Quail had said it, and in saying it he admitted at last to himself that they might not get better. Pathetically he pulled himself round to look at Snyde.

'Brother, what shall I do?'

The hissing quietened and stopped and the crowd waited, uncertain and fickle still.

Snyde looked wildly about for a moment, uncertain too, and then he stilled, and smiled, and feigned calm.

'You are most holy,' he began, the words calming him and the crowd still more.

'I am, I am,' said Quail, 'and I suffer for all molekind. Help me. Take the pains from me with the anointment of blood and the benediction of the flesh, as you promised, as you *said* . . .'

Snyde winced, for these last words of Quail were not quite suitable *now*. But he was, perhaps, on the right path.

'You are most holy, Brother Quail, and worthy for us to begin the Vigil of the Dark Night, for you do not presume to come to this the Stone trusting in your own righteousness.'

'I do not!' cried out Quail, clutching at some hope in this with the same desperation with which he had clutched at Snyde's crooked paw.

'He does not!' cried out one or two of the congregation, though fewer than had hissed. But if any had wondered if a battle of life and death was going on now before the Stone, and one in which all there were engaged, they did not doubt it now.

557

'Therefore . . .' cried out Sturne, seeking to regain the initiative.

'Aye, therefore . . .' snarled Snyde, seeking to retain it.

'Therefore,' whispered Thripp of Blagrove Slide, 'I offer up my body for the blood and flesh of the Holy Sacrament of Paramount and Prime.'

It was nicely done, perfectly done, and his guardmoles did not restrain him from moving forward. Briefly, so briefly nomole-else saw it, Thripp glanced at Sturne and nodded and Sturne came forward and said, 'Thy offer is accepted, Thripp who was once great, but who fell and was abject and then struggled and strived with Snake and Worm.'

'None harder,' whispered Thripp compliantly.

'None harder,' whispered the crowd.

'And therefore, the sacrament offered and accepted, we shall begin the Vigil of the Dark Night,' said Sturne with absolute authority. 'Thy blood and thy flesh—'

'And *hers*, and hers!' screamed Quail, pointing a broken talon at Privet.

'And her blood and her flesh,' agreed Sturne, motioning Privet forward; she came and stanced by Thripp. Hamble seemed to wish to intervene, but Pumpkin, sure now that all he saw was sham, put a reassuring paw to his and shook his head; 'Sturne is on our side,' he whispered.

'But the dawn is too long to wait for their blood and flesh, too, too long, and my pains, I need . . . them, I must . . . she stares at me.'

Quail gabbled and mumbled and moaned and Snyde wriggled at the end of the dark tunnel into which he had led himself, and tried to find a way out. He did not want any more delay.

'Let the sacraments of blood and flesh be made now, that Brother Quail shall have sustenance for his journey unto dawn.'

Snyde raised his cruel talons, and peered at Thripp and Privet with eyes that sought to rend their flesh for that same blood and sustenance.

'No,' said Skua firmly, with a look of pleasure on his face that was only thinly disguised as piety, 'as Brother Snyde has rightly said, thus far Brother Quail has been most holy. Let him be holy unto dawn! And let us all be holy, with Brother Snyde to be an examplar for us and the supplicant's sponsor throughout the night.'

The crowd only half understood the terms he used, but their meaning was plain enough: neither Thripp nor Privet was to be touched until the light of dawn, Quail was to prove his worthiness by waiting

558

until then, and Snyde, as his friend, was to stance by him and help him through.

'Yessss . . .' sighed the crowd in agreement, and perhaps with the beginnings of triumph, for to some it seemed that the 'Yessss' ended with a hiss.

'Begin the liturgy of the Vigil,' commanded Skua of Sturne, and Sturne did not delay.

'Almighty Stone, hear our prayers now for your servant Brother Quail who would be Paramount and Prime and whom you have summoned out of this world . . .'

It was the ancient prayer spoken over the body of the departed, but Quail was not departed, and he muttered and he whispered that he was not, clinging to Snyde, weeping piteously, and screaming weakly of his mortal agonies.

'. . . but who struggles and strives still with the Snake and the Worm. Be with us, O Stone, at the start of this Vigil, comfort us as you lead him through the portals of death and to judgement.'

'I . . . am . . . not . . . dead!' said Quail.

'Does he not struggle?' interjected Skua in his best inquisitorial style, a style taught him by Quail himself. 'He does! Does he not strive? Oh, he does! Blest be that we are witness to this suffering for all molekind!'

'Blest be!'

Sturne resumed the liturgy, his voice drowning Quail's cries.

'Great Stone, you pursue us with the power of thy love and dispel the shadow of death with thy glorious Light . . .'

'I . . . am . . . not . . . dead!' sobbed Quail.

'Blessed are those who have died in the Stone: let them rest from their labours for their good deeds go with them.'

'I . . . am . . . they . . . are . . . I . . . COMING.'

But he could not finish telling anymole that he was not dead, or whatever else it was he tried to say. They are? *Who or what?* Coming? *Where . . . ?*

For though he was not dead, the pain suddenly became too great for him to speak. As a strange and awesome darkness began to overtake the Stone, which until then had been visible enough and, with the stars, had even given out a certain light, Quail began to struggle and to strive in the night, and to tear at himself as he screamed, as if to pull out the Snake and the Worm from his own body.

Then the Stone seemed to fade, the night grew black and blacker still, until all stars were gone, and the Vigil of the Dark Night began as Quail begged to die and whispered, 'I do not want to be Paramount and Prime.'

Chapter Forty-Three

Of that Vigil towards dawn no words, no description, no record could be adequate. Those who have meditated upon Longest Night, and witnessed the mystery of the seasons' turn, which is a progression from darkness back to light, may have a glimmer of what occurred.

Each mole present held his own thoughts; none could see another, nor even their own paw if they held it up against the night sky. The black of night was palpable as Quail's odour had been.

Aye, *had* been. For one thing all noticed was that with the disappearance of the Stone into the black of night Quail's odour was gone, to be replaced by nothing but his screams and groans. But for those, indeed, a mole might almost have thought he had gone as well. But they heard him, and some pitied him, for in the absence of the merciful Stone his pleas to die, to be released, went unheard.

Yet though it did not seem quite possible, he had worse to come. Something so foul, so spiritually noxious, that each mole without reference to the next raised a taloned paw towards the blackness where Quail was, as if to keep at bay an evil the very touch of which could taint them for ever.

It was Brother Snyde, that was what it was. And he was . . . purring in the dark.

Then they heard Quail's screams intermingle with sighs, and sensual gasps, and for one moment – nearly the worst of all – with a snatch of laughter, the cracked crying out of Quail's voice.

'NOOOOO . . . !'

Quail himself had often heard that final wretched hopeless 'No!' from the victims, young and innocent, yet his cry that dark night sounded just the same.

Then, after that chilling laugh, Quail screamed again, and it was absolute, rending, mortal, into and out of a nightmare come true.

Then, after that – and here if those raised talons had faltered they were raised more strongly in the dark, and pointed more severely at the heaving monster in the night – there were the grunts and gasps of effort, rhythmic and thrusting, and as Quail's screams mounted

561

so did the filthy sounds of the unseen congress in the dark.

Until, at last, there came a scream of release which should have been the end, but was not. For it continued, faltered briefly, seemed surprised and then as suddenly as Quail had cried out at the final horror of defilement by Snyde, that cry of release changed into a scream of shocked and unbelieving pain, and Snyde in his turn cried out, 'N . . . N . . . NOOOOO . . . !'

And Snyde began to beg for death, as out of the darkness there came a new scent, not malodorous, but clean – the scent of a thousand nettles, crushed.

Dawn light came quite suddenly, first upon the Stone, and then across the shadows that besieged it. The trembling crowd of moles slowly let their taloned paws slip towards the ground, and stared at what lay dead, and what crawled, in the centre of the circle they had formed on all sides but where the Stone rose straight.

'See where the White Mole is, Paramount and Prime,' whispered Sturne, and the horror in his voice spoke the horror in all their hearts.

For Quail *was* white, white with the crawling of a thousand talon worms whose struggles and strivings glistened in the November dawn light. Out of his body, from the sacs on his head and rear, from his mouth, from his eyes, from his hinderparts, and from out of his cracked paws they came, departing from what could serve them no more.

All about the clearing Newborns departed too, backing away in horror, their dream, their faith, all dashed.

Squelch scrabbled away, and Skua, and Fetter too, backing off with their minions, and the guardmoles who had sustained them so long, departing from a horror that was theirs and which they could not face. Departing into the warriors, and the followers and the pilgrims who, in the night, silently, without reference one to another, had advanced little by little, step by step up from the cross-under, up the pasture slopes, and thence into the High Wood.

No blows struck. No commands given. Nothing but the slow advance of moles of liberty like a rising dawn, and the retreat through them of moles of doctrine and restraint, who had been the night.

While Snyde, alive still, his face filled with pain and agony, lay gasping on the ground, staring at the worms that still crawled out of Quail's body towards him; powerless to stop those that already crawled over and into him, and the many more that followed.

'But . . . I . . . am . . . not . . . dead,' he whispered. He was unable to fend them out of his eyes; they entered even those, and he began to know the meaning of dark night.

Nearby, Privet held Thripp close where he lay. The night had weakened him, its stresses too great for his frail body. His eyes had been on Quail and Snyde, and on the worms that crawled between them. Now he lifted them to the Stone, and the light of the sky beyond it.

'It is done,' he whispered, 'it is done, my dear. May I be forgiven for the harm I did, and remembered for . . .'

Privet held him silently.

Behind them in the still and silent crowd of followers all about the clearing's edge Pumpkin reached out towards her, wanting to help yet not knowing what to do. Then he turned in mute appeal to Hamble, and together they looked among the crowd, in which there were so many moles they knew. Maple was there, Rooster, Weeth, Rolt, so many more. Fieldfare was among them, and, and . . .

'Which is Chervil?' whispered Pumpkin.

Hamble pointed and Pumpkin went quietly over to him where he stanced, dark and still.

'Go to them,' said Pumpkin, 'go on, mole. She needs you, *they* need you.'

Chervil went out into the Clearing, stared briefly and dismissively at the foul sight of Quail's dead body, and Snyde's still living one, and stanced down with Privet and his father.

Thripp reached up to him as he continued to whisper: '. . . remembered for the love we found, and the promise to Privet that I honoured.'

One paw held Privet's, and the other reached out to hold their son's.

'Chervil, call Brother Rolt to me,' he whispered.

But Chervil had no need to look for Rolt, for he had come, and looked into his beloved Master's eyes with love.

'It is done, all done, Master, as you decreed,' he said. 'You have honoured your love for her, and redeemed the wrongs committed at Blagrove Slide. There is no bloodshed now, only peace across the High Wood of Duncton, and spreading out beyond.'

'Not as *I* decreed, good Rolt, but as the Stone decreed. Now Chervil, listen, and you Rolt . . .' But suddenly he said no more, and his clear eyes looked upon the Stone again, and saw a vision simpler but greater than any he had ever had.

'Not I, but the Stone,' he whispered again, his voice at peace. 'And it will help you now, and her.'

'Help her, Master?' whispered Rolt, glancing at Privet, then at Thripp once more.

'Find the Book, mole, find the Book,' said Thripp with a touch of his old impatience that a new vision he had seen was not yet understood by others.

'The Book of Silence,' said Chervil.

'Yes,' said Thripp firmly, and if he saw the Light and the Silence before him then, it was not at the Stone he looked, but into Privet's eyes. Then he was gone from them, like a breath of wind at dawn.

Yet near them Snyde still heaved, still he died, and still Quail's ruptured body desecrated the Clearing by the Stone.

None would touch them or go near. Not Privet, not she. Nor Chervil. Nor Hamble. Nor any one of the followers who stanced so still, and stared, and wished to cast out what had come among them, and befouled them. Nomole had the courage to touch that defiled corpse, or the corpse-to-be.

But one.

A warrior, as true to the Stone as anymole there, yet flawed in himself by a single act, and needing, as he thought, absolution: Maple.

He had led the followers to the Duncton Stone and now he led them one more time in an act whose courage and significance will for ever be remembered and debated by moles who ponder the story of the coming of the lost and last Book.

Maple came forward, slowly and steadfastly. He gently moved moles aside. He stanced above Quail and Snyde and whispered some prayer to the Stone that rose above them; he looked down at them, and then, with a roar as mighty as a thousand moles', charging the vilest of enemies, he bent down and took Quail and Snyde up together in his great paws, white talon worms and all.

He turned from the Stone and ran roaring with them out of the Clearing, out to the west side of the wood, out as others followed, out into the light of the new day and on to the western pastures beyond.

'To the river,' somemole shouted, and down the long way to the river they went, down and down, thundering down, the dead paws of Quail limply flailing, the living paws of Snyde clutching at Maple's thick neck, and the worms, the worms, clinging on to Snyde.

They reached the river and Maple turned from it, swung, and with a final roar he hurled the bodies far out into the dark flowing water.

They turned, they sank, they bubbled, and they surfaced once again, drifting away in the cold, cold water of the Thames.

Quail sank once more and was gone; Snyde seemed to try to swim, seemed to try to rid himself of that which clung to him, seemed to try to scream. But he could not, and nor could he rid himself of any of the worms, struggle and strive though he might. He drifted and they saw come glistening out of his body one bigger than the brood. Fat, puckered, legged, with head of Snake and body of Worm, in Snyde and out of him, the mother of them all. Once Quail's; now Snyde's.

And if any creature alive could ever be called Paramount and Prime it was she, as she curled on Snyde's drifting living body to survive. Then the river moved them on, and they were gone away for ever from the sight of Duncton Wood and the Stone.

Of all the wonders of that day, none is more satisfying than this: not a single Newborn was killed by Maple's followers, not one. Many were buffeted, many hurt, many came close to death before the anger of the crowds.

But not one died. Rather, battered and taloned, scratched and scorned – which even Maple's leadership could not prevent – they were cast out from Duncton, and sent wandering. All but one, that is. For him there could surely be no forgiveness, nor any pity, nor help at all.

Wandering by the Library he loved, and had served so supremely in the long moleyears of darkness that had beset it, the followers found Sturne, unknowing what he really was.

He who was of Duncton and had betrayed them, and had been ever at the flanks of Fetter, ready with the cold eye and unforgiving stare.

'Kill him,' somemole said. 'But not quickly.'

And so, while peace began to reign elsewhere across the High Wood, Sturne was taken and battered, pushed and shoved, harried and hounded to the Wood's edge and then down the south-east pasture slopes, the blood of his wounds the only blood upon the grass. He spoke not a single word. He stared up at the trees which seemed to rise above him as he was pushed further from them and down the slope by a crowd of angry, vengeful moles.

'Take him to the cross-under! He is not worthy to have his blood spilled within the system's bounds. Let's kill him outside it!'

Perhaps he called for help, or whispered Pumpkin's name. Whatmole-else knew that he was innocent, and one of the bravest of them all? If any guessed they were not nearby.

So, torn and helpless, he reached the cross-under and was thrown against its walls, first to one side and then another, torn and taloned by any that could get near enough to hurt him.

'He's the mole Sturne! He betrayed Duncton! He's going to die. He's . . .'

They did not quite get him out of the system before they raised their talons for the killing blows. The crowds pressing to come in were too great, and anyway their bloodlust was up; pathetic and vulnerable, he lay unable to defend himself in a dark and puddled far corner of the cross-under.

'Pumpkin,' he whispered, and he even tried to smile, for this, he supposed, in the painless place to which he seemed to have gone, this was . . . well . . . jocular. After all they had done, such an end was either mad or . . . mirthful. And Pumpkin and he might have laughed, not at it, but at the idea of it.

Somewhere on the slopes above the word went about, 'They're killing Keeper Sturne! They're killing Sturne!'

And Maple had heard it, horrified, for there must be no more killing, not now. Even one was a defilement, as he knew too well. And Pumpkin had told him the truth of Sturne.

'Stop them!' he roared, leading others down the slopes, running ever faster but seeing from the crowd, and hearing from their roar, that he must be too late.

'No!' a voice cried at Sturne's bloody flank. 'No!' it screamed.

The killers paused and stared at the female who had dared raise her talons in Sturne's defence.

'No,' she said more quietly, moving in front of him, to stance boldly between him and their talons. 'Whatmole is he? And whatmoles are you to judge him?'

By then few knew who he was, but one there did and then another.

'That's the bastard Sturne, and he deserves—'

'I don't give *that* for whatmole he is,' said Myrtle, mate of Furrow, who had died heroically at Buckland, 'you're not killing him. It's not what Maple would want.'

'Mole, get out of our way.'

'You're *not*,' she screamed, the very image of righteous anger. 'We didn't fight for *this*. We fought—'

'Get out of the bloody way, you bitch,' cried another of them, who, far bigger than she, was in the act of pulling her bodily aside when a strong paw stilled his own, and a mole came to her flank, and stanced by her.

'No,' he said quietly.

'And whatmole are you, for Stone's sake?' said another, raising his talons to strike.

'My name is Whillan of Duncton Wood.'

'Whillan!' gasped one of the crowd.

'Whillan like hell!' said another.

'Aye, Whillan of Duncton Wood!' said Whillan, his eyes calm and clear, and his shoulders strong, his paws sure, his face mature.

'Whillan,' whispered Sturne.

'Leave him be,' said Whillan with authority, 'and let this female go. And . . .'

The crowd of killers became but a crowd of moles once more, uneasy and retreating, and parting too, for Maple came then and others with him. And after him one more, bigger than the rest.

'Whillan,' said Rooster, and in that grubby, echoing, crowded, puddled place he took Whillan in his paws and held him so tight that tears came to his son's eyes.

'Bad place to meet again,' grunted Rooster.

'Not so bad,' replied Whillan. '*This* is where I was born.'

They tended Sturne. Later they could climb the slopes once more, go through the High Wood, and make their way to the Stone, and Privet; and talk as they must surely do. But for now they cared for Sturne.

'Pumpkin knows it all,' whispered Sturne, 'but you can't blame them. I *do* seem a little severe at times. But we succeeded where we might have failed.'

'You talk less and you'll recover more,' said Maple. 'Why, if Whillan had not come . . .'

'It wasn't me!'

'It wasn't him,' said Sturne. 'It was . . . she . . .' He looked round at the crowd and to his dismay saw her disappear into it. 'Her,' he said. 'It was her. What is her name?'

But she was gone, and Maple, the only one there who would have known her, did not quite see her face.

'She saved me,' whispered Sturne again, when they got him back to his austere quarters up on the Eastside. 'I must thank her.'

'Sleep, mole,' said those who cared for him, and, protesting, he did.

Then Whillan and Rooster and many others made their slow way to the Stone to find Privet, and tell Pumpkin of how near his friend Sturne had come to death, and to talk at last to Privet. And so they might have done, had not Hamble come to meet them looking just a little lost.

'Privet? And Pumpkin the library aide? You won't find them by the Stone now. They're not there. They've gone.'

'Where to?'

Hamble shrugged helplessly. 'Into the Ancient System, somewhere there. Wouldn't let me go with them. They just slipped away.'

'For what?'

'To find the Book of Silence, I should think.'

'You think right, mole,' said Rooster. 'Frogbit! Frogbit!'

'Sir! Ever ready at your flank, through fair weather and foul!'

'Mole,' said Rooster, 'we have work to do. Hamble, you know the High Wood?'

'As well as anymole by now, Rooster,' said Hamble, glad to be with his old friend again. 'I know the parts of it that moles can get into without dying of Dark Sound like the back of my paw. As for the rest . . .'

'It's the rest we go to,' said Rooster grimly. 'Now. And you Whillan, you come. May need your skills.'

The High Wood seemed to have darkened again, and its great trees trembled. Somewhere, far off, there was a cry or scream. Not much, but enough to echo in the gloom all about; it seemed to tell of tunnels deep, and chambers dark, and a female who strove to reach a place beyond them all.

'Needs us,' said Rooster, Master of the Delve, a mole who had journeyed as far as anymole through darkness, and was ready now to come into his own.

'All of us!' said Frogbit.

And Hamble led them into the echoing, threatening tunnels that ran beneath the High Wood.

PART V

Book of Silence

Chapter Forty-Four

Privet had not uttered a single word since taking her vow of Silence at Wildenhope; barely any sound at all, indeed, but for sighs and moans when she had been ill, or lost in nightmare sleep and crying out for help.

But of her long journey into the far recesses of her heart and mind, and her lonely grappling with her own errant spirit, we may reasonably guess. Many before had tried to trek the same path, and have given enough accounts of it to leave us in no doubt that nothing is harder for a mole to do than be still enough to hear the silence of the Stone within.

But we need no texts to know this truth – only a few moments with ourselves. Try it, mole, and you will know. Stance quietly where you cannot be disturbed, and discover what the real disturbance is; it is yourself . . . whatever that may be!

At Wildenhope Privet saw that if she was to find the Book of Silence she must give up all she had, including all she held most dear. Which for her was three moles most of all, all of whom were present there: Thripp of Blagrove Slide, Rooster of the Charnel Clough, and Whillan her adopted son, offspring of her sister Lime and Rooster.

Each had taught her different kinds of love and brought her nearer to the Stone. But faced by the horror that was Wildenhope, which was moledom too and therefore something of herself, and with Quail demanding that she speak and chose between those she loved, she could find no words to say.

In that terrible moment she saw something of the truth in the Stone's Silence, which is simply this: saying nothing might say most of all. She was not fool enough to confuse her own silence with the stillness she would need to discover if she was to know the Stone's Silence, but a mole must start somewhere, and so she started with the simplest of vows, which is the hardest to keep: silence.

The first agony was immediate, for in choosing her new path she saw that she seemed to turn from the ones she loved, and even from searching for the Book itself. She saw Whillan's face, she knew he did not understand, she saw his loss, and felt it as her own.

'Stone,' she prayed, and it was the first of a hundred thousand prayers as she journeyed into the un-silent void which was herself, 'Stone, help him understand.'

How many times she nearly died the death of spirit on that long journey, which led her by degrees back to Duncton Wood, we do not know; nor how many times she was tempted to give up and break her vow.

Yet always, when she seemed near to doing so and near spiritual death, or when some new turn threatened her mortal life, there came moles to help her, sent by the Stone. That mole who guided her to safety from the dangers of Wildenhope and Snyde's plots. That mole from the Community of Rose who brought her out of the fastness of the Midland Wen and gave her space to learn that the best healing of a mole's spirit may lie in the healing of another's.

Then at Leamington, where Thorne aided her, and later Hodder and his sister Arliss, who led her off to safety once again. Then Ross, who set off in pursuit of her as a Newborn, but had to become a pilgrim to find her and lead her back to Duncton Wood.

And lastly, and *now* . . . Pumpkin, guided by Stone knows what insight and bravery to venture out on to the surface and so make his way to the Stone Clearing to be with her that Dark Night, ready to serve her once again as library aide.

'Pumpkin!' How near she came now to saying his dear name.

Now . . .

Now, with Quail and Snyde cast out, and Thripp gone to the Silence, a kind of chaos reigned about the Stone. Maple, unaware as yet of the danger Sturne was in, had the task of ensuring that the High Wood was secure, for though the Newborns had mostly fled, a commander never rests. Insurgence, counter-attack, treachery – this is the language a commander must know. He and Ystwelyn had to protect the followers and Duncton against such things, and negotiate with Thorne.

While Chervil, now the most experienced and commanding non-military mole alive, sensed that if peace was to be maintained, he had things to see to there and then. Peace, he felt, does not grow on trees. It is made by mole, and maintained by mole, so he immediately became busy too.

But failing them, what of Rooster her beloved, and Hamble, her oldest, dearest friend?

Many have wondered about Rooster. Should he not now have stayed close by? So long apart had they been that could he not have spent more time up there by the Stone?

The truth is that he knew it was too soon to come back to Privet. Alone of all the moles, except Thripp, and he could not now help, Rooster understood that Privet's journey to find the Book, which must be made alone, was incomplete. He knew it, and so did she. Their love, which was still as sweet and sure as it had been up on Hilbert's Top, if never yet fully expressed, could wait a little longer. It was enough for him that she was near. It was enough for her to know he cared and understood. So, Rooster-like, he wandered off, Frogbit at his flank.

As for Hamble, he had no wish to be anywhere but by the Stone and in the presence of two moles he held so dear: Privet and Pumpkin. So he tried to stay with her, he really did.

'I'll get you some food,' he said, when the crowds and rush had abated somewhat, and few moles were coming up and saying, with a certain disappointment in their eyes, 'Er, is it true, *she's* Privet? The thin gaunt one stanced with that raggety old male?'

'It is,' said Hamble.

'Oh . . . And the Book?'

'No Book,' said Hamble, 'not yet'.

'Oh . . .'

Their disappointment was palpable, and few seemed to want to approach her directly. There was something about her that was distancing, some look in her face, some sense she gave out of being alone and unreachable.

So Hamble went off to find some food and Pumpkin said, 'Madam Privet, do you *want* some food?' She looked at him and he said, 'You want some peace and quiet, don't you? I know you do. I know a place . . .'

Then Pumpkin led her off; although there were so many moles about, rushing here and there, chattering like bluetits in a bush about all that had happened, only one noticed them go, and he got it wrong.

'Went that way,' he told Hamble, pointing quite by chance towards a spot which Hamble knew led to an entrance into the Ancient System. So it seemed reasonable that they had gone that way. He searched for them but naturally he did not find them. At first he thought they would come back; then he thought they would stay safe, and *then* he began to have some doubts and so set off to find Rooster to see what they should do.

Pumpkin did not immediately take Privet into the Ancient System, but led her instead by ways he had been unable to trek for so many molemonths past, across part of the High Wood and then down the Slopes a little way to that unremarkable and so often unnoticed place where his own modest tunnels lay. They were in poor shape, the entrance portal having been ruined by the Newborns in some vengeful act against him, and his main chamber's roof broken in.

'No matter, it is still my own!' he said cheerfully, 'and if you know where to look there's worms aplenty for a couple of thin old moles like us! Now you settle down there and I'll tidy up a bit.'

It was what Privet needed, and she slept a little, waking to find the place tidier than before, and some food ready.

They ate, and Pumpkin began to tell her what had happened in Duncton since her departure nearly a full cycle of seasons before. He told the tale simply, beginning with the cleansing of the Library by the Brother Inquisitors, and then of Sturne's great courage, and how the two of them helped Master Librarian Stour porter the six sacred Books to the Chamber of Roots.

Of Stour's death he told, and his own later tribulations, which ended with the escape from the Marsh End, and leading the rebels into the Ancient System.

'Can't say I ever got used to the place at all, Privet, for the Dark Sound is ever present there, you know. But, well, I know you're going to have to go there, and it's no good me trying to pretend otherwise. My duty as library aide precludes that kind of deceit! Got to show you where texts are, and give my best advice, haven't I?'

Privet smiled.

'So it's no good me going on about it, the fact is there's only one text you're interested in now, and that's the lost and last Book. I'll tell you what I know, and what I don't know, and you can decide what's best. I'm only here to help.'

He told her of the difficulty all of them had had with Dark Sound, and how in certain places in the Ancient System it was so bad that a mole could not go on without risking his very life.

'Wanted to go on you see, carried forward by curiosity. You know me, Privet! I've a snout for oddities, for finding answers to old questions, for searching things out and putting them back in their right place. I *am* a library aide, and Master Librarian Stour trained me himself!'

Privet nodded, and smiled again.

'Dear me, your silence is a thing, it is! Makes a mole talk. Makes a mole think! Makes me say this: my snout tells me that the

574

Book's waiting for you to find it, Privet, right there in the heart of the system, which is protected by Dark Sound. I can lead you some of the way but you'll have to go on alone. So there, that's what I think.'

He crunched at a worm ruminatively and when he looked up again Privet was on her paws waiting at the portal.

'*Now?*' he said.

She did not answer and he knew she could not.

He looked about his tunnels ruefully. 'We've only just got here, Privet. Does it have to be now? Hmmph! I can see it does. Scholars are so impatient!'

He went past her and out on to the surface and looked about again and suddenly 'now' was all about them, and everywhere.

Now was *now*.

The tunnels of the Ancient System were as still as ever he remembered them, though he knew that would mean little when they reached the difficult parts. They might be as silent as death, but Dark Sound was still Dark Sound when it began.

'What was that . . . ?'

He started and paused as their pawsteps ran ahead of them into tunnels he had never quite reached, and he heard a cry, or scream.

'Dear oh dear, Privet, we're too old for this. This is a young mole's task.'

Privet now began to lead him on, and on, on through tunnels that grew deeper and darker, and felt undisturbed by time. Echoes all around, fearful shards of sound, and the armies of long-forgotten moles that roamed the ancient tunnels were all about them, charging down on them, hurrying them along, ranked before them and unpassable. Unaccountably, Pumpkin felt suddenly cheerful, wildly so.

'Well, we're still aliv—'

His voice was snatched from his mouth, his paws turned under him, the dark walls closing.

'Priv . . .'

She held him still, calmed him, let the ghostly moles rush by, but he knew that if she left him now he would be for ever lost.

'We could turn back,' he said hopefully, dread coming into him.

But silently she led him on and he began panting and gasping, seeming to have to run to keep up.

'All right for you, Privet mole. I think you've been here before.'

She had, many times and in many places and knew this for what it

575

was, which was but a noisy beginning to something that would be unexpected. Always that.

'This is the place I was trying to tell . . . TELLTELLTELL . . .'

The echoes of the word thundered back at him like talons out of night. In the darkness Pumpkin frowned and stopped.

'This,' he repeated calmly, challenging the tunnels to answer him, 'around here, *this* is the place where Cluniac and I could not reach before. This is where things are. This is where even Mayweed never came. But here we are and it hasn't taken long.'

Privet laughed.

'You still have a voice, Privet,' he said.

The Dark Sound was sonorous about them, and he peered at the shadows and forward to the turns, back at the bends, and sideways into chambers, which . . . the chambers which . . .

'Privet! PRIVET!'

She stopped, turned, came back to him, looked the way he pointed, which was into a side tunnel no different from many they had passed, but that they saw light, and felt fresh air on their faces. The former was a glimmer, subtle and changing, and the latter had the scent of spring.

Privet led him into the tunnel, which trembled with sound as they entered it, and the light, away ahead of them, caught at the ancient indentations upon the walls they passed.

'Pri . . .' whispered Pumpkin, who found it hard to breathe, and had a dread of what they might find ahead, though the air was good.

'PRI . . .' rumbled Pumpkin's voice, then sharpened, then swung viciously and turned back on him, and, to his ears, the sound was as sudden and as sharp as the rake of gleaming talons across his snout. This was a place where a mole did well to keep quiet!

They went on, close together, Privet herself showing signs of reluctance to go round the next bend, and then the next, and most of all the last – for last it felt to be. Beyond, the tunnel widened to a portal, the sound seemed to shake the walls and floor, the light to fade and then brighten so fast it made them giddy and unsure.

They reached the portal, entered in, and found themselves stanced still in a chamber that seemed to stretch to their left flank, on and on, and whose soaring walls told them how deep they were in the earth. Roots hung free high above, translucent in the light that came from here and there, and seemed to change, making the distant glimmer they had first seen.

The walls had recessed arches and were most marvellously delved, though how Pumpkin had no idea. By giant moles perhaps, for what-mole-else could reach so high, and delve a line so delicate as that which ran and soared, and turned, and crossed another, and then a third, to split out into two more which deepened and never seemed to end?

Pumpkin felt Privet's paw tighten on him, and trembled, and he looked where she looked, through the light to what had at first seemed the far end of the chamber, but which he now saw was its centre. What lay beyond he had no idea. There, raised a little from the ground, caught in light so bright it was almost lost, was a dais of a kind he thought he knew.

'Privet,' he whispered – and looked nervously about, for that whisper raced away, grew, and threatened to become something uncontrollable. Why, poor Pumpkin could hardly speak at all, so consuming of him was that almost-sound.

'Privet,' he said softer still, 'I know what this place was. It is like the Main Chamber of our Library, and that . . . that dais, why there's one like it all lost and hidden among the stacks and texts. There is! It is an ancient scribing place and this is a chamber where holy moles once worked.'

There, he had said it and got away with it. The sound did not quite swell again, though it threatened to, before it faded away and died.

Neither moved, each held on to the other, each stared, and saw that on the dais was a book. Then each grew as still as ice at what they saw nearby.

As the light glimmered and glistened at the soaring walls and in among the plunging roots above, and back to them again, they saw stanced near the dais, a pawstep or two beyond and to one side of it, reaching towards the dais, ready and waiting, the form of mole who seemed almost alive. His form was black, but what had once been fur was dry; what had once been black talons were pale and caught the light; what had once been eyes were shadows, yet still benign. He might have waited there five hundred years, or he might just then have arrived.

'Privet . . .'

She touched his paw to indicate that he should stay where he was, which he had every intention of doing. This was far enough. But that mole . . . he knew that ancient, waiting mole. He knew that stance. He knew what – or rather whatmole – that mole was waiting for.

'Privet mole, he . . .'

Privet turned back to him, her eyes full of fear, for she knew too.

577

'He was a library aide, he had a task to find a book, and having found it he brought it here as he was told and now . . .' whispered Pumpkin, filled with awe and apprehension, 'the book is there. I have done such a task many times myself. He was waiting for his master to come. But this was no ordinary book, and the mole he has waited for all these centuries through is no ordinary mole.'

Pumpkin's eyes widened and the chamber began to swim and soar about him, and the aide-that-was almost seemed to move.

'Privet,' said Pumpkin, grasping at words to bring himself back to where they were, grasping at duty. As brave a mole as ever was . . .

'Privet, let me fetch the Book for you.'

She shook her head and smiled again, bleakly, afraid, suspecting something he did not. She turned towards the central place, and the mole, and the Book within the light, but this time did not restrain him from following her.

Slowly, how slowly, they approached the centre of the chamber, pawsteps running and racing all about its edge, which only made the impression all the greater of a silence that should not be disturbed, greater still with each step they took.

Then into the light went Privet; she mounted the dais, glanced briefly at the aide, as a scholar might who has come to work and nods her thanks for a text fetched from some distant stack, and reached out a paw to touch the Book that had been placed there for her so long ago.

Pumpkin saw her touch it, he saw her lower her head towards it, he saw her peer, examine, pause and then open it. One folio turning in a great arc of light, and then another, and then a third, and more, faster and faster, the sound louder, the chamber beginning to threaten with sound.

'Privet mole,' he called out, for whispers would not do. 'Privet!'

'Nooo . . . !'

'Privet!'

'NOOOO . . . I cannot!' she cried out. 'I CAN *NOT*!'

And her cry became a scream out of a place that went back before that ancient aide had come, before the Book was brought, before this great chamber was ever delved. Back and back, back into the earth, and from out of it. Hers was the scream primordial, which is the pain of birth.

'I CANNOT DO IT, STONE!'

And then she turned, blinded by an existential fear of what the Stone asked her to do, tumbled into Pumpkin's paws, broke free of him, turned and looked again at where the Book lay open, her silence broken, the chamber roaring now with sound.

Pumpkin caught her paw, righted her, held her, and supporting her, began to help her flee.

'I cannot do it, Pumpkin. I cannot, I cannot . . .'

Out of the chamber, away from its light, back through the tunnels, too weak to run, dragging, pulling, shoving, step by step, both desperate, as if the Book was pursuing them.

'It is, Pumpkin, it is,' she said.

'Yes,' he said gently, aide-like, for he knew it was and that it would find her and she could not get away from it. But they could try.

So on they went, away and away and away, knocking into walls, bumping into bends and turns, dust on their fur, bruises on their snouts, until exhausted, trembling and she still whispering, 'I cannot, I will not even try, it is too much,' they ran into a wall that lived, and had paws enough to hold them, and voices to reassure them.

Rooster, Hamble and Frogbit stanced in their path.

'What was it, Pumpkin? What did she see?' said Hamble.

While Rooster held her, and let her whisper and mutter out her distress and, again and again, absolute refusal. Frogbit stared at the light that glimmered just ahead, and the portal into the chamber.

They had come no distance at all. They were still there. It was Rooster and Hamble and Frogbit who had run to them. The Book was waiting still.

Rooster eased Privet from him and let Hamble take her to his paws. Then, signalling to them all to stay where they were, he went back through the portal and stared and saw what they had seen; and understood.

'What is it?' asked Hamble, puzzled and perplexed.

'It's Privet,' said Rooster. 'She knows. Pumpkin knows.'

Pumpkin sighed and nodded and said, 'She's the one must scribe it. I *think* that's it. Privet's the mole will scribe the Book of Silence.'

All was still and quiet, the Dark Sound retreating into peace.

When she was ready, she turned back into the chamber of her own accord, with Pumpkin at her left flank, Rooster to her right, and Hamble and Frogbit just behind. Together they went to the centre of the chamber and into the light, but she alone mounted the dais and took up the Book. It looked new-made, or untouched by time, and when she turned its folios to show them, they saw no scribing there, nothing at all. All to come, it seemed.

'The lost and last Book,' whispered Hamble.

'Not lost,' said Pumpkin, 'but never scribed.'

'I cannot,' whispered Privet, but though the Dark Sound mounted about them at the word 'cannot' she did not let go the Book, and to her eyes returned the resolution of a mole who has ascended many a mountain, only to find the crest was false and there is more and knows she must go on.

'Like delving, I expect,' said Frogbit, 'hard all the way. Very hard.'

The Dark Sound grew louder and they began to look concerned, yet Privet dared to smile.

'Hard as being born,' she said.

Then she placed the Book on the dais once again and commanded Pumpkin to open it anywhere, which he did, and to hold it so she could scribe.

'If I don't begin now I never will.'

'What will you scribe?' asked Frogbit, genuinely curious.

She raised her paw to the folio, frowned in thought, smiled, and slowly scribed her name and spoke it out aloud: '"Privet",' and that was all.

'There! That will do for now . . .' She seemed lighthearted, but then her eyes grew serious. 'Help me, Stone,' she whispered, and the Light was on them all as she left the Book in its safe place ready for her to return to and begin.

Then, together, they all left, close by each other, as if fearful that the rumbling Dark Sound might reach out and snatch one of them away.

But when they had gone, the Light glimmered on, to shine brighter still upon that unknown, nameless, aide who so long before had brought the Book and with steadfast faith began to wait the long centuries through. Whilst the draught of air was enough to tug at the Book's folios, and shift them this way and that silently, until they stayed open where Privet had scribed her name, and the Light shone brighter still, soft and white and eternal as the Silence that came all about.

Chapter Forty-Five

Duncton slowly began to settle to a new life, and new concerns. It must be said at once that moles were disappointed that the Book of Silence was neither lost nor really found, but rather was in the process of being scribed.

Real Holy Books, the ordinary mole and pilgrim were inclined to feel, were not scribed *now* so much as *then*, or at a pinch, at some time yet to come. But *now* seemed a little dull compared to the nostalgic contemplation of the awesome past, or the hope for a better future, which were ideas a mole could get his imagination into. But *now*, well . . . !

Then again, Privet herself was something of a disappointment, *wasn't* she?

'Come on, be honest, mole, she's not what we expected . . .'

'Well, I don't know about that.'

'She's just a thin and scraggy old female scholar, nothing more nor less. We hardly ever see her down here in Barrow Vale, do we? As for this so-called Book she's scribing up there in the Ancient System, what use will it be to anymole, when all is said and done? Eh? But whatmole cares? After all, the Newborns are nothing now, nothing at all, and that Quail and his Snyde, they got their come-uppance, and as for Squelch and Skua . . .'

Once the initial excitements of the liberation (as it became known) of Duncton were over, it was such conversations as these that were the norm among pilgrims and followers throughout November down in Barrow Vale.

Quite early on a good many moles, principally those from nearby systems who had answered some call they never did quite articulate to come when they had, began to leave. Then, as December loomed and the weather turned colder and worms were scarcer, more moles from further off began to drift away. They had fought the fight, they had completed their pilgrimage, and though Duncton was all very well, they rather missed their home systems and so thought they'd set off once more.

In the last few days of November a whole group of moles from the Wolds, who reckoned they could make it home in time for Longest Night, before winter weather set in, departed, and the system seemed suddenly empty, though in fact it was still temporary home to far more moles than it could really sustain, and certainly more than at any time for several decades past. Of these many were hardened campaigners, like Ystwelyn himself, who were not complacent about the 'victory' over the Newborns and knew it would be many a moleyear yet before they were completely vanquished throughout moledom. With this Chervil agreed, and he and Thorne and Ystwelyn, all allies now, began to plan a systematic re-education of moledom for the moleyears ahead.

They would have liked to include Maple in this, but he would have none of it. Of what had happened in Buckland when he killed Sapient, and the talon worms had entered his wound, none of the witnesses to it spoke, though the leaders knew. Loyal Weeth stayed at his flank, and spoke for him when, as he soon did, he chose to return to his old burrows and live quietly for a time.

The wound he had suffered at Buckland did not fully heal, but festered, and refused all treatment.

'As for the talon worms,' Weeth said to Ystwelyn, Thorne and Chervil, 'I think they don't trouble him, and I hope that they will die. He is a healthy mole, he . . .'

But though Weeth was a consummate liar, he could not fool such moles. Maple was not himself, and might never be again. He had made a supreme effort, he had led the followers not so much to victory as to peace, a far greater thing, and he would be remembered as the mole who rid Duncton of the pestilence that was represented by Quail and Snyde.

Now, if he needed peace and quiet and time to recover he must have it – and Thorne and Ystwelyn discreetly posted guardmoles on the routes to his tunnels, to gently dissuade the many moles who wanted to visit him, and praise him. Apart from Weeth, only a few moles were allowed to visit him, and two in particular – Hamble and Fieldfare. The first understood Maple's malaise, and as a former warrior himself could talk Maple's language, and share the quiet hour.

As for Fieldfare, why, she had known Maple since he was a pup, and had stories to tell which he liked to hear, of her adventures at Seven Barrows, of the friends she had made, of heroes like Spurling and Noakes (whom she had regarded almost as a son) and of the journey with the surviving rebels back to Duncton Wood, when they had been among the first to join Maple's army.

All this Maple enjoyed, saying little, sleeping much, and submitting patiently to the different treatments and remedies that were offered him to heal his festering wound, and purge him of the talon worms, if that was possible.

'He's suffering, Fieldfare, he really is,' confided Weeth one late November day, 'and sometimes he grows sharp and irritable with me.'

Weeth was suffering too, and Fieldfare could see it.

'What else?' she asked gently.

'It's nothing,' said Weeth unconvincingly.

Fieldfare knew well when to be silent.

'It's his fur,' said Weeth eventually, 'it's growing thin about his head and shoulders. I don't know if he knows it himself but I can see it day by day. Fieldfare, I'm frightened for him. He's a good mole, a great mole, and though he treats me as his friend I see him also as the master I shall always serve. He led us all, he fought for moledom, and now I shall do my best to fight for him. Except . . . I don't know how to fight this fight. Talon worms! Why, they're what Quail had, but he was evil. They entered Snyde, but he was evil too. But Maple! A worthy mole like him. Why did the Stone allow it? What can I do?'

'Care for him, mole, as you do already. Seek out remedies, as you also do. Let friends like Hamble and myself visit him.'

'Perhaps Privet will come.'

'Privet!' exclaimed Fieldfare, not entirely approvingly. 'We barely see her these days she's that busy scribing. But I'll have a word with Pumpkin and maybe he'll get her to come down here to see Maple. Now, there's nothing else you want to tell me?'

'Nothing,' lied Weeth, and Fieldfare knew it was a lie but she felt it best to say no more. There were things it was perhaps better not to mention.

'Well, then, try not to worry, we'll all see him right!'

'Yes,' said Weeth heavily, watching her go and then turning back down into the tunnels where Maple stayed most of the day. Maple was there, and had been listening, but turned away when Weeth came, and would not talk. His head was low and Weeth went to him, and put his paws to him and said, 'What is it, Maple?'

Maple turned slowly to him and his face was wet with tears.

'Mole,' he said in a shaking voice, 'I can . . . smell myself. It is the odours that come with talon worms. It is the beginning of decay. Have you not noticed it?'

583

To Maple, Weeth could never lie.

'I have, Maple.'

'What can I do?' said Maple, his voice full of suffering. 'If it was an army of moles I could see, I would know what to do. But something inside . . . I feel helpless and defiled.'

'Master, I don't know what we can do. But there'll be something, there will be.'

'Weeth, you have no need to stay with me now. No need . . .'

'I'm staying with you, Maple, and it's as simple as that!' said Weeth sharply.

Maple nodded his head as if he had known Weeth would stay but was glad to have it said.

'For now, you'll stay,' he said.

'I'll always stay,' said Weeth, his eyes full of a fight and determination that Maple himself had once had, and must surely find again if he was to live.

Yet Maple was not the only suffering mole in Duncton Wood. Indeed, beneath the surface excitements of victory and release from the Newborns, many a mole seemed now to suffer much. It was as if in finding new life moles found space to feel their ills of body and of mind. Many were the moles who wept in those winter nights, for losses they had suffered but not grieved for before: of kin, of home, of friends, all lost, and of their youth and innocence that were ravaged by what were called Crusades. Such moles often found comfort in activity, and some no doubt were among the many who left the system. Others, perhaps nearer to their own true heart, stayed where they were, reclusive as Maple was, quiet, seeking nothing more than to live from day to day, and share community from time to time.

In this way, Barrow Vale became the centre of Duncton once again, and moles would drift there of an afternoon and talk, and laugh, and shed a tear. What pilgrim tales were told then! What fierce stories of the fighting followers! And what sad tales, too, of loss and of slow recovery.

The damp Marsh End remained unvisited, for there, held out of sight, were moles like Squelch and other such Newborns, whose crimes had been too great for them to be tolerated, but whom the new regime under Chervil allowed to be arraigned but not killed. Many, including Skua and Fetter and other Inquisitors, were removed to Wildenhope, there to serve out their time away from worthy moles, and if they suffered the remaining years of their lives in that bleak place, well, there was justice in it, of a sort. Forgiveness was all very well, but those who have suffered at the paws of evil need sometimes to know that evil moles do not go free. Retribution has its place.

A few such moles stayed on in Duncton Wood, partly because their crimes were minor, and might have been committed by anymole under the thrall of Quail's regime, partly because they had use as scriveners in the Library or as aides to the old and infirm. While a very few, and Squelch was among them, were too ill at first to move, and then stayed on.

Squelch's story was most strange, though then almost unknown. For vile though he had been, and complicit in much that his father and Snyde had done, yet none could deny him this – his gift for song and melody was as near to genius as living moles had ever known. Nor could there be any denying that he had a way of organizing others to sing, such as few moles have ever heard.

Yet, even so, many demanded that he die, and so he might have done had not two things happened. One was that Whillan pleaded for him – Whillan who had survived, Whillan whose own tale was so extraordinary (moles surmised, for none had heard it yet), and Whillan had authority and was not easily denied.

The second thing that saved Squelch's life was his own voice – for, refusing to answer any charge against him but with 'I'm guilty of it all, and more, much more,' he had giggled (as was his way) and then sung to all of them, a song of sad remorse, which told of a mole that had been warped and moulded by Quail against his will, but who despite it all had retained a sense of beauty none could deny. A mole who suffered now genuine remorse for all he had done, and whose obesity was dying on him as he suffered, so that bit by bit he became less fat, and his true form, which was not so bad, and even had a kind of faded elegance, began to show.

So they let him live and he was grateful for that. He found a task down in the Marsh End, tending other Newborns who were ill, with a care and love beyond questioning, for it was the care and love he had longed for as a pup. In all this they did right, for it is easy to kill, much harder to reform.

Squelch sang no more, but sometimes, of an evening, he scribed down the songs that were born inside his head. At first this was hard, for he had never been trained in such things, and knew no easy way to do it. Later, at Whillan's suggestion, Sturne himself came to show him a way of notation that mediaeval scribemoles had used, which once learned Squelch found easy to use.

'I don't know why you're kind to me,' he told Sturne.

'It was Whillan's idea,' said Sturne, as brief and chillsome as ever.

'Then do you know why he's kind to me?'

Sturne shrugged, his face impassive. He had guessed why, or half of it, but he would never say. That was for Whillan to reveal.

As for the songs Squelch noted down, and what their purpose, he would say nothing at all, except this: 'They're for a mole I loved, and who loved me. Long, long ago, when I was bad, when I . . .' But Squelch could rarely say much more than that, for he was lachrymose and as his songs had once moved moles to tears, so he was often moved himself.

'Whatmole was that, Squelch?' those who knew him, and saw him, would ask. He would not tell them, but once, in floods of tears, he did tell Sturne whatmole it had been.

'Her name was Madoc. I wronged her but she forgave me. Now, every day and in my head, I sing to her and wonder how she is and what happened. She . . . she . . .'

'Mole, 'tis better you don't say.'

'I *want* to say because it is inside me and unbearable,' he said. 'Anyway, I trust you, Sturne. I know you'll not tell another mole. She . . .'

Sturne sighed, and heard.

'She had my pups, I think. But because of what I am and what I did she'll never visit me, nor contact me, nor will they know whatmole their father was. But Sturne . . .'

Sturne stared.

'. . . I miss them, moles I never knew. I, who have been so bad, so cruel, so vile. I feel tender towards them. So I make my songs for them, and harmonies. Here, let me show you, here, see . . . !'

Which Sturne did, and was amazed. A chamber full of texts of songs and euphony scribed in a notation few could understand, which none, in all probability, would ever hear.

'See! But don't tell another living mole my secret. I don't know why I told you! Don't tell them a mole I violated is my muse. They'll think I'm mad and kill me after all!'

But another already knew, and that was Whillan, who had told Sturne something of Madoc's story.

'Who was she?' asked Sturne.

'A mole I once loved,' said Whillan cautiously. 'Have you ever loved?'

'I love Pumpkin,' said Sturne, 'but he's male. Of females . . . well, I have never known any that way. I am a scholar first and last. But . . .'

586

Whillan saw a look bleaker than usual in Sturne's eye.

'You have, Sturne! Come on, you *do* love some female or other!'

Sturne frowned and shook his head and said he did not, he . . . did . . . not! And tempted though Whillan was to laugh at the thought of Sturne suffering the pangs of love, he was sensible enough not to.

Sensible indeed, for these were rather more than the pangs of love of the manageable kind that youngsters suffer in the spring. These were real racking thoughts and yearnings of a kind that poor Sturne, who had suffered so much for so many moleyears, had no idea how to deal with. His world was texts, and if that was all he had known he would have died, if not happy, then at least not much disturbed. But the Newborns had come, and wise Master Librarian Stour, seeing a strength in him that nomole-else but Pumpkin saw, gave him a most formidable task, which was to pretend to be one thing while being the other.

It was a task Sturne most gloriously and courageously fulfilled, but at terrible cost. He had seen friends die, and had been unable to speak of it; he had seen moles tortured, and had to go along with it; he had seen the Stone abused, and had had to keep his silence; he had seen the system he loved defiled and nearly destroyed, and in none but Pumpkin had he been able to confide. All that he might have lived through without saying much afterwards; it was, after all, of a piece with his unemotional and arid life. He might afterwards have simply kept his own counsel, and found outlet and satisfaction as Master Librarian among the texts he had done so much to honour and protect.

But it was not to be that way. Instead, after the death of Quail before the Stone – a death which was part of a bloodless subversion of the Newborns under their very snouts for which Sturne was largely responsible – he was attacked, not thanked; he was nearly killed, not praised.

It was not fear that Sturne felt as he was battered and bruised and harried down towards the cross-under that day, but betrayal by the Stone itself. Not that he did not understand why moles might have made the mistake they did; but he could not make out why the Stone did not help him.

So he had said nothing as he was attacked, nothing at all, and suffered the buffets and talonings, suffered the jibes, and finally suffered the knowledge that he was about to die *without uttering a single word*.

But to the Stone he cried out in those last moments when he thought his life was over, cried out with a passion he had never ever dared show in life. He wanted to say farewell to Pumpkin, whom he loved. He wanted to say a last goodbye to the Library he had lived for for so long. And – and this was a surprise to him – he wanted to wander one last time among the old trees of the High Wood and the Eastside, for now, as he lay with his back to concrete and about to die, he saw that he loved his system as truly as any Duncton mole, *even if he had never said so, or even thought so.*

Something in Sturne awoke as he was about to die; he found that he had feelings too, real, and deep, and passionate, and he knew that, after all, he might have learned to express them if only he had had a chance.

But there was more. He cried out to the Stone in those final moments and the Stone answered him. It sent a female to save him, Myrtle, dead Furrow's mate. He did not know her name but how he remembered her! Her fierce cry of 'No!', her stancing with her back to him and facing all those raised talons on her own; and her purpose and her courage.

Then Whillan had come, and she, before Sturne had a chance to speak to her and find out whatmole she was, had slipped away, and nomole knew her name. Not that he had not tried to find it out, but nomole seemed to know who she was or could have been. Perhaps he would not have cared, but in all his life, from the very first, nomole had ever protected him as she had done, not even his own mother. Just the opposite . . . Why else was he so severe and lacking in all molish warmth, why else?

Unused to love, afraid of it, never risking it at all, Sturne discovered that day a mole who cared for him, and he, poor mole, found that though his wounds healed his heart did not. On the contrary, his heart had opened to the feelings he had denied for so long, and in the unknown Myrtle – or rather the dream of her, for he could have no more than that – they found an outlet. Love, loss, infatuation, confusion, self-pity, anger, and a yearning gentleness – these were the sufferings of Sturne throughout those November days, and they were terrible.

To make them worse, Pumpkin was so pre-occupied with Privet's great task that he, who alone might have counselled Sturne and helped him find the object of his love, if only to express his gratitude and realize that she was, after all, but a female among many and there might be others . . . Pumpkin was unavailable. So poor Sturne suffered his wild feelings all alone and in silence.

Yet it need not have been like that. For at the end of November, when so many moles left the system, one at least came back. She did so diffidently, having made the trek from Rollright. It was Myrtle. She too had not forgotten that wild day at the cross-under, when some spirit whose name she knew not made her fight for the life of a mole she had never seen before. But there he was, battered and broken before her, set upon by a mob of moles, and something in his eyes that spoke of loss, rejection and nobility called to her.

She stanced before him, she shouted out her rage, and if she was all the louder because she had not been able to do the same for her beloved Furrow at Buckland, it did not matter. She saved him, and when Whillan came she slipped away, embarrassed, and certain that such a mole would not want truck with an ignorant mole like her. Anyway, was he not Newborn? So she had set off on the lonely way back home.

But at Rollright her paws slowed, and she could not go on for thinking about that mole's eyes, the look in them, the need in them. She told herself that if she only knew he was all right and well it would be enough. So she turned back, shy and diffident and unsure what she would do. For days she dallied outside the system, sure that he would have forgotten who she was, or would feel obliged to thank her if she introduced herself. Then she thought of a plan; she would go to see Maple, for he had always been good to her, ever since he and Weeth had found her group north of Caradoc.

Yes, she would go and see him, and ask after his health, and say she had come to say goodbye, and, well, did he know of . . . had he ever any dealings with . . . a mole called Sturne. That was what they said his name was: Sturne, a Newborn librarian.

Newborn! And Newborns had killed Furrow. How could she even think . . . !

But sometimes the heart guides paws more truly than the mind, and so she had dared venture back up to Duncton Wood.

But Maple she never reached. She nearly did, but guardmoles about the place where he lived turned her back, saying he was ill and could see nomole. Then could she see Weeth, for he would remember her and might be willing to help?

'Not seen him about at all, my dear. No, you best leave them both alone for—'

Just then, along the way where she had been stopped, *he* came, large as life, severe, formidable: Sturne.

589

'Evening, sir!' called out the guardmole. 'He'll be glad to see you I expect!'

Myrtle hid away from him as he went past, her heart pounding in her chest quite painfully.

'Who is he?' she asked, amazed to see him there, and to hear him called 'Sir' as well. More than that, amazed at how she wanted to run to him, to put her paws about him, for that look in his eyes, why, anymole could see it was still there. But worse. Her heart wept for him.

'Him? That was the Master Librarian himself, Sturne. A hero if ever there was one. A great mole.'

'Master Librarian?' faltered Myrtle, who could not even scribe. A hero, a great mole . . . well then, it was no use.

'Mole! Come back! I could tell Weeth that you were here and give him your name. What is your name? Mole!'

But Myrtle slipped away, back by the path she had come down, for she knew that so great a mole as a Master Librarian would never want to be embarrassed by her coming to him and asking him if he was well. He had probably forgotten all about that day. He would not want to know.

So Myrtle slept in some scrape that late November night, shivering and miserable and never knowing that not so far away, as miserable and shivering as she, a hero lay, a great mole, a Master Librarian no less, who would have given his all to know her name, and to know that even so late in life he could be understood and loved, and that he, too, had much to give.

November and December then was a time of suffering. But suffering is not always so plain, or harsh-seeming, as this. More often it is subtle, insidious and so unrecognized that it masquerades as the opposite to what it really is.

Privet was suffering, though she did not know it yet. She had found the Book, she had understood that she was chosen to fill its folios, and so, with vigour, she had begun. With vigour she had continued. With vigour reached December, working day after day at her task, scribing of the many journeys that moles had undertaken in the name of Silence – some historic, some recent, and one of them her own.

Day by day she scribed, and often into night, with Pumpkin servicing her needs of food and conversation, and Sturne providing her with the reference texts she sometimes used. A time of austerity and effort, but one she seemed to much enjoy.

Of course she enjoyed it! The words flowed from her talons, clear as light. Words, names, places, incidents, ideas, beliefs . . . all leading towards the Stone's Light and Silence. And as they came she saw ahead towards much deeper things, of which she would in time scribe too. Insights she had had, truths she had never expressed, feelings and senses that she knew – she *knew* – no other mole had ever scribed down before.

Yes, she could complete the Book of Silence if only the Stone would give her time, and health.

So what was the suffering in that?

She did not know. She would not have understood the question yet.

But Pumpkin did, and one night, as December came, and winter cold shivered at his flanks, he took himself up to the Stone he loved, talking to it as he daily did, saying things he could say to nomole at all.

'Stone, it's too easy for her and I am afraid. She scribes and scribes as if she fears to stop. I may be wrong, I probably am . . . but I feel her winter has not yet begun. Forgive me if I'm foolish and presumptuous. But if I'm not, help her, Stone, because I feel that beyond the scribings she has made, and will make yet, is a whole winter of suffering, and it will be Privet's alone and nomole will be able to help her. Not me, not Rooster, not Hamble, though we all love her. Therefore, watch over her, Stone, and see that she comes home to us safeguarded. And if the Book is not to be, well, Stone, remember it's her we love, not what she scribes.'

But Pumpkin's prayers were rarely over so quickly and often as not, having seemed to have finished his supplications before the Stone, and having turned away to go back to his daily tasks, he would remember some other issue or other which he wished to draw to the Stone's attention. So on this occasion . . .

'And Stone, forgive me for troubling you further, but there's Whillan, isn't there? For, as you know . . .'

Pumpkin's concern then, as on many other prayerful occasions through November and December, was Whillan's absolute unwillingness to talk about what had happened to him after Wildenhope. Of even what occurred *at* Wildenhope he would say nothing, though from things that Chervil and Rooster had said, Pumpkin had a shrewd idea how Whillan had got away to safety.

Even more so after he had put his theory to Hamble who, as it happened, had passed through Wildenhope on his circuitous journey from Caradoc to Duncton Wood and had been reluctant witness to some drownings and worked out how Whillan might have effected his escape.

Pumpkin's interest in Whillan was more than idle curiosity, for it troubled him that Whillan, like Rooster, barely spoke to Privet, though Stone knew how much they must mean to each other. For her part, Privet seemed wholly indifferent to Whillan, as she did to Rooster, so absorbed was she by the process of scribing the Book.

While for *his* part Whillan was silent and obtuse to the point of obscurity, and a very changed mole indeed. As Hamble himself had rightly said, whatever Whillan was before he left Duncton it was a formidable mole that returned.

'If he has returned,' Hamble continued darkly, 'for he's a look in his eyes that suggests to me his heart's somewhere else for now. You mark my words, Pumpkin, he'll be off before he comes back, if you see what I mean.'

Their conversation took place in December, and its context was one dear to Hamble's heart and something of a puzzlement to Pumpkin – how it might be that weak moles can sometimes triumph over strong.

'For I'm weak,' said Pumpkin with genuine modesty, 'but we triumphed over the Newborns, didn't we, Hamble?'

'We certainly did, and you're right, you're not the strongest mole I've ever seen.'

By way of illustration of weakness versus strength the conversation turned first to Myrtle's startling intervention at the cross-under on Sturne's behalf, though they did not then know her name.

Anger, conviction, surprise and a loud shout will take a mole a long way, Hamble pointed out, if not always *all* the way. So, for example, Myrtle's initial success in stopping the moles who were about to kill Sturne was relatively easy to understand, without in any way taking away from her achievement.

But the truth is that had not Whillan come when he did, taking his place along-flank her, and turning his calm gaze upon the many moles so eager to strike the first death blow, more than likely not only would Sturne have died, but Myrtle as well.

So therefore, Hamble reasonably asked, how it was that so many moles, all so eager to strike a blow, should have been stilled by Whillan, and then have retreated when faced by no more than his stance and his calm voice, and finally slipped away.

'I might almost say *fled* away, as if they had seen something they recognized as far stronger than themselves. In fact, I *do* say that, Pumpkin!'

It was certainly a reasonable question and only went to show that Whillan was a changed mole. So startling a change indeed that many would say that that young mole, frightened, uncertain, deserted by all including his adoptive mother (as it seemed to him as he was roughly taken to the river by Chervil, Feldspar and the others), *had* died, and was no more.

This much Whillan often said himself. But though it is true that he 'often said himself' this is not to say he often spoke. He did not. Never loquacious, the new Whillan was rather less so on his return. He said little and observed much, and resisted all attempts, even by moles who knew and loved him, like Fieldfare and Pumpkin, to make him tell his story.

Others, most notably Rooster, did not even ask him, sensing that when he wished to talk he would do so. As for Privet, the two met briefly soon after his return and her commencement of her great task, and found that they had little to say to each other.

All that Whillan said was this, to Fieldfare: 'Privet and I are both still travelling, and as we are on different journeys we have nothing to say to each other. At least we both know it, and that's a comfort!'

Fieldfare could not make him out at all, and even less could she understand why he seemed prepared to spend time with moles like Squelch, or 'that Frogbit' – a mole whose brevity and unwillingness to answer virtually any question she asked she found most frustrating.

All this was made worse for her by Privet's preoccupation with her scribing, which meant that she was rarely seen, and when she was she seemed in a world far removed from anymole-else's. That much of what Whillan had said at least Fieldfare understood!

'But Hamble, my dear,' she said later, for he was a mole she could talk to normally, 'it is as if the whole of Duncton Wood was occupied by moles who don't want to say a single thing worth hearing.'

Hamble grinned. He and Fieldfare got on well, and they had a common bond in Chater, at whose death Hamble had been present, and in whose life Fieldfare had found so much love and comfort.

'Your trouble, Fieldfare, if I may say so, is that you like a good gossip and you feel that if moles won't join in they've got something against you. But—'

'Not a gossip, a chat! That's what I like. And dear me, didn't Chater used to tell me off for chatting away to a mole and, afterwards, making two and two add up to five about something they had said?'

'Or six, more like,' growled Hamble. 'Give 'em time.'

'Who?'

'Moles,' said Hamble. 'Most of us here have been through hard times and not all of us have your resilience. But things will improve, you see if they don't. Duncton will be itself again one day I daresay, though I don't suppose I'll be here to see it.'

'Not here, Hamble! And why not? You're not leaving too, I hope, like so many others?'

'Maybe I will and maybe I won't. There's nothing much for me here now, except some of my oldest friends of course! But seriously, I miss the Moors, strange though that will seem to a Duncton mole. But I do. I'd like to have seen the purple heather again, and heard the curlews call, and seen the water in the cloughs racing wild. It's where I was born and raised, Fieldfare, and I miss it.'

'Ahhh . . .' purred Fieldfare, '*that* is what I miss!'

'What—?'

'I don't mean the Moors, my dear, I mean moles talking as you were then. Moles *talking*. There's nothing like a winter's night, and a chamberful of well-fed and well-watered moles, some friends and some strangers, sharing a tale and a joke and a song. That's how Duncton was when I was young, and it was at Longest Night, in a friend's tunnels not so far from here, in just such company that I met my beloved Chater.'

Hamble nodded sympathetically and said, 'Well, Longest Night will soon be on us, and you can rest assured that I'll tell you a tale or two then, and gather a few moles together willing to do the same.'

'Why, Hamble, that's very . . . thoughtful of you,' said Fieldfare, genuinely touched, her snout shading towards pink as she shifted her ample but still comely frame about a bit in a pleasurable and anticipatory sort of way. And, as one thought leads to another, not always in a way that moles understand, she asked, 'Tell me, have you never had a mate? I mean – a long-term mate?'

'No, I haven't,' said Hamble a little shortly, 'no time. I can't say I regret it, for I've had an active life. But then I've never felt the need. Now I must be off, Fieldfare, I must get going. These nights are . . . cold.'

She had regretted the question the moment she asked it, and regretted it even more when he set off into the bitter night, not looking back as he usually did and giving her a wave.

'Oh dear,' she said to herself, 'oh dear!'

A few days later he visited her again in reference not to her too-personal question about his not having had a mate, but about Longest Night.

'Been thinking,' he said, 'and even better, been doing. And better still . . .'

Fieldfare felt the delicious thrill of the promise of a coming treat.

'. . . better still, I've arranged something.'

'What, Hamble, what?'

'Ah, well, I wouldn't want to disappoint you, Fieldfare. You mean a lot to me, you see.'

She did not miss the sudden quiet in his voice, and the gentleness. Indeed, after their last meeting she had begun to think that Hamble might become rather more than a friend. The thought of him leaving for the Moors, and that look in his eyes when he said 'I've never felt the need' – which told her that he *had* felt the need – had set her thinking thoughts she had denied herself for a very long time indeed, namely, that she was not so old that she could not find another mate. More particularly, that she was not too old to take *Hamble* as a mate.

Spurling, Stone bless him, had been something very different, and had that brave mole survived Buckland she would have stanced by her word and taken him into her burrow. But she had always known that it would not have been right. But Hamble was a different proposition altogether. He certainly was . . .

So she let him tell her that she meant a lot him, though when he suddenly spoilt it all by saying that she was almost like a *sister* to him, why, she felt cross and was very short indeed.

'I know I've offended you in some way,' declared poor Hamble, 'and I'm sure I didn't mean to.'

'No you haven't! What gave you that idea?'

But Hamble was not a mole patient with such play and he did not give her the satisfaction of trying to find out what was wrong.

'I never did like it when moles don't speak their minds!' he declared. 'So either say what's up or be quiet.'

'Hamble!' she said feebly.

'Well?'

He frowned at her and did not smile when she did.

'I . . .' But she was at a loss for words. How could she say she thought of herself – or had begun to – as rather more than a *sister*?

He shrugged indifferently and said, 'Doesn't make any difference to what I've arranged.'

'What *have* you arranged?'

'I was going to tell you but now I won't, because it might not happen.'

'What might not happen?'

Hamble grinned and said, 'Look, mole, what did we talk about last time, apart from mates?'

There was a twinkle in his eye, or a certain resolution, and she almost quivered at the sight of it. She couldn't make him out at all.

'We talked . . .'

'We talked about Longest Night, that's what we talked about, and about how you liked a chamberful of moles telling tales and what have you. Well, I agree, and so I suggest that come Longest Night you make sure the place is spick and span, and you have a plentiful supply of worms, because I'm going to bring back here, seeing as your place is more comfortable and larger than mine, seeing as you're an ample mole—'

'Hamble, I'm not that ample!'

'Ample enough for me!' he said shamelessly and chuckling. 'Anyway, you be ready to welcome a good few moles.'

'*What* moles?' she implored him.

'All right then, I'll tell you one, and I'll be honest with you: it's as much a surprise to me as it will be to you. But it was his suggestion, not mine.'

Poor Fieldfare felt sudden disappointment. This was not Hamble's idea at all. This was somemole-else's. This . . .

'Here we go again, Fieldfare, I can see it in your face, I've said something I shouldn't.'

'I hoped it was your idea because you cared!' she blurted out, almost tearfully.

'I do care,' he said, suddenly taking her in his paws. 'I do care,' he whispered, 'and that's why when Whillan said that come Longest Night he might be willing to talk about all that's happened to him, seeing as a certain mole or two might be coming to Duncton Wood, I said that I knew a mole would provide a burrow and be only too happy to hear such revelations, and her name was Fieldfare.'

'Did you?' said Fieldfare softly, not letting him let go, and him not wanting to.

'I did,' said Hamble, his back paws beginning to ache from the awkward position they were in, 'could we stretch out?'

'Just like that, Hamble?'

'Just like this,' he said firmly.

'Moles might find out,' she said sleepily, much later.

'Might,' said Hamble, 'and probably will.'

'Hamble?' she whispered, but he was asleep, and all she could do was to touch his broad shoulders, and caress his scarred face, and to shed a tear of gratitude that there was one thing she knew and that was that Chater would not have minded, not one bit. He would never have wanted her to be alone, but nor would he have wanted her to be with a mole who was not worth something. This mole was worth a lot!

'Chater . . .' she whispered, her tears for him wetting Hamble's fur, and soon she slept too, and needed to grieve no more for the mole she had loved so much.

'Fieldfare,' whispered Hamble sometime in the night, his voice rough, his touch gentle.

'Hamble?' she replied, with growing love.

'Mmmm?'

'Something's occurred to me.'

'Often does,' grunted Hamble.

'You said Whillan suggested coming here at Longest Night. Whillan!'

'Mmmm, I did.'

'But you said he'd have other moles with him. What moles? *Tell* me.'

'If I tell you, do you promise not to say another word and let me sleep?'

'I promise,' she said promptly.

'Right. He said that he wanted to bring three moles to witness Duncton's Longest Night. When I asked him what moles, he said, and I quote, and here I'm going to remind you of your promise and assure you I know no more than what he said, "One of them is the mole I love, and the others are moles who would like to meet Rooster."'

'The mole he loves! Two moles to meet Rooster! Hamble, and all you want to do is sleep!'

Hamble growled and put his paws about her and said, 'You promised.'

'But you didn't tell me it would be so intriguing,' she wailed.

Hamble chuckled and held her, and Fieldfare had the good grace, and the love, to laugh and say not one word more until . . . well, at least until daybreak.

Hamble was as good as his word. On Longest Night, after a celebration by the Stone, somewhat subdued on account of the continuing malaise that seemed to affect allmole at that time, as if it would need

597

the whole of winter and a little bit of spring to recover from the moleyears of trouble and strife just past, a motley but cheerful collection of moles assembled in Fieldfare's communal chamber.

She had cleaned it all out, expanded it a little, spread the sweet-smelling dried sprigs of fennel about, and got as fine a store of food together as any of them had seen in moleyears.

Rooster was there, of course, and Whillan. Privet, somewhat quiet, came too. Maple would not come, but Weeth looked in and said he could stay for a while, and then even Chervil came, back from his most recent journey. Pumpkin came along with an unwilling Sturne, who said he was never much good on such occasions but had yielded to Pumpkin's suggestion that it would do him good. Elynor was there, somewhat aged, and Cluniac, back from some mysterious journey he had been on with Frogbit, neither of whom would say a word about it, though the glances they cast at Whillan made it plain enough that it had something to do with him.

The only disappointment was that whatever moles it was that Whillan had hoped would come were not there, which in Fieldfare's view made it likely that he would not say much, or tell them what they all wanted to know, which was . . .

'How *did* you survive Wildenhope, mole? You know we all want to know!'

It was Hamble who asked the question, and from the deep silence that settled over them, there could be no doubt that he was right, they *did* all want to know, even if some of them were unwilling to ask.

Whillan glanced at them one by one, his face grave, but his eyes clear and sure. Then he nodded and said, 'I did want to tell you before, but there's a time and place for things, and as Cluniac and Frogbit here know, there were a few things to sort out which were better done by them. Well, that's been settled and I'm as ready to talk tonight as I'm likely to be, and especially in this company. All the moles I've ever loved but two are here tonight. You, Pumpkin, who taught me to scribe. You, Privet, who raised and loved me. You, Rooster, my father, and the mole it's taken me longest to get to know and love. You, Fieldfare, who told me tales in this very chamber when I was young, and taught me what it was to be a Duncton mole.'

'My dear . . .' whispered Fieldfare, eyes filled with tears.

How different Whillan looked, how still, and how strong. Not just in body but in spirit, and more than one of them saw then, perhaps for the first time, how like Rooster's his eyes were.

'In the old days they used to begin tales like this: "From my heart to your heart I tell this tale . . ." Well, that's how I want to tell it, and will try to tell it . . . and I'll begin with that terrible moment at Wildenhope when . . . '

Chapter Forty-Six

The talon blow that Chervil delivered to Whillan's right flank after his sentencing and before taking him down to the river was bad enough, causing him to gasp and collapse: but it was the indifference in Privet's eyes that killed his spirit. Rooster was more important than he was, then, and all those moleyears of love, all that care, seemed as nothing, and as he collapsed his world collapsed as well.

Chervil's guardmoles hurried Whillan down Wildenhope Bluff, across the meadows, their paws and voices rough, but he hardly seemed to care. They drew nearer to the river ahead, and he was thinking he must try to resist, yet he did not seem to care.

'Mole,' rasped Chervil in his ear, 'listen to me . . . LISTEN!'

His head was low, the river almost at his paws and he about to be thrown into it. Death, he saw, was a confusion, like life. Death . . .

'LISTEN, dammit, you're not that badly hurt. It had to look worse than it was . . .'

Whillan began to listen.

'It's the best we can do, mole. There's a steep drop and for a moment you'll be out of sight. We'll seem to throw you but we'll let you down as lightly as we can. *Listen* now. There's corpses there, Stone help them.'

Whillan came round all right then, not from mention of the corpses, but from sight and smell of them. He retched.

'You must throw one in, so the moles watching on the Bluff see it and think it's you. Now there is no more time – do it, mole, and then Stone help *you*, for you're on your own. It's the best we can do.'

He was lifted up, hurled outwards, restrained at the last moment and swung thumping down, down into slippery mud, down into the smell of death with the dangerous rush of water no more than a paw's breadth away.

'Throw a body in!' a voice shouted down.

'MOLE, DO IT NOW!'

He did it, tugging and pulling at the greasy swollen thing, shoving and pushing it, and at last heaving it into the racing water. It sank, floated up again, turned in the eddies and was suddenly torn away out into the flood.

'Stay out of sight until we've gone. Then . . . then . . . shit!'

It was, as Whillan later realized, Rooster charging down, over and out, a huge black shadow against the sky. Rooster taken in the water, taken under it, along with it, grasping at that corpse, and then turning, roaring, looking back and seeing *him*, and knowing he was alive.

And Whillan knowing Rooster, his father, who had tried to save him, must surely die.

'YOU . . . !' Rooster had roared when he saw him huddled clinging to the base of the bank, alive among the corpses, and he even seemed to laugh. Then as suddenly as he came, he was gone.

'Disappear mole, that's the best you can do!' It was Chervil looking down at him. 'Leave Wildenhope, go far from here, go to . . . Mallerstang. Thripp says go *there*.'

With that last strange unforgettable suggestion Chervil moved out of sight, leaving only the wind fretting at the vegetation on the top of the embankment high above. Darkness came, and bleeding, hurting, shocked, Whillan found himself alone.

He did not dare climb up the bank, even if he could have done at so steep a place, for fear of being seen. So he clambered along its slippery base, slipping into the water, chilled and desperate, along and round and into the smaller stream. Then, he slept, woke, then slept again, shivering.

Finally, a day later, hurting and aching, confused, he crawled at dusk to drier land and hobbled away into anonymity.

Or nearly so, for there was one place he could go where he was known and might be safe: Hobsley Coppice. There he went, and old Hobsley cared for him until the wound in his body had healed, if not the wound in his heart.

Spring came among the trees, but it seemed sterile to him. He saw the buds, the leaves, and heard the birds, and felt the first warmth of the rising sun, and yet he knew none of it. It was closed to him, or far off down a tunnel whose end would surely take him moleyears to reach. Hobsley advised him to go north, saying that if he had heard of a place called Mallerstang at all, northwards was where it had been. Somewhere or other.

But Whillan chose to go west to Siabod, like Bracken before him. If there was anymole left with whom he could identify it was Bracken of Duncton Wood. So, one day, after a brief farewell and not even looking back, though he knew he would never see Hobsley again —

but what did he care, nomole and nothing meant anything to him – Whillan set off for Siabod.

It was mid-May when he reached there and he barely remembered a step of the way, or a single one of the moles he had talked with, or fought with, or stayed with. Not one.

Then Moel Siabod was before him, dark and well-guarded, and he found the first gleam of light in the tunnel he was in, in the sense that here he would find something alive in himself again. He stayed for molemonths, and one day a mole he knew came to him. Female, beautiful to him but unreachable now, and with pups running about her: Madoc, once his love, once the mole the rest of his life was for.

'Whillan.' And he remembered afterwards the way she said his name.

Whillan . . .

'That's not my name now.'

'You're fleeing from the Newborns. Stay here.'

He shook his head and said, 'I have no name.'

'What happened to Privet and Rooster and—'

'They died, they all died at Wildenhope.'

Madoc smiled and shook her head. She had heard a different tale. Whillan was not himself.

'Whatmoles are these?' he asked, pointing at her pups.

'Mine own,' she said, her eyes steady on his, 'by Squelch and yet mine own.'

'What are their names?'

She whispered them, one by one, all Welsh, and all but one quite unpronounceable.

'Morwenna,' she said finally, naming the darkest one with the brightest eyes and the most beautiful form.

'Morwenna,' he said bleakly, looking at the youngster, who looked at him.

'She can sing, just as her father could. Sing for him, Morwenna.'

Morwenna said bold words in Welsh and Madoc translated them: 'She asks who you are.'

'Who am I?'

'A mole I once knew.'

Morwenna sang and though he did not understand a word he thought it the most beautiful song he had ever heard, and it made him weep.

'It's a song of Siabod,' said Madoc.

'It's a song I'll not forget,' he said, for of all the things he had seen

602

and heard and experienced since Wildenhope, this was the first that made him think that living might be better than dying.

'I heard your father sing,' said Whillan.

'When, when, *when?*' the youngster asked imploring, pleading, angry, weeping when he would not say. Angry and wild and passionate at him.

'You had better leave, Whillan; we are the past to each other now. Our futures are different.'

Through that summer he wandered as in a dream, north and ever northwards, often in systems that knew nothing of Newborns, nor much of followers. Old, isolated, forgotten places where whatever name he used others accepted. To some he taught scribing, to some he told tales, and just occasionally, of an evening, he might try to sing the song Morwenna sang to him as if there was something in it more real than anything he knew. But his voice was cracked, he did not know the words, and gradually, as time went by, he could barely remember her young face.

May passed by, and he began to ask for Mallerstang.

'Mallerstang? No, mate, never heard of it.'

'Mallerstang? Can't say I have.'

'Maller-what? Rum sort of name, and you don't even know why you're going there. Rum sort of bloody journey you're making!'

That was the first time Whillan discovered he could laugh again. It *was* rum.

Then, days later . . .

'Mallerstang? Of course I know where it is. Was up that way before Longest Night.'

Whillan was south of the Western Dales and had asked the question automatically and for the thousandth time, and here was a mole who had been there.

'Historical sort of place, you know. Suffered decades ago under the moles of the Word because its moles stanced up for worshipping the Stone their way, and when a Mallerstang mole confronted you, you knew it, so they say. I'll tell you something about that place: a mole called Merton who was raised there went south and became a holy mole in Uffington.

'Tell you what I'll do, I'll give you some names of moles I met, though they're a taciturn bunch. Not unfriendly, but they don't say much. The moles of the Word virtually massacred the lot of them and those that survived did so by taking to the fells, and that makes a community cautious. Shadows of that kind have a way of lingering.

But they gave me a welcome, and they'll give you one seeing as you're Stone-fearing.'

'I'm nothing.'

'Well, then, seeing as you're not a Newborn.'

Whillan was back in territory that knew about such things, but generally avoided mentioning them. The Newborn Crusades had not reached so far north.

'I'm certainly not Newborn.'

'Where are you from then?'

'Nowhere.'

'You'll get on with them like a wood on fire, chum. You're as taciturn as they are!'

Mallerstang lies on the western side of Ribblesdale, and Whillan reached it at the beginning of June, and as he climbed up its dry grassy bluffs, and scented the clear air, and saw the fells of Pen-y-ghent to the east across the dale he knew that somewhere here, and soon, he would find some light at the end of the tunnel he had been in. This was as far north as he would need to go.

They said little, took him in, gave him clean quarters, and set him to a task, which was delving a new communal tunnel along with other passers-by, and a couple of old Mallerstang males.

He worked hard and long, quite unaware that he was being watched and assessed, and judged to be a worthy mole. Nomole asked him questions, and nor did he volunteer answers. He was happy to have found a place to stop awhile.

By the end of June he was the longest-staying visitor there, and by July he found that the Mallerstang moles were inviting him back of an evening to their communal chamber, which few visitors ever saw. They talked quietly and shared what news there was, which was not much. The Newborns were distant and in another place, the followers like part of a family that had not been in touch for many years – familiar but strange, their world almost unimaginable. Sometimes the names of moles he knew came up – Stour, Privet, Maple – they were all mentioned in their turn, almost as legends. But Whillan never said a thing.

One day, one of the elders turned to him and said, 'And what of you, mole, have you a tale to tell us?'

He knew it was an honour, and a sign that they trusted him, and that he must tell them something. A thousand possibilities went through his head.

'I . . . I . . .'

A thousand tales and he could not choose one to tell.

'Tell us what's in your heart, mole,' the elder said to him.

'I . . . I think I have been lost, and I don't want to talk about the past. It turned from me and I from it.'

'You can delve, mole, better than anymole we've ever seen. Some-mole must have taught you that.'

'A mole did,' said Whillan quietly. 'I could tell you a tale of that.'

'Tell us what's in your heart, mole.'

He told them the tale of how the Stone rose at Hobsleys Coppice, not mentioning the names of the moles really there, and when he had done they were silent.

'What's your name, mole, that you tell a tale like that?'

'The name I gave,' said Whillan firmly.

After that he often told them tales, many tales, always anonymously, never giving the real names of moles or systems, though sometimes he might slip in the name of a mole he knew, for it gave him a sense of veracity. Fieldfare, Husk, Lavender, Bantam, Firkin, Copy Master of Duncton. These names he used, but the ones that mattered or they might recognize he avoided and never used. As for Duncton, well, he located his stories somewhere in the south, with enough variation to confuse anymole, and if sometimes they tried to guess he shook his head and frowned, and they respected that and fell silent.

He got to know only a few of their names, for the Mallerstang moles really were as taciturn as he had been told, and many were no more than faces to him, which was as he liked it. Even then it was only the males he knew – for in their community the females kept to them-selves, appearing only on holy days and festivals. So it was that he first saw most of the community together at Midsummer, for like most systems he had ever heard of, they celebrated it as the time when pups born that spring passed through the portal into maturity.

He was made welcome, very welcome, yet not a part, for their rituals were much different from Duncton's and, though evidently ancient, seemed lacking in a certain warmth. But he watched and listened, and was surprised to see that he himself was an object of interest to many of the youngsters and females, most of whom he had never seen before.

He felt lonely that evening, and began to feel he should move on. The tales he had told stirred memories and yearnings in him, and one in particular, one that had come to dominate all others. Though he had never talked of the Moors he wanted now to journey to the Charnel Clough and see where Rooster had been born. Perhaps he had not talked of it so far because Rooster's background was, in a way, his own. But that Midsummer's night, when the rituals were done, and moles gathered on the surface of Mallerstang, he found himself drawn in to tell a tale.

If, as he began, he noticed a good many there draw closer, and the attention of them all grow deeper, he did not let them know. He guessed it was because they had heard he could tell a tale better than most, and once he started nomole could quite tell where he would end. They had never known a mole like him.

It began simply enough with the previous tale-teller turning to him, as was their custom when one tale was done, and saying, 'I'm sure there's moles here would want to know how you celebrated your first Midsummer, mole, all the more so since here in Mallerstang this is the first occasion youngsters are allowed into the community at night, to hear us older moles tell our tales.

'So, seeing as you're the only visitor here tonight – and a welcome one, for we know you as a worthy and serious mole if somewhat of a mysterious one' – there was laughter at this, and nudges and winks – 'tell us how your home system is celebrating this holy night.'

Whillan was silent for a time, which was his way with tales, remembering always the elder's injunction to speak from the heart.

'In my heart tonight there is sadness,' he found himself saying, 'because the system where I was born and raised is under the thrall of the Newborns.'

Their silence grew deeper, their eyes more serious, and parents took their youngsters to their paws and settled them. They could sense more than a tale coming.

'We have a Stone in our system, which rises in the wood's highest part, and at Midsummer that's where we gather, family by family, kin with kin. The elder in my time who spoke the words was called Drubbins, and he was old and wise like . . .'

Whillan nodded towards the Mallerstang elder who laughed and said, 'I'm old all right, but as for being wise . . .'

'The words *we* said were these,' continued Whillan:

> *We bathe their paws in showers of dew,*
> *We free their fur with wind from the west,*
> *We bring them choice soil,*
> *Sunlight in life.*
>
> *We ask they be blessed*
> *With a sevenfold blessing:*
> *The grace of form . . .*

As he spoke the Midsummer Invocation he did it not from memory of Drubbins' rendition, but from Privet's, learned in her turn from Fieldfare. He spoke it clearly, and let himself linger over the seven graces of form, of goodness, of suffering, of wisdom . . . linger as Privet had lingered, teaching not just the words, but the silent meaning between them as well.

> *We free their souls with the talons of love,*
> *We ask that they hear the silent Stone . . .*

The moles who heard him were hushed and silent when he came to these concluding words, and he himself was lost in a memory that intermingled Privet and her tales – tales that he had repeated so often in the days past – with the Stone.

'When I learnt how to scribe,' he continued, quite unaware of the stir this caused, or the way one or two there seemed to come closer and peer more intently at him, 'those were the words I practised on. Pumpkin, that was the mole who taught me to scribe though my mother Privet could scribe as well . . .'

There, he had said her name, and try as he might to pull back from it, and to talk of other things he could not deny the name he had used.

'Privet, you *did* say Privet?' an old female said to him later.

'I did,' he answered uneasily.

'And you did mean Duncton Wood, didn't you?' said the old male with her.

'Did I?'

'We think you did. That invocation of the graces you spoke, that's of Duncton, I've heard tell.'

'Yes,' said Whillan.

'Yes,' said the two moles almost as one and looking at each other. 'Privet of Duncton, formerly of Crowden in the Moors. Was she your mother?'

'Adoptive mother,' corrected Whillan.

'Well then, there's a thing! There *is* a thing.'

'Why?' asked Whillan.

'Because . . . well, let's just say it's not entirely a surprise, shall we?'

'What isn't?' wondered Whillan.

'Were you sent?'

'Who by?'

'Hmmph! We'll talk more of this, mole, more before . . .'

'Before *what*?' asked Whillan, as exasperated as he had ever been, and yet as still as well. 'Yes, I was sent,' he said impulsively. 'I was sent by a mole called Chervil.'

They looked suddenly afraid, almost lost.

'Mole, we had best talk.'

When there were fewer moles about they began to talk, with the elder as witness, and though Whillan said nothing more of Privet then, he told them something of his tale, until at last they said, 'No more for now. Tell *them* to their face.'

'Who?' he asked again.

'You don't know, do you?'

'I know hardly anything,' he said.

'And the name you go by, "Morren", that's not your real name, is it?'

'No,' he confessed.

'Well then, well then. We'll sleep on it, and in the morning you can tell them to their faces, for they have a right to know. Rolt always said—'

'Brother Rolt? Thripp's Rolt?'

'Yes.'

And suddenly, like dawning light, Whillan knew who 'they' were.

'Loosestrife and Sampion,' he whispered, 'daughters of Thripp. *That*'s who you mean.'

'Yes.'

'They are here?'

'In the morning they will be, for we'll fetch them. They live on the slopes above the system, for safety's sake. And, mole, tell nomole who they are, for only we know. And mole, what is your name?'

'Whillan,' he whispered, 'Whillan of . . .'

'Wildenhope,' said the elder, looking deep into his eyes.

'The same,' said Whillan, knowing that he had guessed long since.

'Then sleep, mole, sleep.'

But Whillan could not, for he had spoken his own name again and it felt new and good, and he wanted to be up and about and once again of the world he had been lost to for so long.

It was a perfect summer's morning as the sun rose across the dale and cast its rays over the slopes of Mallerstang, and Whillan saw them coming with the moles he guessed must have been their guardians. He stanced firm, watching them as they came towards him, as alike and yet different as flowers on a single stem of wild dog rose.

'You're Whillan, aren't you?'

Loosestrife, the bigger of the two, darker, the more lively one.

'Whillan,' said the other with less passion, a shade suspicious and resentful.

Sampion, smaller, paler of fur, eyes disconcertingly clear.

They introduced themselves and Loosestrife said, 'Which of us looks more like Privet?'

'Sampion,' said Whillan.

'You're serious, and you don't look like what I expected at all!' said Loosestrife.

'What did you expect?'

'A younger mole. They always talk of the Whillan who drowned at Wildenhope as Privet's *son*. Sons are young.'

'Were you really at Wildenhope, and if you were, how did you survive?'

It was Sampion, and her voice was cooler, like her gaze.

They settled in the sun, and he began his story, and talked as he never had before. They listened and asked him questions, and their guardians, the moles to whom Rolt had entrusted their lives years before, did not interfere.

'I remember Rolt,' said Loosestrife. 'He was nice.'

'I remember Chervil,' said Sampion quietly. 'His flank, not his face, and being warm against it.'

'Tell us more and more and more,' Loosestrife implored, making Whillan laugh. 'About Privet, and about . . .'

'About *him*.'

'Thripp?'

They nodded but did not say his name. Whillan told them what he knew, and then spoke at last of how . . . and then somehow he understood so much, so very much – guessing then what their guardians confirmed – that Privet's 'Brother Confessor' at Blagrove Slide was Thripp himself. Yes . . . so he told them how Privet and Thripp had first met, and how they had dared to love, and how their pups had been born.

Loosestrife wept. Sampion was dry-eyed and quiet.

The sun reached its peak and then seemed to float in the sky all that day, the dales soft all about them, the air warm, and their lives being re-made for them all.

'I've had pups, Loosestrife hasn't,' said Sampion. 'They've more or less left the nest now. Would Privet be pleased?'

'I don't know,' said Whillan.

'Are you still angry with her?' asked Loosestrife.

'I didn't say I was.'

'Oh, but you are, you are. Are all Duncton males like you, or are some of them . . . light?'

'Light? We haven't had much to be light about. We've had it hard, not like you up here in the Dales away from it all.'

'No,' said Loosestrife, suddenly serious. 'Sorry.'

Their meeting had come to an end, for the moment. But in the days ahead Whillan saw them again, travelling up the slopes to where they lived some way above Mallerstang, hearing their story, and seeing for himself how wise Rolt had been in his choice of system in which they might survive unnoticed by anymole.

July came and Loosestrife said, 'You're leaving, I can see it in your face.'

'Another mole said something like that to me once,' said Whillan.

'Madoc,' said Loosestrife matter-of-factly. 'Did she really . . . you know . . . with Squelch?'

'She didn't have much choice.'

'Do you still love her?'

'No.'

'You're very unemotional, Whillan, like the males in Mallerstang. They're the same. When a system suffers, or moles do, they get like that, don't they? I'm not like that.'

'I've noticed. Maybe you haven't suffered.'

'When are you going?'

'Soon.'

'Very soon,' she said. It was a statement, not a question, and it was true.

'Where are you going? No, don't answer. I know. You're going to the Charnel Clough. Back to your roots.'

'How do you know?' he asked, genuinely surprised.

For the first time she reached a paw to his. It was firm and good.

'I know you, Whillan. You're like I imagined Chervil would be. Like a brother, a half-brother, a cousin in fact. Sampion envies you because you were raised by our mother. But I don't. I don't know her. I don't know what I'd think if I met her.'

'You're not like her, so you must be like Thripp,' he suggested.

'Him,' she said.

'Him,' he laughed. 'Your father.'

She sighed and said archly, 'I don't think you should go to Charnel Clough alone.'

610

He said nothing, and wondered when and from where he had begun to feel so still.

'Shall I tell you something,' said Loosestrife, 'something you don't know?'

'Go on.'

'You look like Sampion. Same eyes. Same stance. Bigger, nicer in a way; happier. But you do. Do you think that's strange?'

'No,' said Whillan.

'You didn't answer my question.'

'Which one?'

'About Privet and what I would think if I met her. What would she think?'

He looked at her for a long time: at her eyes, at her dark glossy fur, at her bold paws and warm face.

'Privet would be surprised, I think.'

'Why?' whispered Loosestrife.

'You're what she's not. She's timid, and shy, and thin, and diffident in lots of things. She'd see you weren't.'

'So what would she think?'

Again he was silent; then he said, 'I think she'd love you, Loose-strife, with her whole heart, just as she did when you were born.'

Loosestrife stared at him, eyes wide and filling with tears. 'And Sampion, and Mumble alias Chervil, and Brimmel who died.'

'All of you. But *you* are what she wanted to be.'

'Whillan,' she said a little later.

'Mmmm?'

They were stanced down looking across Ribblesdale, the sun out of sight behind them sending its red evening rays upon the western face of Pen-y-ghent. They had been like that for what seemed hours.

'I'm coming with you,' she said.

'I know,' said Whillan, and still he might have felt all day, but now his paws shook like autumn leaves.

They reached the Moors in September, travelling cautiously, for now there were Newborns about, and stories of a Brother Commander Thorne, and of Chervil himself, who it seemed best to avoid, all things considered. Nomole knew what was apaw at all, and they adopted the guise of pilgrims, though as Loosestrife said, 'That's what everymole we meet claims to be, and very unholy most of them look.'

They travelled well together, as if they had always known each other, and Whillan had never been as happy. But as they climbed up

611

into the Moors the summer began to fade away and winds came, and rain, and the going grew hard.

Crowden, where Privet was raised, was a disappointment. Ruined now, half flooded by the nearby lake, and barely a mole about, and those they did meet unfriendly and wanting to be left alone. They could find nomole to guide them across the Moors to Charnel Clough, but one at least pointed a stubby talon north-east and said, 'Go by the Withens, if you're going at all, and you might not get lost so soon.'

It was a name that Whillan remembered dimly from Privet's account of her own journey this way, though more did not come to him until, climbing up the long and tiring length of a brook towards what they hoped was Top Withens, a scraggy old mole, fierce-looking, ragged of fur, large, stanced in their way.

'Going far, strangers?'

'To Charnel Clough.'

'You're fools. And you're not from these parts.'

'Do you live here?' asked Whillan, looking about the miserable rutted place.

'Always have, always will. Chances to leave don't come twice.'

The mole was not unfriendly, he just was not used to mole. To Whillan there was something about him, something about the place . . .

'Is that Top Withens up there?' he said, pointing to the coming rise.

'It always was and still is.'

'Are you . . . are you Way . . . Waythorn?' asked Whillan suddenly, amazed that he remembered the name Privet had mentioned in her tale told so long ago. 'Son of Turrell!' That was it.

'I am,' he said, frowning and puzzled. 'How would you know?'

'My father came this way once,' said Whillan, looking about again, sure of himself, pleased to feel his paws on this rough terrain, pleased that Loosestrife was with him to witness it.

'Yes?' said Waythorn. 'And whatmole was he?'

'Rooster of Charnel Clough,' said Whillan steadily, uncertain what the response would be.

Waythorn stared at him astonished. 'Rooster?' he said faintly. 'Ratcher's Rooster? Delver Rooster? Rooster of Charnel Clough?'

Whillan nodded, grinning. The wind tugged at his fur and watered his eyes, and he said, 'Well, Waythorn, we could do with some food.'

'You're small to be Rooster's, though not that small, I suppose.'

'I'm only half Rooster's, the rest of me is Lime's.'

'Ah, yes. Remember *that* shenanigans. Well. Well. And who's she?' Waythorn nodded at Loosestrife.

'Another mole came this way,' said Whillan: 'Privet of Crowden.'

'Remember her,' said Waythorn. 'Like a twayblade those two were when they came down through here. I remember it like yesterday. Like spring itself they were, and it was spring too. What of it?'

'She's Privet's daughter, Loosestrife.'

'Hit me, go on, hit me, and I'll fall down.'

'I *am*,' said Loosestrife, laughing.

'Rooster's too? Brother and sister like?'

'Kin. Not siblings.'

'Clear as peat this is. My mind's clouding fast. Not so sure I want to know anymore. But . . . WELL! Rooster's on one paw and Privet's on the other! Worms, that's what we need, and *days* to hear the story.'

He showed them to his tunnels, which were the same as Privet and Rooster had been in, and Hamble too when he had first come up this way with Privet and her father Sward.

And they talked, long and fervently, and Waythorn told them as much as any mole could about the Moors as he had heard of them in Red Ratcher's time, and later when Rooster gained dominance; and later still when times changed and moles left and only the wind and rain, and the curlew stayed behind. And he himself.

'You'll not be safe trying to get to Charnel Clough by yourself, so I'll guide you there,' said Waythorn some days later when they wanted to get on. 'Come to that, you won't be safe when you get there.'

'Why not?'

'The place is haunted by old Hilbert himself. The Charnel is cut off of course, and has been since the day Rooster, Samphire and the others made their escape. The Reap rages still, tumbling down the Creeds, filling the sun-forsaken Clough with mist and spray so you can't see much but shapes, and rockfalls; and you can hear nothing at all above the roar of water, but the sound of moles long dead wailing and calling their loneliness.

'Aye,' continued Waythorn in a low voice, 'it's a cursed place now and the only moles who go there are ones like me who travel the Moors and look down into the Charnel from the heights above, and shake their heads and move on. But seeing as Rooster was raised there I can see you might want to visit it, Whillan, and pay your respects.

'But you'd do better to go over the Moor to Hilbert's Top, where those two lovebirds lived alone awhile. It's high and it's bleak but

613

it's the nearest this part of the Moors has got to a holy place. And Chieveley Dale below it is a spot I like on a summer's day. I go there and remember things, and thank the Stone for giving me health and sanity, and then I come home.'

He led them first across the Moors to look down into the Charnel, guiding them skilfully through treacherous bogs and among peat hags that loomed out of the chill mist that blotted out all memory of summer.

'Does the sun never shine up here?' asked Whillan, his fur wet with mist.

'In winter sometimes,' said Waythorn with a wry smile.

The sheer edge of the Creeds came out of the mist quite suddenly. One moment the Moors seemed to be going on ahead for ever, and the next the ground fell away into the rocky cliffs, and wild winds, of an impenetrable void.

'There's the Creeds,' shouted Waythorn over the roar of the wind from below, 'and all have streams tumbling down them from off the Moors. Here, I'll show you.'

He led them away from the edge, over a rise and they found themselves looking down into the rocks and rough bracken of a steep clough.

'You can't see the water from here, but it's there all right, and more than you might think. It's white and dangerous at thaw-time, or after heavy rain, for it flows off the Moor tops over there.'

He raised a talon against the wind, and pointed into the mist.

'The Creeds join up lower down and their streams become a torrent, and it's that which is what they call the Reap, which roars through Charnel Clough and makes all wet and dark.'

They moved back to the edge once more.

'That roaring you can hear, that's the Reap. Nomole ever fell in that and got out alive, and in Ratcher's time moles who displeased him were hurled into it and their bodies, or what was left of them, were found way down in the dales, the terror of what they saw before they drowned still scrivened on their faces!'

Waythorn rolled his eyes dramatically, and Loosestrife, morbidly fascinated, clasped Whillan all the tighter.

'They used to say that a Master of the Delve would come out of the Charnel by way of the Creeds, but you can see for yourselves that that would be impossible.'

The mists shifted, they saw first one Creed steep and dark and filled with ever steeper and deeper gullies down which the streams

614

tumbled and grew white, and then a second beyond it, and then, briefly, the third in the distance. As if a giant mole, trying to escape from the Charnel, had reached up his huge talons to pull himself up and having failed and fallen back to his death had left three huge scars behind.

'No, the way in and out is way down in the valley, up along the treacherous slippery way alongflank the clough. You can see why Red Ratcher used it as his hideaway! Now, do you really want to go down and have a look? It'll take half a day, mind, and all you'll get is cooler and wetter and hungrier than you are now.'

Whillan stared down into the shifting mists, and to his right at the Creeds when they showed themselves, silent and thinking. It was from out of here that his father had come. But . . . that was in the past like all else. What use would it be now to go and stare across the Reap at the Charnel?

'Living moles were left there after the Span collapsed,' he said, 'crippled moles, or moles blind and deformed and unable to travel.'

'Aye,' said Waythorn. 'All dead now, all gone, with only their ghosts to haunt us now.'

'Glee and Humlock were my father's puphood friends. Glee was an albino, and white as snow. Humlock couldn't speak, couldn't hear, couldn't see . . .'

Loosestrife signalled to Waythorn to let him talk, though it was bitterly cold, and she wanted to get down to lower, more sheltered ground. But she knew how much this part of their journey meant to Whillan, and if this was how he must say his goodbyes to what had been and find a way to move on, well, they could suffer a little cold and wet while he did so.

So he talked, telling them all he had been told, and they nodded and gritted their teeth against the wind, and nodded some more as the rain began, and ran in little runnels down their fur.

'No, Waythorn,' said Whillan at last, 'I don't want to go down there. My father went back once after he defeated Ratcher, to see if he could get over into the Charnel, but it was cut off, and all signs of life were gone. He said his farewells to his old friends, and I'll say mine to their memory now. Let's go to Chieveley Dale and then to Hilbert's Top. What I really want to find is there.'

'What's that?' asked Loosestrife.

'I'll tell you when we're dry and fed.'

They turned from the edge and trekked away, though it was a long time before the Reap's roar faded from their ears. They found shelter, got dry, ate, and slept, and when they woke the mist had gone and they began the trek to peaceful Chieveley Dale. As they went Whillan told them about how Privet had first gone to Hilbert's Top and how, up there, Rooster had made a delving for them both.

'She put her paw to it at his suggestion and scribed her name and his – but some way apart from each other. When he sounded it they heard the sound of Silence. It was there she buried Wort's Testimony in the wall, and he sealed up the place. Well, we ought to go and take a look!'

But for all his excitement at this prospect Whillan grew very quiet when they got near Chieveley, upset no doubt by the thoughts provoked by the sight of the Charnel Clough. They stayed a day or two in the Dale, and then made the ascent to Hilbert's Top and found the tunnels and chambers in which Rooster and Privet had first discovered their love. The tunnels seemed to disappoint Whillan at first.

'Needs wind to sound them,' he said obscurely.

Many of the tunnels had been ruined by wind and rain, and the delvings sounded in them only poorly when Whillan reached his talons to them. But as they explored they found deeper passages and Whillan grew quiet again. Waythorn, sensitive to their need to have time alone, and needing a little space himself, made his excuses and said he would wait for them down in the Dale where they had found some wormful tunnels, and a pleasant brook.

Whillan and Loosestrife spent two days and nights up on the Top. By day Whillan explored the deeper tunnels that they found, and marvelled at the delvings there, which were part Hilbert's and part Rooster's.

'How do you know?' asked Loosestrife.

'Every delver leaves his own marks, and his own sound,' said Whillan. 'Listen . . .'

But she could not hear the difference when he sounded the delvings, wanting instead his paws about her, and for him to be still.

On the second night the wind grew strong and shifted direction, and the tunnels they were in began to sound.

'I'm frightened, Whillan,' said Loosestrife. 'Let's go down to the Dale and be with Waythorn again. He'll worry for us.'

But Whillan was awake and tense, listening to the wind-sound.

'What is it?'

'Another mole.'

'Here . . . ?'

'Not alive, another talon in the delving, another sound and one . . . I . . . know.'

He looked somewhat apprehensive, and then, without seeming to be interested in anything but the sound he heard, he began to wander almost aimlessly about the dark whispering tunnels, touching a wall here, delving at another there, sounding, listening, perplexed, and searching.

'What is it, my dear?' she asked.

'Sshh!' he said gently, raising a paw and continuing on his way.

Then, as suddenly as he had started his search he seemed to end it. With a cry of excitement, his paw stopped at a place on what seemed a part-delved wall.

'It's a sealed-up portal. And beyond it is where the sound came from.'

He turned to Loosestrife who had followed him throughout and said, 'Mole, come here!'

He looked suddenly powerful and sure.

'Now listen. If you're not used to the sounds real delvings make then be ready to feel fear. I'm going to break this seal and Stone knows what we'll find beyond. Stay close to me, and keep quiet.'

He raised his paws, and crashed them on to the seal-up, once, twice, and then a third time. There was dust, and an avalanche of sound, and they were through into a chamber, richly delved, and humming with the wind.

Whillan snouted at the walls, and said, his voice full of awe, 'Look, look, Loosestrife, these are the delvings my father made. These are . . .'

He reached out his right paw and softly sounded the delvings, which turned and swirled with love about them.

'My father, your mother,' he said.

'So gentle, so nervous, so unsure,' whispered Loosestrife.

'There's more,' said Whillan, pointing to deeper delvings to right and left, and arching overhead. 'These are serious and speak not of love but of need.'

'Wort's Testimony is buried here, somewhere.'

He explored the delving minutely and then, suddenly, pulled away and said, 'Look! There! Hidden until you see it.'

'What?'

He took her paw and touched it about a lighter delving.

'Scribing,' he said. 'It's Privet's name.'

Loosestrife sighed at the touch of it and wept.

617

'And Rooster's name is here, for she scribed that too.'

He pointed to a deeper scribing far away from the first. Deeper, darker, and then lost among the delvings he had described as more serious.

'Here, I think she buried it here!'

Impulsively, Loosestrife dug at the wall before Whillan could stop her. There was a mounting of sound as the soil fell away, a sound which grew even deeper as she cried out that she had found a text, the one Privet buried so many years before.

'Whillan! Look, my dear!'

It was too late, for her voice and the sound of the digging provoked the delving, harried it, and it deepened and grew more savage so that Whillan had to reach up into it, to sound it his own way, to control it, to bring it back to where they were.

'Whillan!' she cried out, reaching out to him.

Dark was the sound, like the rush of a torrent, and strange the shapes, and bitter the wind that seemed to tear at their fur; and desolate the deep cry of a mole in distress. Desolate and lost as he reached across the torrent he could never cross. Melancholy, lost, with the roaring, raging grief of a mole who has saved his life but lost something of his heart.

'Whillan! Whillan!'

She held him as the sound retreated, called out to him as if he was lost himself, and touched the tears that filled his eyes, and begged to know what caused his sudden grief.

'It was for me he made this delving,' he whispered. 'He knew that one day a mole would come who could sound it, and hear it, and know that he must do what Rooster could not do himself.'

'Do what, my love? What do you mean?'

He rose from her, ignoring the text, which she took up, and led her out of the tunnel to the surface of Hilbert's Top.

'What *is* it?' she cried into the wind after him.

He turned back to her and said, 'Go down to Chieveley Dale and find Waythorn. Tell him to guide you back to his tunnels below Top Withens. I'll come there when I'm done, for what I must do I must do alone.'

'Whillan!' she cried again. 'What must you do?'

He stared at her from such a distance that she knew he was already lost to her, and might never be found again.

'I must go to where Rooster could not return. I must go to the Charnel Clough.'

'Whillan . . . !'

But he was gone, off among the rocks of Hilbert's Top, through them and beyond, so that by the time she reached the other side of them, he was far, far across the Moor and on his way back to the Charnel Clough.

Chapter Forty-Seven

A day later Whillan stanced alone in the dark heart of the Charnel Clough, facing the broken ruins of the Span, across which Rooster had come so many years before with Samphire and those able to travel out of the Charnel itself. The place was far worse than Waythorn had described, or Whillan imagined.

The Reap made a roar so loud that even when Whillan dropped rock on rock the sound could not be heard. The spray was savage on the errant winds that blew and tore about the narrow place, and caught at his eyes when he raised them, higher and higher, trying to make out the very top of the forbidding cliffs on either side.

As for the Charnel itself, a jumble of rockfall and dark green verdure that lay unreachable on the far side of the Reap, it was visible only through gaps in the flying spray, and looked as isolated and lifeless as anywhere Whillan had ever seen.

He trekked up on the Reapside towards the soaring Creeds, which were so large and formidable that they looked much nearer than they were. Hours later, when he reached as far as he could go and the Creeds rose almost vertically before him, he was wet and tired and cold. The three streams of the Creeds joined forces far above, and crashed down together into a yellow-white pool of wild water which surged off downslope and back the way he had come to from the Reap. There seemed no crossing-place, none at all, and Whillan could see why Rooster had turned back.

Yet he searched on, driven by the sound his father's delving need had made, crawling down the treacherous sides of rock and scree to the water's edge itself, seeking a way across.

'There is none, there is . . . none,' he whispered.

The wind buffeted him, the waters raged, the cold ate at his flesh.

He looked upstream – or, more accurately, up-torrent, for it plummeted down from an overhang of cliff far above his head – and saw the fall of rock into which the waters broke and split before they crashed into the pool, rocks brought down from higher up by the waters themselves.

He clambered up among them, water all about, his talons slipping on the slimy surfaces; sometimes he fell back, or forward, sometimes sideways towards the dangerous waters. A great plume of spray mounted, turned, caught him and winded him against sharp rock.

He cried out in his frustration and rage, and clambered on, out among the rocks, out over the rushing flows of water, with the Reap roaring off below him to his right, and the rocks rising up towards the towering fall of white water to his left.

The noise and isolation reached suddenly into his mind, and Whillan forgot his fear. He raged, he clambered, he swore, he moved slowly on; the slightest slip, the smallest hesitation in any move and he would be torn from his precarious holds and rushed into the torrent.

'It is not possible!' he shouted, and still he clambered on until, astonished, he found himself in the middle of the roaring falls of water – and mortally afraid. If he stayed here he was safe enough, but any move – forward, sideways and down, sideways and up, back – seemed too dangerous now to risk.

He huddled against the rock as if it were his last friend on earth. He stared down at the tumbling yellow Reap. He was assailed by noise so loud that he fancied he heard silence. And then he saw what he would do: go on.

'If I fall I strike out for that rock into which the pool's water is channelled before it flows down into the Clough itself; *if* I fall . . .'

A huge thundering came about him, all vision was lost in water, the rock that was his friend shifted and slid, and he pulled his paws away to stop them being crushed until, slowly, unstoppably, he felt himself slipping down, faster, caught by water, caught by wind, and then flipped suddenly upside down and lost into white boiling nothingness.

He surfaced, reached, strove, sank, was winded once more by a rock at his chest, saw the rock he had thought of as a haven rushing at him, then past and beyond him, reached out, caught hold of some underwater projection, and scrabbling, slipping, screaming, pulled himself up and up above the torrent, up on to grit and wet moss.

It gave way in his grasp and he began to slip back, but then, with a final surge of strength he scrabbled up again, dragging himself, crawling, his snout full of grit, his breath all gone, until, safe at last, he lay on the Charnel side.

Later, how much later he had no idea, he rose to his paws, aching and bleeding, and stumbled downslope and on to the greenest, lushest grass and spread of dwarf fern that he had ever seen. Then on down

621

towards the Charnel itself, down to where, he guessed, moles once lived.

He passed among fresh-fallen jagged rocks from the cliffs high to his left, among taller ferns and giant versions of plants he had only ever seen as small, down to where the Span had been, on whose opposite side he had stanced half a day before. He found worms enough and a drier place, and slept. He woke in the night and slept again until the dawn and wondered why he had come to this bereft, forgotten place and how he would ever get away.

Refreshed at last, he began to explore, and found evidence enough that once delvers had lived here, for the scree and rocks had shifted, and whole chambers were exposed, huge and beautiful, like shadows of a glory that once was. He found tunnels exposed to the wet raging light and entered them, his paws slipping and slopping in the water there, the sound echoing ahead. Whilst all around this ruined surface huge rockfalls were scattered as they had fallen from above, and plants lay freshly torn and uprooted to show that here the rocks and ground shifted continually. It was no place for mole to be.

A roar, a spattering of sound, and off to his right flank rocks spewed down the lower reaches of the cliff. A sharp report, louder than the Reap's roar, and somewhere a single rock crashed and cracked.

Night came once more and he slept again, fear rising in him as he realized how many were the falls, and how easily he could be killed. The very rock under which he had made his scrape was hit from above, and the scrape he had made had half fallen in on him when he awoke, it was so sodden with the spray.

'I've been and now I'll go,' he told himself at dawn, 'and by the Stone's grace I'll—'

He stopped and stilled, certain suddenly that he was being watched by mole. He turned and looked about, but saw nothing. Then, movement in the corner of his eye: he turned and all was still again.

Ghosts, Waythorn had said, and ghosts they must surely be.

'I'll go,' he whispered to himself, shaken, and he turned upslope to go back the way he had come and as he did so felt his heart stop and freeze with fear.

Ahead, stanced across his path, was the largest mole he had ever seen – or what seemed a mole, at least.

It had no eyes that he could see, yet, eyeless, it stared at him. Then it shifted, snouted at the air, and came for him quite fast. He wanted to run but could not. The Reap's roar seemed to mount in his ears. He had never been so afraid.

The mole – for mole it was – had a snout, but it was huge; it had paws, but enormous ones; it had fur, but wiry, and black as night. It stopped before him and was still.

Whillan tried to speak but could not.

The mole snouted slowly forward, nearer and nearer, its great snout trembling, filthy with grit and slime, and then it raised a paw. Slowly that paw came towards him, slowly touched him, and Whillan saw for sure the mole was blind. Its eyes were folds and in the folds were glints of white.

'Mole . . .' said Whillan, but he knew it could not reply.

'Mole . . .' he said once again, but he knew it could not hear.

The mole's paw touched him, felt him, head and shoulders, belly and rump, and then his snout.

And then the mole uttered a sound such as Whillan thought he could never have heard, broken, high in places, a sound that was a thousand cries; a sound from a void beyond imagining.

'Mole,' whispered Whillan involuntarily, for in all his life he had never heard so bleak and so hopeless a cry for help; and Whillan raised his paw, and touched the mole's face, and then took his huge paw to his own.

The mole's head slumped and he seemed to listen to the ground. He snouted noisily. He raised a back paw and thumped it down. He raised his head and gave a broken roar. Then he turned quite quickly, and moved upslope and paused. Whillan followed and the mole moved on again, always pausing and always seeming to know when Whillan was close behind again.

Into a tunnel they went, though Whillan barely noticed it, and then down it and through a portal, and along an echoing, much-delved gallery, on and on until the mole began to slow and move with a gentleness quite out of proportion to his size. Just ahead Whillan caught a glimpse of a huge shaft of light that came down into the depths they were in, which told him that whatever lay ahead was half exposed to the sky. The roar of the Reap could be heard as well, and somewhere high above, among the cliff-tops he supposed, was the raucous call of raven, and the rumble of falling, shifting rock.

The mole had paused, and now he turned towards Whillan, who sensed that he should stop. For a moment one of the eye-flaps opened and a white eye rolled and the mole uttered a curious mewing sound, which, to Whillan's surprise, for he had really observed nothing at all of where they were, was subtly caught by delvings, and echoed softly ahead of them towards the light.

These were delved sounds of reassurance, and Whillan recognized in them not just that mewing the mole had made, but elements of the strange sound he had uttered when they first met. Whillan looked about and saw that the huge tunnel they were in was delved a hundred thousand ways, more rich and subtle than any he had ever seen.

The mole sounded some of the delvings with his talons and new echoes and sounds went forth and ahead, and that mewing once again, made soft and vibrant by the wall. The mole stilled and waited, Whillan remained motionless, the sounds died away towards the light ahead of them, and silence came, but for the wind and the distant roar of the Reap.

Then, so faint that Whillan would not have known to listen for it had not the mole had his own head tilted near a wall, and the pads of his paws to it as if waiting for some vibration, there came a response.

It was weak, and hurt, and striving to be loud but not quite succeeding. It came towards them, whispering along the walls, and it was a call not just for help, but of reassurance too, as if to say, 'I am still here, I am . . .'

'I am alive . . .' whispered Whillan, feeling a sudden urgency to answer that weak and fading sound.

The mole turned to him once more and Whillan went to him and touched his paw, and then they went on again.

The light he had glimpsed earlier flooded into a caved-in chamber, which was half filled with new-fallen rocks, and through the gaping roof he could see the vertical rise of the cliff, and ravens floating high against a grey sky.

The chamber was deeply delved, but its sounds were fractured and broken and Whillan wondered at that gentler sound he had heard but moments before. He looked and saw that along the unbroken side of the chamber to his right a recent delving had been made, its lines most strange, most fine, and he knew the mole had made them.

They went on, down another tunnel, through a chamber whose roof was dangerously fractured and from which a tiny stream of water fell, and then once more there was light ahead, and another caved-in chamber. But this time the chamber was almost all gone and a great mass of jumbled rock from the cliff above slewed across it, almost up to the inner wall.

The mole turned, took Whillan's paw, and led him towards the base of the fallen rock. Somewhere above them rocks shifted, somewhere else nearby stones spattered down, and one rolled away into darkness. Water dripped on Whillan's face, icy cold.

The mole headed for a narrow gap, which by the nature of the fall, and what remained of the walls and roof, was in the darkest part of the ruined place, paused and turned again and reached a paw to Whillan. Gently, for the rocks all about gave the sense that at any moment they could shift and slide and crush them both, he pushed him through the gap.

He saw her but a little way beyond it, face down, her left paw trapped by rock, her white fur filthy with mud and grit. The other paw reached out along the ground and just touched the wall, and Whillan saw that the recent delving began and ended where her talons were.

'Humlock?' she whispered, straining to look round, touching the delving as she spoke.

The mewing came from beyond the gap, a shimmer of sound, communication.

'I'm not Humlock,' said Whillan, 'he brought me here. You're trapped. No, no, don't try to move . . .'

She strove to turn her head to see him and as she did so pulled at her trapped paw. She began to panic. There was an ominous shifting of rock and Whillan looked up at the massed and looming rockfall, heard it groan and scrape, and knew how near it was to moving once again.

'Whatmole are you?' she whispered, shivering.

'Sshh!' he said, as quietly, 'don't talk. We'll get you out of here, Glee.'

He used her name as naturally as if he had known her all his life: Humlock and Glee, of course he knew their names, and what they were. These moles were once his father's friends.

'Mole, who sent you?' she whispered. 'Let me see your face.'

He moved round where she might see him and he saw a bloodied face, and black eyes that might in other circumstances have been bright and cheerful. Now they were fatigued and wan, and yet held warmth.

'Rooster sent me a long, long time ago. I am Rooster's son,' he said, and wished he had not, for she gasped, and heaved, and broke into the most terrible cries.

Whillan felt himself lifted bodily from her, and Humlock took his place.

'All right, it's all right, my love, he's of the Stone.'

She spoke the words though Humlock could not hear them, but at the same time her talons ran and played across his face in movements

625

that Whillan guessed was her speech to him. He touched her in reply and seemed to wait.

Astonishingly, Glee laughed. 'He wants to know whatmole you are, but I can't tell him what you said. Now listen, Rooster's son, if that's what you really are. I cannot move and he can't move me. If he tries the rocks shift. He might hold them back while I escape, but then he would be crushed. If he leaves me I die. If he stays with me we both die, which is what we thought was best. He lay with me, and fed me . . .'

'How long?' asked Whillan.

'Days and nights now, days. Humlock's fed me, cleaned me, warmed me, just as I did him over the years when he's been ill or lost.'

'Lost?'

'In himself, deep in his silent self, sometimes he gets lost and cannot find his way back to me. Now, mole, the Stone's sent you and you must do the Stone's work. Listen, for it will take you too long to find out for yourself. On past here is a delved chamber, the last of the great ones to survive.'

'I understand,' said Whillan.

'Yes, of course you would, you would. Rooster sent you! Oh mole, oh . . . You'll need to sound the delvings there. Can you do that?'

'I'll try. And then . . . ?'

'Sound them, make them true, sound them hard, and then he'll raise the rock as the sounds of the delvers of the past come here to help us before they're lost for ever in the shadows of the rocks, and the light of the grey sky.'

'There are other moles . . . ?'

'None living as we are. But generations live on in their delvings,' whispered Glee, with such conviction that Whillan almost believed it might be true.

'Listen. Humlock will raise the rock, they will have a little time to hold the rockfall back and I shall . . . crawl, I expect, crawl as fast as my hurt paw will allow, and you will be ready to reach out and guide him over to us. For remember, the rocks will move, and the delvings break, and only you will be there to guide him out of here, and only I can guide you out of the chamber, and only he can raise the rock.'

It was a roundel of destiny and Whillan could not doubt that it was true; whatever it meant, she had worked it out as it must be, and he had trust in her.

'I'll go and look . . .'

'But hurry, mole, for the Stone has sent you, and the Stone moves on. We are the last moles and I wish to live! Don't look, do!'

Whillan went through the far portal into the chamber, which, so long before, Privet had described when she told Rooster's tale. Huge and dark it was, but dripping now, shifting, full of wind yet still integral to itself as Whillan reached up to the richest and most ancient delvings he had ever seen and without more ado began to sound. Round and round he ran, and swooped, and up he reached, to delvings that sounded, up to more, higher and higher towards the arched heights above.

'Rooster's son . . .' she cried out, and he ran back in time to see huge Humlock, made dwarflike by the fall of rocks he strove against, reach his talons to the rock that pinned her down, and unfortunately held them all, and begin to raise it. Even as he did the sound in the chamber became a vast furore of noise and thundering paws that spiralled down through time and swept from behind him, through him, over him, and out towards the broken light and rocks, out to where Humlock heaved, to help . . .

His back was to the rock, his forepaws stretched under it, his back paws pushing as his shoulders bulged and his belly stretched out and up with effort.

'Now!' Glee cried.

Then Whillan, forgetting what he was meant to do, the dark and light sound all about, ran to her, grasped her good paw, pulled and pushed her towards the portal into the chamber and then turned and saw the rock that Humlock had raised fall back, Humlock lift his paws to his ears as the delving sounds were lost and he 'heard' only chaos. He staggered, confused and lost in space and time as all about him the rocks began to roar and move and crush down against him, pushing him forward in dust and noise, unbalancing him and he not knowing where he was and slumping down, head lower, body curling, down, down out of this world and into his own lost place where he could only wait to die.

It was Glee's shout that shook Whillan from his horror and reminded him what he must do: 'Go to him, mole, guide my beloved out of there!'

Whillan went, grasped Humlock's paw even as the first rocks rained down on him, savagely pulled him clear and brought him into the chamber, whilst behind them the rocks poured down, and mounted up and rolled after them in terrible pursuit.

'Now, follow me!' cried Glee.

627

As the chamber's walls shook and vibrated ever more violently, and the delving sounds cracked and broke and generations of moles cried out their last lost cries, they followed her up and away through tunnels wide and narrow, through chambers dark and light, up and up, away from the sound that followed them, away from the walls that crashed after them, each place they had run through breaking into ruins behind them.

Up and out to the light of day and the roar of the Reap as the Charnel rocked and broke about them.

'Up to the Creeds!' cried Whillan, grasping at Humlock's paw again as if in the hope that he would understand. He seemed to, for then, half carrying, half pushing Glee, they ran from where the rocks crashed down and the cliffs slid and heaved, up to safer, more secure ground, if any there was safe. Up until they fell, far short of where the Creeds rose darkly ahead, but clear of the crashing dangers below.

Of what happened next the memories came only slowly back to Whillan later, in flashes of light which gave him only incoherent glimpses of the three of them, chasing upwards, and the cliffs coming nearer, and then the Creeds, and then an ascent into a void that was above them making all seem reversed and upside down.

A torrent; the rush of raven's wings; slipping down and looking down and turning back; Humlock defying gravity to climb on up and push them on; Glee suddenly screaming out into some gullied place, not from fear but for release, to make the darkness echo, to remind them that they lived.

The Creed (which one Whillan never knew) took them unto itself and it became their vertical, terrifying world, and they its pups, clinging on to its flanks, seeking out its safe depths, fearful when it rose and swung on them; and sometimes looking down, down to the rocks below them, down beyond them to the screes, and beyond even them to the Reap, yellow-white and rushing far from them down into the Clough.

Once they sheltered under a fall of water and found green ferns as beautiful as flowers; another time, upon a ledge, trembling in the winds that never ceased, three white starry saxifrage waited for them, as if summer were still there, and signalled them on. When they looked back the flowers had gone, swept down by rockfall, that way no longer passable.

Time they forgot, and finally fear as well, for this was all their world and to it they cleaved and knew only the never-ending upward push of paw on rock, and pull of broken, blunted talon in the crevice, and

628

the swing of paws across a void to scrabble for a hold in another cleft.

'Hilbert came down this way,' were the only words that Whillan afterwards remembered being spoken, though whether it was he who said them, or Glee, he never knew.

Night came. Day followed. Rain came. Sun shone far from them. Winds blew. Silence reigned. Then noise. Then night, another and another and another before day.

They ate, Whillan remembered that. Red worms. Dead raven. The soft green roots of mantle-flower. And they drank of the chill, clear water of the Creed.

Then one day when they had forgotten about the life that lay behind them, and were too weary to believe that anything could lie ahead, they reached up their paws and the rocks fell away and there was green grass ahead; and light, endless; and an horizon, frighteningly far off.

There, in this new and dangerous world, two old moles, withered by rains and mists, harassed by worry and doubt, stanced waiting for them.

One was Loosestife, almost as exhausted as they were; the other was Waythorn, sniffing at the drizzle on his snout, staring at the ghosts that finally came alive out of the Charnel Clough.

'She said to wait!' he said. 'Privet's did.'

'And he said to wait, because Rooster's would,' she echoed.

Then she was in Whillan's paws, never wanting to let him go, or to forget what it felt like to lose the mole she had only in the days past realized she had come to love.

Whillan had left her on Hilbert's Top as friend and kin; he returned to her as a mate. All of that, and a future, was in their long embrace.

Nor was Glee unmindful of her own one and only love, who, sensing the strangeness of where he was, and that his life and world would never be the same, and likewise exhausted from the days of climbing, began to hunch up into himself like a huge frightened rock. She touched his face and paws again and again, whispering words of reassurance he could not hear and he began to relax. Then she turned round and stared down through the mists out of which they had climbed, and turning for a moment to the other three said, 'Leave us be for a time. Leave us be . . .'

They did, making a scrape nearby, getting food ready, and saying nothing when the two strange moles came and slept and then went out together again to stance above the world which had been their only life. One day. Two days. Five days, before at last Glee said,

'We've said farewell. Humlock is confused by the wind and the vibrations which do not come back. He wants to know where this place stops.' She waved a paw across the distance that was moledom.

They tried to explain what moledom was, and where they were, and how they must travel to get anywhere, but none of it made sense to Glee and Humlock. Without the confines of the cliffs, and the roaring of the Reap, they had no place to turn. Nor did tunnels help, not even when – as they always did – they delved to make the place their own.

'Whillan, they seem so lost and sad,' said Loosestrife on the third day after they left the Charnel heights, and rested in Waythorn's place.

He nodded and went out on to the Moor alone to think, and was gone until nightfall. When he came back he called them to him, including Waythorn, and said, 'It's time we travelled south. We're going to Duncton Wood. Waythorn, you'll come with us, for we'll need your help and skills.'

'But what of the Newborns, and what of—'

'It's time, that's all I know,' said Whillan wearily. He turned to Humlock and reached up to his face and touched it, and then said to Glee, 'Tell him that this place *will* stop, but when I don't know.'

She told him and then said, 'He wants to know where it stops, not when. He's afraid of getting lost where there are no cliffs or delvings or Reap to guide him.'

'Tell him,' said Whillan finally, 'that this place will stop at Rooster.'

Humlock stilled at Glee's next touch and then raised his great head and for a moment his white eyes showed. He roared, he seemed to seek the very stars, and then, as gently as a pup, he touched each one of them, and roared again, a strange unearthly Charnel sound.

'Is he weeping?' wondered Whillan.

'No,' said Glee, her white paws to Humlock's, who grew still again. 'That's Humlock's laugh.'

Fieldfare's chamber was hushed as Whillan's voice stopped, and the dawn light after Longest Night began to fill it.

They were all still, all touched by his tale.

'Rooster's!' said Rooster finally, buffeting Whillan with a chuckle. Then his face was serious: 'Where are they?'

'Near Rollright. We travelled south, we took the high route of the Chilterns but there was Newborn confusion and danger about. We heard a rumour from some pilgrims of Privet's coming and so I found them a safe place and left Waythorn to watch over them, and came on alone more quickly. I felt I was needed here.'

'What of Loosestrife?' Privet and Chervil looked at each other and smiled, for both had spoken at once.

'Loosestrife is well,' said Whillan carefully. 'She . . . won't come yet. I sent Hamble and Frogbit here to see that they were safe and they say they are, and they led them on to Cuddesdon, nearby and secure. Loosestrife is not ready to see Duncton or the moles in it. She's curious, but wary. She'll come when she's ready.'

He spoke dispassionately, but it was evident that in some way he agreed with her. It had to do with Privet. Loosestrife, it seemed, was not the only mole who chose to be 'wary' – Whillan was as well.

'When they come? Humlock and Glee?' asked Rooster.

'Tomorrow or the next day!' said Frogbit. 'Humlock's big as you, Rooster, and bigger.'

Rooster smiled. 'Can delve with them. Can delve things long forgotten. Can delve the grief of years away. And will.'

'And Wort's Testimony?' said Privet in a strange dry voice.

'Brought it back and gave it into Pumpkin's care,' said Hamble.

'It waits for you, Privet, near the Book,' said Pumpkin. 'It seemed the best place for it.'

The tale was done, but they were not yet a community again. The Book was what separated them all now, or Privet's distance; and Whillan's. Which might all be the same thing. There was much to heal and the only comfort was that all of them knew it, and all had faith to wait.

'Come, Pumpkin, dawn is with us and I am tired,' said Privet. 'Today we have work to do. Tomorrow, and the day after that: work!'

She said it almost bitterly, nodded to them as if they were not kin and friends at all but passing acquaintances, and left, Pumpkin following her.

'Miss her,' said Rooster, 'that mole I knew at Hilbert's Top. Loved and lost her. But friends come back and she will and then will delve for her again.'

A beautiful smile of peace and patient love came to his face, and, as touching, a look of pride in Whillan.

'Did well, mole,' he said. 'You knew what to do. Now Glee coming here, and Humlock. Loosestrife will one day for Privet when she's done. Not before. Will delve cliffs for Humlock and Glee, and the Reap, and they will want to stay.'

They came three days later, on the Night of Rising, which commemorated Pumpkin's leadership of the rebels into the Ancient System a full cycle of seasons before.

Humlock, Glee and Rooster together by the Stone.

'Never be far apart again but when we die,' said Rooster, and their coming set a tradition that on the Night of Rising, wherever it was commemorated, strangers were made welcome into the system to which they came. Then they celebrated until dawn, a time enjoyed by all but Privet, who was not seen at all.

'Where is she, Pumpkin? Not scribing through the night?'

'She's not scribed a word since kenning Wort's Testimony. Maybe I should go and see . . .'

But he dallied, for the night was convivial and a welcome respite from the winter, which would be upon them soon enough once more. But then he thought he would stretch his paws in the night, and just see that Privet was all right . . . just see.

The look on his face when he returned told them she was not.

'Why, Pumpkin . . . mole, what is it?'

It was Hamble who asked, and Sturne who went to him.

'What is it, Pumpkin? What's wrong? You can tell any one of us, or all . . .'

'It's the Book,' Pumpkin whispered, his face expressing puzzlement and shock. 'She's begun to destroy all the scribing that she's made. It was nearly done, all the folios filled, all there waiting for her to simply say it was done. But now . . .'

'Now, *what*, mole?'

'She's scoring out every single word she's scribed.'

Chapter Forty-Eight

'Place the folio there, Pumpkin,' said Privet, irritably waving a paw at a pile of jumbled folios strewn across the awesome chamber where the Book had been found, and where she now chose to scribe.

'Privet, I think perhaps that *this* folio—'

'Stop fussing, mole.'

'But Privet, I really must insist, I must!'

She stopped her frantic work at the Book, paused, turned to him, and a weary, patient look came across her face. Reluctantly her scribing paw relaxed, though she kept glancing back at the work she was doing, as if it must be done, and now.

'What season is it, Pumpkin?'

'Mid-January, Privet, and it's cold down here and I really wish—'

She coughed, and for a moment had difficulty drawing breath.

'It is cold, you're right. I shouldn't be here. I should be in that snug burrow you and Rooster made for me.'

'You've never used it, Privet, and it's really not that far. There's moles aplenty will bring you food, and if you want company—'

'Company!' she exclaimed with a dismissive laugh.

'. . . or peace and quiet—'

'Peace? Quiet?' Her eyes were as sharp as her voice, and as she looked about the draughty echoing place, in which the ever-present wind-sound threatened always to turn dark, a haunted look came into her face.

'I'll have those things when I have finished this. *Finished* it. The Book . . . cannot wait.'

Pumpkin stared at the Book, once pristine, now worn and torn, some of its folios already falling out, and its covers stained by what he was quite sure were tears.

'No, no, Pumpkin, I'll stay here for now. I must, you see. Bring me worms, and later you can help me to the surface for some air. January, you say?'

'Snow has begun to fall. All is quiet across the High Wood.'

'Quiet!' she repeated, the worn smile returning.

Her eyes went to the folio he had brought, which was so scratched and scored that it might as well have long since been thrown away.

'I am . . . afraid of it, Pumpkin,' she whispered. 'Bring it here.'

He went to it and, with evident difficulty, quite out of proportion to the scrappy thing's seeming weight, he took it up and carried it to her, panting.

'Was it so hard to bring it from the Library?'

'Master Librarian Sturne helped me. It was where it had been left, and Light was there, Privet, and I was so much afraid.'

'Yet you brought it to me?'

'I am your aide and I shall always be, even if I disapprove of how you scourge yourself.'

'"Scourge", now there's a fine old word . . . "Forsoth he scourgith euery sone that he receyeuth", as the scholar Wyclif once scribed. There, I have not forgotten everything!'

Her eyes wrinkled with some remembered pleasure of study and scholarship when she was young, but looking at her Pumpkin thought she had never looked so old, or so ill. She *was* ill: she coughed, she stared at nothing, she saw nomole but him, not even Rooster, and . . .

'Look! I'll scribe it in the Book! There, see, behold!' She scribed the word 'scourge'. She laughed, but bitterly and with terrible sadness. 'How is my Rooster? Does he miss me? Does he ask after me?'

'He does, and alone of them all he understands.'

'Yes, yes I know he does,' she said. 'And Hamble and Fieldfare?'

'They are well together.'

'And no word of Whillan?'

'None since the last. He over-winters at Cuddesdon with Loose-strife. The moles Humlock and Glee are back there now as well.'

'Have you seen Loosestrife?' she asked eagerly.

'I have been at your flank every day, Privet, since you started this scribing.'

'Unscribing,' she said.

'Since you started . . . Loosestrife has not come to Duncton Wood. Whillan will bring her in spring.'

'When the snow has gone?'

She paused, idly reached out her paw and whispered, 'Scourge.' She scored out what she had just scribed.

'So, you brought the last folio of the Book of Tales to me, which I believed was the first folio of the Book of Silence. Well, perhaps it is. Whatmole knows? I don't. I am lost, Pumpkin, lost and lonely.'

'I know, Privet. Come with me to the burrow we made, rest for a while, a few days, then—'

'Then I shall never have strength to begin again and complete my task.'

'Nomole can work so hard. No scholar I have known worked so hard as this and made a book worth half the name.'

She laughed with real warmth at this. 'Listen, mole. I went to the surface today.'

He looked genuinely surprised.

'Oh, I did, while you were gone for the folio. I went up into the High Wood and saw the snow begin. I also saw Weeth. He was going to the Stone. Why? He's not one to pray.'

She looked at him as sharply as ever she had.

'It's Maple. He was praying for him. He is not well.'

'He is dying, mole. Therefore . . .' She paused to think, weighing something up. 'Therefore, bring him to me.'

'But Privet—'

'You want me to have company. I shall have company. And anyway, I have advice to give, which shows how ill I am, for moles should avoid giving others advice – which you would do well to remember, my dear. But . . . Pumpkin?'

He came closer and she reached out to him.

'Stay with me, mole, for all the days ahead,' she whispered with sudden fearful urgency. 'Stay close, for I shall have need of thee!'

'I shall.'

'So!' she exclaimed, her mood suddenly lighter. 'You shall take me to this burrow you and Rooster made for me, I shall sleep a little, and you shall bring Maple. And Weeth. Then I shall return to work. There! A compromise!'

'Privet, Maple is not well at all.'

'I know how he is, Pumpkin, I know it well. That is why I should see him now.'

He helped her slowly down the tunnels back to his own tunnels.

Nor was Maple well, as was plain when Weeth brought him to her. His head was bald now, as Quail's had been, and his paws were swollen.

And he smelt.

'Maple,' she whispered when Weeth helped him into the burrow, which was off Pumpkin's own in the Slopes, on the edge of the High Wood.

635

'Privet,' he rasped. 'I did not want to come. But for you . . .' He looked at her with eyes that spoke of suffering.

'Listen, my dear, I have a task for you. Will you do it for me?'

'For me?' he growled. 'I can do nothing for anymole. I am dying and I know it.'

'But will you do this for me?'

Somewhere in his face there came the faint look of purpose that he had once had when he was well, and leader of the followers. Then it began to fade.

'Well?'

'I am not Maple now.'

'No, mole, I know what you are and where you are. Yet still I have a task for you, for the mole you are now.'

'If I can, Privet, for you I'll try.'

'Then listen, and you too Weeth, for you're to go with him. Go to the Redditch Stone, which lies south of the Midland Wen. There, many years ago, a mole who helped heal me, herself was healed. Her name is Sister Caldey. Go to the Stone, ask for its help, and if you have faith it will guide a healing to you.'

She fell silent, and looked intently at Maple.

'And that is my task!' he exclaimed with a hollow laugh, as if he had never heard anything quite so ridiculous. 'Go to the Redditch Stone, Weeth, in my condition, that's all we have to do! Oh, thank you, Privet! What a simple task!'

'No, my dear, that is not your task. Your task is to return to Duncton Wood, or send a messenger, to say that you are whole again. I need to know you'll do that for me.'

The laugh fled from his face as a look of self-pity replaced it, and he would have wept if he had not been angry. He tried to speak, winced from some internal pain, turned away, shaking his head in disbelief, and was gone.

Weeth remained a moment more and Privet said with a smile. 'He is not the mole he will be, Weeth. I remember when we first met you near Evesham you talked of opportunity.'

'I did, Privet, and it was true. There is opportunity in all things.'

'Then help him find the opportunity in this. Caldey founded the Community of Rose. Find her, mole, he has only to ask for her help and she will give it. But he must do the asking.'

'Madam,' said Weeth in his old way, 'you are peerless but not perfect. In fact, you look awful. Thin of flank, gaunt of cheek, red of eye, and wilting of snout. Therefore, I trust before Maple or his messenger comes back from Redditch you will take some of your own advice and get well!'

For a moment Privet looked genuinely startled, but then, and just as genuinely, she laughed aloud and would have continued to do so had she not begun coughing.

'Wee . . . Weeth . . . mole . . . mole! Oh dear!' Her eyes streamed as she controlled the cough and caught her breath, but she was still smiling. 'Gaunt of cheek! Thin of flank! I am not a—'

'Young mole any more? But you could be, Privet! Let opportunity be your word of the day! And . . . thank you. I shall see him safely there despite the winter weather.'

Then with a mischievous grin Weeth was gone, and the following morning, the first in which Privet awoke in a warm snug burrow away from the Ancient System for many a molemonth, Pumpkin reported that Maple and Weeth had slipped away out of Duncton at dawn, with only himself to say farewell.

'Let us pray that no more snow falls, and that worse winter weather is delayed, or their journey will be too hard. Maple looked so ill, and his paws are so swollen. I love him, Pumpkin, and I love Weeth. I have missed moles . . . so much.'

'Well, there is no need to go back to the chamber and your task today.'

'No, none at all, my dear. Tomorrow, perhaps; but today I would like to talk with Sturne.'

'He will be only too pleased!' declared Pumpkin, astonished at this transformation in Privet and hoping that 'tomorrow, perhaps' might be more perhaps than tomorrow. 'I shall go and get him now.'

Pumpkin hurried off towards the Library, himself feeling something of a new mole, for it was many a morning since he had done anything other than make the long trek through the tunnels of the Ancient System, whose Dark Sound might now be a little easier, but always left him oppressed and exhausted.

Halfway to the Library, however, doubts set in. Would she still be there when he and Sturne got back? Or would the obsessive urge to scribe, or unscribe, which was even worse in Pumpkin's view, get the better of her?

'Mole! Mole!' he called out, spotting a pilgrim wending his way over the surface of the High Wood towards the Stone.

'Hail, Brother, and hallelujah!' cried the pilgrim.

'Yes, well, that's all very well but I have a task for you.'

Pumpkin gave him directions to his burrow, and told him to go and watch over the mole he would find there, and, since she was inclined to wander off, to keep her talking.

'In the name of the Stone shall I do it!' declared the pilgrim with such cheerful enthusiasm that the moment after they had separated, and Pumpkin set off towards the Library once more, he began to worry that he might have made things worse.

He need not have worried. When he and Sturne arrived back at his tunnels they were filled with the sound of chatter and laughter, and the unlikely sight of Privet surrounded by five pilgrims and wanderers all talking away at once.

'Good Brother!' yelled the mole he had first spoken to, 'I met some friends and brought them along so that our frail sister here felt even less like wandering off!'

Pumpkin sighed, Sturne frowned, and the visitors stayed far too long for all but Privet, who listened to everything they said, laughed with them, answered their questions about her 'illness' and her 'brother' with equanimity, and was almost tearful when they left.

'You wanted to see me, Privet,' said Sturne when they had gone.

'I wanted to look at you, mole, and I have done so since you came. You did not join in.'

'I am not good on such occasions,' said Sturne tersely. 'I like the peace and quiet to study and order texts.'

'Ah, peace and quiet again, Pumpkin. It seems in somewhat short supply. I have heard of all you did during the Newborn occupation, Sturne. Pumpkin told me. He tells me everything.'

'Pumpkin talks too much,' said Sturne drily.

'Do *you* not smile too little? I know that is a fault of mine as well.'

'Smile,' said Sturne, unsmilingly pondering the word. 'It happens to me sometimes.'

Pumpkin laughed. 'Incorrigible, but my friend,' he said with a shrug.

'Pumpkin smiles for me,' said Sturne, in all seriousness it seemed.

'Well, mole, in the months ahead we must learn to smile together.'

There was a lost look in Sturne's face, a dry and bitter look. Followed by a yearning. And Privet, who knew that sterile landscape of the heart from whence such looks come, saw and understood to what aridity Sturne's life had brought him.

'We could pray,' she said simply, adding with a light laugh: 'Today I am doing all those things I find no time for while I stick to my task, which makes a mole think, doesn't it? So . . . we could pray.'

Why did Pumpkin feel a tremor of apprehension in his heart then?

First Maple, now Sturne. Whatmole would she next want to see, and talk to? It felt as if she was saying goodbye.

'I leave the praying to Pumpkin, like the smiling,' said Sturne coolly. 'Not that I don't have faith, but words—'

'Well then, we won't pray, Sturne, but invoke,' said Privet, cutting across his explanations. 'You can ken Whernish, can you not?'

'Well enough, Keeper Privet,' he said.

'Let me see if I can remember "well enough",' she replied.

''S mithic teàrnadh do na gleannaibh
O'n tha gruaimich air na beannaibh
'S ceathach dùinte mu na meallaibh
A' cur dallaidh air a léirsinn.'

She spoke the words so lyrically that even Pumpkin, who had but a few words of Whernish, caught the rhythm, and perhaps something of the sense.

'Well, Sturne?'

He was still and silent as he thought about the invocation she had spoken and then, without faltering, he said, 'It is time now to go down into the dales, for gloom is fallen on the tops, and mists shroud the hills, darkening our vision.'

He fell silent, and Privet did not speak, nor Pumpkin move.

'. . . darkening our vision,' repeated Sturne, looking to the light by the portal, not into their eyes at all. 'I cannot smile. Not before, less now. I cannot.'

Faced by their silence he could not but speak, and speak he did, telling them of wild desert winds in his heart since he had lost sight of the mole who had saved him at the cross-under.

'I never knew, Sturne, I never guessed!' exclaimed Pumpkin at the end of it, angry at himself.

'Why should you know? I never spoke of it, though I might have had you been less pre-occupied – but no matter. It is over and done with. She has gone and thinking about her was no more than a wish to avoid the resumption of my work in the Library.'

'Which is?' asked Privet.

'Restoration of what has been lost through cleansing by the Newborns. There are ways . . . And, too, the collection of texts scribed in the era of the Newborns, which are many and varied, including, though I hesitate to say it, some remarkable records kept by Snyde. In his way he was a true scribemole.'

'And that is all?'

'It is all I can hope for, Privet,' said Sturne frowning.

'As you are an honest and Stone-fearing mole, Sturne, will you do something for me, and answer me a question?'

'If I can.'

'The request is this. See if you can find in any of the old texts in the Library the name of library aides in Dunbar's time. Pumpkin is of the opinion that the mole whose body lies near the Book was an aide, and that chamber, so Rooster says, was delved in Dunbar's time.'

'Ah! Yes! I have been working on that, as a matter of fact. I have two or three names that are possibilities. It would be good to name that mole, though, of course, at best it can only now be conjecture and surmise.'

'Really?' said Privet evenly.

'But why is his name important?' asked Pumpkin. 'I mean, he was only an aide after all, and it is the Book that matters.'

'Is it?' said Privet evenly once more.

'I shall bring the names to you here this evening, Privet.'

'Thank you, Sturne. A name might help me now. It is easier to make a Book for one, than for many. So much for my request. The question I have for you comes to this: your good friend Pumpkin here, feeling that I work too hard, and hearing my winter's cough get worse, feels I should rest for a while. Weeth, whose qualities are many, told me yesterday that I should follow my own advice and "get well". What do you think I should do?'

Sturne turned his icy gaze on her and said, with little hesitation, 'You should complete the task that you began. That is your first duty.'

'The Book?'

'Yes. You should finish it.'

'I try, mole, and it is hard.'

'The best deeds are hard.'

'My mother Shire said such things as that. But now I begin to think that she was wrong. It is not that the best deeds should be easy, simply that they should not be hard. A good smile is not hard.'

Sturne's gaze softened a fraction and he glanced at Pumpkin. Pumpkin grinned and shrugged as if to say, 'That's Privet for you.'

'I shall try,' said Sturne a little too earnestly, 'as you should, madam.'

'And we shall help him, Pumpkin,' said Privet when he had gone. 'The Stone sometimes needs a little help from its friends. We shall send a missive out by way of the moles who you say still leave Duncton Wood regularly, feeling that they have seen what they can, and no

640

Book worth the name will now be found. We shall seek this mole Sturne has lost. And we shall see if Sturne will smile.'

'Hmmph!' said Pumpkin. 'I have been trying to make that mole smile all my life. In fact, the Master Stour himself adjured me to make Sturne happy if I could. Even if we find this mole he's certain to be disappointed.'

'The truth is never disappointing, Pumpkin, and anyway, do you think he can smile before he has grieved and wept? He cannot, and will not. Meanwhile, he is quite right; I should complete my task.'

'But Privet!'

'Tomorrow, mole, or the day after,' smiled Privet, whose snout had turned from grey to pink as the day had progressed. 'There's another mole I should see.'

'Shall I fetch him?'

'He'll know to come,' said Privet, 'and until then I'll sleep.'

'Rooster?' wondered Pumpkin.

Privet's black eyes shone in the gloom of the January day.

Perhaps Privet had guessed that word would get out that for a time she had emerged from her onerous task of making the Book of Silence and was resting awhile in Pumpkin's tunnels. For it certainly had, and other visitors came before Rooster did.

Fieldfare for one, sent ahead by Hamble who guessed that the two might want some time alone together to remember once again Privet's first coming to Duncton, and for Fieldfare to tell of her days up at Seven Barrows. Then, too, they might talk softly of Chater, and Privet repeat the story of how he had died, and Fieldfare tell how she had been guided by the spirit of Mayweed himself among the Stones of Seven Barrows to say her last goodbye to her beloved.

Then Hamble came, and the three talked into the afternoon about everything but the Book, put out of mind for those precious hours. Yet the Book's shadow was on them, and when other moles came quietly to pay their respects to Privet and crossed the portal, the moles already there felt suddenly uneasy, as if the newcomers' shadows might be the folios of the Book themselves.

Hodder came up from his temporary tunnels – as he had long called them – down by Barrow Vale, which were near those occupied more permanently by Arliss and Rees. Old friends, old memories, the blood of old wounds dried and gone leaving only scars.

Elynor, she came, fetched over from the Eastside by Pumpkin, but aged she was, and growing blind, and missing Cluniac who had left Duncton in the company of Chervil, Thorne and Ystwelyn, to help bring peace and security to those areas where Newborn doctrines had lingered on, and former Brother Commanders needed to be subdued.

'My dear,' faltered Elynor, 'where are you? I cannot see as well as I could. Let me feel your face. You're thin, too thin. And your paws, worn out with scribing, so I'm told. A Book of Silence should need no scribing!'

There! One of them had dared mention it and then all did, and their voices were a babble of sound, all offering advice, all questioning, all concerned that Privet was working too hard, all relieved now that she had come out among them once again. Those dark moments passed as dusk came and they told each other tales, and laughed, and Privet felt their love.

So much happiness . . .

'So why do I feel such fear, Stone?' muttered Pumpkin to himself.

So much peace . . .

'So why do I feel so confused?'

So much light among those friends . . .

'So why is it the shadows that I see?'

Unable to bear such apparently unnecessary doubts and fears Pumpkin went up to the surface and snouted about, and was surprised to find that since he had brought Elynor, others had come who did not know Privet personally, but felt it was a time to be present, and witness some moment whose importance they sensed, but for which they had no name. They stanced in the shadows near his entrance, silent and respectful.

'Is she well?' one asked eventually, speaking for them all, 'we heard that she might be ailing, and that was why . . . ?'

'Never better, moles, never better,' said Pumpkin.

'And the Book?'

'Not yet complete.'

Oh! The moles began to drift away after a time, almost disappointed it seemed. Privet never quite seemed to do what they expected.

'Library Aide Pumpkin?' said a grizzle-furred mole from out of the dusk.

'Yes, that's me.'

The mole came forward and Pumpkin knew him by sight quite well, and by name too: the pilgrim Hibbott, a worthy mole.

'I was by the Stone earlier today,' said Hibbott, 'and I met five moles, all pilgrims like myself. Indeed, I may venture to say that apart from myself they were the only pilgrims remaining in Duncton

Wood of those who came when the Newborns left.' Hibbott's choice of words was delicate. 'Now they have departed . . .'

'Departed?'

'Yes, they were on their separate ways to the Stone when you stopped one and asked him to come here. He brought the others and after their sojourn here they went to the Stone to ask its blessing for their departure. They asked me to join them in leaving the system, saying there was little here for them now, and I confess I was tempted. But . . . well, when they talked of whatmole they had been with earlier I guessed, though they did not seem to know it, it was to Privet they had talked.

'Something whispered to me. I have journeyed far since my pilgrimage from Ashbourne Chase began, far further than the distance between the Chase and here.'

Pumpkin warmed to Hibbott, and saw the reverence in his face.

'I felt concerned. I felt there was another farewell in the system today, and it was Privet's. I cannot tell you why, but so it was. I prayed for her by the Stone, and for the Stone's guidance in the journey she is on. That done I came here with no expectation other than to pay my respects up here on the surface and go on my way.'

'You are leaving Duncton too?'

'No, mole, I am not. I came in pursuit of a dream, which was to see Privet. I saw her and then my dream changed to a desire to see the Book. The Book has not come to ground and so my pilgrimage is not yet complete.'

'Do you want to see Privet?' asked Pumpkin, Hibbott's words seeming to confirm the growing worries and doubts he had felt all day.

Hibbott shook his head. 'From the sound of laughter and talk, she has more than enough moles to keep her company. No, I have made my prayer to the Stone and I shall see her again when it wishes it.'

'Are you the mole who called out her name beyond the cross-under, and came with Hodder and the others?'

'The same, to my regret. But perhaps I shall find forgiveness for my indiscretion.'

'Come now, mole, and she will give it.'

Again Hibbott shook his head. 'No, her journey is not done. May the Stone grant that I shall be there to witness the joy when it is complete and the Book comes to ground at last.'

'Mole . . .' urged Pumpkin, for he did not want to let Hibbott go, as if to do so was to lose Privet all the sooner. For it was the sense of losing her that loomed in the night.

For the third time Hibbott shook his head, and then he turned and quietly left.

Rooster was the last to come, and he was alone.

'Where's Frogbit?' they all asked, for Frogbit was Rooster's shadow.

'Sent him to Cuddesdon to learn. Glee and Humlock are there now. Whillan learning and teaching. All discovering. Delving will be good in Cuddesdon.'

All this was said before he greeted Privet, to whom he now turned.

'Better be getting along then!' declared Fieldfare, looking meaningfully about the company, feeling that Rooster and Privet might well wish to be alone. 'Come on, Hamble, you're feeling tired, my dear.'

'Am I?' muttered Hamble, who was stanced down most comfortably next to Elynor and sharing a fat worm with her. 'Er . . .'

'You most certainly are tired, dearest!' said Fieldfare, turning for the door.

'He's comfortable,' said Rooster grinning. 'Know his comfort when I see it.'

'It's all right, Fieldfare, Rooster and I do not need privacy,' said Privet. 'We found it long ago within each other's heart.'

She looked at Rooster, as he at her, with such profound love and ease that none could doubt the truth of what she said.

'Heard you were out of tunnels and here, Privet. Came to say things. Things all can hear. Time of Silence coming to Privet and me, if . . .' He paused, and sighed, and stabbed his paws at the floor. 'Sturne's coming. Sturne knows things. We'll wait.'

They did wait, and somewhat uncomfortably, most of them, since the conversation had difficulty getting started with Rooster stanced down in the middle of the chamber and staring at his paws. Privet, closing her eyes for a time, dozed. There was desultory talk here and there, two or three of them went to the surface to stretch their paws, and all were much relieved when Sturne came, texts under his paw, every bit the busy Master Librarian.

'Make room for him, Hamble, there's a good mole,' said Fieldfare, who all her life had been impressed and intimidated by texts and anything to do with scribing.

Hamble looked weary, winked at Privet, grinned at Rooster, and made way for Sturne.

'Now then, earlier today Privet asked me a question and I have come to try to answer it,' began Sturne, starting a long dissertation, which nomole dared interrupt, about the early Rolls and Registers of Duncton, and the reliability or otherwise of such texts, not to mention

644

the difficulties in spelling, and reconciling present molish time with mediaeval time, which as allmole knew . . .

'What it comes to then,' he said finally, and to the great relief of everymole, 'is this: in all probability the dead library aide who appears – and I emphasize the word *appears* – to have been the bringer of the Book to the chamber where Privet found it, almost certainly *made* the Book, for that was part of aides' tasks in those days.'

'It still is, mole,' said Pumpkin, grumpily.

'Ah! Quite so. Also the mole was almost certainly the personal aide to Dunbar himself, which narrows the field to two, one of whom, Cheyne of Fulham, we can immediately discount, since a reference to him as living and dying in retirement at Uffington in later years is beyond dispute.

'Therefore, the second contender, if I may call him that, is a mole who came to Duncton when quite young and served Dunbar for several moleyears at the end of that great mole's life. This library aide was named Collis of Sedlescombe.'

There was a blank silence.

'What do you know of him?' asked Privet finally.

'Ah, yes, I thought you might ask that. We know nothing of him, nothing at all. Just his name, and that of his home system, which is in the south-east.'

'Nothing else?' asked Privet.

'No, nothing. Except, of course, that he knew how to make a book, if not a Book!' A glimmer of a smile stirred on Sturne's face at what he obviously thought was a nice conceit, but it was shared by nomoleelse, and it soon died.

'Nothing, we know nothing,' said Privet mysteriously. 'It makes my task a little easier then.'

The conversation turned to everyday matters for a time until Rooster raised a paw and said, 'Want to say this. Not much, but something. Privet leaving us now. All has been preparation for what's to come. Have said before and say again: I delve with paws, she delves with words. What do I make? I make places where nothing seems to be until moles come, except wind-sound. True? I made this chamber here with Frogbit, but it wasn't until Privet came, and you all now. And after she has gone? Nothing? Or many things, each in your memory. True? When we die and memory of this chamber now is gone? True? Was it ever?

'So I delve now, not yesterday and not tomorrow. Most delving in Duncton's done now, so I sent Glee and Humlock and Frogbit to

Cuddesdon, where delving waits to be. That's why Whillan's there with his love, to delve. He is a Master now . . .'

There was a stir at this, for whatever a Master of the Delve might be, most there had assumed there was only one.

'No, no, no, many Masters, living and dead. Masters live on in the delvings they made. Gaunt was my mentor, but Hilbert was my Master though long dead. But Privet, whatmole is her Master?'

He shrugged, for having asked the question it seemed the answer did not matter.

'Listen. For many moleyears I did not delve. Hamble knows. When I began again I was better, simpler, because was delving in my mind all that time, clearing – cleansing! Ha!'

He laughed as he often did these days at some joke he saw in what he said. And moles about him laughed as well, less at the joke, which often they did not see, more that he was so at peace.

'Not chance that Privet and me came to be same time, or that we love. We love because we know each other's heart. I knew her heart on Hilbert's Top, and she knew mine. Wanted to love her then with everything but was not to be. Too timid, eh Privet?'

'Too timid, Rooster,' she agreed.

'So . . . trouble, sadness. Lust. Fear. Dark searching ways. Yes, Privet?'

'All of those things and more, my dear.'

'Long long time ago Privet said to me, "Delve me tunnels, delve me a place" and I promised that I would. My whole life is working towards that place of Silence which shall be ours and all. Nearly there. Have missed you very much, Privet. Have missed you with my heart and body. Have missed your love. Yes, yes, have been to lonely places.

'But Gaunt said, "One day you will delve the Master's way, and when you do all past hurts and all future longings will be gone, and you will only know the bliss of now. So Rooster, delve each day with discipline of heart and mind and spirit, and that day eternal may come."

'Ha! May come, not will. Certainty isn't delving but staying still. Certainty is dying because it takes life out of now and tries to fix it then or in time to come. So, have come to tell you Privet all these things. My words jumbled up but true.

'Hurry, Privet, hurry. But take time! Winter's a good time to delve with words. All before you to start with, all the words that ever were, like untouched earth. When you choose some and cast out many

646

others which you didn't choose. That's the earth I cast up with my paws. Then you choose more, but cast out even more. So delving begins and words get less. First was all words, finally is no word. None. Hurry and find it Privet, that last word and cast it out for us!'

He had finished in a burst of words and strange gesticulation, breathing heavily, stomping at the ground, and finally bearing down on her and staring into her eyes, which softened as she reached to him and he to her.

'Now,' he whispered, and grinned, and grimaced in mock madness; chuckling, he turned from the chamber and was gone.

Hamble sighed, words utterly failing him.

Fieldfare shifted, peered about, started to speak, and then thought better of it.

Elynor got up and taking Pumpkin's proffered paw, said, 'I'll be off to somewhere comfortable.'

Then, without more said, except goodbye and farewell, they all drifted away until Privet, in Pumpkin's absence, was alone.

She smiled, and slept; and in the morning, in her own time, and asking Pumpkin not to come until a little later, she went back into the tunnels of the Ancient System, back to the Book, and back into Silence.

Pumpkin resumed his daily visits to Privet, to bring food, to clean the chamber, to tidy the folios, to tend to things. In the short intervals when he was not there, he was over in the Library to share Sturne's quiet company; or in his own tunnels at peace; or fretting at his prayers by the Stone.

For all of them he prayed, especially two moles: Privet and Maple. The rest, it seemed to him, with the possible exception of Sturne, could help themselves, though he hoped an occasional word to the Stone on their behalf would not go amiss.

The weather stayed mild as Privet had hoped, at least long enough for Maple and Weeth to have the chance of getting a good way to the Redditch Stone. Then, in February, cold snapped down again and put hoar frost in the trees. Snow fell, thawed, and foul rain drove down. The High Wood became a shivery, bitter place. And still Privet worked, scoring out more than she scribed. Casting out words, as Rooster had put it, and seeking the last.

'Stone, there'll be no Book left if she continues the way she is,' grumbled Pumpkin to the Stone. 'Or no words left at least. She scores it all out like Husk used to do at the end of his long life, scribing, re-scribing, scoring and finally unscribing. It's not the way it should be, and she began so well! Oh dear, oh dear – I suppose she knows what she's doing, but I don't!'

Rooster's words had given Pumpkin comfort initially, but as time went on, and the winter grew steadily worse, and a mole did well not to stay on the blizzardy icy surface for more than a moment or two, all Pumpkin's doubts returned. She was growing more tired, she was eating too little, there was nothing left on her flanks at all so her ribs were beginning to show; and her eyes had the gleam of a dying mole about them.

Her cough had become a steady rasp, and was the first sound that greeted him as he entered the tunnels near the chamber, and the last he heard as he left. That and her groans and mumblings as she scratched and scored and scrivened.

Then early in March she began to clutch the Book to her thin chest when he came in, and to speak to him – or rather shout at him, in a thin and frightened way – in Whernish; and she laughed sometimes. Her eyes grew frightened and when he came near she would often stab at him with her talons.

'Take him away!' she cried out one day, breaking her silence and pointing a paw at the dead aide. 'Collis speaks to me and tells me . . . there is no Silence.'

'Privet . . .'

But his words she did not hear; and he did not remove the dead mole.

'Privet, come to my barrow and rest again, come—'

'Noooo!' she screamed, 'I shall never be able to start again if I do.'

'Privet . . .'

And she wept like a pup, her voice so weak it was no louder than the scribing of her talon on birch-bark. Then she forced him to leave her. Day after day passed like that.

Heavy snow, a sudden thaw at night and waking to the drip, drip, drip of water in the tunnels.

Even as Pumpkin lay aburrow, the wind shifted and the cold returned, and deepened into the crippling thrall of the worse freeze in Duncton in living memory. He begged Privet to leave her icy chamber. She refused. He begged her to let him stay. She refused – and followed him, shouting and railing when he tried to hide in the tunnel outside the chamber that he might keep watch on her.

Next day he returned to a most terrible scene. She lay half-conscious, mumbling, the Book's folios scattered, food he had left half-eaten and strewn about; while above her there hung down, like talons of death, great icicles amongst the frozen roots.

'Privet, this cannot go on,' he said, when he had warmed her, and she had revived and eaten a little.

'No, but it is not finished. One more night and one more day. There is so little left to do, look!' She almost laughed as she proffered him the broken, battered Book. 'Look, my dear, is it not nearly beautiful? Is it not peaceful now?'

He turned its loose folios, though with considerable difficulty, for the Book was strangely heavy, strangely unmanageable, and he strived and struggled with it, panting with effort and feeling a dread.

Yet he pressed on, putting back in place those folios that slipped out, and seeing that one after another after the next all the words she had scribed on folio after folio were scored out. She had made new scribing between the lines of the first, but that was scored out too. And along the margins, and upside down, and everywhere, the scribing was scored out. He could not bear to look at all the folios. This was not scribing, this was a death of words.

'It told all I knew, Pumpkin, everything – but I had to take it out. Bit by bit it had to go. Husk did the same with Tales, but I did not understand. He knew, as Rooster knows. But I . . . I have not the strength to score out everything.'

'You seemed to have nearly done so!' Pumpkin exclaimed.

She sighed. 'Give me another night and day. I shall try one more time. And don't fret so, Pumpkin, I shall not die quite yet. What season is it?'

'March, winter, freezing,' he said.

Reluctantly he agreed to leave her, eyeing the icicles above her as he went, as if they were an enemy.

'I shall be back at midday on the morrow,' he promised. 'And Privet, I swear that if you will not agree to come with me I shall drag you out!'

'Pumpkin!' But even as she exclaimed at his threat, her eyes wandered back to the Book, her paws reached out towards it, and he saw fear and apprehension, and age, creep over her, like shadows, like death.

He went to the Stone before returning to his burrow and his prayer was simple and direct.

'Stone, release her. Let her be free of this! Thy Silence cannot be so terrible that seeking it kills a mole. Release her now . . .' And he wept into the icy, unyielding ground.

He slept but fitfully, imagining he heard her screams and that she called his name; he must go back to her! He rose to do so, felt the bitter bite of cold, thought again he heard her call and slipped back into sleep. So tired . . . But when he woke he knew he was too late. He knew it as certain as the prick of thorns.

'Privet . . . !' and he hurried out of his burrow up to the surface and . . .

And she was there, fallen, her paw reaching out, calling his name in a voice that he could barely hear.

'Privet . . .' he whispered, appalled, helping her down into his tunnel, and putting her into his still-warm sleeping chamber.

'I called your name, my dear,' she whispered, 'but you could not hear. All night I have called your name.'

All night! Her paws and face and flanks – all thin, almost nothing now – were icy, her voice insidiously soft and sleepy.

'Pumpkin, the Book . . . I could not, I cannot . . .'

He held her, warmed her, wept for her, and wondered what to do.

'Pumpkin, fetch the Book for me. Fetch it here. It will help me to have it now, unfinished though it is. Fetch it, mole.'

He warmed her more, settled her, saw that she ate a mite of worm, which was better than none at all, and he began to think she might recover.

'Fetch it, mole, now, now . . .'

It was then that he saw she was beginning to die.

'I cannot leave you. I must get Rooster. I must . . . I . . .' He stanced over her, shaking, muttering, uncertain.

'Fetch it, Pumpkin. For me . . .'

Then he settled her into the warmest place, his own sleeping chamber, and turned from her and ran from the burrow, panting and gasping up the frozen slopes, slipping and sliding on the ice and then down into the Ancient System, down through the icy tunnels, on and on into the heart of all that was lost and forgotten and so long forsaken. Running for his life, and for hers.

He turned towards the chamber, saw the glimmer of light, heard the icy whisper of Dark Sound, and ran in, his pawsteps racing ahead of him.

He stopped dead at what he saw, the echo of his pawsteps fading about him as he took in the scene. The chamber was filled with that light they had seen when first they came. And the chamber was clean and clear, or almost so. The litter of folios was gone. The bits of worm, the nesting material once strewn about had been removed; the chaos she had made about her, all was gone, all tidied away, all cleared.

Even the floor was clear and cleaned, as if a library aide had come after the mole he worked for had left, and had ordered things once more, and made them as they should be.

Only the Book was there, back on the dais where she had first found it, its folios neat and tidy and all made right again. Perhaps then, with one last effort, she had worked to leave things as she found them, and placed the Book back for another to find. Perhaps she had finished it.

But he felt that was not so. Nor did he believe that she could herself have cleared the chamber: it was more than she could have done.

'Much more,' he whispered; stancing now in the light about the Book, he looked around him. It was then that he saw that the body of the aide had also gone, his paws outstretched towards the dais no more, no mark of him left: his part of this awesome task complete.

Pumpkin felt awe and wonder, and knew then what mole had cleared the place, and made it whole again: Collis of Sedlescombe, the unknown aide.

'Mole,' he whispered, his voice echoing forward to the Book, and then to where the aide had been and then beyond, though whether back or forward he did not know.

'Mole,' he whispered in gratitude, for the aide had been there to watch over her, 'mole . . .'

'Mole,' that whisper came back to him, back to the now where Pumpkin was, back in gratitude, aide to aide, mole to mole and Pumpkin understood that *now* had come, and here he was, to do what he must do.

'Stone,' whispered Pumpkin, and the answer came back to him with the clinging of an echo:

'Mole . . .' whispered the aide.

Pumpkin went to the Book. He opened its time-worn covers, and turned its ruined folios, and saw such scorings that no single word on page after page could he ken at all. Not one word seemed left.

Then one he found. Untouched, unscored. As perfectly scribed as it had first been. He turned further on and then to the end of the Book, but all else was ruin and lost words, and nothing at all. He turned back to the single word that remained, and the unscored space about it that was white with light.

He reached out his old paw and touched the scribing she had first made.

'Privet,' he kenned aloud.

651

It was her own name she could not score out, her very self. That alone she could not let go. It was the last word she had found, and she could not let it go.

Privet . . .

And Pumpkin wept for the mole he served. He took up the Book, and felt how heavy it was, how hard to carry, and he turned from the light where it became harder still.

'Help me bring it to her, Stone, help me now.'

At the portal from the chamber he turned back, for he heard a new sound, a clean and steady sound. He put the Book down to see what the sound was. It came from the dais where the Book had been, but it started high above, where the light was bright as stars.

The sound again, deep, sudden; then again.

He looked down at the dais, up at the light, and seeing the great white icicles that hung there pointing down, he knew the sound for what it was.

Drip!

Drip!

And Drip! again.

A sound as old as time, the sound of a season's turn, when winter ends, and spring begins. The water dripped upon the dais that had held the book, and the dais began to crumble and erode away before his eyes, and meld back into the earth from which it had been formed.

He took up the Book again, though it was a struggle to do so, and then, his paws dragging, the tunnels seeming endless, he began to carry the Book out of the Ancient System. And if, sometimes, in that long trek he felt the Book grow lighter, and a paw at his flank, and heard words of encouragement, he fancied that another aide was there to lighten his load a little, an aide who had served, as he did now; a mole who understood.

'Privet,' he whispered as he came to the tunnel end and towards the light of the High Wood, 'I am coming. Wait now . . . wait.' And as best he could, but like a mole who is sure he is too late, old Pumpkin reached up towards the light of day once more.

Chapter Forty-Nine

With a final shove of his back paws, and clutching on to the Book, Pumpkin almost popped up into the light of day, and was astonished to find that spring had rather more than sprung.

For one thing, the grey drear light of winter had fled away completely, and in its place was that softer, warmer, brighter light under which new buds, unnoticed before, shine fresh, and through which breaks the busy brilliant sound of song – of bird, of insect, or so many creatures long lost to light.

Pumpkin paused, startled and confused, bewitched by the fresh and eager scent of spring, his paws caressed by the softness of the leaf-litter underpaw, his ears delighting in the sounds of new life, his eyes dazzled by the burst of beauties long forgotten.

He whiffled his wrinkled snout in the air, put down the Book on a surface root of a beech tree to keep it from the damp leaves, and caught his breath. Time seemed to be running amok about him, and something more than spring sang to him, and took the trouble and the stress from out of his old heart and replaced it in a trice with wonderment.

'But it cannot be!' he exclaimed, peering at the woodland floor and seeing snowdrops and yellow winter aconite, not bursting forth, but fading fast.

'Fading already, and giving way to bluebells and wild daffodils!'

He rubbed his eyes in disbelief and then . . .

'Stone,' he whispered, as he might to an old friend who had journeyed at his flank, turning a corner and seeing something that had taken them both utterly by surprise, 'what's apaw?'

There was quick movement behind him, or so he thought. He turned and looked back to the dark entrance from which he had just emerged, for he was sure there had been a mole there, a mole so close to him he might have been himself, and that mole – or aide – had paused with him, wished him well of the world to which he had now returned, and, laughing like wind-sound in a well-made tunnel on a summer's day, had left him to go on by himself.

'Stone . . . mole . . . I do not understand,' he faltered aloud, except that he *did*, and his heart, so long oppressed, was filled with joy and certainty.

Wherever he had been, it must have been longer than he thought. Had the hours then been days, and the days . . . ?

Sun shone across the trunk of the beech tree on whose surface root he had laid the Book, and the lichen on the bark was green and fresh, and up beyond it the pointed beech buds were beginning to grow full, while the sky beyond was blue.

Bewildered but content, sure that in some way the Stone had been watching over Privet in his absence, though unsure what the nature of that absence had been, Pumpkin bent down and lifted the Book once more. It was so heavy, so very hard to carry, but he could manage now down the slope, and with some strength to spare he could feel the energy of change and growth, and believe they were enshadowed in Duncton Wood no more.

'There you are, Pumpkin!' called out Fieldfare from the entrance to his tunnels, where, to his increased bewilderment, she was busying herself cleaning and making all orderly.

'What a day, what a day!'

'Privet . . . ?' he began, utterly unsure.

Her face clouded and she said, 'Ah, well, she won't stance up on her own paws yet, but she may yet, she may yet. There's nothing wrong that common sense won't put right, but don't try and tell her that. You and her – what a to-do! Books! Scribing! You can't live on words alone! Look at you, Pumpkin, thin as old grass stems. But at least you're up and about again, and doing. Doing with books, it seems.' She eyed the Book under his paw with disapproval. 'Books is for libraries, not for comfortable homely burrows like I've made yours since you've been . . .'

Comfortable? Homely? Pumpkin's heart sank. But wait . . .

'I've been what?'

But she had turned tail with a 'Must get on!' and was gone before he could get an answer from her. What had he been? Ill, like Privet? He had no idea.

But he scented the air once more, felt the bliss of spring and all the joys of which such a day as this was the cheerful herald, and followed Fieldfare down.

Privet now lay in her own chamber, the one he and Rooster had first prepared for her, not in his own sleeping chambers where he had left her. Whatever fears he had about her dying fled away before the look that came upon her face when she saw him.

'Pumpkin!' she called out the moment she glimpsed him.

'I got the Book as you asked,' he said, feeling he had never made so gross an understatement in his life. 'Got the Book'! Why, he had nearly died getting it! Yes, that was it. He had nearly died.

'Put it there, my dear, not too near and not too far. No, no, behind me here where I can touch it if I must, but others will not notice it. We'll know where it is!'

She laughed half nervously, half indifferently, as if it was something she felt she ought to think about, but preferred to forget if she could. He looked at her and saw that though she looked less near death than when she had come to his burrow that dawn – and already that dawn seemed many, many dawns ago – she was very frail.

Her eyes, her face, the way she looked sometimes beyond him at the chamber's portal, belied that smile upon her face, the cheerful words. Plainly, she was very ill.

'Privet, I saw—'

'No, no, my dear, don't tell me what you saw in the Ancient System. I saw things too but was not strong enough to stay; whatmole could be? The Book will wait, and one day, one distant day perhaps, some-mole will have the strength to come and finish it.'

'You will have the strength, Privet, and then you'll find the strength to live again.'

He did not know where his words came from, but he felt them to be true.

'I might "have the strength" as you put it, Library Aide Pumpkin, but I do not have the will. I looked into the void of Silence and felt the nothing I would be. It is not strength I need, but an ability to let go, and that I don't have. It is . . . so hard, so confusing, and my mind was in such a whirl of scoring, and scrivening, scratching and scribing, words and words and words until there was hardly anything left of me at all.'

'Your name, Privet, that was left.'

'Ah, yes, that: what I am. Well, mole, the Stone cannot ask *that* of me and I fled when it did, and, as you see, am much better now for doing so! It was killing both of us, and look at us now. Why, mole, you've ventured forth on to the surface day by day and the warm weather of spring is well and truly here, and now you've even brought the Book. For old time's sake if nothing else!'

She laughed that thin uncertain laugh, and again glanced at the Book in the shadows behind her.

655

'Privet,' he said, with terrible resolution, 'you say "look at us now" and I look at you and I see—'

'Happiness! Contentment! Release at last! No, no, don't say what you were going to because it is not true.'

'I am your library aide, and I must—'

'You must do as I say then, my dear, and leave me be!'

Her voice had begun sharply, but it ended soft and slow.

'There now!' cried Fieldfare from the portal. 'That's enough, Pumpkin. You get worse as you get older. Leave her be she said, and she was right. Got to feed her now, got to let her rest, for visitors are coming.'

'What visitors?' asked Privet querulously.

'Hamble, for one. Rees is coming again today, and Sturne might look in, Stone help us all.'

'Fieldfare, don't be unkind. Sturne is a great mole in his way.'

'A great deal too serious to be visiting a mole who needs sunshine, and rest, and time.'

She turned from Privet for a moment and Pumpkin caught the expression on her face nomole was meant to see. It was full of doubt and care.

'Loosestrife, will she come to me at last, will she?'

Privet was growing more weak and tired by the moment, and more tearful too. As Pumpkin slipped away he heard Fieldfare say, 'Soon, when her pups are a little older, and you're a little stronger. She's been ill and tired with rearing, and they've been sick as well. Whillan will bring them all over from Cuddesdon when the weather's warmer, and you'll take them up on the surface and play with them as their grandmother should.'

'It's Loosestrife I want,' sobbed Privet into sleep.

It was Sturne who later told Pumpkin how things were.

'Found you wandering in the ice and snow myself, and took you to my burrow,' he said. 'You were as near death with cold and hunger as anymole could be, but all you could talk of was that Privet needed help in your tunnels, and you needed to get the Book. But you don't remember any of it?'

Pumpkin shook his head.

'Well, mole, I thought you were going to die. I . . . I really . . . I just didn't know . . .'

Sturne almost allowed himself to weep.

'It's not for me you should feel sorry,' said Pumpkin finally, 'but yourself.'

'Hmmph!' said Sturne, dabbing at his face-fur and frowning. 'If I wept for me I'd never stop.'

'Yes, you would, Sturne, and you'd feel better for it.'

'Well, that's as maybe, and unlikely to happen now. I'm too old for tears.'

'You just nearly wept at the thought of me dying!'

'That's different. You really are an irritating mole, Pumpkin. Obstinate, I'd say.'

Pumpkin laughed and asked what happened after he had been found.

'Well, I got Fieldfare and Hamble to go down to your tunnels, and there was Privet in no better state than I found you, except that you'd had the sense to tuck her up in your own sleeping chamber with some food. We thought you'd both die, but you haven't, though, Privet—'

'She's weak,' said Pumpkin.

'Getting weaker in my view, and not a thing a mole can do about it. And what's most strange, Rooster won't help at all. Been to see her, talked about Silence, and voids, and so on and so forth which only got her agitated, and then left her to think about what he'd said!'

Pumpkin smiled to himself, imagining the scene. Rooster might be many things but he was not a healer, or not in the normal sense of the word.

'So now she's fading away before our eyes and all Rooster does is gallivant about the system delving tunnels and burrows.'

'Delving?'

'Other moles' tunnels, not his own. One's enough for him, thank you very much. No, he goes and helps others out, which is to say the moles who have settled back in the system down by Barrow Vale, and over on the wormful Westside. He's helped a lot of the old moles who you led up into the Ancient System, I'll say that much for him, including Elynor. He may be a Master for all I know, but all he does with his skills is make moles tunnels.'

'Are they happy with what he delves for them?'

'Happy? Of course they're happy, Pumpkin! Wouldn't *you* be happy if a great big brute of a mole came and delved out your springtime tunnels for you? I know I would!'

Pumpkin grinned. 'Ask him what he's about then!'

'Hmmph!' muttered Sturne.

'Perhaps he's keeping his paw in.'

'He could keep his paw in in the Library, which is falling to rack and ruin and needs a delver. More than one in fact. But no, he won't do it. Says the Duncton delving's done, whatever that means. But at least he went over to Cuddesdon the moment the spring came.'

'When was that? When did I go back to my own tunnels?'

'Oh, that,' said Sturne vaguely. 'It seemed moleweeks ago now, yes . . . but you remember!'

'Yes, maybe I do,' said Pumpkin, giving up. What did it matter? 'Privet was saying that she wants Loosestrife to visit her.'

'Ah, well, I don't know all the ins and outs of that. She's had pups by Whillan and they've all been ill, that much I heard from Rooster himself. That's why Whillan won't leave Cuddesdon. Naturally Privet would like to see her daughter, never yet having done so, which seems hard even to a mole like me who's never had a family. I would have thought that Loosestrife could have made the trek from Cuddesdon if she wanted.'

'These things are sometimes best left until the right time,' said Pumpkin.

'Like when?' said Sturne.

Pumpkin looked about the High Wood, scented the balmy air, settled his belly into the warm litter more comfortably, and said, 'Well, a day like this, only a little warmer. When April comes.'

'It *is* April, mole.'

'Well, then,' said Pumpkin, trying not to let his astonishment show, 'later in April, when pups can travel a bit in safety and their parents don't have to fret. If it was me I'd not let *my* pups travel till May-time.'

'Well, anyway, that's how it is. Now I've work to do, mole, and though I need a lot of help I won't ask you in your weakened state.'

'Come on, Sturne, you know it's work that makes me well. Privet's in good paws for now, and has visitors today, so I'll come to the Library with you and see what you've been up to – Master Librarian! Well, then, it really came to pass.'

'Aye,' said Sturne, 'it does seem to have done . . .'

But still, even now, even on a day such as this – perhaps especially on such a day, and with many more in prospect, Sturne looked bleak, and much alone.

'It's good to have your company, Pumpkin, it really is . . .'

Sharing his tunnels as she now did, Pumpkin saw more of Privet than any other mole, and more privately too. The ready cheer of moles like Fieldfare, the rough good nature of Hamble, and the quiet faith of Arliss and Rees were well and fine, but *they* did not see how Privet collapsed the moment they had gone; nor did they hear the sighs and moans night after night, when she slipped into fretful sleep, and seemed to live again all those unimaginable days of her long and lonely spiritual quest for Silence, which being incomplete, seemed nothing but a failure to her now.

She wept sometimes, and held his paw, nodding in the evening light, staring, worrying about shadows only she could see. The coughing, which had gone for a time, came back, a dry hacking thing to which Pumpkin would sometimes wake at night, and listen to wearily, until, unable to sleep, he would go to her and help her to the surface, to drink where the rain left water in a treetrunk cleft nearby. She would not go out by day at all, but on those nights she would sometimes linger for a moment or two, and stare up at the stars.

Then, at the end of April, there came a night when she was too weak to move, and the coughing went on and he was unable to help her with it. On and on, dry as a scab, painful to listen to.

'Pumpkin . . .'

He woke to hear her calling his name, knowing as he did that she had called it several times because he could hear the echo of it in his troubled dreams, and went to her. Dawn had come, and somewhere not far off the first birds were beginning their songs.

'The Book, my dear, reach it over to me.'

The Book, which no visitor ever asked about. The Book, the quest for which had brought her so near death. It was only just beyond her flank, in the dark angle of the floor and wall, and yet she was too weak to reach it. He bent over her and put his paws to it. It was as heavy as ten moles. It filled him with fear.

'Privet . . .' he gasped.

She reached out to it to help him, and between them they placed it in front of her, panting together as if they had run up some great mountainside.

'Turn its folios for me, my dear.'

He did so, one by one, and in the gloom the scoring seemed luminous and rich, yet he knew it was unkennable. Lost words, scribing she had made and then destroyed.

'This first folio is the last folio of the Book of Tales on which Keeper Husk worked all his life, and then, towards the end, began to unscribe and simplify. I wondered why at the time. Now I know. Well, he made a great thing, didn't he? The first folio of the Book of Silence. Not so bad, Pumpkin.'

'No, Privet.'

'Turn another folio . . . and another, mole . . . go on . . .'

He turned them one by one, and at each she had him pause while

659

she reached out a paw to touch what she had unmade, smiling sometimes, or shedding a tear.

'Past history, mole, all gone, all gone. So much. Rooster was right after all. He knew you see, he understood. And he still does.'

'He's gone to Cuddesdon once more, Privet, to see if Loosestrife will come.'

'She'll come in May and bring her pups for me to see. But Pumpkin, turn on, mole, turn on.'

He turned the heavy, awkward, obstinate folios, sweating now, fearful of nothing in particular, seeming to see light glimmer on the walls, and imagining dangers.

'This . . .' and she held her paw to a folio for what seemed to Pumpkin far too long.

'Thripp,' she whispered, 'I loved him so. Ecstasy, Pumpkin, he and I . . .' and she even laughed.

On, on he turned the pages, struggling with them as he might down all the tunnels of her life, until he reached the folio on which so impulsively she had scribed her name when she first found the Book.

'Ah . . .' she sighed, lightly touching the one perfect unscored folio, and peering at her own name, which seemed dark and shadowed, though it was surrounded with the light of untouched birch-bark. 'My beginning and my end. How can I score it out? Pumpkin, it is too hard and too much to ask.'

She shivered suddenly, eyes closed, but when he moved to put the Book back where it had been she held on to him, opened her eyes and told him to continue to the end. He turned the last few folios, all scribed and overscribed, all scored, all lost to whatever she had made.

'Why?' he gently asked.

She looked at him and said, 'Sometimes I was lost in the beauty of what I became when, the words unscribed but their meaning and their memory remaining, I was one with them. I was, Pumpkin, as one with them as Rooster in the delve. But if . . . No, no, don't tempt me. I could score out my name in a moment, and all the Book would be undone. It must be done truthfully and almost without thought. Each thing I cast out I did with struggle and with striving to reach the place where I could do it without thought. Quail talked of worms and snakes. Do you remember? Well then, these words of mine, these were the worms, these the snakes, and each one was hard. But that last one is hardest of all, and all the long way from Wildenhope to here, through landscapes I never knew were mine until I ventured into them, I tried to kill that worm, that dreadful snake that is harboured by my name. But I could not. I cannot.'

'Do you still struggle, Privet? Do you still strive?'

She started at his words and tone, which were not benign, and he was surprised himself.

'I mean . . .' he stuttered.

'Yes,' she said, 'I do, mole, and I am not strong enough. I don't know how to do it now. For this the Stone needs a different mole than I can be. Now, put it back, for I am very tired, and very weak. No visitors today.'

He knew then that she was dying now, and that the Book had been too much. Such a thing was not for mortal mole to make.

Visitors were turned away, all except Fieldfare who washed and cleaned her, turned her, and begged to stay with them.

'Is she coming, is my Loosestrife coming?'

'Soon, now, she'll be with you soon.'

The last day of April passed, night came and the stars shone, and all in Duncton knew that Privet was fading fast. A day more perhaps. Two at the most. And after that, well, at least she would suffer no more.

'At least she seems to have no physical pain, Fieldfare,' whispered Pumpkin, outside his tunnels that night to take a breath of fresh night air. 'But she is much distressed. The Book . . .'

'It was not worth it, mole, it was a dream,' said Fieldfare firmly. 'But no matter! Hamble will be back from Cuddesdon in the morning, and with more moles than just himself.'

'How do you know?' asked Pumpkin.

'I sent him there myself the night before last. "Hamble, beloved," says I, "enough is enough. I was the first mole to greet Privet all those years ago when she first came, and I reckon that gives me some rights!"

'"So what do you suggest I do?" says he, tears in his eyes, bless him, for he loves her just as much as I do.

'"You go to Cuddesdon right now, dark or no dark, and you don't dawdle because she's near her end. You get that Rooster and you tell him Fieldfare says to get back to Duncton Wood immediately. And bring Loosestrife, because she can't be as ill with birthing and pup-rearing now as her mother is with dying. And don't forget the pups!" That's what I said, Pumpkin.

'And Hamble said, being Hamble, "What *about* the pups? Aren't they still too young to travel?" Well, Pumpkin, I'm not a swearing

661

mole in the normal course of events, unlike Chater used to be, but it would seem Chater taught me words I thought I had forgotten, because I said, "Look, Hamble, if the pups get tired, carry the little buggers!"'

'Carry them?' repeated Pumpkin, reeling from this outburst. It was as if Fieldfare was suddenly her old self.

'By the scruff of the neck!'

'So when do you expect them to be here?' said Pumpkin faintly.

'I told Hamble that if him and the others aren't all here, and I mean *here*, not at the cross-under, by midday May Day, which is tomorrow, he could forget all about sharing a burrow with me any more. This cannot go on! Grandpups'll do the trick. Always have and always will.'

'Grandpups? Here?' said Pumpkin uneasily.

'*Right* here,' said Fieldfare. 'And when they come, make yourself scarce, Pumpkin.'

'Scarce,' said Pumpkin unhappily. 'She doesn't like noise and lots of moles.'

'They're *hers*, mole, and that's all that matters. Should have done it molemonths ago. I don't know what Rooster's playing at. You're all the same – you and Sturne, and Rooster, no knowledge of pups and females at all. Whillan should have known better but then look who he was raised by! Privet! And you!'

'You had a part in it, I seem to remember,' said Pumpkin.

'Not a big enough part, it would seem!'

In this kind of mood Fieldfare was not worth arguing with, as Pumpkin well knew. Many was the occasion when Chater had come to his tunnels for a break from her. And lately, Hamble too . . .

'You're right, of course,' said Pumpkin.

'You'll believe that as well as just say it, before long.'

She left then, muttering as she went, but when morning came that was all forgotten. Privet would not eat, would hardly talk.

'I think they may be coming today, Privet.'

No reply.

'Loosestrife's coming, I'm sure she is.'

Silence.

'I hope they do.'

Privet stared, and seemed so tiny.

'Won't you take some food?'

She shook her head.

'Or try to come outside?'

She shook her head again, the slightest of movements.

'When?' she whispered suddenly.

'I'm not sure,' faltered Pumpkin. 'Perhaps midday, perhaps in the afternoon.'

'Midday,' she sighed hopelessly, as if it was too far off to wait, 'midday.'

No morning was ever so slow in Pumpkin's whole life as that morning. Never before had he gone back and forth to the surface and down below so many times as on that morning, nor started at sounds across the wood so often, nor looked to see how high the sun had risen so many times; nor had he ever felt so sad.

Sturne came by and was sent off at once, Pumpkin almost pushing him.

'Who must I tell to hurry? Why, mole, why?'

'Do it, Sturne, do it for your old friend Pumpkin. If you see Whillan and Hamble and . . . oh, just tell them to get a move on, will you!'

'I will!'

Then, before midday, the sun not yet at its height, but the day a good warm May Day, Privet turned away and into sleep.

'Privet!'

But she didn't answer him.

'Oh dear. Oh dear . . .' sobbed Pumpkin, 'I don't know, I'm not sure . . .'

'Where?'

'*There.*'

'Here?'

Their voices came drifting down into the burrow. One was Hamble's, and sounded irritable. The other was a female's and unknown to Pumpkin.

'Oh! They're here!' he said with relief. 'I better go and see. Privet, there's moles come.'

She did not move, and for a dreadful moment he thought she might be . . . but on close examination her flank moved in, and out.

'Well then,' he muttered feeling foolish. 'Well . . .'

'Mole!' the female's voice called down.

Pumpkin hurried up into the light and there she was, stanced right by the entrance. Beyond her were several moles: Rooster, looking ferocious; Hamble, being lectured by Fieldfare; Whillan, crouched down by two pups, and another one snouting about here and there the way pups do on a day in May when the scent's good, and the place feels safe.

'Loosestrife,' he said, smiling. She did not look like Privet, being

663

larger, and with paler eyes. Thripp . . . she had his look about her. But warmth as well, and a look of concern.

'You're Pumpkin, the library aide,' she said, and took him in her paws. 'Fieldfare said to do this,' she whispered in his ear, 'said you'd like it! I hope you do!'

How is it that some moles can win others' hearts so quickly? Pumpkin's was won in her embrace.

'She isn't well, not well at all,' he said.

'I would have come sooner but I've been ill, and the pups all unwell, but suddenly, this last two days . . . and Hamble came. Where is she?'

'I can show you. Or perhaps you should go with Whillan.'

She shook her head and smiled, and suddenly he saw something of Privet in her.

'No, I said I would go to her by myself at first. You show me where her burrow is, and then . . .'

He showed her down, took her in, bent down to Privet and put his paw to her shoulder.

'Loosestrife's come,' he whispered. 'She's come to see you.'

He stanced up and looked at Loosestrife who was staring down at Privet with horror in her eyes.

'She is so small, so thin, and I thought . . .'

'She is unwell,' he said softly, 'and she needs you. Now, I shall leave you.'

He turned from them, and as he left the chamber how could he not look round, if only for a moment?

Loosestrife bent down as he had done, she put her paws to Privet's hand, and whispered, 'Mother,' and then she wept and held her close.

As he left them Pumpkin heard Privet whisper, as only a mother can, 'It's all right, my dear, it's all right . . .'

He paused in the shadows by the entrance to his tunnels, embarrassed by his tears. Then, having wiped them away as best he could, he emerged into the light.

'How is she?' asked Whillan, a pup at each of his flanks.

'Better,' said Pumpkin truthfully.

'And she'll get better yet,' growled Rooster, fighting off the third pup, a male. 'She'll be stronger than us all by Midsummer.'

'She's been very ill,' said Pumpkin, beginning to wonder if he had dreamed it all.

'What's your name?' asked a female pup at Whillan's flank.

'Pumpkin,' he replied. 'And yours?'

'Rose.'

'That's a good name,' said Pumpkin.

'I'm Hawthorn, Pumpkin,' said the other one with Whillan.

Whillan grinned, and had trouble holding them both still.

'And what's his name?' asked Pumpkin, turning to the other male, who stared at him with big eyes from the protection of Rooster's huge right paw.

'That's Brimmel,' said Rose.

Pumpkin stared at the youngster, who stared back. If ever a mole had his grandmother's eyes and face, Brimmel did. Black eyes, and a thin face whose expression was a shade uncertain.

'Where's Loosestrife?' asked Brimmel.

'With Privet,' said Pumpkin. 'I think they need some time alone together.'

'Will you show us your tunnels?' asked Hawthorn.

'Not just now, no,' said Pumpkin firmly. 'But I could show you the way up to the High Wood if . . . well, if . . .'

Whillan nodded his consent. 'I'll go in a little later,' he said. 'And Rooster too.'

'But I can't take them alone.'

'You showed me the High Wood alone,' smiled Whillan, 'and I'm sure you can show them.'

'But Fieldfare could help.'

'Fieldfare's off home with me, Pumpkin,' said Hamble, and she was too, only it was Fieldfare who was leading the way.

So it was that Pumpkin and the youngsters went exploring the Wood: looking past roots, staring up at the trees, shaking the red flowers of campion. Playing hide and seek amongst the violets and dog's mercury.

'Pumpkin? Is the Stone near here?'

'It's not far, but I'm not taking you there. Whillan and Loosestrife will do that.'

'Which way is it?'

It was Brimmel who asked, and that was almost the first time he spoke.

Pumpkin pointed a talon through the trees. Hawthorn and Rose peered for a moment and then wandered away, but Brimmel stared for a long time, and took Pumpkin's paw.

'The Stone's big, isn't it?'

'Yes,' said Pumpkin.

'Is Privet dying?' asked the youngster. 'I heard Hamble say she might be and that's why we travelled all night. It was very dark and I was scared. Is she?'

'I don't know,' said Pumpkin.

'Will *you* take me to her?' asked Brimmel. 'My father said you were her aide.'

'I'm not sure that *I* should,' said Pumpkin gently.

'Rose will go with Loosestrife. Hawthorn will go with Whillan. That's how it always is. So I want to go with you.'

'I'll ask,' said Pumpkin.

'What are you two talking about?' asked Rose inquisitively when she and Hawthorn came back.

'It's . . . a secret,' said Pumpkin, feeling a tremor of gratitude in Brimmel's paw as he did so, and thinking that it was a very long time indeed since he told any mole that something was a secret.

By the time they went back down the Slopes it was mid-afternoon, and Whillan was calling out for them. They scampered to him, and then to Loosestrife who was resting in the sun. She looked drained, but strangely happy. Rooster emerged from the tunnel, growling at the youngsters, playing the fool.

'She'd like to see the pups,' he said.

Rose went first, with Loosestrife.

Hawthorn second, with Whillan.

And Brimmel had a choice, and chose Pumpkin.

Down they went when his turn came, paw in paw: Brimmel, quiet and serious, Pumpkin unsure what to expect. It had been a long, strange day.

'How are you, Privet?' asked Pumpkin.

'Tired,' she said. 'So many moles today, and now another one.'

'Last one,' said Brimmel.

Pumpkin saw that she looked better; her eyes seemed a little brighter, her snout shinier than it had been.

Brimmel went to her and they looked at each other seriously.

'My mother called me Brimmel,' he said, adding very reluctantly, 'in memory of her *sister* who died a long long time ago!'

'She told me,' said Privet, smiling at him. 'Brimmel's a Moorish name used for male and female alike. It's a good name.'

'Are you going to die? Hamble said . . .'

Pumpkin tried to shush him but Privet waved a paw to let him be. 'What did Hamble say?'

'Said you were dying. Also, he said he's known you longer than any living mole.'

666

'He has. He's my oldest friend.'

'I didn't want you to die.'

'Why not?'

Pumpkin would have left them to themselves, but he felt that if he moved, other than to the shadows of the chamber, he might disturb some special communion he sensed between them.

'Because.'

Privet smiled.

He went on: 'Because Whillan said you would teach me scribing like you taught him. And that mole Pumpkin, he would teach me too.'

Privet glanced briefly to where Pumpkin stanced, her look as soft as the way she reached out and touched Brimmel's paw.

'He will, if you ask him.'

'Will *you*, Privet?'

'When?'

'Now!'

Never had Pumpkin felt such a silence. Nor, as he thought, had he ever held his breath so long.

'I could . . . begin,' said Privet, 'but we have nothing to scribe on.'

'Oh!' said Brimmel, disappointed.

'Except . . . Pumpkin, where's that book?'

She said it as if it was any book.

'It's just by you,' said Pumpkin.

'I'll get it,' said Brimmel eagerly.

'But you can't, it's too—'

Privet waved a paw to tell Pumpkin to stay where he was.

'You get it then, Brimmel.'

The youngster climbed half over her to reach it, put a paw to it, and pulled it into the light as easily as if it were almost nothing at all.

'Can you scribe anything at all?' asked Privet.

'My name, of course,' said Brimmel.

'Well then, Brimmel, let's start with that. Open the book.'

It was big for a youngster but he managed it, crying out in disappointment when he saw how old and used the first folio was.

'It's full!' he said. 'And this one, and this one, and this . . .'

He turned the folios as if it was a game, which to him it seemed to be. He went right through the Book and then turned back the folios.

'There's only this one with any space to scribe *my* name,' he said. 'What's that?' he asked.

'My name,' she whispered.

'Oh!' he said, disappointed once again.

'I'll score it out, and put a scribing right round it so you've got clean places to show me how well you scribe.'

'All right,' said Brimmel.

She reached her right paw to her name and without any hesitation and with swift clean strokes she scored it out. Then, with a single fluent circling of her paw, she scribed around it, and it might never have been.

'There,' she said. 'It's gone. Now, my love, you scribe *your* name for me.'

He did so, again and again and again, each time with increasing pride and pleasure, his scribing a little awry, the first attempts clear of each other, the last ones on top of each other so that it became impossible to make them out individually at all.

'Privet,' he said, when he was tired and had finished and closed the book, 'what book is this?'

'It's the Book of Silence,' she whispered, the light of the Book shining on her face, and on Brimmel's too.

'Is it a secret between you and me and Pumpkin, what we've done?' asked Brimmel.

'The Book isn't, but I think that what's inside must always be,' she said. 'Now, Brimmel, put the Book back where you found it, because it's late and I am getting tired.'

Brimmel lifted the Book and put it back by the wall near Privet.

'It's heavy,' he said panting. 'Can Pumpkin bring me to see you tomorrow?'

'Yes,' she said softly, her eyes closing. 'Goodnight, my dear.'

'Goodnight,' he said, turning from her and taking Pumpkin's paw and whispering loud enough that she heard him too, 'she's tired and wants to go to sleep.'

'Then we'd better let her, hadn't we?'

'Yes,' said Brimmel, scampering away through the portal, and pulling Pumpkin with him out of the chamber, which glimmered now with Light, and was soft with Silence.

Chapter Fifty

In those contented, balmy days from May Day to Midsummer, Pumpkin was a truly happy mole. From the coming of Loosestrife and her youngsters, and particularly of Brimmel, Privet's recovery continued, with none but she, and Pumpkin and young Brimmel, guessing at its deepest cause.

Unless Rooster did, in his ragged, mysterious way. But if so, he never asked about the Book of Silence, and nor did any other mole, so that there it lay, half-forgotten as it seemed, untouched by anymole, there where Privet slept.

For she was not well yet, and stayed at Pumpkin's whilst her health improved, and, as Fieldfare put it, nature put some plump back on her bones. Which meant that for a time at least, few tunnels were as busy as Pumpkin's, nor were anymole's quite so welcoming.

Moles came from far and wide to visit Privet, and pass the time of day, and to see Pumpkin as well, for he, along with Sturne, was as great a Duncton hero as ever lived, for they had defied the Newborns, kept the old ways alive, and would be an inspiration for evermore.

Mind, the visitors that came had to like it or lump it if youngsters were about, for there was something about Rose, Hawthorn and Brimmel that brought others along too. Up from the Barrow Vale they came, the youngsters of that spring and early summer, to play in the Slopes' shadows, and to wander up to the old High Wood.

Gone were the fears of the Ancient System, for the Dark Sound now seemed light, and moles knew that the great Stone was nearby and would always protect anymole who had faith in it, and courage to live true.

A new kind of pilgrim began to come towards the end of May – quieter moles than those who had given such formidable support to Maple's great army of followers in October and November. Thinking moles from near and from far, who had been stirred by those deep impulses that first drove Hibbott to take the route southwards so long before.

The hopes and intentions of these moles varied, some wishing to tell Privet what an inspiration her journey into Silence had been – even if (as they thought) the Book of Silence had not been found. No matter, the Newborns had been vanquished, and more important, a new spirit of faith in the old way of tolerance and trust been found. Thripp's original vision of a new moledom had been a long time coming, but it *had* come.

Nothing gave Pumpkin greater happiness in those slow days of early summer than to see such moles arrive in Duncton Wood, and make their reverent way up to the Stone. Then afterwards, of a warm and lazy evening, to hear the tales they had to tell – for Duncton was a place where old tales *could* be told, and new ones made, for there were moles who knew how to listen, and how not to interrupt.

Sometimes Pumpkin himself might be induced to tell a tale, though being a modest mole it was not something he did willingly. But with the right encouragement, and especially if moles he liked and knew, like Hamble, and Sturne, were thereabout, he would talk of his long life, and of the many famous moles he had known and loved.

None more so at the beginning than Master Librarian Stour; and none more so at the end than Privet. Though, it must be said, she had a rival for his affections, and that was Brimmel. By mid-May, when her recovery was well underway, Whillan and Loosestrife took their leave and returned to Cuddesdon, promising to come back again in June so that their young could take part in the famous Duncton Midsummer ritual.

Meanwhile they took Rose and Hawthorn with them, but they yielded to Brimmel's entreaties that he might be allowed to stay behind and live with Pumpkin and Privet – to help the one aid the other while she recovered fully, and to learn something of scribing too.

So Pumpkin's tunnels were busy, more than they ever had been, and Brimmel brought life and love and laughter to them both. As for Rooster, he came by almost daily, and began to teach the youngster something of the delving arts. Or rather, he would talk and thrust his talons about, to Frogbit's promptings, and Brimmel, sensibly silent and attentive, would take in all he could.

'Way to learn, eh, Frogbit?'

'Best way!' agreed Frogbit, whose skills were becoming much in demand.

Of the many comings and goings at that time, a few gave Pumpkin very special happiness. None more so, perhaps, than the afternoon a shy and diffident female appeared asking for Privet.

'She's sleeping, mole, but you're welcome to rest here yourself until she wakes. You're dusty and you've travelled far.'

'Yes, I have,' said the female, who looked over her shoulder from time to time as if afraid of whatmole might come. 'Will she sleep long?'

'You could talk to me if you wished,' he said, for she seemed to have something on her mind.

'No, it's Privet I've to see, so I'll wait here in the shadows if I may.'

Moles came and went. Brimmel brought in some friends, and Rees happened by and the female kept herself out of the way, always looking a little nervous when new moles appeared, and then relaxing when she saw they were not . . . well, whatever mole it was she seemed afraid of.

But Privet did not wake until late afternoon, and by then a good few moles had come to visit for the evening, since it felt a good one for telling tales. So that when Privet appeared and the mole came forward to talk with her, she found that, Duncton-like, there were many eager listeners to hear what she had to say.

'We can talk in private, mole, if you prefer,' said Privet.

'Well, it's about Maple that I've come.'

'Maple, *our* Maple!' cried out everymole.

'Yes, the great commander, him,' she said.

'This sounds like a tale worth hearing,' declared Pumpkin, 'and since there's many a mole here knew Maple, and they are much concerned for him, well perhaps . . .'

'It's all right,' said the female, 'I don't mind. It's just that Maple promised to send a messenger and, well, I'm the messenger.'

'What's your name, mole?' asked Privet.

'My name? I'm Myrtle of Broseley, and my mate was Furrow who died in the battle of Buckland.'

'And you've been sent by Maple?'

Myrtle nodded.

'And he's . . . well?'

'Oh yes, he's well.'

'Tell us, mole, tell us in your own way.'

Which she did, and held them all enthralled by her story of Maple's recovery at the Redditch Stone. Telling them how, with great difficulty, he and Weeth journeyed there, not reaching the Stone until March. There they waited, and there an old mole came.

'Sister Caldey,' said Privet.

'How do you know?' asked Myrtle, and others too.

671

'I knew her once. She's a mole *would* go to the Redditch Stone when she was needed. Why, she had been there herself when she was as ill as poor Maple became. Tell them, Myrtle.'

She did, and told how she herself, for reasons she did not divulge, had gone to the Redditch Stone with the intention of joining the Community of Rose.

'I had this idea I could be most useful to moles as a healer, and heard that the Community was meeting together again sometime after spring. As it happens I was wrong in that – they were not to be there until June. But I don't need to tell Duncton moles that the Stone works in strange ways and when I got there I found a good few moles. You can imagine how shocked I was to find among them two I know – Weeth and Maple – moles to whom I owe my life, with whom I served in the Wolds, along with my mate Furror, Stone rest his soul. Well now, Maple was pitifully scraggled, all sores and odours and swellings. 'Course nomole would go near him but Weeth, so I tried to help as best I could . . .'

'You did not worry about your own health?'

'Worry? With Maple? Why that mole gave new life not just to my mate Furrow and me, but to all moledom too. If he'd had contagious murrain it wouldn't have made any difference at all to me.

'But Weeth explained it was talon worms for which, as allmole knows there's no known remedy, so we made him as comfortable as we could and started praying – it was all we could do. He only had a day or two to live at most.

'Then, the second evening, like a mole out of mist, only it was out of the evening sunset, there comes this old female called Sister Caldey who founded the Community of Rose years back. She came up to Maple and she laid her paws on his head and started talking to him, soft as petals her voice was. Talked to him and he began to cry like a pup and Sister Caldey said to me "Mole, will you help?" and to Weeth the same.

'Well she led us all to a bright clear stream nearby and we went into it. There we went to him and we laid our paws on him too and then the others who had been afraid came and soon he had all of us touching and praying and weeping, and splashing about. I can't say how long it went on but he cried out for a long time like thorns were being pulled from all over his body.

'Sister Caldey called out invocations and prayers in the Stone's name, saying for the Stone to help him as he was grieved with sickness and needed help and then . . . well and then . . .'

672

'Then what, mole?'

'The worms,' said Myrtle grimly. 'He was purged of them like sickness from a pup. Out of him they came, from every part of his body, but we kept on in faith and that stream cleaned him and protected us and it took them away. After that he slept.

'Sister Caldey was gone next day as easy as she came and she said as she went, "Now you are a community once more, and he whom you healed will be a leader among you and a good one too, for he has suffered worse than most, and understands suffering . . . " She came with the sun and she went with it.

'In the molemonths after that Maple recovered and his fur grew back and all his strength. Some stayed in the Community, some didn't. I decided not to because I had things to see to. Anyway, Maple told me that I should go to Duncton Wood and I could be his messenger, which I hope I have been . . . So now the the Community of Rose is in good paws, and their work goes on, ministering to the many moles who suffer and are ill, whether of spirit or of body.'

'And Weeth, did you meet him?'

'I did, and liked him a great deal. He told me to tell you, Privet, that he wishes to watch over Maple until he is sure he is settled to his new task and then, as he put it, "I will take the first opportunity to return to Duncton, in time for Midsummer I hope!"'

'And you, mole?'

'Well, I wanted to serve in the Community, but Maple said I was not suited to so silent and dedicated a life, and I think he felt I had gone into the Community for the wrong reason.'

'Which was?'

But that Myrtle would not tell, only adding, rather lamely, 'Well, that's all I have to say.'

It was a tale well told, but it left Pumpkin unsatisfied.

'Mole!' he said, calling her over to him, as the evening's conversation moved on to other things. 'What is it you've not told us? What-mole is it you seem to fear, and keep looking over your shoulder for? Is he or she here? Eh?'

'There was a missive went out, asking for the mole to come forward who stanced up for Keeper Sturne; well . . .'

'You!'

She nodded her head, and her story tumbled out of how she came back to Duncton and tried to seek out Maple and then had been too intimidated by Sturne's position as Librarian, and, and . . .

673

'Well, we had better see about *that*!' said Pumpkin.

'But he's so important, and I don't know what to say to him, and all I want to do is see him just once more because, well, things were not quite finished. I—'

'Now!' said Pumpkin.

'Now?' she gasped.

'Now is best,' said Pumpkin. 'Follow me and we might get there before nightfall.'

'But he'll be working.'

'Of course he'll be working, he does nothing else but work, does Sturne. It'll do him good to . . .' and here Pumpkin might have said many things but he confined himself to the tamest of all . . . 'to have a chat to the mole who saved his life. He would want to say thank you!'

'Oh! Well, perhaps it's best we get it over with. I won't sleep well until I do.'

Without more ado, and eager to reach the Library before twilight, Pumpkin led Myrtle off by the quickest route he knew.

'Are you sure this is the right thing to do?' she said, as they reached an entrance and went down into the echoing tunnels.

'I am. Nomole knows Sturne better than me, not one. This is the very *best* thing to do.'

They ventured into the gloom of the Main Chamber, Myrtle staring up in awe at the great stacks and rows of books, and into the places of study and scholarship.

'Who's there?' called out Sturne's voice from the Master Librarian's gallery. 'Speak up, it's echoey up here and I'm busy.'

'It's me, Sturne, and I've brought a mole to see you.'

'Oh!' said Sturne, still not appearing at his study cell portal. 'If it's some mole or other who wants to study, tell him to come in the morning and I'll be much obliged.'

For Sturne this was relatively affable, but it was not quite what Pumpkin had in mind.

'It's not "some mole or other", Sturne,' Pumpkin called up, 'it's a female come to see you.'

'A female? I don't know any females, not one. Never have, doubt I ever will.'

'Sturne,' called out Pumpkin warningly, 'I'm getting on in years, but I tell you if you don't put down whatever text or folio you're studying and come down here this instant I shall . . . I shall . . . drag you down!'

There was silence, and finally, and slowly, Sturne appeared, looking over the gallery down towards them.

'I can't see very well from up here.'

'Then come down, mole, for goodness' sake. Or we'll be off, this female and me, to have a merry evening together.'

'What female is she that she claims to know me?'

'Sturne, you may be clear-headed with texts, but you are dungle-headed in all else. You met her, you may dimly recall, in the cross-under in November, when she saved your life.'

Sturne was suddenly silent.

'Perhaps we better go and come back another time,' whispered Myrtle, much alarmed by all this.

'Go? You'll go nowhere! You'll stay right where you are and he'll come down here. Won't you, Sturne?' he called.

With that Pumpkin left them, and tempted though he was – very tempted indeed – he did not linger to find out how Sturne made his acquaintance of a female who had occupied his thoughts every day of every molemonth in the long long terrible times since November. But later, through the services of Fieldfare, who heard the story at first paw from Myrtle herself, he learnt what happened.

Sturne came down the slipway from the gallery like a mole about to face his doom. Nothing had ever frightened him so much, and each step was hard to take. But there she was, staring at him, and as frightened as he was.

He reached her and stopped, and stared.

'You!' he said.

'Yes,' she replied.

'I wanted . . .'

'I wanted . . .'

What did they both want? They wanted to talk. They wanted not to be alone. They wanted to share.

If getting down to where she stanced was hard enough, words proved nearly impossible.

'I . . . really . . . I don't know what to say,' he said. 'Your name?'

'Myrtle,' she blurted out.

'Myrtle,' he muttered.

Why, he thought to himself, it was a lovely name, a beautiful name, the finest name he had ever heard. But could he say such things? He could not.

'I'm Sturne,' he said.

'Master Librarian,' she replied.

If there was a moment when their nascent relationship might have stumbled, and veered into something inconsequential, ending in polite words and a farewell of moles who did not know how to reach each other, that was it.

But some distant sense of what was fitting came to Sturne's heart and he found the right words to say.

'No, no, not Master Librarian,' he said. 'I am . . . I am just . . . well, a mole. That's all I am and all I really ever wanted to be.'

He looked at her then with such appeal in his eyes, as if to say 'Help me, for I don't know what words to say and never have, but now more than anything I want to learn to say them,' that she could only stare, and not care if slow tears trickled from her eyes.

'I came back to see you,' she sniffed, 'because after what happened, I couldn't stop thinking about it and then, well, and then . . .' and it tumbled out, every bit of it.

'You came back here to Duncton?' he said, dumbfounded. 'You slept rough in the Eastside, when I was . . . well, *nearby*! And I didn't know!'

She nodded, and she could not doubt from the lost look in his face how welcome she would have been, and how much he had needed her.

'I don't know what to say, you see,' he said, frowning and really not knowing at all. 'I, well, I'm not used to talking to females, I just have never . . .'

He stopped, unable to go on, as bewildered and lost in the world of feelings as she might well be in the world of texts and folios.

'My dear,' she said, coming to him at last and taking him in her paws, 'you need say nothing at all, nothing.'

'But I . . . I don't . . . I . . . mole . . . I am so afraid to cry.'

Then poor Sturne, who had so rarely cried, began to cry his heart out as she held him. Tears born not of molemonths but of moleyears past, hard years, when he had been so much alone, and so lost.

Twilight gave way to dusk, and still he cried. Dusk to darkness, and still he sniffled and snuffled. Darkness to night, and finally he stopped.

'We better move,' she said.

'Mmm, we had, I suppose,' he mumbled.

'Can you find the way out?'

'I . . .' Bump!

'Perhaps . . .' Crash!

'Take my paw . . .' Wallop!

676

Suddenly, in the pitch black of the Library, she found herself in *his* paws.

'I'm lost in my own Library,' he confessed.

'We could stay here until dawn.'

'It wouldn't be right,' said Sturne, not moving at all.

'It would be very right indeed,' said Myrtle gently. Then, 'What are you doing?' For he was doing something.

'I'm smiling,' he said, 'I think that's what it is, at any rate.'

'I can't see your smile at all,' she said, 'it's too dark.'

And quietly, perhaps a little diffidently, for he was unused to such excess, Sturne dared to laugh in the darkness; and in all his long life the Main Chamber of Duncton Library had never felt so right a place for him to be as it did then with her.

Other strangers came to Duncton who brought happiness to others as Myrtle did, and when Pumpkin heard such tales he was well pleased. This was Duncton after all, and such things *could* happen there, and each one that did made the darker memories of recent moleyears easier to bear.

One such visitor gave him unexpected pleasure, and confirmed his long-held belief that if moles are tolerant, and don't jump to hasty judgements, the Stone will put things right in its own way. She was dark, and she was most beautiful, and she appeared at Pumpkin's portal like some exotic creature that floats through a woodland glade on the wings of the summer breeze.

'My name is Morwenna of Siabod, and it's Whillan that I seek.'

Well, now, here was a thing! Whillan's mysterious past come to haunt him no doubt, and she not a mole to give a single thing away, but rather, to curl up in a male's burrow and treat it like her own, and not many males mole enough to stop her!

Of Siabod too!

She waited languorously until Whillan came over from Cuddesdon, and many a mole wanted to be there when they met.

'Well!' said Whillan. 'Well!'

She embraced him, her glossy fur making him look almost old, and she whispered to him. Then, with no explanation given – and nomole daring to seek one, for together they made a formidable pair – they set off for the Marsh End.

Later, much was revealed.

'Squelch's *daughter*?'

Well . . . what *could* a mole say? Nothing, it seemed.

677

But away from their stares, down in the dank paths of the Marsh End, she was a different mole, and a nervous one.

'Madoc didn't want me to come, but I did all the same. Maybe she did really. She loved you, Whillan. Then after she had us she didn't need to love you any more.'

'Yes,' said Whillan.

'And now?'

They talked with an affection born of having a common bond in Madoc, and the free spirit that such journeyers share. He told her everything, of his past, and of his present happiness. She told him but little, for the past mattered not to her, nor the future.

'How is he?'

Whillan told her Squelch worked and worked at his singing and melodies, and that he had learnt mediaeval notation and made things nomole-else could understand.

'He sings still?' she asked softly, her eyes eager.

He shook his head. 'Morwenna, there's something you should know. The notations he makes, they are for you. I have heard him say as much.'

She accepted it as if it were her right.

'Well then, let us go and see him.'

'He's grown old.'

'Madoc said he was horribly fat.'

'No more.'

'Take me to him, Whillan,' she said, taking his paw, and for that short journey to Squelch's modest tunnels, he might have fancied that he went with Madoc once again.

Squelch *had* aged, and when they found him he was hunched over some scrap of bark, humming loudly to himself and stabbing at it, making marks as he did so. His tunnels were a chaos of folios, and odd texts that he had made for himself.

'Squelch! It's me, Whillan.'

'Ah,' sighed Squelch, peering round, 'a friendly voice. You are welcome, mole. You have somemole with you?'

'I have, Squelch. It is your daughter, Morwenna.'

'Morwenna,' he exclaimed, darting out to see and too astonished to seem surprised. It was hard to say at that moment what his feelings were. He seemed perplexed.

He stared at her and she at him, and then she laughed and said, 'You're thin!'

'Not fat now,' he conceded with a rueful smile.

678

'What are all those?' she asked, moving past him with grace and waving a paw at his work.

'Melodies, songs, and other things,' he said.

'Whillan said they are made for me.'

'Did he? He's right – not you in the body, you in my head. In the body you may be a different thing.'

'Madoc said that the one good thing about you is that you could sing. Whillan says you don't sing any more, so things don't sound promising.'

'He's right. Better not sing. My penance for wrongs done. I put it down here instead,' and he picked up a pawful of folios.

'Sing to me,' she said.

'Well then, perhaps I will. Perhaps I will.'

He would not for a time, only looking at her, getting them food, fussing about, and trying to order his tunnels and chamber, which proved quite impossible.

'Sing to me,' she said.

'Well, I could I suppose. There's a lifetime of singing here. Just one, perhaps.'

'Sing to me, father,' she said passionately. 'It is why I have journeyed from Siabod, so that I may one day tell my pups that I heard you sing.'

He looked at her, and at Whillan, and went to the back of the chamber. He touched one folio, and then another, turning them over, peering at them, seeming unsure quite where to begin.

But then, softly, he began, his strange, high, haunting voice filling the chamber, filling their hearts. Of her coming he sang, and of dreams, and of all there could be when moles came together whom life had pushed apart.

'And another,' she whispered when he had done. 'Another,' she breathed.

He sang then of torment, and loss, and reunion.

'Another.'

He shook his head, and said his voice was cracked and old and not what it once was.

'I know,' she said, 'I know . . . but it is the song I shall remember, not the voice. Sing of my mother Madoc.'

A dark look came across his face, a look of shame.

'My voice is not good enough for that,' he said.

'Sing,' she whispered, and it was like the command of wind and sky.

679

He began, and then, as his voice did break, did crack, she began to sing softly too, gentle as the wind, embracing as the sky.

'You?' he whispered.

And then she sang for him, of loss and of forgiveness, of the light that comes after darkness with the seasons' turn.

'You . . .' he said, tears coursing down his face, for she sang with the beauty that his own voice once had.

'You are my daughter,' he said.

Then she sang for him, and for the first time in his life he knew real joy.

So Morwenna came for a time to Duncton Wood. She stayed with Squelch and he taught her what he knew. The melodies he made, the songs, the great works which he called 'other things' she understood and she learnt from them all she could. Perhaps nomole has ever given moledom so rich a legacy of moving song and chant as Squelch, and that great collection that he made, at her request, was taken not into Duncton Library, for she deemed it not quite suitable, but to Cuddesdon, where Whillan was.

At his end, which was when June came, but before Midsummer itself, she nursed him until he died, and she sang a lament which was his own, made for allmole, but never sung as beautifully again as that first time.

Then, as mysteriously as she had come, she was gone, and Squelch's great legacy was left safe for evermore.

At that time, too, Elynor passed away, and Pumpkin began to grow old as well. As Privet finally regained her health, he declined, all his great tasks fulfilled; and surely there was nothing more for him to do. Now, as he had cared for her when she had seemed near her end, so she cared for him.

'Midsummer's coming, my dear, and I wish you to be there to witness it before the Stone,' she told him many times.

'Aye, Pumpkin, we all wish for that,' Sturne agreed, for when Privet was not near at paw, Sturne took her place. And, if Sturne had been called away, why, there were a hundred moles who would have been there to watch over Pumpkin in those last days.

Two days before Midsummer Weeth appeared, just as he had promised he would do; and, to everymole's amazement, he had a mole with him who had come from the far side of the Wolds: Dint, Frogbit's adoptive father. Tales, stories, arrivals and delights . . . that was ever the way the days before Midsummer *should* be, and that blessed Midsummer was no exception.

As indefatigable as ever, Pumpkin rallied on Midsummer's Eve and declared that nothing would stop him going up to the Stone for the ritual: 'Even if it's the last time I ever go there. Aye, I'll get there!' So he did, with Sturne to help him on one flank, and Hamble on the other, and Brimmel tagging along behind. The trek up the Slopes and across the High Wood was slow, and Pumpkin had to make a good few stops.

'Not what I was, am I?' he said. 'Brimmel? Where's that mole! Brimmel, you see that tree there? Well, that's where Bracken nearly got caught by Rune a century ago, and if he had been, how different things would be! Eh?'

'That's right, sir!' said Brimmel, who had spent many a happy hour with Pumpkin in the days before he was confined to his tunnels, being shown the old places, being taught the old lore.

'Got a taste for it, he has,' Pumpkin had told Privet, and so it seemed.

So now, on what few could doubt was his last trek, Pumpkin was still wanting to show Brimmel things.

'Wait a moment – what do you mean, "That's right"?' said Pumpkin.

'You told me about the tree before. And how Rune didn't catch him, and Bracken ran all the way—'

'Did I? Repeating myself, Sturne. Time to go!'

'There's a whole summer yet, Pumpkin,' said Sturne.

'No, mole, there isn't,' said Pumpkin simply. 'Now, let's go on.'

Their route seemed lined with moles, all cheering Pumpkin on, all sensing that this was a moment they would remember and cherish all their lives.

'How many moles have come!' he said, delighted to see so many new pilgrims, so many youngsters, so many kin together once again. 'The Stone will be well pleased.'

The sun shone in the Stone Clearing, moles chattered and greeted one another, and when the time came the youngsters were gathered round the Stone, Loosestrife's three especially close to Privet. There were not as many yet as there would be in years to come, but it is not numbers, but faith and trust that count.

Fieldfare told of how she had first come when a youngster, and how she had been afraid and hid behind the bulk of Elder Drubbins, who few there now remembered. Others talked, and the youngsters heard the tale of how Hulver, at this very Stone, defied Mandrake of Siabod and spoke the Invocation of the Graces, whose words lie at the very heart of the Midsummer Ritual.

681

'Well, then,' said Fieldfare, 'I think somemole had better say it. In the old days it was one of the Elders did it – a mole loved and respected by all the community. These days we don't have Elders, so . . .'

All eyes turned to Pumpkin.

'No!' he protested. 'All I am and all I have ever wished to be is a library aide. No, this is a task for Sturne, our Master Librarian Sturne.'

For all Sturne's new-found happiness, and his heroism in the face of the Newborn Crusades, it cannot truthfully be said that his name yet inspired as much warmth as it might, and there was a certain lack of enthusiasm at Pumpkin's suggestion.

'No, no,' Pumpkin protested, when Sturne riposted that he say the ritual after all, 'I am not up to it. I do not feel as well as I would wish. No, no, it is nothing, but it would give me great happiness to hear Sturne say it, it really would.'

Even then, moles might have hesitated, had not Privet come forward and said, 'Perhaps, after all, it would best for Sturne to say the ritual. We would not want to tax Pumpkin's strength at such a moment as this . . . and anyway,' and here she smiled at Sturne, and at Myrtle too, 'the last time Sturne spoke before this Stone, why, he was most formidable. It would be good for us to hear him in gentler vein.'

'Aye, that's well said!' cried out many a mole. 'You're one of us, Sturne, and there was never a truer, more courageous Duncton mole than you, excepting your friend Pumpkin, of course!'

Which gave pleasure to them both, and was a heart-warming prelude to the ritual itself.

How awesome Sturne seemed as he took his place before the Stone, and how the youngsters' eyes widened as he indicated that they come forward and form a group about him, and everymole-else a circle about them.

He spoke of how all moles reached a point when they must begin to think of leaving their home burrows, and that when they did, if they had come from a burrow of love, and had faith in the Stone, they had little to fear from the trials and tribulations they would face when they journeyed forth into life.

Then he spoke the words of the Invocation itself:

> 'We bathe their paws in showers of dew,
> We free their fur with wind from the west,
> We bring them choice soil,
> Sunlight in life.

We ask they be blessed
With a sevenfold blessing.

   The grace of form,
   The grace of goodness,
   The grace of suffering,
   The grace of wisdom,
   The grace of true words,
   The grace of trust,
   The grace of whole-souled loveliness.

We bathe their paws in showers of light,
We free their souls with talons of love,
We ask that they hear the silent Stone . . .'

Yet though the sun shone on all of them, it seemed at that moment that it shone on one in particular. Who could doubt, as they looked on old Pumpkin, surrounded by the friends he loved, and the moles whose faith and life he had done so much to protect, that he had been blessed with that sevenfold blessing?

In him was the grace of form, and of goodness. In him there had been suffering redeemed by wisdom. He spoke true words, and had faith and trust in the Stone always. Truly, he was a mole whose eyes shone with the grace of whole-souled loveliness.

Now he stanced before the Stone, weak and growing weaker and the Light was upon him and the Silence called.

'I tried,' he whispered, 'to do all that was asked of me. You youngsters do the same, and if you suffer doubts and difficulties along the way, remember this: the Stone is always there to listen to your doubts, and your grumbles, and your moans – and to your joys as well. There's many of those to find, if you look for them. So many of those . . .'

'Brimmel!'

It was Privet's voice, and it was authoritative in the old way. How could she speak so, and now of all times?

'Brimmel, Library Aide Pumpkin has one more task to perform. Go to his tunnels, mole, and fetch the Book. No need to hurry, mole, the Stone will wait. But don't be too long either!'

The Book! What Book! As others wondered Brimmel turned, and was gone, down the paths that Pumpkin himself had shown him, across the High Wood, and then down the Slopes to Pumpkin's place.

Others followed him some of the way, wondering, puzzled, awed. There had been a light about the Stone, and it was the same light

Brimmel found when he entered the tunnels, and went to find the Book. It was just where he had placed it himself, when he had first come to Duncton Wood. It shone upon his face as he reached down to it, and it was heavy, heavier to him than before. But no matter, he was carrying it to Pumpkin, and nothing and nomole would stop him doing that.

He took it from the chamber, up to the surface, and then began the trek back to the Stone. Whatmole who witnessed it will ever forget that trek? A youngster, not fully formed, carrying an ancient Book, battered by time, worn by care, glimmering with light. Heavy it was, but though many a mole offered to help him he carried it upslope alone. Through the High Wood, alone. And then, towards the Clearing, between two lines of moles, who knew what the Book must be, and understood what they were witnessing was the lost and the last Book, coming now to ground.

Only as he entered the clearing did Brimmel stumble and slip; the Book fall from his grasp and open at a pilgrim's paws. That mole alone saw what was in the Book, and picking it up and righting Brimmel, that good mole, who was Hibbott of Ashbourne Chase, closed the Book and gave it back to the youngster.

'What did you see? What was scribed there?' asked a mole at Hibbott's flank.

And all were silent, and heard the question asked.

'It was *your* name in the Book, mole: your name that I saw!'

'Mine?' whispered the stranger.

'Yours,' said Hibbott, looking at them all.

Then, turning to Brimmel, he said, 'Take the Book to Pumpkin and he will know what to do with it.'

Brimmel advanced across the Clearing and placed the Book by Pumpkin's front paws, where its Light, brighter now, shone upon his face.

'Take it where it should go,' commanded Privet, 'for with you, Pumpkin, will it always be safeguarded.'

Pumpkin stared at the Book, and reached a paw to it. He stanced up in its Light, his eyes shining with faith and trust and love as they looked first at the Stone and then at the moles gathered about him.

'Well then,' he said.

Well then . . .

And he took up the Book of Silence, and went towards the Stone and prayed there one final time. The Book seemed as light to him as laughter, or as a prayer of thanksgiving.

Then he went around the Stone, beyond it into the High Wood, and down into that tunnel which leads to the Chamber of Roots. Privet and Sturne went with him first, and his friends all followed, and the great trees of the Clearing grew motionless and their roots stilled as Pumpkin passed down and then among them into the heart of the Chamber.

To the base of the Stone he went, where the seven Stillstones waited, and the six Books which had been put there by his Master Stour. Then he placed the Book where the circle had gaped so long, and now was made complete, and then blessed Pumpkin, library aide, went on by himself into the Light and the Silence beyond.

EPILOGUE

Mole, I have done my best to tell the last part of the tale of the coming of the Book of Silence to Duncton Wood as my Master would have wished me to, and as he might have, had he lived to tell it for himself.

One promise I must keep, which is to tell you his name – if not my own!

Well then, it was Brimmel of Cuddesdon, son of Whillan and Loosestrife, who first welcomed me by the Stone all those moleyears ago, and set us on this journey. And whatmole better than he who showed Privet the way to the last secret of the Book, and was part of its final return to its place beneath the Stone?

Others have told of the events after the coming of the Book, and I shall not begin to do so here, except to say that after that Midsummer, Duncton entered into a most happy and joyous time in which it found peace once more, and slow forgetting of the shadows that besmirched its past.

Of Rooster and Privet nothing needs to be said at all, though moles often ask. He delved tunnels for them to share, and moles said they never saw such harmony, nor knew such love and gentleness as where those two lived. Love was their other name.

Rooster had said that Duncton's delving days were done, and so they were. Time moves on, and as one system fades away to memory, others come forward to prominence and there's not a mole in Duncton then or now would regret that one little bit!

But it was in Cuddesdon that a new age in delving now began, as Whillan carried forward Rooster's Mastership, and with Glee and Humlock, and Frogbit too, fostered and developed the delving arts. From there Whillan and Frogbit went out all over moledom to help delve the old places anew, and new places which had the atmosphere of old.

The summer passed and autumn came, and brought with it change.

Many a mole came to Duncton, to find Privet, who had scribed the Book of Silence, and to seek out Rooster, Master of the Delve. But

Duncton moles gave them privacy now, and rarely told a stranger where to look.

The High Wood? Perhaps.

The Westside? Maybe.

The Eastside? Sometimes.

The Marsh End? Worth a try.

The Stone?

'Oh yes, you'll find them there, mole, if you know how to look. It's as good a place as any to begin . . . or to end.'

How often, as old Brimmel told me the tale of the Book of Silence, had I had a yearning to tell him *my* name. But he did not want to know it, and in that he taught me much.

I was not born in Duncton Wood, and nor, after I had finished scribing this tale, did I stay in it. Yet long ago, in Dunbar's time, so old kin of mine have said, there was a library aide served in Duncton Wood who bore our name. And my father's father told me once that he was one of those pilgrims who journeyed to Duncton to be witness at that Midsummer.

'Did you *see* the Book?' I asked him when a pup.

Maybe he did, and maybe he didn't, but one thing he told me before he went to the Silence was this: 'Hibbott himself told me that my name was scribed in the Book, which means yours is too. Your name is scribed in that great Book.'

That's what my father said, and he seemed to mean it, and the memory of what he said is what first sent me wandering moledom to find the truth of this tale.

Since I have mentioned Hibbott, he seems a good mole with whom to end. Here are the last words of his *Pilgrimage* and they are a fitting conclusion to the journey we have made: 'I had journeyed far, and learnt much, and I believe I found the object of my quest. But of all the things I saw on my great journey, excepting the Book itself, none filled me with greater joy than that day in the autumn after that Midsummer when I saw again the vale that leads up to my beloved home system of Ashbourne Chase. I had come home.

'Moles must have heard I was coming, for many were there to greet me. Some old familiar faces were gone, but many there I knew, and others, new to me, soon became my friends.

'So many were the questions they asked that the time came when I decided to scribe the tale of my pilgrimage, as an inspiration to some to make such a pilgrimage themselves; and for others to share at leisure in my trials, and in my joys as well . . .'

So did Hibbott scribe, and I can scribe no better. So now I shall journey on, and wish you well, and hope that when the time comes, you too, like Hibbott, will return home safeguarded, and know something of the Silence of the Stone.

AUTHOR'S NOTE

The two Duncton trilogies, of which this is the final volume, have taken fifteen years to write. Only one of the books, the first, has a dedication: 'To Leslie, with love.' Since 1978 our lives have gone different ways, yet our love remains as deep and abiding as ever it was.

Sometimes, during the writing of *The Book of Silence*, I have thought that there is another person to whom I would have liked to dedicate one or other, perhaps all, the books. It is relevant to say that my mother died but days after I began *Duncton Tales*, and that what was to have been one volume became three . . . Her death made it possible for me to find out who my father really was. I never knew him, nor his full name, only that his first name was Robert and that he had a family. Somewhere in Britain, like Whillan in moledom, I have kin I would like to find.

I would have liked to take my father's hand and show him Duncton Wood. But I never could, and *The Book of Silence* is about the long journey we all must make to come to terms and live beyond whatever enshadows our particular life.

One more thing, and then I'll really go . . .

There are three places in Britain which, more than any other, I journeyed back to in my heart again and again when I was writing these books. The first is White Horse Hill, Uffington, Wiltshire, where my mother fell in love, or said she did: you could never be quite sure with her . . . But early on, it claimed my imagination and later my heart. The second is Castell y Gwynt, Castle of the Winds, near the Glyders in Snowdonia. The third is Wytham Wood, near Oxford, and a glade of ancient beeches where I have found great peace. The last is perhaps the hardest to visit and find, but perhaps we all need a place like that to call our own. The first two . . . well, it would give me pleasure to hear from any reader who has read all six books and visited both those places.

Though the reader who would get *most* plaudits would, just for good measure, for the the walk is strangely grand and informs large sections of the Duncton books, visit Buckden Pike, Great Whernside, and go then by the high route down to Grassington in Wharfedale and have cream tea. The best of ways to clear the head for tasks anew . . .

PUBLISHER'S NOTE

Since *Duncton Wood* was first published in 1980, William Horwood has received thousands of letters from readers asking about the conception and writing of what has become a fantasy classic. Readers who would like more details of his work should write to William Horwood at P.O. Box 446, Oxford, OX1 2SS.